Dear Reader:

Just what influences your decision to make a selection when you are searching through the shelves of a bookstore for a book to read? Should you not have anything in mind or a referral, you would undoubtedly want a selection that will keep you intrigued enough to hold your interest until the last word is read. Sometimes you may want one that makes you laugh, or sometimes you may appreciate one that strikes up your anger...enough to raise the hair on your arms. That would be exciting. Also exciting is a thrilling crime story. A good one can also raise the hair on your arms. What about a unique love story that includes all of these subjects?

    Enclosed is a unique, true story about a relationship between two men that travels through eighteen exciting years. It is an adult story and one that should be read...not only for the laughter...or the sexuality...or the drama...or the anger, but because it will enlighten your prejudiced and ancient heart and mind.

    Maybe this little bit will influence your decision?

Sincerely,
The Author

Why Has All the Music Gone?

by

Richard D'Ambrosia

DORRANCE PUBLISHING CO., INC.
PITTSBURGH, PENNSYLVANIA 15222

All Rights Reserved
Copyright © 2013 by Richard D'Ambrosia

No part of this book may be reproduced or transmitted, downloaded, distributed, reverse engineered, or stored in or introduced into any information storage and retrieval system, in any form or by any means, including photocopying and recording, whether electronic or mechanical, now known or hereinafter invented without permission in writing from the publisher.

Dorrance Publishing Co., Inc.
701 Smithfield Street
Pittsburgh, PA 15222
Visit our website at *www.dorrancebookstore.com*

ISBN: 978-1-4349-1855-0
eISBN: 978-1-4349-2090-4

This novel is lovingly dedicated to my children, my family, and to Dennis, in appreciation for their love and understanding.

Acknowledgements

My sincere thanks go to Dennis for his assistance in editing, and to my nephew, Gino, for his continued praise and encouragement, which proved instrumental in leading me on the path of publication.

I also want to thank Harry Cornelius and Dan Rezek for their professional assistance.

And if it had not been for Margot Logan, I may never have completed this novel. I thank her for her excited anticipation each time I brought a chapter to read.

Lastly, my thanks go to Hallmark Greeting Cards for creating the perfect butterfly verse. It was the perfect description of the man the memorial quilt honored.

Foreword

I remember when the author first told me that he was writing this book. He said that it would be the story of his relationship with his late lover, Juan, who recently died of AIDS. As a social worker working with AIDS patients and their families, I thought that this would be therapeutic for Mr. Mella. Little did I realize what a powerful work it would be.

The author and I agreed that I would read his story as he wrote it. I agreed to give him my honest opinion of the work. We both had some trepidation about this. What if I were forced to tell him that the book was no good?

Much to my delight, the book is terrific! The author usually brought me a chapter or two at a time, and I devoured them! It was difficult to wait for the next installment. This is not merely a *gay* story, or an AIDS story, it is an emotionally moving love story that transcends these narrow boundaries. As I read each chapter, I felt that I knew Juan, although I had never met him. I found myself wishing that I had met him while he was living. This book is a testimonial to a love that is strong and everlasting. I am honored to be the one person who was chosen to preview it before it was shown to anyone else. And I know that the love that Richard felt for Juan lives on in this moving tribute.

Margot E. Logan
June 6, 1995

Introduction

I often have wondered how it was possible to write a biography spanning so many years, and to recall actual words from conversations when diaries were never recorded. I always figured they were concocted in order to make it interesting. But now, I find the same thing happening to me! The last eighteen years have flashed into my mind as quickly as they passed, in as vivid a picture as yesterday when the closest and dearest person in my life became terminally ill and eventually died in my arms.

Never in my life did I imagine I could be this sad, this lonely. Was it because I refused to believe he would die? Was it because I was sure a cure would soon arrive, and refused to talk of his illness and eventual death? I have read many books and articles on death since, and have come to believe that *acceptance* is clearly the most important stage the one dying and the survivor must reach. Only through this acceptance can one find peace within himself. Perhaps, then, God has blessed me with memories as clear as yesterday's so my heart will finally accept it as final. Lonely and empty I will always be, but it is possible that the reason these eighteen years are still so vivid is that they will fill the emptiness in my heart.

I asked myself how these memories could last as I grow old and forgetful. The only possible way was to record everything I remembered of this unique man. I wondered—would I be able to capture the memories racing through my mind night and day? Would I find the words? And will these words faithfully mirror the fabulous character of this man? It then occurred to me that my grief might be protracted in my writing. But, somehow, I found that once I was writing, I did not feel as lonely. It was almost as though I could feel his presence guiding my every word to be sure I was accurate. His smile approved each date as I recorded it. I discovered that this writing was something I needed to do—and to make it right, be faithful to his pronunciation. The hard *a*, for example, was not in his vocabulary. Hat became "hot." That became "thot." I could then construe a log of memories that would last! I realized if these words could capture the beauty of this man's warmth, charm, wit, and intelligence, as well as intransigent stubbornness and boyish character, and especially the laughter he was king of, then he would surely be loved by all those fortunate enough to read this story.

I was apprehensive at first, for it meant confessing the truth about our relationship to my children and family. Would it be an embarrassment? I gave it a considerable amount of thought, and finally decided that, above all, I had a story to tell, and to me, it was beautiful. I was sure they would honor the sincerity of my endeavor. We were two men who loved and respected each other. We had neither shame nor regret in those eighteen years that passed so quickly.

We had never been ones to boast about being gay; we knew society was kinder to the straight world because we had been part of it for so many years. One thing we were proud and sure of was the love we shared. Granted, there were events in our life together that we regretted, but I think one faces that in most relationships. Furthermore, these regrettable and outlandish acts eventually led us to an understanding of life's real importance.

Our eighteen-year journey follows a bizarre path filled with crazy people and hilarious moments, but always manages to allow time for love. However, as it sometimes happens, egos and stubbornness create a multitude of wrong decisions, which eventually lead to heartbreak! It tells how, in spite of all the problems, two people can eventually jell into one! Here was a man of many charms. One such charm was his endless capacity to make me feel special by personalizing every phrase with my name. In this way, he showed his love, and he was so contagious that it was not long before I was doing the same.

I decided to use only our first names and to change those of family and friends to avoid embarrassment. Their privacy and anonymity ought to be preserved. In the same vein, I thought it right to change some locations.

So here at last is the story of a man who was not by any means a saint—an individual who could be unyieldingly stubborn and embarrassingly frank, and who could also be just one nasty bitch! Above all, however, he was a tremendously charming man, full of wit, compassion, and laughter, and one who would easily apologize for his behavior. If you find yourself seeing him, laughing with him, or even loving him, and then if you feel you really know and suddenly miss him, then I will have accomplished what I needed to do—to have Juan live again!

Prologue

The time was almost 10:30 in the evening, July 21, 1992. I had arrived home after an all-day outing to Galena, Illinois, a quaint and picturesque town near the Mississippi River. Quite a tourist attraction, the town boasts countless antique shops and restaurants all set in the middle of what was once a mining town. The view is spectacular as one drives into the main part of town because there it is sitting below a panorama of hillside homes. One almost feels as though they are viewing the past come alive.

I had been quite apprehensive about going that morning, but shared none of my fears with Matt when he asked if I would like to join him for the day. He had been continuously urging me to get away from the hospital for a bit; it would do me good to be away from all the stress. I really didn't want to go since I had accompanied him the day before on another outing after returning home from shaving and feeding Juan in the morning. I would then not be able to return to the hospital until late that evening.

As I waited in the car for Matt to cash a check before leaving, a terrible lonely feeling passed through my body. My throat felt tight and my nose began to swell, and then the tears started. It was nothing new; I had come to tears before, especially on days and nights when I left the hospital and Juan wasn't doing well.

Juan was fine when I left the morning before, and when I called his nurse that afternoon, she told me he was okay but quiet. That certainly should have eased my mind, so why was I reacting like this now? Why was I feeling so low? I certainly didn't want to spoil Matt's day, especially since he was on vacation. I knew I had been with Juan at every opportunity—two, three, and sometimes four times a day, to feed him, to bathe him, to walk him, and just to be with him. So I guess my feelings were just a reaction to the fact that I was going to be away from him for a total of a day and a half. But nothing was going to happen to him. After all, Daniel had been reassuring me it was nowhere near Juan's time. Yet, these ominous feelings consumed my thoughts throughout the day.

It helped me to know that, in my absence, Daniel promised to spend time with Juan. Daniel's cheery personality was exactly what Juan needed, especially since I never felt he was receiving enough visitors to keep his mind active. Daniel was my friend, and after meeting Juan, he appreciated him for his charm and wit. During the eighteen years with Juan, I knew he never liked to be alone. Even when he wanted to sleep earlier than I, he still needed to have me in the house. And he still hasn't changed. So it wasn't surprising to hear, "I'm gonna rest for a while, Recharred, so will you please wait for me?" Wait I would. In all of those years, I can't think of a time that I was bored being with Juan. No, not even when he was sleeping!

This had become Juan's longest stay in the hospital since his illness, being admitted March 27, 1992. Shortly after, he asked something I'll never forget. Lying in bed on his side, he said, "Recharred, please don't leave me…keep me well." He surely knew I would never desert him, but it was good to hear him say it, because it confirmed his deep feelings for me, which were, of course, matched by my own for him.

All through the day, I could think of nothing but Juan and I repeated to myself, "He won't look like others! He'll be shaved. He'll be well fed and look good! He will not die of AIDS!" These thoughts lingered throughout the day.

Upon entering my condo, I immediately called Daniel to find out how Juan had been that day. I couldn't detect any alarm in Daniel's voice; he indicated that Juan was doing well. "Richard, he was just a little quiet today," he said, again reassuring me, "It is nowhere near Juan's time to die. Don't worry." Daniel also related that Amanda had received a call from Juan's nurse, Jenny, who thought I should be with Juan. I informed Daniel that my intentions were to go anyway. He said, "Richard, you really shouldn't go now; it's too late." Nevertheless, I insisted that I intended to see Juan, no matter what time it was. I became disturbed once I hung up. I couldn't figure out why Jenny would call Amanda if Juan was well. Suddenly, the phone rang, and upon answering, I heard Amanda say, "Oh, good, Richard, you are home…I was afraid you were going to be gone overnight, and if you didn't answer, I was about to call every hotel and motel in Galena to find you." She reiterated that Jenny felt I should be with Juan. I explained that Daniel didn't mention that Juan was doing poorly, but that I still intended to go to the hospital. We hung up and I was confused…a little concerned…but in no way frightened. Nothing would happen to Juan.

With no traffic, Hines Hospital is less than a ten-minute drive. I phoned Matt to tell him I was going to see Juan, and left. It never entered my mind this could be something serious since Juan had already won so many battles. I had originally intended to stop for cigarettes, but my mind suddenly began telling me, or maybe it was my heart—get there now, get to Juan! The few minutes seemed like an eternity as I sped to the hospital, and my mind kept repeating, *Nothing can happen! No, not to my beautiful Juan! Not after eighteen years!* My mind flashed back to the first time I laid eyes on him. Never in my wildest dreams had I ever imagined that so beautiful a love and closeness could develop between two men. Especially after that first bizarre meeting....

Chapter One:
The Meetings

When I recall that relentless rush of blood that coursed through my body and created the enormous appetite for sex, I'd like to blame it on the heat. Others would say I was just horny. So there I was on a sultry June 9, 1974 evening, driving downtown to see what I could do about it. The Trip was one of Chicago's more popular gentlemen bars. It stood on Ohio Street off Rush in a Victorian mansion next door to Pizzeria Uno, and featured three floors of varied entertainment. I had been there a few times and found it much to my liking because not only were the majority of customers attractive, high-caliber professionals, but I truly enjoyed the female singers who performed there.

Since I was recently divorced, and because my place was too small, a graduation party for my two daughters was held at my sister Deena's. Martina was a high school graduate, and Jacque had graduated from grade school. My twenty-year old son, Michael, had driven the girls and my sixteen-year-old son, Nicky, to my sister's, which worked out great since I had planned on going out afterwards, and especially because The Trip was only a half hour drive.

It had been wonderful seeing my father and the family, and I chuckled as I thought of Deena and Pa's comments after I had said, "Well, everyone's gone and I am off to party because I do not have to work tomorrow." Deena, innocently naïve about the ways of the world, couldn't understand why I wanted to go out so late, while Pa complained at length, finally remarking, "Richie, you a crazy!" As usual, my brother-in-law, Dino, just winked.

I felt I needed this playtime since the divorce and the whole chain of events had left me in a tremendous depression. Coupled with this was a creeping feeling of uncertainty and anxiety, for I had consented to the divorce because I felt it would give me a chance to find out about the other me I had fantasized about. I already knew mine was not one of those everyday divorces. Eleven years earlier, I discovered that my wife had been having an affair with Remo, my sister Geena's husband. At the time, it caused quite a blow to my closely-knit family life. Geena and I tried to make our marriages work during those years by avoiding each other in order not to discuss the infidelities of our respective spouses. My father actually knew about the affair when it was exposed, but turned a blind eye to it. Family was always very important to him. I'm certain that my mother, who died years after, never suspected. Friends told me that in some Italian families, people would have been shot for this, or at least have had their legs broken, but not in the Mella family.

I was aware that my personality could never accept something as final, and that it would take something very drastic to make me realize the tragedy that had befallen me. My failure to accept the situation only meant it would prey on my mind until the pain became unbearable. I actually tried to believe our divorce was only temporary, giving us a chance to get our heads together. Then I would realize that the other life had only been a fantasy, and not for me. We would certainly remarry. My rude awakening arrived the day after our divorce had been granted when I discovered that my lecherous brother-in-law, who had already divorced Geena, moved into my home. I immediately called my ex-wife, demanding an explanation for submitting my children to such an arrangement, only to throw the phone against the wall once she had nastily informed me that I no longer had any say in her household! And now they were soon to be married.

I had had sex with men before, but it confused me because I always hated myself afterwards. I couldn't stop thinking that, had Joan not been unfaithful, had she paid attention to my sexual needs instead of thinking only of her own, I might never have turned to those desires, or even thought of them. Nevertheless, I needed to be wanted, to be loved, and the fantasy of this other me allowed a brief moment of how it might be. Yet, I always found it to be a pocket of cheap, empty tricks. However, the desire grew stronger and drove me on. I'd ask myself why I was doing it, and swear it wouldn't happen again, but never able to sustain that oath.

I wanted to believe there was someone out there. Someone who'd make me realize that it wasn't wrong. There had to be; otherwise, why had God given me these strong desires? I had certainly prayed hard enough to stop them, if they were stoppable, but whenever I asked for the strength and will power to shake them off my mind, they only became more intense.

Being a Sunday night, parking was no problem, and when I climbed the long staircase of the once ornate mansion and walked into the bar, I found it to be as deserted as the street had been—quite a contrast to the standing room only Saturday night crowds. Only two couples were in the place, and they were seated in the loft of the main lounge. On busy nights, there'd be an entertainer performing on the loft. To the left was a small dance floor; I had always assumed that it was purposely designed as a rectangular gazebo since parson benches were facing each other along the two trellis-lined walls. It was never surprising seeing a few making out on the benches, while others danced to the music they had chosen on the jukebox located at the far end of the gazebo. Tonight, the benches and floor were empty. My last alternative was to head for the third floor bar.

Things looked a little brighter upstairs; every spot was occupied along the large, oval-shaped bar, a smattering of patrons standing in various areas. Still, it seemed very quiet. I ordered a Coke, and ended up leaning against a pillar of the entranceway. As I glanced around, it became obvious that my chances of tying up with someone might be slim since everyone seemed to be already paired off. So there I was, facing another disappointing night, realizing that I would be too afraid to talk to any of them for fear that they would not reply. So why was I there? I didn't want to drink alcohol since I had a thirty-mile ride home ahead of me, and I wasn't a drinker anyway. I surmised that if I had a drink or two, I might loosen up a bit, and not just stand like a zombie.

It was the same every time I went out! I would have to hope someone was attracted to me, and that he would do the pursuing. I was confused. I was the life of the party whenever I was with my family, and I never had to drink! Why was I so nervous and tense in a gay bar?

Despite sporadic outbursts of laughter, the room was still a little too quiet. Thoughts of Monday morning prevailed. I nursed my Coke. Suddenly, on the other side of the bar, I spotted someone who certainly didn't appear to be bothered that the next day was Monday. Glowing like a star, he was definitely shades of Saturday night! His happy movements made it immediately apparent that he was feeling no pain. He had a way of raising his arms slightly above his shoulders to make him appear to be dancing to imaginary music. I was mesmerized. He seemed so happy, moving mischievously from one person to another to chat. Though I couldn't hear a word, it was apparent that he was talking up a storm.

However, I could hear his laughter, and it was a nice laugh, a catchy one that brought others to laughter, too. I didn't know where he had come from because I hadn't seen him when I first scanned the bar. Yet it was obvious that he had been there for some time.

I could not believe the glow from this man! The lighting was low, and I had to be at least twenty-five feet from him, yet the fantastic light blue of his eyes and the deep cleft in his chin stood out like Emerald City! Of course, the wonderful laugh and smile only added to the enchantment. He looked so regal! As I took in every part of him, I became convinced that he was the perfect man. His straight, brown hair parted on the left and grown slightly over his ears was right in style, along with his longer sideburns. High cheekbones on a square-shaped face, with an oh-so-slightly upward tip to his nose, completed the incredible impression that this man made. I found myself completely captivated; his full lips seemed so playfully mischievous when he smiled and laughed. He appeared at attention, but at the same time looked so relaxed. Very well built, he looked a bit shorter than me, at about five foot ten and a half. Blue had to be his color because the light blue jeans and navy shirt really brought out the sparkle in his light blue eyes.

I couldn't believe the feeling going through my body! Here was someone I had to meet! He was having a grand time, and it was rubbing off on me! His laughter continued as clear as a bell. Every now and then, he'd happily raise his arms and move them, sometimes to the music, sometimes unaccompanied. What I found appealing was the fact that those movements of his came off as being masculine, with a bit of daring.

I had to meet him, but how was I going to do it? He was so busy having a good time. How was he going to notice me? I certainly couldn't raise my arms and sway to the music; I'd never come off looking as good as him. If I stood on my toes to be seen, I'd undoubtedly look like an idiot. So how was he going to notice me? After all, I knew I was not unattractive, with my slightly receding, wavy brown hair, dark brown eyes, and warm smile. At forty-three, I still had a boyish look. In fact, it was often guessed that I was ten or more years younger, and I certainly acted it. If one wanted to compare me to someone well known, it had been said I was a cross between Jack Lemmon and Burt Reynolds. Though it seemed like such an unlikely combination, it was probably because my boyish charm reminded them of Lemmon and my build of Reynolds. Frankly, it never mattered to me; I was satisfied with myself. However, I still had not changed to the current mode of dress; there I was, the ultimate suburbanite—polyester, powder blue pants, contrasting shirt, and blue and white dress shoes. And I guess I thought I looked sharp! Despite my apprehensions about looking like an idiot, I stood on my tippy toes and swayed to the music, but to no avail.

He was charming the hell out of me and he never realized it! Then it happened! He was talking with one guy, a rugged, bald-headed type whom I felt to be unworthy of him. *Aw no!* I thought, *he's too old for him*, although the guy was probably younger than I was. The fact was that I was jealous because he was giving him so much attention. I wanted the attention, but he didn't even know I was in the room. Then, feeling as though my prayers had been answered, I saw him head for my side of the bar and towards me! To my wide-eyed disappointment, he continued toward the restroom, and never looked my way. At least now, however, it was possible to make myself known; all I had to do was get up the nerve to follow him into the restroom. I took a deep breath and took off after him.

The restroom, which I had never been in before, was extremely small. A sink was immediately facing me, and a stool and urinal were just to the right, making it a tight, cozy area. There he was, standing in front of the stool, relieving himself and appearing quite content. He seemed oblivious to my presence, though I was no more than a breath away. I suddenly became very nervous since I had not expected such small quarters, and I almost left in spite of the fact that I had met my objective.

But I realized that would seem even more conspicuous, and since I was there, I should do what was expected—face the urinal and do my own business. I kept my eyes fixed on the wall in front of me, listening to his soft sighs of relief, and careful to keep my head from turning in his direction.

I felt there was time since he had been drinking a lot of beer, yet I became more nervous with each second. I realized I had to speak before he left the room, but I didn't know what to say. He finished his business, zipped up, and turned to leave.

Still oblivious to my presence, it was now or never. Without thinking I said, "I bet if you were sober, you wouldn't go with that guy." He turned in my direction, stepped up to me, and planted a big, long, sloppy one, smack-dab on the lips. After taking his lips from mine, he stood back and stared into my face, still without uttering a word. Then, almost in an all-in-a-day's work stride, he left. I couldn't believe it really happened, until I tasted beer and cigarettes and looked down and realized that I had wet my pants! I tried to pat it dry, but gave up. I couldn't lose him now.

I ran out to the bar; disappointment and gloom descended upon me as I looked for him. He was gone! And to make matters worse, so was the bald guy! I'd never see him again, I was sure of it. But then as I thought about it, I felt he was like a beautiful butterfly or bumblebee lighting beside me briefly, and I smiled….

Rushing to the hospital, my mind flashed to the Saturday evening, two weeks after that bizarre meeting and I smiled as I recalled how beautiful it had been….

I was angry with myself as I drove to The Trip after the performance. I couldn't believe I had forgotten so many lines in the play. I tried to appease this anger by telling myself I didn't really forget them because I didn't know them in the first place. I really hadn't had enough rehearsal time. I had been cast to replace the lead only one week before appearing in it, and had won the part on the merits of my recent performance in the title role of *Man of LaMancha*, for which I received rave reviews. I didn't receive the script until three days before I was to open, and had only been allowed one afternoon for rehearsal.

Taking all those impediments into consideration, I had ample reason to go easy on myself, but it still bothered me. So I had decided on spending the entire next day working on my lines. But tonight was Saturday evening, and I was going to party!

It was June twenty-second, and because of my preoccupation with other matters, I hadn't really given much thought to that bizarre kiss, but I did chuckle upon thinking of the pants. In fact, I was happy that I was kept busy, because I certainly did not want the sensations of lost opportunity to prey on my mind. I knew that my chances of seeing him again were very slim, and if I started to obsess about finding him and didn't, I would only have more depression, and I certainly didn't need more of that.

The show lounge was packed, and I realized why when I saw that Andie Cahill was the night's singer. Each time she performed, guys went wild after every song, and this night was no aberration from the pattern. I finally made my way to the bar, but found it impossible to get the bartender's attention. I finally gave up and began moving behind the customers seated at the bar to get a better view of the show.

Tonight, I wanted a cocktail. I was just about to yell out to the bartender when the guy seated on a stool directly in front of me turned his head to watch the show.

Oh, my God! I thought, *It's him!*

I couldn't believe it! It *was* him! The bartender finally nodded for my order, but I found it impossible to speak. There was a mounting sense of mystery in the air, and I was certain that the spell would be broken if I so much as called for a bourbon and water. I did realize, however, that I had to eventually open my mouth if I wanted a drink.

He was wearing light blue jeans and a navy shirt again, and it was evident that he was totally unaware that I was next to him. And there I was, wearing my suburbia best polyester, white pants and flowered shirt, and white dress shoes!

I began wishing for a drink to control my nerves; the trembling throughout my body was as severe as it had been that night in the restroom. I finally thought, *For God's sake, you did it that time, and you got a kiss*, and that thought encouraged me to remark, "It looks like you're sober tonight." Somewhat bewildered, he turned completely around to face me, and asked, "Why do you say *thot?*"

His response added another dimension to him. Not only was he the best-looking guy I had ever seen, but he also had a beautiful accent, and a deep resonance in his voice.

He smiled, waiting for an answer, and I explained what had happened two weeks earlier. Not wanting to scare him off by being too talky, I shut my mouth and waited for his reaction. He glared at me rather teasingly as he slowly placed his hand to his chest; his expression indicated that this was his playful manner of appearing embarrassed, and finally, almost in coquettish awe, he asked, "I did *thot?*"

I smiled and nodded. His hand remaining firmly on his chest, he continued with his facetious innocence, "I don' believe *it!* I did thot?"

I laughed and answered, "You did! In fact, I tasted the beer all the way home and got drunk on it. Or maybe it was your kiss." He seemed to be pleased and entertained by that, and began laughing with that catchy cackle in his throat that I remembered. I joined in, and as the conversation and laughter continued, I soon discovered that he had a gift for charming and making people laugh. He got me to laugh as long and as hard as him at each joke, even when it wasn't funny.

The drinks I had ordered arrived, and as I reached for my wallet, he motioned for the bartender to take from his change on the bar. "My name's Rick, what's yours?" I asked.

"My name is Juan," he answered, pronouncing the *j* as a strong *h*.

What a wonderful-sounding voice he has, I thought, as we shook hands, *I could listen to him forever!*

His handshake was firm and manly, yet smooth and warm. I actually found myself getting drawn in merely from listening to him talk excitedly about the style and personality of the singer. He spoke quickly and gestured continually; it was impossible not to be fascinated by the excitement that he generated. I felt very comfortable since hand gestures had always been part of my conversational style, too. The joy I experienced from simply watching and listening to him was amazing; he was like an excited little boy.

He proudly told me that he was from Buenos Aires, Argentina. "First, we moved to Philadelphia in 1960, ond one year later, we come to live in Chicago," he explained, his wonderful accent lending excitement to each word.

I explained that I had been raised in Chicago, and that I was now living in a western suburb. "My name is really Richard, but Rick stuck after some girls in grade school began using it. My family stills calls me Rich or Richie."

"Well, I will call you Recharred because I think it is a better name," he said with a smile after a moment of thought, "Is thot okay?"

"It's fine with me," I replied, happily thinking that he had a friendship between us in mind. I also noticed that each time he said my name, he emphasized the *chard,* almost saying *charred,* and pronouncing the *i* as a long *e*… Re-charred! I liked it! In fact, I loved it! It quickly became apparent that he had no hard *a's* in his vocabulary.

I ordered another round of drinks. It was obvious that he was a fast drinker; four beers had been downed since I first found myself standing behind him, and now he was showing a buzz. He flashed a big smile and asked if I would like to dance, which took me by complete surprise! I explained that I had been dancing since six years old, but that I had never danced with a man. "Aw, Recharred, you got to dance," he pleaded, "It is so much fun! C'mon, let us go up ond disco!"

He wouldn't give up, even with my obvious reluctance. "Do you know thot they took out the big bar on the third floor, ond now thar is a large disco floor instead," he said excitedly. "I am anxious to see it because tonight is opening night."

I had not been this excited about being with someone since I had dated my wife, and I certainly was not going to mess it up by refusing to dance just because he was a man. "Okay, let's go up and see what they did."

He jumped up, absolutely enthralled, and while raising his arms in the same manner I remembered seeing him do so often that first evening, shouted, "Cha, cha, cha!" His smile continued, as well as the gestures, going up the stairway.

Amazingly, the enormous oval-shaped bar was gone; instead, against a wall, a small service bar now stood. In the middle of the new slick dance floor were *go-go boys,* dancing on a raised, round platform. Everyone glowed from the black lights hanging from the ceiling. Though there were quite a few people on the dance floor, it was not overly crowded. Juan continued his happy chatter once we settled on the sidelines.

"Rock Your Baby" began playing, and Juan beckoned me to dance, commenting that he loved the song. So out to the floor we went. I was a bit apprehensive, but once we got into the rhythm of the music, I felt very much at ease. This was the first time I danced with a man, and this comfortability probably stemmed from pride at having Juan as a partner, especially since he was very handsome and not in the least feminine. Besides, hand and body contact was not required in disco dancing. I was amazed at how beautifully Juan's eyes lit up from the black lights. They were shining like stars! And he appeared to look just as happy as I was.

The inviting mix of songs kept us on the floor for some time, and I was pleased that his rhythm complemented the intricate steps I came up with during "Don't Rock The Boat." He had a way of turning his head from side to side, and holding it to show his profile, and I almost felt he was teasing me with it. In fact it was working, especially during "Rock Your Baby." There I was, actually dancing with a man and I wasn't feeling guilty!

We had to be a hysterical sight since both of us continued with hand gestures throughout the evening. I had never been with someone as funny and witty as him. Everything he had to say was interesting, so much so that I wanted to hear more. He especially brought me to hysterical laughter once he began mimicking people. The nellie queens were mince-meat for him. He had such a talent!

Juan then mentioned that he was presently going through a divorce, and that he had a four-year-old daughter named Svetmana. I then related to him my story. When I recounted the infamous saga of my wife and brother-in-law, he again placed his hand to his chest and exclaimed in awe, "She did thot...I don' believe it! She really did?"

Following my bit of confession, Juan admitted to an equally tragic marital situation. His wife had been cheating on him, but especially with a particular Colombian fellow. Though he was deeply engrossed in telling his tale, he still insisted we go out on the floor once "Rock Your Baby" played again.

The evening continued with dancing, drinking, and a tremendous amount of fun! I had never drunk so much in my life, but I was doing fine because the dancing was wearing off the effects. I was certain that Juan was having two drinks for every one of mine. I also noticed that, as he drank more, his voice changed to a different tone and quality. Instead of resonating with that deep romantic energy and quick pace, his voice slowed down and sounded almost boyish. In these moments he became *adorable*.

The evening came to an end much too soon as last call came over the speaker. Juan insisted on having one more. However, the lights came up and the music stopped just as we got our drinks and we immediately heard the disc jockey's voice wishing everyone a safe trip home. Juan quickly began downing his beer, but I figured I should pass on mine since I wouldn't have a chance to dance it off. Juan was a bit reluctant about leaving, and voiced his objection to it, but when the announcement sounded again, we were forced to head for the stairway. It was apparent that when Juan was having a good time, he did not want it to end.

I desperately wanted Juan to come to my house, but I didn't know how to ask. I remembered, however, as we were walking down the stairs, that he had mentioned that he did not have a car, so I offered him a ride. "Yes, I would like a ride, Recharred. Thot will be very nice of you." I had to think where I had parked the car, once we were out of the building, and began edging in different directions, trying to get my bearings. Finally, I remembered, and beckoned him in that direction. Juan was feeling no pain, and continued to raise his arms in that inimitable way of his, moving to an imaginable beat. He actually made me want to join in, but I realized that I'd never be able to do it as well as him. He had a charming, yet mischievous way of moving his body. And he definitely did not come off as effeminate. He was sort of a mix between the *Zorba* and *Fiddler* characters.

Arriving at my car, Juan said, "Recharred, I 'ave to pee bodly!" So *pee* he did, right there in full view! I tried to make it not look so obvious by standing back to back with him, but that looked even more ridiculous. He could have cared less if anyone saw him.

I was glad when we finally got into the car, and as I drove out of the lot, I finally got up enough nerve to ask, "Would you like to come over to my house tonight, Juan?"

"I thought you would never ask, Recharred," he answered, "but you know you will 'ave to drive me home tomorrow morning because I 'ave somewhere to go with my parents." Relieved and content, I told him it would be no problem, and we were off on the thirty-five-mile homebound drive.

I wasn't happy that I was living in such a small place, especially since I had been so used to the grand manner of my eight-room Dutch Colonial home with two fireplaces. This new dwelling, however, which I termed "the dungeon," had served its purpose during the divorce proceedings. I had just bought the building for my barber shop and it conveniently included a small apartment in the basement. The two miniature bedrooms reminded me of prison solitary confinements; solid concrete walls and floors adorned them. Together, they did not measure as large as the bathroom and kitchen. In fact, the bathroom was arguably the most pleasant room in the place since it had a window overlooking the gravel pavement of an alley. I did have another window in the kitchen, but an air conditioner occupied all the light area. One of the amenities was that at least the concrete floors in the kitchen and bathroom were covered with tile. And I hastily had placed carpeting in the cells. I had been using one cell for a closet, and the other constituted my living and sleeping quarters. A thirty-inch daybed, a small table, a lamp, and a television adorned this room. My beautiful cherry wood chest, a piece from my marital bedroom, was placed in the so-called closet.

I had been irked when my wife said it was wonderful and convenient that I had an apartment in the building, and that it would be perfect during the divorce proceedings. I had decorated the place fairly well, but after living in the beautiful house I had built, it was as though I had moved into the slums. And I soon discovered that there is nothing worse than lying down on a narrow cot looking up cement walls and a six-and-a-half-foot high ceiling! But on this night, I did not want to think of the nights and days I lay there, crying, after my divorce. No, tonight, someone was coming home with me that made me forget these problems.

There wasn't a lapse in conversation as we talked about the evening, and it was wonderful listening to Juan's squishy slur. "May I put on the Spanish station, Recharred?" he asked. "I love the music so much because it reminds me of my 'ome in Argentina."

"Of course, I love Spanish music," I answered. His musical movements resumed while explaining the meaning of the words, that is, until the alcohol began taking its toll, and he started dozing off.

I felt a bit apprehensive approaching my building for fear someone would see me coming home late with a man. Complications were unlikely, however, since I lived in the business area, which was dead after nine o'clock. Juan awoke after I nudged him gently, and, like a little boy popping up in bed, brightly exclaimed, "We are 'ere ot last…good, Recharred!"

He followed me to the door, holding his arms up over his shoulders and moving in that happy manner of his. I felt certain that he'd have some kind of comment about the dungeon once we got inside. Instead, he continued talking excitedly and happily. Suddenly, he stopped talking and looked into my eyes. After a moment, he moved slowly towards me and gently put his lips to mine. This time, it was different from the first time. This time, it was not pretentious or impulsive; there was meaning. A broad, manly chest, with just the right amount of hair working itself out from the center, revealed itself when he took off his shirt. I rubbed my hand slowly and gently over his arms, and as firm as his body was, his skin was as smooth as velvet. I did not feel it was wrong; I felt God had sent Juan to me, and that it was right….

I lay myself down on the soft carpeting, cuddling my pillow. Juan had fallen asleep, but I was wide-eyed. There I was watching as he lay on his stomach, so peaceful. He slept so quietly that I began leaning towards him to be certain he was breathing. I was astonished at how good I felt. Totally absent were the usual feelings of guilt, the impending, pervasive desire for that sleeping partner to be gone. I was bewildered; this was the first time I had ever felt good after lovemaking with a man. I didn't know what to make of it; I just continued to watch him sleep, so quietly…until I must have fallen asleep, too.

It seemed as though I had just closed my eyes when I heard, "C'mon, Recharred, it is time to wake up!" Juan was at the doorway, dressed and smiling. I realized it had to be morning because I could glimpse a stream of daylight reflecting from the bathroom window into the kitchen.

"You are up already," I said. "Did you take a shower?"

"I took one while you were asleep, Recharred," Juan answered. "I am going somewhere with my mother ond father today ond I did not want to get up too late."

I quickly slipped on my pants, concerned he might feel somewhat apprehensive in my dungeon now that he was sober; I had to somehow prove to him that I was not Jack the Ripper. "C'mon, Juan, I want to show you my place of business. It's just upstairs."

I had just bought the building and moved my shop into it from a rental location that I had been in for years. I had remodeled these new quarters into a beautiful, quaint four-chair barbershop, and had also combined an arts and crafts gallery with it. I had already been displaying works from members of the local art league in my other shop, and decided upon utilizing the extra space and making it into a real gallery. I had color-coordinated everything: Matte black for the shelving, which had been left behind by the old shoe repair shop…cork-designed wallpaper for the gallery area…earth-tone carpeting…green porcelain, vintage chairs with golden brown Naugahyde…green sinks…a beautiful back-bar with green silk plants across the cornice of it, and golden brown mosaic-designed linoleum in the cutting area.

Juan was enthralled, and sighed, "Recharred, this place is absolutely bea-u-ti-ful! You did all this work?"

"Well, I did the decorating, not the artwork. I invite local artists to display their work and get a small commission if they're sold. I don't really make any money to speak of, but it's good exposure for them, and gives my customers a chance to do something other than read."

"Thot's a great idea, Recharred," Juan remarked, pointing to two pen and ink abstracts. "I would like to buy these two pictures."

"You would? Great!" I exclaimed, "I'll deduct my ten percent because I don't want to make money off you."

I took a shower while Juan prepared breakfast. He had insisted since I had all the ingredients needed for his special omelet. He seemed especially anxious for me to taste its moistness and its flavor. I was transfixed in watching his meticulous manner of preparing food once I came out of the shower. Each time he chopped an ingredient, he carefully wiped up the entire area. And by the time the meal was ready, it looked as though we had sent out for breakfast. If I had been doing the cooking in a hurry, the stove and counter would have been a disaster area.

I was amazed at the pleasant mood he was in! I certainly would not have been able to get out of bed if I had drank as much as he. There he was, moving to the Spanish music on the radio.

His careful blending and seasoning of potatoes, tomatoes, onions, eggs, cheese, mushrooms, and sausage reached new culinary achievement. It was a mouth-watering delight. What also fascinated me was his manner of eating; his mastery in handling a mere fork and knife was remarkable. Besides captivating me with his non-stop conversation, I had never seen such a masculine person eat so elegantly. I felt privileged just to sit at a table with him. It was even a treat watching him do the dishes he had insisted on doing.

A beautiful, bright, and sunny day was there before us as we hurried out, absolutely perfect for the beach in Chicago to study my script. I certainly didn't want to go back to my apartment, especially since I knew how gloomy it would seem in comparison to how bright it had been with Juan there. After telling me that he lived around 4300 south in the Lithuanian neighborhood of Brighten Park, we were on our way.

Juan appeared to be puzzled while looking out at the unfamiliar landscape, and asked where we were. I explained that we were in Staterville, and informed him that we had about a thirty-mile drive, assuring him that it would not take long since I was taking the Stevenson expressway.

"Whot are those papers you 'ave thar, Recharred?" he asked, pointing to the bunch I had placed on the rear seat..

Recalling my fiasco at the theatre, I replied, "That's my script and I'm gonna spend the entire day at the lake working on my lines. I don't want to screw up again tonight. I hate putting on makeup; at the lake, I can get a tan while working on my lines."

After a moment, Juan smiled. "So you are on actor!" he said, emphasizing the "tor."

"And a singer," I boasted. I told him I had always dreamed of becoming a movie star, and that my wife and I agreed that I should pursue a singing career since that often led to the movies. "We'd frequent cocktail lounges that held talent competitions in hopes I might be discovered. Of course, we'd get home in the wee hours, and once Joan got pregnant and began suffering from morning and evening sickness, she had no desire to go sit in a bar to hear me sing." I told how I tried going on my own, that is, until her mood swings and verbal abuse made it impossible.

"It's true, Juan, as I was going out the door, she'd actually scream until drool began falling from her mouth! It really affected me; I couldn't concentrate on my singing when I arrived at the bar. So I stopped going, and gave up my dreams of stardom. In fact, Juan, the only singing I did for twelve years was at family parties and church choir. And she even managed to make me miserable every time I was about to leave for choir rehearsal because she despised the reality of my one-hour weekly commitment. In 1964, she finally agreed to allow me to audition for *My Fair Lady* at a community college production, and I was cast in the chorus." I went on to explain that the director needed someone who could dance, and cast me in the character role of *Karpathy*, which was right up my alley.

"The musical had not yet been released to professional stock companies and a producer from an outdoor theatre had come to see our production because he had received the rights to do it that summer. So you know what happened after our production closed? Our leading lady called. She had auditioned for *Eliza* at the professional company but failed to get the role. She then told me the producer mentioned that he was only interested in one person from our show—namely, me! Well, you can imagine my excitement since I knew Ray Milland was scheduled to do the lead. I decided not to tell my wife that I was going to the auditions. And then the producer recognized me immediately and offered the role before I even auditioned! So, Juan, I had to think of what I was going to tell her. I finally decided to say that the producer had called my director for my number and then called the shop to offer me the role. In a way, it was the truth, for our leading lady had called me. I can't tell you how much I had to beg before she finally agreed."

I again excused myself for going on about myself. "No, no, Recharred, it is very interesting, especially hearing thot you were in a play with a movie star," he reassured me, rolling those *R's* again. I continued, explaining that I would hire a sitter so Joan could accompany me to all of the performances during the three-week run.

"She really hit it off well with the producer. They played gin rummy backstage every night during the show. Do you know he really thought I was star material? In the program, it read: *a man that has many grains of stardust sprinkled over him!*" It's true, Juan! In fact, about seven years later, my wife told me that she had to tell me something that had bothered her conscience for years."

It was apparent Juan was hanging on my every word because he kept egging me on. "Well, she told me that Herb had begun praising my talent during one of their games, truly believing that I was star material, and that he then went on to tell her that he was selling the theater after the season and heading out to California to produce. He then told her he was taking one of the young singers of the chorus along, and that he would very much like to take me too! He bluntly asked if she would allow me to go after informing her that it meant I would have to leave her, the kids, and my business for a while. She explained that he promised to promote me to the best of his ability, but could not give any guarantees. So, her answer to him was an emphatic 'No!'"

Juan glared at me in disbelief.

"I don' believe it, Recharred! You mean he never asked you or said anything about it to you? Aw, Recharred, really?" Juan shook his head in disbelief and sighed, "Aw, no, Recharred, she should 'ave allowed him to osk you, so you could make the decision, especially since both of you had agreed upon it before you were married. I con understand thot she probably did not like to be separated because I also would not like a separation, but she should 'ave allowed you to make the decision."

"Exactly, because she knew me, that I would have somehow made sure my family came, too. They were too important to me!"

My wife's long-term affair came to mind. Suddenly, something dawned on me. "That's it, Juan! I never thought of it! This all happened after her initial affair with my brother-in-law had been exposed! She realized I would insist on taking the family because I had always been talking about going to California. Yes, she did not want to go because it meant she would have to leave him!"

Juan looked at me coyly and asked, "Whot did you do when she told you?"

"What was I to do or say? It was seven years after! If I had been aware of the whole truth then, I may have strangled her, especially if I had known that she was still carrying on with my brother-in-law."

Juan laughed, and because of the contagious catch in the back of his throat and his repeated imitation of my words, I could not help joining in. I had never seen anyone laugh so hard and so beautifully!

After calming down, I asked if his divorce was final yet. "It is in the process now, Recharred; we 'ave not yet settled everything. My wife, Endira, is from

Honduras ond was here on visa to go to school. I met her in the library of the university because I am a librarian thar. Well, I fell in love with her ond just before she had to leave, because her visa had expired, we got married. So then she did not 'ave to return to Honduras because I am a citizen of this country now."

"Why did you decide to get a divorce, Juan?" I asked.

"Well, Recharred, Endira likes to spend money even if she does not 'ave it, ond only likes to buy from expensive stores. So she bought all her clothes ond the furniture from these places, ond I did not make enough money to pay all the bills. But whot really bothered me was not thot, because I also do not know how to manage money."

A noticeable trace of anger became apparent.

"But whot really bothered me was thot Endira was cheating on me continuously. I could not take it anymore, especially after we had a big fight ond she left the house, ond I found out later thot she spent the night with a guy she had been seeing, someone from Colombia!"

"How did you know that she slept with him?"

"It came out from one of her girlfriends, ond then she finally admitted it," his voice wavering. "Thot is one thing I cannot take, Recharred, disloyalty. It gave me continued doubts!"

I decided to change the subject, especially since I did not want us to part on a down note. Our time together had been too beautiful. "Well, my wife is finally marrying my brother-in-law this coming Friday, and she is gonna have a wedding dinner at a hotel for her family and my kids. I know, because my youngest daughter, Jacque, is all excited about getting a new dress.

There was silence for a moment.

"Can you imagine, we were a family all those years, and they didn't even think to invite me!" We burst into laughter, and I was glad that that seemed to pick up his spirits. He laughed even more when I said I considered calling their hotel to cancel the dinner reservations.

"You know, Recharred, I will soon be going on a trip to visit my sister ond her family in Quito, Ecuador," he said after giving final directions, "ond I am gonna take my mother ond daughter, too." Apparently a commodity broker friend had given him money to invest, and twenty thousand dollars was made on the stock. He then added that money was made to be spent, and that he was going to enjoy himself in doing it. "Besides, my mother ond I 'ave not seen my sister since she moved thar after having her baby boy. Her husband was from thar, ond she has never seen my daughter." I felt happy for him, but disappointed that he would be gone for a few weeks.

I asked him his age, and he replied that his birthday was the very next day, the twenty-fourth, and that he was going to be thirty-one. I was a bit reluctant revealing my age; I usually took off four years whenever someone new asked me. However, I had said so many dates and ages already that I had to tell the truth.

Sensing my self-consciousness, he said, "Recharred, whot is the matter with forty-three? Don' be ashamed of your age. You should be proud thot you don't look it. You look *my* age; besides, I prefer mature people to young kids!"

We exchanged phone numbers. I explained that my phone was an extension of the shop, "So you can reach me during the day, too."

Above his work number was his last name. "Sur-se-di-ci-us," I said slowly, a few times, trying to get the right pronunciation. Then, in a sudden burst, I had it—"Sursedicius!"

"My dear mon, I don' believe it!" he exclaimed, holding his hand to his chest in awe, "You are the first one, the very first to cor-rect-ly pronounce my last name!"

I told him I was also proficient in detecting national origins by listening to accents.

But his name puzzled me. "Your name ends in *s* and I could easily think you're Greek, but you're not. You're from Argentina, yet the name doesn't sound Spanish."

"You're right, Recharred, I was born in Lithuania," he replied. "My mother ond father fled Lithuania when I was a baby, when the Russians marched in. My father hurried home from work one day and told my mother we had to leave right away for Germany!" Pausing, and then chuckling, he added, "My mother always told me we left with a pot boiling on the stove!"

He continued, "We fled to Italy ond lived thar for six months, then Switzerland for a short time, ond finally to Germany. My sister was born in Germany ond we stayed thar for over four years. Finally, Recharred, we moved to Argentina ond thot is where I started school. I loved it thar ond did not want to leave my friends, but my father was 'aving so much trouble finding work. The economy was as bad as the politics, so we came to America ond lived with some relatives in Philadelphia for almost a year ond a half. Finally, Recharred, we came to Chicago in 1961. My father was a brewmaster, but found it impossible to get a position here. Finally, he got a job at a printing machine manufacturer. You know, Recharred, for a long time, I was the only one working in the family."

I was amazed! "Boy, you really have had quite a life, living in so many countries! That's so wonderful! How many languages do you speak?" Besides English, he spoke fluent Spanish and Lithuanian, and a little Russian. I had taken two years of Italian in high school, and I still could not speak it. "Everyone in my family always answered my parents in English whenever they spoke in Italian."

"Thot was too bad, Recharred. Do your parents still speak Italian?"

"Well, my ma died in 1968. She and my dad hadn't spoken it regularly for years. Only a few lines here and there. You would've liked my ma. She was a very warm woman, and a fantastic cook! She was completely devoted to her family. I was the baby of the family, and there were many times I stayed home with her when she was sick, and from her bed, she'd call out the ingredients that I had to add to a pan. Between her and my wife, I really learned how to make a great spaghetti sauce.

"My dad lost his strong accent, but she didn't, and probably because she never learned to read or write. Because of this, she could never get interested in many of the things going on in the world, yet she was the moving force of the family, and could never do enough. You know, Juan, I will never forget the times I'd ask why she didn't go to school in Italy. I'd always hear the same thing—'Wella, Richie, the day the schoola she starta, she was a snow.'" Juan cracked up.

Juan told me to turn left and let him out across from the church. "I con walk the couple of blocks to my house, Recharred." Mass had just ended; the street was swarming with people. I double-parked the car and looked at Juan, smiled, and said, "Well, it has been nice, really nice!'

I wondered if I'd ever see him again, understanding his reason for getting off at the corner. I knew, however, that I probably would have done the same.

"Thank you so much for your hospitality, Recharred," he said, taking hold of my hand and shaking it as though we had just completed a business deal, "It was very generous of you, ond I had a wonderful time!" He reached into the back seat for his pictures and started for the sidewalk. I called out, "Have a happy birthday, Juan!"

He turned, smiled, and waved, but it was apparent that he was a bit nervous someone he knew might see him, and he hurried on his way. I wanted to follow him to make sure he hadn't given me a fake address, but I realized that would not be right. I watched him walk down the sidewalk—his shoulders back, his arms swinging to and fro! He had a nice walk, a nice build, and I sat there mesmerized until he disappeared into the crowd; at the same time, I was trying to figure out why I was not feeling guilty, when I was startled suddenly by a loud beep of a car. I drove on, turned at the corner, and went on my way.

I could not believe the reality of it all, that I had spent an entire evening and morning with someone as handsome as Juan. The thought of his eyes glistening in the sun lingered on in my mind. What had made it even more thrilling was that with all those good looks, he was also the funniest and most charming person I had ever met. Not only was he sexually wonderful, thinking of my needs as well as his own, but I wasn't sorry afterwards. Most importantly, he had erased my depression. Throughout the day, I wondered if I'd ever see him again.

Prologue: Continued

As I entered the parking area of Hines Hospital, I refused to believe that Juan was in critical condition. In fact, I was sure that if anything was seriously wrong, it would certainly pass, as all the other alarming moments had. Parking was no problem late at night, and I managed to pull into a space near the entrance. As I headed for the emergency entrance, I found myself almost running. A terrible feeling of apprehension came over me as I quickly headed towards the elevator, and it grew more intense as I pushed the fourth floor button.

What if something is really wrong with Juan, I thought, but dismissed the feeling from my mind, trying to take comfort in the fact that he survived all the other crises. This was not Juan's time; Daniel had been so sure of it!

I decided I had to be certain that Juan would come through this as always…I would stay with him all night. It would make him rest better knowing I was there with him; he had asked if I was going to stay the night so often.

However, I had never seen any reason to stay; after being with him late at night, I'd usually return early in the morning to find him still fast asleep. So I'd awaken him with a gentle pat, and, as in all the years that I had known him, he'd awaken with a smile and say, "Aw. Recharred, did you just get out of bed?"

"Oh, God, let him be okay," I prayed as I hurried out of the elevator, heading towards 4 East. Juan's room was directly across from the nurses' station, and I was there in seconds. And there he was, looking so weak and helpless, cuddled on his side, the bed raised to a quarter sitting position. Jenny was at his side, her back to me, and appeared to be feeding him. A terrible ache clutched my heart as I saw Juan's beautiful blue eyes, so watery, as though they were begging for help. I wasn't sure he saw me, even though his eyes seemed to waver in my direction, and I managed to force my usual happy greeting, but in a choked up voice.

"Oh, good, Richard, you're here," Jenny sighed in a tone of relief. I stepped to the sink to wash my hands as I always did when I entered his room, my mind swimming with thoughts of why I had left him alone for over a day. In my anguish, I recalled the crying I had done while waiting in the car for Matt to cash his check that morning. The apprehensions I experienced throughout the day had to be telling me something also, but I did nothing about it!

Jenny moved aside in order to give room to take Juan's hand, informing me that he had not eaten any of his dinner because he was having trouble swallowing, sometimes choking on solid food. "So I have been slowly squeezing water through his lips with this medical syringe, and he seems to be taking it very well. He seems to be really eager for each tube-full."

I held Juan's hand gently, but I wasn't certain he could see me because his eyes were so watery and weak-looking, so I anxiously asked, "Can you see me, Juan?"

My heart swelled as he gave me a definite nod of his head! I wasn't sure he was aware of who I was though, and my heart stood still as I asked, "Do you know who I am, Juan?"

I repeated it several times, saying the words very clearly to be sure he understood. He then looked at me with as much surprise as he could muster, and in that same manner he usually expressed whenever I foolishly doubted him. He struggled giving me a look that said, *Of course I know who you are, you idiot*, but finally managed to utter, "Recharred!"

It felt so good to hear him say my name, even though he had difficulty getting the word out. He was responding and that was all I cared about! I felt sure that everything was going to be okay, since it was apparent that he was glad that I was there! I wanted to take him in my arms and tell him how much I loved him, and to assure him that he was going to pull through this crisis, as he had done so many times before.

He was responding, which made me feel that he might even want to eat. Speaking very distinctly, I asked, "Are you hungry, Juan? Are you hungry?" An emphatic nod of his head filled my heart with joy!

Never had he been this anxious to eat in all the months he had been in the hospital! It was as though a heavy weight was lifted from my heart, but in my excitement, a sudden surge of trembling passed over my body. I tried desperately to control it, especially since I wanted to conceal it from Juan, but it continued.

At that moment, Carol, who often went out for drinks with Jenny after work, walked in. After a quiet "Hello," she approached Juan and patted his hand.

"He's gonna be fine," I assured her, "but he hasn't eaten anything tonight, and he just told me he's hungry. Do you think you could run out for something? I don't want to leave him."

"I don't think Juan should have anything solid to eat," Jenny insisted, "because he's been choking. I'm afraid, especially since there isn't a doctor here tonight. I don't think we should take any chances."

I agreed, but felt that Juan should have some soup, so Carol went to the canteen.

I realized that he needed more nourishment than that which a small cup of soup could provide, so I pulled his tray table over, opened one of the cans on it and told him I was going to feed him *Ensure* before the soup arrived. Juan nodded in approval. Despite his weakness, he still managed to display gratitude. He was glad to have me there; it showed in his eyes. I was angry with myself for not being there since the morning prior. The other nurses were not like Jenny; they lacked her compassion. However, she was only on duty for dinner, and I was never certain whether or not he had eaten if I did not visit at breakfast or lunch hours. The realization of this fact compelled me to be there as often as possible. I had told the staff that I was going to be gone for more than a day, and they promised to make sure he ate. However, I still had apprehensions, because I recalled the times I arrived late for breakfast or lunch, to feel my heart aching when I saw his food sitting on a tray getting cold, and not a nurse in sight!

My hand trembled as I squeezed the syringe through Juan's lips and tried desperately to steady it with my other hand. I couldn't help but think, *Oh, my God, he looks like a desperately hungry baby!* His eyes looked so sad and watery, and I prayed, "Please, God, make Juan well, please, don't let anything happen to him!"

I continued squeezing the syringe slowly in order to control Juan from choking. He continued to suck hard, however, and my apprehensions were somewhat relieved. I then thought that he might be able to use a straw since he was sucking hard on the syringe, but when I inserted one into the can, he was not able to draw the liquid up! My heart ached at the thought of Juan being too weak to use a straw!

I continued with the syringe, when suddenly the terrible trembling started again! I tried desperately to control it, and finally found that the only thing that helped calm my nerves was to continually assure him that he was going to be fine. Somehow, assuring Juan helped convince me that he would rally.

Carol brought the soup as I squeezed the last syringeful of *Ensure* into Juan's mouth. It encouraged me to see him eagerly opening his mouth for more food. I told him that the *Ensure* was finished and that I was going to start on the soup. Juan's eyes always told me all, and even though they were drifting and swimming in tears, it was apparent that they were telling me how content and grateful he was to have me there. And he eagerly accepted, without any difficulty in swallowing, every spoonful my trembling hand fed him. He was eating, which finally gave me some relief.

We were like one person, yet never had I felt this close to Juan. I was his lifeline, and his adoring eyes made the moments so precious. Never *in all the years that I have known him*, I thought, *have I seen him this helpless*. And my heart ached....

Juan opened his mouth after the last spoonful, eagerly wanting more. Excitedly, I asked if he was still hungry, and again he nodded emphatically. My heart swelled when he put his finger into his mouth and began sucking it. *Oh, my God*, I thought. *He isn't able to talk, yet, like a baby, he is showing me he wants more!* At that moment, Carol entered and I asked her to go for more soup. Juan's smile of gratitude was precious once I told him that more soup was coming.

He lay contentedly on his side, as I had seen him do so often throughout the years. His regal stature was always in a class all his own.

Juan cradled his pillow; I took hold of his hand and continued assuring him that he was going to be fine. He needed this assurance as well as I did to keep his spirits up, and as I gently squeezed his hand, he listened, completely aware of what I was saying, his face glowing with appreciation. He needed to hear that I was going to stay the night with him, and I repeated it several times to be certain he was aware of it.

A smile of relief came on his face, almost as though he had been waiting for those words. Slowly, he settled on his back, and almost instantly, his eyes began drifting and closing. Realizing the rest would help, I assured him that it was fine to sleep. Carol returned with the soup, but it was too late, Juan wanted to sleep.

Jenny came into the room to say goodnight, and before leaving Carol, informed me that she had spoken on the phone with Amanda, who inquired if I wanted her to come and stay the night, too. I saw no reason for this since I felt that Juan was doing fine, and replied that Amanda should come in the morning instead.

I held onto Juan's hand, while he moved restlessly, assuring him that the sleep would do him good. It didn't occur to me that Juan never slept on his back; perhaps, I was subconsciously pushing it *out* of my mind.

I let go of Juan's hand momentarily to pull up a chair, and he turned his head slowly in my direction, barely opening his eyes. It was almost as though he was afraid I had left, but once I took hold of his hand and softly assured him of my presence, he settled down and slowly closed his eyelids again. "I'm still here with you, Juan. You know I will not leave you."

I continued holding his hand, gently squeezing it, and repeatedly assured him of my presence. And then he did it again, slowly turning his head in my direction and barely opening his eyes to focus on me. I'm sure he was finally assured that I was with him to stay when he fell into a deep sleep.

Only a few minutes had passed when suddenly, his breathing became heavy and laborious. A terrible chill touched my heart as I remembered my father doing the same five years earlier, eventually dying two weeks later. "Oh, God!" I prayed, "He has to overcome this...please, dear God!"

I sat there terrified, holding onto Juan's hand firmly, not wanting to believe this was happening, my mind swimming with confusion! I had never believed Juan would come to this when he had been diagnosed with the HIV virus back in the fall of 1986. For almost six years, I had refused to talk of death in regard to Juan because I could never imagine that he'd no longer be with me! How could I possibly believe it now? Though there he was before me, struggling to breathe, I still wouldn't believe it!

I suddenly felt a presence in the room, and upon turning saw Mariana, the night nurse. She remained silent, and finally began gently rubbing my shoulders. I could only focus on Juan's struggling to breathe, and barely acknowledged her presence. My fear would not allow me to ask why this was happening. After a few minutes, she finally said, "I'll bring you some coffee, Richard."

Juan was still struggling to breathe when she returned with the coffee. She resumed rubbing my shoulders, and finally said, "He's doing well, Richard. He's not like the others; everyone usually perspires very badly." I wasn't sure what she meant, but I was afraid to ask. After a moment, Mariana left the room.

Suddenly, like a miracle, Juan began breathing normally! I leaned over apprehensively to listen, and the tugging at my heart finally subsided when I realized that his respiration was normal. Juan was sleeping in his habitually quiet manner, like an angel!

I assured myself that Juan did not look like an AIDS patient. He had weighed one hundred and seventy pounds two weeks earlier, slightly below his normal weight! Much of my worry was relieved, but I was still trembling, and I did not want Juan to be aware of it as I held his hand. Jenny had left me a pack of cigarettes, and I decided to go into the nurses' room for a smoke. I felt it would control the terrible shaking surging throughout my body.

I only stayed for a couple of drags, because I felt the need to be with Juan. I did not want him to awaken and find me gone.

I took hold of Juan's hand again upon returning to the room, and sat there looking at him sleep so peacefully. I could only think about how strong he had always been—how full of life and laughter, and how unfair all of this was! And I thought of the wonderful eighteen years I had shared with him—the trials and tribulations, but mostly the joy, laughter, love, and music he had brought into my life....

Chapter Two:
The Surprise of My Life!

I had my lines down pat when I arrived at the theatre that Sunday night. The fact that I had been able to concentrate on them surprised me, especially since my meeting with Juan kept coming into my mind while lying in the sun that day. I was also bewildered because I had felt no guilt. Then, to my complete dismay, I was confronted with a notice on the bulletin board: "This evening's performance is to be the last. Due to the lack of attendance, we are forced to close."

My shop was closed on Mondays, but I was heavily occupied with phone calls concerning Joan's upcoming marriage to my ex-brother-in-law, Remo. I couldn't comprehend why they were having a reception, especially since it actually forced my children to condone tacitly their adultery by attending.

I was particularly disturbed when my daughter, Jacque, talked excitedly about dressing for the wedding. I realized, though, that she was only fourteen and did not understand the depression I was going through, but why was her mother doing this? Why did she have to flaunt it and include my children? Was it an attempt to justify her wrongdoing? My sister Geena's kids were not attending, so why were mine?

It had been about three months since our divorce, and I realized that I had undoubtedly rushed her into the quick marriage by objecting to his move into my house on the day the divorce was granted.

Even at that, my flare-up did not condone such an action. I went berserk when I heard he moved in, and my phone conversation with Joan was not a quiet one! Subjecting my children to that arrangement seemed to legitimize their years-long affair, which had now become common knowledge. Of course, she retaliated in her usual screaming fashion, hysterically insisting that I no longer had any control over the household, and arrogantly claiming that she had nothing to be ashamed of. Devastated, I hung up. I had not wanted to believe our divorce was final, especially since I was always a believer that once I married, it was forever.

I then phoned my son, Mike, and asked him to boycott the reception and be with me instead. Several months earlier, he had moved from the house after a severe battle with his mother, and settled in an old farmhouse with his girl and a couple of buddies.

I will never forget that fight. Joan was on his case, as she often was, for something he had done. Kids should be reprimanded, but Joan never knew the meaning of *enough*!

She went on until their argument became violent! In her unceasing hysteria, she began spitting drool, and because she refused to listen to my pleas to calm down, Mike became equally violent. He started up the stairway to his bedroom, and at midpoint he stopped, and pointing an accusing finger at Joan, he shouted, **"I'm leaving here, and I will never come back because I know about you!"**

Joan went into a rage, and it was evident that she was about to explode when Mike shouted, **"I know about you and what you did!"**

Infuriated, Joan had demanded to know the meaning of this insinuation, but he just continued to his bedroom, yelling, **"You know! You know!"** Completely enraged, she tried desperately to grab him, but he evaded her grasp and fled the house.

I later discovered that my sister-in-law, Genevieve, in an absolutely idiotic move, had actually revealed the adulterous scandal to her children when it came out ten years earlier. So they had keyed Mike in. I often wondered if her stupidity had ever impelled her to tell them that she had also succumbed to Remo's advances.

Although Mike never returned home to live, he had made amends with his mother. I think he just adjusted to the reality of the despicable happenings, but we never talked about it.

"Dad, let me make up my mind about whether I should go to the wedding or not," Mike answered. "I don't want the relatives telling me what to do. Auntie Dee should let me decide; let all the kids decide for themselves!" I begged him to be with me that night, though, and he finally agreed to meet me at a cocktail lounge.

Another thing that was eating away at me was the following statement that Jacque made when I called her. "Dad, there is nothing wrong with Uncle Remo's living here because he is not sleeping with Mom. He's sleeping in the family room!" It preyed on my mind, and the only thing that pacified me was her innocence.

Martina and Nicky, however, were past that stage; they understood.

My anguish was so intense that Monday and Tuesday that I never had time to think of my wonderful meeting with Juan.

Finally on Wednesday, June 26, I called the Actors' Equity office regarding the closing of the play, and found out that an actors' night was scheduled for the dress rehearsal of a new play that evening. I immediately thought of Juan after being informed that I was allowed one guest. I knew I had to get out, and it had to be someone other than family.

I needed someone who was capable of forcing me to forget my depression completely, and who could do it better than Juan? Just thinking of him made me feel better. However, was the number he had given me really his? False numbers were common after one-night stands. I held my breath, dialing the number he had written.

The ringing continued for some time, and a bad feeling hit me; a work number should be answered. I was just about to hang up when I suddenly heard, "Allo, Stevenson Library." There was no mistaking that wonderful, rich resonance of Juan's voice, but wanting to be certain, I inquired, "Is Juan Sursedicius there?"

"This is Juan," he politely answered, "whot con I do for you, please?"

"Hi," I answered, "this is Richard. Do you remember me? Richard Mella!"

"Of course I do, Recharred! So good to hear from you," he answered.

"I know it is the last minute, but I was wondering if you might like to come with me to see the dress rehearsal of a new play?"

I gasped nervously in anticipation, waiting for an answer. After a brief moment, he replied, "I would love to go with you tonight, Recharred, but a co-worker is taking me out for a belated birthday dinner."

In an instant, a black cloud hovered over me. However, it lifted when he said, "You know, Recharred, I am going to dinner immediately ofter work, so I should be able to meet you thar in time for the play." I gave him the directions, and after hanging up, I stood there, overjoyed. It was working! He was what I needed!

It was apparent Juan had had a few drinks when dropped off at the Ivanhoe Theater, and it didn't take long for him to talk me out of staying to see the play.

He smiled broadly, extending his hand to me. "How are you, Recharred? It is so good to see you again," clasping onto my mine firmly. After I explained that there was a delay because the set still needed to be finished, he asked, "Do you really want to sit and watch a play?" And with a bit of mischief in his tone, he added, "Wouldn't it be fun to 'ave me show you a few bars in the area?" I couldn't resist his approach, and we were soon off to find my white Chrysler New Yorker, which, in my anxiety to meet Juan, I had sort of misplaced.

Juan insisted that the Snake Pit be our first bar, and I comprehended the reason for its name the moment we walked in. It was shades of *Halloween*! Paper streamers were hanging from the ceiling everywhere. In fact, *everything* seemed to be hanging from the ceiling, such as...skeletons, zombies, and shrunken heads. It also looked like it had never been cleaned, but a fun place to be.

The crowd was small, but the blasting jukebox made up for the lack of noise.

"Isn't this crazy, Recharred!" exclaimed Juan with a giggle after asking what I wanted to drink. My mind swam with reasons why I shouldn't drink, particularly since I had just recently resumed after abstaining for more than two years after a severe bout with hepatitis. I didn't want to be a party-pooper, however, and ordered a drink.

The evening raced by; I began to see that being with Juan was never boring. He was king of conversation and laughter, which I badly needed. The third bar had a disco floor, and as small as it was, we managed to work off some of the alcohol. Of course, Juan probably drank twice as much as I. Never had I met anyone so full of life! He was a complete joy because he'd talk about any subject while maintaining his mischievous fun. And his tremendous charm made me feel like I had known him for years.

Again, Juan wanted to stay at closing, but cha-chad to the door once I convinced him it was time. After inquiring if he wanted a lift home, he teasingly replied in his high-pitched, elegant voice, "Of course I do, Recharred. You would not leave me all alone here, would you?"

Instead of falling asleep as he had the first time, Juan moved to the radio music, raising his arms and chatting. God only knows how I made it safely to his house. "You are going to come in, Recharred, are you not?" he said when we arrived.

"I can't imagine anything better," I said, and we laughed. The noise continued as we approached the door, but he didn't seem worried about the neighbors hearing us.

Juan's apartment was directly behind a grocery store, and the owners lived on the second floor apartment. I found myself in a large, neat kitchen.

"How do you like my place, Recharred?" he asked, taking me by the arm to show the rest. He obviously took pride in his belongings. His bedroom was adjacent to the kitchen, and along a short hall leading to the living room was a second bedroom. The bath, which began looking kind of fuzzy, was just across. My head suddenly began spinning and I lost my focus.

I don't remember anything but the morning after. Our sudden awakening, with both of us jumping up at the same time, was almost straight out of a comedy film. There we were, lying not length-wise but width-wise on the bed. The happenings of the night were a total blank. Juan, however, showed no signs of a hangover. He insisted that I take a shower while he prepared coffee and toast. We were late, and had to get going.

Yet I managed. We called in late to work, and hurried along. I offered him a ride to work, and there was not a single moment of silence during the drive to the *university*, which, I was certain, meant there were no regrets. I dropped him off, and watched as he walked swiftly up the long concrete staircase, disappearing into the building, and I thought, H*e's so nice...someone to finally make it right.*

Chapter Three:
Getting to Know Each Other

Juan called the following week. It felt like an awakening hearing his voice after being consumed in thoughts of the disastrous weekend. There was no mistaking that deep resonance when I heard, "Is Recharred Mella thar?" It was amazing how much warmth I felt hearing those words. He quickly explained everything that had kept him too busy to call, and after taking a deep breath, he asked, "If you are not doing anything tonight, Recharred, would you not like to meet me for dinner ot *Orso's* in Old Town"

"If you knew what happened this weekend, you'd understand why this call is like a shot in the arm," I sighed in relief. "I'd love to meet you for dinner!" He asked what had happened, and I explained that I'd fill him in on the details that evening. We arranged a time, and when I returned to my customer, I'm sure I was glowing.

I thought for a perilous moment that Juan might possibly not show up after parking my car. I had really lost all confidence in myself. All of my doubts were snuffed out upon entering the restaurant, however, because, there he was, seated at the bar. And I actually heard bells chiming for me as I walked over. Suddenly, as though he had felt my presence, he turned around and smiled broadly. For a quick moment, the sunlight streaming through a small exposed area of the window caught his face and the wonderful light blue of his eyes. That alone was enough for an evening!

His handshake was a hardy one, yet still conveyed a warm sense of caring. I wasn't too keen about indulging again so soon after my catastrophic weekend, but ordered a cocktail when asked so as not to come off as a nerd.

"I love Italian food, Recharred," said Juan, explaining that he had eaten it many times at his best friend's house in Buenos Aries. He explained that the most populous ethnic group there was the Italians, and we laughed as he mimicked their excitable personalities. He proudly answered, "Julio Rafone," giving a distinct *h* sound to the *j* when I asked his friend's name. "We were friends since we started school, Recharred, ond we hated thot I had to leave to come to America."

"Do you write each other?" I asked.

"We did for a while, but you know how thot goes. Ofter a few years, the letters got fewer ond fewer, until you don't write anymore," Juan answered. Noticing a bit of melancholy, I placed my hand gently on his shoulder to assure him I was there for him. It was evident friendships were very important to him.

The hostess seated us in an intimate booth, which, to my pleasure, allowed us to talk freely. After we ordered another round of drinks and our dinners, Juan anxiously inquired, "Whot happened this weekend thot was so bad, Recharred?"

I took a deep breath and explained that my son, Mike, never showed up at the hotel on Friday, the evening of Joan and Remo's wedding reception, and that I turned to Manhattans as my depression deepened.

"Then, since I knew from my youngest daughter where the reception was, I mischievously picked myself off the bar stool and drove there! Believe it or not, I actually went into the hotel and stood in the foyer of the dining room. There I was, peeking in on the reception while trying to hide myself behind someone! Unfortunately, when my eyes located the wedding table, I saw Mike sitting there!"

"You mean he was thar when he said he was gonna be with you, Recharred?" Juan gasped.

"Exactly!" I said. "But wait until you hear the rest. Joan and that lecherous Remo rose from the table and headed my way, and I ran out of the place like an idiot! They were probably just going to the restroom, but I had no way of knowing. It was just like a movie, Juan! Like Cary Grant peeking in at Irene Dunne while she's with another man! Everyone in that lobby must have thought I was a nut from the way I was sneaking around!"

"You know what I did then? I was so angry that I decided to look for his car. I had seen it parked near the house enough times when I came home unexpectedly to ever mistake it! I found it, but there was no way it could be rammed into, as intended; there was only enough space to pull in alongside of it. There was enough space, however, to angle my car and sideswipe his with my front bumper, which in my savage state I managed to do several times."

Juan gasped, "You did thot, Recharred? I don' believe it!" But after laughing hysterically, he confided, "Recharred, thot is probably whot I would 'ave done."

Juan continued in stitches while I went on. "That really didn't appease my anger, and I drove to my sister Geena's house like a wild maniac. My family was there to console her, and I realized I needed some, too. You know how Italian families do when there is a crisis?" Well, I managed to get there in one piece, and there they were—all brooding as though it was a funeral!"

"Just like an Italiano family," Juan cried out.

"Exactly, Juan, and I became as bad. I continued drinking and even cried on my sister-in-law's shoulders. I was so drunk that she and my brother insisted I sleep at their house, which was only a few blocks from Geena's. Well, once I arrived at their house, I suddenly got the urge to do another nasty thing, but this time to do it to Joan…I had to tell her off! All sorts of nasty things began racing around in my dizzy head, and I quickly told my brother that I was going up to the second floor apartment to say hello to my niece. I staggered up the stairs, asked to use the phone, and since I assumed they would be spending their wedding night at the same hotel as the reception, I dialed information for the number. Well, Juan, my assumption was correct once I asked for their room. The phone began to ring! But then, *he* answered!"

Juan's eyes were popping out of their sockets, waiting for me to go on.

"I wasn't prepared to talk to him, but I knew I had to say something before he hung up. Almost like magic, the perfect words befitting the occasion suddenly slurred out. "Well, how do you like fucking my wife now that it's legitimate? Or are you licking her twat? I hear you like licking her twat, because she told me so ten years ago."

Juan exploded with laughter, gagging even more when I tried to explain that I had shocked myself since profanities had never been used in my family. I was infuriated telling the story, but as Juan laughed, I couldn't help but join in. "You did thot, Recharred? I don' believe it! Shame on you, but I would 'ave done the same. Aw, thot is so funny, so funny! Whot did he say?"

"He called me a cocksucker."

Now Juan was wiping away tears, gagging even more when I explained that I hung up quickly once my brother came up. Juan's laughter increased as he repeated my words. I might have been hurt with anybody else, but his catchy laughter made me realize how ridiculous and funny I must have been. His assurance that he would have done the same since he despised disloyalty also made it easy for me to laugh.

"Well, I made it to work on time the next morning and since it was Saturday, I was quite busy. I happened to look out the window, where I had parked my car, and there was Remo, standing in front of it. It dawned on me that he was checking out my bumper for signs of brown paint from his car, of which there had to be plenty. He then returned to his car and sped out of the lot—in the direction of the police station!"

Juan was hanging on every word. "I realized I had to clean my car before he came back with the police, and excused myself from my customer. I ran down to my apartment for some Brillo pads, and then flew like a bat out of hell to my car so no one from the shop could see me. My timing back in the shop was perfect; four squad cars followed Remo into the lot just as I stepped up to my customer. I can't tell you how good it felt to watch the policemen shrug their shoulders."

Juan wiped the tears from his eyes as I went on. "Then he drove by the shop, blew his horn, and shook his fist violently in my direction." Juan almost fell under the table. "Well, anyway, later that day, my daughter, Jacque, called and asked why I did all that? Can you imagine how badly I felt when she told me that because I did all those nasty things, Mom and Uncle Remo had a fight and didn't go on their honeymoon!"

Juan went into a laughing jag. "Well, actually I did later feel guilty about bashing his car and called my insurance agent. He was a friend and I felt I could tell him the truth. He laughed as hysterically when I explained that I accidentally smashed into my wife's husband's car four times. I finally sighed, "Enough of that! Let's enjoy the evening, Juan!"

"Aw, Recharred I am enjoying the evening, believe me. It is so funny!"

Our salads were placed before us at that moment, and I then had the pleasure of watching Juan dine. His manner was so elegant, unlike so many men who shovel food into their mouths. He ate slowly; eating was an art to him. The very manner in which he handled silverware was fantastic! I was dumbfounded because I had never thought that watching someone eat could ever be anything but mundane and unremarkable. And in all his delicacy, he still retained an absolutely masculine aura. He even managed to enhance the magic with his gift of conversation.

"I haven't smoked in eleven years, Juan," I replied to an offer of a cigarette, and after another round of drinks we were on our way to The Trip.

I was quite drunk when we headed to Juan's place, and fortunate to get us there safely. However, nothing has ever sobered me up so fast as when a tiny woman confronted us at his opened door. There she was, screaming in Lithuanian! I immediately thought it was his mother, and that she was incensed because he had brought me home. *Oh, God!* I thought, standing like a zombie as Juan plunged into a frenzied discussion with her. He finally calmed her, and as he led her out, she nodded an acknowledgment to me.

Amazingly, Juan did not appear disturbed, but I was beside myself! Though the heavy weight of the episode was lifted after he explained, "Thot was Mrs. Rumsas, my landlady. She had a fight with her husband and came into my apartment to get away from him. Con you believe thot she wanted to stay here all night, but I made her realize she should go bock upstairs—con you imagine thot, Recharred? I 'ave no privacy. I just 'ave to get out of here ond move to another apartment. Thot is whot I 'ave to do because everyone knows your business here!"

Our eyes met and we smiled in realizing that the incident had sobered us both.

Unlike the previous night I had spent at Juan's, this one was not lost in gin-nurtured oblivion. It was beautiful! After driving Juan to work, I realized he was capturing my heart, and I felt, though a bit bewildered, absolutely fantastic!

Chapter Four:
Interrupted Courtship

We began calling one another frequently after the dinner date at Orso's, and each time I heard Juan's voice, a wonderful feeling came over me; I imagined him as a permanent person in my life. However, I was also consumed in thoughts of the finality of my divorce. The realization that Joan and I were not going to reconcile still bothered me. I had found it hard to believe that she lied to me about the real reason to divorce. It supposedly had nothing to do with Remo, but now she was married to him!

I eventually realized that when I was with Juan, or thinking of him, my depression disappeared. His talent for making me feel important and wonderful soon changed my whole outlook. My only regret was that I couldn't share this feeling with my family. Only that I met a new friend who makes me laugh so much.

So the courtship began. Juan said that he could, on occasion, borrow his father's car. I decided to invite him to my place for a Saturday evening dinner and to prepare an entree I had learned from Joan—Italian pot-roast. My plan was to have a candlelight dinner and to spend the evening at home.

I started the roast during shop hours and it wasn't long before customers began commenting on the savory aroma filling the air. I wanted to shout and let them all know that a miracle man was coming for dinner, but I knew they'd never understand.

Juan arrived right on time, and once dinner began, he raved, "Recharred, this is the best pot roast I 'ave ever had! It is superb!" I discovered that the previous meals I sat with him were not flukes; beautiful conversation and his elegant table manners still prevailed. However, my plans for an evening at home fizzled when Juan said, "Why do we not go to *The Trip*, Recharred, ond do some dancing!" The wine I served had put him in a party mood to dance.

We began dating often, and our times together were not only to drink and party. A true friendship was growing, as well as the fact that I began falling in love with him.

Though I already discovered so many of Juan's qualities, another appeared. A childlike joy radiated from him over the simplest things in life. I hadn't imagined that I could feel this wonderful merely from being in the fallout of another person's happiness until this first time of many times.

Juan called and was extremely excited. He had just purchased an entertainment center and insisted, "Aw, Recharred, you 'ave to come over ond see it tonight! It is so bea-u-ti-ful, ond I want you to see it so badly! Please, would you not come over tonight?" Of course I went, and it was beautiful—a black tubular shelving unit with wide, chrome banding. He was really excited.

"How do you like it, Recharred, is it not bea-u-ti-ful?" Without waiting for a reply, he excitedly began listing things he felt were needed to finish the room perfectly. He was like a kid with a new toy! There, however, was a definite difference since he had an inner excitement that somehow conveyed that he'd always cherish it, and at the same time a magic within him had the power to excite me as well.

We spent the evening listening to his records, and once he played an album by Sandro, a Spanish singer, I was captivated. It wasn't long before I bought one too. In fact, that seemed to be all I listened to while at home alone, besides a song by a new singer from Australia. "I Honestly Love You," by Olivia Newton John, explained my exact feelings for Juan in the short time it took to play. I'd even play them for Geena on her visits to the studio I had moved into in order to be closer to Juan's apartment. And I wanted desperately to tell her that they were my love songs to Juan.

My family had wondered why I moved twenty miles from the shop, so I merely explained that since I was going to the city to party so much, the chances of falling asleep at the wheel were less.

The day was nearing for Juan's trip to Ecuador, and I became a bit anxious. He'd be gone for almost three weeks, and the fear of another depression began haunting me. The thought that I had not been on a vacation for some time finally occurred to me, and I began inquiring about a place that would be exciting enough to keep me occupied. It was four years since my wife and I had gone to Spain; a trip I believed would save our marriage. Of course, I didn't realize that she never discontinued her relationship with my brother-in-law.

Club Med in Guadeloupe was chosen after being highly recommended for singles by my travel agent. I especially liked it because my flight would leave from New York. This allowed me several days to take in some Broadway plays. It would work out perfectly. A total of eleven days; Juan would be back by then!

I managed to see five plays, and even contacted Barry, a young actor that I had met while attending a dinner theatre seminar a couple of years earlier.

After spending the afternoon together, I invited him to join me for a play that night. I had had a little thing going with him on my last trip there. Unfortunately, though he seemed happy to hear of Juan, his tender manner still managed to seduce me into having sex, which didn't say much for my will power. I tried to appease my guilt with the excuse that my wife had neglected me for so long, and the fact that I was just plain horny.

Club Med turned out to be a blast! Yet, though I met people from around the world, not one of them hailed from Chicago. Everyone seemed to be married. There I was with straight people, and again I was the life of the party. All sorts of activities were going on every hour of the day, and it kept me from thinking of Juan constantly. Nighttime was a different story. After my friends retired, I'd find myself yearning for him, and wondering if he was thinking of me as well.

I'd never been one to participate in every sport, but since I needed to be active, I found myself signing up for almost everything. And I played hard at most of them because I hated losing.

Agnese Biogetti, an absolutely elegant, beautiful woman from Rome, Italy was the only single person I met, and that meeting didn't happen until mid-week. Well, she took to me like glue! Since the policy of the club was to promote relaxation, along with the fun, shorts or anything cool and casual seemed to be the dress code for dinner. However, Agnese always appeared wearing a fabulous silk gown, which quickly earned her the title of *The Contessa*.

I'll never forget the evening I escorted her to her room. We were walking the flowered path and she politely asked, "Ci-ga-retta? "I wanted to refuse, but since her accent sounded so romantic, I felt compelled to accept. I had almost felt as if we were shooting a scene in a movie, and although I hadn't smoked in eleven years, I politely took one. One puff and my head was spinning.

It was obvious that she didn't want me to leave once we reached her room, especially since the longing in her eyes seemed to be telling me that she needed to be loved, making me think, *But where? She has a roommate, and so do I*. I should have carried her off into the bushes, but I didn't, and probably because I was a little gun shy since I hadn't had sex with a woman for so long. Then again, it could be an embarrassment should I be unable to perform.

There was an evening prior to meeting Agnese when a similar incident occurred, but with a man. One of the married couples I spent a good deal of time with was from New York, and if I recall, on their honeymoon. On that particular night, the staff of the hotel had obliged our gang by setting up a cook-out on the beach in lieu of dinner in the dining room. The mood was merry since they had also supplied us with as much rum as we could consume. As the evening went on, I became concerned because the young honeymooner, Mike, suddenly became all too attentive, touching me at every opportunity. And once, he volunteered to accompany me to my quarters for more film, I was certain of his intentions. He insisted even after I had said it would be faster going alone. I was determined that nothing would happen, especially since I didn't want to be pointed at as *one of those*....

My suspicions were confirmed once he lit up a joint and insisted I take a few hits and stop by his room. Marijuana wasn't something I used. It never really affected me. However, after a few drags, I had a little buzz going. So I sat at the foot of his bed while he fiddled in the bathroom, and prayed that I would not succumb to his sexy talk.

Since we had been wearing bathing trunks, I was quite relieved he hadn't removed his when he returned from the bathroom. Though he managed to stand directly in front of me while sighing one sexy comment after another, making me sweat like a madman! The temptation became greater when he moved his body closer, placing his hands on his hips. His trunks were only a few inches away, and he was desperately trying to seduce me with his dirty talk while pushing his torso to and fro. I felt as if lava was running through my veins and realized I needed to stop this rush. I finally managed enough will power to rise from this servile position and say, "I think we better get back to the party because everyone will wonder what happened to us."

I was feeling a bit low the last day, spending my final hours at the pool. I finally had met a group of singles...all schoolteachers from New York. Audra and Adrienne were sisters, and came to the club with Mark. Then there was Colleen, a divorcee. The thought of Agnese actually showing displeasure over Colleen's attachment to me gave me a chuckle.

"Richard, I got something for you," said a friend of mine.

"What? Did you all decide to chip in and buy another week for me?" I asked. It was almost as good once she explained that she had just talked with a girl who was looking for someone who was interested in trading their plane space for an extra week of vacation. I quickly agreed, and it was quite apparent, during our meeting, that the girl was a lesbian, as my friend had insinuated. I chuckled at the thought, *Little do they know*. And before I knew it, six days passed and I was on my way home, savoring the trip yet realizing I would soon be seeing Juan.

My brother, Tony, picked me up. My car was parked at his house. I headed for my apartment immediately after enjoying a breakfast with him and Carmela, thinking only of the sound of Juan's voice I would soon hear in the privacy of my apartment....

However, I was told he was at a meeting. I quickly took off for the shop, hoping he had called there on his return and left a message, At the same time, I was afraid he may have forgotten me.

Chapter Five:
Making Up for Lost Time

The fear of Juan forgetting me ended once I arrived at the shop to find a message stating he called, and that he was told of my delayed return. I had not yet rented the apartment and decided upon the privacy of that phone to try him again. I held my breath with each ring, and once I heard, "Stevenson Library, this is Juan," the gasp of relief certainly had to bellow throughout the building.

"Well, I practically lived in the sun during the day," I explained once Juan remarked on my tan that evening. It was so good to see him; his eyes glistened even more than usual against his own tanned face. I gave him one of the conks I had smelled up the plane with, and the box containing a shirt I bought for him in New York.

"Aw, Recharred, thot was so good of you," he exclaimed, his eyes widening and brows raising from obvious surprise at my thoughtfulness. "I love the conk ond will put it on my entertainment center." He stood back, and after a moment, exclaimed, "It looks great thar, Recharred! I will cherish it for always!"

"Of course I deserve this," he boasted while opening the box, bringing us to laughter. "Aw, Recharred, this is very bea-u-ti-ful," he said, holding the dark blue, embroidered shirt. Some time later, however, I inquired why he never wore it and was told, "Because, it was too fancy a shirt—too suburbanite. I like shirts thot are more mod. So I gave it to my father. I hope you don' mind?"

I was a bit hurt at the time, but quickly learned that he was an honest and frank person about everything. He never got any clothes from me, thereafter, that he didn't like. A change in my mode of dress also began at that time; his constant comments about my polyester clothing drove me to the younger *mod* look.

Juan brought out a couple of beers to toast to our reunion while I described the first roommate I had at Club Med. "Juan, it was so funny because he'd sleep flat on his back with his hands folded on his belly. Whenever I came in late at night, I felt as though I was walking into a funeral parlor. The room would be so hot and I'd put on the air conditioner. And though he'd look dead to the world, I'd hear a voice bellow out that the sound of the motor was waking him."

"You know, Recharred, you should 'ave put a lily in his hands when you came in ot night," Juan chuckled in delight after hearing the paths were filled with flowers.

"Well, why did you not fuck her, Recharred?" Juan calmly asked after hearing the details of the evening with Agnese, "You should 'ave. My brother-in-law took me to a whore house because he felt I needed to 'ave a woman, ond I did." I hid my distress upon hearing that bit of news.

"Recharred, the plane trips were wonderful! Thot is the only way to fly…first class! So much room! We had steak ond all the cocktails we wanted. Aw, Recharred, you should 'ave seen my mother. She got so drunk coming home ond was so funny!"

We laughed after I quipped, "I wonder who takes after her?" I realized the expense it had to be to fly first class, and mentioned it to him, only to hear him quickly reply, "It is only money, Recharred, ond besides my mother is a big woman ond it was more comfortable for her." It was my first introduction to the fact that Juan was not one to save money.

Juan spoke about his sister, about how beautiful and voluptuous she had been as a young girl. "But now she does not seem to care anymore. She was very much like Anita Eckberg with big tits ond blond hair. Do you know thot she only had four dresses in her closet, ond her husband has one suit ofter another! They 'ave a bea-u-ti-ful house on a hill, but she dresses like a peasant! She even has missing teeth in the front, ond hasn't replaced them. It doesn't seem to bother her ot all!"

I went into hysterical laughter as he imitated her appearance by placing his lower lip over his top one. "Yes, Recharred, she is so big ond fat now thot her tits just hang on her belly!" And once he stood up and contorted his body to mimic hers, I went bananas! He then explained that he and his sister had never really gotten along well during their childhood. "Do you know thot I got so angry ot her one time ofter she scratched me badly," he boasted, and we laughed once he added, "thot I got a knife ond chased her all over the house!" I tried controlling my laughter as he continued, "My brother-in-law was really cheap. He conveniently always forgot his wallet every time we went to a restaurant, ond I had to pay. You should 'ave seen the bill the time his mother ond father came with all their relatives!"

"Well, I guess he has to pay for all of his clothes, Juan," I commented.

"Ond all of his mistresses," Juan remarked, quickly raising his arms and sighing, "C'mon, Recharred, let us go cha, cha, cha! It has been much too long since we 'ave danced ond had a good time!" So off we went to another fun-filled evening.

I wasn't prepared for the surprise I received at Juan's after dressing in the morning, and I thanked my lucky stars that it happened when it did. I hadn't heard the knock on the door, when a short, robust, baldheaded man walked in. After a smile and a quick hello, he began conversing with Juan in what I assumed was Lithuanian. *Oh, not again*, I thought.

Though Juan quickly introduced him as his father, also mentioning that he had just begun his retirement, I still felt a bit awkward. I was sure he never thought of saying we were on the same bowling team. His father was pleasant enough, yet I was uncomfortable; I could talk easily with anyone at a first meeting. I wasn't even sure he understood when I remarked that it looked as though it was going to be a nice day? Though it didn't appear to bother Juan that he had walked in without knocking.

Chapter Six:
Learning About the Man

Our relationship flourished, though Juan began causing me some concern; many of his lone outings seemed to be mysteries. I knew he was still seeing George since I drove him there to drop something off. One Spanish party after another always was on the agenda, and it bothered me to realize that when Juan began drinking, he wouldn't stop. This obsession had him going to the bars afterwards, and the fear of him meeting someone was always on my mind.

Juan finally bought a new car, a red 1974 Fiat, and it allowed him to do those things easily. I was hurt because he was doing them without me, and there was no reason for lone outings if we were in a relationship. There were countless times that I'd sit in my car in front of his apartment, hoping he'd come home soon. It finally forced me to volunteer to babysit his daughter, Svetmana, whenever a Spanish party was going on, realizing I'd, at least, see him when he got home. I'd also keep myself available by refusing to visit relatives because he had implied that he might stop by. It was always very late, but he'd make it over. I never complained; I was crazy about him, and the anguish I had experienced didn't matter once he was with me.

"Now, Recharred, you sleep in thot bedroom ond I will sleep in mine," was a phrase I sometimes heard when spending the night at his place. Similar rulings occurred on weekend trips, too, whenever there were two beds around. If that were the case, I'd push the two together, only to hear Juan laughing at my action. Of course, he'd accept my romantic effort, at the same time reminding me to not forget to separate them before the maid arrived. I realized Juan had a sexual identity hang-up, but so did I! However, I had accepted it because I really thought God brought him into my life. It had to be right! Otherwise, how could I know such happiness and satisfaction? Besides, I no longer harbored any guilt after being with this man!

Although I was in a furnished studio, I still had room for my chest of drawers and the antique dining table I was awarded in my divorce. Two daybeds were placed on opposite walls of the living area, which made up as divans once throw pillows were tossed on them. Of course, whenever Juan was staying the night, I'd push them together, only to hear him teasingly ask, "Why are you doing *thot*, Recharred?" I eventually realized he needed me to yearn for him, at the same time needing the assurance that I was jealous.

Oddly enough, though he was extremely handsome, he still lacked confidence in his looks. It did not matter that heads turned his way on the street. He'd concentrate on his bad features; I felt there were none. He'd look at his chest in the mirror forlornly, commenting, "I am gonna 'ave a doctor cut off these tits so they will not look like a woman's!" I'd laugh since there definitely were no similarities, and though I'd tell him he was crazy, he still insisted he'd have it done one day.

I believe the only time he felt handsome was while drinking; I'd often catch him looking at his profile in any mirror available. It occurred to me he just might have needed the reassurance that he wasn't as bad as he thought. But it was always funny to watch his expressions.

Juan began to put on weight, primarily in his tummy. The heavy beer consumption was taking its toll. It was not noticeable when dressed; Juan had mastered the art of holding his body erect. I hadn't noticed it until one morning I awoke in his spare bedroom. He wasn't aware I was awake as he stood glaring out the window, mesmerized. I kept silent, admiring him while he continued to scratch under his shorts. It was then that I noticed the excess baggage.

An evening just before Juan purchased his car comes to mind. He telephoned, complaining because he could not use his father's car. I had then found myself speeding to his place after hearing his repeated threats to kill himself. And there he was, pouting like a child, and drinking a beer. I could tell what was going on just by hearing his childlike pouting about his father confiscating the duplicate keys to his car. It was obvious Juan had done quite a bit of drinking already, which would be reason enough for his father to do what he did. My assurances that his father was right fell short of spectacular. Instead, Juan paced the floor anxiously, holding the phone. He dialed a number and ranted on in Lithuanian. I had presumed it to be his father.

"Con you imagine, Recharred, my father took away my set of keys for his car when I was told I could use it tonight," he screamed after slamming down the receiver! "I am gonna call the policia! Yes! Thot is whot I am gonna do...'ave him arrested!" I chuckled once he grabbed the phone again, pouting like a child. Surprisingly, I managed to convince him that it would do no good, and to hang up. I had yet to realize that his childish tantrum was another facet to this man, and quite unaware that it would be one to grace my presence many times in the years to follow.

Juan's belligerency continued. Amazingly, I had actually found it funny. More amazing, he was so adorable! I wanted to cuddle him, to love him. I already knew that once he began drinking at home, he wouldn't stop. It was his usual prelude to a night at the bars. Of course, I agreed to go out, even with a busy Saturday at the shop ahead of me. His mood change was well worth it; that broad smile of his while raising his arms was something to cherish.

It didn't take long to realize that Juan's daughter was a peculiar four-year-old. No matter how well I treated her, I couldn't get close. An unseen barrier seemed always to separate us. Besides a personality completely opposite of Juan's, she bore no physical resemblance either. Her dark complexion, eyes, and hair were inherent of her mother, and Endira certainly favored her Central American Indian mother. Juan's comments about Endira's infidelities with a Colombian man, inevitably, came to my mind, too. However, I'd never mention it to him. He idolized Svetmana, and I wouldn't spoil that for anything. He'd grant her every wish but insist that Endira was the one responsible for her bad behavior and attitude.

Svetmana was with Juan for as much as a week at a time since Endira's job took her out of town quite often. When spending the night, I'd usually offer to drive her to nursery school on the far north side before heading west to my shop. It was a chore but I'd manage to get her to sing along with me on occasion, as I had done so often with my children. I really thought the sing along would strengthen our relationship, especially since I also babysat while Juan partied. But it never happened. She merely continued in her same cold manner. I was baffled because I treated her so well, trying to love her. My only reward each time I spoke to her was a smart aleck remark. I was bewildered at the thought of a four-year-old child behaving like this. The fact that she was still in diapers took a while to register that this was a disturbed child.

I later realized that Endira was the cause for Svetmana's miserable attitude and personality. It was evident she spoiled her rotten with material things instead of showering her with love. It was also apparent that Endira wasn't one to teach respect and responsibility. I had heard enough of Juan's telephone conversations with her to know she had a way of making him feel guilty about the divorce. This guilt forced him to cater to every Svetmana demand. However, I had figured from the start that Juan was her only example of love.

I think Svetmana resented me even more later because I was always the one to criticize Juan for spoiling her, insisting that she didn't need to have her way all the time. Of course, it would only make him angry and he'd snap back at me, especially when I brought up her nastiness. So I became used to her smirks each time she felt her actions were acceptable. I accepted his angry retaliations because I realized what Endira was doing to him.

Even my daughters didn't like sitting with her on evenings Juan and I went out. I had realized Juan needed to party, and it didn't necessarily have to be with his Spanish friends. So why not with me, especially since he preferred my company. Inevitably, I'd hear them complain, "Oh, do I have to take care of her again?" She is such a brat!"

That summer, Juan's parents rented a cottage in Union Pier on Lake Michigan. Juan would drive them Friday in his father's car, taking Svetmana along for the week; he'd be home Monday. I was surprised when he asked if

I'd like to take the train there after work Saturday and stay until Monday. "In this way, Recharred, you con keep me company driving bock to Chicago, ond it will be so nice to 'ave you thar with us ot the cottage. My father does not drive the car while he is thar. Would you not like to do thot, Recharred?" Of course, I accepted.

I had met his mother once when Juan took me to their apartment, a block from his own. I had realized then that he had inherited her personality. There was the language barrier, but there was no mistaking her witty quips. Each time she spoke, Juan would end up in stitches.

I decided upon bringing my Italian pot roast as a token of appreciation, and honored to hear their raves when it was served that evening. It was wonderful being there because it got us acquainted. However, English was not one of the several languages they spoke fluently.

I was a bit apprehensive at the thought of sharing Juan's bed. What if his mother walks in and my arm is over him? But to my surprise, he was the one to start the lovemaking.

The weekend was unbearably hot and humid but Juan, with his happy chatter, made every moment enjoyable. I quickly learned he idolized his mother and adopted her opinions as his own, especially those involving their likes and dislikes for movies and movie stars.

One evening, we drove to Saugatuck. Juan had heard that it was as beautiful as Cape Cod, and almost as gay. We weren't disappointed; the harbor and the many shops along the waterfront were magnificent! We did come across a gay bar, but didn't stay long since he was not in the mood to drink. I was glad because it would have been a big letdown after sharing the excitement he projected while taking in the panorama of boats in the harbor.

I attended my twenty-fifth high school reunion in October, spending that evening renewing friendships with classmates Vita, Ginny, and Peter. Vita and Peter had dated back to grade school days. Geena came along as my date, and had fit right in. I had had the shock of my life when Vita introduced her husband, an extremely handsome guy. "Well, I am finally meeting you at last, after hearing about you for twenty five years," he had said to me.

I was somewhat puzzled, not comprehending such a statement. While dancing with Vita, I asked if she could explain. I stood wide-eyed as she confessed to falling in love with me since seventh grade after we kissed all night at a party! She had actually held onto that memory for over thirty years! I was stunned; I had never given her any indication that she meant anything to me during our four years at high school! I finally asked why she never let me know of her feelings for me, only to learn that she was afraid of rejection. "So you held a torch and talked about me to your husband for twenty five years!" I exclaimed.

"Not only to him, to my kids, too," she confessed.

Not wanting another twenty-five years to pass to see them all again, I extended an invitation for a party in two weeks. Juan exploded with laughter at hearing the story.

Why Has All the Music Gone?

That Monday, I received a call. "Mr. Mella, I'm Vita's daughter and my mother asked me to call to tell you that she will not be able to attend your party because my father died yesterday."

However, Vita showed up after all. It was a bit eerie because it was as if Vita's husband, after learning I was divorced and available, decided to make her available. A few drinks, however, livened up the party of an otherwise uncomfortable beginning. I had also invited a girl I knew from a community theatre group, and it was apparent she had eyes for Juan. Of course, I did too. Though no one noticed it, they were all focused on Vita's constant attention to me instead.

Juan just laughed when I explained my reasoning for Vita showing up. I believed she had felt obligated because I paid my respects at her husband's wake. "Aw c'mon, Recharred, wake up ond smell the coffee," he remarked, glaring at me with his owl-type stare.

I saw Vita several times, but because the whole thing seemed so spooky, I never felt comfortable. Besides, I couldn't pretend to love her. I was in love with Juan, the joy of my life!

Juan planned a Spanish party and invited Geena, too. Friends from his married days were going to be there. However, only two others were there. Everyone had been invited to another Spanish party. Nancy was a co-worker of his, and the other a Latin spitfire by the name of Matissa. Though extremely tiny, she'd stand out in any room no matter how crowded. What a build! Geena and I were certain her dress had been sewed on wet! How she managed to move in it was baffling, but those vibrating hips of hers moved as though they were powered by high voltage!

Matissa left when we did; her husband didn't want her to get home late. Of course, Geena wasted no time in commenting, "Boy, that Matissa is married, and she's out at another man's house." She then asked, "Is Nancy gonna stay the night with Juan?"

I sadly replied, "I guess."

It upset me to be told by Juan the next day that Matissa's female perception had caught my constant attention to him and had asked, in Spanish, if I were gay.

Juan enjoyed taking trips to nearby cities, and I can't remember him ever not liking any of them. He was always appreciative, and never displayed disappointment at any attraction we ventured to. He had a rare enthusiasm, comparable to the excitement one would see in a boy off to a new adventure! The difference being Juan's enthusiasm didn't fade away. He never tired of it. His excitement would only grow! That was one of my greatest satisfactions, actually feeling like I was given the privilege to share this man's joy and excitement! I'd always hear, "You know, Recharred, I don' think I would mind living here," or "You know, they 'ave some really nice buildings in this city," even though there may have only been a few. Juan loved nature, and driving to the country was another of his favorite pastimes.

I'll never forget our weekend to Louisville. Juan had just got the Fiat, but insisted I drive the Chrysler. I really didn't want to take my car since it had been overheating. But he said, "Why don't you take it to the garage ond 'ave them fix it, Recharred, because it would be so nice to drive thar in the big car. It has to be fixed anyway." I did so and was assured the problem was resolved.

I hadn't been driving an hour when steam began escaping from the hood! It took an hour for the engine to cool enough to continue on. Two more pit stops and three hours later than anticipated, we arrived in Louisville. To put it mildly, I was pissed! Especially since I didn't want to drive the car in the first place. I was also irritated with Juan because his only concern seemed to be that we were late in arriving. The fact that the car might be seriously damaged didn't even concern him! But I held my lip because I didn't want to spoil his excitement at being in a new city. Besides, I had learned before that he could charm me into doing things against my better judgment.

Fortunately, we found a downtown motel near a gas station, which was great since it was obvious we might not have use of the car the next day. I was still irritated, and my only way of hiding it was by remaining quiet. I certainly didn't want to spoil that gift of excitement that was his.

It was too late to really do more than walk the downtown area, and it didn't take long for my anger to disappear. Juan's contagious excitement rubbed off on me in a matter of minutes. I had to face it. He was such a joy to be with that it was impossible to stay angry.

The morning was sunny, somewhere in the sixties, and perfect for our light jackets. Juan's excitement over my jacket quickly persuaded me to trade. After dropping off the car at a station, we headed to see the sights. As expected, Juan made everything a thrilling event, but I must admit his pronunciation of *Ollie's Trolley* when we stopped for a hot dog was truly a highlight for me.

After dinner that evening, I suggested we check out the bars, and since the car wouldn't be ready until morning, I figured we'd hail a cab and ask the driver to take us to one. "Aw, no, Recharred," Juan gasped, "I could not do thot, ond I would not want to be with you if you asked. I'd be too embarrassed!" I was disappointed; my chances for lovemaking were stronger when he drank. Now, I'd undoubtedly hear, "Recharred, two men do not sleep together you know."

A reason for turning down my suggestion was obvious once he mentioned the movie *Texas Chain Saw Massacre*. He had seen that it was in town when we passed a theatre that afternoon. I really didn't care to see it, especially after I came out sick when he dragged me to see *Last House on the Left* back home. But he pleaded, "Aw, Recharred, it is supposed to be so scary! C'mon, let's do thot. Please?" I finally agreed, realizing I didn't need to go drinking anyway.

It didn't take long to realize why there were only twenty in the theatre. It wasn't exactly an after dinner treat, watching people chopped with chain saws or hung onto meat cleavers, or stored in freezers! We were the only people in the theatre once the remains were served as sausages for dinner! Juan wouldn't leave! As gentle as he was, Juan was intrigued with horror films.

We decided to take off right after Sunday breakfast to give us some weekend time at home. Something told me that I should lift the hood after starting the engine once we were told the fan belt had been the problem. Well, we were greeted with a big surprise. It appeared as though a sprinkling system had been installed instead! Water was spraying in all directions, and coming from various spots in the radiator! The attendant finally conceded to my screams, admitting that they had probably punctured the walls of the radiator when installing the belt. However, he could not repair it because he was not a mechanic. We'd have to wait until morning.

"Aw, no, Recharred, we con not stay here until morning," Juan quickly shouted. "I 'ave to be ot work early tomorrow." I tried to explain that it would be impossible to go far before we had to stop from overheating, and that my motor could possibly burn out, but it did not matter. Juan knew nothing about mechanics, and his logic was that we got there with a bad radiator, so we could get back. No matter how I tried to convince him we were stuck, he still insisted on leaving.

So, we were off and running. I kept silent for some time, trying to understand his stubbornness. This was my first exposure to the demanding side of Juan, sober. Neither the fact that material things didn't matter to Juan, nor the fact that the only important thing to him was simply the joy living was just then becoming apparent. So I sat in silence waiting for the steam to rise along with mine as Juan chatted on. However, I finally realized I loved him too much to stay angry, and joined him in discussing the weekend. I lost count of the stops to cool the engine and to put a stop leak fluid in. I do remember that it was extremely late once we arrived at my place.

How I managed to see through the black cloud erupting from under the hood while driving Juan to work the next morning is a mystery to me! I was actually driving blind down Lake Shore Drive! Yet I made it up the ramp without a collision. A gas station was just across, and I made it without blowing up the gas pumps. Juan got out of the car, explaining that he'd have to take off because he couldn't be late. After hearing his well wishes I merely sat back in the cloud, brooding.

I waited half the day, only to learn that the motor had burned out. I made my way home and called Juan with the bad news. He offered his regrets, but also mentioned that I shouldn't worry since I had almost fifty thousand dollars from the divorce settlement. Yes, it irked me that he didn't seem at all concerned, but then I remembered that material things were not important to him. I figured, "What the heck! He's more important to me than any six–year-old car!"

I rode the train to the shop the next day and went to a nearby car dealer as soon as possible. There in the showroom was a new 1974 Gremlin in shades of orange. I liked it and bought it on the spot. The final price was to be determined after my car was towed there. When that happened, I was told that it was worth a whopping twenty-five dollars.

"Well, Recharred, it looks as though you bought yourself half a car," Juan teased after meeting him the next evening in front of the Snake Pit. It was obvious he'd already been drinking when he danced across the street to the bar. But no matter, he looked great doing it.

I was worried when we left because Juan was staggering, and I insisted that he leave his car and drive in mine. There he was with that little boy aura, insisting, "Don' worry, Recharred, I will be all right. Jus' follow me to my house."

"As if that's gonna help," I remarked, "me following you in another car." Completely ignoring my warning, he got into his car and sped away! Luckily, my car was behind his and I got in and took off after him. He was racing but I kept up with him.

Juan entered Lake Shore Drive, and for a moment I lost sight of him! I realized why once I spotted his car about fifty yards ahead—GOING SOUTH IN THE NORTHBOUND LANES! "Oh, my God," I had screamed, "he's gonna kill himself and anyone else that comes along!" I couldn't imagine how he managed to get where he was, but I knew I had better catch him! I floored the gas pedal, and once I was near his car, I began honking and shouting out the window to get his attention. However, he was oblivious to my intentions for getting his attention. In fact, he must have thought I wanted to race; he went even faster! There I was fifty yards behind again. I felt helpless when, suddenly, I saw his car swerve through an opening in the median. My heart stood still as the car teetered from one side to the other precariously! I was certain it was going to flip over! My terror subsided when, miraculously, the wheels of his car settled on the road and were on their way in the right direction.

Juan didn't remember any of it when we got to his place. "I did thot?" he sighed in complete wonder. "I really did, Recharred? I don' believe it!"

Juan and I usually went out twice a week, though a week or more might pass before we partied. There were times I'd feel nauseous with the mere mention of alcohol. Much like I had experienced years earlier while recuperating from hepatitis, but we still partied on.

I managed to switch Juan from beer to bourbon and water since I could then eliminate the alcohol in his drinks whenever I felt he had had enough. By then he didn't know the difference anyway. I thought I was doing him a favor, but as time passed I wasn't sure. The only logic to console my feelings of guilt had been when I realized that Juan undoubtedly would have switched himself; he had already been drinking hard liquor at parties, sometime even picking up a stray drink at the bars once he ran out of money. Smoking became a habit, and that could have been fine while drinking. However, when I purchased a pack during the day, I was once again hooked.

The Spanish parties began to spring up again, and since Martina was off at college and Jacque couldn't be out late on school nights, I found myself babysitting Svetmana again. To keep my mind off Juan while sitting, I'd take Svetmana to visit my relatives occasionally. However, my hope that their chatter would keep my mind from thinking constantly of Juan never worked. So our talks were usually a bit one-sided. And once I returned to his place, there'd be a long wait. Though the wait was always well worth it, he'd come in glowing, excitedly going on about the party, and especially raving about the dancing he had done. I'd feel like I had been there, too.

I had already realized that Juan needed to eat at the conclusion of a night out; we had been stopping off for breakfast, or cooking it ourselves at one of our places. White Castle sliders were carted home, too. Inevitably, if I cooked, Juan played his records or the radio with the music blasting! He'd talk continually and laugh while dancing if he was not too drunk. I'd realize whenever he had had too much; he'd be very quiet, moving to the music as though it was some sort of ritual. He usually insisted I dance with him, and I'd always be sure to lower the volume. He'd never say a word, but always managed to maneuver in position to turn it up blasting again.

I hadn't thought that Juan might be an alcoholic; he couldn't look at a bottle the morning after and sometimes weeks passed before he drank. But when he was in his party mood to dance, he had no bottom!

Juan stopped at a Mexican grocer to buy the ingredients needed for tacos while returning from one of our many trips to the record stores for new releases in American or Spanish songs. "Recharred, now you will taste how tacos should be made because these are all authentic ingredients. Here, start on this one," he boasted after patiently and meticulously preparing one, "Don't wait for me because I want you to enjoy it while it is nice ond hot!"

I tried my first bite, and forced a smile. Juan was waiting for my reaction. I didn't know how to tell him it chewed like gristle. Fortunately, he took a bite of his at that time, and shouted, "Aw, my God, Recharred, this is ter-ri-ble! I think instead of the steak, they ground the bones!" After a good laugh, he vowed, "I will never go thar again…never!"

Juan always made me feel special; the way he personalized every statement was a wonderful feeling for me. I would've been bothered had he stopped saying my name repeatedly.

Juan's middle name should have been Music; it surrounded him almost always. Latin ballads and rhythms—disco and country were only a part of his likes. Music of the twenties was a favorite, as well as classical. He had grown up in a family devoted to ballet. In fact, any music with melody, he loved. Music was his life!

In fact, Juan loved all the arts, especially the movies! Besides horror flicks, the 'oldies' from the thirties and forties were high on his list. He loved slapstick, and thought Lucille ball was a genius. He'd often quote while reading about the stars, or anything else, and unfortunately, I found it difficult to understand since he had been taught to pronounce every syllable in his Spanish teachings. I'd have to ask him to read it repeatedly, and still I would not understand every word.

"Recharred, do you know I 'ave a very famous cousin?" Juan said proudly. "She was a prima ballerina with the Royal London Ballet. Unfortunately, she became an alcoholic, ond now she is just teaching. Do you know thot she had a command performance for Queen Elizabeth, ond she never showed up! They finally found her in a nearby pub, drunk out of her mind! Her father, my Uncle Nicolai, was, ond still is a very famous choreographer in ballet. He travels all over the world directing ballets." Finally, in a suddenly burst of pride, he exclaimed, "Do you know, Recharred, thot I was taking ballet lessons until I was about fifteen years old, but then my father made me quit because he was afraid it would make me a fag." Of course we howled!

That is the reason he has such poise, I thought, *and why he holds himself so well while dancing!* It was especially apparent in the Latin steps because his movements were so defined, so quick, and especially when turning his head from side to side. It confirmed why dancing was always so important to him, and why he walked so proudly! Yet, his walk still had more. We laughed once he mentioned that a guy had stopped him on the street to say that he walked like a proud cat, and especially once Juan innocently asked, "Recharred, do I walk like a cat?"

Juan was spending Christmas Eve at his mother's, and I was somewhat bewildered when he mentioned that Endira was bringing his daughter and staying herself. My plans were to spend Christmas day with the kids, which left only about an hour to spend together on Christmas Eve. "Aw, Recharred, you know whot I love!" he exclaimed upon opening my first gift, a book entitled, *The Movies*. His eyes lit up like stars upon discovering what was in the smaller package. "Aw, Recharred, this is so bea-u-ti-ful, so bea-u-ti-ful! I will cherish it forever!" He set it on his new coffee table, and while standing back to admire it, sighed, "It will always be where I con see it!"

I never thought it would make the impression it did when I ordered the brass bumblebee paperweight from a magazine. I figured it would make a perfect gift since I always kidded him about being as flighty as a bee. Remembering my jest made it mean all the more to him.

One would think I had given him the Taj Mahal! Juan expanded my new mod wardrobe with his gifts.

A depression came over me as I drove to my brother's house. This would be my first Christmas Eve in twenty-two years without the wife and kids. Plus, I wouldn't be seeing Juan for a couple of days. I cried uncontrollably.

Chapter Seven:
Forcing the Tables to Turn

It was now 1975, and I was still trying to deal with Juan's little "outings." It hadn't occurred to me that maybe my jealousy was something he needed for his own ego. Here was a practically flawless individual…someone who was extremely handsome, yet he was always critical of his face and body. Had I wanted to nitpick, it could only be that one front tooth of his. It never grew in properly, and since it was turned slightly, it appeared to protrude a bit. Juan did, however, master his smile to make it barely noticeable.

Still unsure of Juan's commitment to me, I thought of getting away for a while. My new friends in New York had begged for me to come visit. Juan was surprised when I told him of my plans, but didn't say much on the subject, possibly believing I wasn't serious. In fact, I really wasn't at the time. I couldn't bear the thought of being away from him. However, I needed to build my own self-confidence and finally made reservations for the end of January. Juan was silent when I told him I'd be leaving on Sunday, but did offer to drive me to the airport. "I'll be gone for four days," I explained, managing to add, "Of course, Colleen has the hots for me, so who knows!"

My flight was at ten, and of course Juan was at another Spanish party that afternoon. My bag was packed and I became antsy since it was near my time to leave. However, Juan was right on time, and in his usual happy manner, he began raving on about the party.

I picked up my bag, only to hear him sheepishly sigh, "You don' really want to go, Recharred, do you?" There I was, ready to go, with Adrienne and Audra undoubtedly about to leave to get me at the airport, and Juan implying that I really did not want to go!

"What do you mean, Juan?" I asked, dropping my bag. "They're gonna be at the airport to pick me up. I already have my ticket."

47

"I don' want you to go, Recharred," he replied, glassy-eyed and in a somewhat pleading manner, "because I will miss you ter-ri-bly!" There was no mistaking his seriousness by the expression on his face, and especially since he was trying so hard to smile. There was no way I could resist, and I grabbed the phone. Adrienne and Audra were still home. I gave my regrets, explaining further that something very important had come up. We never spoke of it again, and I never regretted not going. It was the turning point I had prayed for in our relationship.

I had been serious about going, thinking Juan was too involved with other activities. Although he became more attentive, there were times I was kept guessing, but I realized he wouldn't be Juan if he weren't mischievous. He did stop seeing George and the Spanish parties were now less important.

Walter and Fred came into our lives; a well-to-do couple that Juan knew for years. Walter didn't share my opinion when it came to fidelity. That caused us each to be at the other's throat. I felt like he had appointed himself as Juan's pimp because he'd keep reminding him that a Latin hunk was arriving and they just had to meet. After hearing the offers of infidelity, I'd strongly object, only to hear Walter's candid displeasure to my preaching. Our carefully aimed sarcasm, inevitably, brought Juan to hysterical laughter, and especially when motivated by my jealousy....

They had been together for almost twenty-five years. It was apparent, however, that faithfulness was not part of their relationship, at least for Walter. Juan had told me that when Fred went on a business trip, Walter would take off for some Latin country and bring home a hunk to wield away his idle hours. I had no cause to suspect that Juan ever took up on any of his offers, especially since Walter seemed to despise me more as time went on.

Fred was a large man, and very masculine. Walter, a bleached blond with a rather pasty face, was very feminine. His makeup and walk confirmed that even before he opened his mouth.

I'll never forget the night of their twenty-fifth-anniversary party. A collection of gays and straight comprised more than fifty guests. Juan had told me their parties were very boring, and that they only played chamber music. "Don't worry though, Recharred, I will make sure thot some disco or Spanish music is played," he assured me, chuckling suddenly while recalling, "Wally got real angry ot me ot one of his parties when I turned on some lively music, but I did not care. I was a guest ond I wanted to 'ave a good time."

It was quiet in the outer foyer of their penthouse. We wondered if we had the wrong night. We soon learned why it was quiet once the door was opened. We stood in the inner foyer, and as we glanced in, it appeared as though a mortician's convention was in process! Walter scurried over to us, decked out like the queen of the Nile. He hugged Juan, and when he finally took my hand, it was as though it was a smelly piece of fish. After placing our gift along with the others, he took off as quickly as he had come. I remarked, "Well, it looks as though it is the survival of the fittest!"

I was always one to easily strike up a conversation while sober, more so than Juan. These stone-faced people, however, showed no interest in small talk. Our alternative was to drink, and make our own good time. As always, once Juan began drinking, he lost interest in eating. I prayed he would not get too drunk.

Juan managed to convince Walter to let him play some dance music, and the place livened up at last! That was until Juan began to carry on with a Latin woman. Then my good time ended. She was so taken by him that she wouldn't leave him for a moment. I drank more hoping it would make me feel better. But I only got more depressed. I knew that Walter was aware of my agony, merely from his pleased expression each time he looked my way. I wanted to take his face and smash it into his hypercritical anniversary cake!

Juan was drunk as a skunk, and completely unaware of anything going on around him as he continued with this woman. I could tell how drunk he was when he began caressing her breasts with one hand and feeling her rear with the other in full view of everyone. If that weren't enough, he started rubbing his groin into hers! Their motions appeared to be synchronized! My temperature rose with every movement of their hips! I could no longer control my jealousy, and finally walked up behind her to whisper, "If you think he is going home with you tonight, you have another guess coming! He came with me and *we* are going to leave together!"

She probably thought, *What a queen!* Yes, if looks could kill, I'd be dead. I don't know how I managed to get him out of there. I must have dragged him out of the place after pulling him out of her arms. And I'm sure she started screaming because we didn't hear from Walter for a long time after, and then the party was never mentioned.

Le Pub was designed to resemble a Parisian street scene and featured French cuisine as well as a disco bar. It fast became one of our favorite hangouts. Beef Tornadoes, smothered in blue cheese, quickly became a favorite to order. "Aw, Recharred, we are gonna 'ave to come here again for dinner. Would you not like thot?" Juan had raved that first time. Of course, we went again, many times, and Juan repeated his raves each time.

Juan was a waiter's delight; each time we had dinner, he'd praise the waiter about the meal. In fact, I never heard him complain about any meal. I was the one to complain if something was not as expected. Juan hated to hear my complaints, even though I was discrete about it. He'd reprimand me for embarrassing him and often mimic me, in an exaggerated manner, as a fussy old woman. Still he was so funny, I'd have to laugh. And neither of us changed.

Juan was a cut up and flamboyant while drinking yet quite the opposite in public when sober. He would be the first to criticize if he thought I was acting too gay, and I appreciated it since I didn't want to come off that way. I loved Juan because he was a man, and I wanted him to love me as one, too. Though Juan drank to excess while partying, he was sober ninety-five percent of our other times together. Any less and I would never have been proud enough to introduce him to my family. He also couldn't enter a gay bar when sober; we'd need to stop in a straight bar if we hadn't had drinks before leaving. Then, should he need to relieve himself before arriving at our destination, he'd do it in the first available vestibule even though we were only a minute away.

It was March 3, my birthday, and that evening will be etched in my mind for as long as I live! "I am gonna take you to the Tango, Recharred," Juan had said. "I 'ave heard thot it is rated as the best seafood restaurant in Chicago."

Tango was elegant and tastefully decorated. I had hoped to be seated in one of the intimate booths when we were escorted to our table instead of the one in the middle of the dining room we were given. However, it turned out fine; the surrounding tables were not occupied.

The waiter had just left with our cocktail order when Juan took out a small, gift wrapped box. I was surprised since I knew that he wasn't one to give presents for birthdays or Christmas; he preferred to give them at random. "Here, Recharred, happy birthday to you," Juan said, handing me the box. My face lit with joy upon seeing a silver cross and chain.

"I did not 'ave enough to buy you a gold one, Recharred, so I hope you do not mind silver?"

"Of course, I don't mind, Juan," I quickly answered while smiling broadly. "Why would I mind? It is so beautiful! I'm gonna put it on right now and wear it over my heart always!" Juan's eyes sparkled as I struggled with the clasp and it was clear they were as glassy as mine. The spell broke abruptly once the waiter brought our drinks.

Juan decided on the special fish entree, but I needed a detailed description before deciding. It sounded great as the waiter described Whitefish stuffed with mushroom sauce and baked in a pastry shell. I agreed to it. The waiter returned with a tureen of soup, serving each of us, then leaving the rest on the table. It didn't take long before the tureen was empty once we tasted an ambrosia for the Gods!

After a salad that tasted even better than the beautiful manner in which it was presented, our entrees were served. I couldn't imagine that the main course could equal in appearance what had already been served. But there before us were two magnificent creations! Juan's smile and the sparkle in his eyes confirmed that he was as enthralled as I was. The flaky pastry had been formed to resemble a fish, and beautifully placed around it were colorful vegetables!

Juan held his fork in his usual elegant manner, and after tenderly placing the first morsel through his lips, a sigh of passion escaped from within him. "Recharred, this is the best tasting fish I 'ave ever had in my life!" he exclaimed with a smile. A flick of his brows confirmed his approval. I apprehensively took my first bite knowing that Juan always showed an over appreciation for food. He wasn't exaggerating this time. It was the best tasting thing that I ever had the good fortune to put in my mouth! Perfect in every way, the crust melted in my mouth, enhancing the flavor of the stuffing, which in turn complimented the light, moist Whitefish. We savored it all.

I didn't need an excellent meal to merit excellent conversation with Juan; that evening, I had both.

What better words could I have wanted to hear after so beautiful a dinner? "Recharred, do you know whot I would like to do," Juan announced, "I'd like to move from my place, because you already know thot I do not 'ave the privacy thot I want. Would you like to move into on apartment with me? We con maybe find one here on the north side."

God! I thought, *my prayers are answered. Juan is the only man that I would ever think of living with!* Without a thought to the fact that I would be driving almost forty miles to the shop, I emphatically agreed! We did nothing more than smile at each other, and we knew exactly what our smiles meant.

Chapter Eight:
The Dream Apartment

On Monday, I called Juan after responding to an ad we had seen to tell him I made an appointment with the agent for that morning. He was excited when I mentioned she had several apartments, and reminded me, "Recharred, be sure you do not pick one without me; I want to see them, too, before we decide on one." I assured him I wouldn't, but he still reminded me again.

I felt great driving to the office on north Halstead Street, but I couldn't help but wonder about the excitement I was experiencing. It was a strange feeling to realize my whole life was changing with this move. I had always thought myself a family man, and I was content with it; I loved my wife and children very much. Now here I was planning to move in with a man, a lover! I was somewhat anxious because I wasn't crazy about the idea of being pointed out as a "fag" or a "queer," especially since I didn't consider myself one. Juan could never be pointed to as one either. He and I had found love and understanding from another man, and it was very probable that neither of us would have ever considered this lifestyle had our wives been true. I was certain that I would have never ventured out if my wife had considered me more during our lovemaking. No, never. The only reason I wandered was because she neglected my needs for so long and I turned to fantasy. I was married to Joan for twenty-two years, and only after she committed adultery did I consider the idea of cheating. And then it was with a man! The guilt I experienced afterwards was tremendous, and my only solace was the church and to ask God's forgiveness.

I thought of the many times that I never had had a satisfying ejaculation while making love to Joan. Her climax was always her main objective; it didn't matter to her whether I had one or not.

I thought of how passionately I made love to her those years, and how she did nothing but take. I realized that the hours she required to be fully satisfied could have been a great situation for most men to be in, but only if they had satisfaction themselves some of the times. I always knew that if only she had given more to me during my lovemaking, it wouldn't have taken her so long to get off, and I would have then been more fulfilled. Instead, one slip after another left me with nothing. I thought of the many times I would complain of a headache.

I searched for more reasons why I was now content with a man. I recalled desires I had always had in the morning, especially on Sundays when the kids were still asleep. I recalled the few occasional times Joan finally submitted to my pleas, the only times I can remember getting total satisfaction, and that was only because she wasn't a morning person and wanted to get it over as quickly as possible. Her contribution to the scene would be to remain in an almost comatose position, and let me have a go at finally having complete satisfaction.

I'd be so content lying next to her afterwards, finally rising to shower. I'd then go down to the kitchen and fix breakfast, leaving her to sleep. The kids loved French toast and sausage. I'd call to them to get dressed and ready for breakfast because we had to hurry off to church. Joan almost never joined us. I thought of how good I felt preparing everything, even singing to myself. I remembered how each time that I felt that way, Joan would suddenly enter like a raging bull, screaming wildly with drool flowing from her mouth!

"Why are you making breakfast, Rick? No one wants to eat!" and she'd continue raging, "You smell the whole house up with grease in the morning, and then rush the kids to leave me with the mess and the dirty dishes!" Her ranting and ravings would go on endlessly until my enchantment turned to anger and forced me to turn and whisper to myself, "Oh, why, oh, why did I ever make love to her!" The ironic thing about it was, because she didn't know when to stop, no one enjoyed breakfast anyway.

My mind recalled the week my mother came to stay with us. She had been ill for some time; early signs of hardening of the arteries caused the family much concern, and I thought it might do her some good to spend a little time with us. My thinking, however, backfired. Joan went into one warpath after another with the kids and me. The rages finally got the best of my mother and she cut the week short, insisting I drive her home. My heart ached as I drove her home. "Whatsa matter with that woman?" my mother cried out nervously, "I think she's a crazy!" I made up one excuse after another in Joan's behalf in an effort to try to calm my mother; her nervous fidgeting while going on about Joan was worrying me.

Never during those years had I ever given a thought to this assumption. Joan was so frustrated and unhappy with herself because the affair with my brother-in-law had been going on for most of our marriage, and she'd take it out on us.

I felt bewildered by finally realizing, "God, this went on for twenty-two years and I put up with it! I even put up with her split personality the times she wouldn't hesitate to belittle me in front of the kids, or anyone. And I still loved her even knowing she never stopped cheating!"

Something Joan said the evening before filing for divorce began pondering my mind, and once I weighed it all out, I assured myself that I was making the right decision in this move. She had practically given me an ultimatum by saying, "Rick, if you make love to me tonight, I will not file for divorce tomorrow." There she was, sitting in bed, actually expecting me to jump at her cold invitation! She had to know that I was a romanticist, and that I needed to be aroused with sincere passion. I had loved her, and all that would have been needed was to have shown me some desire. Twenty-two years of my devotion and it had come down to that…an ultimatum. All those years dependent on one night of cold sex? Never able to make love on demand, she filed the next day.

Nearing my destination, I was consoling myself with the thought that it was Juan who got me out of my depression—that it was Juan who made me remember the joy in this world. It was Juan who made me realize two men could be in love. A woman may have done much the same had she been all Juan was. But it was Juan who entered my life and with him brought a whirlwind of happiness. I knew I was doing the right thing! Yet, little did I know that even with his faults, he was a gem that I had found!

I fell in love with the first apartment I was shown, and after seeing the other two, it still was my choice. I would need to put a deposit on one, and that would be the only one she could hold. I didn't know what to do until she mentioned she had no other appointments and that I could transfer to another apartment if my roommate didn't like the one I chose. I chanced upsetting Juan and paid the deposit on the one I liked, praying they'd all still be available.

On the drive back that evening, I excitedly explained the features of each apartment. Naturally, I embellished on the one I liked, only to hear, "We will 'ave to see, Recharred, we will 'ave to see." To my delight we arrived to hear that all three apartments were still available.

I purposely asked to see the other two before the one I put a deposit on, and it didn't take long before Juan charmed her completely. His exuberance in describing how he'd decorate each apartment had her smiling, and his attempt to hide our relationship by calling me "Buddy" every time he addressed me was practically futile. I'm sure she had us figured out; we were commonplace on the north side. Nevertheless, it was funny watching her eyes shift from his eyes to the cleft in his chin, and then to his broad chest. Finally, she couldn't control herself and remarked about the beautiful blue of his eyes, which naturally embarrassed him.

We finally arrived at the three-story graystone. It had been renovated, yet retained its vintage charm. I prayed that Juan would love it as I did. My apprehensions were somewhat relieved when we entered the common foyer of 811 Oakdale because Juan seemed more impressed with it than the others. I was then certain he was overjoyed once we entered the apartment; the expression on his face told it all!

The living room was to the left and the dining room to the right of the small foyer, and separating them was a brick wall. Built-in shelving in this wall faced the foyer, and quickly brought favorable comment from Juan. The light brown tones of the brick gave warmth to the living room as well as the huge formal dining room. In an almost dancing motion, Juan moved into the living room, completely enthralled with the built in seating below an impressive bay of windows. His excitement peaked when he turned to see that there was a fireplace.

Juan stood in awe, holding his breath while hunching up his shoulders, and when he began slowly exhaling, it was like he was in ecstasy! He turned away from me to take in everything again. Enthusiastically, he pointed both index fingers to the floor. He hadn't even seen the rest of the place, but it was clear that he was showing me that it was his choice, too.

He began rattling on with such excitement that I thought he would have a coronary, and with every turn he made, he'd stop to exclaim, "This is bea-u-ti-ful! I love it!"

She then led us through the dining room to a short hall leading into the kitchen. A modern bath was to our left. The cabinet kitchen flowed on continuously beginning with the refrigerator, followed by a hooded range, sink, and more counter top that extended to an "L" shaped breakfast bar. Juan sighed, "Aw, Recharred, this is great! We con put bar stools thar!" I was already excited about the place, but watching him made my excitement even greater.

The rear entrance was behind the bar and next to it was another door leading to a bedroom, which I knew to be as large as the master bedroom. Opposite the bar, on the left of the kitchen, was the master bedroom, and in the corner of it another modern bath.

Juan pivoted my way and asked anxiously, "Whot do you think, old buddy, do you not like this one the best? Because I definitely do!"

"Of course I do, Juan, because I already put a deposit on it today." He almost split a gut!

Juan didn't ask about the rent until we returned to the office, and gasped loudly after being told it was three hundred and seventy five dollars. It was hard to swallow, especially because apartments were renting for about one hundred and fifty a month. We felt a little better once we reminded ourselves we would be splitting the rent. The girl left the room for more papers after explaining to Juan that a two-month security deposit was required. Extremely upset, Juan whispered, "Recharred, I don't 'ave enough money to put down a whole month's rent. Whot are we gonna do? I want the apartment so badly!" I was surprised to hear that he didn't have the money since he had made twenty thousand in the commodities market. However, not wanting to embarrass him, I assured him I would put up the entire amount. "You will! Recharred, thot is so wonderful...so wonderful!"

After almost breaking off her arm by joyously shaking it, we stepped out into the street. He raised his arms in that manner of his and shouted, "Aw, Recharred, is thot apartment not bea-u-ti-ful! Aw, I am so happy...so happy!" Oh, yeah, we were both happy!

After taking stock of our belongings, I was certain we wouldn't have enough to fill the place, but Juan assured me that, with a little time, it would be beautiful. I had the chest and the table, but no chairs. My son, Mike, had been storing the casual, wood framed family room furniture I was awarded from the divorce, and that would work in the living room. Juan's living room furniture belonged to the landlord. After describing the set to Juan, he excitedly exclaimed, "Recharred, they will be perfect because I love thot homey look." Juan had a bed and a small dresser, his entertainment center and stereo, an Oriental rug, an antique floor lamp, and a glass top coffee table. Besides our televisions, that was it.

We searched the want ads for chairs to match my table. Dee offered a bed frame, mattress, and boxspring. While refinishing the headboard in her basement, I spotted my mother's utility cabinet and knew it would be perfect for the kitchen, and with a little spray paint, it looked great.

An antique dining table and chairs were among the items to be sold in an estate sale listed in an ad. Only chairs were needed, but I figured if the price was right that I'd buy the set. When I left the shop to go there that day, I found the table to be magnificent. The uniquely carved apron complimented the base of the table. In actuality, there were two bases. There were two tremendous butterfly wings, separated by turned dowels. The chairs, however, were old English, and quite massive with high carved backs and pineapple shaped legs. I felt they'd overpower my table, so I decided against them even though the asking price of the whole set was a mere seventy five dollars.

We were invited to Fred and Wally's that evening to watch Cher's program. I mentioned my act of the day just as Wally was drooling over one of Cher's costumes, and he almost choked on his words criticizing my stupid behavior. "Richard, that was a steal! Each chair had to be worth at least a hundred! And if your description is correct, that table is something you should store for later. It sounds fabulous!" Of course he continued his antagonizing criticisms until Juan interjected, "Why don' you call thar now, Recharred. Everything sounds so bea-u-ti-ful." I explained that I left the phone number at the shop. For the rest of the evening, I couldn't help but notice Wally's smug expression. It bothered me because looking at his face, I figured if anyone knew an antique, he would!

I was told the set was still available when I called the next morning, and my offer of sixty- five dollars was quickly accepted. The table ended up at Mike's farmhouse, and I took the chairs to Geena's basement for refinishing.

Moving day turned out to be a sunny, seventy-degree Saturday in March 1975. With help from my kids as well as Deena, Dino, Geena, and young Dino, it still took most of the day because furniture had to be collected from different places. I'll never forget our excitement, and how Juan kept calling me "Buddy," that both Juan and myself were experiencing, and especially how he continually referred to me as "Buddy."

Everyone was moving so quickly that everything was dropped in the first available spot, and becoming quite a mess. It was apparent that Juan was frustrated because he was so organized. I'll never forget his surprise when everyone said, 'Okay, everything is here. Good luck with the place, but tomorrow is Easter and there is so much to do." Poof, they were gone! It was impossible to find a spot clear enough to move to each other. So we froze in position, waved, and laughed.

We finally pushed ourselves along to eventually stand face to face. Juan took my hand and again my heart as he looked into my eyes and sighed, "Recharred, we are finally home," adding, "You know it is late now, ond we 'ave not eaten. Why don' we just leave everything until tomorrow ond go out to dinner, ond then we con go dancing. Ofter all, we 'ave to celebrate our new home together!" So we celebrated! But this time we came home to *our* home!

Juan had to pick up Svetmana in minutes for an Easter brunch at his mother's and I had an early dinner invite at Dee's. We decided not to even think of beginning the work that needed doing after getting up so late. Juan understood when I explained that I couldn't just eat and run, but managed to mimic me by rambling on with, "I know, Recharred, because like all Italianos, you 'ave to mangia, mangia all day long!" This was perfect, our first day together and he had me laughing.

Driving to my sister's, I couldn't help thinking of the wonder of it all—that I was now living with another man! Suddenly I yelled out, "Not any man! Juan!"

I cut my day short but still left later than I wanted. Juan had told me he would be leaving his mother's after they finished eating because he was anxious to get everything in order. Like Juan had predicted, it was mangia, mangia all day long. I got home at seven thirty.

As I opened the door, there was Juan on his side, lying on the couch, reading a book and watching television. Everything was in order! It looked as if we had been there for years! Juan smiled and asked, "Well, Recharred, how do you like it? This is our home!"

I was stunned; there was not even a box in sight! The pictures were on the walls as well as books and knickknacks on the foyer shelving! The Oriental rug was under the cocktail table, and on top of the table was the brass bumblebee among other things. Dee had decided I should have my mother's inlaid tables, and they too had found their place much to my delight. He had even managed to use my fun-fur bedspread under the dining table and chairs. There was the conk I had given him, arranged nicely on the entertainment center, which was placed against the wall.

My biggest surprise of all was that Juan wasn't the least bit disturbed that I hadn't been there to help. "I told you, Recharred, that I know the way Italiano families are. Besides, then I got to arrange everything the way I like!" I assured him his decorating was perfect.

"I see you put the flighty bumblebee on the coffee- table where we can see it all the time," I pointed out.

"Of course, ond it will always be thar so I con see it whenever I am watching television or reading. I love it, Recharred."

There he was—that same glow on his face as the day I had given it to him. What a gem! How could I ever forget his brows flapping up and down in delight, and how he was bashfully trying to deny that he was as flighty as a bumblebee, yet realizing that I had thought of a perfect gift to give him. Being flighty as a bumblebee somehow had been a way of proving to himself that he was truly handsome because the responses would contradict his belief in himself. Though I reminded him that he was better than a carbon copy of Jeffrey Hunter because the movie star had not had a deep cleft in his chin or possibly even the charming personality, he still couldn't accept it.

He then excitedly beckoned, "C'mon, Recharred, let me show you whot else I did in the house?" It was amazing! Everything was in order, including the kitchen. Amazing yet was that the boxes were gone. Of course, he reminded me of the things still needed to make it really perfect, finally swelling my heart with, "Recharred, we now 'ave a nice, bea-u-ti-ful home!"

Juan talked about that apartment for years, even after many others. 811 West Oakdale would always be his favorite. "So bea-u-ti-ful—So elegant!" And our first place together.

Chapter Nine:
A Snowstorm after Easter?

We were excited because Juan had invited a friend from work to dinner on the Wednesday after our move. Win Parke was the one who had dropped Juan off at the theatre the night of our first date. We had run into him at the bar a few times, and I found him to be very pleasant with a great sense of humor. So, I was looking forward to a nice evening with our first guest.

Snow flurries began to fall as I walked to the store to buy mixes. It surprised me since it had been so beautiful on Saturday. I shook my head to the fact though, thinking it might be nice to have some snow because we could have a glowing fire for our guest. It was three o'clock, and the weather report was calling for hazardous road conditions. I decided not to chance staying until six o'clock, and headed for home.

The usual five-minute ride to the tollway took me an hour and a half. That should have been enough to warn me that I was in for a big surprise, and to spend the night at Mike's. However, I was determined to be at home with Juan for our first guest. My car, along with most back then, didn't have front wheel drive. I turned down the ramp to the tollway, and was greeted with a sight of what appeared to be a sea of cars, and not a wave of movement in that sea! There I was at the point of no return, completely frustrated, and moving at a snail's pace.

Had I wanted to exit and spend the night at Mike's, it would've been impossible because the exit ramps were at complete standstill! However, I still wouldn't have ever thought of doing such a thing! I was prepared to go through hell and high water to get home to Juan, but it was now six o'clock and I wasn't even half way there. I was sure he was already home and worried about me.

At least the gas tank was full, but so was my bladder. I really had to pee! But how? The bottled mixes suddenly came to mind! Why not empty them, and use them! I had to go so terribly that I never thought to look out the window to see if anyone might be watching, and it was too late to stop once I noticed a big grin on the woman in the car directly to my left. I tried to assure myself that she was just smiling at something said by the driver, and went on sighing with relief. It wasn't until about an hour later when another attack forced me to repeat my bottle trick that I realized she knew exactly what I was doing. There was no denying it as I caught her big smile again.

I was finally a block from the house! In all, it took seven hours to drive thirty-seven miles! Parking spaces were scarce in the neighborhood and I was lucky to find one on the next block. No one, evidently, attempted to park in the spot because of the high snowdrift, but I had had enough and just plowed in. Half the car was still sticking out on the street, but I didn't care. I let it be.

I figured Juan would be home entertaining Win, so I hurried along. A feeling of gloom hit me once I reached the corner to see that there wasn't a sign of light coming from our windows. *How could that be*, I thought, *it's ten thirty and Juan isn't home yet?* I had struggled on the road with thousands of others, yet I could not comprehend the same thing happening to Juan.

I felt so lonely entering the apartment, especially after I had been greeted so warmly by Juan the night before. I began to worry, realizing that he could be stuck somewhere, and it startled me when the phone rang. Assuming it to be Juan, I picked it up quickly. It was Jacque. "Oh, you are home, good! Are you okay, Dad? We were so worried because the news reports have been saying that people have been dropping dead in this storm!" I assured her of my well being but because Juan might be trying to reach me I cut her short.

Juan came storming through the front door as soon as I hung up. I was relieved, but knew at once that he was in no mood for a warm greeting this evening. "Do you know thot I left work early today because Endira was dropping off Svetmana ot my mother's to celebrate her birthday," he went on to say, "Svetmana's fifth birthday was the day we moved, but thar was no way we could celebrate it then! Do you know, Recharred, thot it took me four hours to drive home from my father's house! Ond my car was giving me so much trouble! I think the transmission had to be slipping because thar were times when I had it in gear ond it wouldn't move! Ond, Recharred, Svetmana was so crabby all the time! I did not know whot to do, the poor baby." His pace quickened as he excitedly went on, "I finally arrived ot Endira's ond had to listen to her go on endlessly about all the calls she had made to my mother's worrying about Svetmana. I then told her to call my mother to tell her I was okay because I did not feel like talking to anyone. Ond do you know, Recharred, thot when I began to pull into this spot, thot my car went completely dead! So, I jus' left it thar! Sticking out! I don' care, Recharred, if I get a ticket. I don' care!" I assured him that they probably wouldn't be ticketing judging from the number of stalled cars I had seen, but he still could not calm himself.

Why Has All the Music Gone?

He finally began to laugh when I explained the details of my journey, and after informing me that Win had told him he wasn't going to attempt the drive to our house, he added, "I called the shop to let you know but you had already left."

"You should have bought a Fiat with a stick shift," I went on to say, "instead of the automatic because they were designed to be operated manually. ."

Still, he insisted, "Recharred, I will never learn to drive a stick shift! No, I will not learn!" I knew he meant it; I was already aware of his determination whenever he stubbornly insisted that he wouldn't do something.

Instead of the Colombian chicken Juan had intended to prepare, I decided on sandwiches. Juan had loved the way I made them, always raving how moist and tasty they were. "Be sure you make them open faced, Recharred, because then I con 'ave more of the meat ond cheese," he yelled out as I headed for the kitchen, "Ond please put on lots of oonions."

We heard on the TV that thirty-one people died in the storm, and were thankful for the warmth of the fireplace in our home. The next morning, we decided to stay home. It would be our first full day there together.

It was a sunny day after the snow melted enough for us to re-park our cars, but it was apparent Juan would have more problems with his.

We ventured out to purchase barstools and a few throw rugs for the beautiful hardwood floors. Juan prepared his chicken with rice, and it was superb. He still needed the assurance that I liked it, and asked repeatedly, "Do you like it, Recharred? Do you really like it?"

It was a pleasure watching him cook. He was so meticulously neat in his preparation, that there was absolutely no mess, wiping up after each splash. In contrast to the dumping manner I do things, he was like an artist at work. From then on, I'd be certain to hear, "Recharred, why don' you clean up as you go along like I do?" I tried, but I never changed. I'd explain that my meals were several courses, whereas his were almost all one dish, but that never mattered to Juan. He was capable of doing it, why not me?

The black, furry bedspread looked so elegant under the dining table, we decided to stay with it. I had painted some of the carved areas on the backs of the chairs with black because I had already done the apron of the roundtable that color. Everything blended so well against the grains of the flooring and furniture, especially since the entertainment center was black, too.

Our first day at home turned out fabulous and it was a pleasure watching Juan act like a little kid with a new toy! He was so happy, and had good reason since his family had lived in one room for all the years they were in Buenos Aires. "Yes, though my mother always kept everything so neat, it still was only one room," he had said, "So, Recharred, I would like to 'ave a big apartment one day ond really fix it up bea-u-ti-ful!" Well, he got his wish because our apartment had to be one of the finest in Chicago.

As I learned more about Juan, I found that he didn't need the *Taj Mahal*. He was happy with the basics, as long as he was able to pay the bills and make his home look rich and inviting. I also discovered he loved to stay home and enjoy it…a true *Cancer*.

Chapter Ten:
The Birthday Mess

Friday evening rolled around, and after dinner, Juan's ex-wife stopped in to see the apartment, and to drop off Svetmana for the weekend. I had met her once. Endira was a very attractive, dark-haired woman with a deep olive complexion. Her father was English, while her mother was a Honduran Indian. She definitely had her mother's heritage, and it was apparent that Svetmana would soon be a carbon copy. She seemed to be very nice. After several meetings, however, I somehow sensed she wasn't—though my good nature allowed me to accept her exaggerated friendliness as sincere. She was an intellect, so I found her conversations somewhat tiresome. I wasn't sure when to laugh whenever she told a joke. Juan had told me she was a very boring person, and that he'd think about something else whenever she went on endlessly.

After raving about the apartment, she asked Juan if she could use the party room to hold a belated birthday party for Svetmana and her pre-school friends the following Saturday. Of course, Juan agreed, but specifically stated that they were not to come down to the apartment. It was okay with me, though I felt ignored because she had continually referred to the apartment as "yours" each time she raved about the place to Juan. It was as though I wasn't living there. It was apparent that her daughter felt the same since Svetmana refused to acknowledge my presence, too.

While driving home, I wondered why Juan hadn't called after the party that Saturday. It was scheduled until three, and I expected him to call to hurry me home for a party we were going to that night. So I assumed he was busy cleaning the party room.

I heard Spanish music blasting as I opened the foyer door, figuring Juan was getting in the mood to party. However, I was shocked out of my wits upon entering our apartment to see what appeared to be the aftermath of an all-nighter! It looked like someone had cleaned up the party room, putting everything into trash bags, then dumped them in our living room! Paper cups, plates, plastic spoons and forks, dirty napkins and cake were strewn about the room! Svetmana was sitting on the window seat, playing with a friend, and again ignored me.

In the middle of all this mess was a bigger mess, Juan, drunk as a skunk, dancing with who I thought was the little friend's mother! He appeared to be making his own music, and it looked like she had been feeling everything that he owned by the way that he was rubbing his groin into hers. As he continued this rhythm, his hands displayed perfect timing by caressing her buttocks in absolute syncopation! Similar to the time at Wally's, Juan showed no awareness to my presence, and likewise, the woman. I innocently blurted out, "Hi, Juan, I am home!"

When he finally noticed, he turned majestically and slurred out, "Hi, mon, 'ow are you? Aww, Recharred, we had such a good time!" The woman said something in Spanish, still holding onto Juan tightly. I assumed she was asking, "Who the hell is this guy butting in?" Juan finally let go to introduce me, falling into my arms in a state of drunkenness instead! It was quickly apparent why he was so close to her. She had been holding him up! He slowly straightened himself, only to make a mad, dash to the bathroom. I said hello, and took off after him!

There he was on the floor, head over the toilet, trying to vomit but without success! Oh, was he sick! I knelt down beside him to support his head, and encouraged him to vomit by prompting him to stick his finger down his throat since the dry heaves persisted, but he wouldn't do it. Then I tried, and began sticking my finger down his throat; afraid I might choke him but also scared that he might bite my finger off! I got him gagging, and he only barfed out liquid. That confirmed that he hadn't eaten all day. In a sudden drunken surge, he managed to raise himself and scurry to his bedroom, falling across the bed! I had heard the woman talking in Spanish during all of this, and figured I should explain before tending Juan, but by the time I returned to the living room they were all gone, including Svetmana.

Juan wanted no part of the food I fixed, and was out like a light in a moment. After struggling with his clothes, I sat next to him and began to reprimand him for ruining the evening. But I was talking to myself.

The kitchen was as big a disaster area as the living room, and my anger increased. I didn't know where to start, but then I thought, *No! I'm not cleaning it! He's gonna do it! If I clean it, he'll never know how badly the apartment looked when he gets up in the morning!*

The irony of it was, remembering the day he called at the shop after arriving home from work. He gave me a thorough scolding. "Recharred, do you know thot you left two crumbs on the counter next to the toaster when you made your toast this morning!" And he went on and on about it. So I spent the evening fuming, trying to concentrate on television.

Juan was as chipper as ever in the morning, and gave no indication that he might be angry that I hadn't cleaned the mess. I still hadn't cooled off and asked why the party ended up in our apartment, reminding him that he had been so emphatic about staying in the party room. Juan quickly responded, "Recharred, it was Endira's idea. We were in the party room, ond then she insisted we come down because she wanted the adults to see my bea-u-ti-ful place. I did not want to come down ond I whispered thot to her, but then she made me feel guilty for refusing."

"Yeah, like she makes you feel guilty about everything concerning Svetmana."

"I know, Recharred, thot is why I started to drink," Juan sighed. "You know Endira is very ambitious. She likes to 'ave luxury, ond to show everyone thot she has money, she spends more than she has. To Endira, money means power! Do you know, Recharred, when we got married, she was jus' finishing college, ond I was not making thot much money ot the library. Do you know ofter the bill came for the expensive furniture ond clothes she bought ot Field's thot she went to my parents ond osked them to pay it!"

"Did they pay it, Juan?"

"Of course not, Recharred. They did not 'ave thot kind of money! It was over five thousand! My mother told me she angrily stormed out ond slammed the door hard ofter herself!"

So what happened, Juan?"

"I had to pay it a little ot a time, ond I jus' paid the last payment. Do you know thot she also insisted I buy a house, even though I could not afford one? Just to make on impression on her friends because they had homes. I finally had to sell it because she kept spending money on clothes, ond I just could not make the payments." After a moment he added, "You know, if she did not cheat on me by fucking everyone thot had a big cock, I probably would 'ave been in the poorhouse now, because I am just as bad when it comes to saving money. I just cannot hold onto it. But, Recharred, I cannot stand for anyone to be disloyal to me. I was going crazy with her fucking around. Yes, Endira likes a big dick in her twat! Now she has another boyfriend ond I know he has a big one!"

"How do you know that, Juan?"

"I con tell jus' by looking ot the basket he carries in his pants, Recharred!" We both laughed very hard, and his cackle was so contagious I laughed harder and longer than usual.

Juan confided that he was happy he went through with the divorce, though his dream was always to have a family. "I 'ave had a hard time accepting my sexuality, Recharred," he confessed, "ond if you had not come into my life, I would still be very unhappy because I know I would not be able to go back to a straight life, ond I would be miserable." He smiled after a pause, adding, "Now, Recharred, you 'ave come into my life ond my entire attitude has changed. Recharred, even though I may sometimes get angry ond take it out on you, I really am only angry with myself because I still 'ave trouble accepting it ot times. Please forgive me because I don' mean whot I sometimes say to you. Honestly, you do make me feel thot it is so right. Ond do you know thot if I was to ever go straight again, or if you did, you still would always be my closest friend...for always, Recharred, because I love you so much!" I was silent and completely touched; he had again tugged at my heart.

After shaking the choked up feeling he had brought on, I went on to explain that I had felt the same about the difficulties of gay life, and that my love for him was equally as strong. We talked about how nice it would be if we could hold each other's hand in public, but, realized it was something we'd never be comfortable with.

After hearing my complaints about the nerve of Endira leaving the mess, he agreed, adding, "I knew Endira would never clean it, Recharred, because she never had before when we were together. Recharred, she thinks she is a queen, ond she expects everyone to do everything for her. Ond, Recharred, she will never teach Svetmana to clean up ofter herself, or to ever offer help to anyone!"

Juan was so charming I forgot my anger. I decided to prepare breakfast while he cleaned. One would never suspect he had been so drunk hours before. There he was, dancing to the stereo the whole time it took to clean, besides keeping a conversation with me!

We had had breakfast, and once the house was back to normal, Juan asked, "Recharred, would you not mind to take me for a drive? I feel very closed in, ond I need some fresh air. Would you not mind?" It wasn't the first time, nor was it the last time that he asked to go for a drive after a night of heavy drinking.

Chapter Eleven:
Adjusting for Juan

Our first year together proved to be a learning process and quite a challenge for me. We knew he had a drinking problem when he wanted to party, but Juan didn't have to drink every day. In fact, he'd go for a week or two, even more without the desire. But when he was in the mood to party...*Geronimo*! So, I had the challenge of getting to know two different personalities. Each one was unique, faults and all; I loved them both. Fortunately, the two shared some of the same qualities, and I always knew it was Juan. When drinking, he was elf-like, full of fun and laughter! A very talkative sprite who cared less what others thought of him. His devilish manner could easily cause embarrassment because we never knew what he might say or do next. And there was no way to reason with him. Yet, he was so devilishly adorable that I couldn't really get angry. In fact, he was like a lovable, little boy I wanted to hug.

As wonderful as that adorable boy and elf were, I still didn't want them on a full time basis. So, along with the many fine and sober qualities that were his a majority of the time, I found a combination that brought richness to my life. He was stubborn when sober too, and still very talkative. Yet he was well read, so his conversations were intelligent and interesting. But charm and wit were his finest attributes as well as his power to rub off the magic of a little boy's excitement. Juan laughed so easily and often when sober too; something I might not have laughed long or hard at became a hysterical event in his hands. I would have been crazy to look elsewhere.

Landscapes and skylines were a big joy for Juan. These were the times I'd see the enthusiasm of that little boy within him. The wonderful thing about it was that he shared them with me, and my appreciation for the simple joys grew. He had a gift!

Though Juan was stubborn sober, insisting on things his way, it never matched his adorable stubbornness when drinking. I'd usually give in, but there were times I balked. My face would tell all, and he'd finally give in and go my way. Those were times I realized how much he loved me.

It didn't take long to realize that his compulsion about things being neat and orderly all the time was not a phase. It was with us to stay, and I found it overbearing at times, especially since tidiness never mattered when he was drinking. However, the love and joy he gave me outweighed it, and I finally realized what matter if he had that quirk.

Had I not loved music, I would have been out of luck since it was a necessity in Juan's life. Our lives were filled with it, and it was wonderful! As long as they had beautiful melodies, we loved them! I never ceased to be amazed each time he named the singer who was performing on the radio. Another thing that amazed me was that he could watch television, listen to music, and read at the same time, and still keep track of all of them.

Patsy Cline was a favorite of his, and he always raved about Loretta Lynn's *Stand by Your Man*. I began believing *music* to be Juan's middle name. It may sound contrived but even his presence created the beautiful sound. The funny part of it is that as much as he loved music, and had a beautiful speaking voice, he couldn't carry a tune. I'd be hysterical with laughter each time he tried to sing a few lines of a song he wanted me to remember. He'd plead, "Aw c'mon, Recharred, don't you know it?" once he finished singing it in one note. Then he'd try again.

So, besides the bars for disco, we were taking in musicals, symphonies, and ballets. Of course, we also managed to see *Dracula* on stage. Count Dracula had always fascinated him. We also took Jacque and Svetmana to see *The Nutcracker*.

On occasion, Juan continued his preaching. "Now, Recharred, this is your bedroom ond thot one is mine. Two men do not sleep together you know." It bothered me that we only shared my bed on the nights we went out drinking, and I began doubting that he really loved me. I found myself wanting us to go out after dinner on some evenings. Sometimes, driving home from the shop, I'd almost hope to hear the stereo blasting when I got there.

It was Monday, and I decided to fix a meal I had seen in Juan's cookbook. *Matambre* was a South American dish served with a refried bean sauce, and one thing about it was that beer was suggested to accompany the meal. Not only would it be a surprise dish but he'd be having beer as well, and I knew what happened after that!

The recipe called for a flank steak garnished with vegetables and spices, then rolled and roasted. Since most of the vegetables called for were those I hardly ever used, I decided to shop Treasure Island; ethnic foods were a specialty there. I needed to call Juan to be certain he'd not stop off at his mother's, as he often did.

"Recharred, be sure you do not make a mess," Juan quickly reminded me after I told him I had a surprise dinner. "You know I will be able to tell if the stove ond counter are not clean, Recharred." I told him that I'd be extra careful, and before he could say any more, I hung up.

On my walk to the store, I could think of nothing but that the recipe included refried bean sauce and should definitely be followed with "beer!"

As usual, my shopping took longer than anticipated, and I had to rush preparing dinner. The Matambre was in the oven, and the bean sauce took so long that I didn't have a chance to clean the mess I had made chopping vegetables. I was frantic! The counter and stove looked like disaster areas, especially because the bean sauce wasn't exactly spatter free while cooking. Juan would be home in ten minutes, and the kitchen looked like a tornado hit it!

I began to move like a dynamo and managed, how I'll never know, to polish the last bit of the stove as Juan walked in! Being the lover of food that he was, and a gentleman, he commented on the wonderful aroma. However, that didn't mean that he wouldn't walk in like the Inspector General. I chuckled to myself when he scrutinized every spot and finally boasted, "See, Recharred, you con cook without making a mess if you try hard enough."

Juan raved about the dinner, and as a treat, we ate in the dining room. He reminisced about Buenos Aires, and how he'd like to see it again and take me. He brought up his childhood friend, Julio, and how wonderful it would be to see him again. He began laughing hilariously, and once he caught his breath he sighed, "Recharred, do you know thot I was a devil when I was in school," which brought a chuckle from me since he had said it so innocently. "I would make one of those things…umm…you know whot I mean?" I didn't, and it wasn't until after he made several hilarious pronunciation attempts, and physically demonstrated the action that I knew.

"A slingshot!" I declared.

He chuckled at hearing the name, his sweet melancholy continuing as he smiled and went on. "I would shoot stones ot someone's ass," he said, the mere recollection of it bringing him to laughter. "Do you know the teacher caught me one day ond took me by the ear ond brought me out in the hall," he sighed as though confessing to a terrible crime. "I had to bring my mother to school before I could return to class!" His laughter continued so hard that I found myself on the floor, helplessly trying to control my belly laughs.

That night we went out, and we stopped for breakfast, and when we came home, it was to the same bed.

Juan couldn't tolerate it when I was drunk, or anyone else, if he wasn't drinking. When Nicky graduated from high school, I used the party room to celebrate with my family. He wasn't pleased that I decided to serve alcohol since he had to be up early the next morning for a meeting. He surprised me completely by being very quiet that evening. I finally attributed it to the fact that it was his first time meeting my brothers, as well as nieces and nephews. I couldn't believe it when he suddenly told me he was going down to read in his bedroom. Then again, it could have been one of his rare bad moods and he didn't want to embarrass me.

I did not drink, as I promised Juan. Geena made up for me instead. Since she wasn't much of a drinker, it was always apparent when she had reached her limit. She'd start laughing, and shortly afterwards a hysterical crying jag would follow. She'd be a blast after two or three drinks, and be really funny. Any more than that amount eventually led to the jags.

When Geena noticed that Juan was nowhere around, she decided to seek him out. They had become great friends and always had a good time when we partied together, and she wanted to party with Juan. This wasn't an evening he wanted to party, though, and I tried in vain to explain that to her. She stubbornly headed out of the room, stumbling down the stairs to our apartment, ignoring my pleas not to. I followed, my nephew closely behind.

"Juaann, are you thar?" Geena shouted playfully, pounding on his door. "C'mon ond 'ave a good time with me like we alwaaays do…pleeease come out, will ya?" I could faintly hear Juan making excuses about his early meeting, but I'm sure Geena heard none of it; her laughing jag began. Her laughter continued while leaning her back against the door, only to slide slowly down into a sitting position. The crying followed as usual. My nephew lost no time hoisting his mother over his shoulders, and headed for the front door, Geena screaming all the way! It was funny to everyone but Juan.

We had never seen any Gay Pride Parades held on the last Sunday in June, and it was going on a few blocks from the house. We decided to see what it was all about. Not being flag wavers, we agreed to appear as though we were just in the area. Juan became even more uptight once we arrived at the parade route. I was a very fast walker but his quick pace through bystanders made me look like a turtle. I tried slowing him down since it was so hot and humid, only to hear, "Recharred, I do not want anyone to think we are faggots!"

Into the fourth month, Juan became very comfortable in our relationship, and shared the master bedroom with me. It was "our bedroom." His bedroom was for Svetmana whenever she spent the night. At times, he'd sleep with her, but most of the times he'd explain, "I am gonna sleep with my friend Recharred tonight so you con 'ave the bed for yourself my darlin.'"

We tried new bars but The Trip and Le Pub were our favorites, as well as one on Broadway. Two lesbians owned the Closet, but patrons were mostly male. It was the friendliest, and we especially liked it because we could socialize with men and women. Another bar, Knight Out, was a block from the apartment and we often used it as a starting point for our nights out.

My jealousy began to get the best of me again because Juan seemed interested in the manager of Le Pub, a good-looking blond guy. El Rubio (the name Juan referred to him by) always saw to it that Juan's requests were played by the DJ. Juan would constantly tease me by raving about him. I thought of it as just infatuation, but I was still sensitive to it. Then, one day, he called the shop to tell me he was having dinner at his mother's. "I am gonna stay for a while tonight, Recharred, because my mother says I jus' eat ond run all the time. Why don' you go see *Towering Inferno* tonight ofter work. You know I saw it with my mother, ond it is excellent, Recharred." I agreed, but felt a little bit uneasy.

I couldn't enjoy the movie because my one-track mind kept wondering if Juan was really at his mother's. I decided to drive past Le Pub on my way home, and when I spotted a red Fiat parked outside the entrance, I was certain my suspicions were right! Clark was a very wide street, however, and I couldn't make out the license plates from the opposite side. By the time I parked and walked back, the car was gone.

Juan got home shortly after I did. I decided not to question him because love must be built on trust. Besides, I wasn't positive it had been his car. I tried to erase it from my mind, figuring that even if it was his car, he couldn't have been up to anything since he was home shortly after me. Or was it his way of keeping me jealous?

Chris was a short, hefty, blond gal we met at The Closet. Though her face had the natural beauty and freshness of a young girl, she acted like a truck driver, and drank like one, too. It was apparent she never wanted to come off as feminine. We would usually see Chris if we went to Knight Out or The Closet. "You know, Recharred, I think Chris drinks three times as much as I do," Juan remarked, "Yes, I think so, but I really do like her. She is so cute ond funny, especially when she stands ot the bar ond challenges all the men thot she will drink more than any of them. Ond she does, Recharred, she really does, until they carry her out!" We'd laugh, and when it subsided he'd imitate her butch manner, and we would start up again.

Pat and Gloria, a lesbian couple we met at The Closet became good friends of ours. Gloria, an attractive Syrian, was the feminine partner in their relationship. She confided that she was still living with her husband, which confused us. Pat had been married, and was raising a daughter. She was tall and blond and, like Chris, she had a pretty face. She moved like a football player, but it was obvious she had a good figure. Her protective manner towards Gloria revealed her role in their relationship. Juan and I couldn't figure out this role playing, but we liked them and just accepted it. Nevertheless, we were baffled because we loved each other as men. We were happy with the friendship because we found it almost impossible to make friends with gay, male couples. Usually, one or the other would make passes at Juan, and sometimes me.

During an evening at The Trip, I spotted Bruce, a guy I had tricked with near the end of my marriage. In mentioning it to Juan, I went on to say, "The following Tuesday morning, I was about to leave for the shop and the phone rang. Joan was still in bed and I answered in the kitchen. It was Bruce, and without going into detail, he said that he had the "bug." Juan, I didn't know what he meant, and he finally said the word—gonorrhea! I was in shock! I think I thanked him for calling, but then I was afraid that Joan might pick up the extension and I hung up. I didn't want to go to our family doctor, Juan, and it took all day to find one that could take me. The doctor assumed that I was already infected, so he gave me two shots in the behind and said no sex for two weeks. Well, that was no problem. We were not having it anymore anyway."

Juan chuckled and said, "You are ter-ri-ble!"

We eventually ran into Bruce that evening and spent the balance of the night talking. Bruce was tall and good-looking, while, his lover, Jim, was short and husky with less than average looks. We began doubling quite a bit after that evening.

Fred and Walter were starting with Spanish lessons from a tutor, and I became intrigued when I heard that she lived a block from our place. I had longed to learn the language because I always felt out in left field when Juan was talking with someone at a Spanish bar we were frequenting. Fred was sure she'd be happy to have another student after I inquired if she'd mind if I joined them. By the expression on his face, Walter wasn't too pleased I'd be tagging along.

It was funny when Fred left the room. Juan shook his finger teasingly at Walter, and slyly asked, "Why are you taking Spanish lessons, Walter…hmmm? So you will be able to communicate better with all the tricks you bring home from Latin countries…huh? Really, Walter, you do not 'ave to worry about using your mouth for thot reason!" Juan then looked at him in that owl-eyed stare and finally roared with laughter. I knew if I had made that statement, I would have been shown the door. With Juan, he just joined in laughter.

So my lessons began. I had hoped Juan would help me study, but found that he lacked the patience. Each time I sought his help, he'd say, "Recharred, you do not pronounce your words cor-rect-ly. You pronounce everything so Italiano!" And then he'd imitate my pronunciation and roar with laughter. So, after about seven lessons, I quit the group. I did manage to learn many words, though the only ones put together were, *"Por favor, chiaro un cigarillo?"* which drove Juan crazy because I was giving up cigarettes every other week.

Walter and Fred had introduced a plush new nightclub, The Inner Circle to us, and we loved it. The lounge had a giant square bar with booths along the walls, and a staircase on one side of the room brought in view an elaborate, terraced nightclub. The stage of the nightclub was raised enough to see the performer from wherever one sat in the lounge. This same stage served as a dance floor between shows, and that could not have pleased Juan and myself more.

Craig Russell, a female impersonator of many famous Hollywood women, was the featured entertainer, and when he got going, he was hilarious. We returned with Bruce and Jim another time and this time, we were seated in the nightclub, up close. I'm certain Craig Russell was pleased Juan was there; his contagious laugh assisted in bringing the house down each time the performer went into one of his impersonations. We never returned, however; it was torched.

While married, I had purchased a filler type hairpiece. It was virtually undetectable because I'd lay it slightly above the part and comb the hair over it. My kids weren't aware of it for some time. When I started going out after my divorce, I didn't like for anyone to touch it while I tricked, and I'd quickly pull it off and stuff it into my pocket upon entering their place.

Juan didn't realize it, and when I confessed to wearing one, he roared with laughter and remarked, "Why are you wearing a hairpiece? You look good without it. You just 'ave thot bald spot in the back. I tried to explain that it gave a fuller look; he still insisted that it wasn't needed.

I also told him that I had had a series of hair transplants, but that I never completed them because of my wife's antagonism about my vanity. I went on to explain that she had even put a plaque on the kitchen wall, which read—*His All Consuming Ego*! After settling down and clearing his choked up laughter, Juan remarked, "She did? Aw thot is so funny, Recharred, I don't believe it!"

His choking laughter continued, but I went on, "So, since I needed to preserve the transplants I did have, Juan, I didn't tape the back of the hairpiece for fear that the ones there would be pulled out while removing the piece. So, the piece was prone to rising with the wind!"

I never wore my hairpiece while with Juan, especially after one particularly windy day. We were walking up Broadway when a gust came up from behind. Juan nudged me and shouted, "Jesus Chris,' Recharred, your hairpiece is standing on end!" I immediately reached to hold it down. By this time, Juan was at least ten feet ahead. When we later talked of it, we laughed hysterically. Juan finally insisted, "Recharred, for Chris' sake, get rid of thot rat!" Still I refused.

Then the first of two incidents happened. Mike and his girl, Sue, had me out to the farmhouse for Sunday dinner. After dinner, we went out to watch Mike play touch football. The October wind was quite gusty as Suzie and I sat in the lower seats of the bleachers, and suddenly I felt my hairpiece standing on end! I quickly put my hand up to hold it down, and I stayed in that position the entire game because the wind wouldn't let up. I was afraid to turn my head for fear of seeing everyone laughing, and as soon as the game ended, I raced for the car.

I never expected it to happen the second time because there wasn't any wind. I had taken my children, as well as Suzie, to an indoor amusement park. Everyone except Sue had gone on the looping roller coaster. In reality, we had actually been riding upside down for a quick moment. I immediately realized the reason for the wide-eyed expression on Suzie's face as she waited for us. I quickly grabbed for my head, pulled off the hairpiece and shoved it into my pocket! Once Juan heard my story, he laughed harder than the kids did. It never went on my head again.

We planned a party and invited Walter, Fred, Gloria, Pat, Bruce, Jim, and Chris, too, but figured she wouldn't show up. The day before, Juan mentioned he had asked a guy from the Spanish bar to the party. It threw me for a loop, and I tried to bite my tongue at hearing it was the very guy I was jealous about, but I'm sure my face told all. He was an Adonis, and I never knew what they were talking about because they spoke only Spanish. Juan detected my jealousy and remarked, "Whot is the difference, Recharred, you say you want to make friends, do you not?"

I wanted to think God was on my side the night of the party, if only to appease my stupid jealousy. Juan was in the bathroom showering when the bell rang. I couldn't imagine who it might be this early. I was apprehensive answering because it could be someone from my family on a surprise visit, and how would they react to couples of the same sex?

I rang the door buzzer, and after calling out I heard a man's voice ask, "Is Juan, he live a here?" I quickly popped my head over the railing, and there he was—Juan's invite, looking more handsome than ever! Whatever possessed me to do what I did I'll never know? In a stupid and rash decision, I replied, "Juan lives here but he isn't home."

"Well-a, he say he gonna 'ave a party tonight," he called out, rather puzzled.

"Oh, no, it has been canceled," I exclaimed, continuing the charade, "Didn't he tell you?"

"No, I 'ave not a talked to him since a he told me," he answered.

It then occurred to me that Juan might be out of the bathroom, so I said, "I'm sorry but I have to be somewhere, and I am late," and after a quick good-bye, I shut the door. I was relieved; Juan had not yet come out of the bathroom, but a feeling of guilt came over me. I couldn't believe what I had done. My stupid jealousy had gotten the best of me, and I wanted to run after him to tell him I was only kidding. However, I realized it would only be embarrassing, especially since another equally handsome guy was with him. He could be his lover and I would have only stirred up trouble. I finally rationalized that if Juan loved me, it shouldn't matter who was at the party.

My conscience bothered me all night, and when everyone was gone, I confessed. Instead of getting angry, Juan laughed, and when the laughter stopped, he shook his finger at me and scolded me, "Recharred, shame on you for doing thot. Shame on you!" He was glad I was jealous!

At times, when I got home late after spending time with the kids, I could tell when Juan had seen a horror flick. He'd be sprawled on the couch on his side, and every light would be on in the apartment. I'd laugh at hearing him rave on about the bloody picture and how scary it was, and remark, "If they scare you so much why do you then go, Juan?" He'd roll his eyes and bite his tongue, sighing, "Aw, but it was so good!"

Juan had a lot of favorite actresses, but none captured his heart like the beautiful Spanish film star, Carmen Sevilla. I cannot count the times he raved about her. His adoration was so strong that I actually allowed him to drag me to one of her movies. It was some sales talk because the film didn't have English subtitles.

Juan was a *Cancer*, and that meant that he was basically a homebody, and he wanted to enjoy it with me. I was the one who enjoyed visiting, and after bugging him to join me, he'd ask, "Recharred, don' you like to stay ot home ond enjoy it?" So we really spent much of the time at home. If we weren't playing the game, *Scribbage*, we'd watch television, or sit on the kitchen stools as Juan tallied our budget. And there was always music.

Of course, there were times he needed to be alone in his room reading. He wanted me nearby, however. He needed that security. Juan read at least two *Castle* pocketbooks weekly, admitting that they were trashy, but claimed that he needed a diversion from his serious reading. There were times, too, that he called to ask me to pick up one for him, reminding me, "Recharred, look for the ones thot 'ave a woman running away from a windswept castle on the cover."

He kept me guessing at times, and though that jealous feeling would pop up, I don't think I was ever happier being with someone all the time as I was with Juan. He was a joy! He had his opinions, strong ones, and if he didn't care for someone or something, he wouldn't 'hesitate to voice it. His honesty was refreshing. We talked incessantly about childhood, families, and friends. He was proud to hear that I had landed the coveted lead in *Man of LaMancha* at a dinner-theatre after receiving critical acclaim for the same role at a college-community production.

I was surprised and anxious when noticing the marquee of a closed movie theatre around the corner from Le Pub. I had had several disappointments in my quest to open a dinner theatre because of one economic crisis after another, and the words—*Opening soon - Dinner Theater*— rekindled the dream. I marveled at Juan's encouragement to pursue my dream once more—completely the opposite of the discouragement received from Joan each time I ventured into it.

Juan's obsession with a summer tan sometimes got a bit much. It had to be a deep tan, and he always felt it was fading. So an area around the Lincoln Park lagoon usually had Juan basking in the sun while I sat on the shaded part of the blanket I had strategically arranged on the grass. Bearing the intense heat of sunbathing was never my idea of fun, so at least this arrangement allowed me to be with Juan.

Mostly gays sunned in the area, and that often led to some hilarious sights. Juan always kept his eyes concentrated in the direction of his book except when I alerted him to some sex-capades. It wasn't unusual to see some hunk strolling slowly into the bushes, and to see another guy not far behind. The real show was when even more stampeded in after them.

I realized that my love for Juan could almost be hypocrisy if there wasn't also closeness between Svetmana and me. I tried to bring it about desperately, especially the times he asked me to come with them to a nearby kiddy park, but it was always the same—that wall between us. I never called it to Juan's attention but Svetmana even seemed to lack that affection one is so accustomed to seeing in a child for a father so devoted. She never ran to hug and kiss him; it was always he who did the running and kissing. He could not have been a more devoted father, and I was proud of that. Though it was sad to see him treat her like a rare jewel and then her wanting more.

Living with Juan allowed me to hear more of his phone conversations with Endira, and it didn't take long to confirm that he was being continually intimidated to spoil Svetmana equally as much. Yet, he was the only one giving her love. She, however, never seemed capable of handling it because it was apparent Endira was molding her into a spoiled, self-centered child, incapable of loving, or being loved for that matter. Endira evidently thought that material things were more important to Svetmana than love. I never mentioned to Juan but it was disturbing to realize that Svetmana's nastiness reminded me of Rhoda from the movie *The Bad Seed*! No, I could never tell him that. Endira's badgering had given him enough guilt complex.

"Recharred, you do not know how lucky you 'ave been to 'ave been able to raise your children until they grew up. I wanted thot so badly," Juan had said so often.

Many times in attempting to persuade Juan to leave a bar, in order to allow us a few hours sleep on week nights, it was in the pretense of going to another one. "Aw, Recharred," he'd plead in his slurred little boy voice, "I don' wanna go 'ome yet because we are 'aving such a good time!" Invariably, once I did manage to get him in the car, he'd insist, "Let's go to thot new bar we heard about!" and assuming I agreed, he'd raise his arms in that inimitable way of his and hum happily while swaying on his bottom.

I'd try diverting his attention by talking about some nonsensical thing, in hopes that he would not notice that I was making one turn after another onto dark streets instead of the direction of a bar. In reality I'd be heading home, praying that he'd doze off. He'd be easier to manage when sleepy. It seldom worked, though, because he'd be on to me in no time. Once his head began bobbing, I'd turn in the direction of home. At that moment, he'd perk up and notice we were going in the direction of our apartment. So, while shaking his finger at me like I had been a naughty boy, he'd slur out, "Aw, Recharred, I know whot you are doin.' You are tryin' to make me fall asleep so you con take me home! Do you think I am stupid or something!" He'd continue shaking his finger, scolding in his little boy voice, "Thot is not nice of you, Recharred, not nice ot all." Then he'd sit up stiffly, brace himself in a manner one would see in a belligerent little boy, and challenge me. "Recharred, if you do not turn the car ond go to another bar, I am gonna jump out! Do you hear me, Recharred? Jump out of the car!" He'd then fold his arms across his chest, clench his lips tightly, and stare at me!

So, I'd usually abide because he was so irresistibly cuddly sitting there like a stubborn little boy, wanting his way! He was so funny! But there were times I didn't think it funny since it meant that we'd only get a couple hours of sleep before a long day's work.

Sometimes I'd convince him to stop for breakfast instead. Of course, I'd have to hold my breath and pray that he wouldn't talk dirty once we were seated. My prayers were seldom heard though, and I'd hear something like, "Recharred, do you want a big cock tonight? Huh?"

There I was, turning every color of the rainbow, trying to quiet him, but he'd go on, "Well answer me, Recharred! Whot is the matter, are you embarrassed? Are you, Recharred?" Embarrassed couldn't ever have been a strong enough word to describe my feelings, especially when my alcohol had worn off. And no matter how I tried to divert him, he knew my intentions and talked even louder and dirtier. My only consolation was that our late night breakfasts were almost always at the Golden Nugget on Belmont and Broadway, and since it always appeared as though half the bars had emptied into it, his remarks were usually greeted with laughter.

It was amazing. Never did he remember anything he said or did the next morning; yet, he had been sharp enough while drunk to realize my diversion attempts. I can't remember ever staying angry; his approach was so innocent, so cuddly, and there was no way I would spoil that.

There was no limit to Juan's energy while drinking and having a good time. He never wanted it to end, and should I be successful getting him home before the bars closed, he'd continue his dancing with the stereo at full blast! It was a wonder the neighbors never broke down our door. He'd insist that I join him occasionally, and while struggling to keep up, I'd eventually turn down the volume. Juan would merely shake his finger in shame, and then move to raise the volume again. Spanish music usually was his choice, and probably because he could then reminisce about Buenos Aires. He'd be so content, holding himself proudly, his chin up, and turning his head sharply from side to side. He'd be in a world all his own. Yes, I'd hide the liquor.

Often, in an attempt to keep him there once I successfully got Juan home, I'd lay directly on top of him in bed in hopes that the prone position would put him to sleep. It almost never worked. He'd talk on in his little boy manner, always knowing my motive for being on top of him. Of course, he often pretended to be asleep and I'd pass out, waking to find him gone. I'd dress and race for The Closet and there he'd be...standing by the jukebox, a cigarette in one hand and a drink in the other, swaying to the music and wearing a big grin. An even broader smile would blossom when he spotted me. He'd place his hand on his hip and sigh in wonder, "Aw, Recharred, you are here? How wonderful to see you!" Like we hadn't been together that evening! There were times that he was aware that he had successfully escaped from the house, and he'd go on totally carefree. Finally, I realized, to keep him home, we needed to stop for breakfast first.

There was one evening that I will never forget! Somehow, I managed to get us home fairly early, and the only reason I succeeded was because I was drunker than Juan was, and he wanted to be sure that I got home safely. I had Juan laughing hysterically with one mischievous antic after another, and it continued once we were home. Juan was laughing so hard that he started gagging, but he still managed to plead, "Let's go out ond dance some more, Recharred. C'mon, it is too early to come home. Let's go out ond 'ave more fun...pleease?" I could barely stand, yet managed to hold up my finger and shake it at him. "No, no, no, Juan," I slurred out, "We 'ave to work tomorrow. Soooo, no, no, no!"

Juan chuckled at my ridiculous behavior but still warned me he'd go out himself if I refused. I continued with the silly manner of shaking my finger in his face until I lost my balance and fell into his arms. "Recharred, you are drunk! You are so drunk," Juan cried, trying to control his laughter while leaning against the kitchen counter almost helpless. Yes, I was drunk, and I was happy he was enjoying my silly behavior. Still, I realized he'd go out should I pass out, and as he continued chuckling, my mind was searching for a way to keep him home. Suddenly, it hit me! Tie him to the kitchen cabinets! I opened a drawer, and to my delight, found an electrical cord. There I was…tying Juan's hands to the handle, and snickering in the process!

Too weak from laughter to even think of attempting to escape, Juan stood there like wobbly gelatin trying to catch his breath while crying out, "Recharred, whot are you doin?' Are you crazy or something? Recharred, you are ter-ri-ble! I am gonna call the policiamon on you!"

"No, no, no," slurred again from my mouth, "You are not gonna go ou' tonight because I'm gonna tie you to the cabinet! Sooooo, you will jus' 'ave to stay 'ome." There I was, shaking my finger ridiculously again and snickering away like the villain tying a maiden to the railroad tracks! Then, suddenly, things began to spin.

I awoke suddenly to find myself in bed and still dressed! I was sober, yet dazed! My only recollection was that we had gotten home early. I panicked, and near hysterical after checking the other bedroom to find that he was not there either! It was past two in the morning and no Juan!

The tying-up episode finally came to mind when I noticed pieces of electrical cord scattered on the counter and a scissors. Juan's hands were, most likely, sloppily tied, and he used scissors from the drawer. I took off like a bat out of hell!

There he was, next to the Closet's jukebox, a cigarette and a drink, swaying to the music! "Did you finally wake up, Recharred?" he exclaimed, his eyes sparkling with joy. "Wonderful, mon! Let's dance." And we danced, and of course, then there was breakfast.

"Recharred, why are you going bock in?" Juan called out as I ran from the car.

"I forgot my pillow, and you know I can't sleep without it," I shouted.

"Recharred you are just like a little boy thot needs his blanket," he teased on my return. It was early Sunday morning and we were off to a two-week vacation in Florida. Although this would be an alternate trip, we were excited because it was to be our first vacation together.

Two months earlier, we saw an ad in the paper for a reasonably priced round trip to London, and it specified that the fares had to be paid in full sixty days in advance. It sounded great because it was for twenty-one days, and we could see so much in that time. Juan, however, quickly mentioned that he couldn't afford it. He reminded me that he had paid three first-class fares to Ecuador besides the down payment on his Fiat when I asked why he couldn't use some of the twenty thousand he made in the market.

"Well, that couldn't have taken all that money, Juan. Could it?" He hesitated, and then admitted to giving his sister a few thousand before leaving.

That explained it, but I still had to ask, "With all that money your brother-in-law is supposed to have, you still had to give them yours?"

"Recharred, it is only money!" he snapped back. I wanted to say more but held my tongue because I knew how much he hated being badgered about careless spending. "If you remember, Recharred," he went on to say, "when you had driven me to George's. The reason I went thar thot night was to pay bock the money he had given me to invest. Ofter all, he had told me I only had to pay him bock if I made money in the market, ond I made money!" That explained it.

I wanted to go on that European trip badly, especially with Juan, and I had finally said, "Well, whatever I have is yours anyway. So, I am gonna pay for our trips, Juan!" I spent hours planning the trip after securing a *U-Rail* schedule; from the ferry to Paris, we would take the train to Monte Carlo, Italy, and Spain. Then, thirty days before our scheduled departure, the trip was cancelled. I was devastated, and to ease my pain, Juan suggested we drive to Florida instead.

Our one day stop in Nashville to see the *Grand Ol' Opry* proved fruitless after discovering that tickets needed to be purchased months in advance, and there wasn't much else to do since it was horrendously hot. However, Juan raved about it. After all, it was another city in America!

While rushing to leave the next morning, we heard a knock on the motel room door. I took a quick peek through the slit in the draperies, and gasped, "Juan, can you believe it's the guy we were talking to so much last night at the bar!" Juan froze in amazement, placed his hand on his chest in his usual gesture of wonderment, and sighed, "I don' believe it." Though we didn't do any drinking, the guy had been quite mesmerized with our wit. Never did we think he'd take up our invitation to stop by before we left seriously, and we glared at each other in disbelief realizing what he was after. "Aw no!" we both shouted simultaneously.

The pounding continued, and we were forced to open the door. It didn't take him long to realize we wanted no part of him. He, however, was determined to try his luck, and when that failed, he went on to satisfy himself. We cracked up after he left and Juan finally remarked, "I don' like thot ot all, Recharred!" After I emphatically agreed, Juan added, "Boy, Recharred, bar lights really do people favors. He was ugly!"

"Oh? If he had been handsome, you might have considered it!" Juan smiled, winked, and then raised his brows.

Since we envisioned Florida as a palm tree paradise, our long drive through the flat terrain of pine trees left us quite disappointed. We felt like we were driving in Wisconsin without the hills. To add to our woes, the air conditioner in my car just wasn't cutting it.

The tremendous heat and humidity kept us uncomfortable continuously. And there was absolutely no relief from the waters of the gulf or the pool. Juan loved swimming, and though it wasn't refreshing, he still managed to swim as often as possible. I had praised his ability often since I could barely stay up in the water. There I'd be, splashing every which way, and when I did manage to get to a spot I could stand with my head above water, I'd catch Juan giggling. He'd try to teach me, but my mold had been set.

Juan never did set foot into the gulf; the scenes in the movie, *Jaws*, were still vivid in his mind. In fact, I was the one who ventured out into the water. I had to get some relief from the horrendous heat, and it didn't matter that the water I was splashing over myself on my plastic raft was like bath water. Of course, once I heard a splash behind me, I'd paddle for shore like a torpedo! I was amazed, unbearable as the sun was, Juan didn't mind lying in it. No way would he return from Florida and not have a tan.

The heat and humidity were horrendous, but we still managed to see all the sights and parks; any time spent with Juan was a joy. I must recall when he politely asked, "Recharred, would you not mind to drive to my aunt's. She retired here from Philadelphia. She ond my late uncle had been our sponsors, ond even though she had not been the blood relative, she was so good to us while we lived with her. I would so like to pay my respects to her since we are so close to where she lives. Please, would you not mind?" Of course I did not mind, especially once I was privileged to see the joy he brought to this old woman. It was unbearably hot and humid in her place, yet he never complained. Most importantly, his vocal praises made her feel like a queen!

We'd occasionally spend a Sunday afternoon just lying in bed, sometimes talking about the compatibility of our lovemaking. It was something I hadn't gotten accustomed to in twenty-two years, and the wonder of it was a thing to cherish. Mutual and simultaneous gratification was a thing I never thought existed in a relationship, and we talked about it. We were aware that society didn't take to our kind of a relationship favorably, and we sometimes felt ashamed. Yet, we figured that God must have meant it to be, because He brought us together, and we were happy.

Juan said something one of those days that I'll hold in my heart forever. Though it was sweet at the time, I never realized just how beautiful that small wish had been. Each passing year since has brought greater meaning to those few words, and I've held my head high with the realization that I had been so honored. Here was a man who wanted a child to love. A child that belonged only to him and the person he loved, and he needed that person to love him as much.

"You know whot, Recharred, would it not be wonderful if we could 'ave a child together," Juan had wished that day, "One thot would be ours, ond ours alone to love."

I knew Juan loved me, but I still had seizures of jealousy, especially because he seemed to enjoy the idea of keeping me guessing. So, along with the frequent problem of accepting his sexual identity, I was faced with one stressful crisis after another. I was definitely aware of his lack of tolerance for disloyalty, but felt certain it would never be a problem I would cause. But still, I had my doubts about him, suspecting he was not true to me. Juan had a habit of telling little white lies at times, and though they were merely to cover up some of his insecurities, I wondered if he might also lie about tricks. I would get so agitated whenever he expected me to accept his drinking as an excuse for anything wrong that he had done. It was permissible for him to cut up with someone, but God forbid should I. After probing him for a reason why he could get away with it and I couldn't, he'd merely say, "Because I am Juan!"

Chapter Twelve: Retaliation

It was a Sunday morning in late September, and Juan had been invited to an afternoon dinner at the home of an old friend. Virginia was also Lithuanian, and from Buenos Aires. He was to be at her home at three o'clock. I wasn't too pleased about it because I realized she'd serve wine and that would put him in a party mood. Since I was going to visit Martina at college, I worried that he might then go out to the bars. I was a nervous wreck at the thought that I might not be home yet should he decide to leave Virginia's immediately after dinner, as he often did when buzzed from wine. The possibility prompted me to head out early to see Martina in order to be home well before that time. He, of course, assured me he would not be doing any drinking because it was Sunday once I reminded him to call if he was in a party mood. However, from past experiences, I had known better.

Juan had mentioned that Virginia lived nearby, and he had smiled broadly once I casually asked for her address. He obliged, but I felt certain his smile was an awareness of the paranoia that would drive me to check if his car was in front of her house.

It was wonderful having dinner with Martina, though constant concern over Juan was eating at my nerves. I mentioned that I had begun upholstering the dining chairs, and was greatly relieved once Martina said, "I know the way you are, Dad. You won't rest until they are finished. So, if you want to leave early, I'll understand."

I was home before five, and figured that Juan would still be at Virginia's. I tried working on the chairs, but my nerves wouldn't let me. My mind needed to be occupied with conversation, and who could do it better than Gina, a friend who dated back to first grade. Of course, I drove by Virginia's on the way, and was relieved to see Juan's car directly in front of her house.

Gina's gangbuster personality should have been enough to hold my interest, yet I found it impossible to concentrate on anything but Juan. I finally faked a severe headache, and was on my way home. I drove by Virginia's house again; Juan's car was still parked out front.

I decided to try the chairs again, but this only lasted about an hour. My nerves were shot because Juan had never stayed this long at a dinner party! Whenever I had been invited to dinner he'd always remark when I got home, "Recharred, why do you 'ave to stay so long ot someone's house when you go for dinner? Don' you know you con wear out your welcome?"

Now it was past eight, and no Juan! Without further hesitation, I took off for Virginia's. This time his car was gone. Fearing we may have passed each other on the way, I sped home. I began pacing the floor when I discovered that he wasn't home and my hopes that he would suddenly walk in diminished because it wasn't happening! I was livid; feeling certain he had gone to a bar. I began babbling to myself, "Who does he think he is! He can go out drinking by himself, but I can't!" My nerves were so shattered that I was pacing incoherently from room to room, not knowing what to do next. I wasn't one who had to drink when stressed, but I decided to this time, probably to get even. I grabbed a bottle from the kitchen cabinet and poured into a water glass. When I stopped pouring, it was almost full. I never drank straight liquor, but there I was, chugging it down! An instant high hit me, and I was on my way out to find Juan, feeling like I was floating on a cloud! It was a complete reversal! Moments earlier, I was in complete anguish, and now there I was, walking to the bar feeling jovial and mischievous, all from chugging down the equivalent to eight shots of bourbon.

I decided to check the Knight Out since it was on the way to The Closet. I was higher than a kite when I walked in; the fresh, cool air really brought out the effects of the alcohol. I glanced around, but Juan was not among the eight customers there. But Chris was, shouting out like a truck driver, "Richard, what are you doing out alone? Where is Juan?"

I explained and she then asked if I had been to The Closet, reminding me that everyone went there on Sunday nights. "That's my next stop, Chris."

She had just called for a cab to go there. "So after I buy ya a drink ya can come with us."

A tall, blond guy was next to her, and she introduced him. My anger with Juan had to be the force that prompted me to do what I did next. Here was a guy I would never have been attracted to…no great prize, but there I was…kissing him passionately! My actions didn't faze Chris; it was a common sight in the bars. She was so drunk she never realized it was I doing it. Instead, she shoved another drink into my hand while I was still at it. I guzzled it down. I could barely stand but still shouted out, "I have to find Juan!"

I now had the equivalent of ten drinks in less than an hour, and I had never had that much in an entire evening! I couldn't see further than three feet. Everything beyond was a blur. A cabby finally called in, and while staggering out, I again reminded them that I had to find Juan.

Why Has All the Music Gone?

Judging by the noise, The Closet was jam-packed, but all that I could see was one big mass of color, as though everyone had jelled together. If Juan had been there, I would have never seen him. Chris went through her usual Butch mannerisms greeting everyone, then led us to a spot along the wall. So, besides guzzling the drinks she handed me, I carried on with this guy. Then, suddenly, I stopped smooching, and completely ignored him while glancing around the bar, though the only people visible were those that were passing in the cruising parade. I remember feeling very mischievous, not even thinking of Juan. Yet, subconsciously, I was getting even with him by mimicking his behavior while drunk.

I was in another world, barely capable of focusing on the passing faces. The rest remained a rainbow of colors. Suddenly, before me stood an Adonis! I quickly put a hand to my chest, and as only Juan could do whenever expressing awe, I sighed, "Hi, there, do you know you are cute!" While pausing, he smiled, and I quickly slurred out, "You know, I would really like to go to bed wit' you because you are so bea-u-ti-ful!" His smile broadened, but he walked on. I didn't give it another thought since he quickly joined the blur of color. I continued in my dream world.

Only a moment passed and there he was, next to me! This time, it was apparent he had no intention of moving on. I stared at him slyly and, while swaying, I slurred out, "So, you came back to take up my offer!" He introduced himself as Ed, and the only thing I recall of the conversation was that he worked for *Blueboy* magazine because I had asked if he was an office boy. I remember him asking me to dance, but we didn't dance long because I was wobbling all over the floor.

The next thing I remembered is getting out of a cab and this young man taking my arm to guide me up some stairs. He began unbuttoning my shirt and rubbing his fingers through my chest hair once inside, and slowly and methodically taking off my clothes while rubbing the rest of my body. Suddenly, there I was on top of him, kissing passionately and both of us naked.

Then, apparently, the passion sobered me enough to realize what I was doing, and I thought of Juan. *My God!* I thought, and I pushed myself off to lie there stunned! I didn't utter a sound, and since Ed wasn't aware of my dismay, he changed position and began to service every part of my body orally. My human weakness, as well as the remaining drunkenness, wouldn't let me stop. Afterwards, I was racked with guilt, hating myself because I had done the very thing I had repeatedly preached against! I quickly rose and began dressing, explaining that everything had been a mistake, and to forgive me because I couldn't reciprocate. He did not object, and continued talking, but I heard nothing. I apologized again and left.

I stood on the sidewalk like a zombie. Where was I to catch a bus since I didn't have enough money to take a cab? After pacing and turning in every direction, I realized my location and ran for the bus stop. During the wait and the ride home, my mind was swimming with the actuality of what I had done! "Oh, God, how could I have done something like this? Me? Who has been constantly preaching fidelity to Juan and everyone else? What am I gonna say to him? Where could I have been till this time?"

This was one time I wanted Juan to still be out as I opened the door, but there he was on the couch, lying on his side. He immediately shouted, "Recharred, we are through!"

"What do you mean, Juan? Just because I'm late?" I retaliated. "What about the times you leave me in bed and go out to the bar?"

"Recharred, I was ot the bar tonight, ond I saw you leave with thot young guy," Juan growled, ignoring my question and going on with his vicious attack! "Where did you go, Recharred?" he shouted, quickly sitting up, "Tell me, for Chris' sake! If you do not tell me, we are through forever! Where did you go?"

I realized I had better have an answer, and quickly replied, "He took me to the Bistro because they have a large dance floor. Juan, I was so drunk and bumping into everyone at the Closet. Yes, Juan, he did ask me to go home with him, but I had sobered up and told him I had a lover! Please, believe me! You know I wouldn't do anything like that. I don't believe in it!"

Juan's anger finally began to subside after I managed to explain the reason I had gotten so drunk. "Juan, I have never drunk that much in my life, and I was so drunk that I didn't realize where I was until the alcohol began wearing off at the Bistro! And then I told him that I had to leave." He finally settled down; my lies did the trick.

I couldn't live with myself the next day; the guilt kept spinning through my head! I couldn't conceive why I had done such a thing when I loved Juan so much, and to lie about it afterwards? I didn't want to believe that Juan's mysterious escapades subconsciously drove me to it. The entire day was like hell, and I knew I had to tell the truth when he got home. Little did I know, at the time, that he wouldn't want to know the truth…that he would never be able to handle it. Little did I know it would only prey on his mind for months, even years to come? Little did I know that I should have lived with my guilt, and that I'd become a better man because of it?

Juan was livid when I confessed, and lost no time cross-examining me while pacing the floor. I assured him repeatedly that I had only kissed the guy and that once I thought of him, that I pushed myself off and laid there in a stupor, but Juan wouldn't accept it.

"When you realized thot you were doing something wrong…when you said you thought of me…why did you not get up ond leave, Recharred?" Without giving me a chance to answer he went on methodically, suddenly losing all control and shouting, "JESUS CHRIS,' RECHARRED, WHY DID YOU NOT LEAVE?" I just stood there not knowing what to say. "I trusted you ond you 'ave betrayed me," he cried out, trembling with hurt, "I con not believe it! I CONNOT BELIEVE IT, RECHARRED!"

"I don't know, Juan, I really don't know!" I pleaded, "You know how I feel about cheating! But I was so drunk, and I guess I was subconsciously getting even with you for all the times that you have made me jealous! Juan, I just don't know!"

The heated agony went on for hours, and every time I thought he had conceded, his vehement manner insisted on all the details again. He finally settled down, but his acceptance of the situation was now callous. "Okay, Recharred, you 'ave cheated on me, so now it is my turn. We will remain together, but now I will 'ave my turn." Any bewilderment my face expressed quickly diminished when he boasted, "I will not 'ave one trick, Recharred. No, I will 'ave ot least three. You will see, Recharred. THREE!" And he held three fingers up to my face!

I should have never told Juan the guy's name because he never allowed me to forget it. He'd harass me constantly, when drunk, and once he had worked himself into a state, he'd shout, "Why don' you go with Ed, Recharred, I am sure he wants your bea-u-ti-ful body! Is thot not right, Recharred?" Yes, I had told him all the details. It went on for months, and he'd become nasty at the end of a night out instead of that happy guy who never wanted an evening to end. I can't count the shirts he angrily pulled from my back on our way home.

One particular evening, as we were ascending the hall steps to our apartment, he tore a brand new shirt completely off my back. In my blinded anger, I turned to him and shoved a lighted cigarette into his face! It didn't leave a mark but it did leave me with a terrible guilt. When I finally confessed, however, he laughed! He loved me too much to ever stay angry, and I felt the same about him to let the shirts prey on my mind. He was only behaving in this manner when drunk, and besides, I realized he was only retaliating to my hypercritical behavior.

There was one time, though, that he began antagonizing me while sober, and it came on very suddenly. We were watching our favorite movie, *Gone with the Wind*. It hadn't been on for an hour when he began needling me about Ed. His needling was so unbearable that I finally walked out of the theatre. I later figured that his memory was rekindled by Scarlet's desire for Ashley....

My unfortunate episode with Ed caused a switch in our relationship. Juan had now become the jealous one, and I really think I would have preferred it the other way since he was not as kind as I had been. I received cross-examinations every time I went anywhere. I could be talking to a guy at the bar only to have Juan approach and drunkenly snarl, "Recharred, you wanna go fuck with him...go ahead!" It certainly didn't help in making friends.

Yes, Juan got even although he was well aware that I was tormented with guilt. He kept his word by tricking three times. For some reason, it was the only way he could feel justified; he needed to see me jealous to assure himself of my love.

The first occasion almost got me barred from the Closet. Juan had been carrying on with some guy, and he was determined to get me jealous. Each word spoken to the guy was purposely said in a manner to antagonize me, and it worked. I was in conversation with an acquaintance of ours, and once Juan began the sideshow, I lost complete comprehension of anything said.

"Aw, thank you my good mon for your kind offer to buy me a cocktail. Thot is so nice of you!" Juan very clearly exclaimed to be certain I heard every word. So, I walked nonchalantly towards them, and without hesitation, knocked the drink over on its side! Of course, Juan was undisturbed; it was exactly what he wanted me to do!

"Recharred, why are you doing thot?" he exclaimed with a chuckle, placing his hand to his chest in that elegant pose, "Thot is not nice, you know." On the other hand, the guy was none too pleased, and expressed it rather angrily. Instead of dropping the matter, he continued to call me down. My tolerance was already near its end and I quickly put the palm of my hand over his face, and quickly forced his entire body down to the floor! No retaliations followed however; the bouncer was there in a jiffy and escorted me to the door.

"This is not like you, Richard!" he shouted, "If you return tonight, I'll be forced to bar you in the future! So please cool down?"

I was fuming, but realized I dare not go back. I began pacing in front of the door, expecting Juan to follow, but he wasn't coming out. I finally decided to walk to the corner and wait there; anyone coming out of the bar could be seen easily from that point. But then I became concerned since it was a frequent cruising area for hookers. All I needed was to be picked up as a male whore working the area. It would really make my night. Fortunately, a big semi was parked on the side street, and I decided to use it to hide myself from passing cars but still able to see the bar.

I finally spotted Juan coming out of the bar, and to my dismay, the guy closely behind! I was excited because they were headed in my direction and I could easily intercept them. At that moment, as I dashed from behind the cab of the truck, a police car came down the street. So there I was, looking as ridiculous as the hookers, racing behind the truck so the police would not spot me.

Juan was gone after the police had passed! A horrible feeling came over me, realizing how Juan must have felt seeing me leave with Ed.

"Now, Recharred, you know whot it feels like," Juan reminded me upon arriving home that evening, "ond I am not through yet!" He never said if anything happened, and I didn't ask.

There was a second time, but the real topper was the third. We were at Le Pub having a good time dancing. Midway through the evening, I noticed a guy giving Juan the eye, and I was certain he was aware of it, too. He was in his glory; this would complete his trilogy of revenge.

I made certain I included myself in conversation when the guy approached Juan. In fact, we were all having a good time and I felt assured that there would be no monkey business. It didn't bother me when the guy asked Juan to dance; he had already danced with me. Besides, I needed to use the facilities badly, and what better time than now.

It was like shock treatment when I returned. I tried to cope with the fact that Juan and the guy were no longer on the dance floor or anywhere for that matter, and stood there in a trance! I finally realized they couldn't be far and hurried out. My panic state was relieved as I spotted them about a hundred feet away walking towards the corner. I called out, feeling certain that Juan heard me, but he didn't respond! I began running, frantically shouting out his name, and felt relieved once he turned his body to look my way. However, he turned away suddenly and continued on his way. And it was almost as though he wanted to rub a bit of salt on the wound; his hands went above his head in that manner of his as he danced across the intersection!

In a wild frenzy, I took after them, feeling certain I'd catch up to them. They headed for the first high-rise on the next block, however, and my mad dash to make it through the opened glass doors with them failed. There I was, standing out in the cold. My pounding on the glass was futile; Juan never looked back as he danced through the lobby into the elevator. And before I knew, he was gone.

I never knew how I made it home. I do remember the phone ringing about twenty minutes after I got there. When I answered, I was greeted with that familiar, elegant voice. "Recharred, will you be so kind enough to pick me up? I will be waiting for you in front of the building here." I could not believe his brazen nerve! But of course, I went to pick him up because I loved him, as I knew he loved me.

I never forgave myself for giving Juan cause to do what he did. I was never sure whether he had had sex with these guys, and I never asked. I assumed he had since he had no control of his behavior whenever he was drunk. The only thing that mattered was that he loved *me*, and that he never remembered the others. They weren't what he wanted in life.

We talked about it at times, and in an odd way, our love grew stronger because of it. My greatest regret was that, because of that one foolish mistake, Juan could never completely trust me again. He was aware that he was my life, but it still hadn't mattered.

"Juan, why can you flirt and carry on, yet if I do the same it's wrong?" I had often asked.

"Because it is okay if I do it," he always replied, and while shaking and pointing a finger at me, he'd say, "But not if you do, Recharred!"

Chapter Thirteen:
Joy from a Greek Orthodox Priest

Our relationship continued, and though challenging at times, I don't think two people ever loved each other more. Juan had a friend, Mrs. Prestine. They would go to dinner on occasion. She had socialized with him and Endira, and at times, would babysit. My suspicions before we moved in together had led me to believe she didn't exist. So, when he had told me that he was taking her to see Jean Simmons in *A Little Night Music,* I had decided to purchase a ticket for the same night. I wouldn't be sitting with them, but at least we'd be driving together. Juan was aware of my motive, but didn't seem to mind. His reminders not to act like a faggot, however, bothered me; he should have realized I knew how to behave around straight people. I finally realized he was probably afraid I'd cater excessively to him, as I had done the evening the Spanish spitfire called me a faggot.

I found Mrs. Prestine to be an absolutely charming and sweet lady, and Juan's manner of treating someone like a queen seemed well deserved. We stopped for coffee afterwards, and some wonderful conversation followed. I soon discovered that as polite and gracious as Mrs. Prestine was, she definitely showed no tolerance for Endira. Her well-placed comments clearly implied that she also saw through Endira. It was also obvious that she was well aware of Endira's infidelities; she repeatedly assured Juan that he was better off without her. It was obvious that Mrs. Prestine had not had to depend on babysitting for a living. Her adoration for Juan made it clear that he was the reason she'd babysit. I also realized that she too was aware of Svetmana's nasty personality, and that she was concerned about it. After dropping her off, Juan said, "See, Recharred, thar is a Mrs. Prestine," and he laughed.

Juan's Uncle Nicolai was coming in from London to choreograph a ballet for a college production in Indiana, and he insisted I join him for the weekend there. Uncle Nicolai was a small man, filled with the energy of a person half his sixty-nine years. It was apparent that he thought quite highly of Juan, and that Juan idolized him. Unlike Juan's parents, his English was excellent. I'm sure he was aware of our relationship; he had been around the artistic world most of his life. He was absolutely charming during our stay, and in fact told Juan of a bar we might enjoy while he was busy with dress rehearsal. It turned out to be gay.

Juan and I attended a Halloween party at Knight Out and had the time of our lives! But I caught only three hours of sleep before work the next morning. I was surprised with a call later that morning from a man who identified himself as the director of a community theatre in a nearby town. They were doing a production of *Man of LaMancha,* and had one performance remaining. "Your number was given to me by the director of Academy Productions," he went on to say, "Our leading man was in a car accident last night and we were hoping you could step in tonight."

Needless to say, I was overwhelmed. Not since I had been called to replace the same lead at the dinner theatre had I been this excited and honored! It was my all time favorite role. It had been a year and a half since my last performance, though, and I hesitated in agreeing. He explained that should I agree, he'd call in the cast to rehearse with me. I agreed that a rehearsal would be necessary, but that I still needed a few minutes to decide if I'd be able to do the part justice on such short notice. He pleaded with me to give it serious consideration. As added incentive, he offered to pay one hundred dollars. I told him the money wasn't important, only that I could do a good job.

It didn't take long to reach a decision realizing Juan could now see me perform. I had always considered *Quixote* to be my best role, and without further hesitation, I called to say I'd do it. I was relieved that Juan was home when I called with the good news and instructions.

Juan had everything ready and we left immediately. He was as excited as I was. "Ot last, I am gonna see you in *Man Of LaMancha!* Ond, Recharred, I con hardly wait!"

I was more excited that Juan was finally going to see me on stage. I figured the hour it would take to get to the theatre would be just enough time for Juan to cue me on all my lines. He, however, had never cued anyone, and it caused some anger and impatience on my part. In fact, it was probably the only time I got angry with him when he was sober. He kept giving me entire lines when I had a blank, and I finally yelled, "Don't say the entire line when I don't know it! Just give me the first word, and if I still don't know it, say the second word, for God's sake!"

"Jesus Chris,' Recharred, I never did this before," he snapped back, "have some patience!"

"I only told you that four times already, Juan!" That did it; he refused to go on! I finally realized my impatience and apologized, and it didn't take long for him to smile and go on.

We were surprised at the reception awaiting us in front of the theatre. Included in the group was an actor in the play I was doing when I met Juan.

That explained how they knew of me. Seven o'clock arrived all too quickly and I was informed that we could no longer rehearse; the doors needed to be opened for a seven-thirty show.

I panicked! There was no way I could go on that soon! I was near hoarse! I needed more time, and insisted they hold the curtain for another half an hour to give me a chance to recuperate. They obliged after some hesitation, and I'm sure they thought I was a prima donna when I then insisted on some hot tea with honey and lemon. They had to be convinced of it after I made a big fuss when I learned there wasn't a seat for Juan. They quickly found one in the balcony.

When the curtain fell I was elated; I hadn't missed one line or song cue. And I was really proud when the leading lady hugged me and cried, "Oh, thank you, thank you so much, Rick! I was finally an *Aldonza!*" However, my biggest pride came in seeing Juan's face as he approached backstage. I knew he wanted to hug me hard, and I wanted him to since it would have completed my joy. Instead, he was forced to shake my hand vigorously while saying, "Recharred, you are so talented, so talented! I did not even know thot was you on stage!" And my heart swelled!

Juan raved on about my performance as we sat on the couch after getting home, and before I knew it, my eyes were closing. This was the first time Juan was disappointed that I was interested in nothing but sleep.

Chris met a sweet Mexican girl who seemed to put an end to her drinking. Maria was fairly shy, but whatever she had, Chris loved it! "Recharred, do you know whot happened?" Juan cried out coming in, "I just ran into Chris ond she told me thot she ond Maria got married last night! I am not foolin' around, Recharred. Maria wore a wedding dress, ond guess whot Chris wore? A man's white tuxedo! Do you believe thot, Recharred!" I really flipped after he said that the ceremony was held at The Closet, and finally asked why we weren't invited.

"It was a spur of the moment thing. She did call while we were ot the movies last night."

Their marriage must have motivated Juan to ask something I had thought of often, but never seemed to have the balls to ask. He had started out by asking me if I loved him. After reassuring him of that certainty, I added, "Do you think I would put up with all your antics if I didn't? You are my life!"

He smiled, and after affirming his love for me, came the words, "Recharred, would you like to do whot Chris ond Maria did? You know, we could also get married." I was in awe; I assumed he'd have laughed at the idea of two men getting married! And now he was asking me. We were silent for a moment, our eyes reassuring each other that it was something we both wanted, and we embraced.

We asked Chris and Maria to be witnesses, but the only time they were available was during the week. Unfortunately, Pat and Gloria could not make it because of sitter problems. Bruce, Jim, Fred, and Walter all confirmed however. I was happy; our vows would bring an end to Walter's pimping.

A small tear in the corner of Juan's eye confirmed his feelings as we said our vows in the center of the dining room. We stood motionless, our eyes reassuring one another of his intent to fulfill those vows. We had prepared a grand buffet, and after the congratulations, Jim led everyone to it. Juan began drinking heavily, yet managed to say repeatedly, "Now we are one, Recharred!"

Juan's usual desire to go out dancing surfaced towards the end of the evening, but no matter how he pleaded with everyone, they declined; the next day meant work. Even Chris refused. That didn't stop his desire, however. He began raising his arms in that familiar manner after everyone left, insisting, "C'mon, Recharred, let's you ond me go out dancing?"

I didn't want to go because we had to get up early, but to appease him, I said, "Let's get everything cleaned up, Juan, and then see if we still want to go out. To tell the truth, though, I would rather just stay home." I then went into the kitchen with a few things.

Juan was gone when I returned to the dining room, and nowhere in sight when I frantically checked out the living room! Our wedding night and he was gone! I shouted, "That son of a gun!"

Sure enough, there he was next to the jukebox, swaying to the music with a cigarette in one hand and a drink in the other when I walked into the Closet. He was so happy to see me, but he still managed to stun me with something I thought he had forgotten—digs about Ed!

Juan surprised me another time while on one of our evening drives. He changed the subject suddenly to say, "You know, Recharred, we are now one person—a family. Would it not be nice if we had the same last name?"

"Of course it would, Juan, but you know that is impossible," I replied.

Still, he insisted, "No, Recharred, it would not be. I would be willing to change mine to yours. Everyone always pronounces mine badly anyway. If I were Juan Mella they would 'ave no problem, ond we would truly know we were partners forever. Because, Recharred, I want you ond I to be together for always!"

He really meant it, and if I had agreed, I'm sure he'd have changed his name. Yes, he touched my heart again. I think of it often and wish that I hadn't talked him out of it.

It was about two weeks after we said our vows when we heard that Chris and Maria had broken up. Yep, Chris was back on the prowl.

We had been doubling with Bruce and Jim quite a bit, and I was looking forward to a lasting friendship. Then, it happened. I began to notice a bit too much attention paid to Juan by Bruce, and it bothered me. I never mentioned it to Juan, but was relieved once he confided, "Recharred, I 'ave to tell you something. Bruce has been calling me when you are not home, ond I know from whot he is saying thot he wants to get together with me." I inquired if he had a mutual desire.

"Of course not, Recharred, I love you, only you," Juan reassured me. "Do you know thot whenever you ond Jim 'ave been in conversation thot he has been talking very sexy to me?"

"Of course! He wants to excite you!" I exclaimed. "Believe me, Juan, I realized it. I had seen enough times with my wife and brother-in-law to know when something's going on!"

I was disgusted. It seemed as if the whole gay scene was full with guys who had absolutely no respect or loyalty for their or anyone's relationship. Maybe it was only prevalent in the bars…but then why Bruce and Walter? I was confused because we had met so many couples at the bars that appeared to sell their own relationships short by admitting to being on the prowl for someone to have a three-way with! Some of them even boasted to having a night out alone to do as they pleased! Had loving their own mate become so boring? We couldn't figure it out. Needless to say, I called Bruce and spoke my mind. We never doubled again, and our paths never crossed.

A new entertainer was featured at The Trip, a bombshell named Pudgy. She was a short, plump gal who worked the audience over like Don Rickles, and who sang in the loud and boisterous manner of Betty Hutton. Anyone easily bothered from being verbally abused had to be sure to stay out of sight. Juan wasn't in the mood to drink the night we first caught her act, and made sure we were completely out of sight. Juan really enjoyed her, and insisted on telling her so after the performance. From that evening on, she'd be sure to chat with us. She was so much like Juan in her frank manner of taking the truth and exaggerating it a bit, and I think he respected her because she did it with such ease. It was a shame that he couldn't be on stage because he, too, was so funny when mimicking others.

While catching one of Pudgy's shows, we met a couple, George and Ted. We really enjoyed their company, and I was happy to accept it solely for the evening since I had become apprehensive at making new friends after Bruce. Physically, they were also quite reminiscent to Bruce and Jim, and that naturally put me on the defensive. George was short and stocky, while Ted was tall and handsome. *Here we go again*, I thought! George had a beard and, while not really good-looking, he seemed to be a peach of a guy. My apprehensions soon disappeared after noticing the continual worship Ted bestowed on George. And our friendship began.

George told us he was a Greek Orthodox priest, and after hearing we had exchanged vows, he remarked, "You know, you're not really married until your marriage is blessed by a priest. What do you guys think? Would you like me to perform a Greek marriage ceremony for you?"

Juan almost burst with excitement, quickly gasping, "Really? You could do thot? Perform a wedding ceremony for Recharred ond me?" His little boy excitement and charm quickly surfaced, joyously exclaiming, "I don' believe it, Recharred! Then we con really be married! Aw, Recharred, con we not do it?" Of course I agreed!

Juan's curiosity continued, inquiring, "Are you sure you con do thot, George? You won't get into trouble?" And his childlike inquisitiveness wouldn't let up. Enthralled with Juan's madcap excitement, George chuckled and tenderly assured him, "Don't worry, Juan, I will not get into any trouble!"

Juan began anxiously listing the items as George explained the things we needed and their purpose in the ceremony. The candles would symbolize everlasting life together, while the ribbon-attached crowns symbolized a uniting of two people into one…forever.

We were thrilled beyond belief, but it was Juan who emanated a magical glow! I had never seen him so excited and happy! A week from Saturday was chosen to allow enough notice for everyone to attend. "Of course, Recharred and Juan, if you have any special song you want played, that will be fine. Ted will take care of that part during the ceremony." I was certain Juan would crush George once he hugged him and sighed, "You 'ave made me so happy, George, so happy!"

Juan's excitement didn't cease after they left, joyfully sighing, "Aw, Recharred, I don' believe it! We are gonna be married by a priest! We are actually gonna be married ond 'ave our marriage blessed! I am so happy, Recharred, so happy!" He took hold of my hands, smiling broadly, and as he squeezed tightly, I assured him of my happiness, and how much sweeter it was because he truly wanted it. Tears of joy filled our eyes.

Just sharing Juan's little boy enthusiasm was something special. He'd fill every moment with excitement for the coming event. He'd insist I sit alongside him as he went through the details of everything that needed to be done, listing them on a pad to be sure they were not forgotten. Many times, he would exclaim, "Recharred, I am so excited! I could hardly work today because I was thinking about it all day," surprising me with a peck on the lips.

Our circle of friends was small, but in preparing our guest list, he still used a pen to point out each of them to be certain I agreed. We couldn't invite our families; we were closet cases. So Pat and Gloria, Fred and Walter, George and Ted, and Chris and her guest comprised the grand total. And since Chris couldn't be depended on, we asked Pat and Gloria to be witnesses.

Each of us would prepare our best dishes. He was so adorable boasting, "You know, Recharred, I am excellent ot making canapés, ond I con ask my mother to make her deviled eggs! She makes excellent deviled eggs!" We had also agreed upon a small cake, and Juan had beamed when I insisted we have Italian cookies because it wouldn't be a wedding without them.

I thought Juan's bright blue eyes were going to pop from their sockets the day he exclaimed, "You know whot else we should 'ave, Recharred? I just thought of it!" After a savory lick of his lips he sighed, "Empanadas! We con order them from thot Argentinian restaurant." He was elated when I agreed, and immediately began reminiscing about Buenos Aires.

He really shocked me when I returned home from work one day. "How would you like it if each of us has a gold band, Recharred?" And he quickly explained that he felt differently about it after I reminded him that he never liked them. "It symbolizes us as one, Recharred."

"You are off Monday, Recharred, ond we 'ave to get our crowns ond the candles in Greek Town," he went on to say, "So I think I will take the day off because we con go together ond pick them out. Don't you think thot will be nice?" It was all too fantastic; he hardly ever agreed to miss work! Once we agreed, he beckoned, "Come into the kitchen ond see whot I made for dinner."

While removing the lid from the pot, he boasted proudly, "It is one of my special dishes—meatballs with mushroom sauce ond sour cream, and I am about to boil some noodles to go with it. I 'ave the salad cut up ond all I 'ave to do is add the spices, especially *Sazon*." Then, to be sure I wouldn't try to help, he added, "Now, don't touch anything, Recharred, because I do not want a mess. I will do it myself. You con put some music on. You love *Sandro* so much, so put thot on."

"You know, Recharred, I think thot woman knew the real reason we were getting the rings," Juan remarked after leaving a jewelry shop, "Do you not think so, too?"

"I would say so," I exclaimed, "especially after she said we made a nice couple!"

"You know, Recharred, thot was not too bad ot all. I did not mind her suspecting why we were buying the rings."

"And I'm certain it wasn't because she thought we looked like faggots, because we don't," I insisted. "Of course, you charmed the hell out of her. I honestly thought she was going to jump over the counter and kiss you because she didn't take her eyes off your beautiful blues."

While driving to Greek Town, we decided to say that we were brothers, and that we were planning our sister's wedding. I can't recall our answer when she asked why we never learned to speak Greek.

Our frustrations ended after being shown one matched pair of crowns after another; an identical pair was unwrapped. Juan's joy was apparent, merely by watching him clench his teeth and flicker his brows in delight.

"Does your sister have a wedding cake ordered already?" she inquired while placing the wrapped candles and crowns on the counter, "Because we make them up special for you. A tiered wedding cake is beautiful, and each layer is made with many flavors. You know, like a torte cake."

Juan's eyes lit up like stars! I had never especially cared for tortes because they were too sweet, but he loved them. "No, she has not," Juan answered.

I almost swallowed my tongue when she pointed to a two-tiered cake and told us the price. I then smiled weakly after she went on to explain that the cake would easily serve fifty, and hoped Juan would get the message since we were expecting less than ten.

Juan motioned me aside when another customer interrupted, whispering anxiously, "Recharred, I want to get thot cake so badly! Then it will be like a real wedding, ond everyone will know we mean whot we are doing. Please, Recharred, I want it so badly!"

He was so thrilled that I just couldn't argue about the cost. So I smiled and said, "If that is what you want, Juan, then I want it, too!"

Choosing the decoration for the top created another problem; all of them were of a bride and groom. Who was to be the bride, and who was to be the groom? We couldn't explain why none of them would do, and I was relieved when Juan spotted one almost hidden in the corner of the case.

"Look, Recharred, ot thot one," he exclaimed, "It is perfect! Our sister loves bells!" It was perfect. One bell for Juan and one bell for me, and they were joined!

Juan almost danced to the car, bending his knees and raising his arms in that inimitable way of his. My mind flashed to the time just after my divorce, when I realized I was gay but couldn't accept it. I had hated my feelings because no one seemed to make it right. I recalled how I had wished for someone to be out there for me…someone I could be proud of, and happy with. And there he was just ahead of me! There he was, dancing happily to the car and turning back to shout, "Is it not wonderful, Recharred!"

Chapter Fourteen:
United as One

"Is thot you, Recharred? I am glad you are home," rang Juan's voice over the sound of *"Rock Your Baby"*. One glance around and it was apparent Juan had been busy getting ready for the evening's festivities. The hardwood floors sparkled, and the smell of a freshly vacuumed carpet was still in the air. Nuts and candy were already in bowls and placed on the cocktail table, and it just looked so festive!

"Hi, Juan! I see you've been busy getting everything ready," I called out, setting down a bundle of flowers and removing my coat, "It looks great!"

"How I wished you were here today, Recharred, I missed you so much," Juan sighed, approaching with a butter knife in one hand and canapé in the other, and surprising me with a quick, tender kiss, "ond I could 'ave used your help."

"I missed you too, Juan. All day I wanted to be here with you getting ready for tonight. I did leave at two, though, to pick up the flowers, and it's only three-thirty now. So there shouldn't be any problem getting ready on time. Believe me, Juan, I look forward to working alongside you!"

Juan stood there, anxiously anticipating the two steps that would allow me to see the full dining room; the ceremony was to be performed there. "Look, Recharred," he finally beckoned, unable to wait a second longer. I had already seen the table set along the wall, but not yet seen how beautiful it looked. Everything was meticulously arranged on the white linen tablecloth. The white gold rimmed platters were placed in two stacks with the matching cups and saucers set behind them. The gold finished flatware was placed into a perfectly formed arch next to the silver chafing dish. Next to the uniquely placed napkins were two gold candles. I took hold of Juan's hand and squeezed tightly to show how moved I was.

I had yet to turn in the direction of the brick wall where we had placed the antique server-buffet. Juan called me at the shop one Saturday to tell me about a buffet he'd seen at a street sale on our block, and that he loved it. Of course, I told him to buy it; the asking price was only twenty-five dollars. "Don't worry, Juan, I'll give you the money when I get home if that's all you have until payday," And it looked ten times the price after I refinished it.

Juan stood there, a big grin on his face, waiting for me to turn in that direction. "Oh, God, Juan," I sighed upon seeing the tiered wedding cake, "it's beautiful!" Placed on each side of the cake were the crowns with the joining ribbon draped in front of the buffet! The candles were placed directly in front of the cake, as well as a small, white platter holding our gold bands. "Juan, it really looks beautiful! It's too wonderful to be true," I sighed as tears began escaping my eyes.

"It is for us, Recharred. It is *our* wedding cake," Juan sighed, taking hold of my hand. We stood motionless, mesmerized with the beauty of it all when Juan finally beckoned, "Come in the kitchen, Recharred, ond I will show you everything I 'ave done." After showing me the filled trays of canapés in the refrigerator, he sighed, "Are they not bea-u-ti-ful, Recharred?"

His excitement took over, and instead of waiting for my reply, he went into his rapid patter. "I 'ave four different kinds…cream cheese ond salsa…spam ond pickle…cheddar ond olive…ond now I am preparing the chicken salad ones. Recharred, I had to cut the bread into little squares! Ond thar on the bottom shelf are the deviled eggs my mother made! Aw, Recharred, wait until you taste them. They are so delicious! Ond look, Recharred, she even put them in a bea-u-ti-ful silver tray!"

He continued excitedly with the tally. "I bought all the mixes you asked me to get, ond the ice is in the freezer. Ond, as you con see, all the liquor is on the breakfast bar along with the ice bucket, ond I 'ave a basket ready for the chips. Aw, ond wait until you taste the dip I made! I put the tray of cold cuts ond the potato salad you made on the porch!"

He finally took a breath, but his excitement stayed at full throttle. His smile beamed as he proudly clenched his teeth and clasped his hands. He was anxiously waiting for me to ask about something very special. He held out as long as he could.

"Thar they are, Recharred, the empanadas for our wedding reception…just like Argentina! Maybe you con place them in the pizza pan so they will be ready to put in the oven."

I couldn't believe how excited and happy he was, and glad that he didn't seem to mind having to do it all alone! It was all so wonderful, and so new to me since all I had experienced for twenty two years from my wife was grief whenever we prepared for parties or any occasion. I was accustomed to hearing constant screaming that I never thought I'd ever enjoy planning any function again. Now, here I was next to Juan, and completely content! We were rushing, and yet he still managed to keep up his lively chatter. I couldn't help but think of how desperately my children and I longed for our guests to arrive early in order to stop their mother's tormenting rage. With Juan, I couldn't have cared less if anyone showed up!

After fixing a floral arrangement, I placed it on the table, and showed Juan the boutonnieres made up with stephanotis. "Aw, Recharred, I am glad you got them instead of carnations."

The last thing needed was a cassette recorder to record our ceremony. Ted was bringing a cassette player to play all the music. We loved the song "For All We Know" from the movie *Lovers and Other Strangers,* and chose it as the selection of our choice. It was a perfect choice; the lovers in the movie lived together and were also blessing their union with the sacred vows of marriage.

"Oh, Juan, the Italian cookies!"

"How could you forget, Recharred, when you said it is not a wedding without them," Juan teased. I found the two-tiered silver tray I inherited from my wife, a wedding present she didn't want, and once it was on the table, it completed the wedding picture.

It was now time to get ourselves ready. We stood there taking everything in to be sure we hadn't missed anything, but mostly because we were so proud. Our eyes met.

Of course, the meeting of our eyes led to a beautiful break, which meant rushing even more to be ready by seven; George and Ted were arriving at that time to set up the altar.

Juan looked so handsome in his navy blue suit, and I wore the blue one I bought in New York. There was just enough time to pin on our boutonnieres, and I'll never forget the adoration from Juan's beautiful blues as he stared into my eyes while I struggled with his lapel. I was doing fine until I spotted a tear clinging to the corner of his eye, and then my hands began to tremble.

"Why are your hands trembling, Recharred?" Juan teased, pronouncing his words in that explicit way of his, "Are you nervous because we are getting married?"

"I guess I am because I'm afraid this is just a dream, and that I'll wake to find it's not happening."

"No, Recharred, it is not a dream. It is bea-u-ti-ful reality."

Ted and George arrived exactly at seven, bringing up the altar and a bag of items. Comments on our handsome looks and the festive appearance of the apartment followed, as well as a quip about how nervous we looked. "But that's normal, and to be expected," George assured us.

Juan fueled his nervous excitement by asking George about the ceremony repeatedly, and after a display of amusement at Juan's innocent manner, he agreed to go over the details again.

I expected Juan to explode with excitement when George slipped on his vestments. "Aw, Recharred, look! A real priest! Ond this place looks like a real church," he exclaimed, and after a sigh of realization of what was happening, he sighed, "Recharred, we are gonna be married!"

Everyone arrived at the same time except Chris. We had told her to arrive an hour earlier to make sure she was on time, so we figured she wouldn't be showing up. Gloria was as excited as we were. She couldn't rave enough about how fantastic everything looked, and was amazed that we spared no expense.

After hugging us repeatedly, she posed us in front of the cake for a picture. "Juan and Richard, you two look so right together," she sighed, "You are a perfect pair. Don't ever change it!"

The excitement coming from everyone was overwhelming. Even Walter seemed to be happy for me, and I was glad because everything had to be positive!

George finally called the chatter to a halt; it was time to begin. If any sound was heard, it was coming from our hearts. Our eyes met, and we moved to the middle of the room, facing George at the altar. The crowns and candles were now on the altar, along with our gold bands.

I never asked what thoughts were going through Juan's mind at that moment, but mine were about everyone standing behind us. I knew they believed in our love and in the ceremony that was about to culminate it. I remember wanting my children and family to be there with them, and to have them respect the ceremony about to be performed, too. Surely, the joy and happiness Juan had brought to my life was obvious, and there wouldn't be any reason for scorn.

I was certain the love emanating from us was felt throughout the room. Never had we been this serious, and it remained that way throughout the rituals. There was no laughing, no joking around. We were experiencing something beautiful in our lives; a culmination of the love we shared. It was time to hold hands, and I realized Juan was trembling as much as I was. The trembling ceased as our tender squeezes assured us that we were doing the right thing.

Though we couldn't understand the rituals and music, we were completely aware of what was happening. It was especially clear when the crowns were placed on our heads, as we held the burning candles. The only chuckle came from George when Juan gasped struggling to squeeze the ring on my finger. Our moment arrived as our eyes met, listening to the refrains of:

Love, look at the two of us, strangers in many ways
We'll have a lifetime to share…so much to say…

"OPAA!" yelled Ted when the song ended, and the others quickly shouting the same!

George grasped our hands and congratulated us, followed by Gloria. Her eyes over-flowing with tears, she reached out to encompass us both in her arms. "Richard and Juan, I have not been so moved in all my life!" she cried out in awe. "It was so beautiful!"

Hugs and kisses were coming from every direction, even Walter seemed moved. Juan was so happy as we stood there holding hands, and in a choked voice, he finally sighed, "Now we are really married, Recharred! We are one!"

"I know, Juan, I know, and I am so happy!" We stood frozen looking into each other's eyes, trying to hold onto the precious moment for as long as we could.

However, we had to break the spell if we were to be good hosts. We didn't want everyone to think that only Italian cookies were being served. I slipped the empanadas into the oven while Juan began placing things on the table. After I fixed everyone a cocktail, he took hold of my hand to lead me to the table. His charm and excitement was overwhelming! "Does it not look wonderful ond elegant, Recharred! Our wedding buffet!" Even more wonderful was he hadn't yet had a cocktail! In fact, neither of us had a drink in our hands once a toast was made.

"Please, everyone," Juan announced proudly, "a wonderful dish from my home in Argentina will be ready in a couple of minutes. They are empanadas, ond you will love them!"

An emotional stillness filled the air the moment we joined hands to cut the first piece of cake. The evening was a happy one for everyone and seemed to come to an end too quickly. Though we savored the moment, Juan made certain no one left with tears in their eyes. He quickly remarked on how accommodating my big mouth was!

Everyone was gone by one o'clock, and it was probably the first time Juan didn't insist we go dancing. There we were, the two of us, alone in our home, and truly married!

Chapter Fifteen:
Conceding to Ego

We were married, but that didn't mean Juan and I became sedate love doves. Our jealousies still existed, we still hurt easily, and he didn't give up his stubbornness. It was a beautiful culmination of our belief in each other to continue in the same manner though. Going to the bars was still very much a part of our lives, and we continued being confused meeting couples who were willing to sell their relationships short by admitting to extracurricular affairs! And I still felt as though I was a policeman when Juan drank heavily. And yet he was basically a stay at home person. Whether it was television for the evening, or playing the word game *Scribbage*, it was never possible to be bored. Going to the movies twice a week was not unusual, even traveling some distance if it was one we really wanted to see.

We had talked casually about opening a bar, since many of them seemed to be so successful. I insisted on live entertainment should our small talk become serious. Small consolation for my long lost dream to open a dinner theatre. Juan didn't have any money but I had over forty thousand dollars besides my shop building. "Are you kidding?" George remarked when we mentioned it. "Ted and I have wanted to do that for some time, too, but we wanted to include a restaurant since I am also a chef."

That is all it took for our small talk to become serious. We finally agreed we were compatible enough to join forces, and decided to search the north side for a spot. The search finally led to a fully equipped restaurant above an antique store. Though we were apprehensive about the place because it was on the second floor, we realized it wouldn't matter if we offered something special. But after repeated visits, one flaw remained…two separate kitchens. We decided on making an offer nevertheless, and were promised an answer after the weekend.

Juan and I had been planning a weekend to Atlanta; this would be the perfect time. So there we were, the end of November, flying to Atlanta.

This was our first flight together, and I soon learned that Juan was afraid of flying. "I cannot fly if I don't 'ave a couple of drinks before. I am too scared to be so high in the sky."

A couple cocktails in flight after the two before put him in a great party mood when we arrived, and after checking in our hotel, we took off for the one bar we were aware of. The weather was wet, but it didn't dampen Juan's spirit; there was that excited little kid in a new city.

A Victorian house set on a slight hill. This was Club Three. Along a row of windows of the verandah were cocktail tables, and on the opposite brick wall was a window, a service area of the bar in the main room. Looking through the portal into the grand foyer, we were astonished to see an elaborate crystal chandelier hanging above a staircase leading to a second floor. Going up looked like quite a task, though; guys were trying to make out on every step. It was jam-packed as we turned right into the main room, and especially crowded around the exceptionally small bar.

A drag show was in progress, and, after waiting forever for cocktails, I managed to push our way through to a spot to watch. Juan's awe at being somewhere new never ceased. The quality of the show also captivated him. "Recharred, I cannot believe they are really men! They are so bea-u-ti-ful! Ond so many production numbers!"

We had only seen one other drag show…at the Baton in Chicago. And we had not been impressed with it. The boring steps of the impersonators were so reminiscent of the strippers I had seen in straight strip joints, and never seemed to be in synch. This was the South, we discovered.

The evening turned into a fun filled one, especially since it was impossible to get to the bar. And dancing wore off the drinks we did have, making the outlook for the next day great.

Juan actually insisted on messing up the other bed before heading out the next morning. "Recharred, we do not want the maid to think we slept in one bed."

The day was a total joy, and after a fabulous meal at Miss Pittipat's Porch that evening, we were on our way to Club Three again. We would have had to be blind not to notice the cruising going on from cars alongside of our taxi. "I don' believe it," Juan whispered, "This town is so gay, so gay! Ond look ot how handsome they are."

The club wasn't crowded and we managed to get stools at the bar. It was unfortunate though; Juan began downing one drink after another, and there was no way I could tell the bartender to eliminate the alcohol. Nevertheless, he was having a wonderful time, and so was I for that matter because he had me in stitches. Suddenly, I noticed a guy at the end of the bar laughing along with us, finally figuring he was cruising Juan. But when Juan went to the bathroom, he surprised me with a wink.

When Juan returned we were served a drink…compliments of this same guy. Juan raised his, and, in his distinct and elegant voice, called out, "Thank you ver-ry much my good mon for your kind offer." That was all the guy needed, and he approached to introduce himself. Well, Ben was quite good-looking…fair hair and macho. Sort of a Gary Cooper type, and we were enjoying his company because he was giving equal attention to us both.

Laughter continued as well as the alcohol, and Juan seemed to be fine. In fact, both of us were quite witty, keeping Ben in stitches as well as ourselves. But since we were so involved in conversation, Juan only agreed to dance one set.

I finally realized that I should have insisted we dance more; in what seemed like only a moment, Juan suddenly became incoherent. No longer was he communicating sensibly. He was in a world all his own, interjecting with ridiculous remarks that had no bearing to what was just said instead. I was pleased that Ben understood since he continued to direct conversation his way. It never occurred to me that it was his way of earning my respect.

I realized I had to get Juan away from the bar and get some food in him. Fortunately, last call had been made; closing was at 4:00 A.M. There should be no problem getting him to leave. I thanked Ben for the nice evening, but he still wouldn't say good night. I explained that Juan needed to eat, and that we were going up to the after hour dining room as we had done the evening before. Instead of saying good night, he insisted on buying breakfast.

This was the first time I ever saw Juan make a mess while eating, but at least he got some food in him. I was so glad once we were ready to leave; Juan had carried on so outrageously. It didn't surprise me when Ben offered a lift, but I was a bit shocked when Juan quickly accepted.

Then it came, the offer to stop by his place to see the old mansion he recently purchased. "Aw, yes, Reeecharr,' let us go," Juan quickly slurred out, surprising me again, "I wu verrry much like to see on ol' southern mansion."

I didn't want to go, but I did, and probably because my ego was at it again. So there we were, on our way to the spider's web, and I wasn't stopping it. I was drunk, too, but well aware of Ben's motive.

Juan raved about the mansion, though I had found it dreary; but then, he could barely stand, let alone focus. He was so drunk! Of course, he quickly accepted the offer of a drink, but I whispered to Ben to make it water and ice.

Of course, he insisted we see his bedroom on the second floor because he had just recently remodeled it. The details about the remodeling were never mentioned once we were in the room; he began disrobing instead. Without hesitating, he invited us to join him in bed. To this day, I don't remember disrobing. But there we were, the three of us, in bed naked! I remember Ben kissing me, and then whispering that I was the one he wanted. I remember catching the expression on Juan's face; it was enough for me to realize my mistake! His pathos filled eyes were begging, "Whot are you doing, Recharred? How con this be happening when we love each other so much?" I was overwhelmed with guilt and pushed Ben away as he approached again. I turned from both of them and laid there in a stupor.

I was sick at the thought of being in such a situation. "I'm sorry, Ben, I can't do this!" I cried out, scrambling out of the bed, "and I don't want Juan to do anything either because we love each other too much! We can't!" I was almost in a state of delirium crying out to Juan to get dressed, too, and in my anxiousness to get out of there, I hadn't realized he didn't respond. Ben's insistence that it was okay only increased my guilt and confusion, and I hurried out without Juan!

I hurried down the stairway expecting Juan to follow. When he didn't, I began pacing nervously. He wasn't coming down, and I was devastated because Juan had no control when drunk. I trembled at the thought of finding him in a sex act with Ben should I return. I began to cry pathetically at the thought of what might be happening upstairs. Juan was drunk. Might he be subconsciously getting even with me for even thinking of having a three-way?

Only about ten excruciating minutes passed but it seemed like an eternity before Juan and Ben came down. The smile was gone from Juan's face. He was silent as he put on his coat, almost burying himself into it once he raised the collar. I don't remember saying a word...only how sad he looked.

The drive to the hotel was silent, and my only response to Ben when he thanked us for an enjoyable evening was to thank him for the lift. Juan fell asleep as soon as we were in our room, and as daylight approached, I sat in bed brooding.

This was probably the first time Juan didn't wake up in a jolly mood. His usual happy self after a night of heavy drinking was gone. He was quiet instead. It was apparent, though, that he was aware something had happened. But he wouldn't talk of it.

I was quiet because I was hurting. I realized if I had not accepted Ben's offer, it would not have happened. I allowed myself to be influenced by the morals of those we had talked to in the bars...to do something I was strongly opposed to. The thing was to never allow it to happen again. Maybe we could learn from it...maybe the experience would make our love grow.

We both looked like something the cat dragged in. It wasn't until we were at the Swan House that Juan's excitement emerged again. Although the drizzle continued throughout the day, he wouldn't allow us to be gloomy.

When we arrived home that evening, all was forgiven. All that had to be kept in mind was that we loved each other, and that we had a wonderful trip. We were not going to bring up the misfortunate happening again. All we wanted was for it to never happen again! I will mention that Juan did manage to fly home without a cocktail. As we sat on the couch, Juan tenderly said, "Recharred, we are bock home where we belong. I love you."

Chapter Sixteen:
Why Not Atlanta?

We expected better news from George and Ted the following Monday evening when we anxiously asked if they had heard from the club owner. "Yes, we did," George replied, "In fact we went there Saturday afternoon, mainly to ask if the wall could be taken down between the two kitchens. Well, he said it couldn't be done."

"Are you sure?" I asked. "He can't? Or he won't take it down?"

"I don't know which, Richard. He was just very firm against doing it." After an awkward pause, he went on, "Ted and I have talked about it and there is no way I will be able to work in two separate kitchens. It's impossible. So I'm afraid we're going to have to back out of the deal."

We were stunned, and though we made every possible suggestion on using the kitchens as is, they still wouldn't agree. They tried talking us into doing it alone, but that was impossible. We only agreed upon it because their families were aware of their relationship, and we could then keep our names from being listed as owners. I had been excited about the bar and when they left, my depression began building. "C'mon, Recharred, don't be sad," Juan said consolingly. "It was just not meant to be. Maybe something else will turn up."

We finally managed to put it out of our minds, especially once the holiday season arrived. However, just before Christmas, Juan mentioned that he'd been thinking about the possibility of opening a bar in Atlanta. "Remember how gay we found it to be, Recharred," he had reminded me. I called attention to the fact that we would then need to move there, and he said, "Well, you 'ave always said you wanted to move to another place with me so we would not 'ave to hide our love for each other. Ond look how busy Club Three was, Recharred."

That magical charm of his didn't take long to work because I found myself imagining how wonderful it would be not to worry about straight friends and relatives seeing us together all the time. We decided to call Club Three for information since it was the only place we knew of in Atlanta. To my surprise, after explaining my call, I was told that their club was available. Before I could ask why, he asked for my name and phone number for the real estate agent.

We were rushing to leave for Christmas Eve. Juan was going to his mother's and I was meeting my kids at Deena's. We hadn't heard from Atlanta, and sort of dropped the subject. But then, the phone rang; the party identified himself as a real estate agent in Atlanta when I answered, and after hearing that we were still interested in opening a bar, he asked if we could make it down before New Year's Day. Juan guessed who I was talking with by my responses, and was ecstatic when I held the phone to tell him the details. His arms rose in the air, waving every which way! "Do you want to, Recharred, do you?" he pleaded. "Aw, please tell him we con make it!"

So I made an appointment, and as soon as I hung up, Juan shouted, "Aw, Recharred, jus' think, we are gonna be bar owners!" However, we were late and decided to discuss it all later.

I knew Juan would be home early, so I didn't hang around Deena's all night, as was our custom on Christmas Eve. Juan was on his side on the couch when I walked in, and I remember the romantic setting hitting me in the face. The only lighting came from the Christmas tree, and I will never forget the beautiful glow on Juan's face as he looked up at me and said, "Aw, you are home early, Recharred. Good! Merry Christmas, my darling!" He then surprised me with a soft peck on the lips and added, "Now, we con decide about our trip to Atlanta, Recharred!"

We decided on driving straight through; a motel room would only be needed for one night while in Atlanta. If we left on Sunday, the twenty-eighth, there'd be no problem making it back in time to be at the shop New Year's Eve morning.

"Now, Recharred, let us now open our Christmas presents," Juan said anxiously.

"I thought we were going to do that in the morning, Juan," I said, a bit surprised.

"Well, it is morning, ond besides, you know I am too impatient."

"Aw, Juan, you are just like a little kid!"

"Well, I want to see if you spent as much for me as I did for you," Juan boasted, using that put-on arrogance. "Of course, Recharred, more should be spent on me because I deserve it!"

"Of course, I know, Juan, because you are royalty," I sighed with a chuckle while continuing to play his game. "In fact, you are more than royalty, Juan!" If anyone else ever heard him like this, I'm sure they would have thought he was the biggest egomaniac there ever was. The fact was that he was just the opposite…never sure of himself or his looks. It was his way of making me laugh. A little boy pretending to be someone important! He was someone very important—to me!

Of course, Juan opened his gift first. I purchased every piece of clothing he had pointed out on our outings. As he came across each of them in one large box, his awe was truly beholding! "Aw, Recharred, you remembered," he sighed with each piece. "Thank you, my darling."

Then it was my turn. He was thrilled as he handed me a box the size of my hand. I smiled as he waited anxiously for me to open it. A shiny chrome, Seiko with a blue face was uncovered, something I never expected! I was especially thrilled because my good watch had been grabbed off my wrist when I was mugged just before we met. "Do you like it, Recharred?" he asked anxiously.

"You know I do, Juan. I really love it! It even has the date on it!"

"Ond you never 'ave to ever wind it, Recharred," Juan boasted, "Ond it does not 'ave batteries either." Wanting to be certain that I was aware, "You know, Recharred, it was not cheap. It cost me almost one hundred ond fifty dollars."

I was surprised when I turned it to the backside. I never thought he'd have the nerve to inscribe it, but there it was—RICHARD ALWAYS J

I cried and then chuckled, realizing why he didn't inscribe his full name. Like anyone wouldn't know who *J* was.

We were spending Christmas day alone. It was a special day, and we felt good knowing we would share it together! I would be making lasagna for the first time. Juan already loved my sauce and meatballs, but this time, along with the Italian sausage, I was fixing *bragiolle*, thinly sliced flank steak covered with bread crumbs, parsley, Romano, garlic, salt, and pepper. It is rolled and tied, and before adding to sauce, browned. My kids called it stringy meat, and loved it.

I knew the counter would look like a disaster during preparation, and realized I had to try and keep Juan out of the kitchen…yeah, right. He popped in constantly, scolding me for not cleaning up after each step. Yet, even while reprimanding, he still was a constant joy. He was lovable, even while griping. Besides, since he couldn't stand the mess, he'd clean it up!

We decided to have dinner on the cocktail table because the Christmas tree and fireplace were there. The glow was very romantic, and it presented a beautiful picture of a Christmas table set for two. Juan played records all afternoon as usual, so the time flew by. It was as it should be on Christmas—a house filled with joy, music, and love! I was, at last, enjoying something most take for granted—pure happiness, being with my lover and preparing a special meal for a special day!

I don't recall being all that comfortable on the floor. Nevertheless, it was very romantic. We toasted to our first Christmas together, and to our love. Even seated on the floor, Juan still displayed his elegant table manner. I'll never forget how his eyes widened and his brows rose while savoring his first bite. "Recharred, this lasagna is excellent! Superb! It is the best lasagna I 'ave ever had in my life!" I don't know where the day went; suddenly, it was over.

We arrived in Atlanta the evening of the twenty-ninth, and collapsed on the bed after finding a mid-town motel. We were bushed, so after a late dinner, we went straight to sleep. We needed to be sharp for our early morning appointment.

John Howard was a short husky guy, and quite a talker. We felt comfortable after he mentioned that he, too, was gay but married. In fact, he informed us that many businessmen in Atlanta were in the same position, usually keeping some young stud on the side.

I asked why Club Three had closed, voicing apprehensions of taking over a bar that had suddenly closed. His sales ability really surfaced after informing us that another bar had opened nearby when he went on to say, "I'm sure they won't hurt you in the least since your bar will be entirely different." One supportive reason after another by him relieved our apprehensions.

We were totally unprepared for the mess we were confronted with when we walked into the club. It was a disaster area! The crowd and lighting had obviously hidden all of it when we were there, and we were practically in a state of shock. What little carpet remaining looked as if the moths had insisted on staying until the bitter end. The walls wore mud and anything else one might imagine flung in a gay bar. It took a few minutes to get over the shock, but in all it was perfect for what we wanted to do. The place needed some paint, a lot of elbow grease, and unfortunately quite a bit of carpeting. Yet we realized that we only had to sign a lease and pay rent, and that it was fully equipped except for the kitchen utensils and sound equipment. John, however, quickly erased these expenditures from preying on our minds by telling us he was certain the previous owners would let us use their equipment.

Juan was checking out the dance floor and said, "The dance floor is a perfect size to do the show, Recharred, ond to dance on!" My mind quickly began thinking of physical changes, which of course would cost money, but I was sure John would consent to do some build-out. A storage room just below the stage would be perfect for a dressing room. Why not cut through the floor and build a stairway for entrances from the dressing room. He quickly replied that it would be permissible but that the construction costs would be our responsibility.

He was aware of our anxiousness, especially since Juan couldn't hide his excitement, and flatly refused to pay for improvements. As an added temptation, he reminded us, "I'm sure you realize you'll be saving by using the previous owner's kitchen, sound, and disco equipment. That'll be more than enough to pay for any construction." At that point, Juan took me aside and said, "Thar is not any cost to buy the place, Recharred. We only 'ave to pay rent. Ofter all, you were willing to buy a business or start a new one, ond thot would 'ave cost much more. This place is fully equipped. I like it very much!" I melted hearing his words. He really wanted to move to Atlanta! I felt he believed we were sailing to a desert island together. I felt so proud.

John was asking fourteen hundred dollars a month, an amount I flatly refused to pay. I knew he realized we were novices in the field, but there was no way I was going to pay rent far exceeding the current rates, and the bargaining began. I finally made my last offer of one thousand, feeling it was still on the high side, but at least a fully equipped restaurant and bar were included. "Okay, but I cannot give you a definite commitment," he said after a moment of thought. "I will have to present your offer to the owner. I'll write up the lease and contract subject to his approval." At that, Juan's arms flew up along with a great big smile.

After completing all the necessary paperwork at his office, we mentioned we still needed to find an attorney, as well as an apartment. John called in an associate from the adjoining office, and we soon learned that he too was married but gay. He called an agent and made an appointment after we explained what we were looking for. Meanwhile, John had called an attorney and informed us that we could go to his office afterwards because he had said he'd be in all afternoon. On bidding farewell, John thought to nonchalantly mention, "Oh, by the way, don't feel uncomfortable with the attorney. Though Tony is married, he also is gay!" We stood wide eyed.

"The apartment is absolutely perfect, don't you think, Recharred," Juan commented once we had toured the first one. "I don't think we 'ave to look any further." I thoroughly agreed. The ground floor apartment of the small building was perfect, and especially nice since it was the only multiple dwelling on a street of single family homes. It was easy to imagine the trees and shrubs on the block in bloom, and the charming and fragrant path that would be ours.

The living room was huge, and a large bedroom was on either side. Each of these bedrooms had a full bath across the hall. The kitchen was small but workable. Though there was only a dining area, we were certain everything would fit nicely.

The agent agreed to hold it for a week after we explained that our business deal was not yet certain. He also agreed to a starting date of February 15 for the lease, and advised us to contact the phone company immediately.

Juan turned back as we were leaving, and sighed, "Look, Recharred, our new address is now 32-28th Street North West - Atlanta, Georgia!" He was so happy I wanted to hug him!

Our last stop on the whirlwind trip was to the lawyer's office. Tony was a very handsome Italian. We discussed everything necessary to incorporate, and were told that he would check on the liquor license. A check needed to be mailed to him as soon as we were certain.

It was six thirty, and we were on our way home. In the few hours of one day, we had changed the course of our lives.

We didn't get home until seven, New Year's Eve, which only allowed time for me to take a shower before going to the shop.

Juan and I had made plans to meet Gloria and Pat that evening to welcome the new year, but somehow we never connected. They say alcohol has greater affect when you are tired. Believe me, they ain't kidding!

Chapter Seventeen:
The Excitement of Moving to Our Desert Island

As anticipated, the call came from Atlanta. The club was ours! It was Friday, the second day of 1976, and the year was off with a bang! Juan was ecstatic when I called with the news, and insisted we plan the agenda that evening.

It wasn't until that moment that it occurred to me that we'd be leaving in six weeks! Would I find a buyer for the shop in that short time? I wouldn't have cared whether I sold it if two of my barbers hadn't recently left to open their own shop; they would have brought in more than enough money to pay my mortgage payment on the building. I then would only have to get another barber to replace myself. However, quite a large portion of the business followed them and I wasn't clearing anywhere near what I had been. The barber profession had slipped, and I was having problems keeping barbers, and more often than not, only three chairs were being worked full time.

What would we tell our families about the move? Juan had no problem because he didn't have a business. All he needed to say was that he was offered a great position in Atlanta. My situation was different; I had a good business for over fourteen years. Why would I even think of leaving it? It had to be something big, and something I loved!

After days of mind-racking, I came up with a whopper of a story. So it seemed that Juan and I had met this very rich man at a party who was quite impressed with our personalities. And it wasn't long after he returned to Atlanta that he called to offer each of us positions with his company...at fantastic salaries. To make it more inviting, an option to eventually become partners was offered. Everything looked even better after accepting his invite to Atlanta to see the business in action, and we couldn't refuse. Of course, the real clincher for me would be that this company was a broker offering public relations experts to other companies that didn't need full time personnel in that capacity. Juan and I were to head the department. What would make it even more inviting for me was the many occasions that called for shows to be produced.

When I asked what he thought, Juan stood wide-eyed and exclaimed, "You are fantastic, Recharred! Whot on imagination! You are really on actor-r!" I really hated lying, but what else could I do? Juan and I had lied about our relationship, though there were many times I came close to telling my kids because I was so proud of him. Yet I couldn't tell them I was opening a gay bar.

The kids and family were not happy about my move, but accepted it after realizing how thrilled I was, and that it would give them a place to vacation.

Suddenly, we were in a whirlwind because there were so many details to attend to. Juan never had seen me in action with a big project in the making and was astonished by the dynamo I was! My constant reminders of things that had to be done gave him a chance to mimic me. So, from that time on whenever I was reminding him about something that needed to be done, I could expect to see his finger pointed at me while mimicking my face and voice saying, "I know, Recharred, THAR ARE THINGS TO BE DONE!"

We were to leave in two and a half weeks, on Sunday, Valentine's Day, and there finally was someone interested in the shop. I felt somewhat relieved but still concerned; it was the most important thing to be done and would've been a load off my mind if it had.

We were so busy we hardly saw any of our friends. In fact, George and Ted drifted completely out of our lives after refusing the bar.

It was two weeks before our scheduled departure when Juan confided, "You know, Recharred, next Saturday, your kids are gonna give you a surprise going away party."

"Juan, why did you tell me?" I yelled, "Now I won't be surprised!"

"But, Recharred, you are a good actor-r. You will certainly be able to pretend."

"That's not the point, Juan. I've never been surprised in my life and I would've really liked it. Aw, Juan, why did you have to spoil it by telling me!"

However, there was no way he was going to admit he was wrong. Still, I continued on with my gripes. I finally realized he was trying to cover up his foolish behavior, and that he never intended to ruin the surprise for me. It was just the little kid in him unable to hold a secret, and because he was so excited, he was certain I would want to know, too. It was impossible to continue my anger, especially after seeing the obvious hurt come over him because he felt I didn't understand his excitement in telling me. The astonishing thing about it was watching his hurt blend in with a bit of arrogance that he always managed to convey whenever reprimanded.

I wasn't really angry with him, only disappointed, and explained, "The only time I think I was surprised was when I was six. It was the Depression, and I never really had any toys. When we returned home from my aunt's house that Christmas Eve night, I was surprised to find a present under the tree for me. It was a doctor's set, and it was from my brother, Tony. He had managed to buy me something from the little he made shining shoes. Besides the usual dollar I'd get from one uncle and the fifty cents from the other, that was the first Christmas present I remembered ever getting up to that time. I remember the thrill, just knowing I was thought of."

"In another apartment our landlord lived below ours. He was a breadman and always worked during the Depression. I remember going down on Christmas morning and the shock I got after seeing all the toys his kids got from Santa…as many as the kids get now! I felt so bad when I got upstairs. I couldn't understand how Santa went down the chimney and missed our floor."

"Recharred, did you 'ave a fireplace in your apartment?" Juan asked.

"No, I guess I thought Santa came through the wall or something like that. I don't know!"

When Juan's choked up laughter finally subsided he chided, "Just think, Recharred, you would 'ave never met me if you did not get thot doctor's set!"

Naturally, I acted surprised at the party. Though in reality, it was a surprise; I had only expected the immediate family to attend. However, as the evening went on, the big old farmhouse was packed with friends I hadn't seen for some time, even Vita and Virginia. Fifty to sixty friends and relatives were there, and my only regret was that the time went so quickly. However, it was obvious how blue my dad was. I was leaving a thriving business, and he couldn't understand why.

Juan was having a ball, and managed to drink his fair share and more, but I felt proud because he was well behaved. I was pleased that the kids had thought enough of Juan to give him some going away gifts, and to put his name to the cake, too. His appreciation was overwhelming.

Juan had thought ahead by getting a lift to the party from my nephew, Dino, and on the way home remarked, "You know, Recharred, you don't know how lucky you are to 'ave such a wonderful family thot loves you so much."

"I know, Juan, I know, and I love them very much!"

It was quite hectic that week before the move, and to add to our problems, the transmission went out in Juan's Fiat. Totally disgusted because of all the previous problems with it, he decided to leave it at the dealer's for repossession. I told him that he was crazy because it would ruin his credit, insisting I would pay for the repairs. Yet, he held his ground and refused to say more on the subject. However, it did solve the problem of driving two cars and a truck.

We made one last visit to The Trip. There, we could talk with Pudgy about coming down to Atlanta to entertain. We had discussed it with her several times and she seemed quite anxious to do it. She agreed after discussing all the details, and it was decided that the opening date would be discussed on the phone. We stayed just long enough to hear our Charleston. Juan grabbed hold of my hand and sighed, "Just think, Recharred, this time next week, we will be in Atlanta starting a new life together." I smiled and squeezed his hand tightly.

I was busy the day Juan said good-bye to Svetmana and surprised he didn't take me to do the same with his parents. I'd be seeing his daughter quite a bit; her mother worked for an airline.

"Recharred, I forgot to tell you but ot the party, your daughter Jacque told me their mother is very upset because you are moving out of state," Juan recalled. I didn't know what to make of it, so I put it out of my mind. I was pre-occupied with the worry of the sale of the shop.

It was Friday and I felt certain that the prospective buyer would come through. He had no sooner arrived when the phone rang. To my surprise I heard, "Rick, this is Joan. I just called to tell you how sorry I am for making your life miserable. Please, forgive me." I couldn't talk while my buyer was there, so I asked her to meet me for lunch the next day. I didn't want her feeling bad, especially since I was so happy.

My buyer wasted no time giving his regrets. He just couldn't swing it. I was now forced to have a part time barber, one I didn't particularly like, manage the shop. The only consolation was that he agreed to quit his other job and devote all his time to the shop when I called.

"You know, Recharred, I am really gonna miss this apartment," Juan said, gazing around the room once we got into bed, "It is so elegant, so bea-u-ti-ful, ond it has been our home. Are you gonna miss it, too, Recharred?" It was one of the rare times Juan was lying on his back, and once I looked his way, I saw the tears in his eyes.

"Of course I will, Juan, but anywhere you and I live will be home for us!" Yes, Juan loved it and never forgot it; he'd never hesitate to describe it whenever we talked of our first home.

I took Joan around the corner for lunch, and it was apparent she was a little uneasy. I couldn't understand why she had become so repentant, and I certainly did not want her to think I was leaving town on her account.

She was quiet. The only words she spoke were the name of the cocktail and that she didn't want to eat. I tried some small talk but only received one word responses. She sat stirring her cocktail. I'm certain that had it been a cream drink, it would have turned to butter. I decided to ease the tension by saying, "Joan, don't think I'm moving because you made me miserable. I have accepted an offer that I can't pass up, and besides, I'm tired of cutting hair. With this job, I'll also be doing some shows for clients. In a way I'll be doing something I've always wanted to do. It will also be a chance to lay aside everything that happened here and make a new life for myself."

Joan listened quietly, nursing her drink, and finally saying, "You know, Rick, people make promises, and then they don't keep them." She was referring to Remo. "You are the only one I know who lives up to your promises. Really, Rick, you are unique!"

I didn't know what to say. It seemed she was making a pitch to reconcile! I still loved her, but I loved Juan more. I knew also that she would never keep her promises, and that it wouldn't be long before *Jekyll* turned into *Hyde*! Fortunately, I didn't need to answer. She cooked her own goose by remarking,

"See, Rick, now you are moving out of state, and how many times did I beg you to do that, but you didn't want to leave your family."

I smiled in lieu of glaring at her with contempt. I couldn't believe that she was twisting the truth again, while attempting to reconcile! I had always been the one begging! I had talked about moving to California many times! I wanted to pursue my dream to be an actor, but she would never agree! She went on talking, but my mind was preoccupied. I could only think of her telling Herb Roger that she wouldn't let me go to California! Now she was trying to convince me that it was she who wanted to move out of state! I knew then, she would never change. That was Joan—twisting things to make herself appear right. I smiled as she went on talking. She finally looked into my eyes, and from the sad expression on her face, I knew she realized her quest was hopeless. We bid farewell. I was, however, disturbed.

I closed exactly at five, and said my good-byes to the barbers, along with last minute instructions. Juan and Nicky were aware that I was picking up Mike with the truck so I knew they would not be concerned should I not yet be at the shop to move the piano.

My meeting with Joan preyed on my mind throughout the day, and I wanted to be sure that Mike knew I was concerned about her. I learned from my kids that she had been hospitalized twice after battles with Remo, and though I was sure that her temper had provoked the situations, I needed to be sure she was protected. I began to cry after asking Mike to watch over her.

"Dad, consider yourself lucky," Mike insisted. "You know how Mom is! She has a split personality, and I don't think anyone could live with her! In fact, Dad, you two should have never married because all you both did was argue and fight all the time, and ninety percent of the time it was her fault! Dad, I can remember the time she was like a crazy woman, swinging wildly at you. She was hysterical and you just slapped her face to bring her to her senses, and then she told Uncle Frank that you beat her up! Do you know he was gonna come over and beat the hell out of you until I told him what really happened!" To show his support, he patted my hand and said, "Dad, make a life for yourself, and consider yourself lucky!" I still insisted he watch over her.

Juan and Nicky were waiting for us, and it didn't take long to load the piano I had insisted on taking after my divorce. The casters allowed Juan and I to push it easily to the forward part of the van, and after lowering the door, Mike took off for his place. Overnight parking would be a problem for the truck near our apartment, especially since Mike could drive it there in the morning.

Alarming news came that evening when Mike called. "Dad, while I was driving, I heard a terrible crash. I think the piano fell over! But I didn't want to look! Didn't you guys tie it down?"

It was Valentine's Day and an unbelievable, beautiful seventy degrees. The first ones to arrive were Pa, Deena, Dino, young Dino, Geena, and with sweet rolls and coffee.

Mike shouted out for me to come down and check the piano. I embraced Jacque as she came up, and was told that Martina would be calling from school sometime before I left. I really didn't want to raise the door for fear of what I would see. And my fears were as expected once I managed it. The piano was flat on its face, with ivory keys scattered in every direction on the floor of the truck! "It's no good anymore, Dad," Mike shouted, "Let's carry it out to the alley!"

He had no idea how much that piano meant to me, or that we needed it! I was near tears, and had it not been for Juan, I would've undoubtedly obliged. "Recharred, don't feel bad because I am sure it con be fixed. C'mon, Recharred, we con put all the keys in a box ond when we get to Atlanta, we con 'ave it fixed." He fetched a box and some rope.

Nicky, Mike, and I took off for the gas station where I had arranged to use the lift; I wanted to drive together in the truck. On arrival, they insisted I was crazy to think my plan would work. However, the owner of the station insisted it would. So I resumed my plan. I drove the Gremlin onto the hydraulic lift of the grease stall, and Mike backed the truck flush against the entrance. Once the lift was raised, I wasn't happy to see the three-foot gap between it and the van floor, though I managed a smile when my boys gasped. And when I placed two heavy boards between the truck and the lift for the wheels to ride over, Nicky and Mike cried out in unison, "Dad, forget it! Those boards are gonna crack! Drive the car!"

On the other hand, the owner of the station still insisted it would work. I decided I would be the one to back it into the van, though I had visions of the car crashing down between the lift and the truck. I became nervous because I wasn't too good at backing up in a straight line. Everyone was yelling directions at the same time, and as I started, I thought, *Oh, my God, I am gonna go off the boards!* I was so nervous! My breathing didn't resume until I heard cheers. We nailed down the boards at the rear wheels because it wouldn't be too nice to have the car fly out of the truck while we were going up that mountain in Tennessee. "Dad, you've hardly any room left! Where are you gonna put your furniture?" Mike yelled, observing the space left.

It took all morning and afternoon to load the van, but we did it. Besides a couple of other things that wouldn't fit, one thing we didn't have to worry about was Juan's glass top cocktail table; it exploded into a million pieces immediately after Mike set it down on the sidewalk!

We were ready to go; the excitement of leaving for a new life dimmed when I confronted the faces of the loved ones I was leaving behind. I had had a beautiful conversation with Martina, but the reality of my departure was obvious once I saw everyone's tears. Pa was unable to hold back from crying in my arms, and it was not until Juan reassured him that he'd look after me that he finally regained his composure. Jacque was the last, and seemed to crumble in my arms. I held her tightly, finally coming to tears. I handed her Valentine cards and gifts for her and Martina. She held on tightly. "Dad, I am gonna miss you so much because I love you so much!" she cried. I assured her I wasn't going away forever and that she'd be able to visit me often.

As we pulled away the sad faces and the sobbing of my precious Jacque began to tug at my heart. I could no longer control my emotions as I turned the corner. Tears flowed down my cheeks, and if it were not for the compassion of the wonderful man next to me, I wouldn't have been able to drive any further. Juan began rubbing my shoulders and neck, saying, "Please, Recharred, don't feel bad because you will always 'ave them ond they will always 'ave you. You are a man who could never give up his family, ond I would never want you to! Just put in your mind thot you are going to a new place to start a new life, but you will always 'ave your family!" Those tender words made me realize I was doing the right thing. I smiled and I looked into his eyes. There was the man who had the magic to soothe my aching heart! My only peace was knowing that we were on our way to a place where we wouldn't have to hide the love we had for each other.

Trust Juan to come up with something to lighten the air. "Recharred, you should 'ave seen Deena when she carried the box with our wedding crowns! Aw, Recharred, she was so careful, ond she kept asking whot was in it because it was so light. I was so afraid she was gonna open it, ond glad she did not ask to. But do you know whot? I do not think thot she would 'ave realized they were ours. She has such a bea-u-ti-ful innocence, Recharred, ond she is so funny!" My mood improved once he mimicked her manner of talking and the way she held the box. *He* was so funny!

Chapter Eighteen: Atlanta at Last!

Juan couldn't drive a stick shift, so I had him at the wheel only during long runs. I shifted as he desperately tried to work the clutch. Of course, there was a lot of jerking going on. The fact that I had continued my penny-pinching ways by renting the cheapest truck available gave him good reason to call me down; the truck had little or no power and was almost impossible to shift. The hills in Tennessee proved his point; we never knew if we were going to make it up or just roll down backwards. So it was quite a scare going down the decline near Lover's Leap. I couldn't get it into low gear, and our terrified faces would have made a perfect trailer for a horror film as we sped down at high speed. Afterwards, we laughed when he mimicked my expressive face.

Atlanta greeted us with still more hills, but after a few hairy scares, we were finally in front of 32-28 Street Northwest!

The fact that the rope holding our clothes had broken from so much jerking never upset Juan; he was just happy to be at our new home! It took us hours to load the truck but only a little over an hour to unload. As usual, Juan's chatter made the work a pleasure. When I called to let John know we arrived, he gave directions to a dock area we could easily unload the car. He also asked if we could stop by the office.

After dropping off the piano and piano parts at the club, we returned the truck. "Recharred, I am so happy to finally get rid of thot rattletrap," Juan sighed in relief. It was also obvious that he was anxious to get back to the apartment, so I obliged. I knew he wouldn't rest until he could start putting things in order.

My meeting with John took longer than anticipated, and I expected Juan to be angry coming through the door. Instead, he was lying on the couch with a big smile on his face, watching television. One glance around the room told me he had done it again! Everything was in order! I quickly hurried to the bedrooms and the kitchen. They too were in order! And not a box in sight! He stood in the center of the living room when I returned, shifting his weight to one leg and resting his hand on his hip. Smiling, he boasted, "Well, Recharred, how do you like it? Does it not look wonderful! This is our home!"

And the saga of RJ's began, our name choice for the club being our initials. We had inserted an advance notice of the new bar in a gay magazine, never suspecting that it would lead to a cavalcade of con artists, drifters, and losers. Leading the parade was Stuart, a self proclaimed professional sound expert, barely in his middle twenties. Although we informed him we would be using the old club's equipment, he would not give up. He was so overbearing, but our good nature allowed him to go on. We even delayed the start of the remodeling, accepting his invitation for a guided tour of the area that Sunday. A fabulous spaghetti dinner prepared as only his lover could, made it especially inviting. We were still hungry when we got home that night; all of a half pound of pasta, covered with the heated tomato sauce from a can were Stuart's conception of fabulous. We laughed while fixing another meal as Juan mimicked the manner in which Stuart shouted out directions during our tour. "No, no, Recharred, not straight…gaily forward!"

Next on the scene were three guys even younger than Stuart. Michael, a tall likable guy did most of the talking. Kent and Lee were lovers. As Lee talked, we were almost certain "he" was a "she." All doubts were resolved as he explained that he performed live drag, impersonating many of the movie queens. It was apparent that Lee was living as a woman, and was henceforth referred to as "she." None of them were employed, and offered to work for practically nothing, just for a chance to get a job in our club. We liked them and with so much to be done we hired them.

Juan came running up from the restroom choking with laughter. He insisted I come down to the restroom to see Lee. There she was, scrubbing the porcelain drain holes of a urinal with a toothbrush, and pointing up her pinky finger.

There were others who showed up to work, too, only to quickly disappear with a few of our belongings. Mike, Lee, and Kent seemed to be the only ones we could trust. We finally offered Kent a bartender position, and told Lee that she should try out when we scheduled auditions. I quickly learned that a businessman Juan was not! We offered Mike the DJ job, and after I agreed to pay one hundred a week, Juan asked, "Are you sure thot is enough, Michael?"

To improve sight-lines, we decided on raising the entire bar area ten inches higher. The contractor was pleased to add it to the staircase job.

We had to reschedule auditions since the piano keys were still in the box. It was a happy day when the piano tuner told us it could be fixed! We hired the first pianist to audition. He was fantastic, so we figured why look any further. Joe was a master at the keyboard and his queenly manner fit in perfectly! I thought casting the show would be a snap until auditions began; I never imagined there were so many bad singers. We tried desperately to get hold of Pudgy in Chicago, but she never answered our calls or letters.

Why Has All the Music Gone?

I finally managed to cast three guys—Tom, Toby, and Mark. Each of them had excellent voices. It appeared there were no female singers in Atlanta, though, until Candy showed up. Elvis Presley would have envied her version of *Hound Dog*. One down, we still needed two more females, and one had to be a red hot mama. No one came close to the image. Though reluctantly, I hired Lee, merely on the merit of her superb impersonations. Besides two left feet, she had a small singing range that was barely capable of carrying a tune.

Joe's friend, Patti, had been coming along on all the auditions, and we became quite friendly with her. We presumed she was a *fag hag*. Joe finally mentioned that she had done some local acting and singing, and when she arrived, I told her to come prepared to audition the next day. Though short and pleasingly plump, she was not the red hot mama I was looking for.

"Oh, God, she has a flat butt and I can't even tell if she has tits, Juan."

"However, Recharred, you are desperate ond if she's good, you con possibly mold her into a red hot mama," Juan quipped. The next day, I found her voice to be small with no range or oomph, but time was running out. Maybe I could mold her.

Rehearsal began on the nostalgic revue I had written about the music of the century, and I discovered that, besides lacking a voice, Patti also had wooden legs. She and Lee would have been phenomenal had I elected to do *The March of the Wooden Soldiers*. Juan cracked up each time he watched Lee moving to my choreography! She actually looked as though she had boards tied on each of her legs, giving him something else to mimic. And Patti? Well, forget it, she was only interested in looking glamorous, blind to the fact that she was egg-shaped. Even when I physically showed her how to move the beef around, she was hopeless. I finally pulled them out of the production numbers. At least Lee had her impersonations, and could M.C. as a different actress for each introduction. We still needed a red hot mama, but Pudgy had disappeared. I had Candy dance in the background to *Shimmy Like My Sister Kate* as a diversion to Patti's lousy vocal offering. Maybe then the audience would not think me a complete idiot!

Rehearsals were scheduled around the renovations, and that took some doing. We had only contracted the raising of the bar and the stairway jobs, which left all the rest to us. Or, since Juan and the others had little or no experience in remodeling—me! Juan did, however, try to do as well, and at least was alongside to assist in painting, applying wallpaper, constructing and designing an outdoor sign, as well as the thousands of other things that needed doing. And during all of it, Stuart hounded us relentlessly about the sound equipment. Meanwhile, carpeting the place became another nightmare, turning into a major expense and exceeding far beyond our estimate.

At a meeting with our attorney, we were hit with another brick. "Neither of you have lived here a year," Tony advised, "and in order to be issued a liquor license, that is a must."

To soften the blow, he came up with a *most gracious* solution. Corbett Carson, a friend, was willing to put the license in his name. All we would have to do was wine and dine him and his party of friends for the duration of the club! Of course, once out of the red, we'd also be expected to pay him a salary. We had to agree; our hands were tied! "Thot is pretty good, Recharred," Juan remarked once we left, "Eat, drink, ond be paid for it!"

At the same meeting, we met Dan, a young associate; he would be our account rep. Dan was surprisingly not gay! He was a great guy and we three became friends.

The hours were long and the work was hard, but during it all, Juan managed to mix in a lot of fun. He was not the workaholic I was, and was extremely happy when we took a break from the club. My attention could then be on him, and his on me. One memorable day: Because the code for a restaurant-bar liquor license called for twelve more dining places than what we had, Joe took us out to the country to a large antique complex in search of chairs. Though the Sunday could not be more beautiful, it was nowhere near as bright as Juan! He was away from the club and all my badgering to get things done, and his spirits and wit could not have been higher! He kept the three of us in stitches throughout the afternoon.

I had been well aware that Joe's adoring glances were practically devouring Juan, but I didn't mind; I knew he was mine. Juan's charm captivated Joe completely, accepting and laughing hilariously each time he mimicked nellie gestures of his. "My good woman! How con you say thot?" Juan had teased, placing his hand to his chest mockingly, only to flick his other wrist weakly while swaying his body.

We got away from the club on other occasions; Juan needed culture in his life and the diversion of play. Nights at the movies and occasional visits to Atlanta's cultural offerings were a must. "Recharred, a Broadway musical series is coming to the Alliance Theater," Juan remarked while reading the Sunday paper, "Would it not be nice if we subscribed to the series? It is much cheaper then." Of course we subscribed, and at the same time bought tickets for *Madame Butterfly*. We could then experience the Fox Theatre. Of course, there were all the drag show bars. Another bar we particularly liked was Shelly's, on the main level of an office building close to our apartment. It was frequented by young businessmen. It also featured a small dance floor as well as a popular restaurant that included straight clientele.

Svetmana visited almost every weekend once we were settled. She always demanded full attention, and it began to destroy the cast and others who were getting the bar ready.

"She's such a pest! Can't you get rid of her?" were complaints I often heard. I'd keep their complaints from Juan, and though he was needed, I'd let him take her out somewhere. Our lawyer, Dan, fortunately struck up a good relationship with her and offered to babysit occasionally.

I had almost forgotten my episode with Ed until the night Juan came home after disappearing. He had complained all day because I was so busy with the club, and then he was gone. He wasn't at home when I got there and my anxiety grew. When he finally stumbled in, he could barely stand! I had seen him drunk many times, but never this depressed. He began crying uncontrollably, and apparently attacking me viciously again because of my evening with Ed. "How did you li' it wit' Ed, Reccharr'," he bellowed, grasping onto my shirt. "I trusted you, Recharred, ond you 'ave betrayed me! How cou' you 'ave done thot to me?"

I tried to steady him and wipe his face, but he wanted no part of it, pushing me savagely. He was tormenting us both and my heart ached. It reconfirmed the fact that I should have never confessed. It took some time to calm him enough to get him in bed. I sat there upset and confused after finding his Jockey shorts in his pocket. In the morning, he had no explanation. I never asked him about them again.

Most of the gay men in Atlanta seemed to have a female alias. That was all Juan had to hear. He quickly said, "I know whot your name should be, Recharred...*Blanche*! Yes, *Blanche Du Buois* from *Streetcar Named Desire*! No, Blanche deMella!" He laughed 'til he cried. I balked at the thought, warning him he'd be Juanita, but he didn't care. It bothered me at first, but after a while, I got used to it because he only used it when I was overdramatic. And it stuck—this name he conjured up for me.

Juan loved to make me laugh, even if it meant mimicking someone's deformity. He never meant to be cruel, or for that person to be aware. His intent was to make me laugh. He got such a thrill from seeing me double up in laughter. He wasn't out to make fun of them; they merely reminded him that he had the astounding ability to contort himself in exaggerated positions and faces. He was aware that I'd be in stitches after one glance at him! "Was I really thot funny, Recharred?" he'd ask innocently, though I was in helpless laughter. Once assured he had succeeded, he'd choke up with laughter himself.

The mannerisms of nellie queens were his forte. We'd be at a restaurant or store and if some effeminate guy was leading us to our table or to some merchandise, there'd be Juan, directly behind him, over-exaggerating his effeminate walk and manner!

Kent invited us to a party, and though we weren't in the mood to drink, we felt it would be relaxing after a hard day of remodeling. We were quite sedate that night, sharing a beer when they suddenly began passing around a joint. Neither of us cared for them, and though I insisted they never affected me, they continued prompting us. We finally gave in and took drags the two times it passed. I didn't feel a reaction, and from Juan's behavior I was sure he had none either. However, everyone was chuckling at length at us. Yet we felt normal. Even when leaving, we felt no effects. Our only concern was that we'd find our way home because Kent lived on the other side of town.

We apparently were moving along fine; the only thing I recall is when I came to a stop at a downtown intersection. Suddenly, as I looked out the window, the tall buildings were moving every which way and about to fall on us! They were coming from all directions! I gasped and turned to Juan, but he was out like a light! What happened next, I will never know. The next morning, however, we were awakened with throbbing headaches by the piercing rays of the sun. I was behind the wheel of the car and Juan in the passenger seat. We seemed to be frozen in an upright position, yet our heads had fallen backward and evidently stayed that way all night. And, miraculously, we were parked on our street!

John England, a friend of Joe's, began stopping by to watch rehearsals. Juan looked forward to his visits; John laughed easily at his witty remarks. John's casual manner in which he wore his sandy colored hair, as well as his tall and lanky stature, lent favorably to his easygoing and pleasing personality. About Juan's age, John became the first really true friend we made in Atlanta. And though he was an every day drinker, his good nature still prevailed.

Once we met Corbett, we really liked him, and it didn't matter that we'd be wining and dining him from opening day on. He had such a pleasing personality. Originally from California, his blond-red hair and well built body typified a mature all-American guy about thirty. We also had no reason to disbelieve his claim of an affair with a well-known movie actor, especially when the star had inscribed so much love to him on a photo of himself. So he began spending quite a bit of time with us. Joe loved sing-a-longs at his house as well as Patti, and he'd join us. At Patti's we met Don, her husband, and this confused us; he was very obviously into the gay leather scene. More obvious was watching Don's eyes practically undress Juan at each of the parties.

Juan finally persuaded me to have a dinner party since we had been at their places so often. John, Corbett, Joe, Patti, and Don comprised the guest list, and they were in stitches from Juan's wit. He was finally away from the club, and so happy. He insisted I show my family home movies even though I felt no one would be interested; he so wanted them to see how he had changed me from the suburban polyester man I had been. It proved a wonderful choice. Juan was laughing so hard when I ran some of the crazy parts in reverse that they could not help but join in.

Since alcohol was flowing freely, it clearly proved my previous observation. Don was actually cruising Juan, and Patti couldn't have cared less!

How it happened I don't know. But we actually allowed Stuart to come along to check the previous owner's sound and disco system. Of course, he managed to convince us it wouldn't work for our needs, and there I was signing a long term contract for new equipment. Fortunately, Stuart wasn't into dining and kitchen equipment and we were allowed to use theirs. He also conceded to the fact that their spotlight was superb and could be used for the shows.

Since we never connected with the black woman the previous owners claimed as fantastic, we were forced to hire an older guy as chef. We were coming down the line and, after all, he had worked in French restaurants. His nephew, who appeared to be simple-minded, had to be part of the deal as helper and dishwasher. No one had filled that position yet and we agreed, and besides it was apparent they were a twosome.

We needed someone experienced as head bartender, and when a personable, level headed guy showed us a long list of referrals, we knew he was the one. Jim Brent turned out to be our mainstay, totally capable of taking over when we were out.

April arrived and no revenue was coming in, but at least we didn't have to pay rent until officially opened. Svetmana was coming down regularly on weekends, and sometimes for as long as a week. She still managed to aim sarcasm and insults my way and I found it quite difficult to take at times without getting angry. She was now six without a sign of losing her nasty and selfish ways, and Juan refused to hear of them whenever I informed him of her abominable behavior. A bright spot, however, was the fact that Dan, happily, volunteered to babysit. We took him up on it quite often, which allowed Juan to be with me at the club.

Juan and I frequented an all night restaurant, Dunk'n Dine, whenever he managed to get me out drinking. Just after four in the morning, the place would look as though all the bars had emptied into it, which was so reminiscent of the Golden Nugget in Chicago. This place, however, was loaded with drag queens. Of course, *cruising* went on as usual here, too. We always managed to get the same waitress, a short, hefty blond, well into her forties; she didn't seem to mind that she looked absolutely ridiculous wearing a miniskirt uniform. Juan wouldn't let up on her, and it wasn't unusual for me to kid her as much, especially since her good nature threw some our way. "Look, Recharred," Juan often slurred out after she hurried away, "her ass looks like two big balloons sticking out as she walks!" I'll never forget how I laughed the time he actually rose and followed her, contorting his butt to stick out, and miraculously managing to have one cheek going up while the other was heading down!

"It's time," Dan happily informed Juan once he answered the phone. "We go before the judge tomorrow morning!" We were elated; it had been almost two months of concern. We practically overflowed the courtroom because everyone involved with the club insisted on going along in case character witnesses were needed. They were not needed, however, since the license was awarded without any questioning. Still, everyone let out a boisterous cheer.

Friday, April 10, was to be our opening. We'd have a week to get out an ad…print up flyers to pass at Piedmont park where gays frequented…order all liquor and food, and we prayed enough time to receive reservations! I intended on preparing lasagna and chicken rosemary myself for the main entrees opening night, but because so much needed to be done, I gave the chicken recipe to the chef instead.

We had purchased an upright piano when we bought the chairs, with intentions of having singing waiters in the dining room; Toby and Tom agreed to serve in order to make more money in tips. Neither of them had experience in serving, however. Then the piano tuner informed us that it couldn't be tuned because of a birdcage interior, and that meant no singing waiters.

Nina, an extremely voluptuous young girl proved to be quite gregarious when she and a gay companion applied for jobs, and won us over completely.

In fact, we hired Paulie as well. They had experience waiting tables, which would make up for Tom and Toby's inexperience.

"Thot was Lee, Recharred. She said she cannot get a lift ond if we could pick her up," Juan stated after running back in to pick up the phone as we were leaving for dress rehearsal.

I grew impatient after honking the horn several times with no response. She finally came out, and headed down the back stairs in her usual graceful manner. Juan chuckled. His laughter continued watching her walk across the yard so ladylike.

Midway through the yard, however, a German Shepherd came from nowhere, howling and charging after her! The horn had evidently awakened him. . Instead of running like the man that she was, up went her arms while screaming and scampering for the gate.

"Ooh, ooh, ooh!" she squealed, fluttering her arms excitedly! To our relief, she managed to open the gate and get out, locking the dog in! Juan almost choked from laughter recalling her face and actions once she hopped safely into the car! And it was another mimic to do many times.

"Look, Recharred," Juan exclaimed happily, squeezing my hands opening night, "our very first customers!" Of course it was apparent his glow had already begun at the bar. He would be of no help this evening, forcing me to run around like a chicken without a head attending to every detail. I finally realized I thrived on pressure and that he didn't. I let him glow on!

We were happy that the entire dining room had been reserved, and that, combined with show only reservations, would mean a full house for the first performance. However, the joy diminished when our hopes for reservations for the second and third shows never materialized.

We were off and running, and once everyone arrived, there wasn't time to keep track of Juan. It was near chaotic in the dining room; the only ones who seemed to know what they were doing were Nina and Paulie. Toby and Tom were completely bewildered, as well as the derelict chef! Many waited over an hour for their salads. So, my anxiety remained until the last dinner guests were through and seated in the club. The show finally started…and only two hours late.

Happily, my anxieties ended as I witnessed the audience responses. Juan ran to me during their vigorous applause. "Aw, Recharred, Recharred, we are a success! They really love it, they really do!" He was so happy and thrilled as we held onto each other tightly, and it didn't matter that he was completely bombed. He was too precious!

Most of the crowd remained for the completely different second and third shows, a small consolation since we had no turnover. One table quite appreciative of the shows also kept Nina very busy, ordering one round of drinks after another, which made me happy. Juan was at my side when the fellow who appeared to be the host of this party came over and introduced himself as Larry Logan. He had been drinking for hours, yet his pleasant manner seemed to appear so sober. After expressing how overjoyed he was with the show, he complimented the improvements done to the club. Our conversation continued for some time, and I was glad Juan was contributing to it, too.

Larry really didn't come off as gay; his manner was strictly straight and macho. A short Gary Cooper would characterize him perfectly. Here was another friendship in the making. John England, of course, was having a ball, and he and Juan continued to party.

Though receipts were good, we made nowhere near as much as we had expected. We finally remembered that two of the large parties were on the house—Corbett's and the law office.

We had waived the cover charge opening night, but when word got around that we were now charging three dollars, very few newcomers ventured in. It didn't matter that a free drink coupon was given with each entry fee. If it were not for the fortunate first night repeaters, the customers could have taken less than two hands to count. Worry really increased once we realized the impossibility of these opening night guests returning night after night.

We needed a break badly, and being Sunday, Jim agreed to take care of the club while we took in an early movie. Juan had been excited because two old movie classics were on the bill. I had only had about six hours sleep in forty eight hours, however, and was a bit concerned I might not stay awake. Well, *Rebecca* had only been playing for a few minutes when my head began bobbing. Before I knew it, Juan was poking me with his elbow, angrily whispering that I was snoring and disturbing everyone! Realizing he easily embarrassed, I simply got up and went into the lobby; I had spotted a sofa when we arrived and figured I could take a catnap sitting up.

Only a few minutes seemed to pass when I was awakened by a hard nudge. It was Juan. "C'mon, Recharred," he whispered with a bit of ire in his voice, quickly heading for the exit door. There I was, sprawled out on the couch in the lobby, a profound picture that would embarrass Juan easily. Once I finally caught up, he snarled, "For Chris' sake, Recharred, do you know you looked like a derelict laying thar snoring!" I couldn't believe I actually slept there the entire double bill!

Juan and I had been out distributing flyers to nearby office buildings; we were now open for lunch and figured we could possibly generate some straight business. We returned to the club to hear Jim exclaim, "Phyllis Killer came in for lunch and left in a rage because she was served mushy spaghetti!" Now, Phyllis Killer was one of the most influential drags in town, a middle aged queen who wrote a gossip column in the gay paper. If we got a good review from him, it would guarantee a successful restaurant. I inquired how that could have happened, and was told that our derelict chef had served noodles that had been sitting in a pot of water for two days.

As always, the chef and his helper were in the waiter's room, enjoying a smoke when I went up to question his reasoning for doing such a thing. Of course, he had no answer. It quickly brought to mind my dismay when I saw the bill for his initial food and supply order. He had spent over three thousand dollars, and when I checked the bill, I found that most of it was on cases of staples. Here was another chance to harass him about it.

"It certainly could not have been because you didn't want to waste the two pounds of spaghetti you had already cooked for one order the other day, was it? Because, after all, you only have cases of it left. Like all the cases of staples you saw fit to order, even though one small container alone could last a year!" He still had no response, so I continued needling him. "But I understand…you and your helper were just too busy smoking to find time to shop at a supermarket! I'm also certain it couldn't have been because you prepare enough food every day for the entire dining room and no one shows up except Juan and me, and all the rest is thrown out!" I really began wondering in what capacity he had worked in those French restaurants.

Less than two weeks later, we were forced to close the dining room. It was sad; Juan and I had gotten so accustomed to dining like millionaires in our elegant restaurant. So, since all the money was going into the club, there was little left to buy groceries for ourselves. We certainly couldn't eat all the condiments and staples our famous French chef had purchased.

We hit a low when all my capital was suddenly gone. Our only alternative was to seek loans on my life insurance. Juan had none. Met Life was just a few blocks from the club and I will never forget the day I left to apply for the loans. Twelve hundred dollars was all I received, and as I walked slowly back to the club, I saw Juan coming in my direction, his face so sad. Tears were actually running down his cheeks when he asked, "Did you 'ave any luck, Recharred?" And to cheer me after hearing the low amount, he smiled and said, "Well, thot is something anyway."

The amount lasted as long as it took to write a few checks. I decided to call the real estate agent in Staterville to accept the offer for my barber shop building he had written about. I hadn't been receiving much in percentages from the shop; my manager never quit his other job and didn't open until one in the afternoon! So, at the same time, I was forced to take this same barber's paltry offer of seven hundred and fifty dollars for the entire works of the four chair shop.

Customers were so sparse that one show a night was enough. At the same time, we let the drummer go. Paulie and Nina agreed to stay on and work for tips, and though I was glad to have her bubbly personality around, I was still concerned. Her heavy drinking habit only encouraged Juan to do the same, and in order to keep my sanity, I sometimes joined in. However, I couldn't drink regularly and his every day indulgences began irritating me because he was then absolutely no help. I realized he never imagined every moment, other than sleeping, being spent at the bar. He had envisioned an entirely different picture. He was sure we'd only need to be there during the day and that managers took over in the evenings. So, he found refuge in his drinking.

"How con you do thot to a bar owner ond embarrass me like thot, Recharred," Juan cried out pathetically once he found out that I had cut him off at the bar.

"You make me look bad. Like I 'ave no authority ot all!" I felt terrible hearing those words. I wanted Juan to be happy, but still I knew the constant drinking was bad for his health. My only consolation was that he'd admit I had done the right thing whenever he wasn't drinking.

He finally appeared to accept it, though I was concerned that the boredom would be too much; he couldn't tolerate others when they got slobbering drunk if he was sober. So, he began sneaking alcohol from the liquor room. He'd be so funny because he actually thought I wasn't aware. Suddenly, he sparkled, and he'd raise his arms and sigh, "Cha, cha, cha!" I finally ignored it because he kept it at a minimum, feeling assured that he was pulling the wool over my eyes. Besides, I needed that up of his to rub off on me, and it always did. And though we certainly couldn't afford it, we usually ended the evening with our favorite waitress at Dunk'n Dine.

All the mechanics of the business, including the bookkeeping, were now mine to do; several crucial errors in the checkbook by Juan clinched that. Periodically, it would irk me that his only responsibility was to clean the club while I had all the major responsibilities of running it!

"Recharred, how con you say thot?" he pleaded after hearing me complain. "I am cleaning the bar every day ond thot is not easy!" I'd finally drop it because he certainly wasn't loafing. He just wasn't cut out to be the businessman I was. Besides, I loved him for the way he was, and that guy was always there for me. He just never expected it to be this way.

Deena surprised us with a call; they were flying down for a week, and Pa was coming too. It would be great to see them, but we had some worries. How were we to entertain when we had no money, and how could we be away from the club for long periods? However, we finally remembered our so-called public relations jobs. Jim could call from the club with make-believe assignments. It wasn't going to be easy since the bar closed at 4:00 A.M., and one of us needed to be there. Daytime liquor deliveries also meant one of us would have to be at the club to pay for them.

Juan insisted Deena and Dino sleep in his bed; he'd take the sofa since Pa was sleeping with me. We included a visit to the Capitol after our agenda of The Swan House and Cyclorama, and in answer to our prayers, they picked up all the tabs, including groceries for meals at home. And if Mack Sennet comedies were still in production, I am certain they'd have loved a few reels of me chasing to the club and back from wherever we were. A little role playing even confirmed that we were indeed straight. Nina stopped in, posing as Juan's girlfriend. Dino's raised brows clearly indicated he had not missed Nina's voluptuous bust!

My one track mind didn't think of it until Jim held out his keys. "Here are the keys to my apartment, Richard. You know where I live, so why don't you and Juan go there and relax a bit. Everything will be fine here." Juan must have complained of our sleeping arrangements, and I felt lousy that I hadn't thought of this.

"Really, Recharred, you want to go!" Juan happily replied after I asked if he'd like to go. And how happy I was that we did; I had been neglecting someone I loved.

Deena had read that an art fair was going on in Piedmont Park, and asked to go. The park was a haven for gays and we tried to suggest some alternatives instead, but she still had her heart set on it. So we obliged. Juan was especially worried that some flaming queen might approach us. "Recharred, whot if they call out Juanita or Blanche?"

"We'll just have to be on the lookout for anyone coming our way to intercept them," I assured him though certain Deena's naivetes wouldn't allow her to judge anyone as peculiar. So there we were, circling them continually while making quick turns to cover all directions.

It had been nice, and Juan was extremely sad when they left; I'd be back to that grindstone.

The summer heat was with us and Juan talked me into moving to a complex with a pool. He was an avid swimmer, and realizing it'd be convenient for him to swim, I agreed.

Unfortunately, the only one we found that we liked was out quite a distance, all of fifteen miles further. A large dining room, however, besides a balcony overlooking the beautiful grounds of the complex made it well worth it. Juan was happy, and that was all I cared about. He got to do his swimming, and whenever Svetmana was down, I'd tell him to spend the time at the pool with her instead of coming to the club. Of course, I had my fun times in the pool with him too.

I liked Steve well enough, especially since he was a big spender, but yet his continual attentiveness towards Juan began eating away at me. Our singer, Mark, had introduced him as his lover at opening, and he was at the bar almost every night since. *Here we go again*, rolled around in my head, and I wouldn't have given it a thought if Juan didn't seem so pleased with his attention. Steve was tall and slender with dark, thick curly hair, though it was apparent he had been through a severe bout of acne in his life. Initially, Juan was intrigued with the attention only while drunk, but when he began talking about him when sober I became concerned.

It unfortunately happened! We were forced to close the show! No longer could we be indebted to the performers. Patti was the only one who complained, stubbornly refusing to wait for the balance owed her. In fact, she made our lives miserable. Candy asked if she might stay and do her solo Rock'n Roll show, offering to work for door receipts only. We agreed, but as fantastic as she was, they still were not coming in. A little more than a week and she too was gone.

So there we were, the two of us operating a disco bar. Juan spun the records while I tended bar. Everyone had been let go. In fact, Juan didn't have to worry too much about mixing, though he was becoming quite proficient at it. No one stayed long enough to dance.

Chapter Nineteen:
RJ's Becomes a Soul Disco

Things were desperate and to add to our woes, Deena called to say that Pa was having serious colon surgery. He was eighty one and had never been in a hospital.

"Rich, he keeps saying that you are not here and he is afraid he is going to die. He wants you here very badly. Do you think you can be here tomorrow? It will mean so much to him, Rich." I didn't know what to say since we wouldn't have enough to pay our bills if I spent it on airfare. Still I knew I had to be with my father.

"Rich, if you are short on money, Dino and I could come up with a hundred dollars," She said. It was as though she sensed our desperate situation.

"Your face is white as a ghost," Juan said after hearing me tell her I'd go. "Whot is wrong, my darling?" He held me tightly while I explained the situation. "Recharred, you 'ave only one father," he said compassionately. "You don't 'ave to worry; I will take care of everything here!"

Since all flights were booked for the evening, I'd have to take the early bird and arrive after surgery. Sensing my concern, Juan quickly said, "I will call Deena and have her tell your father you are on your way. Then he will know you are with him, Recharred!"

Parting was even more stressful since I had no idea how long I'd be in Chicago. It all depended on Pa's condition after surgery. I had grown much closer to him since my mother's passing in 1968. He was so easy to love because the void in his life was so apparent.

"Recharred, I do not want to come in with you," Juan said softly as we were driving to the Terminal, "I will probably cry, ond how will thot look for one man to be crying because another man is leaving." A squeeze of our hands would have to suffice instead, all the while fighting off tears.

"Pa, this is Richie," I said, taking his hand, "I am here with you and everything is all right. The doctor said you are doing very well." He was in intensive care and under heavy sedation. I wasn't sure he could hear me, but I went on to explain why I wasn't there before he went in for the operation. When he squeezed my hand gently, I realized he knew I was with him. We were told Pa would have a colostomy bag for a short time, and we prayed that this proud man would accept it graciously.

"I am so happy for you, Recharred," Juan exclaimed once I called him. "I am glad your father is gonna be okay! Spend as much time as you can with him while you are thar, Recharred, because he needs you!" Of course, the charming rascal quickly asked, "So when will you be home? I miss you so much, Recharred."

I spent the entire two days with Pa, and since he was doing so well, I flew home the following morning. One would've thought I was gone for a year by our behavior.

It would be an understatement to say business continued to be slow. In fact, many nights we sat alone in the bar, only to have someone walk in now and then but quickly leave. On one of those dreadful evenings, a tall black guy lumbered in. His afro added even more height. After watching him walk through the verandah, I commented on his unusual side to side shuffling. One glance at Juan's face and I knew he was aching to impersonate the walk. But this guy surprised us: he actually ordered a drink.

He introduced himself as Danyle, and though we usually had a problem with Black lingo, his delivery and enunciation made it comprehensible. We were taken by his outgoing personality and by his concern when we explained of our disappointment with the bar. After a while, he asked if we would be interested in making the bar a "soul disco"; his "brothers" were being harassed at other bars and needed a place to call their own. "I'll do anything to bring in business," I replied. This led to more discussion.

It wasn't long before he convinced us, and RJ's Soul Disco was born! Maybe it would save us. However, the change had to be quick; our capital was practically gone. We had barely enough to print up flyers to pass out in Piedmont Park. Juan quickly added, "Recharred, we con also put them on cars parked ot the other bars."

Danyle's smooth manner really surfaced once we agreed on the change. We were both actually agreeing to his every suggestion. We balked, though, when he asked to be manager and explained that we certainly couldn't afford to pay him.

"Ritchard and Juan, if I be manager I don't need to be paid much," Danyle said, "I be happy to work for practically nothing, just so it be a place for my brothers."

Even after offering him a paltry figure, he still wanted it. So we agreed to take him on, and to Juan he was our angel; no longer would we need to be there constantly.

Even before asking, Danyle gave me the number of his employer as a reference. It was busy the two times I called, and because I had so many details to take care of I didn't try again.

Danyle insisted we hire only Blacks because his brothers wouldn't come if 'whites' were working in the place. He would do the hiring. He convinced me that it would be a bad idea should I tend bar and for Juan to collect at the door. This was okay with Juan because he detested asking customers for money.

Everything was falling into place. Danyle's excitement truly earned him our respect, as well as the keys to the club and the alarm code. He hired the bartenders, the waiters, a DJ, and a doorman. It had to work; otherwise, we could not pay them. Plans were to reopen on Friday....

We agreed on a three- dollar cover charge for Fridays and Saturdays, and a one-dollar cover for Sunday through Thursday. The first night shocked us! The crowd was almost as large as our original opening night. We were off and running!

Before long, the place would, at times, be so crowded that in order for us to get downstairs to the office or the liquor room, we needed to go out the front door and walk around to the back door, which was on the first floor. After fetching the liquor or whatever, we would retrace our steps to get back in. We were happy to make the trek because it was all part of turning a profit and we just may be successful. The receipts, however, did not match up to our expectations, and we worried that someone was skimming off the top. We tried making head counts but that was impossible. I decided to stay by the door and count as they came in but Danyle advised us against that.

"Ritchard and Juan, my brothers will not come in if you be standing there." So it would remain a mystery? Why couldn't we do any better than three hundred and fifty dollars at the door on weekends, and even less at the bar?

RJ's was the talk of the town, the busiest, but we were just surviving! In fact, the liquor deliveries were paid for with checks that far exceeded our bank balance. We could only hope that the weekend receipts would cover them. We were forced to hire an off duty policeman for security on Friday and Saturday evenings because the crowds were so large. The other bar owners must have thought we were rolling in money, but the receipts never totaled more than seven hundred for the door and the bar combined. A cash reserve finally began to accumulate in the bank, which helped us to breathe a little easier when paying for liquor deliveries. The relief was shortlived, though, because Danyle would charm us into purchasing more sound equipment or on doing other improvements.

Juan and I were sure we had a good relationship with Danyle; his affection had to be genuine. He couldn't be the one cheating? He'd pat our heads and say, "Ritchard and Juan, you be my favorite people." He couldn't be responsible for anything underhanded. We even socialized with him and his lover when they had us over for an afternoon barbecue on the swimming deck of their building. It was unthinkable that he could be responsible for the low receipts. Juan especially refused to believe it. They got along famously, kidding each other continually. Juan had mastered his mimic of Danyle's walk and even got some laughs from him when he did it. I already realized that he catered to me because I had the final say. Nevertheless, he seemed to truly like Juan and his wit, and that was fine with me. If I would mention Danyle while discussing the low receipts I'd hear, "Why would Danyle do something like thot, Recharred? He loves RJ's! If we go out of business, he will not 'ave the elegant place he wants so much for his brothers."

A number of white guys were now coming to the bar, those with black lovers and those who were attracted to Black men. But eventually, they began to disappear, except for John England and Larry Logan. We didn't give it much thought until we ran into one of the owners from the frame shop next door.

"We wanted to come to your bar so badly since it is the talk of the town," he said, "but once we were harassed for three ID's, we figured we weren't wanted." I approached Danyle about it, but he somehow managed to convince me that he knew nothing about it. I decided to watch the door for any whites, but it was too late already. Word had evidently gotten around that RJ's was discriminating!

We managed to get away from the club on occasion; we felt safe leaving Danyle in charge. He appreciated the honor. Juan simply thought that Danyle was the best thing to come into our lives since moving to Atlanta. He was elated the night we finally made it to Six Flags. I especially recall his joy when I purchased one of those glow in the dark neck tubes for him. He confirmed the love I had for that little boy charm of his when he smiled and asked innocently, "How does it look, Recharred? Does it really glow?"

We may have been thought of as millionaire bar owners, but we were forced to get part time jobs with a catering company to survive. We were on call as waiters for banquets and seldom got called, but the little we did earn helped.

Mike called to say Nicky, Sue, and he were coming to spend a week. Danyle would have to run the club on almost a full time basis. We had to let him because it wouldn't be easy to hide our whereabouts from the kids. Racing to the bar as if in a *Mack Sennet* comedy for the daytime deliveries would work, but we couldn't be gone for an entire evening. They'd surely want to join us and see what our business was all about!

We took them to Six Flags on one of our outings since we had enjoyed it so much. Svetmana was also on hand to annoy everyone that day. Fortunately, she was only around for one day.

Mike and Nicky were curious about our jobs, so to ease our tension my creative mind came up with a solution. Larry was a macho guy, so why not invite him over and introduce him as our boss. That might work in lieu of a visit to our pretend office. I filled Larry in on everything he had to know. We were uneasy when he showed up with Tom, a handsome guy he was dating.

Larry whispered that he had gone over everything with Tom and our apprehensions faded.

It was going well until Larry and Tom began to drink heavily. We were on edge the rest of the night because they were inclined to bicker whenever they drank too much. Juan and I refrained from drinking but there they were, sopping it up! The gags were going back and forth and the kids were having a blast. We finally began laughing, too. However, our laughs ended when they began contradicting each other. Bickering could be expected from a husband and wife, but certainly not between uncle and nephew.

I was pretty sure Mike and Nicky didn't suspect a thing; and they laughed harder as the evening went on. Juan and I were very happy when they left.

"You know, Recharred, Larry ond Tom were too much this evening," Juan sighed after the kids went to bed, "I was so nervous with all their bickering. I hope your sons did not suspect anything." I assured him that I was sure they had not.

"Well, Recharred, Sue suspected something. You know how perceptive women are. While we were in the kitchen, she was very inquisitive. She wanted to know what they were to each other. However, I think she was satisfied once I told her that they are known as the quarreling uncle and nephew in the office."

"See, you are just as creative as me, Juanita!"

We had to work for the catering company that Saturday evening and the kids were convinced even further that we were with a public relations company when we came home with a special floral arrangement we had placed on the dining table we were seated at with our so-called clients.

Mike picked up all of the tabs, which I had expected since he was doing so well in his job. But all too soon and they were gone, and with their departure, I saw the sadness in Juan's face.

Danyle's expertise in persuasion was now second nature. He had actually convinced us that the bar would be nothing without him.

We began to notice a change in the type of clientele our club was attracting. The educated and professionals were disappearing. The club seemed to be full of a low class type instead. And to our distraught it seemed they were all friends of Danyle's. The suspicions I had harbored within suddenly began to surface. Was Danyle responsible for the low receipts?

I began taking the liquor inventory daily, and to my dismay I discovered that our costs were between forty and fifty percent. The only way possible for a bar to operate profitably would be at or around an eighteen percent cost. We figured the clientele wasn't buying a lot and undoubtedly were getting high on drugs or from the empty rum and wine bottles Juan would find while cleaning. Even so, that shouldn't have affected our bar costs. And when questioned, Danyle would always manage to handle it. He'd merely fire the bartender and hire another. The inventory would be fine for a few days, so I'd stop taking inventory. The figures, however, still added up the same for the bar, as well as the door, even though the crowds continued to pack the house.

Danyle would invariably go through the same fire and hire procedures when confronted. My suspicions became even more valid when Danyle showed signs of disgust at the mere mention of an inventory. I was certain he was behind it all and I wanted to get rid of him, but there was no real proof. Juan just couldn't believe that Danyle was guilty of such a thing. Meanwhile, Danyle managed to convince us that he was indispensable. We were actually afraid that without him, the bar would again be empty.

Robert seemed likable enough when introduced by Danyle as a 'brother,' but I was reluctant to take his suggestion to hire him to serve chicken and hamburgers because we couldn't afford another salary. I was sure there wouldn't be more than a couple of orders a night. But he then said Robert was willing to work on percentage only. How could he live on so little when he didn't have another job? Still Danyle insisted we give it a try. So we agreed, even though Danyle suggested Robert could drink for free whenever he was at the bar. The dining room would remain closed however.

My assumption was correct. There never were more than two or three orders per evening, and many times none at all. Robert was only earning about twenty dollars a week, but he didn't seem to mind. Mainly, because he was too busy drinking free booze and cruising, and never thinking to solicit food orders. We were losing money again. We could only eat so much chicken and hamburgers before they spoiled. Still, we kept him on. We certainly wouldn't dare fire one of Danyle's 'brothers.'

The catering company called for Juan to work on Saturday.

"Recharred," Juan called out on returning home, "I do not think we will be working for them anymore ofter whot happened tonight!" Before I could ask why, he went into his fast paced patter. "Because you know, Recharred, this was a very fancy banquet dinner tonight. There were about seven hundred people! So the waiters had to carry a tray with ten dinner plates on them. So I was carrying it with both hands in front of me, ond resting it against the front of my body. When the maitre'd noticed how I was carrying them he came up to me ond said I had to hold it over my head, ond balance it with my other hand."

I said, "Yeah, I know, Juan, but it takes a lot of practice."

"Well, do you know whot 'appened, Recharred?" Juan cried out, suddenly breaking into his cackling laugh, "I was nervously carrying the tray over my head when all of a sudden it slipped ond fell! Recharred, thar was creamed chicken all over the floor!"

It didn't take long for me crack up and we fell to the floor in hysterics. Through his belly laughs, Juan managed to continue. "Recharred, you should 'ave seen it! The maitre'd came running over ond I thought he was gonna 'ave a heart attack! I really did! Recharred, thar was creamed chicken all over the carpeting ond I was so embarrassed, so embarrassed!"

"What did the maitre'd do, Juan?" I asked while struggling to catch my breath, "Did he make you clean it up?"

"No, no, no, Recharred, the busboys came to clean it. The maitre'd took me into the kitchen ond told me I should continue carrying the trays with both hands in front of me. But then he stationed me ot the other side of the big ballroom! Ond, Recharred, I felt so bad because all the other waiters knew I was the one who dropped the tray. Ond it was not funny to me ot thot time."

"I could imagine that it wasn't funny then," I cried out, holding my belly for fear it would break, "but at least he put you on the other side of the room so no one there would know it was you who dropped the tray."

"Yeah, but the crash was so loud, Recharred, ond I am sure everyone in the room heard it. Aw, Recharred, it was so loud!"

"Jacque wants to come down and spend two weeks with you. Is that all right, Rick?" Joan asked when I answered the phone. I would be a nervous wreck, but it didn't matter. I missed her so much. Besides, the thought of rolling those *Mack Sennet* reels again amused me.

Soon enough, my dark-haired beauty was walking down the ramp flashing a happy smile. She may as well have belonged to both of us, because Juan was beaming as much as me. Six months had passed since we last saw her, and at that time tears were streaming down her face. This time, she was glowing! I was overwhelmed, only sixteen but already maturing into the woman!

"Aw, Recharred, Jacque is so bea-u-ti-ful, so bea-u-ti-ful!" Juan sighed, "She con really be a model or movie star!" Never had I seen her so happy! In fact we all were!

Although we took her to the many attractions Juan had raved about on the way home from the airport, she preferred the swimming pool. This was right up Juan's alley because she was just as obsessed with getting a tan as he was. Meanwhile, I did my fair share of racing to the club and back. Once again, dear Svetmana arrived. Jacque had never tolerated her rudeness when she was a child, and had less tolerance for it now that she was a young woman. Surprisingly, Svetmana yielded to Jacque's demands. Juan didn't seem to mind at all whenever she called Svetmana down, and I almost wished my daughter was with us permanently.

"Dad, I am so glad she finally left," Jacque whispered the day we put Svetmana on the plane for home,. "I've never seen such an annoying pest in my whole life!" I just smiled.

Nina stopped by one night to meet Jacque and to keep her company while we went to one of our so-called jobs. We regretted that decision the next night. Larry and Tom stopped by, and while in their presence, Jacque said that she and Nina were going to a party later that evening. I quickly objected, explaining that Nina was too wild, and besides that she was just too young to go with her. Jacque then called my attention to the fact that there was not that great an age difference….

I quickly pointed to the fact that Nina was years beyond her age, and had been around. "You haven't! No, you can't go! I don't know what kind of people will be there!"

Jacque still wouldn't let up, and when Juan saw signs of weakening on my part, he took me aside and whispered, "Recharred, you know how Nina is. So don't give in ond let Jacque go! Knowing Nina, she will probably take her to our bar ond thar we will be with all the faggots!"

Nina called, and I motioned for Juan to keep Jacque in the other room so she wouldn't hear my conversation. "Richard, someone in my office is giving the party," Nina explained, "and everyone will be straight! No gays will be there!"

Her persistence continued, and before I knew it, I was weakening. "Will you promise me there will be no monkey business if I agree to let her go with you?" I inquired, further insisting, "Nina, don't dare to bring her to our bar, and if I find out you took her to any other gay bar…I will kill you! Do you totally understand?" Naturally, she promised to abide.

Against Juan's objections, I agreed to let Jacque go. "Recharred, Nina is gonna get plastered," Juan insisted, taking me aside, "ond she will not remember a word she promised you!" But I insisted she would keep her promise; she'd never betray us after giving her word.

Nina called us at the club and said that her car had broken down, but that the person giving them a lift refused to drive them all the way to our apartment on Buford Highway.

"So would it be okay if Jacque spent the night at my apartment, Richard? She can swim at my pool tomorrow because I am off from work. You and Juan can get your business done at the bar and come over after."

Although I wasn't pleased, I saw no harm in it and agreed. Besides, Juan and I had been drinking at the club and it would be so nice to go out dancing at Hollywood Hots.

"I Go to Rio," "I Will Survive," and the disco version of "Tangerine" were only a few of the songs Juan and I danced our hearts out that night. Whenever we were on the huge, raised dance floor at Hollywood Hots, I always felt that all eyes were on us, and it was no different that night. That special magic of truly enjoying each other was obvious.

"Recharred, I wish you would 'ave told me last night thot Jacque was gonna sleep ot Nina's," Juan remarked as we drove towards her high-rise on Peachtree, "Don't you know everyone calls thot building *Vaseline Valley?*"

My eyes questioned his remark and he said, "Because so many gays live thar! Ond don't you know thot Nina lives with her uncle who is gay?"

"Oh, God, no!" I cried while pulling over to the curb, "Oh, Juan, I hope he was over at a trick's last night!"

"Ond what if he brought home a trick?" Juan gasped, taking hold of my hand.

The girls were already at the pool and I asked Jacque how the party went. After a quick "fine" she changed the subject. Her response gave me some concern. I needed to talk to Nina alone, and I was glad she took us up to her apartment to change.

"No, Richard, my uncle was not at home last night," she told me. I also wanted to hear about the party since Jacque had practically avoided talking about it.

"Now, Nina, tell me the truth. Did anything happen last night that should not have happened? I want you to tell me the truth! It is very important, Nina!"

"Believe me, Richard, everything went swell. It was a great straight party!"

When we got back to the pool, Juan and I were both uneasy. We imagined some nellie guy skipping over to us at any moment. Fortunately, it was a week day and we were the only ones at the pool. Our good fortune didn't last for long. Juan alerted my attention to someone almost skipping over to us. To my horror it was the one male singer in our show that would be the last person I wanted my daughter to meet. Mark was a marvelous singer but had a strong lisp when he spoke, and his flamboyant, feminine body language erased any masculine attributes his body may have portrayed. There he was…coming our way in short, quick steps!

Luckily Jacque was in the water and I hoped I could warn Mark to not mention the club. Before I could ask Nina, she explained that he had just moved into the building because he and Steve had broken up. However, my effort to warn him was quickly squashed. Jacque was out of the pool by the time he arrived. Introductions and the ensuing conversation, to say the least, were a bit muddled with double talk.

Before the conversation got even more uncomfortable, we told Jacque it was time to leave. Just then, Mark saw fit to ask when he could expect the money we owed him. I told him that it wouldn't be long because we were expecting to hear from our client soon. I had expected outrageous and queenly show of temperament, but it didn't happen. And probably because he suddenly noticed someone on the other side of the pool and excused himself.

I managed to bend the truth a bit when Jacque went on about his gay mannerisms and asked why we owed him money. "He probably is gay, Jacque. He's a singer who worked for us when we did a show for the company. We had some problems with him, so we held his pay."

"You know, Recharred," Juan said after Jacque left for home, "just before we left the house, Jacque told me thot Nina took her to the Gallus ofter thot party, ond thot she was shocked to see thot it was a gay bar. I warned you thot she would do something like thot but you would not listen to me!"

"Why didn't you tell me before she left so I could have talked to her about it?" I shouted after coming out of shock.

"She begged me not to tell you, ond how could I 'ave when we were together all the time before she left?" Of course, Nina said Jacque asked to go when I interrogated her.

Jacque brought up the subject of the party a few years later. "Dad, it was one of the weirdest parties I ever went to. You know what happened? One of the girls was telling a story, and while she was still talking she went into the bathroom. Dad, the bathroom was facing the living room and she never closed the door! She just continued telling her story! I couldn't believe it! She was

137

peeing and talking to all of us at the same time! And that friend of yours, Nina, was really a wild one!" I reminded her that I had warned her at the time.

The Gallus wasn't mentioned. Jacque probably figured I wasn't aware of any gay bars. Instead, she waited another fifteen years to tell me things she never told Juan. That so-called straight party had one drag queen tripping over another coming through the door!

We had to laugh when Danyle asked if we'd be able to handle the bar on his first night off. There was quite a crowd that evening for a week night, and things were running smoothly. I had done the payroll that day, and passed out the checks after he left. Robert's commission was only sixteen dollars for the week. Despite the fact that he never seemed to care that he was getting so little each week, especially since he was too busy having a good time, I still felt guilty giving such a small check. So I made the check out for twenty five dollars. What difference would a few more dollars in the hole make!

"Robert, you're not supposed to get this much," I said, handing him the check, "but I made it out for a little more." He seemed to appreciate it.

The customers were enjoying themselves, and we were happy because they were definitely white collar. *The low class bunch*, I thought, *must be partying with Danyle.*

We were watching television in the office as we often did to keep Juan from getting bored when, suddenly, Danyle barged through the door, ignoring the knock-first rule and shut off the television!

"What do you mean, Ritchard, by telling one of my brothers that he is not worth the money you be giving him?" Danyle demanded, standing before us, his teeth clenched. "How dare you be saying that to one of my brothers!"

He was referring to Robert, of course, but my attempts to reason with him did no good; he continued his rage! "And it be said to me that you be telling my waiter to clean a table! You be nothing but a muthafucker! I be the only one who be doing that!" We ignored the profanity; his rage was of more concern. He had to be wacked out on drugs and alcohol to get this crazy, but our attempts to get him to go home and sleep it off were futile. Instead, he became more enraged. He began grabbing papers from the desk and flinging them to the floor, screaming, "You have a gall, Ritchard, to be taking inventory every day!"

Although he was stunned, Juan managed some compassionate pleas, but Danyle's rampage went on, wildly kicking at the papers. I demanded an apology and explanation. It only infuriated him more. My temper was now at the boiling point and I shouted out, "Danyle, what makes you think you can do that? You are not the owner here, we are!"

At that point, he headed towards the door, turned to face us, and screamed out, "THIS BE MY BAR! I MADE RJ'S WHAT IT BE! AND I CAN END IT ANY TIME I BE WANTING." As he left, he shouted, "THIS EVENING BE OVER! I BE TELLING EVERYBODY WE BE CLOSING!"

"Danyle," I called out, "if you do that, you will regret it!" We were dumfounded, and Juan finally said, "Whot is the matter with him, Recharred, is he crazy?"

We didn't think he'd follow through with his threats until we realized the music had stopped. I stormed up to the booth and told the DJ to start the music. Danyle, in the meantime was at the cash register, his voice ringing out, "This mutha-fuckin' bar be owing me all this money!" He raced back to the booth, still shoving our cash into his pockets when the music resumed. I again told the DJ that I was the owner as Danyle demanded he stop the music. Danyle shouted arrogantly, "I be your boss, not him! This be my bar, so stop the music!"

The music stopped and a confused customer on the dance floor asked me if we were still open. I assured him that we were, but Danyle picked up the mike and announced, "This bar be now closed!" In moments, they were all gone.

Juan didn't come up the stairs, and I realized I was alone with a raging Danyle and his staff. If they thought he was crazy, they certainly weren't coming to my aid. They just froze. I told Danyle the club was not his repeatedly, but it only made things worse. I was trembling with fear the whole time, but I really got scared when Danyle's lover rushed in and handed him a gun. Danyle ran toward me, wildly waving this gun in my face! I was terrified as he pointed the gun menacingly from my face to other parts of the room! I thought of Juan, and as Danyle went to empty the cash register, he appeared at the bottom of the stairway.

"Whot the hell is going on, Recharred?" Juan asked, starting up the stairs, "Why is Danyle still screaming?"

"Danyle has a gun, Juan! Don't let him see you! Quick! Go into the office and call the police!" Juan disappeared to make the call and returned to face the same gun with me.

The police rushed in moments later. Fortunately for Danyle, they made quite a lot of noise in the foyer, and this allowed enough time for the gun to disappear as well as his rage. He transformed into an innocent angel. By this time, Juan and I were basket cases, and never gave another thought to the gun, completely forgetting to mention it to the police. Danyle had the receipts and had threatened our lives with a gun, but we didn't think to have him arrested. The thought of future retaliation was prevalent in our minds. All we wanted were the keys to the club, and Danyle to be completely out of our lives. Grateful that the cops presence had subdued Danyle, we were quite disappointed afterwards that the police had also forgotten about the gun after he told them about it when he called. It was apparent that they considered the entire incident to be a domestic quarrel, especially once they told everyone to go home and cool off.

Our trembling didn't subside until well over an hour after we were home. We tried to rationalize everything but, we couldn't come up with an answer. I told Juan that Danyle would probably show up at the club like a puppy with his tail between his legs, and try to smooth talk us out of firing him. "I know he will, Juan. I just know he will do that. He will come up to me, curl my hair and say he did not know what he was doing!"

Juan was sure that he wouldn't have the nerve to do that. "No, Recharred, it is over with him. He will be gone forever!"

Chapter Twenty:
The Difference between Success and Failure

Just what I predicted happened, and after all Danyle's sweet dramatics, we actually kept him on, but not as manager—as DJ. We didn't, however, return the keys to him.

The crowds continued, and Danyle slowly became the same, sweet, manipulative operator. Though no longer manager, he knew how to get his way! His ultra sweet and innocent manner continued to excite Juan whenever he talked about buying new things for the club. Of course, I'd hear Juan's excitement and give in. The door and bar receipts were still the same, which meant we continued playing the praying game each time I made out checks to the liquor companies. Should we happen to build a little reserve in the bank, it would soon be spent once Danyle brought up some new sound equipment. We were sure Danyle had learned his lesson. His hand had been slapped, and we assumed it had changed him.... After two months, to keep him happy, Juan talked me into giving him a raise. We finally conceded that the receipts had to be actual.

Danyle suggested we hold a *Mr. RJ's* contest, which we thought a good idea to make some big money. We chose a Sunday since that was the slowest day of the weekend. The Blue Law required closing at midnight, so we decided to begin the pageant at one in the afternoon in order to have more drinking hours.

The turnout was almost as large as a Saturday evening, and it looked like we were taking in a haul. I was glad Juan wasn't drinking, but he was impatient to get home and it was only ten.

"Would it not be nice, Recharred, if we could get home early ond watch television tonight?" he finally asked. Danyle had been very dependable, and since his suggestion was bringing in a bundle, I agreed. So, I gave him the keys, and he assured me everything would be fine when I reminded him of the necessary details. I must admit there was some apprehension because he had been drinking, but I shook it from my mind. We hadn't had a night home since the gun thing.

"Recharred, this is wonderful, just being with you like we used to in our apartment in Chicago," Juan sighed as we settled on the couch, "ond we didn't 'ave the problems we 'ave now."

Our new life was not what he had expected. He never imagined that each day would find us scraping to pay bills. Never was he able to cope with money worries. He needed to be certain he had enough to pay his bills. I couldn't help thinking back to the many times in our apartment on Oakdale when we would sit on the couch or at the breakfast bar to figure out our budget. We were both bringing home a salary, so there was never any worry. Juan needed that assurance to enjoy life. Now, we were borrowing from Peter to pay Paul, and almost always, Peter didn't have it! So it was nice just sitting together and forgetting our problems.

"It's the alarm company, Recharred," Juan called out after answering the phone. "The alarm went off ot the club." I wasn't too concerned; false alarms were the norm. It was only half past midnight and I figured Danyle had accidentally tripped it. I called to confirm my reasoning, and about to hang up when the ringing stopped. It was apparent that the receiver had been picked up, but no one answered.

"Hello?" I cried out, "Hello, Danyle, are you there?" There was no response, and yet I could hear breathing. I cried out again, but no response. Suddenly, I heard a click!

"Whot is the matter, Recharred?" Juan prompted as I stood there baffled. We realized we had to get to the club after I explained, and it had to be immediately. This was no false alarm! However, we realized we'd have to go into the club and we were terrified.

"Whot if someone is in thar, Recharred?" Juan shuddered as we parked the car, "Whot if they 'ave a gun or knife? We will not be able to do anything!" I never answered. I was too scared. There we were, slowly creeping to the door, and staying as close together as possible, almost as though we were trying to hide behind each other. We might just as well have been Abbott and Costello the night they met Frankenstein. The rear door to the dressing room was the only way in. We peered into the hall leading to our office once we edged through the dressing room, surprised to see the glow of lights coming from the room.

"Well, that's why the alarm went off! Danyle didn't close the office door!" I sighed in relief.

"Why would someone answer the phone if Danyle forgot to close the door, Recharred?" Juan quickly reminded me. We were back to square one!

It was possible someone could be in the office, or in the furnace room, or anywhere! We had to find out! So we crept our way down the hall, still moving as one. We finally got the nerve to peek and saw the liquor room door wide open! We still couldn't be certain someone wasn't in the building so we forced ourselves to check the rest of the club. Fortunately, we were alone.

Making quite a mess, and scattered throughout the office and liquor room, were my inventory sheets! The cash boxes were usually left in the liquor room at the end of the evening; we felt it was safer than taking with us at closing. But only one cash box was on the shelf!

"We 'ave been robbed, Recharred!" Juan cried out after lifting the lid to find the only things in it were pageant tickets and a few coins. "How could it happen so soon after Danyle left?"

My assumption was entirely different. Especially since the inventory sheets had been thrown about the room, and I quickly said, "I really don't believe Danyle was gone, Juan."

"I don' believe it," Juan replied in shock.

The only help we received from the police was a report of the robbery. "I told you before, Recharred," Juan reminded me while driving home, "My mother always said I have the devil's black sign over me, thot nothing would be right for me!" My expression of skepticism only caused him to insist, "She really did say thot all the time, Recharred!"

"That's crazy, Juan." This was our biggest setback yet. Not only were the large receipts of the evening gone, but our banks as well, not to mention the several hundreds of dollars we handed out in prizes. We remained silent. Juan had undoubtedly been thinking the same thing. That black sign had obviously come over my head, too!

Our spirits were low when we returned to the club in the morning. The possibility of taking Danyle for a lie detector test was discussed, but we felt somewhat leery about doing it. During the last couple of months, he had planted another seed of fear into our minds, continually calling our attention to the fact that many of his brothers were filing complaints against white employers with the NAACP after being fired. We had to be sure we were in the right, and not just discriminating.

We didn't feel like doing much of anything, but realized things had to be done if we were to open that evening. Juan started cleaning, and though I was not in the mood to take inventory since the inevitable high figures would only add to the depression, it would keep my mind occupied.

"Juan, c'mon here a minute," I called out holding up a bottle of bourbon, "Does this bourbon look lighter than it should be to you?"

"Recharred, you know I don't pay attention to things like thot."

I quickly poured some into a glass, and after a sip, handed it to him. "Well I know *you know* how it should *taste*!"

"Recharred, I don' believe it!" Juan exclaimed after a sip, "It does not even taste as strong as one of my bourbon and waters! Do you mean thot water has been added to this bottle, Recharred?"

"That is exactly what has been done, Juan!" It didn't take long to find the same in other bottles! We quickly agreed...Danyle had to take a lie detector test!

Since Danyle came in at about three-thirty, we called and were fortunate to get a four-thirty appointment. We decided not to confront him with too many questions, but merely say that everyone would be required to take a lie detector test.

Danyle was right on time, giving an absolutely terrific performance as we described the events of our midnight tale. He also showed no signs of dismay or concern that he was being taken for a lie detector test. So, there he was, in the back seat laughing and joking as if nothing was wrong! We decided to play along, and join in his jovial mood, though I never felt more disgust for anyone in my life! To actually think we were in the mood to laugh and joke! I never wanted to sock someone silly more than I did him! Juan could read my mind, and to keep me from boiling over, he held himself forward so his face could mimic Danyle without being seen by him. As usual, it worked. Of course Danyle thought I was laughing at his nonsensical jokes.

It was obvious that Danyle was the cause for our low receipts and the poorly planned burglary; we'd have to be really stupid not to realize it! I never had been one to use profanity; no one in my family ever did. In fact, I always sounded uncomfortable whenever there was an occasion to use a choice word. Our sound man, Stuart, even joked about my awkward delivery of the cuss words left on his message machine each time the sound equipment gave us problems. Well, I finally got comfortable. Danyle taught me well. There I was repeating to myself, "This fuckin' asshole is the difference between our success and our fuckin' failure!"

Juan and I sat in the waiting room for the test results, almost gloating. All the details were explained to the technician when I made the appointment, so he knew which questions to ask. At last, we would get rid of this cancer, and maybe still have a chance to be the successful bar owners Juan dreamed of. After all, we were the busiest bar in town!

Our hearts, however, suddenly were filled with anxiety when the technician stepped out and led us into another room. His expression was too intense. "I'm afraid I don't have good news for you gentleman," he stated, throwing up his hands in a hopeless gesture, "I cannot get any kind of a reading on this man! I really cannot believe it! I just didn't receive any reaction whatsoever! My only conclusion is that he is a pathological liar. I don't know. It never happened before." He continued, but we heard no more; we were lost in the anguish of it all. Everything was suddenly crashing down on us again.

Danyle sat in the back seat again on our drive to the club. He was laughing and joking. Somehow, I felt the joke was on us!

Except for an evening John England was over for lasagna dinner, we were at the club continually. Juan had raved about my lasagna repeatedly, and after a few hints from John, I finally gave in. And then it turned into a catastrophe! We were going in to close that night, but I still was concerned leaving Danyle at the bar without us that I over-salted the sauce! It was edible, but once you ate a forkful, you were looking for something to drink! John was a perfect gentleman, though, eating every bit in his plate. However, I still had to contend with Juan. "Recharred, why did you make it so salty? Aw, Recharred, it is so salty!" I realized, though, that he merely wanted John to be aware that this sauce was not up to par. Through the years, Juan never forgot it. I'd always expect to see that twinkle in his eyes while shaking a finger at me, saying, "Now, Recharred, be sure you do not put in too much salt!"

Just before Thanksgiving, Juan introduced a guy to me. Quite slender and tiny, Harold Williams seemed nice enough. It seemed he had frequented the club for some time, but I didn't know him. We talked for some time and his genuine sincerity was quite a contrast to the theatrics we were so used to with Danyle. He returned every night, and his pleasant personality began growing on us. We soon learned that Danyle had approached him once to ask for his allegiance as one of his *brothers*, but that he had firmly refused, wanting no part of his game. Our discrete observations of the two quickly proved they were certainly not a big fan of the other.

According to Harold, a conference of black, gay, professional men was to be held at a nearby Mayfair Hotel during the Thanksgiving weekend. Our excitement increased at hearing they were big spenders and liked elegant places. If we could get them to come to our club, we'd be set! This urged me to do something I should have done long ago. I fired the doorman, Ron, and the two bartenders. Ron was the original doorman hired by Danyle, and had constantly been rude to us. We used that as a reason to fire him, and the high liquor costs for the bartenders. Harold was sure the hotel would let us put flyers in their lobby, and if they proved to bring in the group, we certainly were not going to chance using a staff with a history of low receipts.

Don Davis impressed me when he applied for a bartending job, and it didn't take long to convince me that he and I would work the bar in spite of being white. Juan was to be host, and the doorman job was Harold's.

It was obvious Danyle was not too pleased we took this action. At last, the pleasure was ours since we wouldn't have to hear his insistence on things being done his way. We were showing some backbone, and he became a silent man. He knew that one slip and his DJ job would be up for grabs, too.

Boy, did they come! It was packed the night before Thanksgiving, and greater yet was the class of people coming in! "Recharred, I don't believe it," Juan cried out excitedly, "These guys are so nice, ond polite, ond educated! They are nothing like the bums Danyle catered to!"

"Yeah," I agreed, "and these guys aren't getting their drinks for nothing!"

Juan introduced me to the two gentlemen heading the conference, and after talking to them for some time, I agreed with their suggestion to open the bar from noon to five thirty the next day. They were free on Thanksgiving Day, and dinner was not until seven.

Juan wasn't happy with the arrangement since we had planned on having dinner at home. It would be our first turkey dinner. "Tell you what, Juan," I finally suggested, "I'll prepare the stuffing and a couple of side dishes before I leave for the club. You can stay at home, baste the turkey, and relax before getting the table set and the other things that need to be done. I'll close at five thirty and come home to make the giblet gravy before our wonderful dinner together." He showed some enthusiasm when I reminded him that we wouldn't reopen until ten o'clock. He didn't prey on his disappointment, though; he was aware that we needed the revenue desperately.

Four o'clock came very quickly that evening, and I was so proud of Juan because he had done very little drinking. He had been too busy captivating our guests with that charm of his.

Juan, Harold, Don, and myself counted the receipts once Danyle and the waiters left. The totals were fabulous! Five hundred for the door at two dollars a head, and seven hundred and fifty in bar receipts! We were too happy to dwell on the fact that this confirmed that we were being taken for months. Why didn't we ever think to make periodic collections from the door?

Thanksgiving morning was a bit hectic after only four hours sleep. We had gone out for breakfast to celebrate our new found success, as Juan had put it. We were tired, but much too happy to admit to it. I wanted so badly to stay home all day, just as we did in Chicago Christmas day. And I knew Juan wanted that as well, not leaving my side as I prepared the stuffing.

"I wish you did not 'ave to go to the club, but I know you must because we need the money so badly," Juan said sadly. His smile confessed that he truly understood. Of course, he managed to remind me constantly to clean up, finally doing it himself to be certain it got done.

Customers started to arrive shortly after opening. Busy as we were, I still managed a few calls to Juan. When the receipts were counted, the door had taken in about four hundred and fifty and the bar about five hundred. It was like a miracle! I had also noticed how lost Danyle seemed to be, and felt a tiny bit sorry for him.

Upon entering the hall leading to the apartment, the wonderful aroma of roast turkey hit me, and I hoped it was ours. It was good to be home at last.

"Recharred, I just took the turkey out of the oven ond it looks bea-u-ti-ful," Juan called out from the kitchen. "Come, look ot it!"

It was a beauty, but not as beautiful as being home with Juan! His happy excitement was always apparent because he'd talk on quickly. "How does it look, Recharred?" he asked, taking hold of my hand and leading me to the dining room, "Does it not look elegant! I put on the white linen tablecloth ond napkins my mother gave me.

"It's beautiful, Juan. Everything is really beautiful. Especially you, Juan."

Still holding onto my hand, he looked at me the way only he could, softly sighing, "Recharred, it is so good to 'ave you home. I love you so much!"

The gravy was done in a snap, and we were finally seated at our table of plenty. We had had to scrape to buy food, and here we now had enough for at least twenty people. Juan had done a great job following my instructions with the candied sweet potatoes, and gloated happily when I complimented him. Sitting opposite Juan at a dinner table was always the ultimate pleasure in my life, but this time it was extra special. It was a real Thanksgiving, and our thanks to God called for a solid *amen*!

Juan never was a chicken or turkey lover, still he didn't remind me of it, complimenting the moist and tender taste instead.... He did, however, rave about the stuffing, which made me feel great since this was a first for me. I had watched my wife prepare it many times, browning the pork sausage with onions just before adding the mixture to the bread bits and celery—though I wasn't certain of the spices to add. So I sprinkled plenty of salt and pepper along with some sage, hoping it would be okay. Juan never filled a plate with large portions; he always felt it was better to go for seconds and thirds, and he did exactly that with the stuffing. "Recharred, this is the best stuffing I 'ave ever had," he kept repeating, the light blue of his eyes sparkling from the glow of the candles.

The weekend was a huge success, the door bringing in about nine hundred each evening with about the same amounts from the bar. We were ecstatic!

Monday was particularly warm, and Juan and I couldn't be happier as we made our largest deposit ever at the bank. I was behind the bar now and we wouldn't have high percentage costs again, though our take may not hit as high since our regulars were not heavy buyers like the conference clientele. The door receipts, however, would be as high since the crowds were always at capacity. After all, Danyle's chosen doorman was gone now!

Juan began cleaning once we arrived at the club, and I went to the office to work on the liquor orders. A tremendous amount of alcohol had been consumed during the long weekend, and it felt good knowing we finally made some money on it.

"Whot is the matter with the air conditioning, Recharred?" Juan remarked coming into the office, "I am sweating my ass off upstairs ond I cannot feel any cold air coming from the vents." I hadn't noticed since it was always cooler in the basement. Instead of taking valuable time looking into it, I called John to get a service man out immediately.

I continued with the orders after directing the service man to the back room, only to hear him call out for me to join him moments later. I assumed he was about to say that it was not repairable, only to be corrected as he pointed to the top of the hot water tank, remarking, "I don't know if that's where you keep it, but it looks like a cash box sitting there."

The missing cash box? Ten thousand volts of electricity surging through my body couldn't have made as big a shock as I felt once I lifted the lid to see tickets for the Mr. RJ contest! "Juan! Juan, come down here quickly!" I shouted, hurrying to the staircase.

Juan practically flew down the stairs, thinking something terrible had happened, shouting out, "Whot is it, Recharred? Whot has happened?"

Without a word I slowly opened the lid and held the cash box out! His wide eyed expression knew immediately what had happened!

"I don' believe it," he exclaimed once I explained everything, "You mean Danyle put it thar the night of the burglary ond then took out the cash the next day?"

"No, Juan, he more than likely came back that night after the police and us had gone. The staff was waiting for him to set the alarm so they could all leave together, and he didn't want to chance taking all that money with him. This must have been a lone move by Danyle because he certainly wasn't going to share the loot. He must have realized they would have to be blind not to see the wads stuffed in his pockets."

"Thot is right, Recharred," Juan concluded, "because thar had to be ot least a thousand in one dollar bills alone!"

"Of course, Juan, he realized the keys would be taken from him the next day because we had been robbed! That asshole!"

Our eyes met, and in perfect unison we shouted, "We finally got him!" His malice had been so intense and blinding that he completely forgot to discard the box! We called and asked him to come to the club, and to avoid suspicion I explained that we needed his opinion regarding new equipment. As usual, his ego was inflated, replying, "I be down after I shower. I know just what we be needin.'" Juan and I smiled broadly. There we were—two cats ready to pounce! Juan added to my delight with a fantastic mimic of Danyle shuffling in.

We had just enough time before Danyle arrived to finish our chores. After placing the last liquor order, I quickly ran up to help Juan with the cleaning. And there he was deep in conversation with Tyrone, obviously spilling the beans! I didn't want anyone to know anything until after confronting Danyle, but Juan was never one to keep a secret. Tyrone was one of Danyle's original waiters, but had alienated himself from him after the gun incident. I wasn't too concerned because he had sort of hinted that he was no longer one of his followers.

Upon hearing the news, Tyrone enlightened us with some major facts that I had suspected but never imagined to be true. No one could possibly be that low. Danyle had been having after hour parties at the club during tenure as manager, along with stealing from the door! Ron had taken his share, too! They had actually boasted to the staff! We now knew why receipts didn't increase after demoting Danyle. Ron kept up with his pocketing while Danyle sent messages to him from the DJ booth: "Due Danyle—fifty dollars!" Sometimes a higher amount! It all depended on the crowd. As crowds increased, so did the notes throughout the evening!

I recalled a particular evening when I first suspected something, but refused to believe it. No one could show someone so much love and still steal from them. Danyle was on break and approached, giving me an affectionate hug. My hand felt a bulge as it rested near his side pocket, and a fleeting thought flashed into my head, "Could this be a wad of bills from our door?"

"Danyle has an intense hatred for both of you, in fact, for all whites," Tyrone revealed. "He'd be cussing you out continually, boasting he'd take everything he could from you."

"Why didn't you come tell us, especially after you alienated yourself from him?"

"Because, Richard, when I refused to be part of his scheme," Tyrone replied, "he threatened me with some kind of hurt, and I was afraid." I shrugged and told Tyrone to get lost for a while so Danyle wouldn't see him.

Danyle sauntered in a few minutes later in his usual cocky and weird manner. Embracing the two of us, he over enunciated, "How be my two favorite people today?"

I wanted to vomit in his face, but I knew I had to play it cool in order not to warn him of the approaching confrontation. His extraordinary talent could talk himself out of the mess given time to concoct a story. I couldn't help but think that this lowdown scum perfectly described the ugly word…nigger! We had opened our hearts to him, yet he hated us with a vengeance because we were white. We, too, were discriminated against for being gay. Why couldn't he have found it in his heart to join in an alliance, especially after we had been so good to him?

He continued talking nonsense, and an intense hatred began building up inside of me. I was about to explode, and it would ruin our plan. Juan sensed it, and approached to put his hand on my shoulder, whispering, "Blanche, c'mon now, please relax!" The club had become an eternal hell for him, and he so hoped that Danyle would be the one to free us. So his encouragement was well taken since I realized how disappointed he was. I had had my doubts about Danyle for some time, but gave him the benefit of the doubt to maybe make Juan's hopes a reality.

Danyle might become suspicious should we ask him to join us in our office; it would give him the time needed to conjure up a remarkable, mystifying lie. The upstairs waiter's room would avoid any suspicions, especially since he was continually after us to open the dining room.

The cash box was on the table, but he was too excited to notice. Juan and I seated ourselves, immediately asking him to sit on the opposite side of the table. His usual cocky manner prevailed, so we knew that he wasn't aware of the boom about to fall. I was certain that the pounding of my heart was audible; the thought of Danyle winning us over again haunted me. I continued, though, taking a deep breath. "Danyle, do you know what is in this cash box?" I asked, holding the cash box to his face and slowly lifting the cover to reveal the scattered tickets in it.

"Yes, Ritchard, those be the admittance tickets for the Mr. RJ pageant," he answered, not yet aware of the scope of it all. "Why you be showing them to me?"

Instead of interrupting, he remained silent as we explained the dirty facts. I continued, feeling as though molten lava was coursing through my veins, "Your hatred for us, especially for me, had so consumed you that you took the time to throw all my inventory sheets around the room! Didn't you think that would make us suspect it was you, since you hated the fact that I took inventory daily! God, you must have been in a rage since you were still here when the alarm company called, and we certainly know they've never been quick to call on a false alarm! You even had the nerve to pick up the phone when I called! Yes, Danyle, your hatred for us made you rub it in further by picking up the phone and not answering, and to laugh at me once you hung up! I've never come across anyone as low as you in my whole life! You are worse than scum!"

Juan and I gloated as he attempted a feeble denial! We finally had him, and he was aware of it, especially after I added, "You made one big mistake this time, and it is the proof that we need! In your anxiousness to revel in our misery, you failed to dispose of the one thing that would point to you as the one who committed the burglary. You were the only one with keys besides us. A burglar would've never set the cash box in the furnace room, only you! You hid it there so the staff wouldn't see the big bulges in your pockets as you all left. Yes, Danyle, I'm sure you realized the keys would be taken from you, so you came back the same night after the police, Juan, and I had left. Not unlike the early morning parties here that you thought you had a right to hold! And I am certain that you charged for the drinks at those parties, and kept the receipts for yourself!"

"Ritchard and Juan, how could you be saying I be doing something like that?" Danyle shouted in another poor attempt to fool us, "It could be you setting up the box there!"

"Danyle!" I exclaimed, looking squarely into his eyes, "We have a witness to prove it was on the water heater...the service man! We no longer have to worry about the NAACP. We want you out of here, and don't ever return!"

He began crying, falling to his knees and begging, yet not for forgiveness, but that we not fire him because this was 'his club!'

"I be the one that made RJ's! It be rightfully mine!" he demanded repeatedly while begging not to be fired. His ridiculous sobbing continued. However, we were not going to be intimidated again and change our minds. He would manipulate us no more!

It was appalling watching the despicable scum of the earth show absolutely no remorse once we assured him of our knowledge regarding his constant pilfering of the door receipts. The embezzling had left the club in danger of closing. The fact that his brothers would be without a place to call their own meant nothing to him. It didn't even seem to affect him once Juan said, "Danyle, we trusted you, ond were so grateful for your suggestion to make the club into a soul disco. When we ourselves were making nothing, I suggested to Recharred to give you more money, ond he graciously did! If we had been making what we should 'ave, you would 'ave had such a large salary coming to you because we would 'ave been so appreciative...."

"And it would have continued to grow," I added, though our talking did no good; he wasn't even listening! He could only think of RJ's being taken from him, and all too consumed in himself and his hatred for whites!

That was the last time we saw Danyle. He was gone forever. What remained was only the memory of the loss of about thirty-five to forty thousand dollars…the difference between success and failure! Why we had not collected from the door throughout the evenings, I will never know. Of course, whenever Juan wanted to make me laugh, he would simply do his fantastic mimic of Danyle's walk.

Chapter Twenty-One:
Exit RJ's, Enter Chez Cabaret

We decided on a weekend away from the club. Besides providing relaxation, it would be a nice break for Juan and me. He often talked of going to Myrtle Beach and Savannah.

"We are so close, Recharred, and it is such a shame thot we connot go thar."

Larry had invited us for a weekend at his mountain cabin in South Carolina. The weather turned cold, and after a fine steak dinner, we sat in front of the fireplace, talking, drinking too much, and having the time of our lives! The next morning, walking in the woods, Juan remarked, "Recharred, look ot Larry ond Tom ahead of us. How con they still be drinking cocktails ofter all thot we drank last night?"

"That's how real drinkers do it, Juan. Am I glad you're not that way!"

"Thank you so much, Recharred, for taking time off from the club," Juan sighed, pausing to take hold of my hand and adding, "This is whot I love…nature. Ond you 'ave made me so happy!"

"I know, Juan, and we wouldn't have had such a great time last night if not for you!"

"Why, Recharred, why do you say that?"

"Because of the way you were mimicking Danyle's walk. You know how you break me up every time you do it. Last night, you were so funny I thought we were gonna split our sides."

"Really?" Juan asked in his innocent high pitched voice, "I really did thot, Recharred?"

Unfortunately, December brought more woes; a giant nearby bar decided to horn in on our success with the black trade by not harassing the brothers at the door, even lowering the cover charge to two bucks on weekends. Of course, we followed suit. This was a big concern, since Back Street had a dance floor six times the size of ours. Word was out, and we realized it wouldn't be long before our place was a graveyard again. We had to offer something they didn't get at Back Street, and Juan came up with a dandy.

"Recharred, why do we not 'ave a special drag show featuring employees."

Harold and one of the waiters had been itching to give it a try, so why not!

Though nowhere near our old jam-packed house, the show brought in quite a respectable crowd. Harold had his heart set on doing "Ain't No Mountain High Enough" a la Diana Ross, and once he hit the stage, I thought Juan was going to die from laughter! The white gown was fabulous, but it was four sizes too large. Juan quickly remarked, "Look, Recharred, you con see his stuffed bra!"

"And how about that wig, Juan? It's so big it is almost down to his nose!" I shouted.

"Aw, Recharred, he is so funny, so funny!"

The idea did bring in some money, but one night didn't keep it coming. So, we began looking for side jobs. I even began auditioning. Juan and I wanted to go to Chicago for Christmas, and if I could land a part, it would help pay the airfares. Don could certainly take care of the bar.

I was finally cast as temporary replacement for the undertaker in *Send Me No Flowers* for ten days. It was perfect because performances weren't scheduled on Christmas Eve and the holiday. But once we called to change to a later flight after my show on the 23rd, we were told that the only space available was at nine on Christmas Eve!

"Aw, Recharred," Juan cried out, "it is foolish for me to go ot thot time because my family always celebrates with on early dinner thot day. My mother ond father go to sleep early, ond by the time I get to their home, everything will be over. Whot am I gonna do? They will feel so bad!"

We decided to keep him on the original flight. It was the only solution.

I often excused myself from working the bar; the crowds didn't warrant two bartenders all of the time. It also kept Don from looking for more hours elsewhere. Of course, this would only encourage Juan to insist on going to other places to dance. I didn't want to go at times because we didn't have the money, but I agreed if only to avoid a scene. His boredom with the bar only caused him to drink more, and revert to his old accusations that I was cheating on him. I couldn't convince him otherwise when he was drinking, and his continual antagonisms would drive me up a wall. I began to actually want his accusations to come true, especially since he felt it permissible to tease me about Steve coming onto him. Our singer Mark's ex had always been a big spender at the club since the beginning, which influenced me to ignore his flirtations with Juan. Juan's occasional disappearances from the club, however, would only arouse my suspicions. However, I never knew whether the concern was warranted, since his behavior simply may have been testing my jealousy.

Hollywood Hots was an all-night membership club, featuring a bathhouse as an added amenity. It was hilarious watching the dirty old men waiting anxiously for a towel to fall from some hunk on the dance floor. Membership included admittance to the bathhouse, and whenever Juan felt mischievous he'd insist, "C'mon, Recharred, let's go in the bathhouse to see whot is going on!" So we would join the parade of guys walking through the corridors of opened doors. Of course he'd have me in stitches with his comments to each of the occupants waiting on their cots for someone to join them. That was probably the only time his wit wasn't appreciated.

I was certain that I was being cruised by a young handsome guy during our visits to Shelly's, and it definitely boosted my ego. In fact, I would discretely look for him each time we were on the dance floor. Even when Juan was half-lit, he was aware of someone giving me the eye. He never failed to come up with a clever remark, though I tried diverting his attention to something else. I don't know why I was so thrilled at being cruised since I loved Juan so much. Was it because I had been starved for affection for so many years? Or was I getting even with Juan for tormenting me so about admirers?

Greg Burke had worked for the previous owners and was always after us to hire him as DJ. According to him, although he was white, the blacks loved his mixes. A friendship developed between the three of us once the job was his, and it wasn't unusual for him to join us for breakfast at closing. He lived to spin records, and couldn't have delighted Juan more than when he invited us over to see his collection. The amazing part of it was Juan knew every song and artist while reminiscently thumbing through.

Juan could have easily taken over as DJ. He would mix records whenever Greg was off and it was a slow night, and he became quite good.

"How did you like thot mix, Recharred? Was it not great," he'd shout proudly. And whenever a new supply of promo records was ready for pickup, he'd insist we go immediately. It was a pleasure just watching his face once we returned to hear them.

"Aw, Recharred, this is great! I know it is gonna be a hit!" He could predict a hit. I especially remember his excitement the day he played Thelma Houston's "Don't Leave Me This Way."

I began to grow a mustache, thinking it would add to my character in the play. Juan decided to do the same. Everyone said it made me look older, but interesting. I knew better. I preferred Juan without one; I felt it hid the fullness of his sensual lips.

The role of the undertaker was fun to do, and I was certain that everyone, including Juan, was pleased with my interpretation. We were both fairly quiet while driving to the airport on the twenty-third; this would be our first separation since I had gone to Chicago for my father's operation.

"Juan, come to my niece's house after your parents go to sleep Christmas Eve? After all, you say they go to bed early, and we'll be up late there." He agreed and our parting hurt less.

I was feeling blue when I returned to the club after my performance, and began downing one drink after another in an effort to bring myself up. An instant happy high soon took over the blues. I didn't realize I was acting in the same manner as I had the evening I met Ed in Chicago. The alcohol soon gained control, and I wanted more! Before I knew it, I was at Hollywood Hots, higher than a kite! I remember mimicking Juan's mischievous ways, then taking on the baths. There I was, peering into the opened doorways and handing out one witty remark after another!

Suddenly, it came to a halt. I was beckoned in just as I was about to make a comment at a doorway. There he was, lying on the cot, totally naked except for a towel across his midsection, and that began rising slowly. There before me was the Adonis that had been cruising me at Shelly's! A sudden rush surged through my body, and I hopelessly submitted to my weakness. I closed the door and stripped. It didn't matter that he acted like a piece of machinery by quickly lifting up his legs, I obliged heatedly!

I was in a stupor the next day, realizing what I had done, though I couldn't remember driving home. The guilt was unbearable. I needed to be alone and couldn't bear the thought of facing anyone at the club. So I spent the day trying to do some last minute shopping in Lenox Square. I couldn't concentrate on it, though; I could only think how I might confess to Juan, then realizing I couldn't tell him what I had done. It would only destroy him again.

Juan showed up shortly after I arrived at my niece's house, and when I saw the glow on his face after seeing me, I knew I had made the right decision. How could I risk losing that sparkle!

I was to meet Juan at the gate for our return trip Monday since he was getting a lift. So there we were, Martina, Nicky, and I, running like crazy down the concourse at O'Hare Airport. Rush hour traffic had been at a peak. I was certain I would miss the flight, especially since we had my luggage and the bags of goodies that had to be picked up each time we dropped them. I'll never forget the expression on Juan's face once we reached the gate.

"Wait! Please don't close the gate!" we shouted out simultaneously, "(My dad has to get on!) (I have to get on!)"

With a relief, he burst into laughter, and once we were settled, he exclaimed, "Blanche, you are so Italian! So Italian! You ond your kids looked like you were running to catch the boat, ond dropping your rolls of salami on the way!"

We had heard, before leaving for Chicago, that bars were usually very busy for the Christmas holidays. Unfortunately, it was not the case with our club. Word apparently had gotten around about Backstreet, along with a bit of boycotting on Danyle's part.

Another disappointment came when I found myself traipsing to the Alliance to sell the last Broadway series tickets. I had done it for the third and fourth show of the series as well.

I was forced to accept an offer for my barber shop building that I had previously received from an agent in Staterville. Three months into 1977 and we were again broke, and facing still another stint at a *Mack Sennett* comedy. Martina had called while driving home after spending her spring break in Florida, wanting to stop off so I could meet her new beau.

"I know you will like him, Dad," she said, and I did. Though their visit would be only a couple of days, it was nice because we felt real again. Juan was as happy if not happier than me. He always thought the world of Martina. "She is, ond always will be, on absolutely charming lady, Recharred!" There was a bit of longing in his face, and I realized his thoughts were of Svetmana. Would she ever be as wonderful?

It seemed as though they were gone before we even had a chance to blink our eyes. I had acted rather prudish when Martina said they would sleep in their sleeping bag together, and Juan laughed again when recalling what he had said to me at the time. "Recharred, they 'ave been on a trip together. C'mon now, mon!"

The check finally arrived from the sale of my building, along with one for my barber equipment, which I was forced to sell for practically nothing. That money was gone all too soon, and since we were broke, we let everyone go. A scenario was repeating itself nightly. Someone would venture into the club, and then leave immediately.

On one particular evening, we heard the familiar patter of little steps in the outer foyer, as well as that drawl we so associated with Lee Shannon, and were happy that we were not wrong. She introduced us to two of her drag queen companions…Ronda and Terri. Our spirits had been quite down, but it didn't take long for their lively conversation to pick us up.

"Richard, you know how popular drag bars are in town," Lee remarked, "why don't you have them here?" After commending her idea, I quickly reminded her that we'd still be in the same boat since we would have to pay the performers.

"Lee, we just don't have the money! Besides we'd also need a DJ and a doorman again."

"Richard, you can work the bar and Juan could take care of the door!" they exclaimed in unison. "We'd be willing to work for the door receipts because we do make tips."

"Ond all we would 'ave to pay is the DJ, ond I know Nina will be willing to work for tips waiting on tables!" Juan quickly added. My eyes lit up, and Juan catching it, he shouted, "Okay, Blanche, thot settles it. We con do it!" But I insisted on seeing their numbers in full drag.

Terri was about six-foot-three, and didn't make up to attractive, but her comedy flair at performing to party records was hilarious. There was no doubt that Ronda was a bombshell—amazingly, a clone of Marilyn Monroe! We already knew what Lee could do. It could possibly work, and since they were so young, their talent could only grow! Yes, it had to work!

We decided to close the club for a few days, and then reopen under another name. That would officially confirm that RJ's Soul Disco had closed and avoid any conflict of interest. A new name would be chosen and painted on the outdoor sign. Flyers were printed and distributed in Piedmont Park as well as various other places. I even choreographed a couple of production numbers. Greg and Nina were available as Juan had predicted, and so we were off and running!

Several names were thrown about before we agreed on the one we felt perfect. Our hopes were high because we needed a winner at last. Holding onto each other, we smiled and sighed, "Exit RJ's...enter Chez Cabaret!"

Chapter Twenty-Two:
That Black Star

Along with our friends and many old customers, quite a few new faces appeared at the opening. Steve was there as well as my jealousy, but I realized I had to be grateful since he was a big spender and a good tipper to the performers. Though the club showed no sign of filling, there was a respectable number that we hoped would in turn tell others. I hoped the queens would be tipped well, and that the free cocktails they talked me into giving them might also satisfy their needs. It was obvious they wouldn't be making much from the door. The prospects of their satisfaction, however, appeared quite good since their consumption of alcohol seemed endless. The more Lee drank, the funnier she got, though she could be insulting once she had over-indulged. Ronda was a real spitfire, and a queen with a fantastic potential since she definitely passed as a woman. She only had to improve her synch and attitude. She, too, could be quite nasty with curt remarks when drunk. Terri was ugly, but funny.

There was one party in particular that seemed to be having the time of their lives, and most of the noise was led by the guy. His loud, squeaky voice was audible throughout the club. He looked like a dwarf because he had this great big head, short arms, and walked with a hobble. Tom Michaels, as he introduced himself, took an immediate liking to us, especially me. Betty was probably about my age, but quite matronly. She was right out of backwoods Georgia. The young girl, Tammy, was absolutely beautiful and probably all of sixteen. We freaked when Betty told us that Tammy was her son!

"My God, I don' believe you are a man," Juan kept repeating. "You are so bea-u-ti-ful! So bea-u-ti-ful!" And there I was, whispering to remind him that he was not a man, but a boy. Juan could have cared less, making over him like he was a Greek goddess! It was also apparent that Betty was very proud of her daughter, or son. Whatever? And Tom's excitement over Tammy almost gave the impression that he had sired her, but we knew that as impossible. Tom paid all the tabs. They became regulars, and if Betty couldn't make it, we could still expect to see Tom.

I broke down and called Don to tend bar; I needed to be on the floor at times, and available to operate the spotlight during the show.

The crowds were only fair, so at times Don and myself were able to collect the cover. That allowed Juan relief from the boredom. Thursday, Friday, Saturday, and Sunday were show nights.

Greg joined us for a late night breakfast at Dunkin' Dine one evening; I had some apprehensions after agreeing to go since Juan had been quite drunk and devilish that night.

"What can I give you tonight?" our favorite waitress asked.

"A big fat cock!" Juan replied, not batting an eye. Greg and I wanted to crawl under the table, but Juan went on to give his order. In the morning, as usual, he didn't remember, reiterating, "I said thot, Recharred? I don' believe it!" And once I begged him to try to control himself he just stood there in thought, suddenly bursting into laughter. Of course, I joined in!

Since I wasn't one of them, the queens would make me miserable each time I choreographed a number, so I gave in and hired a choreographer, Deva Sanchez, a black, red-hot mama. She was one of them, and had a big following herself. It proved a good move because her fans followed. She was great! Quite often, Juan led the crowd in laughter when she performed one of her party records. Since Deva would be receiving a salary, it was necessary to do the same for the others.

We needed a big night to give us a little cushion, and Juan came up with another gem. "Recharred, why don' we 'ave a Miss Peach State pageant! Thar already is one for Miss Georgia, ond you know how everyone in this town likes the queen contests. Ofter all, this is the peach state. Do you not think thot is a great idea?"

I agreed, and once word got around, we realized it was a brilliant idea! It was the talk of the entire gay community, and we were getting calls from some of the top female impersonators in the city wanting to enter. Juan could not have been more elated.

I wanted to add some comedy to the festivities, finally deciding to do the Andrews Sisters in drag. It was not until Juan and John England were drunk enough one of the off nights that I got them to agree to do it, choosing "Don't Sit Under the Apple Tree" as the number. It was perfect since the three of us had mustaches. Deva made some simple apron type dresses, and for wigs, cheap cotton ones had to suffice. Our own shoes and socks would surely add to the look.

I was faced with the task of choreographing the number while they were intoxicated since that was the only time they would cooperate. Even so, it was a hilarious chore. I was sure that they would be drinking that night, so they may as well learn it that way.

It was no surprise when Tom entered Tammy into the pageant. The only thing surprising was that she had absolutely no talent. He was so excited about entering her that it didn't matter when we reminded him that a talent was required to compete.

"That's okay, Richard, I'll have her work up a number," he insisted. She had never done drag. How was she to perfect her timing in so short a period? We had seen enough of her to know that she moved awkwardly, totally lacking any grace whatsoever. A crash course just wasn't going to do it! Yet, there he was, more excited than a new father, asking one silly question after another. He and Betty were also at rehearsal, with Tom certainly winning out as Mama Rose!

Juan was shocked when I decided to use a song from *Follies* to bring on the contestants, and to lip-synch to the old tenor's voice myself. Don also solved another worry, assuring me that he had two reliable guys to work the bar and the door.

There couldn't be anything more beautiful than the sight of us squeezing through the jam-packed club the night of the pageant! And there was Tom, pestering me with one idiotic question after another until I wanted to climb the walls. Finally, we were ready to begin.

Tammy looked absolutely beautiful, and it was apparent the other queens were very impressed. Juan called my attention to the raised eyebrows of the judges we had selected after her initial appearance. We were completely bewildered because her entrance was about as graceful as a cow. "Aw, my God, Recharred, look ot her," Juan remarked, "Clump, clump, clump!"

Our number was scheduled to open the second half, and there I was scrambling through the crowds like a chicken without a head during intermission, searching for them!

"Reeecchar,' wa are you runnin' aroun' so crazy like?" I suddenly heard, and once I turned, there was Juan with a cocktail in one hand and a cigarette in the other! Smiling along with him was John, and it was a toss-up who was holding who up? It was apparent that neither one could possibly have stage fright since they probably couldn't see beyond the end of their nose. After dressing them and smearing on some lipstick, they almost needed to be lifted up the stage steps.

The spotlight hit, and there we were, all doing something different! Everything I had taught them was completely forgotten. Juan was going one way, John the other. Their lips were useless for any synching, but they did curve into big smiles! One thing they remembered was to shake their finger, doing it throughout the number while I did the choreographed routine! The place went up for grabs; it wouldn't have been funnier if I had planned it that way!

"Recharred! Recharred! Was I not good! Was I not superb!" Juan yelled once we made it down to the dressing room, slobbering a kiss over my entire face, "Did you hear them laugh! Did you hear the applause! Aw, Recharred they were laughing so hard!"

"Yes, I heard, Juan," I sighed, grabbing onto him and hugging tight. "The first time on stage, and you're my star!"

The pageant continued, and three hours later, I was handed the list of winners. After announcing Miss Congeniality and the two runner-ups, I swallowed hard to announce, "The very first to become Miss Peach State of 1977 is...Tammy White!" The audience went crazy, and above all the pandemonium, I could hear Tom's high-pitched screeching! When I came down from the stage, he wouldn't stop hugging me.

We assumed the winner would be someone who had talent as well as grace and beauty. We had to be the only two that felt that way, however. After talking to everyone, even the top queens, they all agreed that there was no doubt. She was a woman, and had to win!

The receipts were the highest ever, even after deducting the prize money. Juan and I talked excitedly about it during breakfast at Dunk'n Dine. He was so happy that he even forgot about talking dirty. "Did I not tell you we would 'ave a good turnout, Recharred! Did I not!"

I smiled and agreed most emphatically. "You know, Recharred," he quickly added in his little boy excitement, "we should copyright the title so we con do it every year!"

I thought a moment, and then winked, saying, "It wouldn't be bad to do it every week!"

Since we had to offer more variety to keep our audience, we hired two more queens. We couldn't afford any of the well-known performers, so we settled for a couple of unknowns with promise. Frank Prescott was a young, very good-looking guy from Chicago using the stage moniker of Cherry Lane, a name we called him all the time. He was a ball of energy, so his numbers all had zip. I never thought his square, masculine face came off very feminine, and it dawned on me that most of the beautiful queens were usually very homely guys out of makeup.

I don't think we ever knew Dana LaMour's real name, and probably because she was living as a woman. We fell in love with her sweet nature, never considering her as a man. Once she had performed her physical rendition of Melba Moore's "Lean on Me," we were sold! The contrast of the sweet beginning and the electrifying climax of the song was sensational! We were certain that her astounding energy in the number was equal to Melba Moore's, and even better.

Though crowds increased, we still had to struggle to keep our heads above water. We just didn't have the track record of Sweet Gum Head or Hollywood Hots, nor the name performers that drew crowds. Hollywood Hots was hosting the *Miss Gay International*, and Juan again had a flash.

"Recharred, Dana is so wonderful ond magnificent doing "Lean on Me," ond she has such grace ond beauty. Why do we not enter her in the pageant? Thot way, if she wins, everyone will come to Chez Cabaret to see her because she will be our star."

Although the entry fee was high, I agreed because the only other expense would be for fabrics. Dana made her own costumes, but managed to pick materials that should have been woven with gold. Our investment had now reached an incredible seven hundred, and she would be competing against the tops in the nation! I don't know who was more thrilled, she or Juan?

There had to be near a thousand packing Hollywood Hots at ten bucks a head!

"Just think, Recharred, if Dana wins we will 'ave all these people swarming to come to Chez Cabaret," Juan exclaimed, sitting nervously across from me. We had had to scrape to even attend, so we were nursing our drinks. It was one of the rare times Juan could not chug 'em down.

The talent segment finally arrived, and Dana looked absolutely exquisite in her lame' gown as she took center stage. In an attempt to settle our nerves, we clasped hands across the table to assure ourselves she was in top form. We smiled; the audience couldn't possibly know what was about to happen. No, she was too sweet, too feminine. Once the moment arrived, Dana was like a bolt of lightning, electrifying the audience as her entire body and facial expressions continued through the emotional and vibrant climax! Our tensions were eased even before she concluded her performance; the audience was too electrified to wait. It was just like the Fourth of July!

It was, by far, the loudest response for any performance, including the ones that followed. We were trembling with joy, and in an attempt to assure me that we were victorious, Juan reached out to pat my shoulder! Dana, at the least, would place as one of the winners! It had to be!

When the winners were announced, we realized that black star had again appeared to haunt us; Dana didn't even place in the top four! The judges must have been bought off. I was certain of it! The title was presented to someone who was very brassy and outgoing in all of the categories. We appeased ourselves by realizing that, even though Dana looked great and lovely in every category, she just wasn't flamboyant enough! After all, this was *Miss Gay International*; the winner had to be outgoing in every category. We had failed to do our homework. Attempting to lighten the mood, Juan finally said, "Well, Recharred, at least Dana got a new wardrobe out of it."

"Some consolation, Juan," I remarked, looking squarely into his eyes.

The fact that Dana's appearance in the pageant didn't bring in some new faces really baffled us, almost believing that, no matter how we tried, we were destined to struggle. Juan continued drinking heavily, and be of little or no help. Since it was beginning to provoke me, I'd be on his back about it, which only caused him to pout. The pouting would eventually turn into nastiness, and he was a master at that. He would always talk logically about it when sober, realizing I had every right to badger him, especially since it was for his own good. However, there was no reasoning with him while he was drunk. I finally realized that he alone had to see the harm he was doing to himself. So I went along with him, in hope that reality would come to him while drinking. But he continued, sometimes even disappearing with the car.

It was Sunday afternoon. Larry and Tom had come to the club, and I was happy because they were not in a drinking mood. Juan would not be influenced to drink. He had apparently been drinking from the liquor room before they arrived, however; he became belligerent, insisting we go somewhere else to dance. I tried reasoning with him, explaining that I was the only one tending bar, but it didn't matter. It only intensified his belligerent manner.

I had been quite busy, when I noticed that Juan was no longer at the table with them. In fact, he was nowhere in sight. I motioned for Larry, asking him to check the office. I became quite nervous when he returned to say that he wasn't there, and like a rocket, I ran to check the parking lot! My car was gone! As I walked dejectedly back behind the bar, I remembered that Juan had had my keys. I had given him mine to drive because he left his in the apartment. I hoped he had gone home because my house keys were on the same ring. I called home several times, but no luck.

I wanted to check out a few places I knew were still open after closing, hoping Larry would realize it himself and take me. I couldn't come right out and ask; he had told me earlier that he had to be up early in the morning. Instead, he offered to drive me home.

Larry asked if I would like to spend the night at his place when we discovered that the car was not at my apartment complex. I couldn't think of getting a key from the apartment manager at this late hour; she had just returned home after major surgery. I really felt that, knowing the predicament, Larry would offer to look for Juan. Instead, he continued to insist that I spend the night at his place. Before I knew it, they were gone and I was alone!

I sat on the floor in front of our door, my concern for Juan becoming more intense with every minute. One terrible thought after another came into my mind, thinking what might have happened to him, and I was going crazy! After about an hour, I heard the phone ringing in our apartment! I was positive it was Juan! He, undoubtedly had not given a thought to the fact that he had my keys. I felt helpless, though relieved in realizing that he had to be okay to be calling. The phone kept ringing, and I was so nervous that I wanted to break down the door! Taking a cab anywhere was out of the question since, in my haste, I never took the bar receipts and I had nothing in my pockets. A premonition came to me after another long series of rings. Juan could be in jail for drunk driving and calling for help! Yet I could do nothing but sit there in anguish.

Six thirty finally rolled around, and I was sure the manager's husband would be up. Once I got into our apartment, I immediately called the Fulton police because the club was in Fulton County, but they had no record of an arrest. Though somewhat relieved, I was still scared, realizing that he may have had an accident.

Oh, God, no! I thought. The fear of confirming my thoughts prevented me from calling hospitals, but I had to find him! We were living in DeKalb

County, so figured I should try their police station. He had to be there, not in any hospital!

"So *that's* the way it's pronounced!" the officer exclaimed after I said Juan's last name, "We've been trying to say his name all night!" I couldn't have heard more beautiful words!

Juan had been picked up on the main drag near the house, driving on the wrong side of the road, the officer informed me when I arrived at the station.

"I think you should know that we gave him a breath test, and that the alcohol level was so high we were amazed he was still alive," the officer added. He assured me that he was fine now after hearing my gasp. The only immediate expense was for impounding the car. Juan would have a hearing in the near future, and any fines to be paid would be due then. I signed the responsibility form, and was then told that an identification had to be made before Juan could be released.

I was led into a room, and in the center of it was a small cubicle about the size of a phone booth. I couldn't imagine it a cell, but yet it was! Bars were across the front of it, and peering anxiously through them was Juan! Never had I seen him look so pathetic, and my heart ached!

"Recharred, you are here ot last!" he cried, "Please, get me out of this terri-ble place!" I was beside myself at the sight of him in something that looked like a cage! I wanted him out!

We were silent on the drive home, and I realized that he was aware of his wrong doings. "Aw, Recharred, I am so sorry, so sorry," he finally cried out, "I tried to call you all night to let you know where I was, but you did not answer the phone. Ond, Recharred, I was so worried because they had put me in a cell with all these guys thot were looking ot me like they were gonna gang rape me! Aw, Recharred, I was so happy when they took me out ond put me in another cell alone!"

"Juan, the officer told me you drank enough to kill a person!" I went on to say after telling him the details of the horrible night. "Why are you drinking that much? Why? If you don't kill yourself with it, you are gonna burn your brains out! Why, for God's sake?"

"I don't know, Recharred, why I do it! I just don't know why! I guess I am so bored when we are ot the bar all the time. I don' know whot to do, so I begin to drink to be happy." In a sudden motion, his head was on my shoulder, something he'd never do in broad daylight. And even more surprising, he started to cry.

"I know, Recharred, thot I cannot be around booze all the time, ond I cannot be around people drinking when I am not! Aw, Recharred, whot am I gonna do?"

I didn't know what to say. I was deeply concerned and yet very angry because this was going to cost a small fortune. Where would we get the money? Suddenly, my compassion overcame the anger building in me, realizing Juan needed my love and support more than a scolding. "We'll get through this, Juan," I assured him, "We'll find the money somehow."

He continued in tears as I silently thanked God that Juan was alive and well.

The attorney fee was five hundred, which was like a million to us, but then Juan wouldn't lose his license. Juan looked so wonderful in his dark blue suit the day of the trial, and after watching his childlike innocence charm the judge, I wondered if we even needed the attorney.

Money was short, and as before, I sent a check for twenty-five dollars to the apartment complex with a note informing them that we'd pay the rent balance after the weekend. The owner happened to be in the office that day and proved to be less understanding than the manager had been.

"No, I cannot accept this amount," she said after I had obliged her request to come to the office. "I cannot wait for the balance! You will have to move today!" We were in a stupor, not wanting to believe this was actually happening to would-be millionaires.

What were we to do? I finally thought of Steve, Juan's admirer, and asked, "Juan, isn't Steve managing an apartment complex? Why don't we call him! I bet he'll wait a few days for the rent!" He not only agreed when we called, but also gave two months to pay the security deposit.

This was the first time we had rented an apartment sight unseen, and since I knew Juan was concerned that it would not be nice, I agreed to stop there before going to the club. Though not as nice as our present apartment, Juan's suggestions with the decorating excited me enough to realize it didn't matter where we lived, as long as we were together. On the way to the club, we rented a truck since we'd be moving that night after closing.

A show wasn't scheduled that evening, and since it was deserted, we closed early. Cherry stopped by just as we were leaving and offered to help. Not only was the help greatly appreciated, working into the wee hours of the morning turned out to be tremendous fun because of the witty remarks flying around. It wasn't until we had moved the last piece in that it dawned on me!

"Juan, she bluffed us! That son of a *B*! We didn't have to move immediately; she had to get a court order!" We were so tired we just plunged onto the couch and laughed.

Deva couldn't stay with us at the salary we were paying, when by chance a well-built black guy from New York happened by. He inquired about work as a drag queen, also mentioning that he was a choreographer. On the merits of his own self praise and a sample of one of his numbers, Belle Starr was hired.

However, Belle did not draw. After all, she was unknown, and her routines were nothing to speak of. The crowds continued to dwindle, and along with Deva's fans that no longer came, the place looked like a bowling alley. If that wasn't upsetting enough, I was also faced with Belle's blatant flirtations with Juan! I finally fired him, giving the excuse that he wasn't drawing.

We needed to get away from the constant reminder of an empty club and closed early one Saturday to go to Hollywood Hots. While waiting in the usual long line to get in, we were suddenly next to Belle, in full drag, on her way out. Her unhappiness about being fired was quite obvious, and after a few of her nasty remarks, I lost control and shouted out the real reason I got rid of her! Fists began flying, and in moments, we were in a wrestling match. Someone, not the bouncer, evidently broke it up since we were not asked to leave. I was embarrassed for creating a scene, and when I asked Juan to leave, he obliged.

When I looked into the mirror the next morning I had a perfect shiner, rounded as though it had been painted on! After a chuckle, Juan exhaled a deep breath and said, "Recharred, you are the perfect, jealous hero," adding, "You should know I would never go with thot guy!"

"I know, Juan, but I was mad because he had the nerve to be so bold about it. It was like I was not even aware!" Continuing to dress, I shouted, "Oh, my God! Juan, my silver cross and chain are gone! It must have been pulled off while Belle and I were fighting!"

"C'mon, Blanche, don' get excited," Juan pleaded in an attempt to calm me as I went on in my frenzy, "It is probably ot Hollywood Hots!" We called but it was never found.

That afternoon, we went to the flea market. We couldn't afford to buy anything, but it was wonderful just watching Juan's excitement. "Would it not be nice, Recharred, if we could buy thot!" It felt like old times when we had nothing to worry about, and it was a joy knowing he was doing what he liked best—to be anywhere with me besides the club. Of course, I wore sunglasses.

Business became so bad that we were forced to close the show and let everyone go. We were forced to run it ourselves again, watching guys come in, look around, and take off quickly. Our only steady was Frank Palmer, who had frequented the show. He'd sit at the lonely bar and chat with us. Frank had owned bars for years, and was currently without one. He was about my age with a laid back personality, and a person who laughed first after telling a joke. He reminded us of the actor, Paul Linde, and surprised us by saying they had been college roommates.

It was obvious he was itching to be involved with a club again, and he confirmed it once he asked if he could tend bar. "I have a big following," he boasted after hearing we couldn't afford a salary. "I'll work for tips just to keep from being bored. You'll find out how much business I can bring in." So we put him on, and it made Juan very happy. His big following, as it turned out, was a grand total of eight guys.

We had sold my piano long ago, and I remembered how I cried when it was picked up once Frank suggested we put in a piano bar. We were game for anything that might be successful, but how could we buy a piano without any money? My credit was not yet tainted, so a lease-buy agreement could work. Spinets were only available on those terms; I immediately began constructing a simulated grand top.

Once again, the black star Juan often talked about appeared above us. Steve was fired as manager of the apartment complex, and in order for him to get a good reference, we had to move because the owners discovered our security deposit had not been paid. Though we offered to pay at that time, they wanted no part of it. He had been doing the same with others as well, and they wanted all of us out. Only two months and we were faced with the expense of another move.

Fortunately, we found a nicer apartment on Northside Circle with a deposit of only one hundred dollars. In fact, it was better than any we had had in Atlanta because of the ultra modern kitchen. A feature we especially liked was the extremely large table-height breakfast counter. There was also a small, separate dining room. A large living room and two large bedrooms with full baths finished off the apartment perfectly.

When we had applied for the piano, we were informed that they were only leased to residences. The timing was perfect because it was delivered to the new apartment the day we moved. We immediately took it to the club with the truck we were renting.

Chapter Twenty-Three:
It Looks Just Like a Little Mickey Mouse

I had always abhorred the mere mention of a rat, and it was not unusual for friends and relatives to come to laughter as I complained profusely if they would mention them before or during dinner. The fact is this squeamishness of mine extends even to mice, pet or otherwise. I never did understand why I became so nauseated. What bothered me, too, was that these ill effects were also prevalent should the thought of one cross my mind; I would then lose my appetite completely. This hatred probably started early in my life while playing in the alleys of Chicago. Invariably, an ill feeling would settle in my throat and stomach each time I'd walk by a squashed rat lying on the alley asphalt. My wishes of not speaking about them were usually respected, but on occasion, someone would look for something to give them a good chuckle and go on about them.

Well, the patio doors of our new apartment were on ground level, and since the building had been built into a hill, our front entrance was at the bottom of twelve steps that led down a concrete retainer wall. The possibility of unwanted visitors had occurred to me when we rented the place, but I put it out of my mind.

It was one of our rare evenings at home, and we were planning to enjoy it to its fullest. A flash of black startled me as I entered the bedroom on my way to the bathroom. I thought it was one of those flashes one sometimes sees through the corner of their eye, but not a reality. I put it out of my mind and continued into the bathroom. Then it happened again as I was leaving. This time, it was a reality! A tiny black mouse was scurrying along the baseboard, and then disappeared!

"Juan, Juan! Come here quickly!" I called out excitedly. "We have a mouse in the house!"

"Where, Recharred? Where is it?" Juan asked anxiously, joining me in the bedroom. He thought I was crazy because the mouse was nowhere in sight. I decided we wait for another appearance. Juan returned to the living room, laughing at my childish behavior, and insisted I forget it and join him there.

"Oh no, Juan, I will not be able to rest knowing there is a mouse in the house! Oh, no, Juan!" He agreed to humor me, so there we were, standing in the hall, peeking into the bedroom. Juan's belly laughs made it difficult to stand still.

Our little visitor finally reappeared, making a quick dash along the baseboard, only this time, it stopped abruptly and stood on its hind end to peer at us. Juan dashed for the kitchen and returned with a broom while I continued yelping! He immediately began batting the broom in futile attempts to hit the mouse!

Meanwhile, I screamed, "Juan, Juan! If you hit him, we are gonna have blood all over the place! And who is gonna pick up a squashed mouse!" Juan continued to swat at the mouse, missing completely because of his hysterical laughter. At one point, the mouse scampered by my feet, and I frantically jumped onto a chair! I must have looked exactly like Lee the day she managed to outrace the dog while fluttering her arms and screaming. There wasn't any doubt about it since Juan was left helpless.

The chase and vigil went on for almost two hours, but I wouldn't give up. I was certain the mouse was enjoying itself, becoming bold, daring almost. It paused to sit in one spot and look directly at us. It appeared as though it was setting itself up as target in a shooting gallery. I begged Juan not to swing at it again. I didn't want the mess, but we had to catch it. I wanted the mouse out, although it didn't look like the ugly gray ones I had the abhorrence for. This little thing had some white in the long black fur.

The mouse began stopping more frequently to look at us, even after Juan's wild swings of the broom, wiggling its nose in the process. I finally came up with a brainstorm. Why not try to spray it with hairspray! It allows us to get so close. I was surprised that it didn't scram when I got the can and aimed. Instead, it fixed its eyes directly on me, appearing to be in that happy manner one sees so often whenever an animal anticipates feeding time. I let out a quick, long jet. The mouse froze in place. I had accomplished my task, but continued to spray just to be certain. So there it stood, the little thing, on its hind end, stiff as a board!

Once we realized it wasn't moving, Juan walked over to it and said, "Aw, Recharred, it is so cute, so cute! Look ot the long, furry hair ond the big ears! It looks just like a little Mickey Mouse. Aw, Recharred, I feel so bad." I must say that I felt even worse.

That had to be the first and only time I had ever thought a mouse to be cute. The episode didn't change my feelings about other rodents. And through the years, thoughts of that little mouse have flashed into my mind, along with a little guilt.

Chapter Twenty-Four:
Could This Be Our Angel?

Although Frank's followers were heavy drinkers, it wasn't enough to survive. The piano bar needed to get going and we didn't have a pianist. So, when I heard that Joe DeWall was available, I decided to see if he'd be willing to return to the club. He happily agreed, never mentioning any ill feelings he may have had. Opening was set for the coming Friday.

Frank mentioned that a newcomer to the club had inquired about the dining room, stating that he was interested in sub-leasing it at half the rent of the entire building. We were sure he was kidding, and it wasn't until he insisted that it wasn't a joke that we listened to more. It sounded too fantastic to be true once we heard that he was willing to pay six months in advance and the balance for the year right after opening. Could he be the angel we were looking for? We wanted desperately to believe it! However, it wasn't likely; luck never seemed to be on our side.

Frank pointed him out later that evening. He had been the new guy always buying drinks for the house! Maybe he was a rich eccentric with nothing better to do but spend money, and that could take care of our black star!

Frank introduced us to Blue Bennet, and though he appeared to be bright, he didn't seem to know the first thing about running a restaurant. He was a bit on the stocky side and fairly bald. The meeting turned out to be the answer to our prayers. He had no personality but we hit it off with him, and we did it by being totally truthful about the sad financial state we were in. He was told that he'd be getting us out of a hole, and seemed pleased to help. And he was determined to open the same evening as the piano bar. We would have the first check in the morning. The other half of the year's rent would be paid in two weeks. We were overjoyed!

That evening, we noticed Blue buying drinks for one guy after another. "It looks like he has to buy his tricks," Juan remarked. "Not only does he not have a personality, he's so homely!"

Only about twenty-five showed up for the opening, though all heavy drinkers who liked piano bars. To our surprise, only twelve were having dinner, and Juan had heard that they were Blue's guests. Since he also popped for all of their drinks, the evening was a total loss for him. I finally assumed he meant it as a promotion.

So we were off to another phase of the club. New faces, as well as Tom, Betty, and John began frequenting the bar on Fridays and Saturdays. Tom and Larry came a few times and then suddenly disappeared off the face of the earth…. I even had occasion to sing, and felt good when someone insisted on it. However, the rest of the week continued to be slow.

Frank's friends seemed to be the only ones coming to the bar during the week nights, and we were pleased to be included in a Sunday afternoon picnic held in one of their backyards. We were a total of ten, and the outing proved to be one we needed badly. Juan didn't like to drink during the day, and even though he didn't indulge, he was still full of wit the entire time.

"My good woman," he'd say, mimicking someone's particularly feminine actions, and they'd laugh hilariously. Just watching Juan play badminton for the first time was a hoot in itself; his hilariously awkward misses of the birdie on the very windy day were priceless.

There was no one as appreciative as Juan, especially when he felt people were being sincere.

"I am so glad we were invited today, Recharred," he said while driving to open the club, "It is so nice to 'ave them as friends! Thank you so much for taking the time from the club, Recharred"

We had to come up with promotions to improve business during the week, and Frank suggested we have auctions, volunteering to be auctioneer. In desperation, Juan brought in some of his personal things. After getting practically nothing for his rocker, he brought in the two pen and inks he had purchased at my shop. It didn't matter when I reminded him of the sentimental value as well as the investment potential, he still insisted.

"I love them, ond they mean so much to me, but I need to get some money because I 'ave been behind in my child support."

They went for a song as well! We inherited some pictures and an antique side table that didn't sell because the owners never came to pick them up.

Juan had brought home some extra crispy fried chicken. I thought I had bitten on a rock while biting into a piece, and scolded him for buying it since he knew my front teeth were capped. I continued to torment him about it because I was sure that I had cracked one of them. I was concerned since I was to do the auctioning that night. Frank had come down with laryngitis.

Something dropped from my mouth the instant I called out the first item! *Oh, my God!* I thought, *it's my cap!* I thought of those inbred idiots in *Deliverance* as I crawled and searched the floor, and all while Juan split a gut.

I found two pieces, and wasn't exactly happy; it meant the cap had broken. The only way I could keep them secure on the spike was to hold my forefinger against my upper lip. This, of course, caused quite a lisp when I resumed with the auction, and left Juan gagging in laughter. He replayed everything I did once I left the stage.

Blue's lack of experience only proved to work against him; he ignored any suggestions we offered to improve business. Two customers each night would not be enough to grow on, especially when Juan and I were usually those two. What baffled us was that he didn't seem to mind. However, it bothered us; we had expected his customers to end up in the club. However, he'd cash a large check every night, and sometimes two, then buy drinks for everybody all night.

We were busy handling one crisis after another, and they seemed to be gaining on us. Auction night was the only week night with some traffic, and weekend business was not increasing as we had hoped. The dining room was a desert island during the week. Juan was bothered that Frank's friends only came to the club on the evenings he worked; he thought that they had become our friends, too. He called my attention to their indifference each time Frank was tending bar.

"Look ot them, Recharred," he said. "They almost look like vultures, waiting for us to die!" And it was true. It was a known fact that Frank was itching to own a bar again.

Juan and I were usually alone in the bar whenever I worked the off nights, until Gary began joining us. He lived next door to the club, and had worked the door several times during the drag period, never wanting to be paid for his time. He was short and good-looking. I had found him to be sensually attractive as well. The three of us would get drunk and raise hell in the place, and Gary would always tease me. I knew that he sensed my attraction, and assuming he wanted me, my ego got a big boost. I had felt that Juan sensed it, too, but he never said anything. Why was I longing for Gary? Could it be because Juan had been so nasty to me every time he drank heavily? Gary didn't mind my groping him, and I'd do it every time Juan was in the DJ booth. However, it never went any further, and he stopped coming in.

Three guys in their early thirties began to frequent the club, and it was apparent they had money to burn. Ron and Terry were the slim, live wires of the three. Chuck was on the stocky side, and somewhat reserved. Ron was Albino. Though never discussed, it seemed that Ron and Chuck had something going.

"You know, Recharred, this bar is not one thot guys like to come to because it is not conducive for cruising," Juan surmised, trying to reason why so many guys always walked out after just arriving at the bar. "Look, we 'ave only tables ond chairs, ond a small bar thot only seats about eight people."

The discussion led me to build a narrow shelf along one wall, which was known as a *meatrack* in the gay world. I also built a free standing counter just at the rise. Bar stools would be the only other expense since guys usually liked to sit on them and lean against the ledge to show off their baskets. We hoped word would get around. Though not a landslide, we noticed new faces and other parts making use of our small improvements.

Juan signed on with a temporary agency, and though the pay wasn't much, it was some help. We also attempted to apply for unemployment assistance against our Illinois wages, but gave up after realizing it was a waste of time. No one in the office knew how to handle it.

"Dad, you won't have to worry about entertaining Jeannie and me all the time," Jacque said when she called to say she was coming down with a girlfriend for a two-week vacation. "All we want to do is swim and sun at the pool."

Jacque was now seventeen, and on their arrival, we discovered that she had become a very beautiful woman. As she had specified, most of their time was spent at the pool. Jeannie was quite an outgoing and forward person, and Juan never hesitated in calling down her sarcasm. Of course Jacque mentioned meeting a very handsome guy at the pool, which caused me some concern.

"And he is an actor too, Dad," she said. It wasn't until later that I realized Clayton was doing the lead in a play about gay activities in prison running at the Sweet Gum Head, and that he was totally naked while on stage. I had assumed it was nothing more than fun at the pool once I had given my fatherly advice, only to hear from Juan after they had left for home.

"Yes, Recharred, Jeannie told me thot he took Jacque thar to see it Saturday while we were ot work, ond thot they then watched the drag show ofterwards. "Well, Recharred, she has to learn about the dirty world sometime," he added quickly after seeing my obvious despair.

"Yeah, Juan, but not that way, and not that fast!"————————

"Is this Mr. Mella?" the person asked when I picked up the phone after arriving at the club in the morning. "This is the NBG Bank, Mr. Mella, and we would like to know why you haven't responded to any of our calls, or the overdraft notices mailed to you?"

Completely bewildered, I explained that I hadn't received any messages or notices.

"Well, Mr. Mella, I don't understand why you haven't received *any* of them," she remarked, obviously assuming I was lying. "The fact is your account is in serious trouble! You have almost four thousand dollars in non-collectible checks that we have been sending notices on!"

I was stunned! There had to be a mistake! She went through the list of bad checks, and once I questioned the validity of the accusations, she agreed to my request to call her back.

"But, Mr.' Mella, be certain that you are no longer than half an hour because this matter needs to be resolved immediately!"

"Recharred, whot is the matter?" Juan asked. "You are as white as a ghost! Whot has 'appened?"

As I explained everything, we realized that Blue was involved. A three-thousand-dollar check was mentioned, and he had just given us one in that amount for the final payment. By chance, my eyes happened to glance down into the waste paper basket and I saw an envelope from the bank. A thorough check proved he had everything to do with the mess; one bad check notice after another was in the basket, and all on his checks! The reason they refused payment on the three-thousand dollar business check…it had an invalid signature.

"For Chris' sake, Recharred, I don' believe it!" Juan said in complete consternation. "He has been opening our mail! Ond he has thrown them in the wastebasket ofter seeing they were notices on his bad checks! No wonder he has been here every morning when we came in! We evidently were too early for him this morning."

We were near hysteria! We had paid for the weekend liquor deliveries with checks and now were subject to arrest! We actually had believed we were building up a reserve, and suddenly, there wasn't a cent to pay the issued checks! Any consolation we tried to give one another didn't help; we were devastated! Completely confusing was the fact that I remembered the first three-thousand-dollar check Blue gave us. I also had remarked about the sloppy signature on it. Juan quickly commented, "Evidently, the first one slipped by someone."

Blue suddenly walked in as we were about to leave for the bank.

"Blue, how could you do a thing like this to us?" I demanded, holding the notices to his face and not giving him a chance to question why we looked so upset. "Do you realize what you have done? We can go to jail! Is that what you want? How could you be so low! I thought we had such a good relationship!" My tears wouldn't allow me to say more.

"Blue, Recharred has treated you so good, ond never once lied to you," Juan interjected once I choked up with tears. "You knew how we appreciated your offer to pay us a year in advance! Recharred never lied about the fact that you were getting us out of a big mess by giving us all thot advance rent! Aw, Blue, Recharred is such a fair person to everyone, so how could you do something like this to him, ond to me? We thought you were our friend!"

Juan finally choked up, too, and we stood in a pathetic state, our faces pleading for some kind of explanation. Though obviously nervous, Blue remained silent. Blue had set his key ring down on the desk, and the thought of taking them before he noticed suddenly occurred to me. I certainly didn't want him to take off while we were at the bank.

He finally came out of his silence, apologizing for his actions and swearing to make good on the checks. He promised to wait for us to discuss everything when I said we had to get to the bank before they pressed charges. He wasn't aware his car keys were gone. So I guess I felt safe.

The bank officers finally agreed to give us twenty-four hours before prosecuting once we convinced them that Blue had promised to make good on all of the checks. Frank was at the club when we returned and quickly told us that the police had been there to arrest Blue; a restaurant purveyor had issued a warrant because of bad checks. Our hopes for resolving the mess suddenly went up in smoke, and we were again devastated! Frank agreed that if the bank didn't have us arrested, the liquor companies surely would! And it seemed his only concern was that his reputation would be ruined because he had recommended Blue.

Juan could only come up with a hundred from his parents, and Mike and my sister Deena would ask too many questions should I ask them. But we realized the money had to come from family if we wanted to stay out of jail. Geena finally came to mind; she certainly wouldn't need details. And that's exactly what happened. Somehow, she'd get the money to wire me after hearing that I could possibly be arrested for issuing checks that were bad. She never asked another question; her only concern was that I was in trouble. The money arrived that very day.

Why we didn't press charges against Blue, I'll never know. Possibly, because he was arrested already. We also figured we had the keys to his apartment and the minivan, and could demand payment for the bad checks once he was released. We decided to check out his apartment to see if anything could be taken and used as collateral until payment was received. We found we easily could have taken Juan's stuffed rocker and the pen and inks that Blue had purchased at the auctions, but we couldn't bring ourselves to do it.

"You know, Recharred, if I take any of his things, I will feel like a thief," Juan said. "I cannot do it. I just cannot." I felt the same, actually feeling as though we had broken into his apartment. So everything was left intact.

We soon learned another lesson. We never thought to move Blue's van somewhere else; it was gone from the club parking lot when we arrived the following morning. We sped to his apartment, hoping to catch him there. One look through his ground floor living room window, however, and it was apparent he was also proficient at night moving! The place was empty.

Blue had bailed himself out with another bad check, so we were told by Frank. We were sure he was pulling our legs, but who knew? Nevertheless, we never saw or heard of Blue again.

Chapter Twenty-Five:
Can Nastiness Trigger One's Ego?

Juan continued drinking heavily, and when he had too much, he'd be nasty to me again. However, he'd remember nothing of it the next day. Tom would call him down each time he was nasty to me. So, since Juan detested being called down, he'd invariably retaliate by saying, "I am sorry, but I am *JUAN*, ond I con say ond do whot I want!"

And believe me, he did. Though I must admit he was funny. His head would cock back in a daring and belligerent manner. He'd glare at us, puffing slowly on a cigarette, and just before saying the brash statement, he'd swallow down half his drink! It was always impossible to stay angry, because he'd then place his hand on his hip and swagger while continuing his ridiculous glare. So, though his behavior had been unbearable, I still accepted it. I had grown accustomed to the fact that it was only a small part of Juan.

Dee surprised us with a call to say that she and Dino were coming down again, and that Geena would be with them. Someone Geena was dating was driving them down.

I found Frank quite likable when they arrived, and it was obvious he liked me, too. Juan couldn't be happier, and it was great seeing how well he and Frank hit it off, too. We were forced to be away from the club much of the time, so Juan didn't need to drink. And since they insisted we eat dinners at home, we didn't have to worry about money. Geena and Dee bought the groceries.

Our struggle with the club had taken many precious things from us, and with their visit, another was about to go. Frank had been admiring the black entertainment center, and when Juan finally asked if he'd like to buy it, my heart ached. He loved that center, and though I strongly urged him not to sell it, he calmly insisted, "Recharred, I need to pay my child support."

A very steep road led up into our apartment complex, and there we were at the midpoint when the Gremlin wouldn't move! That Black Star struck again once it was towed in and diagnosed. The transmission was completely shot! Obviously aware of our financial state, Geena and Dee came up with the money to install a new one.

Amazingly, Frank managed to stuff all the disassembled parts of the center into the luggage-filled trunk. It was four in the morning, and after all the hugs and kisses, they were gone. Geena never had asked why I needed the money she wired me. It had been so nice feeling normal again, and I realized the void Juan felt merely by watching him walk slowly back into the apartment.

Though week nights remained as slow as ever, there was an increase in business on Friday and Saturdays. Nonetheless, we were aware that in order to survive, a balanced growth was needed. To make matters worse, Frank and his cohorts were still looking like a pack of vultures waiting to pick at our bones.

I also had Svetmana to cope with. Dan no longer was available to babysit. He had disassociated himself because we were unable to make payments on the balance owed. So Juan had to stay with her while I went to the club. And with each visit, she became nastier to me, usually causing an argument between Juan and myself once I called it to his attention.

Juan was at home with Svetmana and I was tending bar. An argument because of her had caused me to leave the house angry. I mistakenly thought a few drinks would help me forget how unreasonable he had been. I drank one after another, and towards the end of the evening, the attention given to me by a young newcomer began swelling my ego. He wasn't much to look at, but I was flattered to be cruised by someone twenty years my junior. So I accepted his drink offers.

The club emptied out earlier than usual, and once I called it a night, he was the only one remaining. It wasn't long before we ended up on the carpet of the dining room, kissing passionately. I finally came to my senses, realizing what I was doing, and pulled away from him. However, I was quite drunk and my attempts to rise were futile, especially when his face lunged into my crotch and moved passionately. He had placed an opened bottle of poppers to my nose also and one sniff destroyed any defense I might have had. I was suddenly in a valley of clouds, floating in ecstasy. He had lowered my trousers and his lips and tongue were caressing every part of my groin. I sniffed in deeply as he continued to place the bottle beneath my nostrils, and the ecstasy became even greater once I felt his lips slide over the head and shaft of my erection.

I experienced an extraordinary sensation when he lunged into a deep throat position; it actually felt as though he was about to swallow it! He continued at a slow pace, his lips and mouth sliding over the head and shaft with just the right amount of pressure! I was flying high until I suddenly felt a terrible and continuous pain! He was suddenly wild, his lips slobbering at a furious pace, and I felt I was being eaten alive! I was sure he had spikes for teeth, or had placed a jigsaw in his mouth! I was certain of it because I was in excruciating pain! I was loaded and flying high from poppers, but the realization of what was happening, and the pain, finally managed to give me enough strength to kick him off!

After getting rid of him I was still hurting, and when I checked it actually looked as though someone had been chewing on one side! I was still spinning from the alcohol and the sniffing, not really comprehending the seriousness of it all. It was fortunate I closed early; there was time to get my bearings before going home.

I was in shock once I reached a reasonable degree of sobriety! What had I done again? I had absolutely no desire for the guy, yet I allowed it to happen! How was I going to explain to Juan how the severe scratches got on my dick?

Though I never was proud of my creative lie, I still used it. Only one side was scratched and very well could have been caught in my pants zipper. Juan never questioned my blatant lie, expressing deep compassion instead, though he chuckled. I had to smile and live with my guilt.

"You know, Recharred, I should really go to Chicago for the funeral," Juan said after receiving a call from Endira informing him that her father had died. "He was such a good man, ond because he always treated me so wonderful. His body is being flown in some time tomorrow ofternoon. Besides, I liked him very much."

We couldn't afford it, but I agreed. Juan left the following afternoon to return in two days.

I missed Juan and drank while tending bar in hopes that it would lighten my spirits. Ron came in without Chuck, and began buying me drinks after hearing Juan was gone. Of course, I got quite high, and there was Ron following my car home. I never had even fantasized this to happen, though I had a slight attraction to him. So there I was, bending to low morals, allowing my ego to be inflated again because someone twenty years younger was seducing me!

A strange feeling came over me when we entered the apartment; I loved Juan with all my heart, and yet I was with someone else in our home, about to go to bed! I made a weak stab at consolation by leading him to the guest bedroom instead of ours. Yet we continued kissing passionately, feverishly tugging at each other's clothes and tossing them to the floor. When we broke to take off the last piece of clothing, I suddenly wanted to call it off! Ron was before me, his soft, milky white flesh, and I had no desire to touch it! I felt repulsed at the thought that I was betraying Juan for a man with the flesh and body of a woman! All I wanted was for him to leave!

"I'm sorry, Ron, but I can't do this," I stammered, "I love Juan too much to betray him. I've done it before and I don't want it to happen again because I still haven't forgiven myself!"

He seemed to understand, but it was apparent he was disturbed. I was sure he'd begin to dress. Instead, he merely fell across the bed in an obvious attempt to tempt me.

"Why can't I just give you a blow job, Richard?" he pleaded, "That's not like you're doing anything." I still refused, though the thought of losing his business quickly entered my mind, as well as the possibility that the story would be all over the bar.

"Besides, I have wanted your luscious cock in my mouth for so long," he whispered. My reluctance gave way to a surge of sexual excitement, and I quickly climbed aboard. I straddled his head, and laid my throbbing erection across his hungry mouth. Almost immediately, his anxious lips grasped onto it, sliding over the head and shaft with a warm moisture that had me panting. I thrust in slowly, penetrating deeply! The sensation of his uvula rubbing against it...sensational! I continued the same slow manner until I exploded! And there was Ron, ravishingly attempting to drain it! He barely had nurtured out the last of it when a sudden feeling of disgust came over me, and I quickly pulled from his mouth. It was obvious he was disappointed I didn't allow him to savor it for some time, but he finally accepted my wishes and left.

I sat there in my guilt, not realizing that whenever I consumed alcohol while in a state of depression or loneliness, it only tended to arouse my sexual urges or anger. I obviously was attempting to compensate for the sexual consideration I never was given throughout the many years of marriage.

I showered for a long time. I needed to wash Ron from my body, wanting to wash my sins away, too. All I then wanted was for Juan to return home.

Chapter Twenty-Six:
A Shattered Dream...
Our Desert Island Gone

A camera would have preserved so many priceless moments, but we never thought to have one on hand. In hopes of drawing two big crowds, we held Halloween parties on Friday and Saturday. Surprisingly, Juan agreed to makeup in drag on Friday night! A young fellow who had started frequenting the club managed to talk him into it. Bill had done drag at one time.

Juan was sober once Bill began applying the makeup, not to say that he didn't drink afterwards. I believe the challenge intrigued him. It was something different, and he really was getting a kick out of being transformed into a raving beauty, as he so claimed. The mustache wasn't coming off, however. Gold stardust was applied instead, and it looked quite attractive. Juan continued to be captivated during the entire process, and I was amazed that he hadn't even finished one drink. I had felt certain he'd be drunker than a skunk once the transformation had gotten that far. In fact, his serious expressions with each application had me laughing hilariously.

Juan was such a handsome man, and I assumed he merely wanted to see if he'd turn out as beautiful as the homely guys we knew who made up in drag. I thought I'd burst from laughter watching him sit erect while puffing out his lips to make it easier for Bill to apply lipstick evenly.

"Recharred, how do I look?" he asked, admiring himself in the mirror once the transformation was complete, "I am bea-u-ti-ful, am I not?"

He turned his face and body in all directions, standing very erect while pushing out his padded bosom, an absolute delight to watch! Even more hilarious was when he over-exaggerated the feminine walk he always amused me with while mimicking someone!

"I am so bea-u-ti-ful, so bea-u-ti-ful, Recharred!" he raved, answering his own question. However, he was so funny...an absolute joy!

Ironically, Juan was already handsome. Sharp lines on his cheekbones and jaws left no doubt that this was a man even after all the makeup! I couldn't spoil his illusion, however. I had to rave on about the transformation, especially since his lady-like strutting was so hilarious! There he was, turning every which way, sharply, as though he was modeling!

"Recharred, maybe I should do this for a profession because I am so bea-u-ti-ful, so bea-u-ti-ful," he boasted in his elegant voice repeatedly! The hilarious climax arrived when he slipped into the high heel shoes!

Juan realized that drag wasn't for him, just as I had. He just needed to prove to me that he could do it without being drunk. Then to prove that it wasn't a fluke, he did it again on Saturday. He even shaved off his mustache! The mustache was allowed to grow back afterwards.

Frank finally found an angel to back him and offered a meager three thousand dollars to take over the club. Our only alternative was to accept it. I was about to leave for five weeks in Dallas, Texas to do the role of Paravicini in Agatha Christie's *Mousetrap*, starring Noel Harrison, and Juan didn't want to assume responsibility. To give him some peace of mind from the constant worry of bill collectors, I decided he should have the entire amount of the sale. I'd be earning a decent salary that would pay our rent and other expenses.

RJ's was gone, and now Chez Cabaret was about to do the same to completely shatter our dream! One year and eight months of excitement and fun, almost outweighed with worry, sadly, was coming to an end. No more bizarre people and happenings! No longer would con artists eat us up! We realized, at last, that this wasn't a business for people with soft hearts. The era was over, and we had to get our lives going in another direction!

"Aw, Recharred, I am gonna be so lonely without you here," Juan moaned, quite unhappy that I was about to leave him. "Whot am I to do?"

Though I felt as badly, I still realized we needed money, and that I had no recourse since Atlanta didn't have an abundance of jobs to offer. Juan refused to face it until I heard I'd be housed in an apartment in Dallas.

"So, if you don't get a job, you can come there and be with me. It'll be like a vacation."

He still hurt, and even the reminder that we'd talk daily on the phone didn't help. My heart was aching. I didn't want to leave him feeling that way, but what else could I do when we needed money badly? It never occurred to me that I'd be kept busy with the excitement of opening in a play and making new acquaintances, while Juan would be left home alone. Not until years later.

Our parting was not a pleasant one, and yet I never gave a thought to the fact that my depression disappeared once I began discussing roles with Mary Ellen, a co-actor seated next to me on the plane. Any thoughts of the loneliness Juan was experiencing quickly disappeared, too.

I found a pay phone near the apartment I was assigned, and quickly called Juan. Both of us cried immediately. He didn't want to hear me talk excitedly about meeting Mary Ellen and the others, however. He was miserable and lonely, and resented that I may be enjoying myself.

"Juan, I'll call you collect," I said quickly to change the subject, "and you should refuse the call, and then call me right back. We'll save quite a bit that way."

"Recharred, I love you very much, ond I miss you ter-ri-bly already!"

"Juan, I love you very much too," I tenderly reminded him. "Please take care of yourself, and please don't drink too much!"

After assuring me of it, he added, "How con I drink when I don't 'ave any money?"

Juan found a job by the time we talked the next evening.

It was impossible not to feel comfortable rehearsing with Noel. He was so pleasant. There was one bad seed in the cast however. Joe DiVito, playing Christopher Wren, seemed to think he was the world's greatest actor, and obnoxiously dominated every conversation. He had to be a flaming queen; I had seen enough of them in Atlanta. He was interpreting Wren as gay, and I couldn't tell the difference when he was off stage. Though he was married. Of course, that really didn't matter, looking back at Atlanta.

I was informed of a call during rehearsal, and concerned before taking it in the office.

"Recharred, I went to the club last night to see how Frank is doing now thot it is his bar," Juan's voice shouted, "Ond do you know I saw Ron ond Chuck. You know whot they told me?"

I remained silent; I knew exactly what undoubtedly had been said, but prayed I was wrong!

"Recharred, Chuck told me thot Ron told him about the night he came to our house to trick with you," Juan lashed out, his voice trembling. "Chuck was angry, but do you know thot Ron was boasting! Boasting, Recharred! How could you do something like thot to me! I was in Chicago for my father-in-law's funeral, ond you are in our home tricking with thot albino! Aw, Recharred, how could you be so low? You 'ave hurt me so much!"

Concerned about the secretary hearing him go on in his rage, I held the receiver tightly against my ear. "Juan, it's not what they probably told you," was all I felt comfortable saying. Finally, the secretary stepped away, and in that moment, I whispered, "Juan, I cannot go into it now. The secretary is right next to me. I'll call right after rehearsal and explain everything."

I was miserable when I returned to rehearsal. I was certain Juan was going through hell! *Oh, God*, I prayed, *please, don't let him drink himself blind!*

Our conversation went surprisingly well that evening. I admitted to being wrong for allowing Ron to blow me, but he seemed to understand when I explained the fear I had if Ron had left angry. A fact that gave Juan no recourse but to accept the explanation…Ron had talked about my drunkenness continuously. I somehow felt he'd get even with me.

"Richard, you should really get in touch with a close friend of mine in Dallas," one of our customers had said on my last day at the club, "I'm sure he'd be glad to show you the town. I haven't seen him for some time, but Vince was one of those extremely handsome Italian guys."

When I explained that I had no interest in tying up with someone, he chuckled and quickly said, "On no, Richard, I don't mean for that, just to give you a tour of the bars. Vince had always been a chubby chaser! I mean, enormous men! Do you know he'd even have the passenger seat of his car steel reinforced to accommodate those elephants!"

"I assume that you are a very large man," was Vince's response when I called and said that Brad had told me to call. Upon hearing the contrary, he asked if I was free Saturday night for dinner. His lover was a great cook, and they'd take me on a tour of the bars afterwards.

"Hi, I'm Vince," was called out from the window of a vintage, black, luxury sedan at the designated place I was to be picked up, "Are you Richard?"

After all the greetings, I seated myself in the backseat, and we were on our way. The remark Brad had said about Vince's looks quickly came to mind, and it was apparent his Adonis days had long ago seen their heyday! Since Charles wasn't able to turn in his seat to look at me while talking, I leaned forward. Brad was right! Seated before me was what looked like an enormous blimp! Gelatin, clay or whatever, he seemed to be melting into the seat! I actually thought we'd have to call out the militia to get him out of the car when we arrived at their place!

Steak was the entrée, and Charles had seasoned it superbly. After all, he didn't get his size by eating bland food. Never one lost for words, I kept the conversation going, and the evening became quite enjoyable. They seemed to have forgotten about taking me out to the bars, however, and it suddenly occurred to me that Charles might have other ideas on how to spend the rest of the evening, especially since he had been patting my hands at every opportunity. After all, he wasn't a chubby chaser, and I certainly didn't want to leave looking like a pancake!

"Well, this has been wonderful," I blurted out, "but I'd really love to see some of the bars." Charles's horny intentions were quite obvious when he took some time to agree, and especially since a disappointed expression remained on his face while pondering the request.

My ego began working overtime once we arrived at the second bar; a young guy was cruising me, and it really went into high gear when he sent over a drink and motioned to join him. I quickly told Vince and Charles that I wanted to thank him, and marched over. It wasn't long before my will power collapsed.

"Vince and Charles, I really want to thank you for a wonderful dinner and evening," I said, returning to them. "This guy said he'll take me back to my apartment, so you won't have to worry about driving all that distance." Vince, surprisingly, let out a loud huff, while Charles struggled in his effort to turn from me in disgust. Obviously, they still had intentions of a threesome.

I received a rude awakening once we arrived at my apartment, and I'm sure Juan would've said I got what I deserved, while scolding, "You "ave to pay for your sins, Recharred!"

Always requiring pre-play, I needed passionate kissing before sex. Anyone coming onto me in an abrupt or furious manner would leave me completely disillusioned to go any further. This guy suddenly became a wild man! He actually went into an Indian war dance on the bed, holding onto his genitals and waving them like a lunatic! Worse yet, he expected me to do the same! Fortunately, the drive had sobered me, and I managed to throw him out!

"Recharred, I 'ave ter-ri-ble news for you," was the first thing said by Juan on one of our calls, "I was in on accident on thot steep, curved hill near our house while I was goin' to work!"

I immediately asked if he was okay, to hear he had just been banged up a bit.

"I am afraid to tell you, Recharred," he went on to say, "thot the car has been totaled! It was raining so hard, ond the wheels skidded ond I went off the road into a very big tree!"

"Oh, my God, Juan!" I shouted, "You could have been killed! Are you sure you are okay?"

After reassuring me he was fine except for some scratches on his face, he continued, "You know how ter-ri-ble the transits are here in Atlanta. Thot you 'ave to go all the way downtown to catch a bus thot comes bock this way to go west. Aw, Recharred, it took me so long to go to work this morning ond to come home!"

I didn't know what to say. I just knew he needed to work, if only to keep his mind occupied. It was so ironic; I just had sent in the last payment for the car.

"Aw, Recharred, I miss you so much ond want to come thar to be with you," he sighed.

"Come then, Juan!" I said, after hearing him sound so desperate. "Tell them you have an emergency and have to go out of town. They'll understand."

I received a letter from Juan two days later, informing me of the bus arrival. A vending machine snapshot of himself was enclosed in order to see the bruises on his face from the accident. I, fortunately, couldn't make out any. The letter turned out to be one of the most beautiful love letters I ever had read. Juan wasn't one for schmaltzy words, and yet he somehow had captured the feelings in his heart so tenderly. Tears filled my eyes as I read it. Unfortunately, because I was such a closet case, I threw away the letter for fear someone in my family might happen to see it should I die. The picture is gone, too. I've always been a pack rat, and why I allowed my doubts about my family accepting my love for Juan after I die, I'll never know. There was this man, touching my heart deeply again.

Anna was prop girl for the company. She had a youthful, natural beauty. Everyone called her a tomboy, but I knew better since she had implied that wearing makeup was too feminine for her. The husky voice coming from her short and full-bodied figure also assured me that she was a lesbian. Her assistant, Ginny, was the opposite, using her feminine attributes to the fullest. Her long dark hair always was carefully groomed. Anna, on the other hand, had blond hair, cropped to the head so she easily could manage it with a swift sweep of her hand. They were inseparable!

Once I mentioned that Juan was arriving to stay with me, they finally admitted to being lovers, realizing I'd then admit to the same. Our honesty led to a close friendship, and I spent much of my free time with them. And since I ridiculed her actions each time she sat at the coffee table to sort out her marijuana, I was given the nickname of *Daddy*. I never had seen anyone as attentive to their partner as Anna was to Ginny. She was the man taking care of her fragile wife.

Anna offered to drive me to the station to pick up Juan, and when he stepped from the bus, I couldn't believe the weight he lost in just three weeks. Though there was that expression of happiness, that look of a little boy finally reunited stood out! When I inquired about his weight loss, he said that he never felt much like eating because he was so lonely. I wanted to hug the hell out of him, but settled for a vigorous handshake instead.

Juan's charm and wit quickly captivated Anna, and I knew it was the start of a great friendship. His broad smile assured me he was thrilled when I remarked, "Juan, I'll be free during the day, and we can do whatever we want! Things we weren't able to do in Atlanta! And you can come to the theater every night because I'm certain I'll be able to have you seated somewhere! Oh, Juan, it's gonna be so wonderful!"

He was so happy he even admitted that he quit his job. I realized the job loss didn't matter to me either. What mattered was we were together.

We spent our days sightseeing, and as always, Juan's awe was a joy in itself. Anna took us for drives, too. She and Ginny always seemed to look forward to hear Juan's clever remarks, egging him on at times. And once they heard him call me *Blanche*, they really broke up. They were Juan's kind of people because they didn't put on airs, and because they appreciated his frankness.

One of a top television comedy duo came to see Noel perform before his show was to begin at another theater. Juan came backstage after the show, too, and as we were about to leave, Noel introduced him to us. He was cordial as we shook hands, but once he took hold of Juan's hand, he wouldn't let go. His eyes were actually devouring him! Noel and I were wide-eyed, not knowing what to do or say since it seemed like an eternity. I realized Juan had to be mortified because he embarrassed so easily. There he was, holding onto Juan's hand tightly, staring into his eyes! He finally let go after what seemed to be forever, and we raced out.

"Did you see thot, Recharred?" Juan questioned, grabbing onto to me quickly, "Did you see how he would not let go of my hand, ond how he was looking ot me?"

"I saw Juan, and so did Noel! I'm certain Noel was wondering what the hell was going on!"

"I cannot believe it," Juan exclaimed. "How could he be so bold? Aw, Recharred, I was so embarrassed in front of Noel like thot!"

"Don't worry, they're used to it in Hollywood! And you say you're not handsome!"

Anna informed me of a 1972 Toyota for sale. "You should take a look at it because it is really clean," she urged in her macho manner. I already had the check for the totaled Gremlin and bought it on the spot. The theatre in Atlanta had extended the current play a week, which meant Juan and I could take our time driving back. The airfare compensation would far exceed expenses.

Anna and Ginny were hard to leave, and to brighten my spirits during the drive, Juan said, "You know, Recharred, you 'ave a week before you open in Atlanta. We are gonna be so close to New Orleans; would it not be nice if we stopped thar for a couple of days?" No more had to be said. The stop could make up for so much we didn't do in Atlanta.

I had fallen asleep while Juan was at the wheel, and out of it when I woke up. I thought we had passed the New Orleans exit and quickly yelled at him. I wouldn't let up!

"For Chris' sake, Recharred, why do you 'ave to talk to me like thot?" he snapped back in an effort to defend himself, and when an exit sign to New Orleans suddenly appeared on the road, he shouted, "See, I did not pass it up!" His anger, as usual, quickly vanished, and his charm surfaced as he excitedly talked about being in New Orleans.

The three days and two nights live vividly in my mind, still hearing Juan's excitement at everything we ventured to see. He never liked waiting for anything, yet graciously agreed to wait in a two-block line because he was so anxious to see the *King Tut* exhibition.

"One gay bar is like another. Would it not be nice just to go to the hotel ond enjoy each other," Juan sighed when we ventured into one. The joy of watching Juan savor a bite into a *muffaletta* sandwich at an Italian deli was enough to make the trip something to remember in itself. As usual, his eyes were sparkling and his brows flinching with delight. We laughed ourselves sick picking into tiny shells for something to eat in an inexpensive seafood tray, coming up with smelly fingers instead. He never was one to eat with fingers, yet had agreed to do it to please me.

"See, Recharred, it does not pay to try to scrimp in a city like New Orleans," Juan reminded me. We finally left the mess to find another place to eat.

"Recharred, everyone has to go to the French Market when in New Orleans," Juan said as we were about to take off for home. "You 'ave not been here if you do not go thar!" Once we were there, Juan's excitement and charm made one think we were in the Taj Mahal having an exquisite dinner. Yet we were merely having coffee and benets in a market place atmosphere.

Juan insisted on a lasagna dinner for the cast, and when they arrived, he was like a little kid, thrilled because a movie star was in his home. He played a recording of Noel's over and over.

Performances were not scheduled Christmas Eve and Christmas, and because I was earning enough money, Juan and I went to Chicago. Not wanting to spoil Juan's holiday, I never mentioned that three sister theaters had bid for our show. It was confirmed when we returned. Columbus, Ohio, Austin, Texas, and Indianapolis were booked. Juan was not happy, but he realized I had to agree to stay with the company. We needed the money, and we weren't certain of immediate jobs in Atlanta. I tried to convince him that he could come to all the cities as he did in Dallas, but he just wouldn't buy it. Instead, he decided he no longer wanted to live in Atlanta, to return to Chicago and put our furniture in storage. We'd return to pick it up when the show closed.

"I hope you understand. I cannot be here alone without you," he insisted when I tried to talk him out of it. "Ot least in Chicago, I will 'ave my parents, ond will be able to see my daughter. Ond, Recharred, it will be easier for me to get a job thar. Ond you know transportation is so much better thar!" I understood, but I didn't like it.

We were into 1978, and the last week in January was approaching, the run in Atlanta about to come to an end. I tried to talk Juan into driving with me to Columbus, to leave for Chicago from there, but he refused because it would only depress him to be present while our furniture was being taken out. He would fly out the night before my last show instead.

Juan began drinking himself into a drunken stupor the night he was to leave, an obvious attempt to forget what was actually happening. Tom Michaels decided to accompany us to the airport, especially since he had been spending so much time with Juan while I was in Dallas. The tears and the ache in my heart will always remain vivid in my mind. There was Juan, trying valiantly to appear happy he was leaving. I knew better; my heart was breaking, too! He headed down the ramp, refusing to turn back to look in my direction. And then suddenly his arms raised up in that manner of his, and he danced to the gate. Once he no longer was in sight the sad realization finally sunk into my head. Our desert island had come to an end.

Chapter Twenty-Seven:
True Devotion

After watching the movers take out the last piece of furniture, I headed for Tom's apartment with my baggage. He was putting me up for the night. That evening cocktails flowed freely after the last performance, and my fantasies took over again. I knew they never lived up to my expectations, only adding another trick to an empty pocket instead, but still found myself in a bath house. Juan was my life, so why was I out looking? Afterwards, I'd be completely bewildered why I ever needed them. So there I was sobering up as the parade went by. So I left.

The snow got worse as I neared Columbus, and I drove into a city buried in a state of emergency. I plowed into the motel we were to stay, a miracle in itself since it looked just like big mounds of snow. Opening night was cancelled, and ultimately, the entire week. Of course, the road conditions didn't keep me from checking out the bars.

My first outing was a catastrophe. I was certain the stage manager was a dyke when I met her. My assumption proved to be true when she displayed the contempt they seem to have for men. She had spotted me at that bar and informed the entire cast! It dawned on me that she had been noticeably cold to me during our initial meeting, almost as though she resented me for being a man. Anyone with a reasonable amount of sense would've used some discretion. This way of thinking always mystified me, and this crude action only added to that mystery. I was always careful not to give anyone the impression I was gay and, suddenly, there I was faced with an embarrassment I found difficult to handle.

It didn't seem to matter to Noel and Mary Ellen. Joe DiVito, however, saw it as an opportunity to make me squirm. He thrived on handing me one offensive wisecrack after another. Noel was usually busy with his wife and twins and Mary Ellen became quite friendly with Joe. The others kept to themselves, which left me alone and lonely.

I was never much of a loner, and probably because of my loneliness for Juan I ventured out into that snowbound week seeking sex. However, I found I didn't even have to leave the snow-covered motel grounds to fulfill my desires.. On entering the restaurant on the motel grounds, I spotted Joe having dinner with Mary Ellen. Since I wasn't beckoned over, I sat alone. It wasn't long before I noticed a good-looking guy sitting just beyond them, staring at me. I would never have suspected him to cruise. He looked so macho. There was no doubt about it, he was giving me the eye! Joe and Mary Ellen finally left and I was able to stare back. I was sober this time, and a burning sensation still ran through my body. He finished his dinner and seemed to be waiting for me to finish! And it wasn't until I put down my fork and sat back that he made a move to the cashier, his eyes still in my direction.

I hurried out after paying my bill to find him in front of the motel, puttering around his snow-buried car. I casually commented on the weather in passing, and after exchanging a few remarks, he walked to his room. His quick movement to his door gave me the impression that he wanted me to take note of the room number.

It was a perfect ploy! I had a bottle of Chivas Regal from the club! Perfect for a snowbound businessman! So I called his room and asked if he might be interested in joining me for a drink. He seemed pleased that I called and especially surprised that I had a bottle of scotch, and quickly accepted my invite. He'd bring the ice. He was even more macho and handsome when I opened the door, a real man compared to the queens I was accustomed to in Atlanta….

It wasn't an immediate jump in the sack. Dan, on business from Cincinnati, was an excellent conversationalist. Of course, I continued to pour scotch. After a few minutes, the phone rang. "This is the front desk," the voice answered, "I received a call from a guest, complaining that a great deal of noise from your room is disturbing them." Joe came to mind immediately. He had, undoubtedly, spotted Dan coming to my room. I was feeling too good to let it bother me, and told her it must be some mistake.

The conversation continued, along with the consumption of scotch until early morning. I truly enjoyed his company and conversation, and it seemed likewise with him. No more phone interruptions and soon we were in bed, kissing passionately. Dan surprised me when he sat on top of me as I lay on my back. This macho, handsome man wanted me to penetrate him! We tried but it was useless. I drank too much. Dan, however, wouldn't give up. He worked on it until I had a firm enough erection to slide slowly into him. The warmth and rapture I experienced from this beautiful man pumping slowly on my body was all too short. I exploded! I had never been one to satisfy someone after I came myself. This man I couldn't deny.

In the morning, I knew I'd never see him again and the guilt ensued. As exciting as he had been, I had only added another trick to that empty pocket. But he was one I would never forget.

Juan took some time off from a new job to be with me for a few days. The weather was severely frigid, but his enthusiasm and excitement for the sights of a new city were enough to keep me warm. It seemed like only moments, and he was gone.

Austin, Texas, the next city, was quite charming. It was the end of February and it felt like spring. I was housed with Jerry, a co-actor. He didn't cook, and wasn't interested in sharing groceries. I really didn't care since he and Joe had become very close. In fact, I began to wonder about their relationship. While lying on my bed one evening, listening to a tape of *Gigli* singing the opera, *Pagliacci*, the two of them came in and passed my room on the way to Jerry's room. After a few minutes, Joe poked his nose in to ask if he was okay to close the door to my room. I later went to the kitchen for a snack and noticed that Jerry's door was closed too, and oh-so- quiet!

I spent much of the time at the pool, sunbathing. The temperature was cool and I didn't mind the sun then. I didn't do much with the cast because Joe made me feel uncomfortable. The only time I'd join them was when Noel and his family were part of the group. I was on my own most of the time, and I had never been a loner.

I had a phone installed but didn't tell Juan; I was afraid of the tremendous bill with continuous calls from him, or that he might call to find me gone and assume I was out tricking.

"So, I see you 'ave a phone now, Recharred, ond you did not let me know," Juan's sarcasm rang out once I picked up the phone. "Why, Recharred? Because if you were out tricking, I would then know? Is thot not right, Recharred?"

What possessed him to call information baffled the hell out of me! Other cast members put in phones, so I did the same. After hearing my explanation, he finally told me that he'd be coming down for the last week. I was elated. He could drive with me to Indianapolis! I never recognized the devotion of this man. Four cities, and he managed to be with me in each of the them.

Noel invited the cast to an old Mexican restaurant. I declined because Juan was arriving a little earlier. Noel insisted I bring him along even though I said I didn't want Juan subjected to Joe's wisecracks. Noel, however, refused to accept my regrets, adding "Rick, Juan is your friend, and he is certainly welcome at my party. I wouldn't think of anything but having him join us!"

As it turned out, Juan ended up on a later flight and I attended alone. Noel insisted I return with Juan for cocktails, but it was impossible; we were driving down to San Antonio that night.

There was Juan, carrying his suitcase, in that catwalk of his. He had to be a hundred feet from me, but I could see he had been drinking. There was no mistaking that mischievous elf, his head low, his eyes transfixed on me, and that silly grin! He always needed to behave indifferently whenever we reunited after a separation he disapproved of. So he'd talk in a very formal manner, as if it was our first meeting. It was his way of showing his unhappiness about the situation. I could always see through him. The joy of being with me again was always there in his eyes, and before long he'd be that Juan I knew so well!

"It is so good to see you, Recharred," Juan exclaimed, putting out his hand like royalty acknowledging one of his subjects, "It is so good of you to come pick me up."

He was so funny as he kept up his little act once we were on our way. He knew I was enraptured with his performance, and it only encouraged him.

"Do you know who I was sitting next to on the plane, Recharred? Crystal Gayle!" Juan erupted once we checked into a motel. "Do you believe thot, Crystal Gayle! Ond, Recharred, she is so bea-u-ti-ful, so bea-u-ti-ful!" My patience paid off! That's what I was looking for.

"Aw, yeah, Recharred, she talked the entire trip," he answered when I asked if they had spoken. "Ond you know? She kept buying me drinks! Aw, Recharred, her eyes are so bea-u-ti-ful! They are so blue, so blue! Do you know whot she said to me? She said thot she ond I 'ave the same type of blue eyes! Do I 'ave bea-u-ti-ful eyes, Recharred?" he inquired with his little boy innocence.

"Juan, why do you ask such a silly question? How many people stop you on the street to rave about them?" He still went to the mirror.

Juan felt uncomfortable about sleeping in my bed with Jerry in the other bedroom, but he relaxed after hearing about the door closing episode. There was one incident that week that bothered us. The door to Joe's unit was open as we were going down the steps.

"Oh, look, the two lovebirds are leaving!" rang out Joe's voice.

I wanted to go in and smash his face, knowing it upset Juan, but I kept my cool. Instead, I said, "What do you care what he says, Juan? After all, we are lovebirds."

Juan just had to see my accommodations when we got to Indianapolis. "So I con picture where you are, Recharred." We were housed in the theatre, and bedrooms served as private dressing rooms. With that satisfaction, I drove him to the bus station., and he was gone again.

This theatre proved to be my most comfortable; Joe's overbearing personality came to an abrupt end. He and Jerry were no longer a couple, and he became as quiet as a mouse. His obnoxious domination of every conversation was no longer a problem! Mary Ellen's friendship with him ended, too. He had reported her to the union for being drunk on stage, according to Noel, who detested informants. So Joe was alone by his own doing! Mary Ellen and I began spending more of our free time together.

Joe tried to embarrass me once more by his manner in writing a message on the chalk board. "Rick, Juan called. He's in town and wants you at his *motel!* Call him." I didn't let it bother me.

I never expected Juan at this time. I had asked him to come the last week in order to drive to Chicago with me, which he doubted he'd be able to make. But here was my gem!

"I am starting a new job as a recruiter for the National Guard," he said. "I am so excited about it. Thot is why I came now instead of the last week, ond I am afraid I will only be able to stay for the weekend because I 'ave to start work Monday." We made the most of his short visit, and during that time, he really clicked with Mary Ellen. She even accepted his frankness about her drinking. Best of all, he was his cordial self.

"Mary Ellen, why don' you come to Chicago with Recharred next weekend? My ex-wife ond daughter are going out of town, ond I am sure she will let me use her apartment. You con sleep in her bed, ond Recharred ond I will sleep in her sleeper. Will you please come, Mary Ellen?" And he was off to Chicago.

I received a letter from my sister, Dee, a few days later. She asked if I'd be interested in renting a condo my nephew, Dino, bought in a Chicago suburb. He was willing to give me a good deal. Juan had seen it and wanted it badly. I was touched when I read, "Juan has visited me many times while you've been away, and talks of you incessantly. Rich, that guy really misses you, so I hope you decide to take the apartment together because he is a true and devoted friend!" I called her to accept and when I asked why Juan hadn't said anything, she replied, "Rich, he wanted you to be surprised with my letter."

Mary Ellen's excitement over her first trip to Chicago was nothing compared to Juan's once we got to Endira's. "Would it not be nice if we took Mary Ellen to Punchinello's on Rush Street, Recharred," he suggested though it was after 1:00 A.M. Their laughter was heard throughout the club as they tried in vain to out talk one another. A singer was on the bill, and she quickly embarrassed them with the fact that they were disturbing her performance. With this bit of brashness, we realized it was none other than Pudgy! However, we felt somewhat vindicated.

Juan couldn't get the day off. "I made reservations for 6:30 at the Peruvian restaurant, Recharred," he reminded me repeatedly before leaving for work, "so be certain thot you return here about five o'clock so we don't 'ave to rush, ond so we con spend time together."

Mary Ellen was skinny, but that didn't mean she ate less. On the contrary, she ate like a hungry dog! I never had seen anyone gorge down food so fast. In fact, food hung from her mouth while she shoved in more! Even more amazing, she'd be talking the whole time. After overfilling her plate, she'd clumsily stir it into a mess. Inevitably, half of it fell off the plate. I couldn't wait to see Juan's reaction at dinner. I was certain it would be priceless!

It was time to head back north, but Mary Ellen insisted on eating while in Greek Town. I wasn't hungry; we had eaten lunch in Old Town two hours earlier, but she was my guest. Five o'clock came and I was on pins and needles;

her order was just served. I excused myself to call Juan, and he had a fit when he heard where I was.

"Recharred, how con you do this to me when I do not see you thot much? You see Mary Ellen all the time. You did not 'ave to stay out this long with her while I am here alone!" My attempt to explain did no good. He could only think of us being cheated out of time together. Of course Mary Ellen had finished by the time I returned, and we were off.

Juan didn't allow Mary Ellen to notice his anger. His looks and remarks were directed only at me. But as usual, the anger was short-lived, and he happily rushed us to get ready.

A hidden camera aimed at the two of them during dinner would've recorded some priceless gems! What made the scene even more hilarious was that Mary Ellen was totally unaware of the reason for my laughter. Still, Juan never allowed himself to hurt her feelings.

Martina arrived with Don on the last Saturday of the run and, to my surprise, Juan got out of the car! "Recharred, I 'appened to call Martina last night, ond she told me thot she was coming to see you in the play," he excitedly explained. "Ond once I told her thot I was taking a bus to the University of Indiana to see a ballet my uncle is choreographing she osked if I wanted to drive with them. Now, I just 'ave to take a bus from Bloomington to get bock home"

"I figured we could drive Juan there, "Martina interjected, "I've always wanted to see their campus anyway, Dad." Before we knew it we were saying good-bye. But in our hearts we knew that on Monday, we'd be together again.

Martina and Don intended on leaving after the Sunday matinee, but Noel insisted they come to a garden party he and Maggie planned as a farewell. The day was perfect, and the spread magnificent! Mary Ellen managed to overfill her plate again, but this time she displayed an amazing aptitude in catching the falling morsels to swiftly shove them into her mouth.

Six months had passed, and the stage lights were down for good. It was hard to say good-bye to Mary Ellen, Noel and Maggie, but the anticipation of returning to Chicago and starting a new life with Juan sustained.

Chapter Twenty-Eight: Together Again

This was one time Juan didn't have to fuss getting an apartment in order. There wasn't enough belongings to fuss over. It wasn't his idea of living, but he'd have to suffice until our furniture came from Atlanta. Dee loaned us a kitchen table, chairs and utensils, some cots, and my mother's old couch. The television I traveled with and *Scribbage* were our only accessories. However, all that mattered to Juan was that we were together!

We were in the far suburbs, so Juan needed a car. He bought an old beater that had me up early each morning to jump it. I was no longer bringing in a salary, so times became desperate again. Juan didn't earn enough to support two. Visits to agents for television commercials were fruitless, and it was the same with auditions for plays. I just wasn't a part of the in-crowd. I applied for unemployment benefits but since my income was out of state, it took forever.

I got a job as a waiter, but didn't make enough to buy the gas, so I quit. It wasn't exactly inviting to stay home so Juan often wanted to go out. I wasn't always in the mood and we didn't really have money to spare, but it didn't stop his desire. So he'd mix a drink and then beg me to take a sip, realizing it didn't take much to get me high. It didn't matter if I refused. He'd strut over and press the glass to my chin.

"Aw c'mon, Recharred, drink some so you will be in the mood to go out dancing," he'd beg. If I still refused, he'd slowly tilt the glass upward to force me to drink. He'd chuckle while doing it, and this laughter kept me from getting angry. So I'd finally drink half of it down. Many times I got an immediate buzz, and once detected, Juan laughed uproariously.

"Aw, Recharred, you are such a cheap drunk," he'd say, catching his breath. "Only one drink ond you are already drunk! I cannot get over it, Blanche!"

He'd be elated! After all, he succeeded in getting me to agree to go out. He'd then dance into the bathroom to shower.

The music would blast, and he'd continue his dance while wiping his naked body when he came out. No one could be happier! And suddenly, he'd be in a ridiculous squat, swinging his genitals between his legs to the beat of the music! His smile and crazy expression…priceless!

"You are gross," I'd say, not meaning it because he was only doing it for me! Somehow, he had a way of doing things that never came across as vulgar. He was just too funny and a joy to behold! He loved life, and it showed!

"Recharred, do you not think it would be a good idea to go bock to Atlanta ond 'ave the second Miss Peach State Pageant?" Juan said excitedly on arriving home. "Ofter all, thot is still our pageant, ond I am sure it would be a success. Maybe we can use the Sweet Gum Head. I know we con stay ot Tom's. We con then rent a truck while we are thar ond pick up our furniture!"

As always his excitement rubbed off, and we began making the necessary arrangements. In calling Tom, I learned that Juan had already talked with him. In fact, he also surprised me with the news that he was moving to Chicago, and that Juan had invited him to live with us.

We found an apartment in Forest Park, and since it was neglected by previous tenants, the rent was fairly low. We were sure it would live up to our expectations, especially once the landlord agreed to paint it. Three bedrooms, a large den next to the kitchen, a living room, and a formal dining room had already started Juan thinking of how to decorate them.

I still wasn't happy with the prospect of Tom moving in, and probably because of his technique in picking up guys. Juan knew, as well as me, that Tom cruised the streets for straight guys hitching a ride. After some gifted conversation with a hitcher, he'd offer him a drink. Vodka was standard equipment on his car. Once the guy was inebriated, he'd take him home, hoping for a night of sex! Amazingly, his success with straights outnumbered the gays.

"Tom, you are like a spider and his web," Juan often quipped.

"Tom, if you cannot agree to this, then you might want to reconsider moving in with us," was my warning after sensing his excitement on our ride from the airport. "By no means will you ever be allowed to bring a trick home. We are aware of your style, and there's no way I want Juan murdered in his sleep, or myself. The rent is cheaper than any two-bedroom we saw, so we'd have no problem paying it ourselves. So it is up to you, Tom. We just do not want one of the straight guys that you get drunk to wake up sober and go crazy!" Tom gave no argument, agreeing to abide to the rules. I was still concerned.

We wanted to turn in early that evening; the next day would be hectic with rehearsal and the pageant at night. But I had promised Mary Ellen we'd stop by to meet her boyfriend.

Chuck was quite friendly, and we soon realized that he and Mary Ellen were well suited for each other. Juan and I didn't drink, and yet a quart was polished off in less than an hour. They were both thrilled when we asked them to serve as judges in the pageant.

Tom wanted to go out when we got to his place, and to my delight, Juan refused. Tom was another one who couldn't stop drinking once he started. His overbearing insistence wouldn't ease up, but he finally went out alone.

"Richard, wake up, I need help," Tom whispered, nudging my arm to wake me. I scrambled out of bed in a complete stupor.

"Come with me to the hall, Richard," he beckoned in that high-pitched, excited manner of his, anxiously grabbing hold of my arm and pulling me towards the front door. "I need you to help me carry someone up to my room!"

I stood there dazed, still not realizing what was going on. It didn't register until he hobbled to the edge of the stairs…frantically flapping his short arms in every direction. He demanded I help carry the person his finger pointed to at the bottom of the stairway.

I was mortified! Sprawled out at the bottom of the stairway was someone who had to be at least eight feet in length! I didn't move; I was in shock! Tom went crazy, waving those arms of his wildly, screaming for me to help! Juan was right. He was a spider, trying desperately to drag in its prey! In my zombie state, I actually followed him down and helped haul the comatose giant to his lair! There was no way to stop him; we were in his house. I could only go back to bed and pray that Juan and I were still in one piece in the morning.

We did awaken in one piece, and as I noticed the opened door to Tom's room, I figured the giant had left. After explaining everything to Juan, he insisted we sit Tom down for a long talk. Tom still agreed to our ultimatum after our talk. He would take his tricks to motels.

"Who is gonna help you carry them to the room?" Juan quickly quipped, "the desk clerk?"

We hoped for at least twenty-five contestants in order to collect a substantial amount in entry fees, but there were only fifteen, including Lee and Ronda. We were astounded with Ronda. She was total woman, and her lip-synching had become flawless! It was again a task directing the queens, but I managed to get through it. We decided to use the format from the first pageant.

With almost every seat in the house taken, we were still disappointed. We had expected a huge standing room only crowd. We were then enlightened to the fact that our old friend, Frank Palmer, had boycotted the show, not wanting two northerners to make a killing in Atlanta. I began to pray that we break even. The one thing I was proud of was Juan did not drink, and Tom was doing fine handling the door. We had Phyllis Killer as mistress of ceremonies, a wise move since her ad-libs had the crowd in the aisles.

"Recharred, I 'ave never in my life seen anyone drink as much as Mary Ellen ond Chuck," Juan said after sitting with them and the other judges. "They are gulping them down like thirsty dogs! Aw, Recharred, she is so funny the way she is slurring her words!"

As magnificent as she looked, and in spite of her terrific performance, Ronda placed second. Her curt manner in answering the question category lost big points.

"Rick and Juan, I reeeally belieff the wrong one won," Mary Ellen remarked, approaching with Chuck, the two of them trying desperately to hold up one another. Referring to Ronda, she slurred out, "Ohhh, I reeeally thought that blond shoul' hab won the crown! Ohhh, wen she did *New Yor,' New Yor,'* she wa' grea!'" In a sudden, desperate effort to point to herself she let go of Chuck and mumbled, "Ya know wha,' she looked more li' a womannn tha' I do!" We made no comment.

Receipts from the door hardly covered the one thousand in prizes. One consolation though, was we would have had to eventually fly here for our furniture. If it had not been for the boycott, Juan would have again come up with a winner. At least he was allowed to see one of his proud creations come to light again, and I was glad.

After getting our furniture and as much of Tom's that would fit in the truck, we were on our way. Tom followed in his car. Suddenly, he pulled alongside, motioned for us to follow, and sped off. We followed him into the lot of a roadside store, and when he came out he appeared to be holding a bottle in a bag. He got in his car, and paused alongside our window.

"I'll see you guys tomorrow when you get to the apartment!" he shouted. That was it…no further explanations, leaving us in the dust as he sped off!

"You do know whot he is intending to do, Recharred, do you not. Thot had to be vodka."

"Oh, Juan, I don't know what you got us in to," I sighed, nodding my head in concern.

When I agreed to Tom moving in with us, I had figured my family would never suspect him to be gay; he looked like someone with a squeaky voice. The awkward movements of his arms and the hobble in his walk assured me he would be taken for a big dwarf. But now, this other side had me worried!

Chapter Twenty-Nine:
Joys and Tribulations on Harvard Street

Once we settled on Harvard Street, our apartment turned out beautiful. We had to give Tom the largest bedroom because his bed wouldn't fit into the other two. In fact, we had to get rid of our beds, but Dee came to the rescue again, giving us my ma's three-quarter-size ensemble. One daybed was kept for Juan's bedroom, just off the living room, to add support to our pretense.

"Now, we con call this living, Recharred," Juan said as we resumed our new life together, but with Tom tagging along. As far as we knew, he never brought home a trick, at least, not while we were home. Juan was continually on his tail to keep the place neat and orderly, and it seemed to work. One problem however…he refused to hang his wet bath towel to dry. He'd toss it into the clothes basket in his closet instead. The horrible smell of mildew would drift into the kitchen because his room was immediately off of it. We were nauseated at every meal. No matter how we begged, he continued.

I had no luck with auditions, but Tom got a job as a bookkeeper in a nearby office. He always was broke shortly after cashing his check, however. His life, we discovered, revolved around the bars. He also had a habit of placing long distance calls from the bars when he got drunk and charged them to our home phone. Then he never had the money when the bills came. We finally got wise, refusing permission when the operator called to verify the charge. Tom would call immediately, infuriated with us! He had to be an alcoholic. When sober, he couldn't be more cooperative. But after one too many, he'd be unbearably stubborn. His drinking behavior was very similar to Juan's—absolute fun to be with after a few drinks. However, his aftermath was much too bully and overbearing. Unless he joined us for a movie or anywhere else we might invite him, he was in the bars every night. Nutbush and the Hideaway were local bars, and his usual haunts. One consolation: it did allow Juan and I time alone. On occasion we would join him should we desire a night of fun and dancing, sometimes ending up at the Closet or some other Chicago bar. And there were many fun times.

We did all the cooking, preferring it that way since Juan didn't want Tom getting at the stove to leave it covered with grease. Tom was happy with the arrangement and agreed to do the dishes daily, as well as clean my mess when I cooked. As soon as he finished, he was off to the bars. Those times alone with Juan were precious whether in serious discussions or fun ones. It made no difference. Juan hadn't forgotten Danyle's walk, and if I wanted to laugh, he'd do it for me. Once he'd join in with his contagious laughter I'd be in stitches.

"Aw, Recharred, we 'ave had so many good times together. I hope it will last forever," he'd say, trying to catch his breath.

I will never forget the night we got home very late. Juan didn't want his good time to end, playfully mauling me as the three of us toddled down the alley after parking the car. I was quite high myself and, in a playful manner, began to run from him.

"Recharred, Recharred, wa are you runnin' away from me? "Juan slurred out in his little boy voice. "Aw, I am gonna catch you!" he said, immediately chasing after me. There we were, the two of us, laughing hilariously while he repeatedly called out the same things to me.

My laughter turned to panic once I looked over my shoulder to see Juan trip and fall to the pavement! The sight of his face smashing on the concrete brought my heart to a stop; his drunkenness did not allow the quick thought to break the fall with his hands.

"Oh, Juan! Juan! What did you do!" I screamed, running back to him, afraid that his face was smashed. "Why did you chase me like that when you've been drinking so much!"

Tom caught up and helped as I nervously pulled Juan to his feet. Angry with myself for running away, I prayed aloud, "Oh, God, let him be okay! Please!"

He was dazed but it was obvious that the alcohol in his body numbed all feelings. His face was a mass of blood, but he wasn't even aware of it. He assured me he was fine, but I couldn't be sure! There was no telling if any or all of his front teeth had been knocked out, but at least his forehead hadn't made the initial impact.

I was relieved to find that Juan's teeth were okay after we got him to the bathroom, though a stream of blood continued to flow from the gum line of one of them. The fact that it came from the tooth that was slightly turned and protruded told me it had saved the others.

He had to be hurting, but his only complaint was, "Aw, Recharred, you should not 'ave run away from me. Why were you running away from me, Recharred?" When he began to laugh, I realized he wasn't in the least angry with me.

He agreed to be taken to an emergency room, but he insisted on going to the Great Lakes Naval Hospital. "Ofter all, Recharred, I am in the Army.

Besides, I do not 'ave money to pay a private hospital." So we were off on a fifty-mile drive at three in the morning. Tom drove. Juan should've been really hurting with the alcohol wearing off, yet he continued chatting happily.

The tooth needed to be extracted, and my heart was breaking when the dentist started pulling. I felt sure he'd be very bothered afterwards, convincing himself that his looks were marred forever. However, it didn't seem to matter. After all, he had mastered his way of smiling to hide the protruded tooth, so he merely continued this mastery. Of course, once he received his partial, he was then able to smile naturally.

We suddenly became proud owners of a dachshund, the dog of the week in the Sunday paper. "Aw, Recharred, it is so cute," Juan exclaimed once he saw the picture. "Aw, I would love to 'ave it so much! Recharred, would it not be nice if you were the first one ot the anti-cruelty in the morning." So I was the first one, and there I was driving home with a dog.

Juan was elated when he got home from work. One would have thought we had adopted a baby. Now, the word "cinnamon" has always been a tongue twister for me, and yet it was the name we chose for our new addition. We quickly discovered that Cinnamon had a mind of his own; he took us for walks.

"Recharred, Cinnamon is supposed to be my dog," Juan pouted because Cinnamon was always at my feet, "why is he always next to you?" The only explanation I could come up with was that I was the one who brought him home. He was still hurt.

"Whot a stupid dog, Recharred, he does not even try to chase it," Juan quipped after Cinnamon refused to chase a mouse in the house, "ond I thought dachshunds were supposed to be hunters." It was so funny watching Juan telling the dog to chase the mouse. Cinnamon would just lay his head back on the floor and resume his nap.

Christmas Eve has always been very special to me. It was a night to spend with those I love very much. And Christmas Eve of 1978 I would have the kids for dinner, as well as Juan! He wasn't going to his mother's, and my kids weren't going to theirs! The day couldn't have been more beautiful! I had several entrees to prepare, and since Tom would clean up as we went along, I could experience the joy of preparing for a party with Juan!

"Oh, God!" I thought, Where were you for twenty-two years?"

Our entire evening was perfect, including the finale at Dee's. I had my sisters, my brothers, their families, Pa and my kids, and of course, my wonderful Juan. I couldn't have asked for more!

Juan surprised me by insisting I go with him to a New Year's Eve party given by his old straight Spanish friends. He hadn't seen them for some time, so he was looking forward to partying with them. He couldn't think of leaving me behind. He had always been uptight about going to something like that together, so I considered it a breakthrough and an honor that he would introduce me as his friend. Of course, he managed to give me some last minute instructions.

"Now, Recharred, be sure you do not look ot me too long or touch me."

Spanish music filled the evening, which couldn't have pleased us more. We couldn't dance together or hug at midnight, but at least we were in the same room to welcome 1979. Still, it was a pleasure to dance with a woman again. And I had found an absolutely enchanting one from Peru for most of the evening. Juan got very drunk, but he never lost control. Upon leaving, we were surprised to find over a foot of snow and blizzard conditions on our ride home.

After months of traipsing to the unemployment office, I received three thousand dollars in a lump payment. It came at the right time; I had just organized a musical group with three girls and three guys including myself with a vision of making it big as a nostalgic ensemble.

I had met a good-looking black guy, barely in his twenties, while performing in a children's production company. Rehearsals for my group were just about to begin and when I heard he played piano and had done quite a bit of accompaniment, I asked if he'd like to play for us. Jason accepted. I had a feeling he might be gay; the attention given to me had been far too much to be considered as platonic. He confirmed my suspicions when he admitted to his attraction to me, inflating my ego once again. Rehearsals became hectic so Juan joined us for most of them. He also made it clear that he was aware of Jason's feelings. I assured him nothing would come of it, but it was still on his mind.

"I have no way of getting to rehearsal tonight," Jason called to say, "my car needed some repairs and is in the shop."

I told him I'd pick him up in Chicago. I was going to be there later in the day anyway. There was no time for a sit down dinner, so I called Juan to tell him I'd stop for gyros sandwiches and that I was bringing Jason because he needed a lift to rehearsal. Juan's exceptionally cold manner on the phone left me wondering.

During the ride, Jason talked about sex instead of the numbers that needed to be rehearsed, which confirmed the fact that he wanted me sexually. He was trying to excite me and he was succeeding. Fortunately, though, we were almost home and Juan would be there to light up the straight and narrow path. When we arrived, however, all the lights were on but Juan wasn't there. I figured that he probably went out for cigarettes. Tom wasn't home either.

My ego obviously thought it an opportune time to say, "Well, Juan is not here, maybe we can make *hay*!"

At that instant, the back door swung open, and Juan bombarded in! He had actually been hiding in the rear stairway! He went completely bananas! I tried to explain my bit of mischief, but it did no good. Juan was too hysterical. Jason and I left without eating.

It took some time for Juan to cool down, and I'm not sure he ever accepted my explanations. He did manage to harass Jason with nasty phone calls prior to cooling down, however. Jason had a lover, so he had no choice but to quit as accompanist. My ego had again caused stress. Juan's trust in me was on thin ice. It mattered not that I'd never do anything, the thought was there.

The group finally broke up; one hundred agents had been invited to two special showings, but no one showed up. Ninety-one inches of snow fell that winter, and no one was going anywhere except for a gal by the name of Jane Byrne! So, besides the time, the three thousand in unemployment compensation was spent. On a bright note, Geena and Frank married.

I finally won a commercial shoot in California as a little ol' German winemaker, introducing beer battered fish. I was absolutely thrilled, but Juan wasn't happy at all. I'd be gone for three days, and was worried the separation would make it easy for Tom to talk him into going out. He might then find himself in the mood to retaliate for my episode with the accompanist. As it turned out, he didn't go out with Tom. I called late each night and would've known from the sound of his voice. I made good money, but it didn't equal the prize of Juan's smiling face when he met me at the airport on my return.

My nephew, Geena's youngest, surprised us with a visit, and I was a little self conscious. He was nineteen. What could we talk about? Juan took me aside to explain that he heard that Jacque told him about the bizarre happenings with Neva in Atlanta. We figured that curiosity had gotten the best of him. Our job was to wipe out any doubts, and after some level headed conversation, especially by Juan, my nephew appeared to be relaxed, quite a contrast to the uptight manner in which he had arrived.

"Well, it is late," Juan said, well into the evening, "ond I 'ave to get up very early tomorrow morning. So I will 'ave to be going to bed."

It was not long after that I felt very sleepy, and since Tom and my nephew were engrossed in a sensible discussion, I saw no harm in leaving them to continue.

Juan had gone to his room, and to keep up the front, I retired to mine. I had just dozed off when awakened by Juan tapping on my shoulder.

"Recharred, I just went into the kitchen for some water, ond I could smell marijuana coming from the den," Juan whispered excitedly. "Ond you know how Tom works when he wants someone! Recharred, I am really worried! You better tell your nephew to go home—thot it is late!"

Without hesitation, I hurried to the doorway of the den to say those very words. He didn't object, and followed me to the front door. Tom was right behind and, to my horror, followed him down the stairs! Tom had been drinking as well, and there was no way I could let the stubborn bull make a conquest that night! Juan was just behind the arch, and began motioning frantically for me to do something to stop him! He knew as well as I that Tom had no loyalty whatsoever to us when he wanted sex! He had proved his belligerence many times.

"Recharred, you know whot he is gonna do," Juan whispered out anxiously, "Aw, you better stop him before they get away!"

I quickly called out, "Tom, please come back up because I have something important to tell you." To my great surprise he obliged, and as he came through the door I called out to my nephew to get home because it was so late. At that, I quickly closed the door!

I was furious and grabbed hold of Tom with both hands, pushing him to the wall. My anger was so great that I actually managed to lift him off the floor!

"What the hell do you think you were doing, Tom?" I shouted. "How dare you try to seduce someone from my family!" He didn't deny it! He didn't apologize! He just began screaming in that screechy voice of his for me to stop!

"If you ever try that again, I will kill you!" I shouted, my anger even more intense. "Do you hear me, Tom! I will kill you!" With one desperate surge he finally broke from my grasp and ran hysterically to his bedroom, slamming the door shut! I followed, and began pushing against the door furiously. In an attempt to keep me from doing something hasty, Juan grabbed hold and pulled me away from the door. My shouts and threats continued as did Tom's screeching!

Juan finally managed to calm me, and Tom's room became quiet. The drama had ended for that night, but the memory would remain, especially for Tom. I tried to forgive and forget since it was my nature. Tom, though, became distant. No longer was I his favorite.

Suddenly, Juan began doubting my whereabouts during the day, always implying that I was meeting someone instead of going to the agents. I tried to reason with him, but his jealous accusations continued, driving me up the wall. I couldn't figure out why he was doing it.

Cinnamon's disobedience became too much, and we decided to give in to Svetmana's pleas to have him, but after only two months, he broke from her leash and was killed by a car.

Juan loved the park at the corner. He'd spend hours there with his books and a radio in order to maintain his tan, and I'd sit in a shaded area close by just to be with him. I'd usually stop by his office on my way to the agents, just to spend some time with him. His recruiting partner, Joel, a black guy about Juan's age, was always very friendly with me. I was certain he was aware of our story, and that he accepted it graciously because he truly liked Juan. I also felt he respected me as well. But there was Juan, always greeting me with a hardy handshake one would expect from a bowling teammate.

"Hello, man, how are you doin?'" he'd ask. Even when we were alone in the office, he'd warn me not to talk too loudly. Still he wanted me there, and was bothered if I didn't show up.

I was never one to hold a grudge; life was too short. So I put Tom's attempt to seduce my nephew aside, accepting him as a friend. I honestly thought he no longer was bitter and began including him in many of our activities. There also were times we joined him for a night out.

It was Friday and we were going to the Nutbush for such a night. Juan always was a stylish dresser, but never flamboyant. It also wasn't unusual to hear his honest frankness criticize Tom continually for his ugly manner of coordinating colors and fabrics. I had always thought myself to be a tasteful dresser, but it was Juan's repeated criticisms that made me learn how to maintain my youth with modern clothing.

"Recharred, why do you wear clothes that make you look like a suburbanite thot has been buried in them for years? C'mon now, get with the times!"

So, once Tom slipped on a new shirt and jeans for our night on the town, Juan graciously exclaimed, "Now, Tom, thot is more like it! You are positively with it!" It was merely a plain white knit shirt with an emblem, but it was enough to make the difference.

As always, our drinking began at home, with the usual foolish misconception that it would save money. It never did, however. One drink after another at the bar would be downed anyway. I wasn't doing badly myself that night, managing to keep pace with them.

The evening was turning out to be one of the best we had together for some time, and I was overjoyed. Juan and I had anyone we talked to in stitches. They even accepted his mimics good-naturedly each time he fluttered his hand to say, "Oh, my good woman, you don't say!"

We danced our hearts out, and though Juan's alcohol intake was usually kept at a minimum whenever we did so much dancing, he was drinking more. Nevertheless, I was having a ball.

After a long set on the floor with Juan, I made my way to sit on the doorman's stool, hoping for a breeze to cool off. Juan headed for the bar. Tom was standing there and I wanted to enjoy his company. While engrossed in some happy chatter, I noticed a black fellow before me wearing a stylish, white, loose-fitting African sheath. I thought of Juan and me kidding Tom when we'd see him in his night shirt.

"Tom, you look just like a storybook character. All you need to be perfect is one of those stocking hats," were only a couple of quips Juan would hand him.

I continued in my devilish manner by pointing him out, "Look, Tom, that guy has a night gown just like yours." The remark had to be heard; the guy turned and smiled. I returned a smile, wanting to reciprocate the friendliness. The smile remained plastered on his face as he moved slowly towards me, and while holding onto a cocktail, he began caressing my hair.

"How you be tonight, darling?" he asked in a tone reminiscent of Danyle. I was sure he was aware of my happy mood, and that he merely wanted to share it with me. Still, I felt he needed to know that I meant no offense to him and explained the reason for the comparison. He didn't say a word. He just continued stroking my hair in the same manner Danyle had done so many times. It should have been a sign, but my happy drunk could only think positive. My awakening came when a sudden drenching of ice and liquid came pouring over my head! It was not the cooling I was looking for, and I exploded!

In that moment, I saw red, and grabbed hold of him with the strength of a bull! I dragged him out the front entrance, and in the same quick motion, threw him onto the sidewalk, landing on top of him! I grabbed his head and began beating it against the pavement!

"What you be doin?'" he screamed. "You be crazy?" And I *was* crazy with fury!

It wasn't long before someone pulled me off and he got to his feet. I tried to break loose but they held on. There I was, held in a bear hug from behind. It was exactly what my opponent needed because I was left helpless. He took off a shoe and began slamming it into my face in a wild series of blows! The idea of taking a beating while being held helpless was enough to give me the strength of an Army and I broke loose! I lunged at him but the advantage of his longer arms left my attack futile. It was as though I was attacking a windmill gone berserk and that each of the sails had a shoe slamming into my face! I felt blood streaming down my face. Still, I wouldn't give up!

Suddenly a loud, squeaky, voice kept repeating, "RICHARD! RICHARD! WHAT ARE YOU DOING? STOP IT! STOP IT!"

It was Tom! I couldn't believe it! He had to have been aware of what had happened. He was next to me when I was drenched. And yet he was screaming as though I was at fault! My face was taking a battering and still he kept up! I finally managed one desperate lunge to grab hold of the shoe from the guy, and delivered a tremendous blast to his face with it.

Tom's shrieking continued, and my head was spinning! If only he'd shut up! I finally ran to him, and in hopes of getting some compassion, I put my arms and head on his shoulders. Still, there was no solace, only his continued screams. So I wiped my bloody face against his new shirt; at least that would give him a valid reason to scream. It did the job; he squeaked and screamed more! I couldn't take any more of his hysterics and ran behind the building to the parking lot, out of sight from all of them. I flung the shoe up onto the roof of the building and sped home.

The thought that Juan had been nowhere in sight only added to my furor on the drive home; I was certain he was oblivious to the disastrous events. And Tom's attempt to enlighten him with a screeching description during their walk home would only confuse him instead.

I was in the process of washing the blood from my face and shirt when I heard that abominable voice again!

"Richard, Richard! Look how you ruined my shirt," and he wouldn't stop!

And there was a dazed Juan, asking, "Wha 'appened? Wha 'appened, Recharred?" There was compassion in his voice, however, but my anger was too strong to appreciate it. He wouldn't comprehend anything anyway. And that made me angrier!

Tom's voice reached its miserable peak, and I was going out of my mind! I finally demanded he take off the shirt so I could soak it while the blood was fresh. He obliged reluctantly, and it was working. The blood was rinsing from the fabric. I showed him. Still, his shrill continued! Totally exasperated, I grabbed hold of him! In one violent movement I dragged him to his closet and pushed his face into the clothes basket!

"So you won't shut that miserable mouth of yours," I shouted. "Well, I know what will! I'm gonna stuff it with all these smelly, dirty, wet towels that ruin our dinner every day!"

I was furious as I rubbed them in his face! He never had admitted to the stench. This surely should enlighten him! I demanded he admit it, but uncontrollable hysterics ensued instead! My furor softened with concern for his state of mind and I let go, only to see him race out of the house in a hysterical frenzy!

Meanwhile, Juan was still muttering. "Wha 'appened? Wha 'appened, Recharred?"

There was no need to explain; in his drunken state, he wouldn't comprehend anything anyway. So I continued to wash Tom's shirt, feeling like lava was about to burst from my body!

It wasn't long before I heard Tom's miserable yelps again. Only this time there were other voices too. Two policemen suddenly came in, and there was Tom pointing an accused finger at me! They bombarded over, grabbed hold of me, wrenching my arms up on my back! I was even more distraught when I felt handcuffs snapped on! How could this be happening, and so fast? Tom must have flagged them down on the street, screaming like a flaming, raging queen!

I asked if I could get a shirt from the bedroom when they told me I was being taken to the station on charges of assault. They obliged but stayed directly next to me. Once they took off the cuffs so I could put on the shirt, one of them noticed the souvenir ol' wine maker picture.

"Oh, are you the guy that did that commercial? I see it all the time on TV." I assured him that it was me and he announced suggestively, "Well, how do you like that!"

I couldn't understand why they had to push my arms up so high on my back after they reapplied the cuffs. They were hurting me badly even though I was cooperating. And they continued to do it while leading me down to the squad car.

I can't remember whether Juan was following behind, or Tom for that matter. Only the humiliation of being on display for everyone to see from the corner gas station remains vivid. I was certain they thought I just murdered someone!

The cuffs were finally removed once I was locked in a cell, and when Tom's irritating voice started bellowing throughout the darkness, I realized this was for real. He should have realized my anger was only because a beautiful night out was spoiled, and that my threats were superficial. I could have just as well been rubbing his face with snow. No, he was still angry with me for ruining his night with my nephew.

Though I couldn't make out the words, I knew it to be Tom's voice, and sure he was demanding I be arrested. It continued for some time, and then there was complete silence. The only sound that remained was the sound of the beating of my heart, and each beat felt like an explosion. The silence was broken once an officer came to my cell.

"Well, Sir, we talked your *friend* out of pressing charges," he said. "He kept insisting, but we finally convinced him that things like this sometimes do happen to people living together."

I couldn't believe it! They actually thought that freak was my lover! That was even worse than them knowing I was gay!

"Though we feel you should stay here until morning," he added, "just to cool off."

I sat on the chain link bed like a zombie after he left. The thought of them watching television kept flashing before me. I could almost hear their comments to their wives.

"See that guy? Well, he is a fag and I just picked him up for beating up his dwarf lover!"

The birds were chirping happily as I walked home after they released me at the crack of dawn, but I couldn't have cared less. I was still in a stupor. I hadn't slept a wink; thoughts of Tom and the guy ruining our beautiful evening filled the night instead.

Suddenly, I spotted Tom in his car coming in my direction. However, I continued on my way once he pulled to the curb. I felt bad about doing so because Juan was sitting in the passenger seat, and the grave look on his face showed his obvious concern. I felt even worse after Juan called out and pleaded with me to get in, but there was no way I'd accept a ride from Tom!

"Aw, Recharred, I am so sorry thot I was not thar for you," Juan cried, putting his arms around me once he found me in the bedroom, "but I did not know whot was 'appening! I was so drunk! Ond I must 'ave passed out on the couch."

He continued to hold me tightly while laying his head on my shoulders.

"You know I never wake up thot fast, Recharred, when I am so drunk, but ot the crack of dawn I suddenly was wide awake! I ran to the bedroom, ond once I saw thot you were not thar, I became so worried! I went to Tom's bedroom ond woke him up. When I heard whot happened, I insisted we go to the police station to get you. He would not go, ond I pulled him out of bed!"

Realizing that Tom undoubtedly avoided the full facts, I filled Juan in with all the details. We held onto each other and cried, and finally he whispered, "Recharred, you 'ave to control your temper. It is not good to get thot angry."

"I know, Juan, but I was so angry when our beautiful evening was ruined."

Relations between Tom and I were again cold, and yet I still couldn't hold a grudge. I accepted him as family even though Juan admitted that Tom had been the one feeding him with stories about me taking off in other directions whenever I was on the way to my agents. He'd fabricate these stories because he was home so often sobering up after a night of drinking. Hard as I tried, the closeness we once shared could never be again.

The irony of it all was that I realized he was still feeding Juan with insinuations, and yet I treated him as a friend. I wanted to believe that Juan knew they were stories, and yet there still was that uncertainty. Tom seemed to be out to ruin my relationship with Juan. So, because of the suspicion aroused in him Juan made accusations on occasion, and it took some doing to prove they weren't true. The miserable scenario only led me to want to commit them to satisfy his suspicions.

An obvious conspiracy was when Tom talked Juan into going along with him on a weekend to Madison, Wisconsin. He had been aware that I had a prior commitment with my family that weekend. Juan talked of the trip incessantly, seeming to want me to suffer. I realized his motive though; it was his way of showing me that he still had his doubts.

Juan then raved on about their good time after they returned, leaving me to listen quietly and smile. It was apparent that he wanted me jealous, and it worked again. Satisfied with his accomplishment, he returned to his normal, charming self, sighing, "Aw, Recharred, I missed you terribly! I was wishing all the time thot you were with me."

After informing me that Tom met someone in Madison, he said, "He was really very handsome, Recharred, but since he had recently lost over a hundred pounds, his flesh was hanging in bunches." Hysterical laughter hit me when he contorted his body to show how the guy looked.

In May, we were informed that the building was sold, and the new owner wanted our apartment. We hadn't even lived there a year, which was nothing new for us, but we had hoped for a long stay in this one. We found an apartment in a three-story Greystone on the north side of Chicago, not far from all the gay bars. Tom was elated. The first floor apartment only had two bedrooms, and we were forced to give him the largest one because his bed wouldn't fit in the smaller room. Ironically, the bedroom was just off the kitchen again. My mom's bed could fit in the other room, but how would that look when my family was over? So we were at the trading block again. Dee obliged, returning the two daybeds.

We placed the chest on chest in the dining room since there wasn't room in the bedroom, and it looked great with the woods of the table and chairs. We especially liked the built-in buffet in the dining room. The Formica table and straw-back chairs we had taken from the club worked in this kitchen, too.

Juan wasn't a happy man during the move because I had just been cast to do two shows in Sattomon, Illinois, during their summer season, and they each were to run three weeks. I had to leave the end of May, a week after the move-in. It didn't matter that I could come home after the Sunday shows since Monday and Tuesday were off days, or that he could come down weekends. He remained depressed. He finally got caught up in the excitement of decorating a new place, and our time together was beautiful, especially since Tom couldn't wait to get to the bars.

So the two of us settled into another place. He was aware that I, too, excelled in decorating, and yet it was hilarious to hear him boast that he should be the one to place things.

"Recharred, you know I am the one who knows just where any picture should go! Look ot all of our other apartments!" And I agreed as I always did when he was so proud. The week was wonderful; his excitement was as always. After all, his excitement settling in all of our apartments had to make an indelible mark in my head, especially since this was our eighth in four years.

It was Saturday evening, and the living room draperies were the last thing to do. Tom was out as usual, and Juan and I were enjoying the evening alone. I had to leave for Sattomon early Sunday afternoon. We stood there transfixed once I hung the last panel. We finally began reminiscing about 1975 when we purchased them for our Oakdale apartment. This was another vintage apartment, and Juan stood there in complete joy.

"They look so bea-u-ti-ful, Recharred, so bea-u-ti-ful! Just like they looked on our bay windows on Oakdale. In fact, Recharred, everything looks so bea-u-ti-ful!"

Of course, he didn't forget to say, "Of course, not as bea-u-ti-ful as Oakdale, but almost!" His beautiful blues looked into my eyes, and he sighed, "Let's stay here a long time, Recharred."

Juan wasn't doing well the next morning. I asked if he was all right, and once he gave me a quick smile, I knew that he wasn't. Tom never came out of his bedroom, and I was thankful for that. I was relieved and happy once he began talking excitedly about the things we still needed to make the apartment complete. However, I couldn't help feel that he was hoping I'd change my mind and stay home.

It was time. My suitcases were sitting next to the front door.... I felt a tenseness in Juan as I embraced and kissed him. In fact, a sudden chill came over me from his apparent coldness.

"Aren't you gonna walk me to the car?" I asked when he held fast.

"I cannot, Recharred, I jus' cannot," he answered in a choked voice. Instead, he held onto the door, almost appearing as though he needed it for support.

"You go to your play, Recharred, ond leave me alone again," he lashed out after I insisted he walk to the car with me. "Go ahead!"

Without another word, he slowly closed the door to leave me alone in the hall. I froze in disbelief. I wanted him to be as excited as I was, but it didn't happen. Tears began to flow even though I tried desperately to stop them. So I forced myself to walk out, to merely wipe them from my eyes and get on my way instead of going back in and reassuring him we'd be together soon. I somehow didn't understand what he was trying to tell me and went on my way. He was someone who loved me completely for what and who I was, and yet there I was still searching for that star.

Chapter Thirty:
A Summer of Theater

Rehearsals began that Monday morning with introductions mostly. The stage manager, Don Shaver, was in his early thirties and handsome, and though he looked very macho, I thought he may be gay. That sense prevailed even though the idea should have been dismissed after his wife stopped in to catch a bit of the rehearsal.

"Hi, I'm Bev, Don's wife," she said, greeting me as I sat alone in the theatre watching the others on stage. She was a bit more than pleasingly plump and quite gregarious. A redhead, of course. In our short talk, she informed me that they had five-year-old twins, a boy and girl, and that they were housed in a small cottage for the summer. She wasted no time telling me she was cast as the female lead in *Pippin*.

"I'm a party animal, Rick," she added, before leaving, "so look for one party after another at our place!"

An elaborate opening night party was held at a country club, and any depression I may have had about missing Juan completely disappeared with one drink after another. Don and Bev's friends—three girls and a guy in his late twenties—had come in to catch the opening. Brett's black hair, eyes, and mustache really set him off as one sexy guy, and once I noticed his glares coming my way, my ego was running at full steam. Also fairly obvious sisters were Romo and Jack, two young locals. Romo was quite a joker, definitely the dominate personality. Jack, an Adonis, was quiet, but still managed to send vibrations my way with continual glances. However, I left alone.

Juan came down the first weekend, driving his father's car, as his car had died. As usual, I was immediately greeted with the indifference he was so good at handing out. After all, he had to make me suffer for leaving him, and to show me *he was Juan!* It only lasted about fifteen minutes, however. I needed only to cater to him, and he was his usual charming self.

The only time Juan had seen me perform was when I stepped in to do *LaMancha*, and I was especially anxious for his reaction to this slapstick comedy role. I knew he'd be frank.

"Aw, Recharred, you were definitely the best one in the play," he quickly raved after the performance. "Aw, you are so funny, so funny, Recharred! I laughed so hard! I was not even thinking it was you!" He was the critic that counted as far as I was concerned.

Don was meeting Bev at a nearby restaurant after the show and asked if I wanted to join them when I told him Juan was in the audience.... And there she was, looking eager to party, sitting with a few of the apprentices from the chorus of *Pippin*. Don came in just as I was introducing Juan and shocked me with his behavior. I almost thought we were in Dallas again after introducing him to Juan. He was devouring Juan as they shook hands and it was quite embarrassing because Bev was totally aware of the entire scene. I thought it strange that it didn't seem to annoy her. Then, at one point in the evening, Juan excused himself from the table. Don followed in a flash. I didn't think anything of it until I overheard one of the apprentices whisper, "There he goes! After another one!" I was certain Bev heard the remark, especially after their chuckles brought a smile on her face.

"Recharred, do you know whot happened tonight when I went to the bathroom?" Juan quickly commented when we left the restaurant. "I cannot believe it! Thot Don came in the bathroom right ofter me, ond do you know thot he stood ot the doorway, holding his hand on the door frame so I could not pass! Ond then he said, 'Well, when is it gonna be?' I was baffled, Recharred, ond I osked whot he meant. Well, Recharred, he osked when we were gonna get together for sex! Ond then he told me thot he had to 'ave me because I 'ave such bea-u-ti-ful blue eyes! I did not know whot to say! I could not believe thot he could be so bold! Ond his wife was sitting ot the table when he came into the restroom to cruise me!"

Rather irritated with Don, I sighed, "I don't know, Juan, I really don't understand myself."

I went home after the following Sunday night show, but on my return trip to the theater, the car broke down. Not only did it cost three hundred to repair, but I held up the Wednesday matinee performance. Fortunately, they waived the usual fine, but it still left me apprehensive about driving home again. This didn't fare well with Juan. I tried to explain that I was in rehearsals for *Pippin* and needed to be there on my off days, too, but he still was unreasonable. He then found a new way of spiting me; he didn't come to see me do the role of Charlemagne.

Brett and the girls came down for the opening and stayed a week, and since I was kept very busy spending time with them, I was able to put Juan's distress out of my mind. Of course, the attention given to me by Brett helped me reckon with it. In fact, he and I were left alone many times and I never allowed my ego to submit to the special manner in which he catered to me.

I made it home before the last week of performances and received the same indifference from Juan. He even admitted to meeting some guy and inviting him and his friend over for dinner. He then went on to say that he prepared my Italian pot roast.

"I really do think thot it came out better than when you make it, Recharred," he boasted, aiming to rub in some salt.

This attitude very well may have been my reason for finally making it to a gay bar I knew forty miles from the theater. Then again, it may have been my ego, as well as the adventure. My ego certainly was boosted since I did connect with a young Adonis who took me to his apartment. Still, all I could do was lie back and allow him to service me.

During the last week of performances, the director offered me a role in their final production of the season, *Little Mary Sunshine*. How would Juan react? I finally told the director that I felt sure I could do it, but that I would need to call to confirm once I was home.

I knew Juan well enough to know that he was overjoyed that I was home, though he tried desperately to act indifferent. After all, I had to suffer for all my wrongdoings as he always said. It didn't take long, however, for him to become his charming self again. Tom was gone most of the time, so we were able to enjoy our home alone. Though, every now and then, he still thought to refresh my memory by mentioning the guy he met.

"Juan, wouldn't it be wonderful if we spent the weekend at the *Holiday Inn* on Lake Shore Drive. It will be my treat," I shouted after the thought of avoiding Tom altogether came to mind. The kid was thrilled, though I realized I needed to tell him about the role offer before. However, nervous apprehension kept me from telling him until the day we were to leave for the weekend.

"Whot good will it do, Recharred, for us to go on a weekend to renew our relationship when you will be leaving me again soon," he shouted. "No, Recharred, I do not want to go! Whot good is it to go!"

I pleaded, but it did no good. He was not going on the weekend. I finally realized he was more important and called to inform them I couldn't do the show. Juan had won, and yet I didn't mind. The smile on his face was worth it!

Though I came down with a miserable cold, the weekend couldn't have been more beautiful! We hardly left the room except for meals and a couple of walks. All we needed was each other! We brought *Scribbage* along, and it was hilarious hearing Juan cry out, "You know, Recharred, it is not fair! I should be allowed to make out words in Spanish!"

I actually found myself purposely not forming words just to see that glow and smile on his face once he won.

Juan was a lefty, and yet his hand never looked awkward when writing. He also had the unique talent of writing in reverse, and in the same quick manner. I marveled each time I took it to the mirror to read. Long sentences were written as quickly, and were much more a challenge for me to figure out.

Time flew by that weekend, and though these games were a great part of the laughs and fun, the mutual satisfaction we shared in our lovemaking reigned supreme. Our compatibility was never doubted, but during this weekend, it was even more outstanding! Our sexual compatibility could have very likely fizzled out after five years instead of the explosion we experienced. We were to each other the epitome of the love. There should be no reason to look elsewhere!

Juan took hold of my hand once we arrived home that Sunday evening. While gazing into my eyes he sighed, "Recharred, I 'ave been thinking. I know I 'ave been selfish to stop you from goin' to do the play because I know thot is whot you 'ave always wanted to do all your life. It is not fair of me to deny you the chance. I jus' love you so much thot I am afraid you will find someone else while you are away. I know now thot you love me as I do you! Ond, Recharred, I am so proud thot you are willing to give it up for me! I want you to do the show. You are a great actor, ond I want you to 'ave a chance to show your great talent. So, please, call thar ot once because I want you to go!"

His compassion, his love, and understanding, again, touched my heart.

The part was still available and was mine once I called.

"I am so happy, Recharred, so happy," Juan exclaimed, devilishly adding, "You know, Recharred, I 'ave two weeks coming for vacation. Would it not be wonderful if I come down ond spend them with you." Our eyes met and we laughed and hugged each other tightly.

Rehearsal week went fast; Brett was in and I spent much of my free time with him. Juan was coming in after the opening and I was especially anxious for him to see the show since he loved nostalgia. The camp written into it was definitely his kind of comedy. When he began talking excitedly at the train station, I was assured he was overjoyed to be with me.

"You are not gonna believe whot happened, Recharred," he remarked. "Tom left the apartment yesterday while I was ot work. When I got 'ome last night, all of his things were gone except his bed ond night stond, ond a big mess! No note—nothing, Recharred! He had to 'ave gone to Madison to live with thot guy because he had been talking to him constantly on the phone. Con you believe thot, Recharred? No good-byes—nothing! Just his bills for the long distance phone calls ond his share of the rent!"

Even at that, I had to admit I was relieved that he was finally gone. No longer would there be fabricated stories about my whereabouts.

Juan was enthralled with the play that evening; no one could have raved more. "Recharred, it is so cute—so cute. I jus' love it! Oh, Recharred, I want to go with you every night to see it."

Corn fields surrounded the town, and Juan had me driving the narrow roads, completely awed with the splendor of seeing nothing but stalks that seemed to be reaching for the sky. A few miles from town was a marina, and Juan would dream about us possibly owning a cabin cruiser some day. However, it never was his criteria in life to be rich, always reminding me, "But, Recharred, if we don't—it would not matter. Jus' as long as we are together."

"Recharred, I really 'ave to spend some time with Svetmana while I am on vacation," Juan reminded me. "I promised her thot I would bring her here for a few days. Would you not mind?"

"Of course not, Juan. You can take my car."

"Aw, no, Recharred, I will not drive a stick shift," he quickly replied. "I con take the train, ond I am sure my father will lend me his car. Ond ofter I drive her bock, I can return on the train so I will be able to drive home with you once the play ends. Is thot not okay?"

I agreed. After all, look what he was going through just to be with me.

Remarkably, Svetmana wasn't nasty to me during her stay! She loved the play, and my character especially. It almost made me believe that I was truly a great actor; she raved about how funny I was continually. Obviously, it wasn't me she saw on stage.

Bev asked if we'd like to go with them to St. Louis to see the Archway to the West for the final break of the run. While there, Juan suggested we take in Six Flags. However, they thought it much too expensive on arrival, but accepted Juan's offer to take their kids in with us.

"Rick, if you remember, there's a party tonight by Jack and Romo at Jack's new apartment," Bev reminded me before heading off. "I have a babysitter for the kids tonight so if you want to leave Svetmana at the cottage, too, it's all right with me." After they left, I felt so relieved. Don would no longer be around to touch or glare at Juan.

I had no intention of going to the party, especially afraid that Jack might begin giving me the eye. Juan's perception would certainly pick up on it. However, they were still at the cottage when we arrived to drop off their kids, and Bev insisted we go. Juan quickly agreed, apparently ready for a party night.

We began drinking while getting ready as always and were quite high before leaving. The long day in the sun had obviously intensified the effects of the alcohol. The high helped me forget the possible chaos Jack's glares might bring. It didn't take Juan long to surpass my high once we arrived at the party. It was amazing; as drunk as he was, he still detected Jack's attention to me, though I tried desperately to avoid him. I received one dig after another, and he didn't care if Jack heard any of them. Unfortunately, Jack also made a point of listening after being on the receiving end of the initial words of wisdom and sarcasm by Juan.

"My good woman, if you don' watch out, those eyeballs of yours are gonna pop out of their sockets! Yo' shou' really 'ave someone sew those lids of yours together!"

"Recharrr,' open the door becau' I 'ave to pee verrry bodly," Juan pleaded while knocking on the bathroom door.

My high made everything a bit fuzzy, and I didn't give a thought that Juan had no holding power when drunk as I called out, "I can't while I am going. I'll open the door in a minute."

His pleas continued, and yet he wasn't in the hall once I opened the door. One step into the dining room soon ended my fuzzy world however. There he was, actually standing in the corner of the bare room, relieving himself! Everyone was in the adjoining living room, too busy in conversations to be aware of his action, and for a brief, panic stricken moment I thought it possible to get him to stop, to run to the bathroom before anyone saw him! However, my pleas were futile! We were in the bright lights of the dining room. No way could I block his actions by standing in front of him as I did so many nights on the streets.

Suddenly, my anxious whispers sounded as though I was shouting in a library. The chatter that once sounded thunderous was at an end, and when I turned slowly from Juan I was confronted with the shocked faces of the entire party. It was as though I was in the middle of a silent, slow motion dream; they remained in that still position for what seemed like hours! I tried to give some excuse but my lips were frozen. Instead, I attempted to pray on their sympathy with a feeble gesture of my hand. At that moment, Juan finally finished and turned around. The silent, dreamlike atmosphere continued until Juan discovered he was the center of unwanted attention.

Totally confused, he uttered weakly, "Well, Recharr,' you woul' not come ou,' ond I 'ad to pee verr-ry bodly, verr-ry bodly, Recharr.'" He was drunk, but it was apparent he was crushed when he began pacing helplessly from spot to spot in a futile attempt to avoid their eyes.

Jack came running from the kitchen, raging! Someone had obviously cued him in.

"What the hell do you think you were doing, you bastard!" were his first words. "How dare you piss on my carpeting, you prick!"

His vicious attack continued, belittling Juan with one profanity after another! Juan just stood there in a stupor. He didn't attempt to retaliate, and my heart ached at hearing him degraded so. And yet there wasn't much I could say either. He was plain drunk, though he probably drank more because of the cruising and attention Jack had given me. It shouldn't have happened and I wanted to sock Jack silly!

What made matters worse the others continued their silence, which made me realize I needed to get him out of there quickly, away from their condescending stares. I needed first to try to soak up the carpeting with dry towels to show we cared about the good things in a home. After managing to find a roll of paper towels in the kitchen, I began patting the wet area. It took some time and the entire roll, but it did the job. The carpet was finally dry without a stain.

During the process, however, Jack continued his verbal attack on Juan! My head was swimming through it all. I couldn't understand why someone didn't tell the asshole to shut up, at least Bev. Instead, she seemed to be the most appalled, and continued to stare at us as though we were some kind of freaks! Juan never attempted to retaliate either. He just stood in one spot pathetically, almost as though he just burnt down a house accidentally. So he peed on a carpet, something drinkers at a party probably would have laughed about after the initial shock, especially after I padded it dry. Finally satisfied the carpet was dry enough, I took hold of Juan, and, without a word, we were gone.

There never had been such trauma on his face before when Juan awakened the next morning. Even including the time I picked him up at the police station in Atlanta. The realization of what he did definitely was racing through his head, as well as the humiliation he suffered, and it was apparent he was having a difficult time coping with it. Jack's outrageous outburst had brought about just enough sobriety to know what he actually did. In the past, he always slept out his drunkenness, to awaken to a blank memory. It was evident he didn't want to discuss it; otherwise, he would've brought it up himself. It was best to let him be, to give him the space to work it out himself. But, oh, how I wanted to hug out the wretched misery!

A barbecue was planned for the cast that afternoon as a farewell to the summer season of shows, and Juan surprised me when he said, "Recharred, I want you to go to thot party. It would not be fair of me to osk you not to go to the last party."

He surprised me even further by agreeing to go along. None of the others in the cast were at Jack's party, so he only had to face Bev and Don. And I was so proud as he held his head up high while talking with them in his usual charming manner. Bev finally laughed over the incident.

"Do you know that after you left last night," she remarked, "Romo told Jack, 'Well, at least now you can say that you have a piss-elegant apartment!'"

I was even prouder once Romo arrived; he and Juan talked happily as though nothing had happened. Of course, Jack never showed up, and I was certain it was because of a guilty conscience.

Juan drove Svetmana back to Chicago that night and returned the next evening by train. There couldn't be a more beautiful closure to the summer season than that last week with Juan.

Chapter Thirty-One:
An Unfortunate Chapter

Life ran smoothly for Juan and me in spite of jealous insinuations occasionally by him. The bar scenes continued with his sexy talk at early morning breakfasts, and he still continued to ask politely the day after, "Do you mind, Recharred, if we take a drive because I feel so closed in…I jus' 'ave to get some fresh air. Please, would you not mind?"

The times I laid on him in bed after managing to get him home from the bars in hopes that he'd fall asleep were priceless. That wonderful, slurred little boy voice always tugged at my heart.

"Recharred, I don' wanna stay home. I wan' you ond I to go out ond 'ave a good time!"

We were now sharing the full size bed Tom left behind, which enabled me to remain next to him once he finally fell asleep so soundly. He always looked so angelic, and that was the assurance I needed to be certain he wouldn't awaken until he slept off the alcohol.

Juan actually asked to go home one of our fun nights at the Closet, but this time, I refused. I was drunker than him. I was sure he was kidding when he said he was taking my car to go home. He had to be going to a nearby bar instead. Though near sobriety occurred when I walked there to hear he never arrived. I headed home at once, and was shocked to see the car parked on our street. At that moment, I suddenly remembered that my house keys were on the same ring as my car keys! I also realized that Juan would never hear the doorbell when in a sound, drunken sleep. He didn't, and I was frantic!

I decided to try the window on the back porch; our bed was immediately next to it. Juan was sleeping in his usual sound manner when I looked in. I could touch him if the glass wasn't there. I felt sure that this time he'd awaken after a few knocks on the glass. He didn't, though, even after I began pounding violently! He never stirred. I was going crazy, and finally realized that the only way I was going to sleep in that bed was to break the window. So I found a brick in the yard.

Amazingly, all the sounds of the glass shattering and my grunts squeezing through the window made little difference to Juan. They only added more magic, sleeping dust to his eyes. He was never one to move much while asleep anyway, and it was no different that night. So I simply undressed and cuddled next to him.

"Recharred, why did you not wake me?" Juan asked, laughing hysterically.

Unfortunately the only old friends we managed to see were Chris and Sue. They owned a liquor store just down the street from the Closet. The only time we'd see them was when we stopped in. There'd be Chris in her old glory, setting up shots on the counter for the winos and herself, and then challenging them to see who could drink more. We tried calling Gloria and Pat, but their phones were disconnected. So we never saw them again. Walter and Fred said they'd call after Juan called, but we never heard from them. George and Ted had already disappeared.

We met Vic at the Closet. He was someone I knew while married. He had been in a local production with me. We wanted friends very badly and were happy when he and his equally handsome lover, Sam, became friendly. However, outside of one time that they agreed to come to a party, they never seemed interested in doubling. We soon discovered why…they were only interested in searching for someone to have a threesome with. We were confused. Why would two very handsome lovers want a threesome? I finally asked Vic, only to hear him casually admit to it as the natural thing to do. It seemed to confirm what I heard from so many others, and I began to think that it was the right thing to do in order for a relationship to survive.

Juan had always made the evening a joy whenever we were out drinking. True, he could end up a nasty bitch once he drank too much, but at least he'd always awaken the next day in a wonderful mood. So I was completely bewildered once he began accusing me of exchanging numbers after consuming only one or two drinks. Other assumptions were even worse.

"If you want to fuck, why don't you just leave with the guy," were words he said after storming over and interrupting an innocent conversation I was having with someone we both had just met at the Closet. The guy, of course, departed from my company quickly.

I admit that I was guilty of roving eyes at times. Subconsciously, I had to be retaliating to his constant accusations. He could be in his usual happy mood, and then suddenly be triggered by something I did or he thought of. He'd start with mild accusations. However, before long, his constant digging would be overbearing. A desire to live up to these accusations actually began building up in my mind and, fortunately, disappeared once he was his charming self.

I spent much of my days writing a book musical based on the nostalgic review I produced in Atlanta. The idea came to me while in Sattomon, and I completed the draft at the time. My work on it was interrupted when I was cast in a musical in a far south suburban theatre. Two hours more were added to the time I'd be gone each night. Juan accepted it, though he wasn't pleased.

"It's just another void in our lives, Recharred."

The young stage manager was quite good-looking, and surprised me with obvious cruising. Instead of ignoring them so he'd stop, my ego accepted these flirtations. It was all he needed. There I'd be, waiting backstage in the darkness to make my entrance with him directly next to me keeping tabs on my cue. Amazingly, I never made it on stage with a hard-on even though his hands had been quite busy fondling my crotch. Even more amazing, I began waiting anxiously for his fondling each night, though bad smells always turned me off sexually, and this guy had a terrible body odor! But my ego was growing too much, and I finally agreed to accept an invitation to stop over his apartment the following evening after the performance. I needed a reason for coming home late, and when I concocted one, I even included Juan in the lowdown deceit.

Juan recently had purchased a beater, and could very well drive to a location should I have car problems. He wasn't mechanically minded and would never know if my car needed to be jumped or not. I found a location on the expressway halfway between our apartment and the theater that was walking distance to an exit with an available phone booth in case Juan thought to check. My plan was to call Juan before leaving Stewert's, to tell him my car stalled and ask if he could please come to jump it. I could then leave immediately and be at the spot before Juan arrived. It was uncannily shrewd, and yet the lowest thing I had ever thought of doing in my entire life. And then to do it to someone I loved.

I got the shock of my life once Stewert undressed. I expected him to be well endowed, but totally unprepared for the sight before me! Yes, it was tremendous, but as his erection grew, it actually made a ninety degree turn in the middle!

"What am I doing here?" I asked myself. His cock looked as though some drunken surgeon attempted to sew on an extension but did it in the wrong direction! However, I felt funny to refuse to go on when I made the commitment. I finally asked to take a shower, and suggested he take one too.... At least then I wouldn't have to smell his terrible body odor. He reluctantly agreed, and that's when I should have left. I didn't however. After all, I couldn't break a commitment.

I couldn't touch it or look at it, and turned him around instead. I stood behind him, his body odor still with him, and attempted to push into the crevice of his buttocks in order to get it over quickly but was refused passage. So, to keep him from turning back to face me, I merely rubbed against his cheeks until I came. I wanted to get out of there and felt terrible when I called Juan to pick me up, and even worse when he happily agreed to come to my aid.

My drive to the designated spot was not a happy one. I could only think of the infidelity I committed again. The guilt remained with me for some time.

In fact, it has bothered me to this day. I did realize, though, that he would've laughed and quipped about it if I told him the details of the deceitful act in later years.

"See, Shifty Eyes, you were punished for your sins, ond got exoctly whot you deserved…a guy with bod body odor ond a crooked cock!"

Juan decided on taking Svetmana with us to see the spring ballet his uncle choreographed for Indiana University. He thought the world of his uncle and never wanted to miss any of his productions, and since he grew up around ballet, he always explained every move made to me. My love was opera, and when I said I'm always waiting to hear something come from the mouths of the ballet dancers, he gasped in obvious outrage.

"Aw c'mon, Recharred, how con you say something so stupid like thot!" After a pause to catch his breath, he sighed, "C'mon now, 'ave some class! Please don' ever say thot to my uncle!"

Uncle Nicolai invited us to join his party of guests for some wine and snacks after the performance, and there we were feeling quite honored to be seated with celebrities from the world of ballet. His uncle was seated at the head of the table, and I somehow got the chair at the opposite end. Svetmana was to my right and Juan was next to her. Seated to my left was an absolutely beautiful and exquisite young woman who gave up dancing early in her career, and now operated a renowned ballet school.

It felt wonderful being part of such a celebrated group, especially since I was enjoying a fascinating conversation with the lovely woman. She talked in much of the same manner as I did, using her hands for gesturing as well as facial expressions. So I felt quite comfortable with her.

"You know, Richard, this little girl across from me is making me very nervous," she whispered after some length. "She has been mimicking every word, gesture, and facial expression of mine since our conversation began. I feel as though she is making fun of me!"

I quickly turned to check and saw exactly what she meant. Svetmana was nodding her head wildly about while rolling her eyes, and mimicking the woman as though she was some kind of idiot! At the same time, her hands and fingers were fluttering about at a frantic pace! And she didn't even think to stop after realizing I caught her in the act! I rose and stepped behind Juan who was talking with someone to his right.

"Juan, Svetmana has been making fun of Victoria," I whispered. "It's really embarrassing her. Will you please tell Svetmana to stop!"

So what did he do? He simply turned to Svetmana, and while gently shaking his finger, he said, "Now, Svetmana, please do not imitate people. Thot is not nice to do, my darling."

I felt even more livid when he then cuddled her while she gave me one of her spiteful grins.

It took years to realize why Svetmana made fun of people…. As a child, she tried to copy her father's masterful ability to imitate, but because of her inability to love, everything came off insulting. All the comedy was lost because her intention was to be nasty. And since Juan always was afraid of losing her, discipline was rarely used. Endira, of course, never believed in it.

Auditions were going nowhere, and I finally managed to get a part time job as a bartender in the neighborhood with the help of Domina, an actress friend who lived close by. Domina was pretty and well built, and yet her greatest asset seemed to be the fire and spirit within her.

"Recharred, she is so bubbly ond so cute," Juan said, really taking to her, "a real blond spitfire!" And that was proved once she tried to break up a fight at the bar. My contribution was to stay behind the bar and watch. I certainly didn't want to lose one of my front caps again. She did manage to get everything under control, though receiving a bloody nose in the process.

We began auditioning together, and in the process became close friends. And what was so great was that her friendship with Juan was equally as strong. I was certain she wasn't aware of my true relationship with Juan; her total frankness would've questioned us immediately if she suspected. I felt the love the three of us shared, however surely would allow her to accept it. So I planned to tell her during a slow time at the bar. Then, when I was just about to tell her, a crowd came in. Later, I had second thoughts.

Tears were in my eyes the day I walked into my old home and saw Martina looking so beautiful in front of the fireplace. My little Miss America was about to marry Don. I was in rehearsal for a minor role in a musical at the time and was grateful when the director gave me the day off. Of course, I wouldn't have accepted the role if he didn't. No way would I miss walking her down the aisle. And then after walking her down the aisle, I went up to the choir loft to sing.

Juan suddenly began tormenting me with jealous accusations while sober, and I was completely bewildered since there was no reason for it. It had to stop, but how? I finally came up with a solution, and it undoubtedly initiated from the crazy relationships I heard about at the bars. I thought it would put the accusations to an end. However, I was dead wrong. His shocked expression quickly told me that I was a fool to suggest we each have a night out to do as we please. Not a word was said and yet the hurt in his eyes clearly asked, "Recharred, how con you even suggest such a thing if you love me like you say you do? How can you suggest something like that when I love you so much?"

He remained silent for a while except for the incredible disbelief in his face. I realized my mistake and attempted to fluff it off as a joke, but he could only pray on what I had said....

"Aw, no, Recharred, thot is whot you want to do," he said, finally breaking his silence. His show of contempt for my idiotic suggestion continued at fast speed, "So it is exactly whot we are gonna do! Yes, Recharred, we will 'ave our nights out alone!"

After a pause he smiled slyly and said, "Aw, yes, Sir, are *we* gonna 'ave our nights out!"

The sinister smile on his face clearly indicated what was in store for me!

Nothing happened the first time we went out alone, and I think we both were relieved. It was the opportunity I needed. So I tried to convince him to drop the foolish idea.

"No, Recharred, it is too late! We are going through with it because thot is whot you want! SO THOT IS WHOT YOU ARE GONNA GET, MY GOOD MAN!"

Wonderful times still continued in our lives, though. After all, we loved each other. However, I still realized how quickly he could explode should the plan come to mind. And that was exactly what happened on one of those good time evenings. We were having a fantastic time. The arrangement never was mentioned. In fact, our happy high continued throughout breakfast at the Golden Nugget. Even more sweeter, he didn't go into any of his dirty talk.

"Recharred, would it not be nice to go to another bar," Juan pleaded once we walked out of the restaurant. I was totally unprepared for his angry response after I told him it was too late. He even bypassed his usual boyish manner of pleading.

"Okay, Recharred, so you want to go out with other guys instead! Is thot whot you want to do?" he shouted, the anger in his voice mounting. "Okay, Recharred, then you do not need me!"

As he struggled to remove his gold band, I assumed I was about to get it back. Instead, he threw it wildly into the night! After a moment of shock, I scurried out in a desperate attempt to retrieve it! Juan, meanwhile, turned away and continued crossing aimlessly. I was frantic, but still realized that he wasn't aware of the late night traffic speeding on the street. He was more important than a gold band. So I abandoned the search and returned to him to keep him from getting hit by a car. He was obstinate, but I finally managed to guide him across and home to bed.

As always, Juan was his chipper self in the morning. The entire ring incident was a blank. We were certain we'd find it in the daylight. After hours and days of searching, however, it was not found. The scenario was replayed on a later date with a gold chain I had given him.

The brighter and definitely beautiful side of the seesaw was still very much a part of our lives. Chicagofest was in progress, and Juan was very excited because Crystal Gayle was one of the guest performers. He hated to be in large crowds, and yet he wanted to go.

"Aw, Recharred, we 'ave to go see her! Aw she is so bea-u-ti-ful! Remember when she sat next to me on the plane, Recharred…thot time I came to see you in Austin when she kept buying me drinks! Do you remember, Recharred?"

I smiled, recalling the time. "Juan, how could I ever forget that mischievous look on your face and that catwalk of yours as you came towards me in the airport."

He glowed with pride watching Crystal Gayle perform. One would have thought she was one of his closest friends. There he was…so proud that thousands were appreciating her, and the marvel of it all was sharing it with him!

I was surprised with a call from a director in New York. Months before, I had mailed my resume after hearing that *My Fait Lady* was to be revived with Rex Harrison. I never expected to hear from them. He quickly mentioned that he was impressed with my resume and because I had played opposite Ray Milland back in 1968.

"Would it be possible for you to be in New York tomorrow morning, Rick…to audition for the role of Karpathy? I have you scheduled for eleven thirty."

I should've been excited, but all that was on my mind was the expense. So I asked, "Am I guaranteed the part, and will I be reimbursed for the airfare?"

He quickly told me he couldn't promise anything, but added, "I really would like you to make it, Rick. You seem to be just what I am looking for to do the role."

The fact that the director was calling instead of a secretary or stage manager didn't sink in. This was a Broadway director calling me, and yet I was still apprehensive.

"Give it some serious thought, Rick," he urged, "but please call us by six o'clock tonight to confirm." It never entered my mind that this was the chance I was striving for. So I decided against it after hanging up. I couldn't afford the airfare, and Juan would be upset besides.

"Recharred, thot is big time! You should 'ave said yes," Juan said instead. Completely enthralled, he added, "Is thot not whot you 'ave always wanted all your life?"

I was quite moved with his compassion as he tried to convince me to take the early bird flight, and surprised when he told Domina everything once she stopped by.

"Rick, do you know what that would mean?" she asked excitedly, "Do you, Rick? If you got the part, and it sounds like the director really wants you to audition, which is ninety percent of the battle, you'd make it to *Broadway*! If you couldn't afford the plane fare, why didn't you take off in your car after he called? Aw, Rick, if you don't go, you are crazy!"

And there was Juan, totally agreeing with her, reprimanding me for not going. It was finally settled, I was going. We'd take from Peter to pay Paul.

Juan's positive attitude amazed me, but then he and Domina always had agreed on everything. In fact, they were two peas in a pod…each loving to kid the other. She had kidded the hell out of him about the contents of a bottle of Jack Daniels that he replaced with tea and he just laughed. She and I had returned from an audition and when she spotted the bottle sitting on the buffet, she asked for some on the rocks.

"Rick, this is not Jack Daniels," she gasped after one sip, "It tastes like plain tea!"

I hurried through the horrendous heat of New York only to be told by the secretary that the role was already cast.

"I'm so sorry," she said, "but you never called to confirm and they were anxious to cast all the principals. Oh, it is such a shame because I know he was very excited about you!"

She suggested I audition for the understudy role of Doolittle since I was there. It was still open. She called the theater to let them know I was on my way. So there I was, dressed to kill, headed to read for the role of a slobbering drunk.

Cockney accent never was one I mastered, and since I didn't even have a chance to run through the lines, I felt my chances were bleak. Exactly that happened. My reading was terrible, and yet it felt as though they were laying down the red carpet for me! Surprisingly, he let me sing all of the lengthy *If I Were a Rich Man*, and then raved about my interpretation of the song.

"Rick, why don't you read the Karpathy part while you are here? One never knows when we may need a replacement," he called out, surprising me more. This couldn't be New York!

I was proud when they praised my acting and singing talents, but the only real thing that mattered was when I returned home and Juan sighed, "I feel so bod, Recharred. I would have been so proud if you got to do the role on Broadway, so proud!"

The bridge in Juan's mouth had cracked in half, and he continually complained of pain with the new one the Army dental lab made for him. So it wasn't long before I witnessed another tossing spree in to the darkness after leaving the Golden Nugget. He had to wear something, though, and began using the two pieces of the broken bridge. I'm sure it wasn't comfortable, but it did give him a chance to do more theatrics for me. At any given moment, if I happened to look his way, there he'd be…the two teeth hanging from his lips with a crazy, idiotic glare on his face!

It was odd, but the few times we went out separately, I never connected. So I somehow thought that Juan didn't either. I'd try to get him to drop the idea but he refused. He was determined to make me suffer. I returned home depressed on one of our nights out in hopes of finding Juan there. He wasn't. I sat in the living room darkness trying to comprehend it all when he walked in swiftly. The dim light from the kitchen wasn't enough to see me, however, and just as I was about to call out, I saw the shadow of guy following closely behind him! In that distraught moment, I saw them disappear into the spare bedroom and the door closed quickly!

He brazenly brought home a trick! It wasn't enough to merely tell me about it. The rest of the evening has remained a blank in my mind to this day. I had to have wiped it out of my mind as I did with other misfortunate incidents in our lives! We never talked of it afterwards, though it was obvious that Juan was angry with himself the next day as well as with me.

I wanted the arrangement at an end, and yet I allowed my ego to once again get the best of me. I was cruised continually by one young guy at the Closet but never reciprocated because I realized Juan was always aware of it. Then, on one of my lone outings, I ran into him. We talked and I finally accepted an invitation to go to his apartment. However, we only talked, nothing else happened. Though it preyed on my mind. Why was Juan able to do it, and not me?

He had given me his phone number and insisted I call some time in the future. His plea for a future meeting began to eat away at me, inflating my ego enough to want to see it through.

"Juan, I'm gonna run to the El station to buy some cigarettes," I said after dinner. My intention was to call the guy. So there I was…standing in a phone booth, about to hang up after several rings. And who is standing in front of the booth? There was Juan, glaring at me with a smug expression. Our minds ran as one. How did I expect to hide anything from him?

"Whot is the matter, Recharred, do you 'ave something to hide?" he said sarcastically once my guilt allowed me to open the door. "Why don't you call your tricks from the house? Ofter all, we 'ave thot arrangement you osked for!" I could say nothing but to accept his logic, and his torment went on for days. I never called the guy again, totally ignoring him at the bars. It took some time for Juan's hostility to cool down, but when it did, life once again became a joy.

Juan suggested we be tested for venereal diseases. I saw no reason but agreed. And then the beautiful reflection in our mirror was shattered again; Juan was diagnosed with syphilis! Besides his treatment, I received shots, as well as counseling sessions with him. It preyed on his mind, and he wouldn't let up! It was my doing because of the arrangement, and it did no good to remind him of my pleas to stop it. He continued to torment me. I became racked with guilt at the thought of it. If I never suggested an arrangement, he never would've contacted the disease.

Finally, we agreed to end the arrangement and I was elated. Our life appeared to be back to normal again. At the same time, I realized that the Juan I knew had to have eruptions when recalling disastrous scenarios, especially while drunk. These eruptions didn't matter so long as the beautiful harmony overpowered them going into 1981.

Spring arrived, and then to my dismay, flowers weren't the only things blooming. Juan's elephant memory began sprouting one recollection after another of the arrangement, and the upsetting thing was he said them when sober! He'd accuse me of things I hadn't committed and go into a rage! There was no reasoning with him, and his continued badgering drove me up a wall! The good times were now outweighed by the bad, and I almost believed I no longer loved him.

"Recharred, I am gonna move out," were Juan's first words returning home from work. "I 'ave found on apartment not far from here." I was stunned, but remained silent as he went on, "I think it is for the best, Recharred, for the both of us." I had to realize that he was the love of my life, and I his, and yet I didn't object. Instead, a feeling of relief came over me; no longer would I be antagonized with his vicious accusations. It never occurred to me that this could be another one of his tests. How could I not remember?

Chapter Thirty-Two:
Apart and yet Together

Juan's move in April was an amiable one, and undoubtedly because we were experiencing a needed relief. There were no more doubts; neither of us had to account for every moment of the day. There also was the excitement of decorating a new apartment to occupy his mind. Therefore, because of his stubborn inability to set aside his jealousies and my refusal to insist he stay, we found ourselves in a scenario that totally disregarded all the vows we had made.

Tom had left his couch in the bedroom as well as the base table. So, besides one of the platform rockers and footstool I insisted he take, the living room wasn't empty. He purchased a bed ensemble, and since the place needed so much more, I added the table and chairs from the club as well as pictures and decorative pieces. The brass bumblebee was the first thing he placed on his glass top coffee table. He smiled as he admired it, but with a definite sign of sadness in his eyes.

"Aw, Recharred, I am gonna buy a big entertainment center to fill that wall," he said. "I am so glad because then I will 'ave such a bea-u-ti-ful apartment! Don' you think?"

It certainly wasn't as beautiful as any we had together, but I still agreed. In about a week, he had his twelve-foot wall unit. He appeared to be happy, and I guess I felt the same. After all, we were still seeing one another almost every day. We just weren't living together, though I often stayed overnight. And most important, his jealous rages finally came to an end.

My times alone gave me the opportunity to reminisce. I remembered those times he was so dynamically proud and yet funny…and sometimes humble.

"If you were born in Lithuania, how did you get a Spanish name like Juan?" I had asked.

"Because, Recharred, my name was Jonas, which is John in English and Juan in Spanish. So once we moved to Buenos Aries everyone called me Juan." I had liked it and asked if I could call him by the name and quickly heard, "No, Recharred, do not call me thot because I am *JUAN*!"

And I recalled how I interrupted his conversations habitually at the bars the first couple of years, driving him crazy! Since I always told my life story immediately when asked, I always thought it my duty to correct him if he wasn't telling his as it was. Hearing his accent, everyone would always ask where he was from. He'd always boast, "I'm from Buenos Aires, Argentina!"

Invariably, I'd butt in and say, "Oh, but Juan is not really from there. He was born in Lithuania." When I continued on with his history, he'd maneuver himself next to me…put his arm around me as I continued rattling on, and then surprise me with a hard pinch on my butt! It wasn't that he never told me not to tell his story, I just never listened.

Once we were alone, I always could expect to hear, "Recharred, why are you such a blabber mouth! Let me tell my story if I want to tell anyone! If you 'ave to talk about something, tell them about your background with all the pasta ond salami! Ond you con also tell them about the screaming all of you do when you are together, like you jus' got off the boat!" Though he was angry, it never came off as malicious…just funny!

A recollection of something I never learned not to do had brought a smile to my face. Juan never stopped whenever I called out should he be a distance ahead. He walked faster instead.

"Juan, why wouldn't you stop and wait for me?" was always my inquiry once I caught up to him breathlessly.

"Because, Blanche, I told you never to call out my name like thot in public!" he'd snarl, picking up his pace, "You sound ond look jus' like a queen calling out, *Juuaan! Juuaan!*"

I recalled the time we were living in my nephew's condo. Dee asked me to stay with my father while she, Dino, and my nephew went on a trip to Europe. Pa's colostomy was never reversed because the doctor botched up, and he had been having a difficult time coping with it. Juan spent much of his free time with me. One of the evenings after Pa went to bed, Juan talked me into going out to the bars, only to be confronted by him when we returned.

"What are you doing, Richie, leaving me all alone alla night!" Pa shouted standing in the darkness of the dining room. His finger trembling, he pointed to the area of the colostomy bag, "I 'ave this crutch ona me ond you a leava me alla alone!"

He then surprised me with, "Ond I do nota understand a why you don' a go outa with a woman! You should a find yourself a good woman!" It was dark, and yet I had been certain Juan's face turned every color of the rainbow. Never had he sobered up so quickly! The next day, I realized Pa didn't mean it as we took it. If he had, he would have mentioned it again.

The landlord agreed to allow me to stay and just pay my half of the rent until I finished his apartment. So, if I wasn't working in his apartment, I was busy with my musical. Juan was forced to junk his car, which I considered fortunate since it kept him from driving while drinking. My Toyota then died and I was forced to sell it for a song. I almost cried when they drove away my Lotus Blossom. My brother-in-law, Frank, knew of a clean 1978 Buick Century, and I bought it.

It wasn't unusual to have Juan calling in his slurred, drunken voice to ask to go out dancing, though it suddenly seemed to become routine. Sometimes, he was out at the bars and sometimes still at home. It was hilariously funny hearing him try not to let on that he was already drunk. That lovable little boy voice always denied it once I remarked that he was drunk, immediately chuckling afterwards. Of course, I never refused. Juan always came up with an excuse why I should go to his apartment instead of mine at evening's end. In fact, he never set foot in it again. He obviously didn't want to be reminded of the love nest he wanted us to have for a long time.

Juan became friends with a couple of guys he met at Little Jim's, a bar on Halstead Street known as an easy pick up place for tricks. It caused me a great deal of worry since I no longer was aware of his whereabouts. His calls to go out became fewer and fewer, which meant I never was certain whether he got home safely. So I found myself out looking for him, sometimes waiting in his foyer through the night. Dancing wasn't a feature at Little Jim's, which also meant he couldn't dance off some of the alcohol, and constant drinking always made a vegetable of him…. There were many of these sleepless nights because I wouldn't give up!

Little Jim's closed at 4:00 A.M. and reopened three hours later. If I didn't find Juan in my search at night, I'd realize he very likely would return after tricking or whatever; the alcohol in his body couldn't wear off in so short a time. There were times he never showed up, but the mornings that he did were heartbreaking. He'd be totally wasted, a vegetable! I'd beg to take him home, but his belligerency made it near impossible to persuade him. There were times, though, that I succeeded, and only because I didn't come on too strong. I had to revert to my old tactics, to tell him nicely that we were going out for breakfast. However, sometimes that didn't even work. His keen, amazing sense, though he was absolutely plastered, realized my coy intentions and he'd turn from me belligerently and head for the bar again. I'd lose my patience and walk away in disgust. It didn't matter to him; he'd just continue into the bar. I'd finally be next to him in the bar, trying desperately to wait for that compassion of his and the moment he was ready to leave.

I was baffled after meeting his new friends; how could Juan get involved with such alcoholic, low life? It was especially disturbing since he actually was spending time with Cal while sober. Cal lived only a few doors from Little Jim's, and since he was such a sorry alcoholic, there always was someone willing to see that he arrived home safely. I then realized that Juan, very likely, slept off many of his binges there, too.

I found Cal to be quite nice in his sober state the evening Juan invited me to go along to his apartment, though I realized he'd soon be drunk again with all the drinks he was downing. He also was trying to get Juan to do the same. It was also apparent that he felt more than just a platonic relationship for Juan. I was appalled at the idea of Juan sitting in his apartment in such a relaxed manner. Ma and Pa Kettle's place had to look like a palace compared to the pig pen we were sitting in! That is, once we managed to clear off a couple of chairs.

I finally attributed it to the fact that Cal accepted all the verbal abuse Juan freely threw at him. There he was, giving him one insult after another, "Why don' you take time to clean this place. It is so filthy ond messy, my good woman!" and Cal just smiled!

Dee's call to ask, "Would you like to move into Pa's apartment, Rich?" was perfect timing; I just finished the work for the landlord. They had purchased a house in the suburbs, and Pa had moved in with them. Young Dino was living in their first floor apartment.

"So you want me to be burglarized instead?" I asked jokingly after she explained that a friend of my nephew's was living there but moved out because he was robbed twice.

"No, Rich," she quickly replied, "I don't think you would have that problem because you have such erratic hours and that would keep Dino from being robbed too."

Once she mentioned I wouldn't have to pay rent, I quickly agreed. It was especially great because I just began working again at the banquet facility near her house as bartender.

Meanwhile, Juan's contract with the National Guard wasn't renewed, and in his fear of not being able to pay the rent, he decided to move out of his apartment. I was overjoyed instead of being sorry; it would break the ties with Cal and his gang. I tried to talk him into moving in with me but he felt uncomfortable with it.

"Recharred, how will thot look if I also move in ond don' pay rent? Maybe later, when I can afford to pay." So he moved in with his folks.

It was early summer, and whenever Juan could borrow his father's car, he was over. We hadn't been this happy for some time. Juan loved the backyard to sunbathe in, and of course, I was in a shady spot, pecking away on my typewriter….

Juan and I still shared beautiful love together, and yet we never talked about a commitment again. We were free to do as we pleased without reservations. I knew he had tricked far more than I had because I ran into one constantly in the foyer of his old apartment. So I finally convinced myself that I had as much right as he. A freedom came over me with this apartment, though I needed to be careful because my nephew lived below. So there wasn't an abundance of tricks during those nine months. However, one trick became steady, a young guy who began getting serious. He begged for a relationship, but I refused. I finally stopped seeing him entirely.

Juan was hurting for money because he wasn't receiving unemployment benefits. He talked of it in that fast-paced manner of his constantly.

"Recharred, I can not understond why I am not able to collect! They say it is because I worked for the government ond I am not entitled to any."

I decided to teach him how to tend bar, and got him a job at the banquet hall. It was wonderful since we almost always worked the same bar. Of course, after a few drinks at the end of the shift, we'd be out on the town.

New owners took over the banquet facility, and added bingo games during the week. So we began working the food concession on separate shifts. A friend of Mick, one of the owners, always seemed to be on hand for every bingo session as well as banquets. Don had a slight build with a receding brown hairline, and less than average looks. And yet he walked around as though he was the cat's meow.

"Thot guy has to be gay because he acts ond looks likes a queen," Juan insisted.

Ironically, he still took Juan's insults and mimicking. In fact, they really hit it off well. In the opposite corner, whenever I tried to strike up a conversation with Don, a wall fell between us.

Juan finally got himself a beater, which made it possible to come over often. So he sunned while I kept busy on my musical. I mentioned to him that I was itching quite a bit, and without a blink of an eye, he said, "Recharred, you probably 'ave crabs. Now you know you should be more careful who you go with."

His scolding continued while shaking his finger, "Aw, Recharred, all you care about is thot cock between your legs!"

There were no signs of distress as he searched my chest, and he laughed when I showed embarrassment. It was as though my tricking was now accepted....

The Army reserve finally picked up Juan as a recruiter in the fall, but he still worked the banquets. In fact, he was called more than me. His friendship with Don very well could have been the reason. On one such night, I waited for him to come to the house after work so we could go out to the bars. However, one o'clock struck and he hadn't arrived. Initially, I thought the party might be a late one but when I called there was no answer. I walked over to be sure, and when I found the place dark, I became a basket case! I began trembling at the thought that he possibly was attacked since he always went to the adjacent convenience store to change his tips for larger bills. The neighborhood wasn't the safest, and I had thoughts of someone spotting him coming out while counting his money as he always did. A recent murder and body dumping in the area actually triggered me to look apprehensively into a nearby dumpster.

I remained a basket case even though informed by the police that no violence had occurred when I called. I was about to call them again in the morning when Juan walked in.

"Where have you been?" I asked, "Why didn't you call me to tell me that you weren't coming last night? I was worried sick all night."

The heavy weight was relieved at last, but I still torpedoed one question after another at him! I was especially livid once he laughed it off after telling me that it was an early party and he had gone out with Don and Mick! I was even more outraged when he announced casually that the three of them ended up in Don's bed together!

"Aw, Recharred, thot Mick's skin was jus' like velvet—jus' like velvet!" he boasted. We were no longer lovers, but I was bothered. It took some time to realize his motive for so colorful a picture.

The house had been up for sale for some time, and finally sold to a black family. I stayed throughout the bitter winter, and was content since Juan came over quite a bit. That spring of 1982, I agreed to take Geena's offer to move in with them, though it wasn't conducive for my relationship with Juan. He always was hung up on coming over too much; they might suspect something. So, we didn't see each other often during the week. To keep busy, I typed into the wee hours of the morning until I finally completed my musical.

I was cast in a musical at the same dinner theatre in Indianapolis, and the day I was leaving, Juan called to meet at a designated spot. Since he was also living with his parents, there was never a chance for us to make love during my tenure at Geena's. So it wasn't surprising when he suggested we check into a motel for a farewell roll in the sheets. It was at that time that he said he had been spending much of his time with a crowd he met through Don.

Though our lovemaking was still exciting, I felt a bit of indifference in his behavior before and afterwards. It was almost mechanical, and his abrupt departure convinced me of it. He did, however, manage a bit of sarcasm that clearly insinuated that I was deserting him again.

Ironically, the girl playing the lead was from Dallas, and once I mentioned Joe from the *Mousetrap* cast, I heard, "What do you mean he was married? I never knew Joe to be married. In fact he was my roommate for a while. He was gay, and I never knew him to do anything but *drag*!"

Oh, how badly I wanted that hypocritical mouth and face before me!

Yes, I practiced my sexual freedom with a few tricks during that six-week run without any guilt, though it always was apparent afterwards that they never filled my empty pocket. One night, I somehow drew the attention of a young Greek God! To say that he was tall, dark, and handsome wouldn't even be enough! He was gorgeous, and when I discovered that he was actually cruising me, I was elated! I finally discovered that he was with a group, and all of them using their hands to talk. He surprised me with a motion to dance, and when I met him on the floor, I realized he apparently kept his rhythm by feeling the vibrations.

I knew nothing about sign language, which made it difficult to communicate. So we glared at one another instead. Our awkwardness finally was resolved once he managed to get a pad and pencil to write with from the bartender. We were off to a motel once I read his first words.

There had been no exaggeration! I thought I was in a room with a Greek God once he stripped! A perfectly carved Adonis! His broad, smooth chest and massive shoulders and arms were not overly muscular, which I disliked anyway. Even more exciting, he was endowed like a bull! Words certainly weren't needed. My eyes told all. I caressed his body and was awed with the smoothness of his skin. How could I ever satisfy such a dream man? My nervousness had to show as I watched him lower himself on the bed. There was no doubt, he was a Greek God! Still nervous, I managed to get into position to enjoy him to the fullest. All I could think of was a night of heavenly bliss. And then his body was so perfect I was almost afraid to touch.

My fantasy of slow, beautiful sex came to a sudden, abrupt end, however. There was no need to worry of what to do. He took care of those illusions with one quick, powerful motion! There I was, suddenly on my stomach, and before I could even think of turning myself back I felt the excruciating pain of his enormous erection ramming into me!

I tried desperately to push him off, screaming, "NO! NO! I beg of you, please stop! Please take it out!" His firm pressure on my shoulders held fast, however. There I was, flapping my arms every which way, screaming for him to stop…not realizing he couldn't hear a word!

He had to think my arms were fluttering in sheer delight! Fortunately, his youth turned out to be my only salvation; it was over in minutes. I was in excruciating pain, barely able to move aside once he jumped off, but I knew I had to. I also knew I needed to get out of there, especially after he patted my shoulder and smiled in an obvious gesture of approval. There was no way he was getting seconds and thirds!

I moved into a second floor flat in the suburb of Cicero on returning to Chicago in May, very pleased that the rent was so reasonable. I was also anxious to present a backer's audition of my musical and after assembling a cast, including myself, I rented a north side theater.

Juan was on hand to help that evening. We were further surprised when fifty prospective investors showed up. He loved the show and was so excited.

"Just think, Recharred, if even only ten invest, you should 'ave enough to start production!"

Only two signed pledges, however, and by the time I followed up with calls, they were no longer interested. So I put the show on the shelf and focused in other directions.

I was near broke, but whenever Juan called in his slurred voice, I was on my way to meet him. There were times, though, that he called and talked on incessantly only to hang up suddenly.

"I did thot? Recharred, I don' believe it," he always said in disbelief when I called it to his attention the next day.

I accepted a job to tend bar in an exclusive restaurant Mick purchased on the north side of Chicago. My social life came to an end, though, since I worked until 4:00 A.M., but I didn't care. The extravagant tips of waitresses and bartenders from other restaurants ended eight years of drought.

Juan came to the bar just two times because it was too long a drive. Except for occasional outings together, the telephone became our only means of communication. And then that, suddenly, became difficult because of a Valentine card I had sent him. I had made certain it was not a mushy one in case his parents saw it. However, I hadn't realized that his father opened all his mail before he got home.

"Recharred, as soon as I got home my father was holding up the card," Juan said, calling to reprimand me, "ond he shouted out, 'Whot man sends another man a Valentine's card?' Aw, Recharred, I did not know whot to say!"

When I sent out the card, I had completely forgotten what Juan told me months earlier…that his father found out he was gay through a mutual friend of his and Endira's. She had told him about Juan's real relationship with me. I never knew if he was telling the truth because he always had a way of fabricating stories, and especially since I never even met her. I finally figured that it was it true that Endira told her. She had been at the club in Atlanta in the afternoon a few times, and had to have seen the rack with gay magazines. I never had liked the idea of her being there.

"Recharred, she knows about the club already because Svetmana told her," were Juan's words when I objected to her visits to the club.

Juan had informed me of the verbal harassment his father handed him each time I called.

"Recharred, I feel very bad when he does it! It is a very difficult situation!"

I became aware of that same feeling when I called one day and his father answered.

"Juan no home, you cocksucker!" was his response when I asked for Juan. Of course, I had hung up quickly.

"Aw, no, Recharred," Juan insisted when I told him. "I don' believe it! My father would not say thot word!" I then reminded him that I certainly couldn't have mistaken that word. Thereafter, I was forced to change my voice when calling—Richard no longer existed!

Chapter Thirty-Three: Separate Ways

Don managed the restaurant for Mick, and though he was very courteous, I still felt that wall between us. Barry appeared on the scene one Sunday, assisting Don as host for brunches. He was tall, dark, and quite good-looking, and his affable smile and chuckle made it easy to like him. Since Don was part of the crowd Juan was socializing with, I learned that he and Barry had been lovers and were in the process of moving in together again.

Vera, a tall, large-boned girl about thirty-five years old with long blond hair, never missed a night at the bar. She was a waitress and always showed up shortly after midnight. It was evident that she never fussed with her hair, except to shampoo and sometimes tie it back in a ponytail. She didn't wear makeup, though it wasn't needed since her face had a natural loveliness. She had to have been a tomboy in her youth. And though she drank like a man and had a deep and low-pitched voice, I was certain she was definitely a woman. Inevitably, near the end of the evening, she'd be totally wasted. More often than not, she'd be accompanied by a stone-faced guy, much older than her, a bartender at the same restaurant. I soon learned that they were lovers and had recently split up, and that he was trying desperately to reconcile. Their arguments were so loud that it was a relief once he stormed out. They finally discontinued coming in together, and he'd finally leave after trying in vain to strike up a conversation with her.

It became very apparent that Vera was attracted to me; her eyes never deviated from my direction. And before long, she actually began telling me that she liked me, and that I was very handsome. I was embarrassed, and yet my ego was lifted, and it wasn't long before I actually found myself waiting for her to walk in with that big smile of hers.

I didn't realize it but my life was suddenly heading in another direction. I wasn't going to gay bars, so there wasn't any tricks. In fact, Juan and I seldom went out or, for that matter, talked on the phone. When we did talk, he seemed to relish rubbing in the fact that he was doing so many things with his new friends. And he was too stubborn to invite me along. However, it never seemed to matter; I was too busy making money at last, as well as dealing with the fact that I was being wooed by Vera.

Jacque and Bill married in October, and again, I ran up to the choir loft to sing after walking her down the aisle. She looked beautiful in her traditional hoop wedding dress, wearing her own headpiece attached to Martina's train-length veil. Martina, Don, Mike, and Nicky were all part of the huge bridal party, and I couldn't help but think of what a good-looking family I had.

Juan looked dashing in his dark blue suit, arriving at the reception with Svetmana. We hadn't seen one another for some time, and there was that same feeling hitting the pit of my belly once our eyes met. As always, I ignored it, too proud to admit that I still loved him deeply.

"Why is that bandage on your neck, Juan?" I inquired when I finally approached his table.

"I had a very large cyst on my neck, Recharred," he replied, "ond I guess it was pretty bad because it was touching my throat. So it had to be removed." As always, he lost no time reminding me of my failure to call when I reprimanded him for not calling to let me know.

He looked so regal as he sat at the table, just as he always did once we were seated for dinner, and I swallowed hard. Remarkably, there was that magic casting a spell over us again as our conversation continued. No one else seemed to exist. And yet we lay the feelings aside.

Then it happened: Vera asked to remain while I cleaned and counted the receipts of the bar. I agreed, and wasn't surprised when she asked to stop by her place for a nightcap. Her intentions were quite obvious, and I somehow wanted a try at it. After all, it was years since I went to bed with a woman, but a couple of drinks should build up a sexual desire. So I began chugging them down while I counted the receipts.

Still, "Will I be able to perform?" kept running through my head, especially if I lost my high. There was no chance of that, however. Another cocktail was placed in my hand the moment we arrived at her apartment. And then another, and another as we sat on the couch, wrapped in each other's arms, kissing passionately!

We eventually tore each other's clothes off and plunged ourselves in her twin bed, rubbing our bodies together. I was so drunk and so awkward that I had to be a replica of Peter Sellers as Inspector Closseau. There I was, pumping away on top of her, trying valiantly to get it hard enough to poke it in, but it wasn't happening. The alcohol probably had something to do with it, along with the fact that, though she was full-bodied with broad shoulders, her tits were like fried eggs, and a well-busted woman was what always turned me on. So, no matter how passionate I tried to be, I couldn't get it up. Vera, on the other hand, wasn't even aware of it. She was in complete ecstasy, furiously rubbing herself against my crotch! The passionate kissing finally managed to arouse me enough to feel a complete erection, and just as I was about to ram into her she went into a wild orgasm. Never had I been with anyone who clawed and scratched so wildly, and there I was, limp again and completely turned off. However, Vera was sighing as though she was just laid by a tremendous bull!

I realized if she continued to be that wild each time we made love, it would always turn me off, and yet I went on with the relationship. I wanted it to work, and I finally came up with a solution. I relaxed enough to get it hard and in quickly, and because of my fast wick, I'd ejaculate just before she went into her manic attacks.

Vera loved to pamper me, and I enjoyed it because I never had that much attention from a woman! If I didn't spend the night I'd sometimes drive the long distance just to be with her during the day. She loved to cook for me, and always talked of how nice it would be to live together.

I also must admit that I was pretty excited after the shock of hearing that she hadn't yet gotten her period. The thought of becoming a father again almost felt good, especially since I was aware of how much she loved me. I also felt that I loved her enough to see it through. There was no need to hide this relationship. She did finally get her period, however. Thereafter, we used precautionary measures, though her wild clawing continued to bother me. I found myself hurrying to come, and completely unable to savor the lay once her wild panting and clawing began. And no matter how much I talked to her about it, she couldn't control herself. Still, I liked her enough to give serious thought to the possibility of moving in with her, also spending a great deal of time selecting a Christmas gift for her.

Juan and I didn't communicate much the initial months of 1983, and when we did, I somehow never thought to tell him about Vera. Subconsciously, I still loved him, and the fear of hurting him was always on my mind.

Vera's wildness in bed finally became too overbearing, and along with the realization of my sexual preference, I decided to break off my relationship with her. She was much too nice a person and didn't need someone in her life who'd possibly revert to his gay lifestyle. I saw no reason to mention any of this as the reason, only her wild climaxes, as well as her excessive drinking.

At the same time, I was cast in Mousetrap again at a suburban dinner theatre and had to quit the bar. It was a blessing since I wasn't able to cope with Vera's face once she came in.

Juan called to inform me that he was coming to the theater with Barry and another friend. He already saw the play many times when I toured with it, and yet he was coming to see it again!

He managed to wait after the performance and introduced Marina, a slim blond about six foot five with a deep voice. Her mannerisms were also a bit masculine. In his usual fast-paced manner, and quite indifferently, he went on to say that they were in a hurry to leave because he wanted to dance at the gay disco across from the theater. He never asked me to join them, but it was obvious he wanted me to make the move. Of course, I didn't hesitate to ask.

He continued with his indifferent manner once I joined them, but I knew Juan. His eyes never lied! He was happy we were together again.

Barry, as always, giggled at every word Juan or I said. Marina smiled but didn't say much.

"What 's with this Marina?" I inquired once she and Barry went out on the floor to dance.

"Con't you tell, Rechared?" he replied with a loud, choking laugh, "She had a sex change, but she never completed it because she has no tits! Ond, Rechared, look how she walks! Jus' like a man! But she is really a very nice person, ond I like her very much!" Once he choked on his laughter, I knew he'd warm up, and he did. It was like old times that evening, and yet I went on with my life without him.

"Hi, I'm Daniel Rusk," greeted a smiling face after I turned to respond to a tap on my shoulder at Dandy's. It was Sunday at the very popular piano bar, and especially crowded after the gay pride parade. "I was wondering if you would like to chat for a while?"

The atmosphere was so festive, why would I refuse. I found him to be quite gregarious, and really began enjoying everything he had to say. More enjoyably, after each sentence, his white teeth flashed in a big friendly smile, and looked even greater because of beautiful blue eyes. I didn't think of it at the time, but he was a duplicate of Pernell Roberts once Pernell shed his hairpiece. My only thoughts were that he was not my type…too fat, bald, and with terrible bad breath. He was about the same age as Juan, so the weight had to make him appear older.

Daniel's charm finally won me over, however, and it didn't hurt that he made over me like I was some kind of stud! His expectations were apparently fulfilled that evening in bed. After all the foreplay, Daniel was on his back with his legs on my shoulders. I thrust into him slowly and deeply while moving my body in a circular motion. In this way, he could feel an exaggerated fullness each time I thrust in.

"Oh, Richard, beautiful!" he sighed, "You certainly know how to use that thing!"

I was a bit surprised on awakening. Daniel was dressed and about to leave, and as he hurried to the door he called out cheerfully, "Just push the button on the doorknob when you leave, Richard!" With that, he was gone.

Daniel continued calling and though I informed him I wasn't interested in a commitment, I accepted his invites to go out. It was easy to like his cheerful and extroverted personality, and the fact that he treated me like a king, in or out of bed, kept me from bowing out.

Fate then suddenly turned good fortune my way. The theater I worked in went bankrupt, and when I contacted the restaurant it was housed in to offer my services as director should they desire to continue on with productions, they advised me that they would only be interested if I came up with my own company. A quickly prepared offering managed to raise enough money from friends and family to start up my own production company.

It became quite an undertaking; I decided on a complete makeover of the space. Elevated seating was the most costly. Though Juan was overjoyed with the news of my dream come true, I never thought to ask him for help. And he was waiting to be asked apparently. Stubbornness prevailed again, and it was a shame because his presence would've made the work such a joy.

"Richard, I am gonna quit my waitress job and come work for you," Vera quickly exclaimed when I greeted her with the news. And even though I explained that salaries would be minimal, she still insisted on coming aboard. She wanted to be there when I made it big.

With the help of some members of my family, all the details that needed to be accomplished were finally done. Daniel also insisted on helping and I had him, Geena, and Frank monitor auditions. Vera came on board just before opening and became my girl Friday. Besides taking on the hostess position as well as ticket sales, she was our cleaning woman and costume mistress. She even designed covers for programs. Most importantly, she cheered me up when I needed it.

I told Daniel not to call because the office was so small. In fact, I usually instructed my staff not to interrupt me with calls whenever I was involved. He pleaded with me to call before leaving for home, however, no matter how late. So there I'd be, eating sandwiches he thoughtfully prepared, and fulfilling our hungry desire for sex afterwards. Meanwhile, Vera was leaving one drunken, lovelorn message after another throughout the night on my home answering machine.

I went all out with an elaborate press party for the opening night of the theater. I told Daniel to come the following evening since I expected Juan to be present, and then Juan never showed up. So I was on my way with a schedule of fourteen hours a day, seven days a week with Vera continually after me at the theater while Daniel pursued on the home front. I was so busy I never thought to call Juan. Besides, he never called.

It was necessary to sometimes stay after the performance in order to cheer up Vera. Many times, she couldn't cope with the fact that I wasn't going to resume our relationship, and would go into a crying jag the entire day. At least her spirits lifted with the satisfaction of my company into the wee hours of the night, even though it was only to talk and sip wine. True confessions though always prevailed once the wine flowed too freely.

"Richard, I have to confess to having sex with a girlfriend," she cried out one evening.

Of course, that opened a can of worms. I confessed to having sex with Juan, though only admitting to two times. At the mention of Juan's name, she told me of the countless times he had called when I didn't want to be interrupted. It made me realize the reason Juan was always so cold when we did talk. He felt ignored.

"I hate him! I hate that Juan!" she screamed hysterically even though she never met him.

Daniel's feelings for Juan weren't any better, and he also never met him. Juan was calling after the bars closed, and never failed to beg me to come pick him up. Daniel was always upset at hearing that I never failed to oblige. Of course, I was stupid enough to also tell him about Juan's antagonistic behavior towards me and that he borrowed continually.

So, frustrated because I refused to commit, he'd shout, "I hate that guy, Richard, I really hate him!" It was just as Juan always said…"Recharred, you 'ave such a motor mouth!"

Juan again surprised me by making an appearance with Marina and Barry the last week of the run.

"How do you do, Recharred, so good to see you," he said in his over-exaggerated, elegant manner while extending his hand in a mock gesture of royalty waiting for it to be kissed. I should have slapped it, but I realized what he was getting at.

I always watched the performance while standing in the rear but that evening my eyes were on Juan instead. Unmistakably, his concentration wasn't on the play. I was in the darkness, and yet it was obvious that every movement of his body was a regal performance for my benefit. I lost sight of them once the play ended and they disappeared without a word. Assuming they again went across the way, I hurried over. My assumption, disappointedly, was wrong.

Juan's drunken calls in the wee hours of the morning continued, and though I believed his story of losing his car to be an excuse I'd still go after him. I couldn't chance something happening to him. And then I could always expect to be pestered for sex once I got him to my place and in bed. It never fared well with me since he'd be slobbering drunk, and though I tried to discourage him, I sometimes gave in to his overbearing persistence. Most of the times, I'd be disappointed because his sexual performance had changed drastically. The tender and slow manner of lovemaking I had got him so accustomed to throughout the years had fallen to the wayside with the freedom trail we willingly, and unfortunately, presented one another with. His approach to sex was now obnoxiously abrupt.

"Recharred, I don' know whot I am gonna do! I wrecked my father's car into a lamp post!" were Juan's cries once I managed to wake from a sound sleep to answer the phone. "My father is gonna kill me!"

He was actually crying, and it took some time to sort out all his mumbo jumbo to know where he was—Cabrini Green, one of the most dangerous neighborhoods in Chicago, and especially at three in the morning! The area was infested with dope peddlers and seekers, and I trembled at the thought of him being easy prey for someone who was broke and out for a hit. I managed to get the street location but never thought to ask where he was calling from.

A church seemed to be illuminated as I turned onto the street Juan had said, and it continued to glow as I drove in. As I approached the illuminated area, I discovered the church to be on a cul-de-sac. I also realized why it stood out like a glowing star. Juan's foot surely had continued to accelerate once he hit the light-pole; the front end of the car was resting against at a height of eight feet! The pole, of course, was leaning with the light aimed at the church!

My heart stopped. How could anyone escape serious injury after an impact like that, especially since the force had to be strong enough to tilt an iron post? I became more frantic when I saw that Juan was nowhere in sight! I was sure he was lying dead somewhere in the huge empty lot directly across from the church! In an almost incoherent manner I began to pace the edge of the field, not wanting to venture in for fear of what I might find, and totally unable to call out his name! And yet I realized the field had to be searched!

I ventured in, and in my madness, my searching eyes suddenly caught glimpse of a light reflecting from a building in the darkness of the street I just drove down. It stood out like a lighthouse in a dark sea, and I was sure it was a sign telling me that Juan was okay! I was near slap happy as I ran towards the building.

"Oh, God, please let Juan be there!" I kept repeating aloud.

Halfway House was the name on the hanging sign as I approached the building, and as I looked into the glass doorway and up the staircase through another glass door, I suddenly saw him! There was Juan...holding a cup of coffee in one hand and a cigarette in the other...talking to someone behind an apparent reception desk! And it was obvious that his mouth was going nonstop! He had hit a light pole in front of a church, and yet, once I found him it was as though God, at that very moment, put his hand on my shoulder to assure me, "YOUR JUAN IS ALL RIGHT, RICHARD. I WAS THERE FOR HIM!"

Juan smiled broadly at seeing me enter the lower hall, and I was quickly buzzed in the second door. All my stress suddenly disappeared once I saw him so healthy and happy, and I knew by his expression that he certainly appreciated my presence.

"Aw, Recharred, I am so glad you are here," he exclaimed, clasping onto my hand and giving it the old heigh-ho buddy shake. "Thank you so much for coming to pick me up!"

He had just totaled out his father's car, destroying a light pole in the process, and there he is, thanking me like I just came to pick him up from an afternoon tea!

"This is my very, very good friend, Recharred," he boasted, introducing me to the receptionist. "He is such a good person, ond my best friend!"

After we acknowledged the introduction, she said, "Take good care of Juan because he is a wonderful guy." I smiled in agreement, and once I finally succeeded in bringing his charm to an end, we were out the door.

Of course, the answers again were vague when I asked why he was in that area. Still, I tried to ignore the fact that he possibly had tricked in the area, not really wanting to come to terms with reality.

Chapter Thirty-Four:
Further Apart, Only to Jell into One

Juan didn't come to the next two productions, and since I averaged about fifteen hours a day seven days a week at the theatre, the only times we saw each other were those late night excursions to pick him up. Daniel, however, made certain I stopped over almost every evening, even persuading me to take time off for two outings. Meanwhile, Vera was still at the ranch.

My relations with Juan became even worse once I began production on my own musical, particularly since this had to be the most frustrating period of my life! Undoubtedly, he was calling, but I never was informed because of my instructions not to be interrupted. I instructed Daniel not to call and he obliged, though he insisted I call him at evening's end.

I was forced to cast myself in the role I wrote for myself even though I didn't want to because I was directing and it would be difficult to take on both jobs. However, no one who auditioned for the role came near to satisfying me. I wanted everything to be just perfect for my musical, and yet I was faced with one crisis after another! In fact, directing and acting in the same musical turned out to be worse than I imagined. So many production details kept me busy that I actually had problems memorizing my own written lines and dance steps I choreographed!

Added to these woes, my stage manager didn't like the show. So, since he constructed the sets for each production, these feelings were well read once I was confronted with his slip-shod renditions of my suggested designs. And besides the problems with the costume designer and the musical director, I was faced with an even bigger trauma…the attitudes and egos of singers!

Money was going out in leaps and bounds because of the added costs of a musical and I counted on rave reviews in order to recoup most of my capital. However, we received only two favorable reviews from critics who appreciated the original songs depicting the nostalgia of various eras. However, the others were not easy in their criticisms, also making special mention of the sets. They thought they weren't even worthy of a high school production. I needed Juan so badly! Vera tried to raise my spirits but it was apparent she was hurting as much as I was.

So, while the theatre was near capacity Friday and Saturday evenings, we were still faced with the humiliation of walkouts during intermissions. Meanwhile, ticket sales the rest of the week were low, and to make matters worse, the restaurant wasn't going to pick up their option to renew the lease. We'd be out of business at the end of the twelve-week run since the building was scheduled to be razed as part of a complete mall renovation. My bank balance dwindled quickly.

Juan finally showed up at the theatre again, entering from the dining room in that unmistakable catwalk of his. I never went into the dining room that evening so I was totally surprised to see him. I cannot recall if Barry and Marina were with him but I do remember being introduced to Donald, a big, burly guy with a sarcastic mouth! His rude manner baffled me since we had never met. Meanwhile, Juan's exaggerated attempt at being elegant gave me every indication that he was even more intoxicated than the last time. It also annoyed me since it was obvious he wouldn't concentrate on the show he encouraged me so to write. My heart broke once the second act began; I glanced at the location Juan was seated to find the seats empty. Months later, he told me Donald insisted they leave.

Daniel had always made over me like I was the *Taj Mahal*, only to come up with a decision that baffled me completely! A week before the scheduled closing of the theater, he informed me that he no longer desired to go on with our relationship. He said he went out alone and had sex with someone, and wanted to continue with him and any others who might come along. True, I never committed but he was the only one I was seeing. Of all times, when I really needed someone.

"But I still want to be friends, Richard," he said.

My ego was destroyed, especially after standing up for him whenever one of my friends remarked, "You surely could do better than that, Richard."

My dream ended, I was faced with the chore of finding storage places. Daniel never offered to help, and I don't believe I ever called Juan. Of course, Geena and Frank were on hand, as well as Martina and Don. Vera had already returned to her waitress job but managed to show up the last night of packing. I was sure she was crying on Martina's shoulders once I looked out into the parking lot while closing the door for the last time. Martina later told me that she talked about how deeply she loved me, and that she was afraid we'd never see one another again. I did see her quite a few more times, though, even driving to Wisconsin while she vacationed at her brother's place. I finally realized it wasn't right; I'd never be able to give her a total commitment, and we never saw each other again.

The tables then turned in my relationship with Daniel. I never had wanted a commitment. I enjoyed his outgoing personality as well as the availability of sex but that was all. And yet I found myself chasing him. It became an obsession. So much so that I actually thought I was in love with him. He wanted men who were extremely well endowed, and I was confused once he boldly admitted it. God, I, obviously, had been a *Sabbatical* in his life! I wouldn't believe it, though. So I tried desperately to change his mind by catering to him. He, on the other hand, only ventured after those who were hard to get. Meanwhile, my ego was hurt and I actually forced myself into thinking I loved him. I was actually getting jealous every time he was going somewhere without me, or if he specified that I shouldn't come over because he was expecting a guest.

I became a part of his crowd, and became good friends with Roy Maton, who was my age, and Wally Miller, in his thirties. Wally had been stricken with cerebral palsy as a child, and yet, except for a slight limp and the awkward use of one arm, he lived a normal life.

I finally told Juan about Daniel, though I wasn't able to bring myself to admit to chasing him. In fact, my obsession was so strong that I seldom thought of Juan, and months passed.

Daniel went out on one of his escapades, and to keep my sanity, I asked Wally and Roy to join me for some barhopping on the north side of Chicago. While at BJ's, our last stop, I spotted Juan walking by in that cat-walk of his. *His* new crowd was following closely behind as they entered the bar. I quickly made myself obvious as he passed, and he acknowledged my presence by extending his hand out in that manner of his that almost demanded it be kissed.

"Aw, Recharred, how are you my good mon? It is so good to see you."

I was annoyed after all the introductions when his burly friend, Donald, walked away in a huff after throwing me a nasty remark about my show. I also assumed that Juan would stay and chat a while, and really was disappointed when he took off in that indifferent manner to never return. Wally and Roy had been tuned in about Juan but well aware of my pursuit of Daniel. So I am certain they were totally confused with the excitement I showed at seeing Juan again. I lit up like a light bulb, going on about his handsome looks, and actually wanting them to be as excited.

Juan mentioned, in one of our rare talks on the phone, that he often went to Norma's, a bar on Halstead Street. "You 'ave to remember her, Recharred. We talked with her so much when she worked ot the Closet."

On another evening with Wally and Roy, I insisted we stop there before taking in the bar next door. I was chasing after Daniel, and yet my subconscious mind was hoping to see Juan. And those hopes were answered once Juan walked in with Barry and Don. I hadn't seen Don since I left the restaurant, and discovered that he was as cold as ever.

Juan, however, was the total opposite of all the other occasions! Absolutely charming...the *Juan* I always knew! He was so thrilled to see me that I couldn't help but feel the same. We only talked a short time when Wally and Roy insisted we leave for the other bar....

"Oh, Juan, I wish we could talk longer, but they have been looking forward to going to the bar next door," I said with much regret. I then bid adieu reluctantly and we left.

My excitement at seeing Juan wouldn't cease once we settled at the other bar, and I'm certain Wally and Roy were confused once again.

Not ten minutes passed when Juan suddenly came through the door, walking in that mischievous catwalk of his, and with a big silly grin on his face!

"Recharred, I decided to come over to see you because I do not see you thot often," he quickly responded after seeing the bewilderment on my face.

"They got angry because I told them I wanted to be with you. So I left," he replied when I asked about Don and Barry.

I almost had forgotten the pleasure it was to be with Juan, and was grateful Wally and Roy moved a few seats away to talk on their own. It was just like old times…laughter and wonderful conversation. I was so wrapped up in the marvel of it all that I never gave a thought to the fact that he actually had left his friends stranded just to be with me! Unfortunately, I had driven, and Wally and Roy wanted to leave earlier than expected. The look of disappointment in Juan's eyes once I said good-bye will never be forgotten. However, I did ignore it at the time to pursue Daniel.

This pursuit of Daniel left me in a constant depression, especially since he favored one guy out of all the others he was seeing. I was introduced to Tommy, a policeman, and learned that he liked to boast about the rings on his tits and the head of his yang. He even pulled it out at the bar one night to prove it to me. Daniel invited me to join them occasionally, and on one occasion, Tommy insisted we go to Norma's. A warm feeling surged through my body at the thought that Juan might be there. My continual glances towards the door, however, were all in vain.

I struck up a conversation with Norma while Daniel and Tommy were involved, and was surprised when she mentioned that Juan had purchased a new 1984 Cavalier. He never said a word. She then took me by complete surprise when she mentioned how often he talked of me, and that his manner had always seemed to convey a definite yearning for my company.

"I really should not say anything about what he said to me…that should be his doing," she remarked. Then when I tried to get more information out of her she said, "I'm sorry but I shouldn't have brought it up." And yet, I did nothing about it again; Juan's jealous tantrums were still very vivid in my mind.

Juan called to tell me Uncle Nicolai invited him to Europe and was paying his way.

"He said it is okay to take Svetmana, too," he went on to say. "Is thot not wonderful! Recharred, I am so excited!"

Of course, he then hit me with, "Do you think you con lend me five hundred dollars, so I 'ave some spending money?" I was struggling to survive but still managed to oblige. In fact, I lent large sums to his ex-wife many times, getting her out of one mess after another. Her postdated checks that included large interest amounts wouldn't let me refuse.

"Well, you are finally going on the trip we so badly wanted to do together," I remarked the day he came by to pick up the loan. "Why didn't you ask me to go with you instead? It would have been our trip at last." There was no answer.

I finally got a sales position at an art gallery in October, and Mike married. Joan came from a very wealthy family. I planned a party during the first month of 1985, but I was a bit apprehensive since it was to be the first meeting of Juan and Daniel. My apprehension was quickly relieved once Juan arrived with Barry and Dan. Everyone was captivated with his wit and charm, including Daniel. In fact, Juan kept his alcohol intake at a minimum, an obvious intent to show me that he could remain reasonably sober.

There were so many indications that Juan still loved me, and yet I continued chasing Daniel. So, when Daniel asked if I'd like to move into an apartment with him, I jumped at it. If something was going to happen between us there couldn't be a better place. Juan surprised me when I told him. It didn't seem to matter that I was moving in with another guy.

I moved in with Daniel in June, never realizing that it was also the beginning of a new relationship with Juan, one that would eventually mold us into one! We were on the phone constantly, and he was up to his old tricks of pulling me out of the shower with his calls. He, somehow, always managed to keep me there to drip on the floor.

Daniel was out of town, spending the Fourth of July with his parents. So I decided to have Juan over and surprise him with my Italian pot roast. We could spend the afternoon at the pool while it cooked. The roast was quite big, so I invited a few others to join us. It would be nice. Juan liked parties. Wally was available and Lucille, a gal I was spending a lot of time with socially. We had met at one of Daniel's parties. Lucille was short and hefty with black cropped hair, and with very definite masculine mannerisms. In fact, whenever she called, I almost always thought it was a guy. Hank was also available. We had met at a party. He was in his early thirties and quite hyper, though it seemed to go well with his thin and frail body. He was a beautician and I often wondered how many clients were scorched because of his nervous and awkward mannerisms. He was truly a nut, which made him very easy to like. He also made it clear on our initial meeting that he wanted me. Of course, I eventually took him up on it, which was a thing that lasted a while.

Juan took an immediate liking to him, especially since Hank appreciated his well-placed mimics of his clumsy movements. After they made a feeble attempt at playing tennis, Juan took me aside to say, "Recharred, thot Hank is really stuck on you!"

Again, he didn't seem bothered by it and I wondered. I finally realized that Juan knew my likes…have sex maybe, but nothing serious.

Vic Schmitz and Phil Sitak owned a gift shop. I had met them through Daniel. Vic was four years older than me and looked younger, too. In fact, it was apparent he was quite good-looking as a young man. Phil was over twenty years younger than Vic…very tall with less than average good looks. If he was in the mood, he could be almost as pleasant as Vic, which was in complete contrast to his moody personality when his only contribution to a conversation was a dig at someone.

"Richard, this is Stan," Daniel said as he introduced a guy sitting next to him on the couch when I came home from work. It seemed they had met in the woods. I also learned from the short conversation that Stan was a chubby chaser, and Daniel answered his bill since he had gained quite a lot of weight. I was disturbed but bit my lip.

"He has a tremendous cock," Daniel boasted in response to my critical review of the guy after he left, "and I will never give that up!" It didn't even bother him when I called his attention to the fact that Stan looked like Fred Flintstone. That didn't matter, Stan had met his criteria!

My jealousy continued and only subsided when I was with Juan. Unfortunately, Juan moved into a downtown apartment, and I was in a western suburb. So it wasn't easy to be together often. To keep my mind off Daniel, I spent quite a bit of time with Vic and Stan, as well as Hank.

Juan held a party to welcome in 1986, anxious to show off his new apartment with the furniture he went out of his means to purchase. I was surprised when he showed no signs of regret when I brought someone along. Vic and Phil weren't able to attend but the crowd was a lively one. Marina, Barry, and Dan were on hand, and along with those I never met was Jeannie, a blond bombshell! What a voluptuous, red-hot mama! I soon learned that she was one of the first sex changes in Chicago. In contrast to Marina, Jeannie wouldn't allow you to forget that she was a woman for one moment.

"You know, Recharred, she probably wears her hair in thot old fifties pomp style because she is bald on top," Juan remarked, choking on his laughter at the thought of it. It was apparent, though, that he thought the world of her. She was someone he really could cut up with and talk sexy. It was hilarious because she'd top every remark of his or mine with a sexier one. It was impossible not to like her. She was such a live wire, and once she erupted into laughter it was as though lightning struck.

Juan doubled up in laughter when she cradled her breasts into the palms of her hands and quipped, "Oh, baby, it cost me a small fortune to have these tits pumped up so big!"

"C'mon, Jeannie, let's cha cha," he begged throughout the evening, and once they were dancing, her rocking laughter reigned.

Brent and Cary had been together for twenty years. I had been to their parties several times with Daniel, and it was at one of them that I met Hank. Another one was coming up and I asked Juan to join me. He had previous plans but said he'd try to make it later.

I then couldn't enjoy myself at the party because Daniel and Stan were holding hands continually. It didn't make sense because I was also anxious for Juan to arrive. I finally figured he wouldn't show; it was getting too late for a

Sunday party. Of course, that didn't help my depressed state of mind. However, when Brent approached to tell me I had a call, and once I heard Juan's desperate plea for directions, a sudden calm seemed to settle my nerves.

Brent took me aside after meeting Juan. His brows raised in exclamation as he raved, "Boy, what beautiful blue eyes, and that wonderful cleft in his chin! He's really some handsome man!" Then, while shaking his head, he said, "And you want Daniel? You're crazy!"

As it turned out, Juan consumed very little alcohol, and was an absolute joy to everyone that talked with us. I was the one who did the drinking. That led me to become consumed with jealousy because of the fondling going on between Daniel and Stan. I should've taken up Juan's offer to stop off somewhere with him. Instead, I insisted that I needed to get home. My true reason…Daniel and Stan already left, and I was determined to get home shortly afterwards! If Juan was aware of my jealousy, he never let on.

Lava seemed to be running through my veins on the drive home, and there was no way I could control it! I was obsessed with jealousy. To make matters worse, I had to piss badly.

My mad jealousy took charge when I entered the apartment. They were sitting on the couch very innocently, and yet I lost control when I saw them holding hands. Instead of running to the bathroom, I quickly unzipped my fly, with every intention of pissing all over them. However, a sporadic dribble spattered onto the coffee table that stood before them and me instead. It was a pity a camera wasn't focused on their faces. Daniel, however, lunged towards me like a bull in an effort to grab me, totally disregarding the stream on him to make his way through.

"What the hell are you doing, Richard?" he screamed, punching and pushing me down the hall to my bedroom! It certainly called for return jabs on my part, as well as threats to Stan.

"I'm gonna call your wife and tell her about you!"

Of course, Stan was nowhere in sight once we concluded our wrestling match and returned to the living room.

Of course, it didn't take long to realize how wrong I was. I was a jealous fool. Repeated apologies did no good; Daniel moved out within a couple of weeks. Fortunately, he assured me that he'd pay his share of the rent for the balance of the lease. My one consolation…I finally came to terms with the fact that I was only jealous because my ego was hurt and not because I loved him.

Daniel always had been a broadcasting system, and it wasn't long before Vic and Phil were tuned in. To my displeasure, Juan was also enlightened to all the facts by them. He surprised me, though, by laughing hilariously.

"Recharred, you ond I are the same," he said, "thot is exactly whot I would 'ave done, because you know how jealous I am also!"

Chapter Thirty-Five:
The Crowd

A three-bedroom apartment can feel very empty when the only things in it are a bedroom set, a television, and an entertainment center. I had bought the entertainment center with Daniel and paid him off in order to have something in the living room. So, again, I scurried around to get the pieces stored at various homes. I had already given my daughter, Jacque, the living room couch and chair, and since Juan just purchased a new sectional, I settled for Tom's old couch that he stored in Geena's basement. So, along with my mother's inlaid living room tables and my dining table and chairs, the living room was somewhat furnished.

The thing that really mattered was that my life became full suddenly. Almost all of my free time was spent with Juan. His big burly friend, Donald, had moved to New England, and he wasn't seeing Barry and Dan much. I actually had almost forgotten the joy he always brought into my life with his constant and happy chatter, and his zest to live made life for me wonderful again! Vic and Phil became our constant companions, and if we weren't together, we were on the phone with them. Phil had told Juan about the way I chased after Daniel, and continued to bring it up on occasion, not realizing my feelings for him had died. It took some time to convince him that it was only an ego thing with me. It never seemed to bother Juan that I chased after Daniel, though, and probably because he knew my actual likes and dislikes to know who I'd really take seriously. He felt that I should be friends with him, however, and I agreed, knowing that I was completely over my depressed obsession. Juan had solved that problem by coming into my life once again.

I finally realized that it was Daniel's gregarious personality that I liked, and it confused me into thinking I was in love with him. He always had laughed easily at my witty quips, and now his big belly should shake like Jello with Juan around. He'd have to cool off first, though.

Juan never showed any signs of jealousy even though he was aware that I was going out alone at times. Of course, I knew he was doing the same, but we never talked of it. It was just *understood*. Besides, our beautiful and compatible lovemaking was still there to share.

Ronnie was just twenty-one, quite good-looking, and quite feminine. He supplied Vic and Phil's gift shop with his pottery, and frequently stopped by while I was at one of their apartments. Juan seldom joined us on weeknights, and I could then expect Ronnie to come on to me. Of course, my ego wasted no time arranging three encounters in a row, though I had enough sense to put a halt to it when he began suggesting a relationship.

Saturday nights with Vic and Phil became a ritual for Juan and me, and we often sought out new bars for dancing. Many times, we just stayed at Vic or Phil's to watch a movie on video. Juan's sex change friend, Marina, soon became one of the crowd and joined us on the nights out. I liked Marina, and felt that her feelings for me were likewise. In fact, she sort of adopted Juan's pronunciation of my name, but gave it a twist of her own. Hers was more like *Rat-charred*. She liked her times alone, though, and sometimes declined our invitations to watch a couple of videos. At times, Juan did the same.

"It is too far to drive, Recharred, jus' to watch television. I will stay ot home tonight." I sometimes had my doubts about him staying home, even though he often called there to ask about the movie. I was sure he was going out later.

My Buick burned more oil than gas, and I was glad when my daughter, Jacque, gave me her 1978 Monte Carlo after buying a new car. A trick I was seeing expressed interest in buying the Buick, and I agreed to let him take it for a few days to make a decision. I then became disturbed when he never called, especially after a week passed. When I finally reached him on the phone, I was told he wasn't interested in it. He also refused to drive it back.

Juan and I went out alone the following Saturday and met Wally at the Nutbush. Juan was drinking like there was no tomorrow; he was very drunk. I remember keeping up with him but still sober. I was too consumed with the fact that the guy refused to return my car. The thought finally came to me that we could pick up the car on the way home since I had another key, though Juan wasn't in any condition to drive. However, after explaining the situation to Wally, he agreed to come with us to drive Juan's car to my apartment.

"That is, Richard, as long as you drive me back home." Luck was then with me; Juan agreed to leave easily. Of course, he assumed we'd return to the bar. My hopes were that the long drive home would find him too sleepy to go anywhere.

Still upset about the car, I had no desire to drive the twenty-five miles back with Wally when we arrived at my place, especially since Juan hadn't fallen asleep and wanted to return to the bar.

"Will you stay overnight?" I asked. "I'll drive you in the morning, Wally." He agreed but it took some time to convince Juan. When he did agree, it was apparent he had amorous intentions in mind and I wasn't in a mood to cope with his drunken fondling.

"Wally, you sleep in my bed with Juan," I insisted. "This couch is so short and will be very uncomfortable. I'll sleep here instead." There was nothing to worry about. Juan was always very emphatic when he said, "Recharred, I could never 'ave sex with thot Wally!"

Well, no sooner had I crawled on the couch when I realized something was going on in the bedroom, especially after Wally tiptoed in the darkness to get something from his coat pocket. A condom, no doubt! It was a known fact that he loved to be the *bottom*! I was beside myself, but what was I to do? I no longer was Juan's lover. So I lay there in agony and anger, trying to figure out why he was doing it when he always said Wally was a complete turnoff!

Suddenly, I heard footsteps in the darkness, and the sound of the front door opening. A sudden flood of light from the outer hall spotlighted Juan about to exit. Darkness prevailed almost as quickly as I heard the door pulled shut. I wasn't angry, no…I was livid!

I was really annoyed with Wally while driving the next morning. His lack of compassion for my misery was obvious as he repeatedly complained about Juan leaving so abruptly. He actually had expected Juan to cuddle up next to him afterwards!

Don't you realize that Juan was slobbering drunk, and that you were merely something convenient to poke? I wanted to shout out. However, I held my lip.

"Juan, how could you do that in my bed? And with me in the other room!" I cried out on confronting him, "And especially with Wally?"

Juan remained silent throughout my attack, though his facial expression showed obvious regret to his actions of the night. He was definitely sorry. However, as always, he wasn't going to allow me to continue with my reprimanding.

"Jesus Chris,' Recharred, it was just a fuck!" he shouted. "So whot's the difference!" And he refused to discuss it any further. It was apparent, though, that he wasn't laughing it off as he had so many times before. His stubbornness wouldn't allow him to admit that he was wrong, however. It took me some time to get over it, especially since I was certain Daniel received a flash from Wally, which was the equivalent to front page headlines! I finally dropped the subject when I realized why Juan had left that night. He had sobered up enough to feel guilty, and it wouldn't allow him to face me in the morning.

Vic and Phil became our closest friends. No one, in all of our years together, had been that close. They were not without their faults, though, and being tight with their money was the big one. I was always a giving person, but Juan was the one who really loved to give. Every time the four of us were going out on the town in Chicago, he insisted on cocktails at his place beforehand. Of course, he always included his wonderful canapés. Dinner parties were also always given by both of us, and though they often brought a bottle of wine to me, they never thought to bring one to Juan. In fact, it never occurred to them to buy him a drink or two in appreciation for cocktails and canapés at his place once we were out dancing.

It bothered me more than Juan, though, he often mentioned, "You know, Recharred, they must think I am rich because I live in this nice downtown apartment."

"Don't' you think it would be nice if they brought a bottle of wine ot least once?"

Even more exasperating, Juan and I bought a round of drinks separately, but they did it as a pair.

Juan and I also were always aware whenever someone was coming on to either of us, and we'd quickly call it to each other's attention. It was an extremely frigid Saturday evening in February, and Juan suggested we go to a new disco that featured a huge dance floor as we left his cocktail party. Marina was there, too, and offered to drive. The dance floor was everything Juan had said and we returned several times after that night.

That night, Juan took me aside to say, "Recharred, you do know thot Phil has the hots for you. It is very obvious!" It was something I already was aware of since he always seemed to be touching me. In fact, Juan also noticed it whenever we were all on the dance floor. I'd disco with Juan and Phil would be out on the floor with Vic. Somehow, Phil always managed to move our way and rub against me continually.

"Be careful, Recharred," Juan warned, "you don't wanna cause a problem with Vic." Of course, I assured him that I liked Vic too much to allow it to go any further.

"I'm not attracted to Phil anyway," I said, teasing Juan a bit. "Besides, I love you too much!" Occasional spurts of jealousy were also quite obvious in Phil whenever I catered to Juan's wishes. He'd actually appear quite annoyed. Somehow I always seemed to receive the brunt of the digs he felt he had to hand out to appease himself. I'd put them out of my mind, however; their friendship was too important, especially since Vic was so warm and personable. Besides, when Phil was not in one of his moods, he was great company.

The alcohol we consumed at the disco didn't help to keep us warm once we left. It felt as though we were in the North Pole! To make matters worse, Marina's car had a flat! Juan was quite drunk and oblivious to the problem, and merely got into the car to continue shivering. The rest of us shivered in the cold, looking dumbfounded. Marina always wore jeans and flats but chose a dress and spiked heels for this outing. After our few agonizing moments of looking hopelessly at the flat, Marina finally broke from us and raised the trunk door. Without further hesitation, she quickly hauled out the spare tire, as well as the jack!

There we were, the three of us in a frozen stupor, watching, as she commenced to jack up the car! It certainly had to be a sight for anyone in a passing car. A six-foot-seven woman, in heels, pumping away on the jack while the three of us stood there shivering! Guilt finally got the best of me and I began loosening the bolts on the flat. Vic, meanwhile, apparently motivated with my chivalry, took over the pumping. Marina, however, hoisted the spare onto the wheel once I removed the flat. She gave in to us when we insisted on tightening the bolts and finishing up.

She didn't want to drive without a spare. So the real sight came once we drove into a nearby station. Marina jumped out quickly, opened the trunk, and hoisted out the tire! She began rolling the tire like any man would do just as the attendant came out of the doorway. I thought his eyes were going to pop from their sockets after seeing her and checking us out in the car.

"Please, Ma'am, let *me* help you," he quickly called out, giving us a look of disbelief at the same time. The episode eventually gave us repeated laughs, especially when Juan had done an imitation of Marina hoisting out the tire.

In the spring of 1986, the four of us planned to vacation together, and considered Saugatauk, Michigan, if accommodations were available for the time we wanted in the summer. We had been aware of the *Dunes*, a gay hotel, and made reservations for a Saturday night. We could then check out the area along Lake Michigan on Sunday for housekeeping cottages. It had been the right thing to do because we not only found one, but we got to see it, too. It had been the cottage the owners lived in while their huge home was being built just below on the lake. It had two bedrooms, a kitchen, and living room with a fireplace, as well as a screened in porch overlooking the lake! Of course, Juan became as excited as a little kid.

My lease was finally up in May, and I managed to find a one-bedroom apartment in a suburb much closer to Chicago and work, directly across from a golf course. I junked Tom's old couch and purchased a fantastic neutral colored, L-shaped sectional, as well as a beautiful brass and black glass-top coffee table. I now had a very attractive apartment, and one Juan felt comfortable visiting. In fact, he spent almost every weekend with me.

"Aw, Recharred, you know I am always so excited every Saturday, packing my overnight bag to come here,' he often remarked, "because it seems like I am going on vacation. Ond, Recharred, I love the area so much because it is so green!"

It was never surprising to occasionally hear him say, "Recharred, I hope you don' mind but I osked Marina to come to dinner tonight."

Should I give him an expression of surprise, he'd add, "Aw, Recharred, she is alone all the time. Donald is gone, ond now especially since Barry has moved to California. Jeannie is always on the prowl for a stud, ond Marina is too afraid to go with her. You don' mind thot I osked her—do you not, Recharred?"

"Of course not, Juan. This is your home. I just gave you a look because you never think to mention it until the last moment." Then he'd add that he asked Vic and Phil to come over later to play cards.

So my apartment became the gathering place for the *crowd*, as Juan always referred to the group as. It was fantastic since he usually never drank, and still he was hilariously funny. *Uno* and *Scat* were always played and sometimes

Hearts, and once I introduced a game I played as a kid, *Spoons*, it became the finale of the evening. It had to be because the cards were always mutilated. A set of four of a kind for each person playing were the only cards needed. After shuffling, all the cards were dealt to each player. Players picked up their cards at the same time, and if they didn't have four of a kind they began passing a card to the right simultaneously. When a player had four of a kind in his hand, he'd grab into the center of the table for a spoon. Of course, the others needed to follow suit. This is when the real fun began because there was one less spoon than players. The place would rock with a good deal of hand and arm wrestling, which naturally accounted for the mutilated cards.... A letter of the word "piggy" would be awarded to the person failing to latch onto a spoon, and once he received all the letters, he was out of the game. Believe me, everyone fought to a bitter end just to be the last one standing! Oh, how we laughed! Of course, it was always necessary to pad the table heavily.

Our blonde bombshell, Jeannie, began joining us for some of the Saturday evening fun-fests, but it always had to be a last minute decision. After all, a stud might call. In fact, she tried getting something going with Juan, and when that didn't work, she started on me. So the laughs were even more plentiful with one sexy crack after another breaking up Juan. Juan and I were excellent in egging her on, which gave her the ammunition she needed to come back stronger.

Those evenings at my place are cherished in my heart. They had to be the most relaxed and fun times of our lives! The memory of Juan doubling up in laughter and wiping away his tears were enough to fill the cup, especially after Jeannie just scrambled for a spoon and held out her hand, screaming at the top of her voice, "Oh, my God! My beautiful fingernail is broken!"

The fact that Phil never had anything to say whenever Juan called began bothering him. I attributed it to his infatuation for me, especially since signs of jealousy always were prevalent each time I catered to Juan's wishes.

"Recharred, if I don' ask him a question, thar will be silence. But I do love to talk with Vic! He is like a philosopher!"

Vic and Phil didn't cook daily. In fact, they each had a condo because Phil didn't want his family to be aware of their relationship. So they rotated from one to the other each month, eating all their meals at diners. We joined them on occasion. Juan was raving about the fun we always had at our parties during one of those times, and gave special mention to the times Jeannie attended.

"Aw, she is so funny, so funny, ond such a woman! I love her so much!"

When Vic mentioned that Phil's birthday was about to come up in May, Juan's eyes lit up.

"Aw, Vic, you 'ave to 'ave a party for him! Tell you whot. Why don' you 'ave one ot my place! You con invite anyone you want! Aw c'mon, Vic, it will be so much fun!" Juan's excitement was so tremendous that Vic had to agree.

I was taken by complete surprise once he said, "You con even invite Daniel ond his lover if you like." They had been at Vic and Phil's annual turkey buffet in February, which was the only time in the year that they cooked because they received a frozen one as a Christmas gift. So Juan was thrilled that a party was in the making, quickly offering to prepare his canapés.

Juan then ended up preparing everything for the party, except the ham and cake that Vic brought. He also brought large two-liter bottles of liquor. Of course, everyone felt more comfortable pouring from the smaller fifths Juan graciously set out.

"Jesus, Recharred, I did everything for this party, and Vic asked if I would buy the ice because he did not want it to melt in the long drive," Juan whispered taking me aside. "Ond then he never offered to pay me. Do you know I spent a small fortune today, Recharred!"

"Juan, you should've known it when you begged Vic to have the party at your house," I replied with a chuckle. "You know they never think of reimbursing money."

"I know, Recharred. They are tight, ond if we want their friendship, we 'ave to accept it."

Daniel and Stan did come to the party, and it was apparent that Daniel had finally laid aside his hard feelings. And between Juan, Jeannie, and I, his big belly looked as though it was about to explode with laughter. Daniel's animosity towards Juan was gone. He truly liked him!

Donna, an extremely sexy and attractive redhead, had been a customer of mine at the gallery during the troubled times with Daniel. Her husband had died of cancer just before the time I delivered an Erte bronze he purchased for her. After a bit of conversation, I casually had asked her to be my guest at the annual Christmas party, and was taken by complete surprise when she accepted without hesitation. She was a professional dancer and teacher, and once we had gone out on the floor, we were Astaire and Rogers. In fact, she dressed so sexy that I was surprised we didn't slip on the drool oozing from my colleagues. We dated a few times after that evening, and I had begun to think of a straight life again because Juan and I weren't seeing one another regularly yet. However, I always felt intimidated because she had inherited so much money from her husband. Listening to her talk about taking a trip around the world definitely made me feel like a pauper. So I stopped seeing her. I later had mentioned these feelings to one of my colleagues.

"Why don't you tell her that you want to go along," she quipped, "that you will swim alongside the ship!"

Well, I hadn't seen Donna for some time when she suddenly appeared in the gallery. During the course of our conversation, she said she was producing and directing an original musical for a community theatre. All the parts were cast except one, a fuss-budget husband. Of course, I told her I'd have no trouble doing the character, only to have her quickly run out to her car to return with the script.

"If you don't do this part, Richard," she demanded, handing me the script, "I will never buy a piece of art from you again!" So there I was, involved in a show that demanded time, though I soon found it fun since I hadn't done a show for so long. The only thing that bothered me was Juan, Vic, Phil and I had planned on going to Saugatauk for the Fourth of July weekend as a pre-vacation outing and the last performances were at that time.

Juan was thrilled with the show in spite of the one hundred degree temperature in the theatre. The dance numbers, reminiscent of Astaire and Rogers, really helped him to forget the heat. I felt certain that he'd want to see it again the last weekend and cancel Saugatauk but he surprised me instead. He left with Vic and Phil. And on their return, he raved on about all the hot guys.

I received the surprise of my life the third week of July. I lost my job with the gallery! I couldn't believe it, especially since I was the top salesperson for most of the previous year. True, I never would call in the assistant director to close a sale for me because I'd then have to split my commission with him, but I guess it was reason enough to fire me.

I was devastated! Never had I been fired in my life! I already had a few drinks when I called Juan, and though his compassion was overwhelming, I refused to listen to his pleas to discontinue drinking. Instead, I hung up and went on my way. Besides, his car was in the shop and he had no way to join me, and I needed to drown away my sorrows with alcohol.

The rest of the evening had remained a blank except for the recollection of leaning on the bar in a drunken stupor, and suddenly seeing Phil's face before me. Juan had called and pleaded with them to search me out.

I felt sure a herd of galloping horses was running through my head when I awakened the next morning on Vic's couch, and it took some doing to go along with them to breakfast.

"Richard, he really was so worried about you," Vic said of Juan, "So afraid that you would get in an accident and be killed. He wouldn't give up until we agreed to go out after you."

While Vic spoke, a smug expression was very obvious on Phil's face. However, Vic's compassion and philosophical views managed to take my mind off Phil's jealousy.

"Your talent is too great not to find another job immediately, Richard." And I did find one that week in a gallery on Michigan Avenue. They even agreed on a starting date after my vacation.

"Recharred, my battalion is having an important meeting Monday morning, ond I am required to be thar even though it is my vacation," Juan called to say, "so I will not be able to go with you guys early Sunday morning. I will 'ave to drive to Saugatauk myself."

"Oh, no, you're not," I replied quickly, "I will stay and wait for you so we can go together!"

"Aw, you will do thot, Recharred?" Juan asked in a voice filled with awe. "Aw, I am so happy. But are you sure? You don' mind missing one day of your vacation, Recharred?"

"Juan, the excitement would never be there for me without you." I could almost see his eyes sparkling.

It was apparent, however, that Phil was again provoked because I was catering to Juan. He just couldn't understand why I would want to miss a day of vacation, and I didn't feel it necessary to explain. Juan then didn't disappoint me. His excitement during our drive made me feel as though we were going to the Taj Mahal!

"Hey, you guys owe us four dollars each because we bought some groceries," were the first words said by Vic once we walked into the cottage.

"Con you beat thot, Recharred, they could not wait until they said hello before asking for the money. Like we would not pay them once we saw the groceries," Juan later remarked. He wouldn't allow it to spoil our vacation, however. We were there to enjoy ourselves.

I was the only one who didn't like to lie in the sun, so I brought along my *Jarts* set. It took some doing to get them off their backs to play, but once I did, they looked forward to the competition of the game. The fact that the owners returned home that week was another plus. We had the beach to ourselves. I was aware of dune buggy rides in the area and bugged them to go continually. They kept putting me off but I continued to pursue. I wasn't one to sit and they knew it. Still, I think they appreciated my egging on. Of course, our usual card games were on the agenda in the afternoon as well as the evenings, and the laughter that accompanied the sessions kept their adrenaline running.

The last two evenings were agreed upon to eat out, and outside of one breakfast prepared by Vic, Juan and I did the cooking. We didn't drink during any of the evening card games until the third day. Of course, Juan talked us into going out to the Dunes nightclub later that evening.

Vic and Phil were already down on the beach the next morning while we straightened up the cottage. As always, though Juan did a great deal of drinking, he still woke up in high spirits. His energy always managed to rub off on me. In fact, he was really up. So there we were, in a pillow fight, laughing hilariously! Suddenly, Juan grabbed me in an effort to restrain my swing of the pillow. His gagging laughter brought me to do the same, and we finally fell across my bed in helpless hysteria. Slowly, the laughter subsided, and there we were touching each other gently. Lovemaking followed. Not just sex…beautiful love.

I had asked Juan several times to once again resume as lovers, and his response always was, "We'll see, Recharred, we'll see." So I naturally assumed he wanted his freedom. I never gave a thought that he still may not trust my fidelity. It was obvious that we loved each other deeply. Our friends considered us a couple. So why aren't we committed?

"Juan, why don't we tell Vic and Phil that we're lovers again," I asked, taking hold of his arm just as we were about to go down to the beach, "Oh, Juan, it would be so beautiful, especially since it's obvious we love each other!" I felt sure he'd agree from the glow on his face.

"Not yet, Recharred, let's wait. We are friends, ond friends are more important." The disappointment had to be apparent in my face. I wanted our tricking to finally come to an end!

We did go for a dune buggy ride that day, and I remember the fullness felt in my heart. I had to touch Juan, even if it was just to lay my hand on his shoulder as a picture was snapped of all of us. I'm sure he felt the same. He didn't pull away with embarrassment because the dune buggy driver was snapping the picture.

Juan and I suggested we dine at Sir Douglas at the Dunes Motel for our last dinner. We had heard it to be quite elegant and expensive, and were pleased when Vic and Phil didn't object.

It turned out to be everything we expected. The atmosphere was perfect and so festive. The chatter from a full house, which included many straight couples from the area, made the mood just right. It also confirmed that the recommendation of exquisite cuisine a valid one.

I cannot recall the entree I ordered, though I remember it being excellent. Nor do I remember Vic and Phil's. I do, however, remember the mouth-watering creation Juan had. His brows rose several times and his eyes glowed once the specially prepared Halibut steak was set before him. His appreciation was valid this time! Only one other time did I see a more scrumptious-looking entrée…that wonderful adventure in food at the Tango restaurant years before. The crumbly coating was browned just enough, and the manner in which it was presented made it appear even more magnificent.

"Aw, Recharred, look how bea-u-ti-ful this 'alibut is! I don' believe it! Look ot it, mon!"

He cut into it with his fork in his usual elegant manner, raised the fork just as elegantly, and placed the moist-looking morsel through his lips. Just watching his pleased expression was a joy. He had that gift. I already knew how superb it was before hearing his raves.

"Thot is too, Italian, Recharred. It looks like we just got off the boat," was something I could always expect to hear whenever I asked him to share an entrée. This time, *he* offered a generous portion to taste. After placing it on my plate, his eyes glowed, waiting for my approval. It was all I expected and more! In fact, I was sorry I hadn't ordered it.

Dancing and drinking followed in the disco that evening. Unfortunately, though we had a ball together, Juan and I got quite high and began roaming separately towards the end. A guy suddenly came onto me, which eventually led to a darkened area where we could sit and talk. He seemed quite nice and especially taken with me. My ego began to work again. Fortunately, Vic broke the spell when he approached to say it was time to leave. My ego wouldn't allow me to discard the guy's card when I discovered it in my pocket the next day.

After brunch, and at Sir Douglas again, we were on our way home.

"Well, Recharred, our vacation is over ond it is sad," Juan sighed, "but we had a bea-u-ti ful time! I am so happy we came! Maybe we con all buy some property like we talked about with Vic ond Phil, ond then we con come here every weekend. Ond I think we con get along well with them. I know they feel the same way, otherwise, Vic would not 'ave talked so much about it. I jus' wish thot Phil was more friendly with me."

I assured him that Phil would change, that his fantasy about me would soon end once he realized I wasn't interested.

"I know he enjoys you tremendously, Juan. You make him laugh so hard. So believe me, it'll change. Although you have to stop criticizing the way he dresses. Stop telling him his clothes and shoes are out of style!"

"Recharred, thot is Juan! I always tell the truth," Juan quickly boasted with a chuckle. The ride home took only moments, it seemed. Juan's excitement about the vacation and the possibility of buying property together made the time fly by.

"Would you like to do thot someday, Recharred?" he asked over and over again in that little boy charm of his. "Buy a summer place together even if Vic ond Phil bock out! Would you not, Recharred?"

During the vacation, I stupidly had slammed down the hood of Juan's car without releasing the supporting rod. The hood bent. The three of them were in conversation away from the car and I quickly attempted to straighten it out by hand. It didn't come out too good but somehow no one noticed it. I was too upset and embarrassed to admit to Juan that I did it once he noticed it, My face, however, always told all. Guilt was written all over it, and yet Juan never got angry. Oh, he reprimanded me, but in his usual charming way of shaking his finger.

"Recharred, you know you should not try to hide things like thot! You should never be afraid to tell the truth. Shame on you!" He was a wonder, making life so beautiful because he loved it so much. And I guess he loved me in the same way!

Chapter Thirty-Six:
That Accursed Black Star

I wasn't happy with my new job. Not only because I didn't like the works of the artists they represented, but because their hours during the summer went to ten during the week and midnight on Saturday. We rotated shifts so I didn't have to work the late hours all the time. I dreaded taking the subway so late at night the times I worked the midnight shift. It also meant I couldn't have the card parties every Saturday, although I always met them later when they went out dancing. Juan's apartment wasn't far from the gallery, and I sometimes spent the night there if I commuted to work. Of course, on the weekends I didn't work late, Juan either picked me up or met me in the subway to head for my place for the weekend and the activities with the crowd.

But then there was that card with the phone number of the guy in Saugatauk in my wallet. It began to get the best of me, and I started fantasizing. Why those desires bothered me I never knew. Maybe Juan was right when he quipped, "You are always thinking of thot cock between your legs, Recharred!" Whatever the reason, on one of the Saturdays I was to work until ten, and because Juan hadn't made plans, I called the guy.

There was a one hour time difference so I didn't arrive at his place for dinner until two in the morning. I then realized that it was just as Juan always said. "Alcohol and dark lights do wonders for some people!" So I made certain I blinded myself with alcohol. He proved to be a perfect host with a wonderful steak dinner. I consumed a great amount of alcohol in order to put him in a better light, realizing at the same time that any sexual desires might go limp. His moist lips, however, managed to maintain my erection long enough to slip on a condom. The few pumps into him ended my evening of sex. Quite a contrast to the long fantasizing drive there.

A terrible feeling of guilt came over me once I awakened. I was certain Juan was calling my apartment! Though we hadn't planned to spend the day together, he still might be calling. After a quick excuse to avoid sex, I told him I needed to leave because of an engagement I forgot. He wasn't happy but it didn't matter. I had to get home. The only thing on my mind during the drive was that my phone was ringing continually with calls from Juan!

My concern was in vain, as it turned out. No messages were on my machine when I got home. It seemed as though Juan had gone out on Saturday, too, and that he felt as guilty as I did. Otherwise, he would have called continually. That evening, I stopped over to see him, and as I recall, he was eating quite a bit.

Ronnie, the young ceramic maker, invited the four of us to a Sunday barbecue to celebrate his move out of his parent's home. Unfortunately, I had to work, and there was no way I could change it because of vacations. So, the three of them went without me. Juan came over afterwards and raved endlessly about the great time he had!

"Recharred, this girl was thar, ond she was so much fun!" he went on to rave, "Her name is Amanda, ond she is so cute ond funny! She ond I were 'aving such a ball!" Then, while holding his hand on his chest in a dramatic pose, he sighed, "She is so small…just like a pixie!"

I expressed my regrets at not meeting her, only to hear him exclaim, "Aw you will be meeting her, Recharred. I told her how anxious I was for her to meet you, so we made plans to meet in two weeks ot a bar called The River's Edge. Aw, Recharred, I cannot wait until you meet her. You will love her!"

On the evening we were to meet Amanda, I was scheduled to work again, this time until midnight. However, I was determined to make it, since closing wasn't until three o'clock, and because it wasn't far from the station, I got off. Juan could surely leave the bar to pick me up. However, it was Phil who picked me up in Juan's car. Juan was too drunk to drive.

I felt like a celebrity the way Juan made over me once I got in the bar. He was so excited as he pushed gently to meet Amanda.

"Now, ot last, you are to meet Amanda ond she will, ot last, meet you, Recharred!" One would have thought this was the meeting of royal families. And it felt exactly that hearing Juan's elaborate and regal introductions.

Yes, she was tiny and cute, and exactly the pixie Juan described her to be! I swear I almost read the *tee-hee* caption above her head each time she giggled.

"Boy, Richard, that guy really thinks the world of you!" she sighed once Juan took off to buy drinks, "Ever since I met him, he has talked of no one but you, and with all praises!"

I somehow felt that we had met before, and it wasn't until about a month later that I remembered dancing one set with her at Hunter's. I was there on one of my lone outings when I ran into Ronnie coming in with a group of lesbians. When I mentioned it to Juan, the little boy in him still refused to submit, insisting on the claim of meeting her first.

I really hadn't seen much of Svetmana, and was thankful for it. The short encounters with her only made it obvious that her sarcasm had grown even more profound. In fact, Juan showed a great deal of disappointment each time he spoke of her.

"Aw, Recharred, she is such a mean ond nasty person," was a comment he'd often say. His only wish was for her to change, but that possibility appeared very slim. Amazingly, none of his wonderful qualities were inherited by her, except that she did eat daintily. And even at that, her elegant manner always appeared more arrogant than regal. She also tried to mimic people, a feat Juan was master of, only to come off rude and obnoxious instead. I soon discovered it was exactly how she meant it.

Juan had given her keys to his apartment so she could stay overnight when he wasn't home, and that was often because he was at my place almost every weekend.

"Recharred, I really think Svetmana is 'aving parties ot my place," he said, quite disturbed, "I know she is doing thot, jus' by looking ot the amounts left in my liquor bottles!"

"Juan, she's only sixteen," I remarked. "Something is gonna happen to those kids, and you will be the blame! For God's sake, take the keys away from her!" Of course he said he would, though I don't believe he ever did. The guilt complex had been hammered too deeply into him by Endira. And when he did scold her, it never took long before he took hold of her in his arms to say, "Aw, I love you, my darlin.' I am so sorry!"

He was also confronted with one problem after another regarding her behavior in school. It baffled him, especially since he knew her to be extremely intelligent. It didn't take me long to figure it out, however. I had learned long ago that she couldn't take orders. Endira had never taught her to take them, and neither did Juan, for that matter.

Juan talked me into having a housewarming party, and because I invited bar friends, too, over thirty showed up. It was far too many for my small apartment and impossible to focus as a group as I preferred. So I ended up with the typical cocktail type party I so detested where guests paired off. Before long, it felt like a steam room.

"Who the hell is that guy, and who the hell does he think he is?" inquired one of my bar guests, pointing to Juan. I chuckled to myself once he walked away in a huff. Juan was very drunk, and yet it was obvious that he still managed to catch it each time my bar guest had patted my butt. It was certain Juan had given him a few choice remarks.

Amanda arrived late with Ronnie and had taken me aside to say, "I really never got to finish telling you about Juan and the day at the barbecue. Never have I ever heard anyone talk so highly of someone, Richard! You were included in every conversation we had! It was as though you were part of him! You must feel wonderful to have someone love you that much."

"Oh, Amanda, I wish he'd just come out and admit it to me," I said very touched, "but he doesn't! I know how he feels because I can feel it within my body, and it is exactly how I feel about him! He is the only one I could ever want in my life because no one gives me joy and happiness like he does! But he will not commit to a relationship because he knows I will always be there for him. So he feels it is not necessary."

Autumn arrived and Juan, Vic, Phil, and I decided to take a Sunday drive to Galena to see the quaint mining town that boasted President Grant's home. As usual, the three of us did all the talking; Phil was in another one of his moods.

AIDS had become big news, especially after the shocking reports that Rock Hudson had it.

"Oh, that is that faggot disease," had been one of the ugly comments I heard so many times. So I tried to appear unconcerned when news reports aired while I was with family and friends.

"You know, the Army has decided to test everyone for HIV, ond our company is being tested in two weeks," Juan mentioned casually in the conversation about it during the drive.

"Do you know, I really think everyone should do thot," he added. No one really answered; that was something you only read about others getting.

The streets of Galena were jam-packed, and, as an alternative, we decided to take a river boat ride. However, we arrived there just as the boat took off. I had been there with my family years earlier, and suggested we drive to Dubuque as another alternative to ride the special tramcar up to the highest point. Three states could be seen from the top. I was certain Juan would love it, and he didn't disappoint me once we reached the top.

"Aw, Recharred, this is so bea-u-ti-ful! I am enjoying this better than fighting all those people on the streets of Galena!"

Juan was having money problems again, and was two months late in his car payments. I wasn't able to bail him since I was taking home very little at the new gallery.

"Recharred, I am gonna 'ave to 'ave them repossess the car. I jus' cannot make the payments," he confided one day. "I 'ave too many bills."

"Juan, you can't do that! Your credit will be ruined again for five years! Besides, you have already paid four years. You only have about a year more, don't you?" But he still insisted.

"See, if you didn't buy all that furniture, you wouldn't be in this mess! You didn't need that fancy glass dining table with the upholstered chairs!" I also thought of his extravagant spending on Svetmana, but kept my lips tightened on that one. No matter how I tried to convince him not to, he still insisted. I so wished that my job had not been such a disappointment.

"Please, don' tell anyone," he pleaded once the car was repossessed. One consolation, his office was only three blocks from his apartment, and he wouldn't be driving while drunk. We resumed meeting at the subway station every weekend to ride to Oak Park Avenue, where I parked my car. It was always so wonderful to catch that first glimpse of him with his overnight bag on his shoulders once I entered the subway. There was always that great big smile!

Four weeks had passed since Juan was tested for the HIV virus. We hadn't thought of it until he informed me that the sergeant-major had called him.

"He wants to see me in his office ot Fort Sheridan, Recharred. I don' know whot he wants to see me about. Besides I don' 'ave a car to get thar. Do you think thot you con get the day off ond drive me thar, Recharred?" Nothing was mentioned of the HIV test, but I knew he was thinking of it because he wasn't his happy self. I was sure nothing, could possibly be wrong.

Even though Juan kept the conversation lively, some tension was evident during the drive. The dreadful thought of Juan being HIV positive was ever present in our minds, but we refused to discuss it.

"Recharred, would you not mind to wait in the car for me?" Juan asked once I drove into the fort and parked, "You don' mind, do you not?" I assured him it was okay.

I can't recall how long I waited. I seemed to be in limbo, and the dreary clouds only added to that feeling. It had to be at least two or three hours of nervous twisting and turning within my body. I didn't want to think about the HIV virus and tried to appease myself with thoughts of them discussing his job. It wouldn't take this long to inform Juan that he had the virus.

Finally, Juan came into view. However, once he was near, I noticed that his walk wasn't his usual quick and proud manner. No, his shoulders were slumped. Never had he walked this way! There was also no smile on his face! I felt a sick feeling in my stomach but still refused to believe it had anything to do with the HIV virus! Of course! Juan was a very conscientious worker. He was bothered because he was reprimanded for something at work!

He took a deep breath after getting into the car slowly. My eyes focused on him anxiously.

"Recharred," he said, never looking more serious, "I am HIV positive!" A deadening silence filled the air as I stared at him in disbelief. A dreamlike limbo occurred again because my mind refused to believe it. My Juan was just given a death notice and I wouldn't accept it. This couldn't happen. He loved life too much! I didn't cry; this only happened to others, not Juan!

I truly felt he was kidding when the dreamlike silence ended, and yet the despair in his face was never more evident.

"Are you sure, Juan?" I pleaded once I realized his smile wasn't going to replace the despair. "Couldn't there be some mistake?"

"Recharred, they sent the blood test in a second time," he replied, breaking down in tears, "ond it came bock the same! They also checked to be sure the blood was mine. Ond, Recharred, it was! They are gonna take another test, jus' to be certain, but they feel sure it will come bock with the same results!" I still didn't cry. Juan was too strong, too full of life!

Juan went on, and every word spoken still remains in my heart.

"Recharred, aw, Recharred, the sergeant-major was so compassionate. He even took me in his arms ond cried with me! Aw, Recharred, whot am I gonna do? Whot am I gonna tell my family?" he cried out. "I don' wanna die! How con I tell them I am HIV positive? I won't tell them, Recharred, I won't tell them!"

"A cure will be found before anything happens to you," I said, taking hold of his hand. "No one needs to know anything about it." My firm assurance brought his tears to an end and his eyes appeared to suddenly have some hope.

"They did tell me thot I could live five to ten years, Recharred, if I take good care of myself!"

"We'll make sure of that, Juan," I assured him, "and we know that a cure will be found well before that time! Juan, you are going to live! You're too full of life to die!"

"Recharred, I want you to promise me thot you will not tell anyone," Juan pleaded, squeezing my hand firmly. "You 'ave to promise me!"

"You know I will promise, Juan," I replied. The fullness felt in my heart was tremendous as I continued. "You know I will! And you know you have me forever. You will always have me because we are gonna live to a ripe old age together!"

The drive was not like the others we were so used to once we were on our way. The usual happy chatter and laughter was replaced with the gray gloom of the dreary autumn day instead, and I'm sure Juan was also thinking of that accursed black star!

Thoughts of the evening I had stopped at Juan's apartment after work also flashed in my mind. He had called at work to tell me he had a terrible fever; no cold, but a high fever. I had bought crackers and juice to be certain he received some nourishment, and I remembered his confusion as to why he had a fever. And the next day, the fever was gone.

Last but not least, I remembered my lone trip to Saugatauk. Why Juan had never called that Sunday still baffled me. It wasn't like him. He always called. Did he do as I did? Go out and trick that Saturday night and feel guilty afterwards, too? Was that the reason he didn't call? It had to be because the heavy burden of guilt would never allow him to confront me immediately after.

All of this swam around in my head, searching for an answer to why this was happening to us. Just then, suddenly, a terrible realization flashed in my head!

Oh, my God, I thought, *could it be possible that Juan caught this dreaded disease the same night I went to Saugatauk? All the pieces seemed to fit together, and this sent a cold chill through my body. I wanted answers. Why did I have to fill my ego? Why didn't I insist we get together that evening, even though it would have been late? We got together so many times before when it was late. Why not then?* There were no answers, only the terrible questions running continually through my head.

Chapter Thirty-Seven:
This Unique Man

The tragic news didn't affect me in the same manner as Juan, and not because I wasn't the one diagnosed with the HIV virus. On the contrary, Juan was my life! The fact that Juan was given a death notice just never sank into my head. After all, I was always certain that his creator was so awed with him at creation that he dropped the mold and broke it. Why would so unique a man then be taken from us? No, he wouldn't. I was certain of it. They'd never take Juan!

One never tired of him, even when he was repetitious with things said or done. He had that magic, that gift to look and sound as fresh each time. No one was as giving either. He could have a cherished possession, but if someone admired it, he'd willingly give it to him, just for the joy of knowing a friend he liked had something he loved.

True, Juan was a mischievous elf, and totally frank and honest. To be his friend, one had to accept that honesty. Of course, not all queens could take the honesty.

"If they cannot take me for the way I am, I don't need them as a friend," he often said. "In fact, Recharred, you are all I need in this world!" However, his charming personality and contagious laughter, somehow, always managed to capture them!

He so detested losing that his pride would force him to destroy something we cherished, especially if he felt I had betrayed him. I had learned that with the gold band, and also with our wedding crowns. When I realized the crowns were missing, I had questioned him, and was told that he threw the box containing them away after hearing of my albino episode.

Juan was never envious of anyone or anything, and always was content with the simple things in life. So how could he possibly be taken from us? The music alone that he brought into our lives was something special. Why would anyone want it to end? He couldn't hold a tune, and yet no one could appreciate music more. I wrote a song in 1982 while doing the play in Indy, and he praised it immediately after hearing it. I think he realized it was written with him in mind.

"Aw, Recharred, thot song is bea-u-ti-ful, so bea-u-ti-ful! You should get it published, ond try to get Barbra Streisand to record it!" How could anyone take away the joy of watching and listening to him trying to sing:

Lonely, I find the days without you lonely—I seem to yearn for you only
Why must it be this way, why won't you come and stay?
Instead, you left my heart, so lonely
Dreaming, I spend my nights without you dreaming
I always dream of your scheming, to have it all your way, your love was out to play
You'd always leave me be so lonely.

You tore around with your head in the clouds, searching for new kinds of love. There I was standing around, longing to be all you were thinking of.

Lonely, I'll spend the years without you lonely
I'll long for times when you thrilled me—the way you smiled at me,
Your face so lovingly. I pray I'll one day see the day you'll come to me, so lonely, so lonely.

No, there was no possible way I could accept the fact that Juan was going to die of AIDS.

Chapter Thirty-Eight:
Joy, In Spite Of the Anxieties

Though the news devastated Juan, we still went on with our lives. I sometimes believed that he felt as I did…that the dreaded HIV virus wouldn't kill him. A cure would be found. I never imagined it was possible to be closer than we already were, and yet that virus began to mold us into one! However, I still refused to talk about it. He would not die of AIDS!

Then, the first of many anxiety attacks began. I received a call from Juan. He was in the emergency room of *Presbyterian - St. Luke Hospital*. He was very ill so he took a cab there. He described the terrible feeling throughout his body once I was directed to a cubicle in the emergency room, though he appeared fine. An intern then approached to say that Juan was in excellent shape. Juan's agitation disappeared immediately upon hearing that report. He had to hear the words from a doctor to assure himself that he wasn't sick. He'd then go on with his life until his mind got the best of him again, and each time, I raced to the hospital to hear that he was fine! When I had tried to explain that he was having anxiety attacks, he'd shake his head and describe the pains he was experiencing. Apparently, the worry brought on the pains, and he didn't realize that was the reason it was happening. And though he stopped running to the hospital after a couple of months, it didn't mean the attacks ended. He just finally accepted them for what they were.

It was remarkable! Outside of those anxiety attacks, Juan accepted his diagnosis with grace. He didn't look for pity, though he sometimes asked what so many others had asked, "Why me?" His normal behavior finally prevailed, and it wasn't unusual to hear him accept the inevitable and say, "If it has to be, it has to be!"

Still, I never wanted to hear it. Yes, he had his night sweats and would talk of them, but never in a worried state. After all, they were one of the signs of the disease.

"You know, Recharred, I might only 'ave five or ten years to live," he'd often say. Of course, I'd be upset, especially when he'd laugh.

So the HIV virus became a part of our lives, though Juan didn't prey on it. When he did talk of it, he was very calm, and I truly believe he felt as I did…that a cure would be found before it hit him. Being positive is an important factor in survival, and I was glad he knew it. At least, for my benefit, he appeared to believe it because he needed me to be positive for him.

"Recharred, I am still Juan," he'd say in his elfish way, "I will never change!" So, most of the time his diagnosis was shoved on the back shelf and everything was as always, only more beautiful! My love for him grew as I knew his did for me, and though we weren't lovers, we had something more important. We were becoming one person!

The crowd was totally unaware of the fact that Juan was HIV positive because he never faltered from being his charming and devilish self. Although I was sworn to secrecy, I still felt one of our friends should be aware of the bravery of this man. It would also give me someone to lean on. Marina was the only one I could trust; she never had been one to gossip. She proved to be the right choice because I was positive she held the secret as her own. However, she was never one to show emotion and so our talks regarding Juan's condition were far and few between.

The holiday season arrived, and I decided upon a Christmas breakfast for the crowd. I was spending the day with the kids. Juan was thrilled because we never had Christmas breakfast together. In keeping with the holiday spirit, we had gifts for all of them. Marina thoughtfully did the same, though Vic and Phil arrived empty handed again, though it was apparent that they were finally embarrassed. However, they reciprocated at a later date.

No one could ever show more excitement and appreciation when receiving a gift than Juan, and there was no exception this time. I was the only one capable of detecting a meaning behind his expressions, however, and this one was obvious when his eyes looked my way.

"What the heck are they giving me an electric knife carver, Recharred, when they know all my menus ever consist of is ground meat, cubed chicken breasts, and sausages, exclusively?"

Juan threw another New Year's Eve party, and besides all of us, quite a few of his old friends were there, too. Even Donald Coney, the big guy with the big mouth, came from Rhode Island. I must admit I was a bit apprehensive about seeing him, afraid he'd hand me one sarcastic remark after another again. Finally, after a drink or two, I decided to ignore the situation…to just be myself. It worked. Within an hour, he approached to say that he really liked me, and then apologized for his past rudeness.

Juan was a perfect host, keeping his drinking to a minimum in order to be certain everyone enjoyed themselves. It was hilarious watching his face while dancing with Jeannie. His eyes were bouncing in unison with her boobs and hairdo. And each time she went into one of her happy screaming jags, I thought he'd choke with laughter.

Juan only talked occasionally about his condition as the year moved on. However, the fact that he had not told his parents bothered him, and I never knew what to say when he mentioned it.

"I don' know how my father will react, Recharred," he said, knowing everyone called it the *gay disease*. "You know how he has already harassed me." It also reminded me of my concern should my family know. Through the years, we had done an excellent job of hiding our sexual orientation, and now that was in jeopardy. The bigotry we faced in society actually forced me to be ashamed to tell them! I somehow allowed it to be more important than JUAN'S LIFE! It controlled my logic. We were still the same persons our families loved, and that love could be the wonderful support Juan needed! He didn't need the added grief of guilt, or the fear of more verbal abuse from his father should he agree to take up my offer to move in with me.

"You know, Recharred, I 'ave to go twice a year to an Army HIV clinic, so my 'T' cell count con be checked, ond for counseling," Juan informed me one day. "I con either go to Washington DC or Denver. I think I would rather go to Denver though."

He also decided to fly commercially even though he'd have to pay for it. Flying standby for an Army flight would take too long and trying on his nerves.

"It will cost me a lot of money that I don 'ave," he barked. "Aw, Recharred, it looks like I still 'ave thot black star over me!"

Meanwhile, I accepted an offer for a sales position with another gallery on Michigan Avenue. The move proved a great one once I realized a tremendous increase in take home pay.

"Recharred, I will soon be transferred to Fort Sheridan in an office job," Juan said after informing me that the Army no longer allowed personnel to have contact with civilians.

"Whot am I to do, Recharred? It is my job!" he snapped back after I said I thought it was an absurd rule. "I 'ave to go where they send me! So I will definitely need a car."

Juan finally settled on a cherry red, four-door 1987 Dodge Omni once I agreed to put the loan in my name. It was Valentine's Day the evening we picked it up, and during the drive there, he couldn't thank me enough for agreeing to put it in my name. It was hilarious watching him play the game to the hilt once the salesman handed me the keys.

"Aw, Recharred, I am so glad you picked this color! It is perfect for today's date." And with a quick wink to the salesman, he added, "His girlfriend is really going to think it is for her!"

Almost two years passed since we were forced to admit Pa into a rest home. The crutch of his colostomy bag, which was impossible to reverse, and the sleepless nights Deena was subject to because of his hallucinations had made it the only alternative. Otherwise, she certainly would've ended up in the hospital. She harbored a terrible guilt for some time afterwards, and it wasn't until Pa adjusted to life there that she finally had some peace. Of course, all of us visited him more than when he was home. He was getting along wonderfully until he broke his hip from a fall while dressing. Unfortunately, when he returned to the rest home from the hospital, he was back to square one.

Everyone at Vic and Phil's annual turkey party were in stitches as Juan, Jeannie, and I came up with one sexy quip after another. Daniel had gained a good amount of weight, which fulfilled Stan's desire as a chubby chaser. So, with each quip, his belly shook more.

"Jesus, mon, your belly looks jus' like a bowl of Jell-O," Juan quipped. Of course, that only brought on more laughter from Daniel.

Amanda arrived late, which was a trait of hers we already were accustomed to. She brought along Patti, and the two of them seemed to be quite attached. Juan lost no time asking Patti if she spoke Spanish since she appeared to look so Latin. He missed speaking the language so much. Patti, however, was black. We soon discovered that she, too, had a tee-hee type laugh, though a deeper tone than Amanda's. We liked Patti, and were glad when told they were now a pair.

The only available week for another foursome in Saugatauk was early June, a time not favored by any of us. So we began throwing out alternative places during our card parties. However, every suggestion we'd make was either too expensive, or they just didn't want to go there. It began to sound like a broken record, and we actually felt they were no longer interested in going with us, especially because the subject was always changed immediately. We then decided to drop the subject for a while in hopes that they'd finally realize time was growing short.

"You know, it would be wonderful if we could all go to Boston," I finally remarked at one of the card parties. "I have always longed to go there, and then we could also go to Provincetown!"

They quickly objected to the expense, and in an attempt to arouse some excitement about the idea, I reminded them of Juan's friend, Donald, who lived in the area.

"We could save a lot of money because I bet he'd put us up. Juan said he's supposed to have a big house." Juan's quick assurance and excitement, however, did no good.

Phil replied immediately, "Oh, no, I wouldn't stay there! I don't like him! I just did not like him when I met him at Juan's New Year's Eve party!" So that was that!

"Recharred, I don' think Vic ond Phil want to go on vacation with us again," Juan said unhappily, "because every time we bring it up, they do not say a word. I con not understand? We had such a good time last year." I wondered if they were avoiding the vacation because Phil was still having fantasies about me.

Vic then called to say, "I don't know if we will be able to go on a vacation this year. I have so many old hospital bills that need to be paid." It seemed as though they wanted to break ties.

"Recharred, I am not gonna stay in this hospital next time I come here," Juan's voice rang out once I answered the call from Denver. "I cannot get any sleep because this black guy plays his radio so loud every night!" It was his first trip there, and we hadn't yet talked.

"Well, at least you now know how it sounded to everyone in our buildings, Juan, when you played the stereo at full blast late at night!" Of course he ignored my witty caparison and went on about his dilemma. It was good to hear him go on so strongly though, and especially when he calmed down and said he missed me.

Juan's last call before he returned was the best. He had already informed me that a count of 300 in his "T" count would mean worries. "Recharred, my 'T' count is still high…twelve hundred," were the first words I heard, "ond I am so happy!"

I never celebrated Juan's fortieth birthday because it fell during the time we weren't seeing each other, and since June 24 was approaching, I planned on making up for it with a surprise forty-fourth party. I realized it wasn't going to be an easy chore because he was spending the weekends at my place. Where would I hide the food trays when he came over Friday night? He always went into the refrigerator. After explaining the problem to Marina, she offered to give me her apartment keys so I could put everything in her refrigerator on the way to work that afternoon. She'd bring them over Saturday and set up before we arrived. She'd also pick up the cake.

I ran around like a chicken without a head Friday morning preparing the food, and dropped everything off at Marina's, except two gelatin molds. Those I hid behind several jars in my own refrigerator. I was on pins and needles that evening each time Juan went into the refrigerator. Luckily, he never noticed.

Juan was to pick me up at work after spending the day at his mom's, and we'd get ready at my place because I told him I was taking him out for his birthday. I said I needed to work later to allow time for everyone to get to my house before us. I thought of nothing that day but the excitement that would erupt from him once he was surprised with the party.

When he picked me up, I told him that my son, Nicky, stopped at the gallery for the key to my apartment to get something I borrowed from him. This made it possible to ring the bell several times, as a warning, while he was busy inserting his key into the foyer door.

"Whot's all thot noise, Recharred?" Juan asked as he inserted his key into the lock on my door. I couldn't believe they weren't quiet after hearing my bell warnings, though the worried expression on his face was priceless!

"Aw, it's probably Nicky and his friends, Juan," I quickly thought to say. "The Cub game is still on and they're probably watching it."

"Aw, I can't open the door, Recharred," he whispered nervously, moving away as though he was entering illegally.

"Juan, what's the difference? Nicky knows you're here a lot." Still, he insisted I be the one to open the door. So I abided, but still managed to hold onto him so he'd be the first one seen once I swung the door open. And though I held onto him he never suspected anything. He stood there.

"SURPRISE!" everyone shouted as Juan stood there in shock.

"Jesus Chris,' Recharred!" he gasped, holding his hand to his chest in awe. "I am so surprised…so surprised! How did you manage to do this, Blanche?" It worked! He was truly surprised! Even more joyous was hearing him say repeatedly, "I don' believe it! I really don' believe it!"

Everyone was there, that is, except Amanda and Patti. Juan hugged everyone, and was especially pleased because I thought to invite a couple of friends from the old crowd he and Marina were going with. He then lost no time mixing a cocktail for the two of us to set the party mood.

I had written names of celebrities on slips of paper as a get acquainted game, and informed Marina to pin them on everyone's back once they arrived. Everyone was not to eat before the party, and just as she started to pin one on us, Daniel called out, "Richard, don't worry about that now because everyone has already guessed theirs. Why don't we eat now? I already finished all the snacks and I am still starving!"

Daniel took my kidding about his weight good naturedly, and he accepted it from Juan, too.

"Now, my good woman," Juan said in his high-pitched voice, "you will soon be able to add to your belly!" The table was ready in moments, and just by the festive chatter going on, I knew the evening was going to be great!

Juan never thought of food at a party unless it was a sit down dinner. So, while everyone was busy filling their plates, he was putting on records. He wanted to dance, even if Jeannie had to hold her plate while dancing with him! In between bites, she managed to keep him laughing. I was then relieved when he ate enough from the plate I filled to saturate some alcohol.

Juan hurried to hug and kiss Amanda and Patti when they finally arrived.

"Recharred has done a bea-u-ti-ful thing for me," he sighed. "Aw, I was so surprised, so surprised!" Then with that definite air of elegance, he added, "Of course, I really deserve it!" And of course, this brought out their giggles.

Pointing out a time when Juan was the happiest could be a difficult task because he loved life so much! But if I had to…this would be the time. He glowed like a star! He was so happy he even stopped dancing and agreed to party games. He knew I detested parties with guests pairing off into couples. Party games always kept things rolling as a group.

Goose the Moose was a game I introduced him to years earlier. Of course, I had to put my hand over his mouth to keep him from giving away the climax with his hilarious recollection of it. Fortunately, his gagging laughter muffled his comments enough not to be heard.

All that was needed was a blindfold, plenty of towels, and something I had to be certain no one saw…a jar of Vaseline! I hustled everyone into the bedroom to keep them from hearing any more of his anxious comments. His uncontrollable laughter was certainly going to spill the beans. In fact, it was so contagious that I was doing the same. I finally contained myself enough to settle him down so he could follow my instructions.

"Bring in the first one, Juan, but be sure you hold onto the blindfold so they can't see. Then, guide him to me. Be certain to tell him to stick out his finger, and to moo because he's a moose looking for his mate. Now, remember, even if you have to take hold of his finger to stick it out."

It was a pity the others missed seeing Juan guide six-foot-four Marina my way. His laughter was near hysteria as he led her in backwards, holding onto the blindfold desperately. The fact that her face was almost parallel to the ceiling while her arm and finger stretched out before her made it even more hilarious! He was blinded with laughter, and they finally fell over and onto the couch! Amazingly, he managed to hold onto the blindfold while the two of them scrambled off the couch. Even more amazing, he actually made certain her finger plunged into the jar of Vaseline just as he pulled off the blindfold to catch the expression on her face. Of course, Marina had to take over leading everyone in because Juan fell into the couch in helpless laughter. The game continued, and with each person, the laughter and mooing got louder. I had played the game many times while married, and never came across anyone close to the magic of Juan's. That magic that made others laugh so hard.

The evening went on at its fast and fun pace, and it was hot, hot, hot! However, no one seemed to mind the heat. They were having too much fun. Juan's friend, Arthur, suggested we play *Under the Blanket*, though I decided to use a sheet instead. The sheet was placed over the head and body of a player while the others waited their turn in the bedroom. They were then asked to take off something they didn't need. The players then continued to remove clothing until it dawned on them that the sheet was the item that wasn't needed. Until they figured it out, the discarded items kept everyone in stitches. The highlight of the game was Juan's contagious fit of laughter once Marina handed out her bra. Everyone fell to the couch or floor in belly laughs.

Juan looked so proud sitting in the middle of the room opening his gifts. Sincere gratitude was written all over his face. However, he still felt he had to add more laughter by quipping, "Of course, I deserve this!" And how proud I was that he was still sober enough to really enjoy himself! The alcohol wasn't having the wonderful time…Juan was!

The glow from the candles on the cake caught the wonderful smile on Juan's face, and it was apparent to me that this was one of the happiest days of his life. And once his eyes caught mine, I could almost hear him rave, "Aw, my Recharred, you did all this just for me!"

It was apparent no one wanted the evening to end, but before we knew it, everyone was saying good night. The party was over, and my heart swelled when I realized this was the first time Juan didn't insist we go out dancing afterwards. Instead, he savored the precious moments of the evening.

Chapter Thirty-Nine: Loose Ties

An absolutely orderly apartment greeted me when I awakened the morning after, and there was Juan puttering in the kitchen. And the joyous part of it was that he showed no signs of a hangover. He was so chipper that one would never think he did any drinking the night before.

"Recharred, thot party had to be the best one you ever had," he quickly remarked once I managed to make an appearance in the kitchen. "I laughed so hard ond so much!"

"That was because it was your party, and because *you* were there," I replied with a smile.

"When Vic could not figure out thot he had to pull off the sheet, ond kept taking off his clothes…aw, Recharred, it was so funny!" he remarked, gagging on his laughter. "Ond thot Jeannie when she kept screaming ofter she stuck her finger in the Vaseline! Did you see her face? Aw, ond Marina's bra was the best!" Although his cheerful patter and laughter continued, he still managed to prepare his frittata, and in his meticulous manner.

"Do you know, Recharred, thot Marina has told me thot she never has had sex in her life," he remarked, his tone suddenly becoming serious, "Not even as a man." I was amazed but not really surprised, especially since she always struck me as frigid. It was apparent each time we embraced her; a sudden coldness always came over her. She also couldn't show emotion.

"Recharred, I had such a good time last night, the best ever!" Juan sighed reflectively after breakfast, "ond I cannot begin to thank you enough for doing all thot for me."

He then surprised me placing his hand over mine, and with tears in his eyes, he said, "My darling." He had said that to me on occasion to show how special I was to him, and it never came off as feminine or mushy. He had that quality.

We knew the party was the best ever after receiving calls of praise from almost everyone.

"Recharred, I am going to Boston," Juan quickly announced coming into the apartment. "I already called Donald, ond he says thot he would be glad to 'ave me stay ot his house."

"What do you mean, *you* are going?" I inquired feeling abandoned. "Can't I go, too?"

"Of course you con go, Recharred," he replied with a chuckle. "You know you are always welcome to go with me anywhere!"

"Then why did you say that *you* were going, and why didn't you ask me first?"

"Because I wanted to see if you really wanted to go without me asking," he replied, flashing one of his elfish grins.

"Oh, you and your tests all the time! You know I wanted to go there, and that I always want to go places with you. You always have to be so coy!"

Vic and Phil were no longer calling daily. In fact, we hardly heard from them unless we called. It bothered Juan because he always considered them to be our closest friends. So we did likewise. In order to avoid the discomfort indifference brings, our calls were only when necessary. We could also wait until Patti's party to tell them about Boston.

"We'll meet you at Patti's," Vic responded to my question regarding the time they would meet at my place. Our custom always was to meet at my place before going out on the town or a party. It made the evening more festive.

We didn't have a chance to greet Vic and Phil, who were at the far end of the living room, because Patti took us on a tour of her Victorian home as soon as we arrived with Marina. It would be our last chance to see it before she and Amanda moved into a new townhouse they purchased. Marina didn't join us for the tour.

We were particularly pleased when Vic hurried over to greet us once we returned to the living room, though our anticipation for a joyous greeting was soon crushed.

"I hear both of you are going to Boston in a couple of weeks," he quickly remarked with obvious sarcasm, "Why didn't you tell us? I thought we were supposed to go somewhere together!" They had avoided the subject continually each time we brought it up, and now he's complaining because they're not included? It didn't make sense! And when I mentioned the fact that he called to say that they undoubtedly wouldn't be able to go on vacation because of his back hospital bills, he denied it!

Phil walked over in that cool manner of his that he did so well and didn't say a word as Vic continued his verbal abuse. His smug expression said enough.

"Then why didn't you tell us when you first arrived? It was the least you could do!" My attempt to explain did no good. He continued and when we finally broke away, we avoided them for the rest of the evening....

When we approached Marina, we found that while Patti took us on tour, she told them we invited her to go along. In reality, Donald had invited her, too, when she phoned him but she refused because of the lack of money. This didn't make Juan unhappy.

"Aw, Recharred, I love Marina, but I am so relieved that she did not accept Donald's invite," he had remarked. "Everyone would know we were gay, just by looking ot her walk like a man. If only she would listen to Jeannie ond be more feminine."

"Recharred, they really did not want to go anywhere," Juan later remarked at the party. "They were jus' peeved thot we were going! Ond they wanted to make it appear as though they had intended on going somewhere with us. Thot way we could look like the bad guys."

"Yeah, I know, but did you hear Phil again show his jealousy towards you? He just had to mention that I always did what you want, even though it was me who suggested we all go to Boston in the first place."

"Exactly, Recharred, so don' let it bother you. They were jus' acting like typical queens, which really surprises me about Vic." We finally realized, though, that it was Phil's doings, and that Vic was merely supporting him.

"Phil was jealous because you were going on vacation with me, Recharred, ond I am certain Vic has been aware of this fantasy he has for you. Besides, did you not tell me thot Vic was aware of another fantasy he had for a friend of Daniel's ond thot he allowed him to go out with him to do whatever he wanted thot night?"

"Yeah, I couldn't believe it when Daniel told me."

"Well, thot's whot happened again. Vic was protecting him from being hurt, because he is afraid of losing him. I cannot understand it myself, Recharred. Even though he is over twenty years older than Phil, he still is better looking, ond he has a much better personality! Yet he feels thot he will not find anyone if he loses Phil. It is a shame, Recharred, a real shame."

The atmosphere finally cleared up, but it was apparent that our friendship was never going to be the same again. Those ties that were once so tight were now very loose. We were well aware of it when we attended a party at Vic's place. Old friends of theirs that they had lost contact with completely were all on hand. It was difficult for Juan to accept. How could a sexual fantasy ruin so beautiful a friendship?

Chapter Forty:
A Dream Vacation In Spite Of Donald

"Recharred, why did you 'ave to say we would go thar?" Juan complained when I said Jacque invited us for dinner. "You know we 'ave to get up before six tomorrow in order to catch our flight to Boston. I wanted to jus' stay 'ome ond jus' relax, but all you con think of is filling your belly with free food…*mangia…mangia*! Thot is all you think about, Blanche!" However, he did give way to my demands on occasion. And, again, he was the one who talked on and on, keeping us there quite late.

"I love you, Dad," Jacque called out while I backed out of the driveway. "Don't forget to call that number for the limousine service to pick you up at the airport. They are great!" We had had a great evening talking about the places to see in Boston and though we already called for a cab company for the morning, Juan was excited about the limousine.

"Aw, Recharred, I would really like to try thot one when we return to Chicago, because I 'ave never been in a fancy limousine, ond I want to do it ot least once in my life!"

"Look, Recharred, they look like father ond son!" Juan kidded once he spotted Donald and his young lover at the end of the arrival ramp, and after Tim waved, he gasped and added, "Aw, Jesus Chris,' he is waving like a nellie queen!" I cringed, realizing what was in store for us, especially since I already had seen Tim in action when they stayed at Juan's while visiting Chicago. One would have thought his arms were made of cellophane paper. Juan didn't mind then because they were on their own except for one dinner out with us. Donald was built like a bull, while Timothy was very slim and boyish. Or maybe a better description would be…girlish.

They made over Juan like he was a celebrity, almost ignoring me in the process. I didn't mind, though. Juan should have the attention. After all, Donald was his friend. He was so happy as he talked in that fast manner of his, and that is what I wanted...for him to be happy. I was somewhat disturbed, however, when I learned that our entire schedule was already planned by Donald. All the times were to be spent with them! I was stunned, especially since Juan had said that we'd be on our own most of the time. Otherwise, why would he mention that Donald had two cars, and that he told him we could use one? I finally accepted the fact that more people would make it more festive and Juan loved parties. They'd certainly make certain we took in the historical sites we both loved to see. Would Juan accept being in public with Timothy continually though? Would it cause him stress, and to cringe every time Timothy flicked his wrist while saying, "Well, how do you like that sight, Mary?" I prayed it wouldn't.

"We figured we could leave in the morning for Provincetown," Donald explained, "and stay for two days or so. And by the way, there is a party in your honor, Juan, next Saturday night in Connecticut at one of my friend's house!" Of course, Juan was elated and managed to voice his gratitude with that flair of elegance he did so well.

"Yes, we are going there on Friday, and will stay through Sunday," Timothy thought to add. I wondered if Juan had explained that our intentions were to see many of the sights in Boston and Cape Cod? At this point, none of them were mentioned. And it wasn't until Juan got excited about going to Faneuil Hall as I suggested that they finally agreed to take us.

"Aw, look, Recharred, ot all the wonderful ethnic food stonds, ond the bea-u-tiful grounds!" Juan raved, completely awed with the festive atmosphere of Faneuil Hall. He almost exploded with excitement when he spotted a South American concession.

"Aw, Recharred, look! They 'ave empanadas! Aw we 'ave to 'ave some! Donald, 'ave you ever 'ad them? They are so delicious, so delicious! You 'ave to 'ave some!" Well, even if they hated them, there was no way they could refuse or show dislike for them. No, not after Juan's show of excitement over them.

When we settled on a bench in the park area to eat them, my presence was totally ignored by Donald and Timothy, and yet I felt satisfied just watching the happiness in Juan. He needed the attention and love, and he was getting it. That was enough for me!

Donald lived in Providence and insisted on treating us to one of his favorite restaurants in his neighborhood that evening, a seafood restaurant. Though not a fancy place, the servings were plentiful. I ordered a seafood combination in a cream sauce that was delicious.

Juan's intentions were to tell Donald of his HIV diagnosis, and I agreed because he needed as much support as possible. However, I was somewhat surprised at Donald's calm reaction.

"So what's new," he calmly remarked. I figured he apparently had heard the grave news from his friends repeatedly. When I thought of it later, I realized it was the right thing to do. Juan didn't need the dramatics of someone gasping as though he was already dead.

Providence was a historical city and I was glad when Donald granted Juan's wishes to see the downtown. As usual, Juan was thrilled because he was in another city of the United States, and it again joined the many places that he'd not mind living in.

We planned to leave early in the morning for Provincetown, and I was shocked when Juan confessed to being tired, and that he was going to bed. It wasn't like him to cut an evening short, especially when there was so much to talk about. Two twin beds were placed side by side in the bedroom we were to sleep in because there wasn't enough room to leave space between them. I quickly reminded Juan of the time I pushed the two beds together at the Hyatt Hotel in Atlanta, and we laughed. Somehow, I felt that Juan was thinking the same, wishing we were back there.

"I'm going to bed, too," Timothy said, flicking his wrist. "After all, Mary, I do have to get my beauty sleep, too." Juan, of course, managed to flash a crossed eyed expression in my direction. The scenario allowed Donald and me the chance to get acquainted, and I was grateful since he revealed his concern regarding Juan's condition. Our talk also relieved my apprehensions about spending our entire vacation with them. His appeared very sincere, and I liked him.

"Richard, I cannot begin to count the times Juan talked of you during our times together," Donald remarked, as so many others had said in the past. "You were always brought into every conversation, and always in the highest regard." I was touched, and especially happy because Donald's war against me seemed to be at an end.

I felt so good to see Juan sleeping so soundly once I got into the bed immediately next to him. I could touch him like we were in the same bed…like when we were in Atlanta, and I fell asleep with a smile thinking of how he made certain the beds were pushed apart in the morning so the hotel housekeeper wouldn't know we slept together.

I was then awakened suddenly with severe cramps during the night. The pain was excruciating, and yet I wouldn't awaken Juan. No position gave relief and I wanted to scream out in pain, but I wouldn't. Juan needed his rest. Cold sweats finally forced me to make my way into the bathroom. I really felt like I was in the process of dying and that I needed to get Donald to take me to a hospital when diarrhea and vomiting climaxed each spasm. I couldn't switch fast enough and I was certain the bathroom would be in a mess! The vacation was ruined! I was certain of it! This had to be a severe case of food poisoning and I was going to die! It went on for over an hour, and I felt sure that my moans could be heard throughout the house. Miraculously, as quick as it all began, it ended and I returned to cuddle next to Juan. I told Juan about it in the morning and we agreed not to upset Donald by telling him I got food poisoning at his favorite restaurant.

Provincetown was very much like Saugatauk, but on a grander scale. Though it rained during the drive, it was now sunny and bright. Donald managed to find a gay-operated hotel, much like a cottage arrangement, and we checked in. It was clean and would give us the freedom to be ourselves.

"The show is the rave of Provincetown," the desk clerk said in answer to our inquiry about entertainment for the evening. "You will laugh your asses off, besides loving the food! And I am not just saying it because the same person who owns that place owns this one, I really mean it!"

"Please, then, will you make reservations for tonight," Juan urged excitedly.

Provincetown always was known as the place to go in gay circles, but gays certainly didn't seem to be in the majority in the streets. It brought on immediate concern to Juan and myself because of Timothy's flamboyant and feminine outbursts in public.

"Oh, Mary, look at that hunk," he yelled, waving his arm out of the car window while driving through the busy downtown. The sidewalks were jammed with people and he still continued to flutter his arm like a butterfly while pointing to a guy he assumed as gay.

"Oh, she is cute! Hey, Mary, will we see you at the nude beach?" Unfortunately, I couldn't get my camera focused on Juan's face fast enough.

"Recharred, I hate the way he refers to guys as 'she' all the time," Juan later remarked to me while looking out to sea from the boardwalk of a gay tea-dance, "I hate thot, Recharred!"

"So do I, but that is the way a lot of gays talk, especially the younger queens! Why don't you tell Donald it bothers you so he can have Timothy stop it?"

"Aw, Recharred, I cannot do thot. It would hurt Donald's feeling," Juan replied, surprising me greatly. It had to be the first time he refused to speak his mind. And as we watched everyone dance to the music on the covered boardwalk, I remembered the times Juan insisted on a cocktail in order to set the mood to join them on the floor.

Juan's excitement was overwhelming on leaving the hotel for dinner. He was that little kid again, anxious to see the show everyone is raving about. We were aware of the fact that parking was near impossible in the downtown area and suggested taking a cab. Donald insisted on driving, however. Everyone's mood was up and we didn't argue.

Donald managed to drive into the last available space in the hotel parking lot, but just as we all piled out, a young fellow came running over.

"I'm sorry, but you are not allowed to park here," he shouted. Of course, we told him we were having dinner there, only to be told that parking was for hotel guests only. It didn't matter that we were guests at the other hotel. There were only enough parking spaces for hotel guests. We should have left it at that, but we lingered on instead, griping in the process. It was the wrong thing to do because it only agitated Donald more, and he continued shouting.

The manager of the hotel, or owner, suddenly appeared on the scene to check out the reason for the commotion. Instead of explaining in a humble manner, he immediately cried out for us to leave. All of us accepted his poor business judgment, except Donald. He refused to budge, and began shouting vulgar profanities instead. Unfortunately, the owner followed suit, which only infuriated Donald more! He became completely manic, and before we knew it, we were struggling to restrain him from engaging in violent, physical contact. Juan never liked fights, and pleaded with Timothy to start the car while we coaxed Donald in. We finally succeeded in talking him into the car, though he still shouted out the window as Tim drove out. I never had seen anyone become that wild over so trivial a matter, and was glad I wasn't the one on the receiving end.

Donald continued shouting, not realizing the disappointment he caused Juan. I only had to look at Juan's face to realize it. I was determined though. Juan had come to have a good time, and he was going to have it! I told Timothy to drive further into town while we tried to divert Donald's mind. Finally, he stopped talking about it and was quiet. Timothy followed suit and it appeared as though the evening was doomed. Juan and I, however, were determined to keep the fun rolling.

We ended up at a rundown diner that wasn't air conditioned, and this was supposed to be our night on the town. Still, we continued to be up. Donald, meanwhile, slipped into a shell, and Timothy respected his wishes by doing the same. They remained silent and just accommodated our wishes. It never occurred to Donald to apologize to Juan for his behavior, especially since it ruined any chance to see the show he was so excited about. So we tried to keep the mood up by kidding with the waitress. In the course of our conversation, she suggested we take in the female impersonator show in the lounge just above the restaurant. It wasn't what we really wanted to see, but we realized it was impossible to do anything else without reservations. So we headed up!

Only two performers were on the bill, though one of them turned out to be a black queen from Atlanta…Dena Jacobs!

"Con you beat thot, Recharred, I don' believe it," Juan shouted brightly. "Who would think thot our Miss Peachstate would be here!" And when she joined us at our table between shows, he became that thrilled little kid again! Everything was fine again. The unfortunate happenings in the parking lot were gone from our minds as we joked and laughed with Dena. We tried including Donald and Timothy in the conversation, but it did no good. They remained quiet.

"Everyone keeps wondering when a third pageant will be held," Dena replied once Juan asked if anyone ever mentioned his pageant. "In fact, I would really like to be there to present the crown to the winner if you ever decide on another one."

"Did you hear thot, Recharred?" Juan shouted excitedly, "My pageant must really be important for them to talk about it so much!"

"I know, Juan, but we're not going back again because we lost money last time…remember?" He needed the reminder, and I didn't need the temptation.

"Is it not a small world, Recharred," Juan exclaimed, smiling broadly once Dena left to do her act. "You know, it was so good to hear about all the queens in Atlanta. I don' believe thot Ronda LaRue 'ad a sex change, ond thot she married a rich man?"

Then placing his hand to his chest in that manner of his that showed absolute awe and disbelief, he gasped, "How do you like thot, Recharred? Boy, she was such a spitfire, ond do you know I think she drank three times as much as me!"

"You don't have to remind me of that, Juan. I know how much those queens drank because they were more belligerent than you when I cut them off!"

"Remember the time she was sitting ot the bar, ond telling us thot she had picked up some guy the night before," he asked, his eyes glowing with the hilarious memory. "Remember? Thot she told us thot she was the one who fucked him!"

"How could I forget it, Juan," I answered, trying to control myself once his contagious laughter got to me.

"Remember how we laughed, Recharred, when she said thot she was still dressed in drag! Aw, Recharred, she was so funny when she said thot her wig was moving all over her head ond thot her false tits were falling out while she was pumping away on him!"

"How could I forget it, Juan! It was so gross!" Juan finally collapsed into uncontrollable laughter once I inquired, "Don't you remember that I told her that they should have been in Ripley's Believe It or Not?"

"Jus' think, Recharred," Juan thought to mention after recovering from his gagging laughter, "one time she is fucking someone, ond the next time she has no dick!"

Dena had turned out to be a Godsend.

Our decision to completely ignore the unfortunate episode the next morning worked. Donald was chipper again, and laughed at every funny quip Juan thought to say. We were on our way to the beach, and just as we were about to get into the car, the desk clerk poked his head out.

"I understand that you guys caused quite a stir last night over at the parking lot of the night club!" he shouted sarcastically. It was all the ammunition needed to once again set off a firecracker! And it exploded instantly! Donald flared up like the Fourth of July! He immediately denied any fault. Of course, this provoked the desk clerk, and he continued the rehashing. Donald went into a crazy fit, and again, we felt helpless! We certainly didn't need another battle to ruin the day.

"Wait a minute," I interjected, intending to explain that he and his boss needed to practice some humility and courtesy with customers. "Let me tell you what happened!" However, I never got to say another word. Donald came at me like a bull!

"You keep your fuckin' mouth shut," he shouted, pushing his body against mine while holding his clenched fist to my face, "or I will shove this fist down your throat, you asshole!"

I was in shock, and it didn't matter when I tried to explain. He wasn't listening! He just continued to push me around the lot, shouting profanities and threats instead! It was unbelievable! I had seen some split personalities in my life, but never the likes of this madman! Juan stood there in shock! Timothy finally used some sense by forcibly taking hold of him, attempting to calm him while guiding him into his car. However, his vicious threats continued once he was behind the wheel. My nerves were completely shot, and as I glanced around for some support, I noticed that the idiotic desk clerk had disappeared, obviously grateful that I got the maniac off of his back.

"You are not welcome in this car, you asshole!" he shouted, continuing his rage. "C'mon, Juan, you know you are welcome!" I was stunned! The madman actually thought Juan would leave me and go with him? Juan had never moved throughout the mad episode and I'm certain his hesitation was because he was trying to reel back from the reality of what just happened. Finally, he told him he was staying with me, and with that, Donald sped off!

"Aw, Recharred, whot happened to him?" Juan questioned after a few moments of silent disbelief. "I don' understand it? Aw, Recharred, I am so sorry." I began pacing about haplessly, trying to settle the trembling surging throughout my body.

"I hope you realize, Juan," I sighed, coming to a halt and looking into his eyes, "that we cannot stay here with them now. Even if he should apologize, it will not be a friendly atmosphere, and I doubt that he'll apologize anyway! He never said a word about last night, and he knows your condition! The damn guy is a crazy man! A schizo! I wouldn't want to chance it! He's had two manic outbreaks in less than a day already! Juan, I can't believe how he got! I know that he would've socked me all over the place if Timothy hadn't grabbed onto him to pull him away! The guy's crazy!"

Juan never looked so low. He needed Donald for support, too, and suddenly I was taking it away! He was completely baffled, trying to comprehend how it was possible for someone so gentle to suddenly turn into a violent Mr. Hyde? They were close friends for two years before I came back into the picture, and suddenly he was confronted with someone he didn't know!

I tried to sort it out in my head. I realized Donald thought the world of Juan. So he never acted in this manner towards him. He never liked me from the start…but why? Could I possibly deserve so horrible a treatment merely because he didn't like my show? No, there had to be more! Could Donald's feelings for Juan be more than a close friendship? He was aware of Juan's feelings for me, and maybe that forced him to deny his own for Juan. Could that have triggered an intense jealousy to grow against me? I don't think Juan ever really knew.

I was sure Juan felt uneasy about leaving. He liked Donald very much and this was like betraying him. I also was sure he was relying on my easygoing nature to forgive and forget, but this time, I wouldn't. I couldn't chance another manic outburst. Juan needed to be kept in good spirits, and that could only happen if both of us were enjoying ourselves.

"But, Recharred, whot are we gonna do? We don' 'ave a car, ond the rest of our luggage is bock ot Donald's house."

"Juan, let's just walk downtown because I'm sure there is a car rental place. We should be able to rent one that can be dropped off in Boston. Then we'll come back here to wait for them to return from the beach and make arrangements to pick up our luggage tomorrow night." We were on our way, but it was apparent Juan was feeling bad. He also hadn't figured on the extra expenses we'd incur for hotel and such in Boston. I quickly told him I'd charge them.

The sun was horrendously hot, and the humidity so high that there wasn't much relief in the shade as we continued our search…. To our misfortune, no one had drop-offs in Boston, and the only bus of the day already left. Juan was exhausted and I suggested we give up, but in respect to me, he insisted we continue. However, the possibility of finding one looked bleak.

"You can drop our car off in Hyannisport," was like music to our ears once we inquired at the very next rental office. "I know you can then rent one there that can be dropped off in Boston."

It was the middle of the afternoon when we returned to the hotel to find they were already back from the beach. The hours apparently had cooled down Donald's temper because he looked very calm as they stood on the balcony of our room waving to Juan. However, the car brought a puzzled expression to his face. I didn't expect an apology, and he certainly didn't surprise me with one. I had no intention of bringing up the mess again since attempts to explain my actions that morning only antagonized him more. The fact that I merely wanted to teach the desk clerk and owner some humility had gone completely over his head that morning. Why try to explain again?

It didn't bother Donald in the least that I was leaving because he actually thought Juan was staying. Arrangements were to pick up our luggage the next evening.

I found it odd that even though Donald looked sad because Juan was leaving, he still didn't embrace him, or even say that he was sorry. As I drove off, my mind thought of the irony of it all. We actually had thought our expenses would be minimal, and that there wouldn't be any hotel or car rental expenses for the rest of the vacation. Instead, we had prepaid one hundred dollars for a second day in a room we wouldn't spend the night in, with still more to follow. And not only had we rented one car, we'd have to rent another one, too!

"I know Donald was trying to protect himself by lying to the desk clerk," Juan related in a brief rehashing of the sorry happenings of the morning, "ond when you started to try to explain everything, he thought you were going to tell him the truth, Recharred."

"Juan, you know that is not what I was going to do. I wanted to explain that the owner should've practiced some humility and not lost his temper, too. There was no reason for him to come at me like that! He acted as though I was an enemy instead of a friend!"

"No, Recharred, he should've not acted so violent ot you, so crazy! I always knew he had a temper, but I never saw him thot bod."

"It is for the best, Recharred," Juan sighed after a moment. "Besides, I don' think I could 'ave taken much more of Timothy flickin' his wrists, ond referring to guys as *she* all the time." A fantastic mimic of Timothy followed and this assured me of Juan's approval to our departure even though there seemed to be some apparent sadness surfacing. After all, Donald had been a good friend of his and I was taking him away. The thought of it brought an ache to my heart. So there he was, raving on about the scenery while I thought only of him. I could only think of how wonderful it was to be with him alone, and of the joy he always managed to fill my life with. I wanted it forever, and a lump came into my throat as the thought of losing it all came to mind. My nose swelled and with that, tears followed. I turned my head quickly so Juan wouldn't notice. Juan, however, never missed a trick.

"Whot's the matter, Recharred?" he asked softly. "Why are you crying?"

"I was just thinking how wonderful it is to be with you, Juan." His bittersweet smile held on as he continued to look my way. He had to be sure these were real tears.

"Oh, Juan, I was thinking of everything that happened and how sorry I am that it did because it shouldn't have! I love you so much, Juan, and I never want our times together to ever end." Of course a fresh batch of tears erupted as I sighed, "Oh, Juan, you make me so happy!"

He couldn't be more touched. I was certain he felt honored knowing I'd cry for him.

"Recharred, thar is no one I ever want to be with than you, ond now we are together to do whatever we want. Thar is so much to see! Look, Recharred, how bea-u-ti-ful everything is here!" I told him that I loved him repeatedly, but my tears were what he wanted to assure him of my love.

Hyannisport proved to be everything we expected and more, though our late departure from Provincetown made our arrival much too late for any tours. We walked to the piers after our late dinner to watch the boats coming in instead. It proved to be quite satisfying.

"Aw, Recharred, this is really Cape Cod! Is it not bea-u-ti-ful!? Aw, would it not be wonderful if we con take the trip to *Martha's Vineyard* tomorrow, because, Recharred, thot is really supposed to be so nice." The schedule, however, didn't work for us since the boat didn't return until eleven at night and we needed to be at Donald's by seven. Nevertheless, the day turned out perfect. We took a short boat trip instead. The humidity ended, and as we enjoyed the great fish morsels at a dockside eatery, Juan laughed at reading the sign warning. He couldn't believe the seagulls would actually swarm down and pick these morsels from your hand! We were the only ones on the pier but we didn't need anyone else. Juan made it a party!

"You know, Recharred, I would not mind living here," he sighed happily as I anticipated him to say, "Would you not like thot." Of course I agreed and he continued his happy chatter.

"It was so nice watching all the people coming off the boat from Martha's Vineyard last night, Recharred. They all looked so happy. I wish thot we could 'ave gone on thot trip."

"Well, Juan, we can come back and take it before we leave." He lit up like a star!

We drove the scenic route along the seashore instead of the expressway on the way to Donald's, and were absolutely thrilled with the charming splendor of the Cape!

"This has to be heaven!" Juan exclaimed as we drove into Newport. "It is like we are in a movie," and it was! I almost felt as though we were driving into a beautiful painting, and glad I decided to turn off when the Newport sign popped up. And, again, we didn't have time to take the tour of beautiful homes and mansions. So we settled for a tour of one. Once we were on our way again, we realized the quick stopover was like a sip of rare, vintage wine.

"Juan, there is no possible way I will stay at Donald's, even if he apologizes," I said emphatically as we neared his house, "because I am certain he'll blow up again! I really don't think he'll apologize anyway." Juan gave no feedback and took a deep breath instead as we headed up his stairway.

As expected, Juan was greeted warmly while I was totally ignored. Actually, I could have used a knife to cut through the tension I felt in the room. In fact, it was so thick I thought I'd suffocate. I finally proceeded to pack our things.

I was completely baffled with Donald's behavior. It was apparent that he wanted Juan to stay, which would have to include me, and yet he wouldn't apologize even if only to Juan. He just stood there, depressed. It provoked me and I couldn't refrain from audibly expressing my anger.

"Do you believe this guy, Juan? He still won't admit that he was wrong!" Of course, an outburst of denials shot out of Donald again! And then, exactly what I feared happened.

"Why does it 'ave to be this way? Why can't we all be friends?" Juan pleaded. "Ofter all, I don' know how long I will be around because of this HIV thot I 'ave!"

Juan's plea for peace again touched my heart, and I could probably forgive the worst killer in the world…just to make him happy! There was Donald, however, totally unaffected, still denying any fault! The heartfelt words never moved him, never tugged at his heartstrings to even request that we forget everything and start over again! Instead, he remained the belligerent bully!

"Okay, Juan, if you want to stay with this crazy asshole…stay!" I lashed out, taking my anger for Donald out on Juan. "I will go myself!" I was also a bit bothered because Juan went against his word, even though I realized he only wanted peace in his life. I needed to lay the cards on the table, if only to show Donald! Juan pleaded his heart out for peace, and yet the arrogant bully refused to humble himself! I wanted out, and stormed out the door, and there was Juan directly behind me! I was certain I never wanted to cross paths with the likes of that asshole again!

"Recharred, I would never want you to go without me," Juan said, taking hold of my hand as we drove off. "I would be miserable! I hope you understond why I wanted peace?"

"I understood, Juan, but I don't think Donald was even affected!"

"Now, Recharred, we con do all the things *we* wanted to do," Juan sighed, continuing to hold my hand, "like we planned in the beginning."

"And are we gonna have a wonderful time!" I teased after a slow wink of the eye.

Our stay in Boston began, one that I will cherish my entire life! We never got to take the boat trip to Martha's Vineyard or to return to Newport; still, we never felt cheated. There was so much to see and do in Boston alone. The history and charm of the area already appealed to both of us, and coupled with the excitable awe Juan was king of, I couldn't want more. We managed to see everything we planned on originally, and impossible to point out one as the best. Our tour of The Constitution rated high as did the drive to The House of Seven Gables. Of course, the walk and trolley ride along The Freedom Walk as well the beautiful and elegant dinner we sat down to in the North End could rate the best. However, I must admit that the sparkle of wonderment in his eyes, while in the witch castle in Salem, was a joy to behold.

Only one occasion threatened our joy, and it awakened a fear we had laid aside for some time. We had a couple of glasses of wine during our Italian dinner in the North End when Juan suggested we go out dancing, as he always did in the past. I was so pleased to see him in this mood and especially pleased at the elegant bar we found…a combination of The Trip, Le Pub, and The Inner Circle. It was like old times. However, we weren't there ten minutes when Juan insisted we leave because he was having one of those attacks again.

"I am sorry thot I ruined your evening, Recharred," he cried once he began feeling better during the drive to the motel, "but I got those same sick feelings I used to get."

"You're the important one, Juan, not a bar," I assured him even though I was disappointed and concerned because of the reoccurrence of the attacks.

Our vacation was coming to an end, and as I stood alone on the balcony of the motel that Sunday evening, I savored all the beautiful things we were fortunate to do together. A depression finally came over me and tears came flowing down my face. I didn't want to accept the fact that we were leaving for home the next morning. Oh, how I wanted to stay there forever with Juan! Donald was forgotten and we had a dream vacation!

Yes, we did ride home in the fancy limousine Jacque told us about. We certainly couldn't afford it after spending three times what we expected to spend, but it didn't matter. Juan had never been in one!

Chapter Forty-One:
The Short Move-In

There wasn't any reason to believe anyone suspected Juan of being HIV positive because he remained his normal happy self. In fact, I wondered if Marina heard what I said when I confided in her. She never questioned Juan's condition whenever the two of us were alone.

We savored our trip to Boston, and whenever we brought it up, it always provoked Phil. Endira called Juan again for a loan, which was pawned off on me as always. I'm sure she was aware that Juan never had money to spare. So it had to be her way of getting to me because Juan never failed to suggest that she call me whenever he knew I had money. Of course, I got her out of another financial mess. It still confused me because she was now married, and Dan certainly should've been bringing home a professional salary as well. Juan's concern about Svetmana continued. She refused to find a part time job to earn some spending money.

"She cannot work for anyone, Recharred," he said repeatedly, "because she does not want to be bossed. Do you know thot she does not even like to be instructed about a job. She jus' wants to sit thar like a princess!"

At long last, Juan put his furniture into storage and moved in with me in October. We'd look for a two-bedroom apartment eventually. My closets were overflowing, but I didn't care. Juan was finally living with me. Neither of us would have time to go out cruising, and that was exactly what I wanted. There wasn't a commitment, but it was a start. Especially great, there were no more jealous tantrums. I frequented a nearby forest preserve before Juan moved in, and though I was sure he was aware of it, he never showed signs of jealousy. Better yet, his constant presence quickly diminished my desire to frequent the woods again.

There was an evening though when I got home from work to find Juan gone. It was odd because he always was there before me, and usually preparing dinner. I suddenly remembered that we talked about the forest preserves the night before. I was sure it triggered him into checking it out. It proved to be correct once I drove there. The scenario was a priceless gem.

There he was, seated in his car, reading. His car was backed into the curb as others did so often in order to face the parade of cars cruising before them. I pulled ever so slowly into the parking space next to him. He never looked up and I was glad because it gave me the opportunity to stare his way. I wanted to see his reaction once he felt the feeling of being watched. As expected, his breathing appeared to accelerate and I chuckled. Finally, ever so nonchalantly, he raised his head and glanced over.

"Recharred! Whot are you doin' here?" he gasped, attempting to avoid my eyes.

"What are *YOU* doing here?" I replied. His helpless innocence was so devilishly adorable that I couldn't help but laugh hilariously. We both laughed and then drove out to order our favorite spaghetti marinara with sautéed mushrooms at Rocky's.

"Recharred, thar is talk around the office thot my job may be phased out, ond if it is, I could be transferred out of state. Indianapolis is one of the places mentioned." A ton of bricks falling on me would've been less shocking than hearing those words from Juan.

"Why? Why would they do something like that, Juan, when you are HIV positive?" I continued on excitedly once he merely shrugged his shoulders. "Juan, you are HIV positive! Why would they transfer you out of state to live alone, when you can be here with your family and me? It is crazy, and I don't understand it!"

"Recharred, they do not know about you," he cried out sarcastically.

"That doesn't make any difference! I know they don't! But they do know that you have a family here, and that's what is important! You need to be near your family and friends!"

His temper flared as he shouted out that he had no choice. He had to go where the Army sent him! He stood his ground in his old belligerent way until he finally realized I needed to be diverted from the stress of the subject.

"Recharred, it is only talk around the office. I doubt if it will ever come to pass." It was what I needed to hear and I felt better. I was sure he was only testing my feelings again.

"Recharred, my 'T' count is still over a thousand!" was also something I was grateful to hear about his HIV testing in his call from Denver, "Is thot not wonderful!" He also met a guy at the clinic who recently moved to Chicago.

"His name is John, ond he has a very strange personality, Recharred. He is not good-looking ot all, ond he has a big belly, which I remind him of all the time! Ond do you know thot he has a puppet teddy bear thot he takes everywhere! I con't believe thot he spent his entire career in the Army, because, Recharred, he octs so gay! When we were together with the medical staff, I would be so embarrassed! But, Recharred, he needs a friend, because he only knows two people in Chicago, an old school girlfriend, ond his sister. But his sister is not in good terms with him because he is gay! His 'T' count is much, much lower than mine! Recharred, I want to be his friend, ond besides, he takes my abuse!"

I was pleased that Juan opened up to John, especially since it was apparent he'd have problems making friends. He was too nice, and that definitely made him come across as a phony. And his constant attention to his puppet would certainly have heads shaking. However, as much as I tried be as close to him as Juan, he still remained distant.

Pa was rushed to the hospital near the end of November and went into a coma. We were aware that he no longer desired to live because he refused to eat at the rest home. The broken hip he incurred from falling left him unable to walk, and that alone broke his heart, especially since he had always walked so proudly.

The doctors felt certain he'd succumb immediately since he was ninety-two, and were baffled when he rallied. He went into one coma after another, and each time, we were called to keep vigil. To our surprise and joy, he'd rally.

"Recharred, thot is wonderful," Juan exclaimed when we talked of the phenomenon. "He must not want to die ofter all, because he is fighting to live! Ond if he licks this, maybe he will fully recover. I pray for him, Recharred!" Here was this man so full of heart and concern for me when he was carrying such a heavy burden himself!

"I think you better get to the hospital, Rich," my brother said when I picked up the phone during the night, four days before Christmas, "because it looks like this is it. Pa is really laboring to breathe!" I felt sure the call awakened Juan, but he assured me it didn't.

"No, Recharred, I was awake already. I was thinking of your father. I pray thot everything goes well. But if it is time, I hope thot he goes peacefully. Jus' thank God thot he 'as lived such a long life, my darling!"

The vigil went on for hours, and at one point, I almost thought my father was going to lick it again, especially once his laborious breathing came to an end. No one seemed to realize that it had ended. My nieces had just come and were trying to talk to their grandpa. Still, I wanted to be certain he was breathing. As I went to the foot of the bed, Frank also left the room. My fears were quickly realized once a nurse rushed in to feel his pulse. Frank had called her.

"I am afraid he is gone," she quietly said after turning Pa on his side to check for a heartbeat in his back. Those were the words we were waiting for, but didn't really want to hear. Pa had taken his last breath, and none of us had been aware that he was gone.

The patriarch of the family was gone…the proud gentleman…our father who only had to give us one stern look of his green eyes to make us behave when we were kids. He was gone. So there we were, crying out for him to return, holding and caressing him, realizing it would be our last time to feel his warmth.

This was the first time I was with someone in his final moments, and I suddenly thought of the beauty of it. Pa had to be proud that his family was with him at the very end. His whole life focused on the love of a family. I felt proud that he was my father! He was still on his side, and suddenly appeared to curl up into a fetal position. He looked like a baby about to be born. I smiled because I was sure a baby, at that very moment, was being born.

"I think it is grotesque to stond over someone in a coffin, Recharred," Juan said so often, "ond I do not want to be in one when I die! No, no! I want to be cremated." So I understood when he arrived late at the chapel and never approached the casket. He also told me he couldn't get off for the funeral the next day because he wasn't a relative. I understood but, at the same time, realized that he also wanted to avoid the finality of it. No, he didn't need the sadness the day would bring at this time in his life.

Pa loved to play the harmonica, especially whenever he was very happy. And young Dino, in a touching tribute, arranged for a professional harmonica player to play while everyone followed the casket into the church. While each bittersweet note tugged at our hearts, I felt certain that Pa was smiling, that he was rid of that crutch at last, and happy again!

Marina's mother was in for the holidays, and we were invited for a Christmas evening gathering to meet her. I didn't feel much like partying, but Juan insisted.

"It will be good for you, Recharred, ond for me to 'ave you thar with me." I decided to stop by after spending Christmas at Jacque's. It might ease some of the bittersweet sentiment of the day, besides show Juan I'd always be there for him. Amanda and Patti were also there, as well as Barry Hanson, who came in from California! And there they were, all playing the *Spoons* game. It turned out to be just what the doctor ordered. Who could remain sad after hearing Juan's catchy laughter during their battles for spoons? Not to mention the tee-hee giggles of Amanda and Patti and the silly cackle of Barry's.

I gave Daniel regrets for his party to welcome in 1988. He gave me all sorts of reasons why I should attend, but I still refused. Italians just didn't celebrate after a death. I finally realized I had to go if just to keep Juan's spirits up.

The cemetery was just down the road from my apartment, and as we drove by on our way to Daniel's, the stoplight turned red. To my left was the tremendous mausoleum my father was interred in. My emotions faltered, and realizing it Juan began to rub my shoulders.

"Aw, c'mon now, Recharred. Please do not feel bod? Remember he lived a long life, ond you know thot he wanted to go. Please, my darling." The magic of his touch and voice was all the comfort needed and I drove on. His contagious joy did the rest at the party. Along with Jeannie, the three of us made it a laugh-filled occasion. Daniel called the next day.

"Richard, thank you so much for coming. The party would've never been as great without the two of you cutting up with Jeannie!" And he raved about it for a month.

I received over fifteen thousand from my father's estate, and realized I should invest in a condo before I blow it all. We already were searching for another apartment, though Juan was concerned about the miles accumulating on his car driving to and from the fort. He'd then mention the free apartments available to him at the fort. He'd drop the subject, however, once he saw how upset I got. So I decided to surprise him by buying a condo on the north shore. It would only be a short drive to the fort from there. However, my search soon discovered that real estate on the north shore was completely out of sight for me.

"Recharred, the traffic jams are just too much for me! They are causing me so much stress," Juan shouted out after my distress at hearing he decided to move to the fort.

"Is thot whot you want? For me to get sick!" So I was forced to accept it and hide my feelings. Besides, I needed to realize it was the only time he complained of his HIV condition.

"Recharred, I will still be coming here every weekend, ond sometimes I will drive here during the week," he said in an attempt to appease me. "Ond you con drive there. C'mon. Blanche, be a man!" So he made the move, and he did come over weekends, sometimes staying to Monday morning. I only drove there a couple of times, though. He was always so uptight whenever we walked the grounds together.

"People might think we are gay." He even became obsessed with the fear of someone looking in the window to see us sitting alongside each other on the couch even though it was the only available seating in the apartment. So the phone became our means of communication during the week. Loneliness thus ensued, and chased me out alone to the bars again.

I also knew Juan was going to the bars with John during the week, and it seemed to be quite often, which worried me. Alcohol weakened the immune system. So I didn't hesitate to bring up the fact to Juan as well as John. Of course, this only intensified John's indifference towards me. In fact, I felt certain he only tolerated me because of Juan.

"You know, Recharred, John says you are nothing but a fussy old man," Juan informed me, exploding into laughter immediately afterwards. Juan had no desire for John so there was no fear that way. They only shared one thing in common…the terrible HIV virus!

"Recharred, I went to John's house last week, ond he took me to this bar far on the south side," Juan admitted, proving my point. However, his exciting manner made me forget it.

"Aw, Recharred, we 'ave to plan a party ond go thar. The drag queens were so bod thot they were funny!" As usual, his gagging laughter was contagious.

So we planned a party with Jeannie, Marina, Vic, and Phil, and John cordially invited us for cocktails at his apartment beforehand. He was a perfect host, though we thought it a bit unusual to see pencil labeled snacks and liquors. Vic and Phil were their old selves and the evening turned out to be a ball. Even more surprising, new queens were performing at the bar and they were terrific. It was okay, though. We didn't need them to be bad to laugh. Juan took care of that.

My steady search came down to a choice of two condominiums, and the night I took Juan to see them turned out to be reminiscent of the time he walked into our very first dream apartment. He followed the agent into the second apartment. His shoulders hunched while pointing fingers of both hands to the floor. He, again, chose my favorite with one glance. The spacious living room to the right and a breakfast bar of a charming, open kitchen certainly told him this place was perfect party atmosphere. Though his actions already chose this one, he didn't comment until after he saw the powder room and the two large bedrooms separated by a full bath. It was then that he turned and smiled broadly.

"Recharred, this is the one I love!" He then resumed to charm the saleswoman.

Closing wasn't until late in June. It certainly should give me enough time to talk Juan into moving in with me. Instead, I heard, "Not now, Recharred, maybe later. We'll see."

Temperatures soared into the nineties that spring, and Juan was pleased because he managed to get Svetmana a part time job in a gift shop at the fort.

"She is able to drive her mother's car thar, Recharred. So I am very happy thot she ot last has a job."

"Recharred, I cannot believe thot Svetmana!" were his words in frustration a few days later. "It was so hot today ond the fort had problems with the electricity. So the air conditioning was not working anywhere. Do you know whot she did? She left the gift shop ond came into my office like a raging Banshee, screaming hysterically! Yes, Recharred, she could not understand how they could expect her to work in such a hot place! I tried to tell her thot it was the same for me, but she still continued to scream! I could not believe it!" An expression of concern lingered on his face once my laughter subsided.

"Aw, Recharred, I really don' know whot I am gonna do about her. She is so selfish ond spoiled." He then admitted that Endira was responsible for her miserable attitude because she allowed her to do as she pleased and never demanded she do any chores. Besides that, Endira also gave her a hundred-dollar allowance, as well as unlimited use of charge cards from all the finer stores. Juan could do nothing about it. He tried to teach Svetmana responsibility, but since Endira always intimidated him into a guilt complex, there was no choice but to submit.

"You know, Recharred, today I talked with the owner of the gift shop," Juan stated, coming into the apartment looking quite disturbed, "ond do you know whot she told me? She told me thot it took Svetmana all day Saturday to dust everything on one shelf! One shelf! She could not believe someone could be thot slow! She said thot Svetmana never waited on one customer because she was dusting everything on thot shelf all day, which should 'ave only taken half on hour! So then she said she was sorry but thot she had to let her go.

"Well, Juan, it was her first job, and maybe she learned something from being fired.

"I don' believe she will ever learn, Recharred. All her life, her mother has made her believe thot she is a princess. I am so disappointed in Svetmana. She does not make me proud at all." I didn't know what to say to comfort him, especially since I always knew he needed to be proud of those he loved. That's what made him love them more. It was why he clung to me…why he loved me so. He was proud of my energy…my determination to strive for the things I wanted in life. He knew I never got a big head from his praises, even when he praised my singing and acting.

"Recharred, you are so good," were praises he said so often, "God should bless you!"

"Hi, Ratchard, this is Ted," Marina said, coming into my apartment with her out-of-town guest a memorable Saturday evening. Juan invited everyone that day while I was at work, and Amanda and Patti shocked us by being the first to arrive. Jeannie couldn't make it because she had a hot date, and as usual, Vic and Phil had other plans. Ted walked into the room and an immediate moment of awkward silence prevailed. Here was this jovial, robust guy handing me a cold watermelon and greeting us in a very husky voice. We were speechless because he just didn't jive. His voice and lumberjack manner definitely didn't belong to the sparse, bleached blond ratted hair on his head, and especially to a face adorned with rouge and lipstick. No, it just didn't seem to match, particularly with someone wearing heavy workman's overalls and construction boots! To add to the confusion, Ted's dainty blouse revealed two very busty appendages, not to mention the huge basket he sported in those overalls! A basket that surely would get quick attention in a gay bar. However, we discovered that in spite of his bizarre combination of sexes, he was very personable.

While slicing watermelon in the kitchen, Juan suddenly remembered that Marina had previously told him about Ted…that he was in the process of a complete sex change but changed his mind after receiving breast implants. This sent him into uncontrollable laughter and I almost wet my pants as he lost all control trying to add his last little quip.

"Aw, Recharred, con you imagine? He has tits, ond a cock between his legs! Only it is not someone else's cock…it is his!"

Fortunately, all our laughter was within. No one could hear what was going on and I was glad because in spite of the sexual mess Ted was in, we liked him. He was very personable as well as quite knowledgeable. So the evening was not only entertaining but interesting.

Marina and Ted didn't stay late since they planned on going to the *Magnificent Mile* early in the morning. It took some explanation to unravel Amanda and Patti's confusion, but we managed in spite of our gagging laughter.

"Aw, thot Marina! I love her so much," Juan sighed. "Nothing bothers her!"

"Recharred, look ot my jaws," Juan said, quite concerned about the sudden swelling of his glands just below each ear, "I almost look like a chipmunk for Chris' sake!" It wasn't enough to be noticed by everyone, though it gave a fuller appearance to his face. Of course, a weight gain could do that. That sensuous, masculine jawbone he had turned so often to the mirror to admire, however, was gone. We were certain that the HIV virus was responsible, but lived with it as long as there was no pain or discomfort.

Juan loved snacking during the evening, and enjoyed pizza rolls especially. Sometimes he desired something sweet. Chocolate ice cream or chocolate was then his preference.

"Recharred, if you go to the store for some frozen pizza rolls, I will buy," was a request I heard often, or "You know, Recharred, I 'ave a taste for some cha-co-lot ice cream. I will buy if you go for some.

"You know whot kind of pizza rolls I like, don' you?" he usually inquired as I was about to leave, and in a tone like I was a forgetful little kid. When he wanted ice cream, anything with "cha-co-lot" was fine.

"You really are not thot hungry, Recharred, are you?" was a phrase he loved to tease me with once the pizza rolls were in the oven.

We never went on a picnic together. Two guys sitting on a blanket never appealed to Juan. After all, straight guys would never be seen doing that! Amanda, Patti, Vic, Phil, Jeannie, and Marina, however, were all available when I suggested we have a picnic the Memorial Day weekend. Juan surprised me by being excited about it.

"Jus' think, Recharred," he exclaimed once we chose the nearby forest preserves to hold it, "We con all 'ave fun watching the queens cruise in the woods."

The Sunday turned out to be very cold and windy with the threat of rain, but it never spoiled our spirits since everyone was up and never came down.

"We'll see, we'll see," Juan said, giving Amanda the same response when she inquired if he was intending to move in with me.

"Are you guys gonna resume as lovers?" she teased with a twinkle in her eyes.

"Whot? Me be lovers with Recharred?" he responded, holding his hand to his chest in that exaggerated stance of his, "No, no! Never, never!" Amanda giggled, and yet it was apparent she was aware of Juan's theatrics.

"Richard, thot guy just does not want to admit to any of us that he loves you as a lover," she quickly remarked once he moved to chat with someone else. "He is always trying to cover it up. But, Richard, the guy talks about you and praises you to no end whenever you are not around! And he waits anxiously for you whenever you are arriving late. There is no doubt in my mind, Richard. He loves you very much."

There I was again, allowing my ego to get the best of me. The rain finally began falling the morning of Memorial Day, and I guess I was bored since Juan had to work. I had been cruised in the subway on the way to work by a very young Adonis that week, and the number he gave me was burning a hole in my pocket. So there I was, driving to his place in the pouring rain to once again conquer. The meeting turned out to be a quickie, and I was on my way home with nothing but my guilt and another trick to add to my empty pocket. However, I blamed my weakness on Juan, because of his continued refusals to commit. In fact, I convinced myself that his persistence was only because he had become so accustomed to the freedom.

Early that afternoon, I called Phil and he asked if we'd care to join them for dinner at their usual restaurant. I explained that I'd have to check with Juan since he had reluctantly agreed to return to my place instead of remaining at the fort. After all, he might be tired.

"Recharred, I really do not feel like driving anymore," Juan replied to the invite as I expected. "Would it not be nice if we jus' ordered from Rocky's, ond got a couple of movies? I know they 'ave to eat ot their regular restaurant, so why don' you tell them to come here ofter to watch a movie. Then we con watch one before they arrive. Is thot all right with you?"

While Juan was unpacking our meals, I called to explain everything to Phil, and suddenly there was silence. Finally, after an awkward moment of silence, he agreed. Assuming it was settled, I sat down at the table to enjoy dinner with Juan. At that moment, the phone rang.

"There you are, catering to Juan again!" were the first words I heard Phil's voice shout when I picked up the phone. "Everything he wants…you do! First, you tell us you are going, and because he does not want to go, you change your mind!" I stood there in shock, in disbelief, and once I caught my breath I tried to refresh his memory as to what I actually had said, but it did no good. His jealousy made it impossible to cope with matters as they really were, and he went on in his rage! I never was quite certain, but it sounded as though he called me an asshole for catering to Juan all the time before we were disconnected…and in more ways than one!

"I cannot believe thot, Recharred," Juan sighed after I explained what happened. "He was angry ot that? Jus' because we did not go with them to dinner? I don' believe it, especially since you told him thot you were not sure of going. Aw, Recharred, thot Phil has a problem." I was fuming and began to pace the floor.

"C'mon, now, don' let it bother you. Sit down, my darling ond eat." But it did bother me, and I was getting angrier! I did no wrong, and was battered again! Not wanting the evening ruined, Juan tried to make light of it by joking around, and finally got me to relax.

"Recharred, you know you are so good," Juan said with a smile later in the evening, "ond everything seems to happen to you." And we laughed.

Vic called the next day, and from our conversation, I realized he was well aware that there was no logical reason for Phil's hysterical outburst, but he still wouldn't admit to the cause behind it all. Instead, he merely said that Phil would call to apologize for shouting. It was unbelievable! He had to know that it happened because of obvious jealousy, but there he was, making excuses for him again!

Actually, Phil never did call to apologize, and completely ignored the subject in our cold meetings thereafter. It was a shame because I was never one to hold a grudge. Juan and I were sick because of it. Vic and Phil were always considered our best friends.

Hank and his new lover, Dick, invited the four of us to a dinner party. The message was clear once Vic and Phil said they'd drive separately to Dick's apartment in Chicago. We were the first to arrive and Juan explained everything tactfully once Hank questioned why Vic and Phil didn't drive with us. Hank apologized for inviting them to the same dinner party.

"Aw, don' worry about thot," Juan quickly replied. "We are talking to them. Ond you don' 'ave to worry thot everyone will feel uncomfortable, because we know thot you love a good time, ond so do we." And everyone did, and primarily because Juan kept everyone in stitches, including Phil. He never laughed so hard, especially during Juan's impersonation of Hank's hyper movements. In fact, Hank was on the floor in helpless laughter as well.

God! There was Juan holding his body rigid, and moving about exaggeratedly in a jerky manner, dropping everything he picked up!

"OOPS! I'm so sorry…so sorry!" he kept saying repeatedly.

Chapter Forty-Two:
Fear Becomes a Reality

Juan was anxious for Jeannie, Marina, John, and Hank to arrive, and finally positioned himself at the front window thinking it could hurry them along. It was the Sunday before the closing of my condo and we planned an outing to Cantigny. The war memorial, museum, and mansion of the renowned publisher, Robert McCormick, was always a favorite place to visit. Vic and Phil had declined, and Patti and Amanda were to meet us there. Dick was working.

"Come here quick, Recharred," he shouted. "Look ot Jeannie walking down the courtyard. Look ot her bouncing tits! Aw, whot a woman, ond look how feminine she walks!"

"Jesus, Jeannie, your tits are so big ond bouncy today," Juan teased, losing no time in starting the quips of the day. Jeanne merely stared wide eyed into Juan's face.

"Oh? They look that big, do they?" she asked solemnly while cradling them in her hands, "Well, here, honey, suck on them for a while and make them bigger!" The laughter continued throughout the day, and especially after Amanda and Patti failed to show up.

"Aw, they are probably too busy fuckin'," Juan remarked oh so nonchalantly.

"But how do they do that?" I inquired oh so innocently.

"Aw, c'mon, Recharred?" Juan teased, holding onto that perfect wide-eyed owl expression of doubt he did so well. And captured on Hank's video was Marina chasing after John in those long, masculine strides of hers while calling out in her best baritone, not to mention the mooning Hank surprised us with after asking to focus the camera on him.

Juan arrived as the movers were about done and lost no time getting everything in order. Geena was arranging the kitchen cabinets and was just as pleased as I that Juan finally arrived. Suddenly, it no longer was a tedious chore but a joyous occasion instead.

"I am very professional when it comes to decorating," Juan boasted once all the furniture was in place. "Do you not agree?" Of course, I agreed, especially since everything was arranged as I intended. It was like old times as he went on making sure things looked just right. I wanted the second bedroom to be Juan's, so it was empty. Still, he wouldn't react when I said it. He just stood in the center of the living room, admiring everything.

"Recharred, you know you still 'ave to get so many things to put the finishing touches," and after listing them all, he sighed, "Then you will 'ave a really bea-u-ti-ful home. Here is a new dish drain for your sink, Recharred," pulling it from a bag he had placed in the corner. "Get rid of thot old one you 'ave." As I chuckled, his hand went back into the bag again.

"This, Recharred, is for you from my collection. I want you to 'ave it because they are supposed to bring you luck in a new home." I wanted to hug him as he held up this beautiful pearl white ceramic elephant with its tusks pointed upward because I knew how much his collection meant to him, but Geena was there. However, I'm sure my wonderful sister would have only considered it a gesture of appreciation and nothing more. To my surprise, she also brought a ceramic elephant for luck...the same size but tusks pointing downward. A perfect match from two people I loved.

"Recharred, you know I 'ave to go back to Denver in August to check my 'T' count," were the first words I heard on answering the phone, "ond I was thinking, maybe you con come, too, for a vacation. I only 'ave to be ot the hospital in the morning for four days, ond while I am gone you con sleep late. Aw, whot do you think, Recharred? Do you not think thot would be so nice?" Who could ever refuse such excitement!

Amanda and Patti had bought a summer lake home in Wisconsin, and invited us for the Fourth of July weekend. We had been there earlier in the summer while they were busy painting, and, of course, I helped paint. Juan, however, hated to paint—more got on the floor and him while we were decorating the club in Atlanta. Nevertheless, he had charmed us with wit throughout the day. Of course, he reminded them of his expertise when they were ready for the finishing touches. This weekend, however, was to be dedicated to fun.

We arrived about ten o'clock Saturday evening, and plans were to go to a disco in Madison. We brought a huge cooler of food and a bottle of vodka. I wanted Juan to eat before taking off, but it was near impossible after he downed a couple of cocktails. He wanted to party and was his usual antsy self, raring to go out dancing. I continued to badger him until he finally ate a few bites, but it still wasn't enough to saturate all the alcohol he'd drink.

Their giggles continued throughout the drive because the joy of being with them made his chatter funnier. They decided to stop off at a women's bar beforehand, which led to eventual disaster. Juan downed three quick drinks because the bar didn't have dancing. When we started on our way, I was concerned because Juan was drinking much too fast....

He continued drinking at a fast pace once we arrived at the large disco and I was worried. It was apparent to me that he only wanted to be certain they were enjoying his company. However, at this fast pace, I could be certain the evening would end in a disaster. I was correct, of course. Suddenly, he was the mischievous elf, which would've been okay in itself if his outspoken vulgarities didn't accompany it. Patti and Amanda never had been exposed to this behavior of his, and it didn't set well with them.

When I discovered the bar served food, I suggested we get a table. Maybe I could get Juan to eat. It took some doing, but he finally agreed to order breakfast. However, he continued on with his filthy remarks. It was the first time Amanda and Patti ever became disturbed with his drunkenness. There were no tee-hees this time. In fact, his constant needling of me really bothered them. They saw no logical reason for him to do it, but Juan just ignored their pleas to stop. I tried to explain this trait of his…that it was only harmless words, but this just added fuel to Juan's mouth. As angry as I was, I still didn't want Amanda and Patti to feel the same. So I continued my futile excuses. I wanted them to understand Juan as I did. Whenever drunk, he just had to let the devil out. I was getting nowhere, however. It was the only time since that evening with Ben in Atlanta that Juan lost all elegance in dining. There he was, scrambling everything in his plate and missing his mouth with every attempted forkful.

The music could still be heard coming from the disco, and I was probably the only one who realized what was going on in his head as he tried to rise majestically.

"I 'ave to pee!" he informed us proudly, and with that he marched off. I was certain Amanda's request to head home was never heard. The night, after all, was still young for him because the music had not ended.

I didn't want Amanda and Patti disillusioned with Juan and tried to explain my logic.

"The hell of it is, even when he 's drunk and belligerent, there are so many times I want to hug the hell out of him because his stubbornness is so devilishly funny. Yes, there are times I won't laugh because I'm so angry, but once I think of it later, I'm in stitches!" They giggled, but I still wasn't certain they understood.

"For cryin' out loud, when is Juan coming back?" Amanda cried out after some time passed. I immediately checked out the restroom, concerned that he may have become ill, and became worried once he was nowhere to be found. The thought of him being enticed to leave with someone entered my mind, and I was suddenly in a state of panic! We searched everywhere but he was nowhere in sight. I was in a state of panic as we stood out on the sidewalk staring at the opened front entryway. I felt helpless, certain someone took Juan off!

Suddenly, like a puff of magic, there he was standing in the entryway peering out at us with that mischievous grin of his! There he was, standing in that ridiculous, gloating pose of his…one hand on the lower part of his hip and swinging from side to side in a fast staccato action! It was obvious that he was overjoyed because he had won. I was greatly relieved so to me he was unbelievably hilarious, but Amanda and Patti thought otherwise.

"How could you do that to Richard, Juan!" Amanda shouted as he walked down the staircase towards us, sustaining that exaggerated elegance he did so well. "He was so worried…afraid someone grabbed you and took you somewhere. Why did you do that, Juan?" Juan never answered, which I expected, because he was now satisfied. It wasn't necessary to be nasty any more. He was able to stay at the bar longer, even if it was only to play a game with us. As angry as Amanda was that night, every time she talked of it afterwards, she giggled.

"Oh, that Juan was so funny! I could not believe that macho man doing that hip action!"

The fear I dreaded finally came around.

"Recharred, I am being transferred out of town…to Indianapolis," were Juan's first words coming into the apartment, "ond I start to work thar right ofter Labor Day." I refused to believe it, but the expression on his face told me otherwise. It was as though an ice cold hand just grabbed my heart. I remained silent, trying to comprehend it all.

"JUAN, you can't go!" I screamed once I realized the scope of what he just said. "Tell them your mother needs you…that she is ill!" The loneliness we would endure, especially Juan because he'd know absolutely no one in the city, was flashing before me like a warning signal.

"Recharred, for Chris' sake, whot do you want me to do! Quit my job!" Juan shouted. "I 'ave to go where the Army sends me!"

"Then quit the Army!" I screamed, bringing his temper to a quick halt. However, it was apparent he was about to make a mockery of my statement from the glare in his eyes.

"Aw, quit the Army, huh? How con I do thot ond still pay all the bills I owe?"

"JUAN, I am making more than I ever made in my life! You can live with me!' I pleaded, "and if we need any more money, I am sure you will be able to get some kind of work! They can't send you out of town…away from your family and me when you are HIV positive!"

"OND how will we pay for the expenses of my HIV tests, ond all the medications once I get sick, Recharred?" he shouted, his voice now trembling with rage.

"JUAN, you are not gonna get sick!" I cried out in near hysteria. "You're not!"

"RECHARRED! Face it once ond for all! I am gonna get sick one day, ond die one day!" he shouted, finally taking hold of my hands in an attempt to soothe his pain as well as mine. "Maybe not for years to come, Recharred, but it will happen because thar is no cure. Ond who is gonna pay for all the medications I will need? Do you know how much it costs when a person is sick with AIDS, Recharred, huh? Do you know?"

I tried to reason with him…to explain that he'd then be a veteran and be entitled to hospital benefits, but he refused to listen.

I finally realized he didn't need the stress my anguish was causing. I had to get it in my head that he was accepting this heartless maneuver by the Army, and be there for him. So I bit my lip and accepted the fact that he was moving out of town. Of course, he always managed to lighten my heart with assurances that we would be seeing each other often.

"Ofter all, Recharred, it is only about one hundred ond eighty miles from here, ond either one of us con drive to see the other." I smiled and agreed, though my thoughts could only think of the times Juan might possibly be out drinking. Oh, God, how the heck will I get to him when he can't find his car!

So I was forced to live with an empty feeling running from the pit of my stomach to my heart. For the present, however, I had Juan, and it seemed like that joy would go on forever!

We managed a two-day trip to Indianapolis a week before our vacation to check out apartments, and he ended up renting the first one we saw. Later, Juan admitted that he had called back to exchange the one-bedroom apartment for a unit with two bedrooms. It upset me because it meant he needed more furniture, besides the higher cost in rent. He had sold his beautiful sectional to Endira for practically nothing just before putting his furniture in storage. In fact, it was for nothing because she never had paid him.

"Recharred, all I am gonna 'ave in the living room is thot small sofa bed I bought for my room ot the fort." I quickly reminded him of his glass top coffee table, television, and the end table and lamp. When he still complained of the emptiness, I refreshed his memory about the antique side table from the auctions in Atlanta I had given him, and not to forget his dining table and chairs.

"Aw, Recharred, thot is gonna be nothing in thot apartment!" I tried to convince him that it was enough since he was paying more than he could afford with the higher rent.

"Juan, you're not gonna be there long. I want you back here to live with me before too long." Though he assured me he wouldn't buy anything, I *somehow* felt he'd do it anyway.

As though I didn't have enough depressing news, Jacque filled me in with more. She and my son-in-law, Bill, were in the process of a divorce.

Juan was concerned about ruining my vacation because he'd have to spend some mornings at the hospital. I finally reassured him.

"Juan, you're the only one I want to go on vacation with. A little wait makes no difference to me as long as I know I am going to be with you the rest of the day." His smile assured me that was what he wanted to hear.

A new 1988 black Baretta was waiting on landing in Denver, and since the capitol and downtown were so close Juan insisted we see it all before checking into the motel…. It was perfect since the streets were practically empty on

Sunday. Who needed a crowd, anyway, with the excitement Juan created with his awe! It was impossible not to be impressed.

"You know, Recharred, I would not mind living here," he sighed, doing his usual scan of the skyline. It is a bea-u-tiful city, do you not think?"

It was extremely hot, so we changed into shorts after checking into a motel near the hospital. We then took off to see the hospital and grounds of the fort in order for me to be able to picture where he was in the morning.

After a narrated tour, Juan suggested we drive to The Valley of the Gods, which turned out to be a breathtaking experience. The towering rock formations actually made one imagine the world was turned upside down. Before us was a valley of tremendous cavern stalagmites! These wondrous creations, however, were shooting out from the ground, and appeared to be reaching for heaven! To make it even more spectacular, the colors were dispersed perfectly. Some were orange and cream, some were mauve and cream, while others had just the right amount of yellow splashed in.... And contrasted beautifully with it all were the dark greens of the many evergreens interspersed throughout the park, groomed meticulously in rounds and ovals, while the tall spirals reached for the clouds. I was awed so one could only imagine the excitement coming from Juan. Our vacation was off to a great start.

"Recharred, I don' want to waste time each day deciding on where we will go once I return from the hospital," Juan said that evening at the motel, "This is your vacation, ond I know you do not like sitting around doing nothing when thar is so much to see. So we need to plan out an agenda each night."

I'm certain we would've made a perfect team for a movie comedy in each of our excursions into the mountains. It didn't matter who was driving, the terror and nervousness was plastered on the face and body of the one seated next to him. Of course, the driver refused to take his eyes off the road to view any of the splendor while the other remained frozen in the passenger seat, pressing his foot taunt on an imaginary brake. This doesn't mean we didn't enjoy the trip, we did. We weren't always in a car.

Our trip up the tramcar to Pike's Peak once again proved Juan's dedication and compassion for me. I got very sick from the altitude or from going up backwards, or whatever. In fact, I thought I was dying once we reached the top. So there I was, seated on a bench away from the spectacular scenic view. I insisted he leave me and enjoy the scenery, but he wouldn't think of it. No, he even wanted to see if a doctor was available, but I said it would pass, and it did…once we were on ground level.

We even refused to take the drive up to Trail Ridge Road in the Rocky Mountain State Park when a woman pointed to a spot on the model in the pavilion and said her husband almost passed out after looking over the edge. We walked the low lands and looked up instead.

Another occasion was our little jaunt to see Buffalo Bill's gravesite. The road leading up appeared innocent enough once we started. Signs posted informed drivers of the distance left before reaching the site. In fact, we drove one third of the distance and it was a snap. We were really talking up a storm. Suddenly, the road became very narrow and winding, and I found myself driving along the edge of a long drop down! Chatter ceased immediately, and once the corner of my eye caught a glimpse of Juan, I saw his taunt body and face frozen in terror! Needless to say, I was the same except for the nervous movements of my hands on the steering wheel and the trembling of my knees.

Like a miracle, we suddenly approached a very wide area in the road. I'm sure engineers thought of us when excavating!

"You really don't want to see the site, do you?" I asked, not even waiting for a reply. "I'm gonna make a U-turn and go back down! My knees will not stop shaking." Believe me, there were no objections from him.

"But wait before you make the turn," he insisted, "I want to get out!"

I don't know how I managed to make the turn after watching Juan scurrying sideways to the inner part of the road while looking back like a scared jackrabbit to be certain he was moving in the right direction. My laughter replaced all the fears, and continued once he returned to the car with a big grin of relief on his face.

"Why you laughing, Recharred?" he asked innocently. Of course, this only continued my laughing spasms.

"Thot really made you laugh, Recharred, did it not," Juan always said the many times we talked of it, and after repeating everything, he'd go into a laughing jag. The world was his stage, but I was the only audience he needed.

We had purchased tickets earlier that day for a chuckwagon dinner at the Flying W Ranch, and Juan was extremely excited about it. When we arrived, we were greeted with about a thousand people waiting in a nicely decorated corral. At least, it appeared to look like one. In fact, it had to be just that because we were crammed in like cattle. Juan wasn't pleased since he hated being in tight areas. His displeasure continued after they announced that, because of the threat of rain, dinner would be served indoors. We were then herded in like cattle, which made his mood even worse, especially after ending up in smelly tent with everyone racing like maniacs for places at picnic tables.

"Recharred, this is a ter-ri-ble place. I don' believe it," he complained after we managed to fight our way to two places at the last available table. "This is where we 'ave to eat?"

"They're just trying to create an atmosphere," I said attempting some sort of appeasement, but it did no good.

Our table was the last one given the go-ahead to get into the serving lines, and waiting that hour did not help Juan's mood, especially since there were three separate lines…one for beans, one for roast beef, and one for a plain slice of cake. I thought I'd die at the expression on Juan's face once a tin plate was shoved into his hand.

"It's atmosphere, Juan, atmosphere!" It was even funnier as each of the servers plopped a spoonful in our plates, almost as though they were shoveling manure and had to get rid of it as quickly. Oh, if I only had the camera.

"This looks more like shit than food," he barked. I assured him that it was probably delicious; otherwise, why would so many people be there.

"Because they did not know," he said blandly, "like we did not know, Recharred."

Oh, what I would have given for that camera once he took his first mouthful of beans! It surely wouldn't have captured the same expression I saw at the Tango or Sir Douglas.

"Recharred, these beans are not cooked," he shouted after spitting the mouthful back into the plate. "They are like very small rocks!" I took a forkful from my plate and his, and sure enough, he was right. He also always despised gristle in meat, and it appeared as though it was filled with nothing but that.

"Recharred, I don' believe it," he exclaimed after spitting out that mouthful, too, "this meat is like shoe leather! I can't believe they charged twenty-five dollars for this shit." So he just sat there, fuming. I forced myself to chew hard on a couple of pieces, just to get something in my stomach, but finally gave up. At least a piece of cake would get something in my stomach. After one bite, I was glad Juan refused to try his piece. They actually ruined that too.

Juan insisted we leave to eat somewhere else, but I managed to persuade him to stay for the entertainment, a country group. The food served that evening, we discovered, wasn't out of the ordinary. The spokesman for the group had built an entire repertoire about the beans and gristle served at these chuckwagon dinners, and had the crowd laughing hilariously. Juan remained angry, though, and it was a shame because the group was fantastic. His mood, however, wouldn't change, and I felt we should leave. The irony of it was that I always was the one who complained about a bad meal at a restaurant while he never failed to praise them.

"Blanche, you sound ond act like on aging queen. Keep your trap shut!" were words I could always expect him to say. His complaint of the food was the very *first*, and only because the food was absolutely inedible.

"I'm so glad I was not a movie star, ond to 'ave to eat thot shit," was a quip he often said to keep everyone in laughter while telling the story.

The drive to Central City was right up our alley. We drove low and looked up. We also were fairly calm at The Royal Gorge, since the area was surrounded with high steel fences. So we felt safe and really enjoyed the spectacular views. Riding the trolley over the Gorge didn't bother us, either. However, when we decided to hoof it back on the see-through grid bridge, we became terrified and began running like two scared rabbits.

"Well, Recharred, I will find out whot my T-count is tomorrow morning, ond if you want, you con come with me." This was the reason for the trip, and yet he had avoided bringing up the subject during the week. And no doubt because he didn't want me to get upset. The same scenario prevailed so many times before when he wanted me to face reality! I always refused to come to terms with it, still dreaming of a cure!

"Aw, Recharred, I don' wanna get sick, but you 'ave to face it! I'm gonna get sick one day, ond eventually die!" he'd say, which I always followed with hysterical denials. I was aware of the AIDS death toll; still, I refused to come out of my dream world. It couldn't happen to us…only to others!

"Until they find a cure, Recharred, I am in danger," he'd say, "I jus' wish thot you would talk to me about it because it would be so much easier for me to face death."

"Juan, I know you're going to die one day, and I know I'm gonna die one day," I'd cry out, my eyes flushed with tears, "but we're not going to die for a long time." By this time, my face would be totally wet with tears and I'd scream out, "and Juan, you're not gonna die before me. You can't! How would I ever laugh again?" This always managed to stop his fire. He'd stand there quietly, smile, and then giggle.

"Do I really make you laugh thot much, Recharred? Do I really?"

"Recharred, you cannot believe how nice Doctor Montano is. He has such compassion for everyone. Ond do you know I think he has sort of taken me under his wings," Juan confided while driving to the hospital, "You know, Recharred, this man is so full of heart. He even embraced me when I cried, and he cried himself. He is such a good man. Do you know he wants to tell me my results himself. All the others are being told by the nurse, but he wants to tell me personally. Thot is why he gave me a separate appointment. Is thot not wonderful, Recharred?" This possibly was a broad assumption but I didn't care. All I cared about was that he deserved special attention. His respect and trust for his caretakers was worthy of it.

"Would you mind, Recharred, to wait for me while I go in for my results. Do you mind?" I agreed, and as he walked, I smiled at the thought of him still nursing his hang-up even though the HIV virus was almost considered to be a gay disease.

Well over an hour and a half passed walking the courtyard, and suddenly I began thinking of that gloomy day I waited in the parking lot of Fort Sheridan. I became anxious and began walking quickly, trying to shake off the thought of bad news. Once I reached the far end of the courtyard, I turned to see Juan suddenly come out of the entrance he had walked in. I couldn't see his face. He was too far, and my heart stood still. I could hear the thumping of my heart as I headed his way, and at that moment, he suddenly jumped high into the air, clicking his heels together on the way up! If that wasn't enough to stop the thumping, there were those arms of his going up in that inimitable way of his!

"Recharred, Recharred, my T-count is still near a thousand," he shouted once we met, the sparkle in his eyes never more brilliant! "Aw, I am so happy, so happy!" I wanted to hug the hell out of him! We finally reached the highlight of our trip.

We planned to celebrate on Saturday evening with dinner at an elegant restaurant Juan knew of. It would be our big night on the town.

Early that day, we drove to nearby sights, ending the drive at a beautiful park. Once we settled alongside the lagoon, we were surprised at the friendliness of the geese roaming the banks. Even more surprising was the sight of Juan strolling along with them, and not one of them fluttering away. He was deep in thought, and I wondered what was going on in his mind.

"You know, Recharred, I am in the mood to 'ave a party," he said during our beautiful talk that afternoon. "It is so much nicer to be able to play records of songs we love. I hate thot rap music they play now. So why don't we 'ave a housewarming party for your new place. Do you not think thot would be a good idea, Recharred?" Of course, I agreed.

Juan was not upset that we were seated at an intimate, candlelit table for two…slam bang in the middle of straight couples that evening. He was too overjoyed to allow it to embarrass him. So the beautiful vacation ended with a wonderful dinner, fruitful conversation, and the glow of the candle in Juan's happy eyes.

Chapter Forty-Three:
The Moon as Farewell

Juan stayed at my apartment the remaining week of his vacation, and it gave us time to plan the party. I had taken pictures of him during the vacation, and expected to receive hell since I managed to catch his belly sticking out in most of them. Instead, he merely laughed. At this point in his life, a belly meant he was healthy.

"Recharred, I don' want to ever look like a skeleton," he always emphasized. "I would rather die!" So sandwiches, pizzas, as well as pizza rolls were often called upon, besides "cha-co-lot." In fact, when I noticed his belly resting on the couch while he was lying in his usual side position, I quickly kidded him about it.

"I do 'ave one, Recharred? I really do?" he asked innocently with a chuckle.

"Yeah, you look just like a cupie-doll, Juan." With that, he merely rose from the couch and pushed out his belly even further, and while patting it profoundly, he pranced slowly around the room. Amazingly, he looked like an exact replica of a cupie-doll, silly grin included.

As always, preparations for the party were a joy with Juan, and once everything was ready, he insisted I sit next to him before they arrived while he tallied the guests.

"Thar will be Amanda ond Patti…Daniel ond Stan…Marina ond Jeannie…Vic ond Phil, if they come…Wally ond his lover, Don…John…Hank ond Dick…Daniel's ond your friend, Roy…Lucille…your friends, Julie ond Marva…ond the guy you ond Wally know, Grant. Do you know thot makes eighteen, Recharred? Thot is gonna be some crowd," he sighed, pointing his pencil my way. He forgot to mention Hank's ex, Dr. Guy Strong, and I quickly teased him about it because Guy had actually made passes at Juan when he and Hank were together.

"Aw, yeah, Recharred," Juan replied with a chuckle. "I think he is ofter me because he has even called to ask me to go out with him. But don' worry, I 'ave always refused."

He then lost no time calling out that my drink was ready once I got out of the shower. He always preferred to take a shower before me so he could mix us a cocktail while listening and dancing to the music, and probably to have an additional one or two drinks.

"C'mon, Recharred, dance with me," he pleaded, moving to the music of "Rock Your Baby," his usual cigarette in one hand and his drink in the other. "I cannot wait until Jeannie gets here to dance with her. Aw, she is so voluptuous ond funny. C'mon, Recharred, please dance with me?" How could I refuse, especially since we were perfect hosts and never danced together at our own parties.

The party moved quickly, and though the only game played was my celebrity guessing game, it still was a group affair. Most importantly, Juan had a ball. A howling moment for a few of us was when Julie asked to keep an eye on her cocktail while she danced.

"You will be sure, Richard, that no one touches it, will you please?" Most of us knew she refused to be around anyone infected with the AIDS virus. She actually believed they'd infect her just by being in the same room. Well, Daniel never cared for her opinionated and egotistical personality and came up with a dandy when I told him about her request.

"Gimme that glass…I will pee in it!"

Juan's move to Indy was approaching, and my depression was increasing.

"I know if someone I loved was moving out of state that I'd go, too," Amanda remarked, upsetting me even more. The inner battle I was already having with myself didn't do any good either. The fact that I just bought the condo and that I was earning more than I ever did in my life was reason enough to stay put, but it still bothered me. My one consolation was that Juan also was aware of the economic problem it would cause. I was sure that was why he never brought it up. Somehow, I know I would've agreed to go if he had. Instead, he waited until years later to talk of his loneliness and of his longing for me to be with him all the time. So, for the present, he managed to keep up a good front. The excitement of decorating a new apartment camouflaged all the worries of loneliness that he obviously was harboring.

Juan was overjoyed at the turnout for the restaurant farewell dinner I planned, and beamed with pride because everyone he cared about was there for him. However, I decided not to mention that Vic and Phil were somewhat reluctant in attending. In fact, it turned out to be the last time we saw or heard from them. They disappeared from our lives, never even calling to get together with me or to inquire about Juan. It was so sad, especially for Juan. He so hated losing anyone dear to him.

Martina invited Juan and me for a dinner just before his move, and the memory of that evening will be cherished in my heart forever. A beautiful candlelit table was set in the dining room, and I remember thinking it a bit odd that she would have so romantic a setting for two men. It was as though she was aware of my heart breaking, and it was her way of saying, "Dad, I love you both and know what you are going through."

Martina and Don were trying to have a baby for nine years, and once she announced that I was finally going to be a grandpa, I was overjoyed. The fact that they thought to include Juan in the momentous announcement was especially touching. Of course, his excitement at hearing the news deserved the recognition. He even beat me to her, taking her into his arms.

"Aw, Martina, I am so happy for both of you!" he sighed. "Jus' think, you are finally gonna 'ave a bambino!"

"Martina is such a gracious hostess," raved Juan during the drive home, "ond an absolutely lovely woman, Recharred. I am certain thot she is gonna make a wonderful mother. Ond thot Don is so good. I cannot believe him. It is certain thot he loves her very much."

Our conversation continued while I kept my eyes focused on expressway traffic. Suddenly, in turning his way to answer a question, I saw a moon never before seen in my life! There it was, a moon almost as big as the sky, and it appeared as though Juan's profile was silhouetted in the center of the beautiful glow!

"Juan! Juan!" I shouted, "Look at that moon! Have you ever seen it so big?"

"My God, Recharred, I don' believe it! It is so bea-u-ti-ful," Juan gasped in awe. "Never...never 'ave I seen it so big! It almost fills the sky! Recharred, try to move to the easement ond stop. "I tried, almost losing control of the car in the heavy expressway traffic. Concerned about our safety, Juan shifted his eyes from the moon to the road ahead, keeping them peeled in that direction until we reached the exit ramp. However, to our disappointment, our moon was nowhere in sight once we were safely stopped. We were sure it would pop up again and drove for blocks, circling every which way, but our moon was gone.

We talked about that moon many times, searching the sky to see it once again. Unfortunately, it never reappeared. I was certain then, and even more since, that that moon was for us only. It was meant as a farewell to Juan, and to assure us that, no matter how far we were from each other, we would still be together under its glow.

I intended on driving with Juan to Indy on the day of the move, the Thursday before Labor Day. To my disappointment, he informed me that Svetmana wanted to drive with him, and that he didn't want to refuse. He begged me to understand, and as an appeasement, said he would return Saturday so we could drive back to Indy on Sunday.

"We con finish decorating my apartment. Then I con drive you bock on Labor Day ond stay with you because I do not 'ave to startwork until the following week. Would you not like to do thot, Recharred?" How could I complain?

A lonely feeling kept running through my body the entire day of Juan's move. This separation was not going to be like any of the others; there was no run of the show this time.

"Well, Recharred, I guess I am now a Hoosier," Juan remarked in his call to say they arrived. It felt good to hear the deep resonance of his voice. I saw him that morning, and yet it seemed so long since I heard that beautiful voice. All I had thought of that day was the one hundred and eighty miles separating us and the freedom we again would have for cruising, and I wasn't too happy.

"Ofter I dropped Svetmana home, Recharred, I went to my mother's for the day," Juan remarked on arrival Saturday evening. "I had to tell her I was returning to Indianapolis, because if she knew I was not going bock until tomorrow she would 'ave insisted I stay thar. Aw, Recharred, I really hate to lie to her. It makes me feel so bod, but I know you want me to stay with you."

"Well, Juan, isn't that what you wanted to do?"

"Of course, it is jus' thot I feel bod about lying to her even though I know if I stay thar she will go to sleep early because she gets so drunk. Aw, Recharred, she is so funny when she is drinking. She picks on my father, ond always makes fun of his small cock. Aw, Recharred, she talks so dirty when she is drunk, but aw so funny."

"I wonder who is exactly like her?" I quickly teased.

I was completely surprised on entering the ground level apartment. This was the first time Juan wasn't immediately settled after a move. Unpacked boxes were scattered everywhere. The suspicion that Svetmana was responsible was quickly confirmed once Juan informed me that she had talked him out of doing it because it would be so much nicer to check the city out, and the restaurants, of course. The biggest surprise was the new, white couch suite.

"I wanted to surprise you, Recharred," he confessed after seeing my stunned expression.

"I did not tell you, but I had saved money in the credit union," was his quick reply once I questioned how he was going to make payments since all his money was already allotted for. What was even more baffling…I believed him, though I knew he never could save a dime.

"What did you do, Juan? Go out to buy them just as soon as the movers left?" I didn't have to go any further; the adorable, coy smile on his face answered my questions. The thought of Svetmana also lingered on. She would be visiting him now and then. How was he ever going to pay his bills?

We toasted to Juan's new home with a glass of wine at a restaurant that evening, and after another, Juan insisted on going to a bar to celebrate his arrival in Indianapolis.

The bar was packed, and our excellent spirits made it easier to strike up conversations. In fact, our wit attracted quite a few into conversations, and at the end of the night, one couple was still with us. As we were about to leave, they asked if we'd like to join them for something to eat. It appeared to be a good chance for Juan to make friends, so I quickly accepted. Juan always had the insight to know what people were really after, though, and called it to my attention once we were following their car. I didn't believe it, especially since much of our conversation during the night was about preparing dishes we were good at.

"Well, I hope these guys do not 'ave any other ideas ofter we eat, Recharred...like a four-way. I saw how thot Ben was touching you all evening." I still didn't believe it.

To our surprise, they then drove into the lot of a convenience store.

"Instead of going out to eat, we thought we might buy the ingredients to prepare some of the things we talked about tonight," Ben shouted running over to our car. "How about it? Is that fine with the two of you?" I agreed, even though it was apparent Juan was upset.

"Why did you say yes, Recharred? You know whot they are looking for," he insisted. I really didn't think so and reminded him of our conversations about preparing special dishes.

"They just want to prove to us that they can make those dishes, Juan."

"Recharred, you are so naive."

"Aw, c'mon, Juan, you need friends here, and this is a good chance to make some." Juan finally accepted my decision, though I was sure he was waiting to prove his point once he sat back and glared at me.

To our dismay, an absolute pigpen greeted us once we walked into their place. Only Juan's buddy on Halstead had a place as filthy. The sofa and chair looked as though someone searching for drugs or jewels shredded the upholstery with a knife or saw. To add to the disgust, at least an inch of smelly animal hairs was caught onto the shredded material. The place was in total disarray, and one glance at Juan quickly assured me of his anger. But at least he sobered up quickly, which I was grateful for. In his drunken state, it is certain he'd call them pigs. He did, however, sit on a wooden chair, and I certainly knew he wouldn't dare eat anything. Cats were walking all over the counters. And even if they weren't, the counters looked like they were covered with a mixture of kitty litter and food droppings they never found time to clean up. To add to the filth, stacks of overflowed garbage bags were everywhere.

Ben was busy in the kitchen and nothing unusual was happening, just good conversation with Dave, so I gave Juan one of those *I told you so* looks. In fact, we began enjoying their company again. I was glad. Juan needed friends in town, and once he got to really know them, he'd set them straight about their filthy place. As always, they wouldn't mind his clever criticisms once they got to know him. I wasn't surprised when Juan politely refused any of Ben's concoctions, though I chuckled inside when he said it was because he can never eat after a night of drinking. Still, I felt forced to try them. I then did everything to keep from vomiting, especially once the thought came into my mind that rat hairs may well be included. My reprieve came when Ben admitted that they didn't taste anything like they should because he had to substitute for items the convenient store didn't carry.

"Well, then, I won't have anymore. I'll wait for another time."

It then became Juan's turn for the I-told-you-so looks. Dave decided to change into something comfortable after Ben suggested we watch one of his favorite movies. Of course, it wasn't *Gone with the Wind*. No, the title may very well have been *C'mon with the Cum*. Juan's expression wasn't exactly happy when Dave returned, wearing nothing but a short robe, just as Ben left to change, too. Of course, it didn't take long before Dave, seated across from us, began to rub his basket.

"It is much too late, ond Recharred ond I 'ave so much work to do tomorrow," Juan said politely as he rose from his chair. "So we will 'ave to leave now. I want to thank you, gentlemen, so much for your gracious hospitality. It was great fun talking with you tonight, but now we must go." We were on our way home, and I was so proud of Juan. He didn't lose his cool and proved again that, when necessary, he could sober up.

"Well, so much for making friends," I sighed. Juan just glared at me.

"Recharred, you are so gullible, so trusting. Please, Recharred, I hope you are careful when you are with someone. Please, my darling, be careful." I knew what he meant.

It only took a day to get the apartment in order even though some of the time was spent buying accessories for his bathroom. In fact, he even managed to charm me into buying them for him, reminding me of all the decorative things he had bought for my living room.

"Recharred, I think my apartment looks great, "Juan sighed after putting everything in place. "All I need now is an entertainment center for this long wall. How I wish I still had those bookcase units I gave to Marina because I really could use them now." His eyes lit up when I then reminded him of the black lacquer entertainment center I bought and that he could have the old one when it arrived.

"Thot is right!" he exclaimed. "Aw, how I wish I could 'ave thot new one instead."

"Well, you're not gonna con me out of that. However, it could be yours. All you have to do is move in with me."

The next morning, we enjoyed a beautiful and mutually satisfying love encounter together. These encounters had become rare and I'd forget how wonderful it was to feel Juan's warm, smooth flesh against mine. It was always apparent he felt the same, and yet he wouldn't commit. It made no sense. I could only reason that he still couldn't get it into his head that I'd be true. He knew I'd always be there for him, and for the time being, it was all he needed. We were almost one, and yet we were free to trick. It was crazy. Our pockets were still empty when they should've been overflowing.

Chapter Forty-Four:
The Constant Runs Begin

Two of my co-workers finally succeeded in convincing me to join them in a gallery venture. I had been somewhat reluctant because I finally was financially sound. The venture proved, however, to be good therapy for my loneliness. The business of preparing an offering actually made me forget that Juan was gone from the city, especially since we talked on the phone every day and traveled the highways to see each other on weekends. Dee asked if I wanted to buy their 1984 Ford Escort because they were buying a new one, and I accepted.

I began to go to the bars quite often during the week, more than I ever did in my life because I was lonely. I wouldn't admit to it because I wanted to think I was enjoying myself, relishing in my conquests. In reality, I subconsciously was angry with Juan because he was gone. In the beginning, if I worked on Sunday, he'd drive in. After a few months, however, he realized the mileage was too much to do regularly and I did the driving.

I was transferred to the gallery in the new Bloomingdale mall and was shocked one afternoon going to work when I bumped into Juan with his mother. He had gone to his mother's house first on one of his rare trips in and decided to take her to see the new mall. The meeting turned out to be quite awkward since his mother and I hadn't seen each other for over eleven years! It was certain she was confused as I clumsily took hold of her hand to greet her.

It bothered me and preyed on my mind afterwards. We were two people molding into one, and here we were lying to his mother. I became angry because he refused to stand up to his father's abuse on his sexual orientation. He didn't have any problems confronting him on other domestic matters. I recalled the time I gave Juan an extra television of mine to give to them because their set was shot, and it bothered me because I was sure he never told them it was from me. I became particularly angry since he always said his father put monetary things above anything else. Knowing the television was from me might have put a different light on our relationship. I was sure of it, especially after hearing him repeatedly say that his father always asks him to pay his share when he eats there!

"Do you know, ofter you left, my mother asked if you were Recharred Mella," Juan related when asked about the meeting. "When I said yes, she then told me thot she had nothing against you." For the life of me, I'll never understand why I didn't insist that he take me to see them so they'd get to know me again. After all, we were friends.

Joe was a fellow I met frequently during my excursions to Nutbush, a nearby bar. I didn't have any attraction for him. I just enjoyed his constant conversation. Unfortunately, I made the mistake of telling him I was an actor and singer. His conversations then became quite overbearing. He never had seen or heard me perform, but there he was praising my talents continually. It became too phony and I found myself avoiding his eyes each time I entered. Still, he'd manage to spot me and come running over., putting his big nose and face almost next to mine! It was so annoying but I didn't know how to stop him without being rude.

Juan was in for a weekend and in the mood for some dancing. As always, we had drinks before heading to The Nutbush. Of course, Joe hustled our way once we were situated at the bar. I no sooner introduced him to Juan when he quickly put his face against his, babbling nonsensically about my talents. Juan already was in an elfish mood and just stared wide-eyed at him as he continued. Finally, in that grand mannerism of his, Juan placed his hand on his chest. Simultaneously, his eyes widened even more in amazement.

"You know, you 'ave a big nose," he stated, looking directly into Joe's face. Joe was silent. He surely never came across anyone like the likes of Juan before. Meanwhile, Juan continued his wide-eyed, owl stare until Joe excused himself from our presence. My problem with Joe was certainly solved. I never saw the likes of him again.

The black lacquer entertainment center finally arrived, and it looked beautiful once it was set in the living room. The timing was perfect. Juan was anxious for my old one, and if it took any longer, I was sure he'd go out and buy one on credit. He so hated to live in an apartment he considered as unfinished. At the same time, Martina gave me an extra mattress and box springs for Juan's room, and it was great since he no longer would have to contend with my snoring. I wanted a new bedspread, and purchased one that was absolutely beautiful. The black, white, and bronze colors in the pattern actually looked as though a rattan design was interwoven throughout, and a heavy, black cording at the borders gave it just the right look of elegance. The old one went on Juan's bed.

"Aw, Recharred, I wish you would give me thot one instead of the wooden one!" Juan exclaimed when he saw my new entertainment center.

"Oh, no, Juan, you're not going to con me out of it with your sweet talk. As I have said, it can be yours. All you have to do is quit the Army and come live with me." He said no more.

"Aw, Recharred, thot is so bea-u-ti-ful! I love it!" he then sighed at seeing my new spread. "Aw, thot heavy cording makes it look so elegant because it falls so nicely. Aw, you 'ave to give it to me because it will look so good in my bedroom with my brown carpeting!" Explaining how much I loved it only made him go into his put-on but lovable character.

"Thot is why you should give it to me, Recharred. Because you love it so much, ond because you know I deserve it. Ofter all, you know I am royalty." And as usual, his manner was so lovable I couldn't refuse. It was his. I even included the throw pillow. So I then bought a gray and black quilt with pillow shams for my bed, and two matching geometric designed throw pillows for Juan that I was certain would compliment his spread. I never regretted it because his appreciation was overwhelming. Besides, he was always giving me things.

I was taking Monday and Tuesday off, so we packed the disassembled entertainment center into our hatchbacks and took off Sunday for Indy. Juan put the spread immediately on his bed once we arrived, and it was hilarious watching him fuss to be sure it fell evenly. Thereafter, whenever I made up his bed, I could always expect to be checked by the inspector general. In fact, even when it was perfect, he'd still redo it.

It didn't take Juan long to get familiar with Indianapolis. In fact, I'm certain he knew it better than many who lived there all their lives. Since he was a well-read man, he was aware of the interesting places to see, as well as the special attractions going on. Of course, it didn't take long to know which bars were the most fun and those that played the music he liked. His excitement for the sights he wanted me to see always managed to rub off on me once we were on our way. He was the perfect tour guide and information center.

On many of my Saturday night arrivals, I'd hear loud disco music as I pulled into a parking space in front of Juan's apartment. Of course, it meant we were going dancing. I'd use my key on occasion and really surprise him should he just happen to come out of the shower.

"Aw, Recharred, you scared the hell out of me!" he'd gasp dramatically while holding his hand to his chest. It also wasn't unusual to see him sipping a cocktail while drying himself after his shower, and at the same time spreading his legs apart and waving his genitals to the beat of the music. A silly grin on his face only added to the hilarity. His goal in life was always to make me laugh. I could also expect a scolding whenever I was late.

"Hurry up ond shower because we 'ave to go out dancin', Recharred." I was usually very hungry and would check out the pot on the stove first. Most of the time, chili or ground beef with noodles and mushroom sauce were in it, and I'd dig in with a spoon.

"Thot is all you think about, Recharred…mangia, mangia, ond your belly!"

It was always very evident though that he was happy I was there, even as he reprimanded me for making a mess in the kitchen while trying to eat quickly. This was Juan, and if he didn't react in this manner, I'd feel something was wrong. He had such a way of making me feel so important in his life…of making me feel like the cat's meow!

Juan was Juan, and this meant I was faced with the embarrassment of his dirty talk whenever he insisted we stop for late night breakfasts. Oh, how I wished for a paper bag to put over my head. Finally, I began suggesting that we cook breakfast at home, and he usually never objected. He could then play the stereo and dance while I prepared it. And there he'd be, dancing very seriously while turning his head from side to side. A tireless energy seemed to ooze from him. He never wanted an evening to end. Of course, I'd turn the volume down, only to see him dance nonchalantly over to turn it up again. And, of course, to shake his finger my way in reprimand.

Svetmana didn't visit Juan often, but when she did, Juan always called to tell me not to come that weekend. I understood.

"You know, Recharred, thot Svetmana is something else," Juan said in a call. "She always gets angry ot nothing ot all, ond starts screaming like a crazy woman! Then she runs into the bedroom and slams the door shut. Ond, Recharred, she will not come out the whole evening. This last time, I yelled out thot she should stay the fuck in thar all the time!"

"Oh, Juan, why do you talk to her that way? Why must you swear?"

"I really don' care, Recharred, because you know I really don' like her. She is a nasty miserable person, ond she will not try to change. Aw, Recharred, she has disappointed me so much because she is so mean ond nasty to everyone. She is ter-ri-ble!"

"Just ignore it and show some hurt," I urged in an attempt to get her to feel sorry for her temper tantrums and in turn realize she was wrong. It did no good, however, because he wouldn't take my advice. So it was always he who gave in to her because he really did love her, or at least he wanted to love her. This was what he was all about. He needed a child to love and be proud of, and he wanted Svetmana to be that person so badly because he couldn't see any more children coming into his life.

Almost three weeks passed since we saw each other because of my hours at the new gallery and Svetmana's visit, and it seemed like an eternity. However, a wild time in November showed great promise this weekend because Juan invited Daniel and Stan to come along with me. No one liked to barhop more than Daniel.

To my surprise, there was Juan standing at the curb waiting anxiously when Daniel pulled forward to park. It was cold and there he was without a jacket, just wearing a great big smile! He was so excited! After the greetings, Juan hustled us in.

"C'mon, let's bring your things in! We 'ave to leave right away because I made reservations for dinner ot Jimmy's for eight o'clock ond it is almost thot time." I followed Daniel and Stan in with Juan behind. Immediately, Juan slammed the door shut and to my surprise grabbed hold of me. In one motion, he turned me his way and placed his arms around my waist tenderly. He then smiled and looked at me compassionately.

"Recharred, I 'ave missed you so much ond am so happy you are here ot last! Two kisses on my lips followed oh so gently.

"Oh, look, Stan, isn't that wonderful!" Daniel sighed.

In all of our years together, Juan never displayed emotion publicly. And here he is…tender, caring, and loving. It didn't matter that Daniel and Stan were watching. He missed me! And here he was…touching my heart again.

Juan and I never cared for barhopping because we felt it broke up the fun, and really wanted to stay at Jimmy's to dance because they were the only ones that played 70's disco. He did, however, prove to be a beautiful host again and we were off.

Daniel and Stan never believed when I talked about Juan's bold actions whenever he and I were out, and probably because they had never been to the bars with us. I felt certain that this was the night that Juan would entertain them with his infamous behavior, and almost gloated. As expected, it didn't take long. In fact, we were just leaving the first bar.

"I 'ave to pee," he blurted out as we were about to get into Daniel's car. Of course, he immediately proceeded to do it. There he was, peeing into the weeds of an empty lot standing on the well-lit sidewalk.

"Juan, why are you peeing right there where everyone can see!" I screamed. "Why didn't you walk into the bushes? What if a cop sees you!" Of course, I never expected that to happen. However, at that moment, a police car came driving by very slowly.

"Hey, buddy, what do you think you're doing!" yelled one of the cops sticking his head out the passenger window. "You're not allowed to do that in public!" I felt sure an arrest would be made when Juan ignored him and just continued to pee. Instead, the police car just continued on its way.

"Evidently, he thought I would pee on him," Juan remarked cleverly while zipping up.

The fifth and last bar, Our Place, was wild and hot, and quite a melting pot. There they were…desperate ones looking for a last chance to pick up a trick…those who just wanted to dance…women and straight…as well as those who didn't want to or couldn't stop drinking. It was a perfect place to end the evening because we were in the right mood to dance to anything. Juan, however, did more drinking than dancing.

Juan insisted on breakfast and did exactly as I expected in the restaurant. As open as Daniel was regarding his sexual orientation, I do believe he felt as embarrassed as Stan while Juan babbled his dirty talk. However, Juan's charm still managed to prevail.

I was the last to awaken the next morning, and only because of Daniel's loud voice. Juan was in his usual good spirits and suggested we go for brunch at the Restaurant on the Green, a charming cottage located on the grounds of the Museum of Art. We thought it a perfect choice because their elaborate buffet included a wide variety of scrumptious desserts, which would please Daniel immensely. In fact, we were right on the button. Daniel was in heaven.

After brunch, Juan played his usual colorful tour guide. In fact, the sunlight oozing from him made the damp and dreary day seem bright. Daniel had not wanted to leave any later than six, and the hour arrived before I knew it. One glance at Juan told me he wasn't happy. As always, he quickly asked if I'd stay over and take the bus in the morning. Unfortunately, I needed to be at work early and the bus schedule wasn't cooperative. So he wasn't too happy. In fact, he declined from walking out to the car with us to say good-bye.

Amanda and Patti followed for a weekend just before the Christmas holidays. This time, I drove on my own. Again, it was Jimmy's Place for dinner and some dancing. He also was aware that women liked drag shows and took us to one he had been to recently.

"I was thar last week ond I had a ball laughing because the drag queens were so bad."

This time, the queens were exactly as Juan claimed, in fact…worse! What made it hilariously funny wasn't only because of their terrible lip-synching, but also because their dresses were hanging on them, besides being badly wrinkled. Amanda and Patti couldn't control their giggling, especially once Juan called attention to all the tears and dirt on the dresses. Still, we felt we should be polite, especially since we were their only audience. So we handed them one dollar after another. I was also thankful Juan didn't over indulge as he did in Madison. I'm sure he somehow remembered his actions of that miserable night and because of his love for them took hold of himself, which proved he could control himself when necessary.

We were off on another one of Juan's fantastic tours after enjoying his famous frittata breakfast, ending up at the Union Station Mall. This quaint mall was loved by browsers during the Christmas season because the walkways were loaded with barker demonstrations. A show that really caught our attention was the monkey puppets. The puppets were controlled by a wand attached to one of the monkey's arms. We stayed for some time, amazed because they looked so adorably real. Juan had to be the biggest fan, choking with uncontrollable laughter…I decided to buy one for Mike for Christmas because he really loved novelties and games.

Amanda and Patti decided on leaving at about six, too, so I was glad I decided to drive separately. It'll also allow me to leave in the morning after he was off to work. In this way, he wouldn't feel depressed because I'd still be there when he left.

My children hadn't been to my place for Christmas since the Christmas Eve dinner when Tom was living with Juan and me. So I planned to have dinner at my place. It was perfect because Juan always celebrated at his folks Christmas Eve…he'd be able to be with us. Unfortunately, his mother decided on a Christmas dinner this time round. My disappointment was pacified when he said he'd come after dinner.

"But thot means I will then 'ave to buy them presents ond I don't 'ave the money, Recharred," he then said in a weak attempt to back out. "I know they will buy me something because they did the last time we were together for Christmas Eve. This way you con tell them I am not coming ond they won't buy anything."

"No, Juan, I want you to come very badly. Just give the girls something. In fact, you can give them the chains with the gold-dipped leaves that I bought in Indianapolis." It was settled, and I knew he was as happy as I was.

Once Juan finally arrived, I was surprised to see the princess with him; this forced me to do some shuffling with gifts to be sure Svetmana got something to open. I remember Juan's face as my kids were shouting at the same time while opening gifts. I knew exactly what he was thinking…how Italiano we were! He did, however, fit in well and as always kept them laughing with his wit. Svetmana was quiet, but did manage to criticize someone for something they wore. It didn't make sense! Juan was loaded with charm and yet none of it rubbed off on her.

Chapter Forty-Five:
In Need of Adjustments

1989 arrived and I really believe my relationship with Juan grew stronger, even though we were living miles apart. Still, his stubbornness prevailed. He refused to agree to a commitment, and I was too blinded by my empty conquests to insist on it. In fact, we'd never dare discuss our conquests because we were both aware of our jealousies. So we made one wrong decision after another. It was inconceivable. We were so close and yet we accepted these separate encounters! At times, though, I realized the foolishness of it all and reached out just to touch him. To me, you needed to touch the one you loved. Sometimes, I'd ask him to lay his head on my lap while watching television or try to lay mine on his.

"Recharred, two men do not do things like thot," he'd quickly reprimand. However, it was always he who initiated lovemaking the morning after a night out and he was sober by then. Many times, I'd sit on his bed to say goodnight lovingly as he lay there reading, and after leaving the room, I'd peek in quickly and throw a kiss. In fact, I'd continue to do it until he'd do a fast take and stare at me like an owl.

I finally won a commercial on the merits of my expressive face. The script called for a head chef to direct a regimental march of cooks towards the camera while holding platters high above their heads. The first cook was to place his platter directly in front of the camera. The camera was then focused on me to catch my pompous expression, daring them to try my new delectable entrée. The studio requested I come in for a test prior to the shoot.

"Aw, Recharred, con I go with you?" Juan begged on his arrival in town. "I 'ave never seen a commercial being filmed ond it would be so nice watching you rehearse it." I felt there was no reason he couldn't, especially since I wasn't being paid for rehearsal time. He then asked if he could bring Svetmana and I agreed as long as she was quiet.

The director was very cordial when I said a friend from out of town was with me and graciously had two chairs set up directly behind the cameraman. It was great! There he was, smiling with pride as he watched me go through my movements, and it didn't matter if he laughed out loud because it only confirmed that the commercial was funny. Amazingly, I can still see that smile of his and hear his catchy chuckle.

Juan didn't stop talking about it that day, and thanked me repeatedly for taking him. However, Svetmana's excitement was what really surprised me. She was so nice and actually appeared to be proud of me. It had to be Juan's excitement rubbing off on her as it did when I performed in *Little Mary Sunshine*.

Unfortunately, money wasn't rolling in on our offering to open a gallery. The economy was in a bad state. Months passed and yet only ten thousand dollars was pledged.

Then it happened. Mario gave me some photos of antique art available to him, and I showed them to a client. I explained that I possibly may be opening a gallery, and that the antique paintings would then be available. This type of art was not even offered at my present gallery, but I still requested she not mention it to anyone. However, the customer became very disturbed because the management wouldn't give a refund for a picture she wanted to return. In her anger, she told them about my photos. I was fired!

"Please, do not get drunk like the other time, Recharred! You know you con get in an accident. Please, my darlin'," Juan pleaded after I called. But I did go out to get drunk, if only to pacify the irony of it all. I lost the best paying job I ever had for a wild dream of Mario's. So I was left with nothing but time on my hands and no money. Fortunately, after a court battle with my ex-employers, I began to collect unemployment compensation. One advantage, I was able to visit Juan during the week, too.

Juan and I went to many bars whenever I was there, but favored Jimmy's because they played some of the old '70s disco. He hated the so-called music of the time. Of course, I felt the same. There was no melody…just beat, and you'd tire easily. So we'd dance our heads off whenever a medley of the '70s was played and it was so wonderful watching Juan smile with every move. If we were in the barroom and a medley began, I could always expect Juan to hurry me into the other room, almost pushing so not to miss some of it. One of our favorites to dance to, ironically, came out in the '80s. The disco version of "Memory" from *Cats* was quite lengthy, but because the beat and melody was so great, we never tired. There he'd be, about four to five feet from me, moving to the fantastic beat and holding onto his serious expression while moving his head from side to side. A big smile would always flash on his face once the tempo reached a climax because he could then move at a fast and furious pace.

"Look at him…he is so strong and happy," I'd say to myself watching his strong movements, "Oh, God, thank you so much because I know this will go on forever. Juan is never going to get sick!"

It is impossible to count the many times Juan managed to embarrass me with his dirty talk in a restaurant after drinking, and there was no exception in Indianapolis. I really wanted to cut off my head the evening he insisted we have breakfast at Perkins, a restaurant that catered to the young straight clientele. I said a quick prayer as I pulled into their parking lot.

Juan glanced around and quickly commented on the huge crowd, and I thought I might be safe tonight. However, after placing our order, it was obvious what was about to happen after one look at his mischievous smile. I said another quick prayer but this wasn't heard either.

"Recharred, do you want to fuck tonight?" he bellowed out. I wanted to cut my head off as he sat there with a smug expression, actually waiting for an answer. I tried to whisper to him to stop, but it did no good. I was talking to a wall.

"Juan, please don't talk that way," I whispered in desperation, "everyone is gonna hear you. Pleassse, Juan?" Of course, my pleas didn't faze him. He just laughed.

"Whot's the matter, Blanche? Are you embarrassed thot everyone will hear thot you like cock?" I didn't know which way to look. I prayed everyone was plastered drunk or deaf while he sat there with a silly grin on his face, itching to say more. Our orders finally arrived.

"Look, Recharred, they serve pigeon's eggs here!" he bellowed out after observing our orders. "Perkin's serves pigeon's eggs!" He was right! The four eggs weren't as large as one jumbo! I thought it wonderful though. I was saved from further embarrassment because he was hilarious over the eggs. Of course, he didn't remember anything the next morning. In contrast, Juan wouldn't think of talking vulgar when he wasn't drinking. In fact, he even was embarrassed should I call out his name on the street. I could always expect to be reprimanded.

Juan was well-read so he always knew everything special going on in the city and all the amenities, and insist we see them all. He talked continuously about the construction plans of the new downtown mall, and knew all the stores and problems involved. He always loved the bright colors of Southwestern art and was elated because of the new museum being built.

"Aw, Recharred, I cannot wait until it is finished! Do you know it is gonna be in the shape of an adobe?" The 'Marketplace,' with all the concessions, was another favorite of Juan because it was something out of the past. The tree-lined streets and roads in Indianapolis were also a favorite.

"Aw, Recharred, it is so bea-u-ti-ful here!" were said often. "You know, you do not even 'ave to drive out to the country to see the beauty. There is so much greenery!"

"Recharred, Recharred, I cannot wait until you come to see it!" Juan exclaimed in his call to tell me the museum opened. "I went yesterday with Svetmana, ond I wanna keep going! It is so bea-u-ti-ful, Recharred!" I was quite certain he meant every word when he waited over an hour in line with me without a complaint, and this was his second time there. That little kid in him again was anxious for me to see something he discovered.

"You know, Recharred, I would like to one day do my living room in Southwest colors," Juan said driving home. "I love it so much! Would you not like thot, Recharred? It would not be too difficult to change because I already 'ave white furniture. Do you know I watched *The Rich ond the Famous* on television ond they had Ann Miller's home in Santa Fe. Recharred, it was so colorful ond bea-u-ti-ful! Ond, Recharred, she has white furniture also! Would you like to 'ave Southwest, Recharred? Do you not think it would be a good idea?" Of course, I agreed, but what really impressed me was that I was included in his plans.

"Aw, Recharred, I would really love to go Santa Fe with you! Do you know they say it has the most bea-u-ti-ful sky of anywhere in the country?" We finally agreed it would be our next vacation.

"If we open the gallery, maybe I can go there and buy art and you can be my advisor." Of course, this brought a proud smile to his face.

Whatever Happened to Baby Jane was one of Juan's favorite movies, and probably because of Bette Davis. He loved her guts and played his video copy continuously. In fact, the scene where she locked the door to Crawford's room and childishly refused to open it for the housekeeper brought him to choking laughter each time. He'd rewind to that scene more than any other. Joan Crawford was called Blanche and as hysterically dramatic as Vivian Leigh in *Streetcar*, which solidified his reasoning for my name tag.

Juan loved the new Lambada dance rage because it was so sexy. We returned late one evening after a night out in Indy and I was quite out of it. So much so that I could hardly stand. Juan, on the other hand, could only think of playing his Lambada record and was again his tireless self. Of course he insisted I stay in the living room to watch him dance to it.

I was so tired and sleepy, trying desperately not to fall off the arm of his loveseat as I watched him do his thing. Suddenly, in one grand manner, he swooped me up into his arms! I might just as well have been a Raggedy Ann doll the way he led me around the floor in bold movements. And true to the dance, he began pushing his leg into my crotch! He couldn't be more serious while leading me around like a floppy rag doll.

"C'mon, Recharred, this is the way you do the Lambada!" he demanded, trying to get me to follow and bending me over backward. It wasn't intended to be a joke. He was showing me the dance. Fortunately, in one of his long strides, I managed to collapse into the couch. My dead weight then made it impossible for him to resume his lesson, especially once I passed out.

Whenever I stopped to ask a clerk a question while in a store, there was Juan directly behind them...staring at me with his owl expression and his broken bridge hanging from his lips! I'd have to contort my muscles every which way in order not to laugh in their faces. He'd also do an excellent over-exaggerated mimic of me whenever I sat in a lounge chair holding a finger to my head like *The Thinker*. A habit of mine...holding my lips tight while deep in thought was one he never missed. He'd look just like Mussolini in that mimic.

Juan picked up a habit many would consider as quite vulgar. However, I finally realized he always felt his mission in life was to make me laugh. So, he decided not to hold his gas whenever we were alone, and once I voiced an objection, it left me wide open for more bombardment.

"Whot…whot is it? Whot happened, Recharred," he'd say innocently, holding the bland, owl expression, only to finally laugh. If I didn't laugh, and most of the times I didn't initially, he'd add some theatrics. In one quick movement, he'd walk over…turn his back to me…then lower his pants and shorts revealing his bare butt! Without shame, he'd bend over…spread the cheeks of his butt apart, and fart in my face! I'd be livid! Of course, this only made him laugh harder, especially once I reached to light a match. There he'd be…wrestling to get the match from my hand before I had a chance to strike it. And all while choking with laughter.

"Juan, I can't believe it! You're so elegant and you do something so vulgar like that!" I'd shout. Of course, this only made him laugh more, and as usual his laughter…contagious! We'd get so weak from laughing that neither could win. I'd try to give him a taste of his own medicine on occasion but it did no good.

"Aw, Recharred, it smells so good," he'd say, taking a deep breath, "but do you know I am gonna tell Deena on you…thot you pull your pants down to fart in my face." Of course, his finger was busy shaming me.

I decided to give him some theatrics on one occasion and quickly ran to his refrigerator. I took hold of an onion and came running back holding it to my nose, sighing sweetly. I thought he was going to collapse from laughter. And he never forgot it.

"Aw, Recharred, you were so funny thot time when you put the oonion to your nose…aw so funny!" Only he could get away with something like this and still be the absolute elegant charmer.

"How are you, Reeecharrred…'ow are you doin' this lov-e-ly evening, Reeecharrred?" Juan slurred out in his little boy voice that I heard so often once I answered the phone.

"Juan, you've been drinking…why are you drinking, especially on a week night when you have to work the next day?"

"Whot do you mean, Reeecharrred? Why do you say I 'ave been drinkin?'" he inquired very innocently while chuckling.

"Don't be funny, Juan…you know I have answered enough of these calls through the years to realize when you're drinking!" However, he continued his childlike denials and finally pleaded for me to go out dancing with him even though he knew it was impossible.

"Juan, please don't go out yourself! You know how you get and it is such a long drive to the bars! I don't want you to drive when you're drinking…please, Juan!" He didn't argue. No, he just chuckled and then said a sweet "bye, Recharred"…and hung up. It didn't matter that I called back because he never answered. I figured he was either dancing to his records or that he went out. It undoubtedly was the latter. This was the first of many times and what I had dreaded when he gave me the news of being transferred. How was I to go after him when I was 185 miles away?

The art gallery finally became a reality. A space was available on Michigan Avenue in Chicago and Mario and Victor talked me into investing ten thousand, which turned out to be a third of our total capital. We should have had at least a quarter to a half million but because all the artwork was coming in on consignment, they felt we didn't need that much. I objected to the location because it was on the second floor, but still managed to give in. The landlord agreed to do the build-out of our exquisite plans, and I couldn't help but wonder if we would have received a lease had he known of our small capital? Somehow, he never requested financial statements. Plans were to open in about three months…sometime in May.

"Juan, Martina had a baby girl this morning! And I got to go to the birthing room and hold the baby," were my first words when I called.

"Did you do thot, Recharred…did you really do thot? Aw, thot is wonderful! I am so happy for Martina! How is she, Recharred?" He was as excited as I was.

"Aw, Recharred, I jus' love this family of glass elephants. I don' ave anything like this in my collection. These are so petite ond cute. I am gonna place them right here on the end table so I con see them all the time. Thank you so much my darling, ond also for the wonderful shirt for my birthday. But, of course you know I deserve them."

I arrived at Juan's on a very hot and muggy Saturday evening before the Fourth of July. As I pulled into the parking place, I was certain we were going out on the town. The sound of music blasting through the air always made it evident. Needless to say, I was hurried through his meatball and noodles stroganoff meal and after showering, we were off to Jimmy's with Juan again taking his vodka and diet coke along. We were to meet Larry Kess, a new friend of his.

"I think he likes me Recharred, but I told him I am only interested in being friends. I also told him I wanted him to meet you. Aw, Recharred, I did not tell him about our bar in Atlanta, so please do not bring thot up."

"What difference does it make if he knows, Juan?" I asked bewildered. "Why can't you tell him we had a bar in Atlanta?"

"I jus' do not want him to know, Recharred." It didn't make any sense but I respected his wishes.

Larry was exactly as Juan described…tall with gray hair and definitely distinguished looking. Though he was cordial, signs of resentment towards me showed through. It was obvious he was after Juan and he didn't want any interference from me. It was especially noticeable whenever I mentioned we'd been lovers and that our feelings for each other had grown through the years. He'd immediately change the subject.

I assumed Larry was about my age and surprised to hear he was only two years older than Juan. In fact, I looked younger. Maybe because I colored my hair.

"Recharred, why do you 'ave to color your hair? Why don't you let it jus' be natural instead of dyeing it dark like thot?" Juan had often remarked, quickly adding another dig in order to get my goat. "You look like an aging queen with dyed dark hair…ond on older face." So he'd just continued to laugh and then suddenly take a big whiff of me.

"Aw, Recharred, do you know you smell jus' like on old man? Aw, yeah…you know jus' like old people smell." Of course, he'd be in hysterical laughter while I tried to smell myself.

Late Sunday morning, we joined Larry again for brunch at the wonderful Restaurant on the Green and he insisted we return that evening to his apartment for a light dinner. Though conversation was great, I realized Juan wouldn't stay long. A small portion of chicken salad certainly wouldn't do the job of saturation he needed after a night of drinking. It was nothing like crashing at home with me and just relaxing watching television and eating open faced sandwiches all evening.

"Juan, I will be coming right back tonight after work," I said, getting ready to leave in the early morning darkness.

"Thot is jus' it, Recharred, you are coming right back tonight. Is thot not crazy to do…drive thar ond back again the same day? Why don' you stay, Recharred, because I only 'ave to go into the office for about an hour today, ond we can then 'ave the whole day together." I couldn't refuse. He looked so desperate.

"You know, Recharred, maybe we con go to the anti-cruelty when I get home from work." And we did go that afternoon.

"Aw, look, Recharred, how cute this puppy is. I jus' love him," Juan sighed while tickling its neck. "You know I would really love to get a dog, Recharred, because he con be so much company for me. I get so lonely." This was the first time I heard him say he was lonely.

Juan had done nothing but rave about the gallery and continually said he'd buy one of each piece if he had the money.

"Because Recharred, you 'ave put so much work into it ond really deserve to be a success." While driving on one of his usual tours, he came up with a suggestion he had to know I couldn't swing financially.

"You know, Recharred, you should open a gallery in Indianapolis because thar are a lot of rich people living here."

"Yeah, what would I open it with…peanuts?" This wasn't the only time he suggested I do that, and I really didn't understand at the time why he always asked. He was well aware of my financial situation. It had to be his way of asking me to come live there with him, and I never really realized it until years later. Of course. Otherwise, why did he insist we stop to see model apartments so often. Yes, I could always expect to hear.

"It would be so nice to 'ave you living here with me, Recharred. Don' you think thot would be nice?" However, he never came right out and asked me to come live with him…to tell me how lonely he was for me. I guess, because I had the gallery. So he wanted me to be a huge success. Then I'd be able to open one there.

We talked late into the night that evening, and as always, time flew by. I was pleased to hear that his sister and her two daughters were coming from South America to stay with his mother for the summer. Juan was going to spend his two week vacation there, too. Of course, there wouldn't be enough beds for him, too, and he said he'd have to sleep at my place.

"But I will 'ave to leave every morning to do things with them, Recharred."

"I understand, but it'll be great to have you here every night, Juan. And you don't have to spend every minute with them…do you?"

"Not every minute, Recharred, but I will 'ave to spend as much time as possible." He then went on in that rapid pace of his, worried that his sister would expect him to pick up the tab every place they go.

"Recharred, I cannot afford it. I don' 'ave thot kind of money! I will be on vacation but still only 'ave the regular pay I receive, ond I 'ave so many bills. I know her husband will probably not give her much money, ond whot he does give her will only be enough to buy the things he wants her to bring back for him." He continued, worried that he'd go through all his money, and not have enough to pay his bills. I reminded him of his trip there in 1974.

"Juan, remember you gave her all that money. They probably think you still are loaded, especially since you paid for your mother's trip there again. Just tell her the truth, or be like he was…slow to pull out your wallet."

I was still asleep when Juan talked with Larry the morning of the fourth and never was quite sure exactly what was said. He only mentioned he had to call him back. On Sunday, Larry had mentioned coming to his place to watch the parade. He also wanted us to stay for a fair going on in the afternoon, and for the fireworks as well. From Juan's actions and words, I was aware he wasn't crazy about spending the entire day with him, and probably because he knew Larry had an attraction for him. I urged him to call with an answer, even if it was to tell him we were only going there for the fireworks, but he kept putting it off. Once he did call, there was no answer. No wonder, it was well into the afternoon. He obliged my wishes to call before leaving for the fireworks, and from the sound of his voice, it was apparent Larry was giving him hell!

"Con you believe thot, Recharred?" Juan said bewildered, "he hung up on me! First, he kept yelling thot I was supposed to call him ot ten o'clock ond thot he kept waiting ond I did not call, so he went to the fair ond parade himself!"

"I kept telling you to call but you just ignored me," I quickly reminded him. "He was angry because you told him you were gonna call. Anyone would be angry."

"Well, Recharred, he wanted us thar all day, ond I did not want to stay thar thot long."

"All you had to do then, Juan, was call him and tell him so, but no, you were stubborn. So now you have lost a friend."

"Well, it is just as well because he has wanted to 'ave a relationship, ond I jus' want to be friends. Ond, besides, I am Juan!"

It was too good to be true, having Juan with me in the morning and then at night when his vacation started. I was especially pleased when he told me his sister was paying for many of the things on their outings. I wasn't quite sure, though, because Juan was so good at telling tall stories, especially when he had to cover up heavy spending.

Martina invited Juan to the christening party slated for the last Sunday in July, and told him to bring Svetmana, his sister, and her daughters.

"Recharred, I do not know whot I am gonna do with thot Svetmana," Juan complained before the party. "She is such a nasty, miserable person! You know whot she said to me? She said thot she was embarrassed to be with my nieces in public because they did not dress stylishly…thot they looked like peasants! Con you understand thot girl, Recharred? So I told her to stay the fuck home! If she does not call ond apologize, I swear I will not bring her to your granddaughter's christening party! I don' care if I never see her, Recharred! She is so miserable!" I didn't think he meant it. He always gave in to her. However, she wasn't anywhere in sight when they arrived.

The day was perfect, and the setting under the elaborate tent was beautiful! Martina loved to decorate and entertain lavishly and that was exactly what it was. It couldn't have looked any more professional. A grand buffet…a sweet table…cocktails…were beautifully presented throughout the house.

Juan wore his dark blue shirt, which always complimented his eyes, and Martina lost no time telling him how handsome he was. Of course, he was embarrassed. I felt so proud because he truly looked so handsome and happy.

The party turned out to be one of the most laugh-filled times Juan and I ever had, and especially amazing…neither of us had a cocktail. I felt so wonderful, and probably because Juan was once again sharing a joyous occasion with my family. After all, 'joy when not shared with someone dies young.' I was already aware that Juan was a special someone. My wit was in full bloom, and I kept topping each crack with a funnier one. Juan couldn't control his laughter. His sister and her daughters fell victim also. When my son, Mike, and daughter, Jacque, and her beau, Gil, joined the table, the laughter was even greater.

Juan's niece, Ronica, who was all of about nine years old, decided to teach me Spanish. This turned out to be a hoot because her excitement each time I leaned towards the Italian pronunciation of the Spanish words caused me to be even more exuberant and comedic. Amazingly, we never tired and the laughter continued the entire afternoon. In fact, it seemed like only minutes and the party was over.

Juan's stay in Chicago passed so quickly and before I knew it, he was gone. So I was back on the road driving there every weekend. Amanda and Patti came down on one of the weekends, and Juan was so pleased. Of course, he insisted they see the Southwestern museum.

"Thot Amanda is so cute," he sighed after they left. "I love the way she giggles."

Business continued to be dreary. A second floor shop just wasn't conducive enough to attract customers. We needed more than six thousand to pay the rent and other bills and we didn't have it. So I decided to make a sale happen. I drove out of state with artwork to show the husband of a woman who had come in and loved the works. I returned in the wee hours of the morning, but happily with a check for ten thousand.

"Recharred, do you think you can give Svetmana a part time job ot your gallery? She needs to learn some responsibility," Juan asked. He was aware we weren't making salaries ourselves. He just wanted Svetmana to learn that she couldn't go on doing nothing forever.

"If it is for very little pay, Recharred...thot is fine." At that moment, I remembered we were planning a grand opening. Svetmana could address the invitations.

"Aw, Recharred, thot will be great. Thank you so much."

Juan certainly didn't exaggerate when he said Svetmana was slow. Every move she made was at a snail's pace. I already knew she didn't like to take orders. For that matter, she didn't even like to be instructed. I think she actually thought she was going to merely sit at the reception desk and greet the two customers that might find their way up the stairs. She was, however, fairly nice to me and probably because she realized she had to in order to keep her job. She knew nothing about a typewriter and didn't even seem to be interested in learning how to pick and poke at it! I didn't dare give her any filing for fear we'd never find it again. She also never arrived on time.

The invitations arrived and the job of addressing them should be an easy chore for her. It would also free me of the job, which was great because my fingers cramped when writing for long periods of time. Mario and I could devote the time to getting the gallery ready. However, observing her at work couldn't be more frustrating. A snail moved faster! It was unbelievable! No one could be that slow. After finally writing the full name, she'd study the list for a few minutes. Then she'd take as long to write the address. It took over ten minutes to do one. I'm sure she had to be thinking that the addressee should be proud to receive an invitation addressed by a princess.

"Svetmana, do you think it is possible to write a bit faster because if we don't get them in the mail in enough time, we won't have anyone here," I said in an effort to motivate some speed. She merely looked up with a smug expression.

"Richard, after all, you do want them addressed correctly, don't you?"

I said no more. She didn't write in calligraphy, which baffled me. No, her handwriting was much like mine…letters going in every direction and very juvenile! Mario and I had to finally join her.

"See, I told you so," Juan replied without surprise once I told him. "She jus' does not want to work ot anything. Recharred, she has been such a disappointment to me. I don't think she will ever make me proud of her." There was, however, one thing. She copied an old '30s movie poster in pen and ink and colored it with crayon. She managed some resemblance to the movie stars but it was evident an amateur had moved in slow strokes. In fact, we suspected some stenciling. Juan, however, had it framed and praised it continuously.

"It probably took Svetmana a year to do this, Recharred," he finally admitted.

She volunteered to print name plates for the artists. After two days of very poor attempts, we had them printed up professionally. Well, at least, I felt sure she'd do well as hostess. She could feel like the queen she thought she was. It would give her a definite air of importance greeting guests and making certain they signed the guest book. I also hired a group of starving actors to serve the hors d'oeuvres and wine. Svetmana then surprised me with an offer to make them. I was a bit hesitant until she reminded me of the wonderful spread on the table the Halloween party her mother had invited me to a few years ago.

"Well, Richard, I made everything for that party and others, too." So the two of us went to the super mart to buy everything needed, and this was one of the rare times I really enjoyed being with her. We laughed and joked like two old friends. She had been in my life for over fifteen years and this was only one of rare times she seemed to truly enjoy being with me.

A fairly large turnout showed up for the occasion. Of course, my family made up the majority. Endira never missed anything the rich attended, and arrived early with the hors d'oeuvres. Svetmana would be late and asked her to bring them. When she finally arrived with her girlfriend, she looked striking. Her hair was swept back into a bun and gave her an exotic Eurasian look. Of course, she did absolutely nothing except to drink champagne and act out her princess role. Juan arrived late.

"I had to go to my mother's, Recharred, because she had made dinner for me, so thot is why I am late. Aw, Recharred, the gallery looks absolutely bea-u-ti-ful! I wish you make lots of sales tonight ond always." However, no sales transpired.

"Do you know, Recharred, thot I arrived early this afternoon?" Juan asked once we got to my place. "Well, I went straight to Svetmana's. Ond lucky I did because you would 'ave never had your hors d'oeuvres. I could not believe it because it was already four thirty ond she had not yet started to make them. She jus' kept dancing to her records. I told her she better get started, but she jus' kept dancin.' So I had to make them all. Thot was why I was so late because I then had to go to my mother's. See how irresponsible she is!" It was unbelievable, especially since I paid her to do them.

Juan loved the fact that I joined an *I Love Lucy* video club, and played the same scenes continuously. Of course he'd laugh hilariously each and every time. His favorites were: "Lucy Does a TV Commercial"…"Lucy Gets into Pictures," and "Lucy's Italian Movie."

"Recharred, she was a tremendous comedienne, the greatest! I love her so much!" It was amazing. Usually, whenever I laughed at a funny scene, I'd never find it as hilarious the second time. This wasn't the case, however, while watching a funny scene a second time with Juan. In fact, his magic to make me laugh continued through third and fourth times, even more!

"Really, Recharred, you are gonna come here for Thanksgiving! Aw, thot is wonderful! It will be jus' the two of us like in Atlanta!" He was that excited little kid again when I called to tell him I was bringing a turkey, and it was so wonderful to hear that excitement again. I didn't even mind when he didn't fail to comment on the mess I'd be making.

"I will jus' 'ave to stay next to you to be sure you clean up ofter yourself, Recharred, because you know how I like my kitchen to be spotless…ond you jus' don't clean ofter yourself." Of course, he did make sure I kept everything in order by staying near, but that made it more wonderful. From the minute I arrived Wednesday night through Thanksgiving Day, it was evident he was thrilled I was there. What could be more wonderful. He really had a way of making me feel so important in his life.

I gave Juan two gifts he never expected for Christmas, especially since I was struggling to pay bills in the gallery as well as my personal ones. It didn't matter, though, because I wanted to see that joy in his face. Besides, I only had to pay cost. When he unwrapped the limited edition porcelain bust of an Indian and his squaw, and the framed Rance Hood limited edition print of an Indian and his squaw facing each other sitting on a horse, he was speechless!

"Recharred, these are bea-u-ti-ful…aw, so bea-u-ti-ful!" finally burst from his mouth. "You remembered I loved them." He just stood there shaking his head.

"But I can't let you spend this much, Recharred. You cannot afford it ond I feel bad because I did not spend thot much on you. You 'ave to take them bock." His pleading was futile, however. There was no way I was taking them back. His joy meant too much.

"Of course, Recharred, I really deserve it," he finally boasted, not wanting to break his record, and we laughed.

"Recharred, why don' we 'ave a New Year's Eve party this year ot your house…we con both pay for everything." Of course, we had one and it again was a blast.

"You know, Recharred, you ond I never 'ave a party thot is bad," Juan boasted coming over after a spin on the floor with Jeanne. "They are always so full of fun. Aw, listen to Jeanne scream. She is so funny!" In fact, she had everyone in stitches throughout the night describing how badly she needed a man.

"Oh, am I gonna find myself a real man!" were her words when she left at one o'clock. Juan doubled up laughing, knowing darn well she'd find one.

"Aw, Recharred, I love her so much! Whot a Mae West! Aw, we are so fortunate to 'ave her as our friend, Recharred!"

Fortunately for Jeanne, she did find a real man that night, as we later heard. However, it was unfortunate for us because we were never to see her again. She had called Marina and asked if we would honor her request and never call at her house because she had to disassociate herself from a gay crowd. Juan's heart was broken, and little did I know how much I should have savored that party.

As usual, New Year's day was filled with sandwiches, *I Love Lucy*, and downright contentment because it was just Juan and myself and his fantastic chatter to bring in 1990. I was certain this was never going to end because my Juan was living with HIV.

Chapter Forty-Six:
Max, a Short-Term Companion

The year 1990 was on its way and that black star still hovered over Juan because he was having continued problems with his car, and that was fine with me as long as the problems were limited to mechanical and material things only. I believe that star also managed to find my head, because traffic got worse at the gallery and my bank account was almost depleted. To add to my woes, my car eventually began overheating, causing concern about driving to Juan's. I even borrowed Nicky's extra truck and realized a gas bill four times my usual cost. Sometimes, I'd drive with Juan back to Indianapolis when he came in and return by bus. Each time, I'd sit myself at the window to wave good-bye to him, and each time, my heart ached to see the sad look of loneliness come over his face.

Svetmana was causing Juan a great deal of concern. She'd go through one screaming tantrum after another, threatening to run away and never come back.

"She has changed her whole way of living and dressing, Recharred. Endira says she does not even wear makeup anymore ond never wears a bra. I also found out thot she has been seeing someone over fifteen years older than her. In fact, I am sure she is a lesbian because on one occasion when I was thar, I looked out the window ond saw her stonding next to her car waiting for Svetmana. Believe me, she had to be one. This bull-dyke looked like she could beat the hell out of anyone who looked at her cross-eyed. So, Recharred, I really think Svetmana is gay." One problem after another with her began eating away at Juan.

"Recharred, thar is nothing I con do. She will not listen. Her mother made her this way by spoiling her constantly," and in total despair, he sighed. "Recharred, it is not *my* problem!" However, it was, but because he was so down, he refused to admit it. I also realized he'd never desert her. He had too much heart to desert her or anyone for that matter.

Fortunately, he was still himself. Loud music still greeted me as I drove into his complex. He still waved his genitals happily to the music drying himself after a shower. The first shirt he tried on was still the one he chose to go out dancing in, and we continued to have the time of our lives doing it. The wonder of his elegant manner of dining remained a marvelous treat to behold. He also continued to take me to see rental apartments, and the joy of watching him charm the woman showing them made me regret why I never said the hell with the gallery and the condo and move there with him. Yes, he still went on drives to show me the sights, filling my heart with the charm of his little boy aura. And we were still talking and dreaming of the vacation we wanted so badly…Santa Fe.

"Recharred, my 'T' cell count is ot 500," were his first words when I accepted his collect call from Denver. "So it means it is gradually going down." It wasn't what I wanted to hear but I felt better after he told me one guy only had one 'T' cell and doing fine for over a year.

"So, Recharred, it could take me five or more years to get sick. We jus' 'ave to pray." What amazed me was he said it so lightly, like he was discussing the weather…. As I thought of it later, it was probably his way of keeping me up. I don't know if I will ever be sure!

"Guess whot, Recharred? I 'ave a dog, a very cute Beagle with black ond brown spots on his white hair," were the first words he said on another call. "You remember I told you not to come this weekend because Svetmana was here? Well, this neighbor girl was walking him ond when Svetmana ond I went out, she told us he had been around the apartment complex for some time ond thot he was very dirty. She told me she checked if someone lost a dog, ond because no one knew of anyone, she took him in ond gave him a bath. Then, Recharred, she told me she could not keep him because she already has a dog. So, Recharred, ofter she offered him to me, I accepted! So I finally 'ave a dog, ond he is so cute, Recharred. I am so happy now because he will be so much company for me. Are you not happy for me, Recharred!" How could I not be, but I still told him to have the dog checked.

"Don' worry, Recharred, I will tomorrow because I will leave work early to do it." Absolutely tickled, he sighed, "Aw, Recharred, I am so happy! Recharred, I named him Max!"

The following Friday, I waited anxiously for Juan to arrive. He had stopped at his mother's first. Max was with him and he was anxious for me to see him. It was late so I was concerned. Just as I started to pace the floor, I heard the lock open, and in he walks, or rather…struts! Max was on a leash, and he proceeded to parade him around the room in that very elegant manner he was so good at. He was so funny because I realized he was waiting for me to rave about Max, but I didn't. Instead, I asked why he was so late.

"Well, Recharred, whot do you think?" he asked, ignoring my question. Then, in total exasperation, he sighed, "How do you like my dog?"

"He's okay," I replied. "He does have stumpy legs and I really don't think he's that beautiful."

"He is bea-u-ti-ful, Recharred," Juan insisted. "Whot do you mean by saying he is not thot bea-u-ti-ful?"

"Juan, I never said he is ugly. I guess I have to get used to his looks and then he will look beautiful to me, too." And, amazingly, he did look better after a while.

I didn't want to drive to Indy the middle weekend of July since my car had been overheating, but after Juan reminded me that we'd have the time alone, I decided to go. It was the wrong thing to do because I ended up in a black cloud after an hour drive. Of course, Juan never uttered a word of complaint when I called to be picked up.

So, there I was feeling and looking like a deported bagman waiting. I held tight onto my clothes bag, my barber case, and a plastic bag containing my down pillows. A little after two hours, the red Omni pulled into the gas station. There was Max sitting on the passenger seat and Juan with a big smile of joy on his face.

My usual mechanic offered a token amount to take the car off my hands after hearing the engine cap cracked. I accepted, which really amounted to a total loss. After a few weeks without a car, my kids offered to come up with a down payment for a new car. How could I afford one? They insisted and I purchased a new 1990 dark blue Geo Prizm. That weekend, I drove to see Juan. He was more excited than I was. All I thought of was that I now was saddled with five years of car payments.

Juan was going to Atlanta for a week for an Army course and asked if I'd take Max back home with me. I wanted to go with him to Atlanta so badly, but knew it was impossible since I had no money. So I took Max home with me instead. Max was not the most obedient dog; in fact, he was quite eccentric.

"Recharred, thot Max does not listen ot all," Juan had already said many times. "You know, when I walk him, he squeezes out of his collar ond runs about a hundred feet away. Then he will jus' stond thar ond stare ot me! I will call him ond he will not come, ond when he finally returns, it is about two or three hours later, ond he will be full of mud. This makes it bad when I 'ave to leave for work or somewhere because then I jus' 'ave to leave him out." Of course, I experienced the same behavior walking him in my neighborhood, though I was lucky to corner him in someone's backyard and grab hold tightly. He then did the same Sunday when I accepted Daniel's invitation to spend the day at their cottage in Michigan. I was sure Max wouldn't come back before I left and very disturbed because I felt certain Juan had lost the companion he wanted so badly. Hopes to find him continued to be dim even when Stan's daughter went looking for him. However, to my surprise, she returned with him, holding onto his collar tightly as I did back home.

"Recharred, it is me, dummy," Juan interrupted as I struggled to make out the operator's pronunciation of his last name in a collect call. "Recharred, you would not believe how much Atlanta has changed! It is unbelievable! I could not recognize places we had been to many times because thar has been so much building going on. I 'ave mailed you a card of an aerial view of one part of the city. Wait until you see it. You won't know where it is, but I 'ave marked on X where our club was. It is still thar but is now a Mexican restaurant. Recharred, I will tell you more when I see you because this call will cost too much if I talk too long. You are gonna come this weekend…are you not?"

"Yes, Juan, I am gonna leave from the gallery Saturday because I am bringing Max with me. I'll keep him in the back room. I cannot wait to see you, Juan."

"Me, too, Recharred. Has Max been a good boy?" I quickly.

"I'll tell you when I see you, Juan." And when I got there, he quickly told me he would be going out of state quite often for meetings and seminars.

"Recharred, I don' know whot I will do because I know I will not always 'ave you here to take him home, ond I really don' like leaving him in a kennel. But I think I should try it the next time to see whot happens."

He then surprised me when he didn't seem disturbed at hearing how worried I was each time Max broke loose from his leash.

"If it was meant to be, Recharred, it was meant to be. You should not 'ave worried.

"Recharred, thar are so many skyscrapers now," he then said excitedly, referring back to Atlanta, "in places thot were empty. Everything looked so different! Thar is one outdoor cafe ofter another along Peachtree Street. It is unbelievable! You know, Recharred, it would be so nice to go back thar with you someday. Would you like to do thot, Recharred?"

"You know I would, Juan. It'd be like walking down memory lane. We can also go to Dunkin' Dine for breakfast and see if your favorite waitress is still working there."

"Aw, Recharred, she was so funny," he quickly recalled, "with her big ass sticking out from under her mini skirt." His excitement intensified with an added remembrance.

"Wait until you hear who I saw, Recharred! I went to the Cove ond while I was stonding ot the bar, I heard this screeching voice call out…Juaaan…Juaaan! Ond who is it, Recharred? None other than Tom Michols! Ond he comes running over to me waving those short arms of his in the air, jus' like he always did when he was excited like a crazy queen. I was so surprised to see him…so surprised! He says he is gonna drive to see me sometime."

"That's really something, Juan. If I remember right, that was one of his favorite bars."

"He says he does not go to the bars thot often anymore, Recharred."

"What's he doing now, Juan?"

"I think he is selling cars or something, I don' remember. He still does see Betty all the time, ond do you know thot her daughter…or shall I say son? Well, he is now a real woman! He had a sex change ond is now married to a man. I also went to Frank Palmer's place ond do you know he told me John England died."

"Oh, no! He did, Juan? What did he die of?"

"Cirrhosis of the liver. I really felt bad because I liked John very much, too, Recharred."

"He did drink too much…so much more than you. Remember all the good times we had with him, Juan, especially doing the Andrews Sisters?"

"I do, Recharred, ond I will never forget when you put too much salt in the lasagna."

"Yeah, you never let me forget it even though John didn't say a word about it."

"You know I love to tease you, Recharred, but I love you ond thot is the difference."

"I know, Juan, I know."

"Do you know, Recharred, whot Frank said to me," Juan said after a moment of silence. "He said he always had the hots for me, ond thot he always desired me."

"Him and how many others. God only knows!"

"Was I really thot good, Recharred?" Juan sighed in that little boy aura of his.

"Yes, Juan…really."

Whenever Juan was in a happy mood, he'd call. He needed to share his joy with someone he loved, and I couldn't feel more honored. He also loved to clean his apartment because he'd play his records and dance to the music doing it.

"Whot time will you be coming tonight?" he'd ask anxiously in a call even though I already told him when I'd arrive.

"Recharred, I am cleaning the house ond am playing all the old disco songs we love. Con you hear whot is playing now?"

"How can I not, you have it on loud enough…'Shame, Shame, Shame.'"

"Thot is correct, Recharred. You know I always play disco music while I am cleaning. It is such a shame the bars do not play them anymore. I miss them so much. Well, Recharred, I am tired of talking. I am doing a thorough house cleaning ond 'ave to finish it now. Bye now, Recharred." After a quick click of the phone, I'd call back.

"'Allo? This is the Sursedicius residence," I'd hear in that put-on elegant voice, "ond this is JUAN! Whot con I do for you please?"

"Don't give me that shit, Juan. Why did you hang up so abruptly?"

"Really? I did thot? I don' believe it," was his usual ever so innocent response. And it never mattered that we were on the phone, his contagious laugh had me joining in hysterically.

Tremendous heat and muggy humidity kept us in on one of my weekends with Juan. It also gave him the opportunity to do one of his thorough house cleanings. Max, I discovered, didn't like the vacuum to get too close, and his frantic retreat brought me to laughter. Well, Juan immediately saw the opportunity to make me laugh even harder and commenced to pursue Max relentlessly. I felt I was watching a Mack Sennet comedy because his footing was so like the silent film chases.

"C'mon now, Juan…you're terrible! C'mon, stop it!" I yelled, laughing uncontrollably. But because he was on stage for me and realized I couldn't control myself, he continued, that is, until he was left helpless from his own laughter.

I also got a good taste of Max's eccentric personality, or should I say he got a good taste. Max was leashed and we were walking along nicely, so I decided to treat him to a run even though the heat and humidity were unbearable. We were going along quite fast and I figured he was overjoyed. However, a quick turn in my direction certainly proved otherwise. There he was, biting viciously into my knee, tearing my new jeans in the process.

"I think he must be a little crazy," Juan said once I told him. "He bit Svetmana last time she was here. That makes me worry because I will not be able to trust him, Recharred."

"Well, one thing for sure…don't ever run with him, Juan."

Juan went on his business trip and put Max in a kennel until he returned. A week after Max came home, he was loaded with fleas. So Juan had to have the apartment fumigated. Of course, I had to do likewise because Juan had come in just before Max showed signs of being infested. He then tried another kennel for his next trip out of town. This one proved favorable. Max, however, began to retaliate with stubbornness.

"I think he is getting even with me for leaving him ot the kennel, Recharred. I also think he must 'ave been mistreated by his previous owners because he cowers so much," Juan said in a call to me. I felt bad because Juan needed his companionship. He wanted and needed someone to be there when he got home. He tried desperately to love him…to train him.

"Recharred, I don' know whot I am gonna do!" were complaints I began hearing. "Max has been shitting in the house all the time. I take him out ond he will do nothing ond as soon as he is in the house…he shits!" Still, Juan's patience continued, trying to somehow train Max.

"Recharred, I gave Max to the anti-cruelty society today," was something I was surprised to hear when Juan called. "I was so sorry to do it, but he jus' would not behave. Now I 'ave no one to keep me company."

Chapter Forty-Seven:
Reunion and Separation Process

"You know, Recharred, Marina ond John are coming here this weekend, ond you are so broke so why don't you call to see if they will pick you up ot the gallery. Then you con come with them," Juan said when he called. I agreed to ask, though I didn't know if I could tolerate John's personality during a long drive.

"Marina ond John 'ave become quite good friends, Recharred, ond they go everywhere together. Con you jus' imagine seeing the two of them walk down Michigan Avenue together. Marina with her man walk ond John with his feminine one!" Of course, he roared with laughter.

I could see Marina seated in the back seat as I approached John's car and surprised to notice that another being was seated in the front passenger seat. When introduced to this being, I almost went into shock! I was sure the being was a girl, but then the name Fernando sounded more male. Long, kinky, raven black hair adorned an extremely pot-marked face heavily layered with pancake makeup, rouge, lipstick, and eye outliner. This had to be the drag version of Tiny Tim! I felt sure. The drive was very long, indeed!

"C'mon, Recharred, I will show you where to hang your things because you will be in my bedroom," Juan said after greeting everyone graciously.

"Whot is thot, Recharred," he then asked in a desperate whisper, "another freak of nature Marina ond John accept? How con John do thot to me? Marina wants to go to Union Station tomorrow ond whot am I gonna do if someone from work is thar ond sees me? For Chris' sake look, ot thot makeup ond heavy mascara!" I could only tell him he didn't have any worries for the evening since we were going to a gay restaurant.

"Yeah, but whot about tomorrow, Recharred?"

Juan kept a quick pace Sunday during our visit to Union Station. It worked out well since Marina had a habit of walking slowly whenever she was out to see a new attraction. This kept John and Fernando beside her. However, Juan was still experiencing some nervousness.

"Recharred, whot if someone from work sees me with him?" Juan whispered whenever they caught up to us. "Look ot him...all thot makeup ond he even has a handbag to match those fancy women's boots he is wearing!" So I did my best to keep his mood up.

We returned to Juan's at four o'clock and to our surprise, John wanted to leave for home. I was sorry I didn't drive myself. Juan wasn't happy about the early departure, but there was no changing John's mind. It was also obvious that Fernando was aware of our keep way game at the mall when he slipped quickly into the front passenger seat just as I was about to get in. I needed to pay. To make matters worse, I had to contend with John's miserable sense of humor during the drive, besides one sightseeing stop after another. It took six hours instead of the usual three and a half it took to drive home. I was in a slow burn.

I couldn't control myself once Marina and I left John's house in her car.

"What the hell was John thinking...bringing that freak to Juan's? He knows Juan doesn't admit to being gay! He also knew Juan was planning on taking everyone to Union Station. Juan was so nervous there because he was afraid someone from work would see him with Fernando! Marina, you know he's HIV and that he shouldn't have any stress! He was miserable! I know John is HIV, too, and I have sincere compassion for him, even though he doesn't seem to want it. He had to realize how Juan would feel! Juan has told him enough times that he could never be openly gay!"

Marina didn't say a word. She just remained silent as I continued lambasting their actions of the weekend. When I later thought about it, I realized my remarks lambasted her as well. No wonder she appeared to be hurt. She looked just as she did the night she brought Ted, her rugged friend with silicone tits, to my apartment. In a sense, she was one of those freaks, too.

I reflected back to those incidents many times and thought it very possible that Juan and I were wrong...that maybe we were just as narrow-minded as those who couldn't tolerate gays. These people were Marina and John's friends and no matter how they looked and dressed, they were still their friends. We should not have allowed the so-called society to intimidate us again. After all, we loved Marina...and she was different. Everyone has the choice and privilege to live as they please as long as they are honest and peaceful. However, we were brought up in the straight world and these things were not accepted. It was also unthinkable for a relationship of love to ever develop between two men, let alone to live as half man and half woman. These things were against our upbringing. So we were forced to be ashamed of some of our friends, even though they were beautiful individuals, and in reality...ourselves.

It is truly a shame. If we didn't have to hide our relationship in the early years...if we didn't have to lie to everyone including ourselves...if we could have walked hand in hand, proudly! I'm sure there wouldn't have been a need to look elsewhere for sex. Then Juan may possibly have never contacted this dreaded disease. As it turned out, we were so accustomed to lies to our families and places of employment that it carried over to ourselves. We then became vulnerable to our egos…But then again, there are so many "ifs."

"His All-Consuming Ego" were the words on a plaque placed on the kitchen wall by my wife once I had begun hair transplant treatments, so I finally discontinued them, though she didn't mind that I colored my hair. In fact, she encouraged me to do so. Juan, on the other hand, badgered me continuously and insisted I leave it natural.

"Because, Recharred, you look like an aging queen with such dark hair on an old face!" It never was that dark because I always managed to leave some gray. My face also was always youthful looking so I never looked my age. He just liked to tease the hell out of me. In fact, I let it go all gray most of 1989 and part of 1990, and it looked great. Only when a commercial audition came up did I color it. Juan had come in town on a Sunday and stopped at his mother's first. He was to be at my place in an hour, which was just the time I needed to color my hair for a pending commercial.

I mixed more solution than I needed, and like other times when this occurred, I applied the balance to the hair on my chest. This time there still was more and decided to apply the rest to my pubic hair. After all, it should match the hair on my chest besides looking more natural if a trick happened to come along.

"Recharred, I'm here early," caught me with my pants down when I heard Juan's voice.

Oh, my God, I thought, *he's gonna give me hell!* I looked for something to slip on quickly so he couldn't see the solution on my pubic hair. I finally grabbed a pair of old jeans from the closet. Just as I began tripping all over the place attempting to put my legs through, Juan stood at the doorway greeting me. He quickly observed the solution on my hair.

"I see you are again coloring your hair, Recharred, jus' like an old queen! Why con you not leave it natural, Blanche?" I was still bent over and nervously trying to pull my pants up thinking he wouldn't notice the body coloring when my thoughts backfired.

"Aw, c'mon, Blanche? Why are you putting it on your pubic hair? Is thot for all your tricks to see…pubic hair thot matches the hair you 'ave left on your head? So they will think you are younger?" He continued on with his comments while laughing, and especially after I gave him the excuse that I only did it because I had so much and didn't want it to go to waste.

"Aw, Recharred, wait until I tell Deena thot you color your pubic hair," he shouted, choking on his own laughter! This was something he found to be very funny and said so often. Our wrestling matches whenever he passed gas in my face were the start of it. It was no different this time as the two of us ended up on the floor in hysterical laughter. One thing that always remained clear and apparent, even though Juan teased and insulted, it was always his way of telling me he cared. He was so contagious…not only in laughter, but in life.

I had finally accepted that Juan and I weren't going to be committed to each other, especially after all the times he said we didn't need to be…that we were already one person. So I continued on with my sexual encounters. Grant and George were two steadies I saw separately on occasion. Grant was tall, dark, and good-looking. I met him through Wally and really felt I could fall for him. He appeared to have feelings for me, but his only contribution to our sexual meetings was 'receiving.' Treats for dinner at restaurants and theatre were his obvious considerations of care.

George was also good-looking, but just the opposite in bed. He was excellent and absolutely giving! Sex was the only thing on his mind. Whenever I arrived at his place, there never was any doubt as to why I was there. He'd open the door wearing only his jock strap. So there'd be very little conversation because he wanted to get down to business. I never complained because the setting was very romantic, especially with Ravel's "Balero" as background music. Each thrust into him was like a dramatic and exotic climax.

There was nothing more to that relationship than sex and I was certain of it whenever he was with a certain guy at the bars. He'd ignore me completely. In fact, I was sure the guy was someone I had tricked with a while back. On one of my visits to his place, there were cardboard boxes everywhere…as though he was in the process of moving. I was shocked when he said he was moving in with Matt, the guy I had seen him with so much, especially since he had called to invite me over. I found it hard to believe when he said they weren't moving in as lovers.

"She is okay now, Recharred, because Dan managed to get the pill bottle out of her hands ofter she ran around screaming she was gonna take them," Juan said in his call after initially shouting out that she tried to commit suicide.

"Aw, Recharred, I am so worried about her because she is threatening to do thot all the time. Endira said they are watching her constantly ond catering to her. I guess she is fine now. I am gonna drive in to see her tomorrow. Aw, Recharred, I don' know if this is one of her games again or whot!" I was sure it was. It was her way of getting attention. Of course, I couldn't say that to Juan. He didn't need the stress. But then, Svetmana doesn't know he is HIV positive.

The next evening, Juan arrived after seeing Svetmana and from his calm manner, I was quite sure this was another one of her excellent performances in order to get complete and sole attention. I never knew how to console him on the matter, or to suggest a remedy.

The following weekend, I didn't plan on going to Juan's, but once I thought about his depression regarding Svetmana, I knew I had to go. In fact, I decided to head out Friday evening and skip Saturday at the gallery, and once I called to hear his happy reaction, I knew I had made the right decision.

His joy at hearing Martina was again expecting a baby was as if it were his and yet I could sense a bit of longing.

"You are so lucky, Recharred, to 'ave a family like yours…so lucky."

I remember the weekend so vividly. The emotional and sentimental conversations, again, managed to leave an indelible mark on my heart.

"You know, Recharred, I 'ave never told you how I 'ave really felt about living here alone. I always raved thot I would never live anywhere but here, ond even though I like Indianapolis…it was still a front for your benefit…to make you think I was completely happy here. Only, Recharred, I 'ave been so lonely all the time. Why do you think I would never come out to the car to say good-bye? Because I would 'ave cried once you got in the car…ond I did not want you to see me do thot. So, instead, I would cry once I closed the door. Yes, I had a few friends from work, but you know how I am. I con only take them for so long. I needed you to be with me because you are the only one I want in my life." Of course, Juan knew how to lighten the mood.

"Besides, Recharred, you are the only one who will take my insults ond demands." Naturally, after we chuckled, his true feelings prevailed.

"But, Recharred, you 'ave to know I don' mean any of them. It is jus' the way I am once I love someone very much. I need them to accept me for being JUAN…to accept me for saying anything I want to say. Ond, Recharred, you 'ave done jus' thot all these years…ond it has made me love you even more."

"Juan, I knew you'd be lonely when you told me of the transfer," I sighed, my heart and eyes heavy with moisture. "That's why I begged you to tell them your mother was sick when you told me you were being transferred. Oh, how I wanted to live with you. Why didn't you just come right out and ask me? You knew how many times I asked you to be lovers again. I would've never refused…not that! Knowing myself, I would've probably said the hell with the gallery and rented out my condo. Why do you think I drove here so many times even though I didn't have the money? Being with you has always been so special, especially since I know you feel the same about me."

"You are so right, Recharred, we 'are' like one person ond we will always be thot way. Do you know I con now retire on full disability because my 'T' cell count is low enough?"

"Then do it now and come back to live with me, Juan," I shouted. "I don't know why you're always saying you're gonna live here after you retire."

"Recharred, you know how I am. I jus' wanted to 'ave you ask me so I would not feel as though I was begging. I need you to want to be with me as I want to be with you."

"Juan, you know you are the most important person in my life," I sighed, glaring at him in disbelief that he'd think such a thing. "I'd never desert you and even though we're not lovers, my love couldn't be any deeper."

"Recharred, thot is exactly my feelings, too. All the years I 'ave known you, even if I were not gay, I would still want you as the closest person in my life. You are thot special."

"And so are you, Juan. So very special. You are and always will be the joy of my life!"

Later in the weekend, Juan brought up the subject of AIDS and should he come down with it. I didn't want to discuss it as always, but he continued in order to help me face the fact that this was something serious in our lives.

"Recharred, one day I am gonna get sick. Maybe it won't be for five or ten years, but the fact is I will definitely get sick." My insistence of a most probable cure only made him go on. "But, Recharred, I still 'ave to be prepared in case they do not come up with a cure. Ond, Recharred, I do not want to waste away like I see so many unfortunate others do. I would rather be dead than look like a living corpse, so I am gonna 'ave a living will made out to be sure I am not kept alive when there is no hope. I really am, Recharred!"

Of course, Juan immediately made certain the air was lightened.

"How do you think I will look when I die, Recharred?" he said, quickly distorting his face to look like Lon Chaney's character in the silent version of *Phantom of the Opera*.... "Like this?" There was no getting angry. His capable manner of distorting that handsome face could do nothing but make me burst into laughter.

Juan finally decided upon the retirement and started the process rolling. However, he insisted on remaining in Indianapolis to complete his lease, which was ten months away. No matter how much I pleaded, he would not change his mind.

"Recharred, guess whot? Tom Michols called ond is coming this weekend," were Juan's excited words once I answered the phone. "Do you think you con make it here, too? It would be so nice if we con all go out like old times. He is bringing a friend along, ond I already told him you were coming even though you said you would not be able to come this weekend. Aw, he was so happy to hear you were coming, Recharred!"

"Yeah, I bet," I sighed sarcastically, remembering the icy wall that grew between Tom and I and his abrupt exodus from our lives ten years earlier. I was never one to hold a grudge and could only hope that those years finally helped Tom see the mouth-stuffing episode as a laughable one. So, of course, I agreed to go.

Tom jumped up from the couch and ran excitedly to me as soon as I opened Juan's door, relieving any apprehension I may have had.

"Richard! Richard! How are you?" he cried out, waving his arms in that wild and awkward-looking manner we were so used to seeing him do when he was excited to see us.

"Oh, it is so good to see you again!" he raved, hugging and kissing me. It was apparent that time had healed all anger as I had hoped, and I was overwhelmed with the same joy. Tom had matured into a man, at last, and I could only reciprocate with the same love and care. Once our excitement settled, he introduced his young friend, Chuck. It was wonderful. Tom still was filled with the same excitable traits Juan and I loved so much about him, but had added some pluses. His body as well as his mind had finally matured. His head no longer appeared to be too big for his body, and I was glad for him.

"Recharred, you are late as usual," Juan reprimanded coming from the kitchen. "Here is your drink. Hurry ond drink it because we 'ave to leave soon because I made reservations ot the Varsity this time." After a hug, he hurried me to the usual guest room with my bag.

"Why are you putting my clothes in here?" I asked, "Aren't they sleeping here?"

"No, Recharred, I did not ask them to stay when they arrived this ofternoon, so Tom went to get a motel room."

"Oh, Juan, that is terrible! You should've asked them to stay here!"

"I don' care, Recharred. I did not want all thot extra work of washing sheets ond cleaning the bathroom because I remember whot a slob Tom is."

"That still wasn't nice because you know I would've cleaned it for you after they left."

"Recharred, you know you don' do a good job like I do." I said no more.

Tom still had the gift of gab, we discovered, only now it had matured. His persuasive talents, it seemed, had now made him a very successful salesman in commercial real estate.

"Well, Tom, it looks as though your smooth talking has finally paid off," I said. "Now, you sell them real estate instead of just luring them to bed." Of course, this brought Juan to his throaty laughter.

"You are right, Richard, but I still do well with the other, too," Tom responded after joining Juan in laughter, making him laugh even louder.

Memories and laughter continued while dining and I tried to make Chuck feel comfortable by including him in every conversation, and it was working because he was in stitches. We also were told they were friends, not lovers. After dinner, we went to Jimmy's. I was glad because Juan could dance off the alcohol. Chuck decided to catch up on some sleep and left the bar to do it in Tom's car while Juan and I danced our hearts out. In the meantime, Tom proved he still had the apt ability of persuasion. There he was, seated at the bar, completely mesmerizing a new conquest…a very good-looking young guy.

Juan then surprised me. It was not all that late and he wanted to leave for home. Tom had driven and he insisted I interrupt his conversation to say we wanted to go home. I hesitated, remembering Tom's nasty disposition whenever his technique was disturbed. A lion holding onto his catch from intruders could not be angrier. I finally managed to thwart my apprehensions, realizing Juan's health was more important, and went behind Tom to tap him on the shoulder.

"Tom, I hate to interrupt, but Juan wants to go home. He's very tired." He did not appear to be too happy, and solidified the reaction by continuing on with his hypnosis. Juan wasn't happy when I returned to give Toms' response. He insisted I interrupt again.

This time, Tom merely held out a five-dollar bill and without turning in my direction, said to take a cab home.

"Tom, do you know how much it probably costs to take a cab to Juan's? It's over twenty miles!" However, he never responded.

"No! We are not gonna take a taxi home!" Juan shouted when informed of Tom's response, "We will wait! He does not need to 'ave someone tonight. Why is he thinking about getting a trick when he has Chuck sleeping in his car? No, we will wait, Recharred!" Juan wanted no more drinks. It should have pleased me but I was bothered instead. Never had he wanted an evening to end.

"C'mon, Richard, C'mon, Juan, let's go," Tom said, surprising us by leaving the guy and walking over to us. He didn't appear too happy, so I figured the guy turned him down.

I wasn't sure, however, so I didn't ask, for fear we'd be blamed because of our interruptions. The drive to Juan's was a quiet one, and once we arrived, Tom said he'd return in the morning to go out for breakfast. To our disappointment, they never showed up, and to make matters worse, we never got Tom's new address and phone number…. So we never found out his reason for not showing up. Perhaps, he was peeved because he felt his chances for landing a trick were ruined by us. And yet, maybe he dropped off Chuck at the motel and went back for the guy? With Tom, anything was possible.

"Do you know, Recharred, thot I 'ave to be separated from the Army in Denver because thot is where all my medical records are. Ond it takes two or three weeks to do thot," Juan said in a call to me. "So thot means I will 'ave to be thar all thot time without a car. Aw, Recharred, I am gonna be so bored because thar is absolutely nothing to do ot thot hospital base. So I am seriously thinking of driving my car thar." Juan knew absolutely nothing about mechanics, which gave us much concern. In fact, he didn't even know how to change a tire. I finally talked him into leaving from my house. Then my mechanic could check everything out.

"Recharred, I will try to pay you bock as soon as I con," Juan said as I handed him the four hundred I borrowed from Geena to loan to him. "Thank you so much. I don' know whot I would do without you! You 'ave always been there for me when I need you. God bless you, Recharred, you are so good." Of course, the last statement was delivered in his exaggerated best. However, I always knew he meant it. It was just his way of not sounding too humble.

The car was mechanically sound and I assured Juan that he had enough time to drive at a leisurely pace. I loaded in a cooler with enough food and snacks to keep his mind active throughout the trip. This would also help keep him awake as it did me when I drove from Ohio to Texas while touring with *Mousetrap*. Still, I was worried. He would be alone.

"In case you get a flat, Juan, it will be pretty funny for some gal to stop and see this macho guy helpless, begging for someone to change his tire." This helped lighten the parting.

Juan called midway through the trip. It relieved some of the tension, but I knew I wouldn't relax until he was home, especially after he called to say he had arrived.

"Recharred, I am finally here! Do you know, when I left the motel the morning ofter I talked to you, I drove into ter-ri-ble snow ond ice! I was so nervous driving through the mountains, Recharred. The roads were so treacherous! Ond I think I only drove about ten miles an hour." We prayed that it would be gone for the trip home.

"The first thing thot has to be done is to check my blood count, ond in all probability, it will not 'ave gone up. So the doctor will then 'ave to fill out a recommendation form requesting I be discharged on disability. Ond then, Recharred, it will be a long process because you know how the Army moves. Aw, Recharred, I am gonna be so bored! How I wish you were here with me."

"Juan, you don't know how I wished I was able to go with you, but when I suggested it you didn't think it would look good because you were going to stay in the housing there. And, as usual, you were afraid it might appear as though you were gay."

"I know, Recharred, I know. Whot difference does it make now? I am leaving the Army anyway. But you know 'Juan'…. I always 'ave to hide thot I am gay."

"Oh, Juan, how I wish I could've gone with you…that we could've afforded a motel!" Little did I know how much of a difference it would have made in our lives. My absence from home would've changed the course of events.

"Recharred, my 'T' count is a little lower than 300," Juan shouted in his bravado tone in his call a few days later. It wasn't what I wanted to hear. Over 500 would've been so much better, but this was My Juan as he continued on in his strong bravado.

"I will be starting my separation process. Recharred, they are now gonna put me on AZT. Do you know whot, Recharred, I found out from one of the guys here thot they put him on it once his count was ot 500. So I should 'ave started at thot time, too. You know, Recharred, I really think the Army goofed up on thot. I really do!" I couldn't get over the wonder and marvel of this man. My anger at hearing it shook my stomach, and here he is talking calmly about it? He may as well have been in a restaurant and the waiter neglected to serve him the soup he was entitled to. In fact, that could've possibly upset him more. Instead, he assured me everything would be fine.

After saying good-bye, I couldn't help from thinking how I always insisted he share my multivitamins. I always left a bottle at his house, placing it on the kitchen counter to remind him to take one daily. However, each time I returned, the bottle wouldn't be on the counter, and I'd find it buried in the cabinet. It was always apparent that he hadn't taken any in my absence.

"If you didn't have to have everything so neat all the time, you could leave them on the counter and the bottle would remind you," I'd say. Of course, he'd come up with an excuse why he didn't take them, sometimes even saying that too many vitamins could be toxic. However, he never refused to take them when handed to him. I always felt he loved for me to care of him in this way.

I also glanced around the living room thinking of the many things we had bought for each other and those that we helped choose through the years. Our houses were filled with them, and each of these artifacts and the times we received or purchased them were carved in my heart. Looking into the closet brought even more memories. We had traded clothes so much besides the many gifts given to each other. I remembered the time Juan came home from the fort, a big smile on his face. His were eyes glowing while pulling out a pair of powder blue pants from a bag.

"Recharred, here, I bought these powder blue pants for you today while I was ot the PX…are they not nice? Ond they did not cost thot much." And I could not help from thinking how anxious he was that I try them on, and his elation once they fit perfectly. Whenever one of us gave something to one another, we were more thrilled than the one receiving.

Chapter Forty-Eight:
A Seed Is Planted

Juan had a little over a week remaining in Denver before his separation was completed, and even though we were calling quite a bit, I needed some companionship. It was a Thursday evening in the middle of November and I felt horny. I wasn't in the mood to play games at the bar, and I hadn't been with the sex machine, George, for months even though I knew he no longer was with Matt. Whenever I ran into him at the bars, he'd be tangled up with one or two guys and eventually leave with either or both. It was obvious there was no fidelity in their union, especially since George had me over the day before he moved in with Matt and many times afterwards. It was obvious they had an open relationship. I was sure of it because I'd seen Matt cruising in the woods so many times while they were together. I thought about calling Grant but changed my mind as I picked up the phone. No, his comatose manner in lovemaking wasn't what I needed this night.

Suddenly, I thought of Matt and remembered that we did have a very exciting night after our initial encounter in 1986. At that time, I was sure he thought he was King Farouk, and I wanted nothing to do with him again. Of course, both of us were extremely drunk that second time and could have been the reason why the evening was so exciting. He also had repeatedly asked me to call him whenever we ran into each other at the bars. So, it may very well be possible that he remembered the sexual excitement of our last meeting. I finally decided to give him a call, only to hear his answering machine. So I settled for a night out playing those games. I never gave a thought to how one telephone call could change my world with Juan.

There wasn't much chance for any game playing because Nutbush was quite empty. So I decided to call it a night. Just as I turned from the bar to leave Matt came bursting through the door like gangbusters. He seemed to be so anxious and happy to see me.

"You know, Rich, I could not understand everything you said on my machine, so I'm glad you're here," he said, taking hold of my hand.

Matt was considered to be fairly good-looking…about a half inch or so taller than I was. His brown hair was receding a bit, but what he had was quite thick. I was sure the curls running throughout were applied by a stylist because everyone was highlighted blond. However, the style sort of stereotyped him as gay. His biggest attributes were his broad shoulders, his meticulous manner of dressing, though a bit too flamboyant at times, and especially his very striking…very dark brown eyes that almost appeared to be black. They were very piercing and revealed his every mood. When he smiled, years fell from his age which just reached the halfway mark in a century. This I gathered from our conversation. It was also nice to hear that he assumed I was about the same age. So once I admitted my sixtieth was coming up in the new year, he was quite surprised.

Conversation flowed as much as the drinks he continuously bought for me, and I was enjoying myself. Our conversation went into many avenues of our life. Of course, he didn't hesitate to rub his body close to mine, especially while he talked of his desire to settle down with someone…that he was ready to give up his promiscuous lifestyle. He was charming me and I was sort of thrown for a loop because…here I was out looking for a trick and his statements appeared to be telling me I could be the one to fill that desire! I remember thinking of Juan and the many times I begged for him to commit. How I finally accepted our relationship as friends, not lovers, and yet united as one. Somehow, I didn't feel guilty being charmed by someone else, but still certain Juan wouldn't be hidden from him. Once I explained everything, being certain he was totally aware that Juan would always be number one in my life, and that we were in actuality 'each other,' he surprised me with understanding and compassion. I cannot recall if, at that time, I told him about Juan being HIV and that I'd never desert him, but whenever, I told him.

"Rich, I understand because I recently lost one of my best friends to AIDS and was one of the few who were with him to the end." This made me realize that we could continue to see each other. I also felt the subject should be changed. This would not happen to Juan.

We closed the bar that evening and said goodnight in the parking lot. We didn't jump into the sack together. I headed home, my mind wondering if his intentions were to show me he was not merely looking for a fast trick, but for that that someone.

Matt did call to ask if I'd like to join him antiquing Sunday morning and I happily agreed, knowing it would fill my otherwise lonely day. I learned antiquing was something he did very often. I should have known it from the many times I tricked with George when they were lovers. At the time, I remember seeing the largest chicken and cock collection I had ever seen in my life…hundreds of them, all kinds and sizes!

The day turned out to be very pleasant, talking about everything, including our families. He told me his children were aware he was gay…that he told them. I commended him for doing it, but that I didn't believe it necessary. They didn't need to be burdened with it.

We did end up in my bed that evening, and this time he was not King Farouk. A seed was planted in my mind. He called during the week to see a movie and again, we returned to my place. The seed was beginning to grow in my mind.

I received a call from Juan. He was really disturbed because it was taking so long to get his discharge. He wouldn't leave there until early Saturday morning.

"Ond thot means I would not be in Chicago until late Sunday night. So I think I will drive straight home because you 'ave to go to work early Monday morning. Besides, Recharred, if I go to your place, it will mean so much more driving for me because I then 'ave to drive home." I was very upset because it would be over two weeks before we'd be together.

Matt and I saw each other again that week when he called to ask me to meet him for the cocktail hour at The Nutbush. I learned that he went there almost every day after work and that he frequently returned in the evening. I questioned why he went so often since he told me he wasn't a big drinker and he answered that he merely liked the atmosphere and to socialize.

I couldn't believe once we were in bed, tears began filling his eyes.

"Rich, I am a very emotional person and this is so beautiful and I am afraid of what might become of it!" I didn't know what to say. It was so touching.

I found myself beginning to think of Matt while at the gallery. I remember thinking Juan would like him…that he'd be happy for me because Matt admired the close relationship we had. I felt they could also become close friends. Still, I put off telling Juan. It was yet so new and I still had to be sure.

"Well, Recharred, I am now officially retired from the Army!" Juan shouted as I picked up the phone Friday. "Ond I will be leaving here early in the morning because I do not want to drive ot night in the mountains." He again insisted on fulfilling his lease obligations after I tried to convince him he should move in with me. My anxiety was relieved once he informed me how pleased he was weather conditions were now ideal. Without another word, he happily drawled out, "bye now," and hung up. I quickly thought, *That lovable stinker!*

Saturday, I had something going on with my family. Matt insisted we meet afterwards at the bar. Again, I was greeted with his happy smile in anxious anticipation of my arrival. As soon as I approached, he took hold of my hand and held onto it tightly, keeping it close to his body. It made me feel like I was someone. I was amazed the difference his smile made to his looks. He looked so much younger and better looking…. Once he frowned or was serious, he looked much older than me! That evening, he spent the night and left early Sunday morning. Our sex was mutual again and I must admit a seed seemed to be growing. I didn't make plans to see Matt Sunday because I was waiting for Juan to call.

"Juan, I'm gonna take tomorrow and Tuesday off and drive there to see you," I said when he called Sunday night to say he just got home. "I'm gonna drive there in the morning to be with you because I've missed you so much."

"Recharred, it is only seven thirty, why don't you leave now?" Juan said in that little boy excitement of his. "Thot way, you will not 'ave to battle the rush hour traffic in the morning. Con you not please do thot, Recharred?" Of course, I agreed, and was on my way.

"Aw, Juan, let me go!" I sighed, breaking loose from our hug. "I have to pee so badly."

"Recharred, be sure you sit on the seat, otherwise you will splash all over it." In fact, that had always been Juan's rule.

We stayed up late into the night talking about everything possible.

"Recharred, do you know I am gonna 'ave difficulties paying all my bills because it will be some time before my benefits come through…maybe three, four months or even more? I don' know whot I am gonna do? I know I will 'ave unemployment benefits coming to me, but you know thot will never be enough to pay everything."

"That is why you should move in with me, Juan, because you will not have to help me with bills until your benefits start arriving." I tried to convince Juan he should tell them about his disability.

"Then I will 'ave to show them all the papers ond they will know I am HIV. No! I will not do thot!"

"Aw, she was so much fun, Recharred," Juan sighed as we reminisced about Jeanne. "Was she not?"

"The last time we saw her was New Year's Eve, when she left to find a hunk," I said, agreeing wholeheartedly, "and she found him."

"Yeah, ond now she is married to him," Juan sighed.

"Juan, remember when I called and he answered the phone and once I asked for her, he shouted, 'Who the hell is this?'"

"Yeah, ond then she called Marina to tell everyone we should never call thar again." After a moment of reflection, Juan sighed, "You know, Recharred, I miss her very much."

"Barry called me from California. Did I tell you thot? You know Barry, don' you, Recharred?" I nodded my head in wonder. I had seen him at least fifteen times.

"Well, you remember Don went thar to live with him about two years ago? Well, Don has been very sick ond has been in ond out of the hospital. Ond now Barry says he is bock in again. Ond, Recharred, he is supposed to be very bad. I think he has AIDS, Recharred, but they are not saying. I even called Don in the hospital before I left ond he was so happy to hear me, but he would not say anything about having AIDS." I had never been close to Don, but still my heart shuddered. I quickly changed the subject because I felt Juan needn't dwell on a subject so depressing. But the fact was Juan kept himself up because he refused to allow anything to bring him down. He made me proud because he'd continue to be the wonderful vivacious person he always was, never faltering. But again, maybe this was one of his performances in order to keep me up.

The landlord offered the first floor to us, and even to do the build-out of the gallery. It was unbelievable since we were two months behind in rent as it was. Now, at least people on the street would see us. When I told Juan, he was elated.

"He did, Recharred? He really did? I don' believe it! Thot is wonderful, Recharred!"

"Juan, I even told him I couldn't promise we could pay the higher rent, besides paying the back rent we already owe! But he just said consider it my investment in the gallery. So you see, Juan, I think he's respected me for being honest with him all the time. In fact, Mario has always insisted I do all the complaining whenever there was anything wrong. I guess even though he'd get aggravated, he still respected me for my guts. And I know he likes me, especially since I was always sure he received the rent after he mentioned anyone going into business should have enough capital to pay the rent for two years. Well, he received his rent for two years, and always on time…so I don't have to worry about it anymore and maybe Mario and I can take home some pay instead."

"You are lucky, Recharred, because sometimes you 'ave such a big mouth ond people don' like to hear complaints all the time."

"Yeah, but this time, it worked out well for me, Juan."

Like so many times, Juan and I went to the library and he chose six videos to take home, and once he began to watch one, he always needed to have me sitting there to enjoy it with him.

"Recharred, c'mon now ond watch this with me! Please, Recharred, I want you to be here with me so we con enjoy it together. Please, hurry, Recharred?!" Of course, he also managed to pass gas and while wrestling, he'd laughingly remind me of the 'oonion.'

Remembering these crazy things Juan would do brings to mind one he especially liked to get my goat with, when he would ask, "Recharred, you know thar is gonna be a time you are not gonna attract these young guys anymore. Whot are you gonna do? Still dye your hair dark ond really look like on aging queen with on 'old' face? Or are you gonna pull down your pants to show them you also 'ave dark pubic hair?" Of course, he'd then laugh himself crazy. If this wasn't enough, he'd hold his nose and tell me I smelled like old people. But as I reflect back, even though each of us knew the other was tricking, we never discussed it. So this had to be his way of showing disapproval…by tearing me apart with one insult after another.

"Recharred, be sure you are careful when you are with someone. Please do thot for me?" were words I could always expect to hear him say when he knew I was tricking.

I continued seeing Matt, but when Juan was in, it was understood my time would be with him. It was strange, although I was beginning to be quite serious about Matt, whenever I was with Juan, I was completely happy and never gave a thought to him. That was how special Juan was to me…the magic never ceased to be.

Matt and I were at the Hideaway for cocktail hour and as usual, he was holding my hand close to his chest. He made me feel very important in his life and I was taken with it. I was so taken I hadn't really paid attention to the two women next to us. Suddenly, after taking another look, I realized it was Amanda! I couldn't believe how haggard and thin she looked. After embracing and introductions, I took Amanda aside, while Matt was busy with Fanny.

"Where is Patti? How come you're here with someone else?"

"Richard, Patti and I have been having problems; that is why we haven't been in contact with you recently. I have been so distraught and that is why I am here with someone tonight…to try to relax. I'll tell you more later."

As the four of us chatted, Matt continued to be very attentive to me, holding my hand firmly. During the course of the evening, I took Amanda aside to ask a few questions. I never got to ask them, however, because she bombarded me instead.

"Richard, this Matt is so attentive to you! I have never seen anyone as concerned and caring about someone…that is wonderful because you deserve it! Juan always gives you such problems at the bar and aggravation." I was happy she appreciated Matt, but disappointed she didn't really understand what Juan was about…that he always had to be himself or to realize that even though his friends were gay, he didn't like advertising he loved a man. Before returning to the others, she begged me not to tell Juan.

"Because you know how he keeps secrets." I thought to myself, *Little does she know how capable he is of keeping a secret when he wants*. Amanda went on to explain her story a little better.

"It is just a case of being constantly badgered by her because she doesn't like the way I do things in our business. She is always right and I am wrong. She is sexually cold but still doesn't want to consent to our breakup. The big problem is we own quite a few things together and cannot seem to come to terms in splitting them." I shook my head in regret, especially knowing how this will break Juan's heart.

Juan came in town early December and visited John before coming to my house.

"Aw, Recharred, you cannot believe how skinny John is…he almost looks like a skeleton! All his bones are sticking out in his face. Aw, Recharred, he looks ter-ri-ble! Today, while walking into the restaurant, everyone kept turning their heads to stare ot him!"

"You never said anything to me. Did he just get sick? Does he now have AIDS, Juan?"

"He says no, Recharred…he says he has jus' been losing weight. Recharred, it does not bother him ot all thot people are staring at him. Aw, I never want to get like thot! Never! Never, Recharred!"

"Juan, you're never gonna look like that! You're never gonna get sick! I know you're not because I'll never let it happen!"

No! I'd never want to see Juan like that, and yet my mind realized his 'T' count was going down and I'd get scared. His weight was great. In fact, he was a bit overweight, and mainly because he believed it would keep him from getting sick. He was taking his AZT and those swollen glands in his jaws finally disappeared! This had to be a good sign.

Since Juan wasn't working, I began driving there during the week. I then could spend the weekends with Matt. I never told Juan about Matt, but I'm sure he knew I was seeing someone, especially because of that remarkable perception of his. I wanted to wait until I was sure Matt was for real. I was also sure Juan never told me about all of his affairs, so why tell him if Matt was just a passing fancy. The month of December should be enough time to know if Matt was someone serious in my life. Then, I could invite him to the New Year's Eve party Juan suggested we have. I could tell Juan while we prepare for the party. He'd be in great spirits as always when preparing for a party. I wanted Juan to be happy for me and for both of them to become close friends. However, I was a bit apprehensive. I loved Juan dearly and didn't want him to think this would alter our relationship, because I'd never allow it to happen.

As I reflect back, my subconscious mind really wanted Juan, but afraid he'd die. So I began grasping for someone to be there for me...to love me as Juan did. I don't know!

Chapter Forty-Nine:
Not What I Wanted to Happen

"Recharred, guess whot? I got the job ot Marsh's Supermart! They want me to work in the deli ond I will get from twelve to thirty hours a week!" Juan shouted happily on the phone. I was elated for him. I tried to say a few other things but his excitement wouldn't let me.

"I did tell them I would not be able to work during the holidays ond, Recharred, they were not too happy. But they finally agreed when I told them it was the only time I could be with my family in Chicago. Aw, Recharred, I am so happy thot I 'ave something. It is not thot much money, but every little bit helps. Do you not agree, Recharred?" I couldn't get a word in. He was so thrilled that his fast talking quickly followed.

"You know, Recharred, I may keep this job even ofter my benefits begin, because, ofter all, I 'ave to 'ave something to keep me busy. Do you not think thot is a good idea, Recharred?"

"Juan, I want you to move back here and I know you certainly can find something here," I sighed after agreeing he should keep busy. "I might even have you work in the gallery."

"You would, Recharred? Aw thot would be wonderful! You know, I am a good salesman, Recharred. Thot is whot I had to do in recruiting when I was in Chicago. You remember I received thot plaque as the top recruiter…do you not, Recharred?"

"I remember, Juan. I also know your charm would be perfect in selling art, especially with the exuberant enthusiasm you have for it. I really feel you'd be better than I am once I teach you a little about the art and our artists. Oh, I can just see you charming those rich women!"

"Aw, Recharred, thot is such a good idea to 'ave me work thar because I know I will be able to make some money for you, ond you would not even 'ave to pay me a salary. I would do it so you con finally be successful! Aw, Recharred, you deserve it so much!"

"The way things are going now, I wouldn't be able to pay anything anyway, Juan, but it would be so good to have you there with me. You'd make even our darkest days bright. You really would, Juan."

"Do you really mean thot, Recharred? Do you really like to be with me?"

"Juan, as far as I'm concerned, the sun rises and sets with you because you are my joy."

It was one of those Sunday afternoons one enjoys sitting at home…looking out at the bitter wind blowing gusts of tiny particles of dry snow into corners and cubbyholes. However, we were on our way to Arthur and Jake's party. I hadn't seen them since Juan's surprise birthday party. Juan said I should be prepared for a huge crowd and an abundance of food.

"I hope there are not too many thar, Recharred, because I am not in the mood to be in close quarters." He then went on to explain how his job was going. "It is nice to be with people, ond you know how I like to talk with strangers most of the times…but on one of the days, I was scheduled to work eight hours. Ond, Recharred, I was so tired…you cannot imagine." I suggested he tell them he wasn't able to stand for long periods of time…to split his schedule into smaller periods. Juan immediately answered in his reprimanding and sarcastic tone.

"If I want this job, Recharred, I will jus' 'ave to work the hours scheduled. Thot is the way it is! I cannot demand the hours I want. So, Recharred, if I want to eat…I will jus' 'ave to work the hours they give me. If I do not, then I jus' will not eat. You understand?"

It was a long walk from the parking lot to Arthur's apartment and it felt great to get in and out of the bitter winds. The huge crowd expected turned out to be twelve, including ourselves. Instead of the expected grand spread on the table, it featured one of those giant sub sandwiches, a couple of salads, and a small tray of cookies, which was fine with us.

Juan was on AZT and shouldn't drink and asked if I'd honor him by refraining, too.

Marina wasn't present and we were told she never responded, which surprised us, especially since she had been close to them at one time, too. It was good to see Barry and hear his happy giggle with almost everything said.

"Don is in the hospital," Barry replied when we inquired, "and he is holding his own. I do, however, feel very bad about being here in Chicago while he is alone in the hospital." Barry then confirmed Juan's suspicions by telling us Don did, indeed, have AIDS.

Two of the guests were Carl and Frank. Carl said he was a hairdresser and I couldn't help but wonder if they were the friends Matt told me about. The names were the same and their occupations. Their looks, especially, filled the bill. They also talked about playing pinochle, and Matt had made plans for a game in the near future. I didn't want to ask if they were them while Juan was near for fear of upsetting him. So I waited until they were alone to ask them.

"Then you are the Richard that Matt told me about," Carl responded, "that we are gonna play pinochle with." Before I could respond, Frank bellowed out.

"Oh, why didn't you bring ol' Materino along?"

I was immediately sorry I asked, feeling certain Juan heard everything of Frank's loud tone of voice. So I walked them nonchalantly into the kitchen and quietly told them I was Juan's guest, and that Arthur and Jake were his friends. But even as I spoke, I felt certain Juan was aware of everything we said. His hearing was excellent. So I was pinching myself for bringing it up, especially since nothing was gained by knowing they were Matt's friends.

Juan never mentioned it during the party or afterwards. However, he was fairly quiet and not his usual witty and charming self, especially with Carl and Frank. It wasn't until Matt told me Carl didn't like Juan that it was apparent he had given them a sample of his put-on arrogance. Of course, if someone didn't know Juan, the put-on arrogance would certainly give them the wrong impression. On the other hand, I also realized Juan was capable of doing it purposely, especially if he didn't like them. And yet there was no reason he should dislike them. Unless, he was taking out the hurt he was feeling on them because I was only driving to his house during the week.

Daniel insisted everyone bring something to the New Year's Eve party.

"Because, Richard, don't be silly. You can't do it all yourself. You're not even making any money at the gallery. Everyone can bring something and that is final. So don't argue."

"Aw, Recharred, the party is not gonna be the same," Juan said sadly, once he heard Jeanne wasn't coming. "The only ones who cut-up are Hank, Amanda, and Patti. But it has always been Jeanne who leads the way." When I reminded him about us, he said we didn't count. It certainly wasn't any time to tell him Amanda and Patti might not be coming, especially since I'd have to mention their domestic problems. So I was glad Hank confirmed, though Dick wouldn't be coming until just before midnight.

"You know, it is such a shame he never calls to get together," Juan remarked while talking and laughing about Hank's nutty, hyper, and clumsy personality. "He is so much fun, but let's face it, Recharred, it is jus' like when we meet someone ot the bar who is so much fun. Ofter the bar, you never hear from them. So he is like the bar friends we always talked about."

Matt began sending me thank you cards after each of our outings, always being sure to include a written sentiment. It gave me a feeling of involvement…something I never thought I'd feel except for Juan. The words seemed so sincere. To keep good conscience, I felt I had to tell him about my encounters with George while they were together, and to ease the shock, I reminded him of the fact that I wasn't aware of their true relationship. That fact didn't matter to him. He could only think of my willing encounters with George, and was devastated! He insisted I had to have been aware of their relationship, and because I was a friend of his I should never have agreed to see George. I tried to explain he was never a friend of mine…that I really didn't care for him to even think about declining any offer given to me by George. I even reminded him of the many times I saw him cruising in the woods, which naturally led me to believe his relationship with George was an open one, but it did no good. No matter what I said, it was still my fault…not George's. This was the first time he showed a trait I disliked intensely…of twisting things around, but I let it drop. After some time, I realized his ego was hurt more than anything.

Every year since my divorce, I made ricotta and sausage-filled calzone pies for the holidays as my contribution to the festive tables. I was to spend Christmas Eve at my brother Tony's again and Christmas at Martina's. I didn't begin to make them until Christmas Eve morning and decided on one for each outing. I also decided to have one for the New Year's Eve party and one for Juan to take to his mother because he was stopping by before heading there.

In the meantime, Matt called to tell me he was going to be alone that evening…that he would only be with his kids Christmas Day. I felt bad and decided to cancel with my brother so I could spend it with him. Of course, I didn't tell them the real reason. I also felt guilty since I couldn't yet tell Juan about Matt. I'd have to lie to him, too.

As I took the last of the pies out of the oven, Juan arrived. He quickly told me he wouldn't stop by later because I always returned so late from my brother's.

"I will come here tomorrow morning, though, Recharred…about eleven, to wish you Merry Christmas." It didn't take long for him to spot his packages under the tree, and he insisted we open each other's gifts. My objections did no good.

"Aw, Recharred, I 'ave wanted this one so badly," he sighed after unwrapping a Hollywood movie book. "Thank you so much!" As soon as we finished our gift-giving, he grabbed the pie and hurried out, reminding me to wish Carmela and Tony a Merry Christmas.

My anxiety regarding the lies of the evening were squashed once I arrived at Matt's to find he had been anxiously watching from his window for me to arrive. His gracious attention continued as we sat in his living room, the first time for me, sipping wine and snacking on my calzone. A glow from the fireplace warmed the antique shop look of the room.

Matt was quite a moviegoer and I thought to add a small soft-cover movie book as one of my gifts. However, his lack of enthusiasm when he opened it threw me for a loop. I guess I was spoiled by Juan's excitement when receiving gifts, especially if they were books on Hollywood. Matt presented me with several packages. One gift was a frosted champagne glass and a heart-shaped candle to float in it.

After dinner out, I was surprised to hear him ask if it was okay to stop by the bar before heading to his gay church for midnight service. It was a first for me because I never was in my own bar on Christmas Eve. I didn't want to refuse, however.

Matt left about nine Christmas morning and ten minutes later, Juan's voice rang out from the foyer. I said a quick thanks be to God! I didn't need for them to meet in this manner! I had every right to the freedom, but my bedroom certainly wasn't the perfect meeting place.

"Merry Christmas, Recharred, how was your night?" Juan said in his usual cheerful manner, walking into the bedroom.

"I did not tell my parents thot I was coming in so I will be able to stay over for the whole holiday, Recharred," Juan said on his arrival the day before New Year's Eve. Matt had been badgering me about spending the night after the party and I told him I didn't think it'd be right with Juan in the other room. I began to feel guilty about the entire affair and uneasy about telling Juan he was coming to the party. So, how could I then tell him we were dating?

We did some shopping that afternoon and after getting the house and bar ready, Juan began his usual tally of guests.

"Recharred, thar will be twelve here tonight, including you ond me. Thar is Amanda and Patti, Daniel ond Stan, Hank ond Dick, Marina, Wally ond his zippered-mouth friend Don, ond thot friend of Daniel's, Roy. Except for Amanda, Patti ond Hank, thot is not really a fun rousing crowd, Recharred, especially if Daniel is in one of his moods to watch television." I was certain Amanda and Patti wouldn't show up but didn't dare tell him, especially before I broke the news about Matt.

"Oh, Juan, there is one other coming," I finally said in a nonchalant tone. "His name is Matt and I want you to meet him because I have been seeing him occasionally." I was relieved, even though I didn't mention we were romantically involved. He had to assume it.

"Aw, Recharred you should 'ave told me he was coming, then I would 'ave stayed ot my mother's tonight," Juan replied to my surprise. "I won't be able to go thar late tonight because I told her I was not coming in. Ond you will probably want him to stay over tonight…ond he should." I was somewhat bewildered because he didn't seem to be a bit disturbed, and when he went on about calling Matt to tell him to bring his overnight case, it really confused me. I told him I didn't want him to go to his mother's…his place was at my house, and like a fool, I abided and called Matt. Why would I ever want to be confronted with a situation like that?

There was a couple of hours before the party, which went as always…Juan as excited as a little kid because a good time was about to happen.

"Recharred, I am not gonna drink tonight because I am on AZT," Juan suddenly thought to tell me. "Are you gonna drink?"

"No, Juan, I will honor you like I always do. Now, remember yourself!"

Roy was the first to arrive. He didn't drive so Juan had obligingly picked him up at the bus stop. Juan then went into the bedroom to freshen up. Matt arrived next, dressed in his usual flamboyant manner wearing a bright aqua-colored tuxedo shirt. To add to the flamboyancy, blue and white shoes were on his feet! He carried a jug of wine, but no dessert. I had only told him to bring a desert about four times. Knowing Daniel would have a fit, I took the Christmas cookies Martina and Jacque made out of the freezer.

Any apprehensions I had about the meeting was relieved once Juan came out of the bedroom and reacted in his usual charming self. In fact, I felt all was well because he seemed to take to Matt, which was exactly what I wanted. He even took him aside to say it was too bad Jeanne wouldn't be here because she always got everyone going.

"You would love her," he raved. "Unfortunately, I think we may have a bunch of deadbeats here tonight…I hope not, though." I was happy because Juan seemed to be in very good spirits, which only proved what he always said…that we really don' 'ave to drink to 'ave a good time. I also reminded him that we were the ones who made a party. We didn't need her.

Juan's excitement at having a party began growing with each arrival and I was glad.

"You know, Recharred, I know Matt because I have seen him many times cruising in the forest preserves," Juan suddenly whispered to me. "I will tell you more later."

Everyone finally arrived, except for Dick. Of course, Amanda and Patti never showed up. Everyone seemed in good spirits, so I felt we were off to a good start. However, I made one mistake. However, I didn't realize it until after I lit the floating heart-shaped candle Matt had given me. I sensed everyone's eyes on my action, and when I looked up, there was no denying the despair on Juan's face. At that point, his happy personality and attitude changed. He was once again that cutting personality I had seen so many times when he was angry and drunk. Still, I thought it would only be for the moment. I soon discovered I was wrong and became quite uncomfortable with the scenario. I had never been uncomfortable at my own party!

Hank was his usual hyper and crazy self and seemed to hit it off well with Matt. Matt seemed to like him, too. The others, however, didn't seem to be quite taken with him. Wally then informed me that I had forgotten to buy a special soda pop for Don. I figured Don would insist on going for it, but he just sat back and let me leave a house full of guests. I asked Wally to come along.

"Well, what do you think of Matt?" I asked once we were on our way.

"Richard, I know him," he answered ever so nonchalantly.

"Oh, you have met him before at the bar?" I inquired.

"No, Richard, I mean intimately…I have been with him intimately." I must say I was a bit stunned and I didn't know what to say after hearing someone I might be falling for has been to bed with my plump friend.

"Oh, you have?" I asked very timidly. "Well, I am sure he's been to bed with others, too."

"I am sure!" Wally replied quite emphatically. I was well aware that Matt had been with others because he didn't keep it a secret. I also realized no one should be judged by their past. What really counted was the present and future.

Once we returned, Daniel, Stan, Roy, and Don were watching television. It seemed Daniel insisted on watching the cities in different time zones celebrate the arrival of 1991. Of course, Wally decided to join them. Television had never been turned on at my parties and I wasn't too pleased. So there we were, Juan, Hank, Marina, Matt, and myself huddled around the counter. To make matters even worse, Juan began to drink, and when I tried to talk to him about it, he shook me off by saying it was his business. I then asked him to dance but he refused. Matt and Hank were cutting up together and oblivious to the disturbed expressions aimed at me by Juan.

Matt asked me to dance and I really didn't want to realizing I'd feel as though I was on exhibition, especially for Juan. However, I realized I couldn't refuse and began to disco with him. So there I was dancing when my heart wasn't in it. I never felt so miserable and uncomfortable while dancing in my life. The party had just begun and I was already sorry I had it. My heart felt as though it was torn apart because I was sure Juan was jealous. His expressions never lied. He was hurt, and in his anguish, his expressions were definitely crying out the words, "Why are you with someone else, Recharred?" One could almost say there were two separate parties…Daniel and the others watching television, and four of us around the bar while Juan moved defiantly from the stereo to the bar. Everyone except Matt and Hank had to be aware of the tension in the air. They had gone into the bedroom a few times to smoke pot and were quite high. If the others weren't aware of the tension, then it was my imagination thinking they were because I felt so miserable and guilty!

Juan continued his complaints because Jeanne had not come to the party. He also was careful in directing his face in my direction so I would be the only one to see the hurt and anger in his eyes. I also decided to have a drink to possibly lighten my situation, but it did nothing. Pot had never been prevalent at any of my parties, but I thought what the heck…maybe it will help get me up. So I joined Matt and Hank for a couple of drags in the bedroom, but that did no good either. This was the first time I wasn't enjoying my own party.

If all of this reads like a big mess, that is exactly what it was…a big fiasco! This time, there was no happy beginning to Juan's drinking. No, this time he began with depression and belligerency and there was no way I could control it, or reason with him. Suddenly, Hank approached me, looking very troubled.

"Richard…Juan just took me in the bedroom and told me he is HIV positive! Oh, Richard, I don't believe it! Is it true?" I couldn't believe Juan told him, but slowly nodded.

"Oh, God, Richard, this is terrible!" he gasped finally walking into the bedroom, dazed. If this was not enough, Marina then approached to say the same, with the assurance that she didn't mention I had already confided in her. It was as though Juan was reaching out for some kind of sympathy because of the hurt he was experiencing. It was as though he believed I was deserting him! And yet he had to know that could never be true!

Juan continued his belligerence, insisting we all go to the bar.

"Because no one here wants to dance," and yet he refused and walked away when I asked him to dance. I prayed Amanda and Patti would show up because I felt they'd possibly get him out of this mood. At the same time, I was angry with Daniel because of his insistence to watch television. He was aware that I never turned television on at a party, and yet he persisted to sit there, keeping the others beside him as well. So there was nothing to divert Juan's attention to lighter conversations. It also again proved Daniel's stubborn, selfish ways. 'He' wasn't in the mood to party, so he made others do the same!

Hank had locked himself in the bathroom just before midnight…evidently throwing up. He wouldn't even answer when I knocked on the door. Once midnight arrived, I tried to hug Juan, but he just pushed my hands away, telling me to go to Matt instead. I don't believe I hugged anyone because I was so distraught. Dick arrived shortly after midnight and walked to the bathroom at hearing Hank had been in there for some time. Matt then surprised me with a sexual comment I thought to be uncalled for as Dick left the room.

"Oh, now he is someone I wouldn't mind getting to know."

It was a complete fiasco after midnight! Daniel and the other couch potatoes lost no time getting to the table once I set out the food. It seemed that was all they came for! Dick explained they'd have to leave because Hank was too sick to think of eating anything.

"I never got this sick before but I guess it was the combination of marijuana and booze," apologized Hank, "and once Juan told me about himself, it just finished me off." And as soon as the others gorged down their food, they were gone, too! A New Year's Eve party not even an hour after midnight and almost everyone is gone already…the first flop ever!

So there we were…the three of us…Juan, Matt, and me. A trio I had hoped to be close. That hope, however, looked like a pretty slim dream. Juan continued in his belligerent manner, insisting we go to the bar to dance. I finally gave in, thinking it might possibly put him in a better mood.

He then refused to take off his very heavy jacket at the bar, and insisted on a drink in spite of my pleas not to have anymore. I immediately asked if he would like to dance and he flatly refused. Matt also asked him but he declined the offer. I just wanted to sit next to Juan…to see if I could somehow make him relax with conversation, but then Matt asked me to dance. My heart was breaking and I didn't know what to do. I wanted so badly to erase the entire evening, but that was an obvious impossibility. I couldn't understand it.

Matt acted oblivious to the goings on when he had to know the grief Juan was experiencing, and how his actions were affecting me. And yet he continued to ignore it all. So, being Mr. Nice Guy, I followed him to the floor, but with an ache in my heart.

There was Juan sitting on the stool, his collar pulled up around his neck, and his shoulders hunched as if he was swallowed up in it. He sat there, his tear-filled eyes directed at my every move, almost in a trance of disbelief that I would do such a thing!

"How could Recharred be doing this to me?" seemed to be the words emanating in his face. "How can he be with someone else when he knows I love him ond he loves me? How can he hurt me like this?" I tried desperately to smile, but my heart would only allow an obvious fixation of one on my face. I could only think of the things that were going on in Juan's head. I then tried to justify my actions as well as Juan's, and I couldn't imagine who was right! I knew I had every right because of Juan's constant refusals to commit and yet I felt he wasn't wrong. I would probably react in the same manner should the shoes be reversed.

I was dancing, but yet resenting Matt because I felt he surely knew what Juan was going through. Still, he continued to rub the salt further into his wounds. The music went on forever.

"That's it, Matt, I can't take anymore," I finally got nerve to say. A thought also came to mind that Juan probably never expected Matt to come to the bar. He thought I'd tell him not to come. He had to know I'd never do that. But maybe this time I should've. Maybe I should've analyzed Matt's last two relationships. After all, he hadn't been true to either of them. So what could I expect?

I tried to talk to Juan but it was hopeless, and finally he wanted to go home. I assumed Matt would just drop us off. Instead, he came up. Appearing to be in complete oblivion, Juan walked into his bedroom. I followed to help with his clothes and to get him into bed. By this time, there was no fight left in him…he was like a docile cub. He fell fast asleep the moment he lay in his usual half stomach and side position. I stood there for a moment and just looked at the little devil. Once again, his drinking had made my night miserable, but yet to me he was still the very innocent angel who slept so soundly.

Now I was faced with the task of appeasing Matt because I knew by this time he wasn't a happy person. Yet, I realized he was probably the only one who had a good time. He had been cutting up with Hank…completely oblivious to the torment Juan was going through, which was immediately passed onto me. No, he was enjoying himself until Hank got sick. Also, if I recall, Juan was civil to him the entire evening. Juan made sure his glares and comments were only directed to me. The others were aware of the problems, too, because they knew both of our personalities, and those 'personalities' definitely weren't present at the party.

Matt insisted on going home instead of staying the night. This was exactly what I wanted but I knew the different tones of his voice. He felt sure I'd persuade him to stay, and I should've since I thought we were working on a sincere relationship. However, I couldn't. I couldn't hurt Juan anymore. I couldn't subject Juan to his presence in the morning. So, I'd have to make it appear as though he made the decision to go home.

It took well over an hour for Matt to finally head for home, and I couldn't believe what he put me through before doing so. In the process, I discovered a personality I never knew. He contradicted himself constantly. He talked in circles, and never remembered what he or I just said, let alone two weeks ago. His constant interruptions wouldn't allow me to finish anything I tried to say, besides bringing up the same disagreements repeatedly.

He seemed to be focused on bringing down Juan and I couldn't understand it since he wasn't aware of the remarks and expressions I received all night. There was no call for it because Juan had been very polite to him. And during all of it, Matt got louder and louder. It disturbed me because I thought Juan may awaken and hear him. I asked him to keep his voice down but he only got louder. When he finally left, I knew he had absolutely no compassion for Juan's HIV condition and should've told him I never wanted to see him again, but I guess I was too blinded with…love?

I peeked into Juan's room from the door I had left partially open since he never liked to be closed in. I was happy to see him sleeping soundly, still lying partially on his tummy with his head to the side. I walked to the bed to be sure and there was no doubt. He was an angel, sleeping too sound to have heard any of our conversation and I felt better.

"Tell Juan to shape up so you can live your life!" Matt had yelled out to me during our talk, and I was glad Juan didn't awaken to hear it. No, I would never say that to Juan! I couldn't stay angry with him as usual and stepped closer to stroke his brow, and then bent over and kissed his cheek softly.

Chapter Fifty:
DUI Again, but Why?

I awakened in the morning, hoping for a brighter day than the night before and the start to a glorious 1991. Little does one know what a new year can bring!

From the noises and clatter heard, I was certain Juan was busy cleaning the apartment and putting everything in order.

"Good morning, Recharred," Juan said cheerfully once I walked out of the bedroom. His high spirits continued and I decided not to bring up the happenings of the evening. I realized this was one time he knew exactly what happened and was making amends the best way he knew…being his charming self. Everything that had to be done in the apartment was already taken care of by Juan, which was something I had gotten used to through the years.

Except for savoring the festivities of the evening, we went through the day as always after a party. We ate sandwiches while watching television mixed in with good conversation. Only two mentions were made by Juan regarding the disastrous party.

"Remember I told you last night thot I 'ave seen Matt ot the forest preserves? Well, in fact, I saw him many times, Recharred." I explained that I had seen him also when I used to go.

"So, Juan, does that make us bad, too?"

"No, but I don't mean it in thot manner, Recharred. But on one occasion, I was walking through the woods ond thar he was…leaning against a tree. But ot the same time, his hand was over his head, holding onto a branch. Ond you know whot? His head was raised up ond his eyes seemed to be looking up ot the sky. You know, like some pictures of the Madonna." I laughed and said he had to be exaggerating, but Juan insisted.

"In fact, Recharred, the way he was hanging from thot limb, I would say it was more like a monkey." This brought more laughs and I didn't realize how

Juan had been so right until months later when I heard the stories told by gays frequenting the woods. Matt was known as 'The Tree Monkey.'

"I guess he thinks he looks sexy hanging thar with his eyes looking up to the sky," Juan added. "Well, anyway, Recharred, I 'ave to tell you. I did grab his basket, ond whot did he do? He still continued looking up ot the sky! I guess he thought I would take care of him like he was some kind of king…or maybe I should say queen. Well, I jus' walked away, Recharred." It occurred to me that this was my impression of him after our first encounter.

"Aw, Recharred, are you sure he is not lying because he looks so much older," when told Matt was fifty. "His skin is hanging so much under his chin, ond it is wrinkled, too!" I realized he was trying to discourage me because he knew how important looks and age were.

"Juan, it doesn't really show up when he smiles…only when he frowns or is serious and probably because he lost quite a bit of weight a few years ago."

"A few years ago?" Juan exclaimed in surprise. "Ond it is still hanging?"

I had anticipated some mention about his behavior during the party, but he said nothing. I was disappointed because this wasn't like Juan. He was always truthful.

"Recharred," Juan finally said near the end of the evening, "I wanted to 'ave a good time last night. I had no intention of causing any problems, but once I saw you with someone else, I realized how much I love you. I could not accept it. I knew I loved you so much ond I am sorry thot I did not realize it until last night once I saw you look so happy while dancing with him." I quickly explained the uncomfortable feeling I really had while dancing, much to his surprise.

"Recharred, sometimes thot is whot it takes to find out how much you really love someone." I was touched and yet confused. I knew I loved Juan more than myself, and yet I thought he may just be afraid he'd lose me if I'm involved with someone. I knew that would never happen, but he probably couldn't be certain. So, I felt he may be grasping…to be certain he had someone in his hours of need. I quickly tried to sort everything going on in my mind. There was no way I wanted him to misunderstand my feelings. He had to know how much I loved him and that I'd always be there for him. He had to know that my relationship with Matt was new, and that I wasn't sure it could develop into a lasting one. He himself had told me to find someone who would be there for me.

I was confused because Juan had acclimated me to accept the fact that we were 'friends.' He convinced me that it was richer to be friends than being lovers, and now he is saying this? I had doubts regarding my relationship with Matt. I wasn't sure where it was going because he kept saying we were working on a relationship. With his other lovers, he had committed after only two weeks of dating. At times, it almost made me feel as though he was looking for someone better. Then, a week before the party, he began backing away each time I was near his lips, claiming they were chapped. I didn't know what to think, especially since I knew he had never been true to any of his lovers. I knew I couldn't just tell him to get out of my life because Juan is back. No, especially since he insinuated exactly that in our repetitious discussion last night. It's not me. I couldn't ever use anyone. My conscience would get the best of me. No, I have to see this thing through to finally prove to myself that Matt could never be true and that maybe it's just an infatuation on my part because of all the attention he has given me.

My mind was swimming with all of these doubts and I realized none of it could be told to Juan at this time. Before any of these thoughts were said, I had to convince him of my loyalty.

"Juan, you have to know how important you are to me. You are my life and I will always be with you; besides, we are just what you have always wanted…one person. I'm just going out with Matt. We're not lovers and I doubt that there'll ever be a chance of it. But if I can gain a friend, what's wrong with that? Besides, Juan, he could also be your friend, and that's what I want!"

"Thot is not what I want, Recharred," Juan said while glaring at me in disbelief.

Juan returned to Indianapolis not really accepting this arrangement, but we were talking every day and things appeared to be as normal as always. In the meantime, I began discovering a split personality in Matt, and the new one was definitely turning me off. However, each time he was nice I'd set aside the manic rages, especially after receiving another sentimental card.

Martina gave birth to a bouncing boy just after the first of the year. This became my third grandchild since Mike and Joan adopted a beautiful baby girl in May.

"Aw, Recharred, whot 'ave you done, man! Now, you 'ave three grandchildren!" Juan raved at hearing the news. "Tell Martina congratulations for me. She ond Don are so lucky."

It was well into January and since I had been to Juan's during the week, I made plans to see Matt after work on Saturday. I cannot recall where we were going, but wherever, Matt asked me to come to his apartment directly from work. As usual, he wanted to go to the bar afterwards. He wouldn't let me stop off at home to change into something casual, so I dropped him off and went myself.

While changing, I noticed the flashing red light indicating a call on my answering machine. I realized there had to be quite a few messages because the rewind took so long once I flipped the button on. There was no doubt that Juan had been drinking when I heard his slurred little-boy voice saying he needed my help. I couldn't make out the rest because he was talking so quickly. It was only about ten-thirty.

I replayed the message and this time, I thought I heard the word arrested. I didn't want to believe it and played it again. Still, I couldn't be sure. The tape continued and once a second message came on, Juan's voice was much clearer. This time, my dreaded fear was true! Juan had been arrested for drunken driving! How could it be? It was so early?

He did leave a phone number, which I dialed immediately. However, I got no answer. My nerves started to get the best of me and I began pacing the floor.

"Juan is in jail and here I am in Chicago!" I shouted in near hysteria. "What am I gonna do?" I continued to pace while the machine beeped one empty message after another.

"Richard, this is Svetmana," suddenly rang out from the speaker, "and I am calling to let you know my dad wants you to call him because he is in jail for drunken driving. He called me about one o'clock this afternoon and it is now about two thirty." And that was it. She hung up! She didn't even confirm a phone number in case the one I heard from Juan was wrong! I let the machine continue in hopes she had called back to be sure I received the message. And maybe she'd have more information. There were no more calls, however. I couldn't believe it. I couldn't understand why Juan was drunk so early in the day.

I dialed Svetmana's number in hopes of getting more information but got no answer. I tried again, thinking I dialed a wrong number and this time her machine came on. I left a quick message and sat there in disbelief! I couldn't believe that this self-assumed princess never called back to be certain I did something to get her father out of jail. What if I didn't come home? I finally shook off my doubts because she must have told her mother and that she bailed Juan out. I never imagined she'd go on her merry way not certain I was aware of the situation.

I dialed the number Juan left again and finally someone answered…a police officer. He was fairly pleasant and confirmed that Juan was there. He said Juan had been very drunk, and once I asked if I might speak to him, he politely explained it was impossible. He then assured me that he was fine because he was in a cell alone. I inquired if anyone else had called to make arrangements for bail and he again politely said I was the first to call. He explained everything I should do once I inquired about bail and finally suggested I deal directly with the bail company. I dialed the number he gave me, even though I was somewhat confused because it might be better to go in person. There was no answer so I called the officer again, and he gave me the number of another company. I got an answer this time, and was shocked to hear we'd be socked with eight hundred-dollar cost. A check was acceptable if backed by a charge card, which meant I'd have to drive there.

I told him I'd arrive there about three thirty in the morning, but then realized I had to first go to the bar and explain everything to Matt. It was certain Matt would be irritated to hell. So I told the guy I'd call back in a while and drove to the bar to tell Matt.

I figured Matt was waiting anxiously for me, worried something had happened because I was so long. I felt sure my eyes would meet his as I rushed into the bar, but he was facing the opposite direction. In fact, he was almost face to face with someone laughing away.

"Where the hell have you been?" he yelled as I hurried to him. "It's been over an hour!" I quickly explained everything and instead of some feeling of remorse knowing Juan's HIV condition, he merely flicked his hand in disgust.

"Now, I suppose you're gonna have to drive there tonight and leave me." I didn't know what to say. I wanted to go, though afraid I might fall asleep at the wheel since I had a few drinks during the evening. So I asked him to come along, thinking it might make a good impression to Juan. Of course, he shrugged it off as ridiculous.

I really wanted our relationship to work and knew I had to handle this situation with kid gloves. I was extremely disturbed once he again waved me off.

"Go ahead, Rich…go ahead if you think you have to go. Go ahead…you don't have to worry about me, because I certainly know I'll get a lift home." The sexual intonation in his voice really got to me and I should have told him to get the hell out of my life then and there…but I didn't. Instead, I cowered and talked him into coming home with me because I needed to call the bondsman again. It might be permissible to give them a charge card number on the phone. If so, Juan could be released immediately. However, I didn't mention any of this to Matt because he was being totally unreasonable.

"Why the hell do you have to call the guy again when you already have directions how to find the place?" he demanded.

"Because I'm afraid of driving there alone after having a few drinks." However, I knew if I wasn't involved with Matt, I'd not hesitate one second to drive there…even with the fear of falling asleep. It was as though I was attached to a puppeteer's string.

It took almost two hours to finally arrange everything with the bondsman, and during all of it, Matt complained. He couldn't imagine why it was necessary for me to help Juan. I had explained everything many times, but he still didn't understand the love and respect Juan and I had for each other. It was almost three in the morning, and I felt a little better because the bondsman said he'd leave immediately to post bond and bring Juan home. I paid extra for his time and gas. However, though relieved, I still wasn't completely satisfied because I felt I should've gone there to drive Juan home. This only disturbed Matt once again.

Juan didn't answer when I called in the morning and I became quite disturbed. I was certain something went wrong and wanted to leave for Indianapolis immediately. Matt insisted I wait a little longer and then call again. I was on pins and needles, but agreed to wait a half hour. When I called again, I was so happy to hear Juan's voice.

"Juan, where have you been? Didn't the bondsman drive you home early this morning? He was supposed to because I paid him extra."

"No, Recharred, he did not come until nine this morning."

I wasn't pleased to hear this, but Juan explained that he was okay because they put him a cell alone. I then explained everything, including Svetmana's call, and then questioned why he was drinking when he is on AZT.

"I don' know, Recharred, I really don' know!" Juan replied very apologetically. "I am so sorry for causing you so much trouble all the time. Thank you so much for always helping me, Recharred. I don' know whot I would do without you."

"Juan, you know I will always be there for you, but I don't want these things to happen because I am always so worried about you. I just don't want you to drink like that again! Besides, neither of us can afford another disaster. In fact, I don't know how I'm gonna pay the thousand I put on my charge."

"Recharred, you mean it cost thot much?" Juan responded with a loud gasp. "Aw, I don' believe it…I don' believe whot I 'ave done! I am so sorry, Recharred, ond I will pay you as soon as I can." I explained that seven hundred and fifty dollars was only a collateral…it would be returned after his court date.

"Yeah, but the two hundred ond fifty dollars is lost…right?"

"Right"

"I know I should not do things like thot, ond then I do them." Juan said shaking his head. "Aw, Recharred, I promise I will pay you bock the money…I promise."

"Juan, you know money has never meant anything to me…it never has! You're the one I'm concerned about. I want you well."

"Are you gonna come here, Recharred? I really need you to drive me to pick up my car ot the police pound because thar is no way I con get thar. Besides, I need to be with you." I had every intention of going and told him so. However, since he hadn't slept much, we decided that I should leave in the afternoon so he could get some rest.

I must say Matt kept reminding me all morning that I had to go to Indianapolis and I'd have appreciated it if his tone hadn't been so sarcastic. Instead of wanting a drive home, he insisted I drop him off at 'Nutbush,' and to have a Coke with him before I left.

"I'll be able to get a lift home from there, Rich." I guess he had to make me wonder. I baffled myself that morning because I allowed him to get away with one dig after another about Juan.

I hadn't seen Juan look so ragged since the morning after Sattoman when he confused the corner of the dining room as the toilet. Even at that, his joy at seeing me made up for it.

"Juan you called me early in the afternoon. Svetmana's call was after yours, and that was at two thirty. Did you drink early in the morning?" I inquired while hugging.

"No, Recharred, I went out Friday night and drank." I quickly reminded him of his condition, thinking he drank all through the night.

"Recharred, I don' think I drank all night ond morning. It was probably very early in the morning when I came home ond went to sleep, but then the alarm was set because I had to return something I borrowed from Sergeant Ballard. So, because I only slept about three hours, I was still drunk driving to his house. Well, on my way, I did not stop totally for a stop sign on this deserted road ond was stopped by a policeman. In fact, Recharred, he was not even a policeman but one of these civilians thot help out. I think he would 'ave let me go, but I got smart with him, Recharred."

"Aw, Juan, why 'd you do that? You know you have to be extra nice when you're stopped by a traffic cop."

"Recharred, you know me when I am drunk."

"I'm an expert on that, Juan."

"You know whot I said to him, Recharred?... I osked why are you stopping me? Whot 'ave I done thot is so wrong? Why don' you stop some of the crooks before they rob everybody. Then he immediately gave me a ticket ond drove me to the station to be locked up."

"Oh, Juan, when will you learn something called 'humility' when drinking? No, you're always so stubborn and your mouth is as nasty." Juan just stared at me sheepishly.

"Recharred, you know how I am…you know thot is me." And then with his put-on arrogance he boldly added, "Thot is JUAN!"

"I know, Juan, believe me, I KNOW!"

"Ofter I talked to you, I ran to Marsh's ond bought all the ingredients for my chili," he said, taking me to see it on the stove. "Thot way, I could make it as soon as I woke up, Recharred. I wanted to have it ready for you as soon as you got here…because, Recharred, you are so good to me. I don' know whot I would ever do without you. I mean it, Recharred, I really mean it." He then placed his hands and head gently on my shoulders.

"Juan, that's because I love you as I know you love me," I said stroking his back softly, "and you'd do the same for me…and you have." Of course, Juan had to lighten the atmosphere.

"Besides, Recharred, you know how I 'ave to eat ofter drinking so much," he boasted as he edged me towards the kitchen stove.

"I know, Juan, until you finish the whole pot. That's why we never had any leftovers. You ate every half hour." He then insisted I taste a spoonful from the pot before filling the plates. Believe me, just watching him dip into the pot and putting the spoonful in his mouth was a wondrous and beautiful sight to see. One could never imagine the fascination of this man! To see his anxious anticipation awaiting my approval as he placed a spoonful into my mouth was even more wondrous.

"Whot do you think, Recharred? Is it not the best I 'ave ever made!" Of course, I agreed.

After a great deal of red tape recovering his car, and towing fees, we returned to Juan's.

"Recharred, I was thinking…I do not 'ave to work until Thursday evening. So I thought it would be nice if I drove bock with you tonight ond stay with you. Then, I will be able to be with you longer." It was one of the crazy things we did so often…to just arrive at one of our places and to turn back again. I agreed once he assured me Sergeant Ballard would probably pick him up from the bus depot when he returned.

"Because, ofter all, Recharred, you 'ave taken it so many times, so why not me." Of course, Juan polished off the chili before we left.

The drive home was always a very long one for me, but when Juan was with me, it flew by like the wind. I was aware of the fact that Juan often managed to take advantage of me, but never minded because his appreciation for anything I ever did for him was always overwhelming. Besides, we'd talk of it freely.

"Yes, Recharred, I know you realize I sometimes take advantage of you, ond I truly respect you for never complaining. But, Recharred, I love when you do things for me ond wait on me by bringing me one sandwich ofter another or whatever. I love it because it makes me feel safe…ond so important to you."

"That's because you are important to me, Juan…and what is the most important thing ever, Juan? In all the years we've known each other, and all the times we've been together for long periods of time, there has never been one time that either of us has been bored with the other. And that is what really counts, Juan!"

Juan enjoyed bringing up old times whenever we were in the car for long periods of time. This time, he decided to talk about our breakup in 1981 and some of the crazy incidents. I always knew how to work my dark eyes whenever I saw someone interesting at the bar and because I had such an expressive face, once the party made eye contact, he got the message.

"Do you remember, Recharred, how I would continuously call you down about it…but then once I moved out, I did not mind anymore ond decided to call you 'shifty eyes.' Do you still 'ave 'shifty eyes' in the bar, Recharred?"

"Juan, on that I take the 'Fifth Amendment.'"

Juan wanted to talk about his HIV, and as usual, I wanted to ignore it as though it wasn't part of our lives. As always, he insisted I face the fact that he was one day going to come down with AIDS, and those four and a half years had passed since he had been diagnosed.

"Ond, Recharred, they are no closer now to a cure than they were then!" Juan realized I was uneasy talking about it, but it didn't matter. He had to get it off his chest.

"Okay, Recharred, you refuse to accept whot is happening to everyone with AIDS…ond you will not talk of it! But the fact is…thar is no cure, Recharred, ond I may come down with it any day. I don' wanna come down with it, Recharred, ond we 'ave to pray I stay well. Recharred, I could remain jus' HIV positive for another five years. I jus' want to talk about my death so I con accept it myself." I didn't say a word, realizing it was something he had to do. The amazing thing was, his voice always sounded so calm…so matter-of-fact whenever he talked of it. He never faltered or gave an impression of being down.

"Recharred, I know I owe you thousands of dollars," he said, changing the subject, "ond once I get my full disability pay, I am gonna start paying you something each month. I only 'ave a little over a year more to pay on the car,

Recharred, ond I jus' hope it is running by thot time. I want you to keep it because in thot way if I get sick ond I 'ave not paid you bock…it will at least be a small token payment."

"Juan, I am not worried about that…you know what is important to me…YOU! All I want is for you to be well!"

"I know, Recharred, but I want to pay you as much as I con. I wanted to leave you part of the fifty thousand dollars of the Army insurance…five or ten thousand, but I don't think I con put you down as a beneficiary. I think it has to be a relative. But, Recharred, I am gonna tell Svetmana to be sure to give you the money."

"Juan, please, that is not important to me…only you!"

We were nearing Chicago and I was surprised Juan hadn't brought up Matt. However, that didn't last and it was then obvious Matt wasn't a favorite of his.

"Recharred, I know you are still seeing thot Matt, ond I cannot understand it. Recharred, he looks so gay with thot curly hair thot has all those bleached blond tips. Are you not ashamed to walk down the street with him? Ond the way he dresses, Recharred? It is so gay, so gay!" I was aware of Juan's intentions…to give me doubts, but at the same time my mind flashed to an evening Matt and I were in Chicago. A couple of guys walked by us going the opposite direction. After they passed, Matt told me he heard them call us faggots. I hadn't heard the crack because of my hearing problems. It really bothered me, though I tried to make light of it because it didn't seem to bother Matt. In all the years Juan and I walked together, never did we hear any nasty remarks on the street.

It set me thinking, and I thought of that morning in bed with Matt. He had scolded me during sex! In fact, he actually yelled because he said I wasn't satisfying him sexually! It had made me feel as though I was again in bed with my wife, Joan, and turned me off sexually! I, however, put it out of my mind because I figured it wouldn't happen again. It certainly was something I wouldn't mention to Juan.

Juan said something I really didn't understand at the time.

"Recharred, I would not mind if you took up with someone like Daniel. It would not 'ave bothered me as much." I glared at him in surprise because it didn't make sense.

"You mean if I was going out with Daniel you wouldn't have realized you loved me? That is crazy, Juan!"

"No, no, Recharred, I still would feel the same. I jus' would not feel as threatened." It took some time to realize Juan's reasoning. He was well aware of my likes and dislikes and figured Daniel's weight would discourage a lasting interest. I guess he didn't think personality mattered to me. It was ridiculous reasoning and even with these thoughts, I still never understood it completely. My only consensus was that Juan was afraid once I became interested in someone that he'd lose me as the other half of our one-person relationship. He was used to having me there and I couldn't convince him it'd never change.

Juan was worried because he still hadn't received his first unemployment check.

"Ond besides, Recharred, do you know I will only receive sixty-three dollars a week, ond for only a total of three months! Con you beat thot. I live in a state that has the lowest unemployment benefits in the whole country! So, I am jus' not gonna pay my bills."

"Juan, I don't have much, but you know if I can help, I will."

"I know you will, Recharred, but I cannot depend on you all the time. Aw, how I wish my social security would come through now, but they say it takes about three or four months. I don' know whot I am gonna do!"

Juan drove me to work each of the days because he then had my car to see his folks and Svetmana. He also managed to spend an afternoon with John.

"Recharred, John now has full blown AIDS. Aw, Recharred, he is as thin as a skeleton. I feel so bad for him." He continued talking about John compassionately and again, he showed no signs of apprehensions because this could be happening to him one day. He wasn't concerned about himself, only his friend who was battling a dreaded disease.

Matt respected my wishes not to call while Juan was in. However, though I explained that I truly wanted to be with Juan, he still managed to come up with a curt remark.

"Rich, do what you think you have to do, I will get along." He just had a way of making me feel uncomfortable each time I told him I'd be spending time with Juan. It didn't matter that he told me repeatedly that he didn't care if I was with Juan six days of the week, just as long as Juan knew I was going out with him. He'd constantly contradict everything he agreed upon. In fact, he never remembered any statement he made. He also couldn't understand how anyone could love someone more than themselves. He just couldn't comprehend how two people could gel together, and yet not be lovers.

Juan and I didn't have money to go out those evenings, but it didn't matter because all we needed for a good time was each other.

"Recharred, be sure you do not put in too much salt in the pasta sauce. You know how you 'ave a tendency to do thot," Juan pleaded as I shook it in vigorously. Then, he quickly walked over and insisted on making the salad.

"Recharred, because when you use 'Sazon,' you do not need much salt."

"Juan, I like the way you make a salad anyway." 'Sazon' was a Spanish spice Juan had introduced me to when we first met. It was a combination of garlic and onion, along with other ingredients, and gave a salad a great taste. It also made other dishes outstanding.

Juan was especially attentive and wonderful during his stay. In a way, I felt he was wooing me, and it really felt good. But before we knew it, I was driving him to the Greyhound Station and we were savoring the wonderful time together. The radio was on as always and tuned to a Spanish station.

"You know, Recharred, I really miss listening to this station since living in Indianapolis. You know whot else, Recharred? I am so happy you 'ave liked

Spanish music all these years…thot you never argue to change the station. Thot is wonderful because we are so compatible."

"I have known that for some time, Juan. Besides, I've always loved Spanish music."

"You know, Recharred, you 'ave a voice thot would sound so good singing the ballads."

"Juan, you've told me that for years, yet never have gotten me the sheet music. And I'm certain you'd never have the patience to teach me the proper pronunciation."

"Aw, Recharred, thot is not true…I would."

"Yeah, that's what you say now, Juan."

He wasn't gone a week when I received a note card from him. Pictured on the card were two children smiling and talking over a fence. On the fence post were two birds facing each other, and two mice doing the same on the ground. The caption was perfect…'Happiness Seems made…to be Shared.' It reminded me of the plaque I once had with the caption, 'Joy when it isn't shared…dies young.' I wanted to believe Juan had this in mind when he chose this card and wrote this note:

> *Dear Richard*
>
> *It was nice being in Chicago, although when there is no money, you can't enjoy it as much as wanted, but things will have to get better for everyone concerned. The trip was ok although the bus left hour late and then made a stop for coffee. The unemployment check was not in the mail got very upset, hopefully comes today. Otherwise will have to make a trip downtown. Also will take care of the bond I am sorry to have caused so much trouble. We can't make phone call so little cards like this will save us a bundle. It's only 29 cents.*
>
> *Hope to see you soon*
>
> *Love*
> *Juan*

Chapter Fifty-One:
The Unwanted Inevitable

The year 1991 began well enough until a series of hasty decisions eventually led to a seesaw period, or maybe one might call it a 'Tug of War' era...whatever! It, however, had to be the most confusing and heartbreaking time of my life. It was ironical because what began as a poor example of self-satisfaction for my ego eventually led to the demise of my own self-esteem. How many times have I longed for the beginning of 1991 to be there before me once more...to again have the opportunity to evaluate and list the things in my life in the order of their importance. Who knows? It may then have been possible to change the mistakes and poor decisions made by myself and Juan. Then I'd be able to color everything pretty. Unfortunately, only Juan's science fiction movies returned in time.

January rolled on, and with it, I was experiencing the charm and beauty Juan was so capable of offering. In the meantime, I was giving Matt every opportunity to remain a part of my life, especially after receiving his continuous thank-you notes expressing his love and hope for a future with me. However, I began realizing a tremendous off balance in his obvious split personality and the manic side decidedly outweighed the good. Scolding during sex continued as well as neglect for my sexual needs. Holding my hand was a thing of the past, and instead of facing me whenever we sat at the bar, his eyes were now searching the room. And that winning smile seldom was on his face. I met his friends, Carl and Frank, again to play pinochle and was annoyed to hear him speak maliciously about them after we left their places. He also began screaming endlessly should I make a wrong turn when driving or if I gave him incorrect directions. Also, instead of making it a fun thing should we forget where we parked the car once we left a bar, he'd make me the goat. He'd then threaten to leave and take a cab home. He'd get me so upset I sometimes wished he'd do just that, but he never did.

My daughter, Jacque, worked for a movie distributor and I'd call her for free passes. He'd never thank me or ever think to pay for my ticket in appreciation for the many times I got him in free should I be unable to reach her. It was also the same whenever we went out to dinner. I sometimes had him over two or three times a week for dinner, and yet he'd never reciprocate with an occasional treat to a restaurant. I'd want to go, which meant I had to spend the survival money I received from my kids and sister.

A Sunday theatre outing caused me another disdain. It was bitter cold, the wind blowing enough of those tiny dry particles of snow to make it slippery as we left the theatre. After a treacherous walk to his car, we were surprised to see quite a few of those snow particles collected on the windshield. He had been nursing a bad cold, so I insisted on brushing the snow from the windshield. Instead of taking my offer graciously, he opened the trunk…took out the brush, and began to clean the windshield himself. I demanded the brush, raising the tone of my voice quite high. He should've realized my demands only were in concern for his health. Instead, he lashed out viciously and continued to do so the entire drive home.

These personality changes in Matt were going on for well over a month, and I found myself becoming somewhat disenchanted. I finally realized I had to do something about it…that I really needed to break up the relationship and just be friends. Still, I was afraid to approach him. Finally, early in February, I realized it was over. Juan was in town and I decided to tell him.

"He has been yelling ot you during sex?" Juan gasped. "I don' believe it, Recharred!" He insisted I not put it off if I truly wanted to break from him.

"Because, Recharred, the longer you wait, the harder it will be to tell him."

Juan became quite annoyed when told Matt felt anyone with the HIV virus should completely abstain from sex because they're a menace to society.

"I tried to explain the facts, Juan…to make him realize that a person with HIV isn't a leper! I tried to explain that they need sex like anyone else…that they just need to practice safe sex. But it doesn't sink in."

"I 'ave never seen anyone so narrow-minded thot is 'so gay,'" Juan growled in disbelief, "but yet be someone who talks like a red neck."

"Yeah, Juan, he was shocked to hear I've had sex with you many times since you've been HIV, even though I explained we're always safe."

Matt and I hadn't really acknowledged Valentine's Day, so the timing was perfect. I asked him over and once he arrived it was obvious he knew something was brewing. A strained look of apprehension seemed frozen on his face as he sat on the recliner across from me.

I knew I couldn't beat around the bush and came to the point immediately. It threw him for a loop. In fact, he became quite angry, especially once I said he contributed absolutely nothing during sex. His ego was devastated!

"You never loved me," he lashed out. "You were only using me because Juan wasn't around and because he has AIDS. You are nothing but an asshole!"

"So you're aware…Juan is HIV positive. He doesn't have AIDS! And that's not the reason I went out with you, or why Juan and I are no longer lovers. I wanted to resume our relationship many times, but Juan didn't want to. He always felt we had something better just being friends. We love each other like no one can imagine. I have explained all that to you many times. The love I have for Juan is different from the love I was feeling for you. If I wanted someone to use, I never would've called you in the first place. Remember? I told you repeatedly…AFTER THAT FIRST TIME WE WERE TOGETHER, I DEFINITELY NEVER WANTED TO CALL YOU AGAIN! Matt, I called you in November because I was horny and because you had been constantly asking me to call when we saw each other at the bar. I didn't feel like playing the cruising game that evening, so I figured what the hell…try you once more. I never lied to you about it. I told you that from the very beginning. I also told you my feelings regarding our long and beautiful conversation that November night, and then the lovemaking the following Sunday evening and thereafter. I started to fall in love. But then, suddenly, I'm confronted with the same guy I tricked with years ago…only now he has a split personality!"

No matter how much I tried to convince him, he just wouldn't admit to a split personality, and because I didn't want the night to go on, I let it drop. Instead of accepting my proposal of remaining friends and leaving, he just sat there depressed. I didn't know what more to say. I wanted him to leave in good spirits. So I decided to sit on the arm of the chair and rub his shoulders. It should help relax him. However, he continued to sulk. I felt so sorry for him, and whatever possessed me to do what I did I'll never know? I guess my sexual urges were aroused from messaging his shoulders when I suggested we have sex for a last time.

Much to my surprise and pleasure, I was the main character in this sexual scenario. I lay there hoping for a small contribution to my pleasure. Instead, there I was lying on my stomach in ecstasy. The sensation of his tongue sliding up and down and inside my buttocks seemed like pure heaven. The finale was even better once he turned me over and slid his mouth gently down and over my cock, moving ever so slowly until I exploded. However, he left that evening still appearing to have a chip on his shoulders, and I probably never realized another seed was planted.

Juan came in again the following weekend because I was so busy with preparations for the gallery move into the first floor. We were seated on the sectional, and I remember how elated he was once I told him it was over with Matt.

"Well, Recharred, would you like to be lovers again?" Here was something I had wanted for so long. And yet I probably didn't realize the scope of the statement. We had been so acclimated to being friends and molding into one person the thought of being lovers again never reentered my mind. We were there for each other and I knew that would never change. So why change it? Of course I agreed, but the excitement I should have experienced seemed anti-climatic to what we already had. After all, our lovemaking had been limited…usually the morning after a night out at the bars. However, these occasional encounters were as beautiful as they always had been through the years. So it baffled me. Why did we ignore lovemaking at other times? My only reasoning could be because the excitement and anticipation one experiences from a new attraction wasn't prevalent. Blood wasn't rushing throughout our bodies because the anticipation of a new conquest didn't exist. It was a shame we never gave a thought to the fact that there were no disappointments in our lovemaking.

"If we are to be lovers, Recharred, should we not consummate it by making love now?" This took me by surprise, especially since I never was one to hop into bed at the mention of it. I always needed to be sexually or romantically aroused. So I put it off by reminding him we already knew our compatibility...that we didn't need to make love at a specific time to prove our love for each other. He accepted the reasoning but I don't believe he ever truly understood. It was apparent he was hurt, and it's something that has tormented me to this day. I've tried to make excuses since...thinking he should've approached in a loving manner, though it never appeased me. The thought of the seed planted by Matt always comes to mind.

I knew that a night out was on the agenda as soon as I pulled in front of Juan's the following weekend. Loud music filled the night, and it definitely was coming from his apartment.

"Recharred, I thought it would be nice if we go out ond celebrate being lovers again. Do you not think it would be nice, Recharred?" were Juan's words as soon as I entered the house. I agreed, but reminded him of our low funds.

"Don' worry, Recharred, my mother sent me a hundred dollars so I will be able to treat all night. So hurry ond take your shower while I heat up my special meatballs stroganoff."

It had been so long since Juan and I made love that I almost forgot how wonderful it was the next morning. The mutual concern was still very prominent as well as the simultaneous and beautiful satisfaction we always were so fortunate to share throughout the years. Why did we have to look elsewhere when it was there all the time? The tenderness of his lips and the warmth and smoothness of his body could never be matched, and I knew he felt the same about me. Did our egos need that much? It never occurred to me how much this beautiful morning would be cherished.

"You remember Larry don' you, Recharred? He was the one who hung up on me?"

"Of course I do, Juan. It was July 4, 1989. You were supposed to call him early in the morning and didn't until late in the afternoon."

"Well, Recharred, we ran into each other the beginning of the month ond finally began talking at the bar. He wanted me to apologize...but I would not...so he finally laughed ond now we are friends again. I told him I knew he wanted to be more than jus' friends ot thot time, ond now he agrees to set all thot aside."

"Juan, you know you should've apologized because you were wrong."

"Recharred, thot is me! Thot is JUAN, ond I con do thot!"

"Juan, you're terrible, you know?" Of course, Juan stood his usual ground,

"No, Recharred, I am JUAN!" I laughed as he went on to say, "Well, anyway, Recharred, Larry works in the fine arts office for the city ond gets free passes for plays ond concerts…in fact, for anything in fine arts. Well, Recharred, he said he is always looking for someone to take along ond asked if I enjoyed things like thot, and if I did, if I would like to join him on occasions. Of course I said I would love to go with him anytime. Is thot not nice for me, Recharred? I will be able to see so many things I normally could not afford!"

"Aw, Juan, I think it's great! Why don't you ask him if he can get passes for me, too?"

"Aw, Recharred, I would feel embarrassed to ask him thot." So I said no more because I was glad for Juan since we couldn't afford live theatre. Juan then said that Larry had asked if he wanted to join with him to see a cabaret musical the coming weekend.

"But it is your birthday, Recharred, ond I should be with you." My birthday was falling on Sunday and the kids usually took me out for dinner.

"Well, Juan, I'm not sure if the kids will want to go out Saturday or Sunday. If I come here, I'll only be able to stay for the day. So, why don't you go with Larry. I'll come during the week and we can celebrate my birthday then." So it was settled. However, I didn't know Juan was aware of something brewing for my sixtieth.

We had been up for some time and still hadn't taken our showers, and since I brought along my hair coloring, I told Juan to take his first. I'd then be able to apply the solution to my hair and slip in behind the curtain while he was drying himself. Well, somehow, he caught sight of me entering the shower.

"Whot 'ave you done, man?" he asked, swinging the curtain open. "Huh? Whot 'ave you done, Blanche? You thought you could sneak in the shower without me seeing you, huh?"

There he was…that wide-eyed owl expression!

"Blanche, did you think I would not notice the difference once you came out looking like an old, dark-haired queen?" Of course, this made him laugh harder, and to be sure I remained in sight, he continued to hold open the shower curtain.

"Why don' you leave it natural, Recharred? Aw, Recharred, whot's the matter?" he teased, "why did you not put it on your pubic hair this time?" His spontaneous and choking laughter followed, and continued for some time while I pleaded for him to stop.

"You looked so nice when it was naturally gray in 1989 ond '90," he said once his laughter subsided, "ond then you met thot queen with the blond-tipped, curly-locks. So you started coloring your hair again! So why are you still doing it now, Recharred?"

"I don't know, Juan? Maybe because it makes me look younger…and besides you know it doesn't make me look like an old queen! You just like to aggravate me by saying that!"

"Okay, Blanche, color your hair." And as I thought back, Matt had been the one who asked me to color my hair again.

"So, it's gonna be your sixtieth birthday coming up…right, Dad?" Mike's voice asked when I answered the phone. "So why don't we do something special this time on the day of your birthday?" I knew immediately…something was brewing…like a surprise party.

"Mike, you kids always take me somewhere special for my birthday."

"Well, we'll take you somewhere extra special this time. So why don't you come to my house at three o'clock because I will have everyone meet here…okay, Dad?" So I played along, though I felt sure they were having a party and that my sisters and brothers were invited.

Matt called and invited me out for a birthday dinner. I felt very relaxed that evening because I knew this was just between friends, and that I didn't have to worry about being yelled at for something he did wrong. It was my birthday, and I was sure he wouldn't be curt with me on my day. However, he was very quiet and it sort of made me uncomfortable. So, although he didn't order a cocktail, I needed one to break up the tension. And it did exactly that because it made me realize this was what I wanted…just to be friends. Matt took me directly home and didn't ask if I might like to stop off for a drink. This, of course, was fine, but once he sped off, I couldn't help but feel sorry for him because he had appeared so brokenhearted all evening. Again, I probably didn't realize what he was doing.

"Recharred, happy birthday to you," Juan said, calling me early. "I am sorry I am not with you, but I jus' do not want to drive my car too much." I asked about the cabaret show.

"Aw, Recharred, it was so good…so good! I know you would 'ave loved it because the singers were excellent." We made plans for the midweek and because my phone was beeping with another call, we said our good-bys. Jacque was on the phone and after wishing me a happy birthday, she said she and Gil would pick me up. After hanging up, I thought about Juan and how he sounded so much like the times after a night of big drinking.

As soon as Jacque, Gil, and I got up to Mike and Joan's condo, we were told Martina, Don, and the children, besides Nicky, hadn't yet arrived.

"C'mon, Dad, we got time before they arrive," Mike said in a rather excited manner. "Come with me to the lobby because the condo association is looking to buy new artwork to hang there and I told them you have an art gallery and could probably give us a good buy." I chuckled to myself, though this excuse wasn't really bad. So we surveyed the area.

"C'mon, Dad, now I am gonna take you up to the clubroom because they are also looking to add some art there," Mike said excitedly once I went through the motions of examining the lobby. Now, this was getting to be more obvious and I chuckled to myself.

A large foyer was there before me once the elevator door opened and jam-packed in it were at least forty smiling faces shouting out a big surprise! This was truly a surprise because I had only expected my kids and my brothers and sisters. Instead, everyone was there! Along with all my nieces and nephews and their kids were my partner, Mario, and his wife Jane, and with them one of our woman clients who was very obviously after me. The biggest surprise was the smiling faces of Daniel and Stan. This had to be a first…my gay friends at a party with my family and straight friends!

Daniel was never one to hide the fact that he and Stan were living together, and I was sitting nervously on the edge of my seat as he continuously brought up everything they were doing or sharing. To make matters worse, most of it was directed to my partner and client. I heard later he had been talking to everyone before I arrived.

"Oh, Richard, everyone must know your story by now," he sighed, flicking a wrist in my direction once I questioned him about it.

"If they didn't, I'm sure they do now," I quickly retaliated. Of course, he merely laughed.

"Where the hell is Juan and where is your new friend?" I hadn't talked to him since I broke up with Matt. In fact he didn't even know Juan and I had resumed as lovers, but I felt this wasn't the time to explain. So I quickly told him I didn't know. Then, almost in an interrogating manner, he began inquiring why Wally, Don, Roy, and Marina weren't invited while Amanda and Patti were? I looked at him puzzled.

"Yes, Richard, your daughter told me they couldn't make it because they had previous plans. So why weren't the others invited?"

"Daniel, how the hell should I know?" I answered, glaring at him in bewilderment at such a ridiculous question. "I didn't plan this party. If you knew they weren't invited why didn't you call my daughter and let her know?" He had no answer.

Later on I was told Martina had contacted Juan for a list of names. Then I understood why the list was limited. My kids already knew Daniel, and Juan realized Amanda and Patti could be considered straight. So, since we were still closet cases, he didn't want me to feel uncomfortable.

I was kept quite busy and didn't really have much chance to think of Juan, but once he came to mind, I felt a bit disturbed. We had just resumed as lovers. He should've been there for my surprise party. It began to prey on my mind even more the following day.

"You know, Rich, I'm really peeved at Juan because he didn't come in for your party!" Geena said adding to the disturbing fact. "He is supposed to be your best friend and he wasn't here for a special birthday party given for you." I tried to come to his defense but she went on,

"All you do for him and he can't come? I really am angry with him, Rich!" I made up an excuse because I didn't want Geena angry with him, not her of all people because Juan loved her dearly, and especially because she was totally unaware of the burden he was carrying. Still, I felt he should've somehow made it in, and when I confronted him about it, he didn't want to be reprimanded, even though it was obvious he felt bad. Of course, this was always the case whenever he realized he was wrong. Besides his car having too much mileage, I cannot remember what other excuse he gave. It took me some time to think of a reason, and that just recently came to me. It's possible he didn't want to be present once Daniel opened his mouth?

Juan sat on my couch the day he came in, waiting anxiously for me to try on an expensive shirt he gave me for my birthday. He also raved on about the cabaret show.

"Recharred, Larry has tickets for a show this Saturday to see a group called 'Dance Kaleidoscope' ond they are supposed to be fantastic!"

"So, I guess that means I won't be able to come this Saturday after work, huh?"

"Recharred, I would not want you to 'ave to sit home while I am ot the show. I would feel bad."

"Okay, Juan, I'll just come Sunday or during the week, but that means I have to take off from the gallery again and even though we have no business, I still feel funny leaving Mario all the time." I was happy he made up with Larry and especially glad he was having a chance to see so much theatre, but at the same time bothered since I wasn't sharing them with him…that I was at home and given the opportunity to be on the prowl.

The following weekend, Juan again was invited by Larry to see *Hedda Gabler*, a ballet, and a Spanish play called *Roosters*. This was great because it kept him active and busy. However, as I think back, it was a very crucial time for us because we should've been doing these things together. He should've insisted Larry invite me because we had just resumed as lovers. Whenever I came in, I never saw Larry. So it was possible Juan never mentioned we had resumed as lovers. Knowing Juan, this was very possible because he didn't like to divulge too much information about his life back in Chicago. Once I did begin to see and talk to Larry on the phone months later, I never thought to ask him if he knew about Juan and I resuming as lovers. So, because I wasn't going to Indianapolis weekends, I was available when Matt called to go out. And though we were only going out as friends, seeds were being planted each time he sent a thoughtful card expressing what a great time he had.

Juan called, excited about joining a Catholic HIV and AIDS support group.

"Recharred, I 'ave made friends with two guys who are lovers…Phillip ond Kent. They themselves are also HIV positive. Phillip ond I 'ave become good friends. You know the way I am, Recharred…thot I love to give verbal abuse. Well Phillip takes all my remarks real well. He jus' laughs ond gives me bock the same. I really like him as a friend. Kent is sort of distant but thot is okay because Phillip makes up for him. I 'ave been over to their house for dinner a couple of times. They live way south of the city. I told them about you, Recharred, ond they would like to meet you. Do you think you con come this Saturday ond then we con meet them ot one of the bars?"

I found that they really appreciated Juan's wit and humor once we met, and it was apparent Phillip was the one who really enjoyed Juan. Kent was a very handsome tall, dark-haired guy who was obviously stuck on himself. Phillip was average-looking, but what was important, he made Juan feel like a king. He was about forty, more or less…a Jewish New Yorker. The minute he opened his mouth, you knew it. I couldn't help but think this is what two lovers should be doing…sharing an evening with friends. Juan wanted to dance and since they weren't dancers, we said farewell and went on to another bar.

This was one of Juan's big drinking nights and there was no way I could get him to stop. Our last stop was the wild disco Our Place. Again, Juan decided he couldn't wait to use the facilities, and peed in full view of every passing car. Of course, there I was trying to hide him. The night had been beautiful and instead of worrying about Juan's cracks at a restaurant, I decided to cook at home. And there he was, raising his arms in that inimitable way of his, not wanting the evening to end…not wanting the fun to end! In fact, not really wanting anything to end as he danced in his living room while the music played at full volume! And there I was…truly believing that dreadful HIV would never dare stop his beautiful music!

I didn't think much of it when Juan told me on the phone that he had a severe case of hemorrhoids until I arrived at his place Sunday afternoon. He could hardly walk, and was complaining with every step. I was baffled because he never was one to complain about pain. I thought he might be exaggerating, until he finally pulled down his pants to show me. I couldn't believe it! He didn't even spread his buttocks and they were sticking out…two of them, the size of golf balls! I never imagined they could grow so large! My heart ached because I couldn't understand why this was happening to him. Never had he had problems with hemorrhoids in his life…why now? Was this because of his HIV?

"Oh, my God, Juan, how can you even walk?"

"Recharred, it is ter-ri-ble…every time I move it pains me so."

"Have you gone to the doctor, Juan?"

"I 'ave, Recharred, ond was given some pills besides medication to apply on them, but he did say I should stay off my feet as much as possible. I think I got them from working eight hours a couple of times a week in the deli, Recharred."

"Well, tell them you cannot work that many straight hours! Juan, your health is too important for the little money you're making there!" I insisted he call in sick because he was scheduled to work that evening.

Still, he insisted he was going in. I tried to convince him otherwise, but it did absolutely no good.

I decided upon going to the store after he left to buy some sweet rolls, but mostly because I wanted to see Juan behind the counter. I couldn't get over how handsome he looked wearing his white deli cap. Of course, I expected it because he always looked excellent in hats. There he was, charming some woman and once he spotted me, out came that buddy greeting.

"Hi, old mon, how you doing?" I stayed around the produce area next to the deli for some time just to see him. I felt so proud watching him smile and talking cheerfully without any indication of the pain he was bearing.

I wasn't back at his place an hour when, to my surprise, he came home.

"I told them I was not feeling well, ond besides I could not stond thot you were here ond I was not with you, Recharred." That couldn't please me more.

Juan finally got rid of the large hemorrhoids, and probably because he lost his job. They felt he was off too much. It was just as well because the job was responsible for causing his problem in the first place. The hemorrhoids came back now and then, but never as large.

Juan always smoked but now it was one after another. His ashtray never appeared to be emptied. He was so meticulously neat, and yet the ashtray sitting on his glass top coffee table always appeared as though it was the remains of an all-night poker game.

"Juan, why are you smoking so much?" I asked repeatedly.

"Recharred, whot difference does it make now?" he'd ask, lighting up another cigarette, "Ot least I con still do one thing I enjoy." I had a little black plastic ashtray at my house and when he was over, he'd use it constantly, carrying it from room to room.

"Recharred, don' ever throw this ashtray away because I jus' love it. It is my favorite little ashtray…so keep it always for me. Would you not do thot for me, Recharred, please?"

A decision I made has remained a haze in my mind, and probably because I cannot understand why. Juan and I were continuing our lives in the same manner as we had been for years. We couldn't have been closer, and yet there was no lovemaking. Could I have been hurt because Juan was going to so many theatre productions with Larry and never giving a thought to including me? Could that have given me reason not to pursue intimacy? It's a complete mystery because no two people could be more compatible and completely satisfied than we had always been in our lovemaking. Could his lack of pursuit be because of a fear of passing this dreaded disease to me? Or was it because there wasn't that pre-excitement? Why didn't I insist we talk about it? I think my final logic for doing what I did was a combination of all of it, along with another fact. Matt was out there and he was excellent at baiting a hook, and yet still keep his distance. He was boosting my ego and I began believing I was falling for him again. So on one of my visits with Juan, I opened up.

"You know what I think, Juan? I think you were grasping for a commitment between the two of us when it wasn't necessary, and probably because you thought you'd lose me? That will never happen, Juan, because you have filled every corner of my heart, and I'm certain I've done the same to you. We're one person, Juan, and that'll never change. So I do not think we have to be lovers to prove we love each other more than ourselves. So let's continue as we have done for so long…to be as close as one person." Juan never said anything to the contrary and to this day, I don't know if he fully understood. It wasn't like him. So I think he didn't understand, especially after the eventual chain of events.

Juan continued to rave each time Larry took him to a theatre performance and I was so happy for him. He was enjoying something he longed to do all of his life. In a sense, his excitement in telling me about the shows was a way of sharing them with me. The ironic part of it was he could have actually had me there with him if he were not embarrassed to ask Larry for another pass. Then I wouldn't have been lonely enough to allow myself to get interested in Matt again, especially after being so disenchanted. Instead, I began longing to make love with Matt…grasping for and hoping to have him love me in return as he did those initial times.

Matt was playing his cards well because he once again had me interested.

"I need my space, Rich," he'd say, continuing his refusal to commit. And he was using this space to see others. He even flaunted it when I saw him at the bar catering to some very effeminate guy. There, he totally ignored my presence. Instead of realizing what he really was, it only made me desire him more. At the same time, he was keeping me close at hand with constant calls and invites to accompany him on his antique chicken hunts.

I decided not to tell Juan I was getting serious about Matt since I wasn't quite sure of anything. He'd only be upset and ridicule me for taking up with him again, especially since he was aware of Matt reprimanding me during sex. He'd say I was crazy. I'd have to concoct a few stories so he'd think Matt and I were just friends. He shouldn't suspect anything because he knew what I wanted and Matt wasn't filling that bill. The sad thing was I knew it, too, because Matt only wanted to receive…not give. Still, I continued my pursuit.

Juan had already gone to court for his DUI charge and was required to take a special course for a few weeks. In April, we picked up the seven hundred and fifty dollars collateral from the bonding company, which really came in the nick of time since business became even worse once we moved the gallery to the first floor.

"Recharred, I need to go to the HFC office in the city because there is a clause in my contract thot says if I am disabled, then I do not have to pay my loan anymore," Juan said as we drove from the bonding company. I waited in the car, and when he returned, he was laughing.

"Recharred, you should 'ave seen the guy's face once I told him I was disabled and would die soon." One would think it was a big joke. How could I think this HIV was something serious?

"You know, Recharred, I 'ave been 'aving headaches continuously," he said casually. "They do not seem to want to go away, ond they are ter-ri-ble." I urged him to call the VA hospital. When he phoned, he was told he needed to check into the hospital to stay overnight so the doctor could see him in the morning. At first, he refused.

"Juan, it will not be that bad…this way, you can get a good checkup. And besides, Juan, you'll be able to get a couple of free meals. I was heading home that Friday evening, so we decided to leave for the hospital late in the afternoon. It was amazing because he had to be having pain, and yet never complained again.

"You don' 'ave to stay here ond wait with me, Recharred," Juan said after we waited for some time. "It is probably gonna be a long time."

"Since when have I ever been bored being with you? I don't care how long it takes…I'm not leaving until you are in your room, Juan."

A series of blood tests began and everything needed for admission in a hospital. This was Juan's first admittance and they needed his complete history. When the girl asked for a name of a relative or friend to call in case of emergency, he gave Svetmana's.

"Juan, why didn't you give my name and number?" I asked quickly. "You know Svetmana is never home to take her calls." He quickly added my name. Of course, he charmed every nurse and technician.

After a few hours, Juan was elated to discover he had a private room.

"Aw, I do not know whot I would do if I got someone like you, Recharred, as a roommate…who snores like a machine." Juan finally insisted I get on my way so I wouldn't be sleepy on the road.

Again, we arranged a code for the public phones since VA hospitals didn't have them in rooms. The cause of his headaches was a mystery to him and yet he still was disturbed because he had to stay at the hospital. Then on Monday, April 15, he called.

"Recharred, I 'ave something called CMV. It is a virus thot is attacking my left eye. If you had this virus, it would be no problem to cure it. But because I 'ave an immune system which is so low…it becomes something very serious. So, Recharred, now I 'ave full blown AIDS.…"

I didn't know what to say! He'd just given me news that should have devastated me…but said it as though he was giving the weather report! *He* didn't even sound devastated! I cannot remember being in terror because of his matter-of-fact tone! I never heard of CMV, and he said if I had it I could be cured easily. So I guess I didn't think it was serious, even though his immune system was disappearing. He was so up, how could I be otherwise? I didn't yet believe Juan was going to get sick…and HERE HE WAS ALREADY SICK! Yes, I was shocked, but, to this day, I don't remember if I realized the scope of what he had just said!

"Recharred, they want to give me a new drug called Gancyclavir ond it has to be administered intravenously," he continued to say in that fast paced manner of his, "and thot means I will 'ave to take it for as long as I live…ond every day."

"Well, that doesn't matter," I assured him, "as long as it's something that will help."

"I know, Recharred, because if I do not take it, I will go blind! Do you know, Recharred, I will 'ave to 'ave a tube inserted into my chest thot will lead to my main artery so the solutions con be administered without 'aving to stick into my vein all the time? I think they call it a Hickman, Recharred." Then with a sudden show of sadness he added, "Aw, Recharred, thot means I will never be able to swim again, ond you know how I love to swim."

This seemed to be devastating to him than being diagnosed with full-blown AIDS and I was upset.

"Juan, what difference if you don't swim! What's important is the treatment." He then went on to tell me they still weren't sure he needed to have the Hickman. I told him I was coming down, only to hear Svetmana was already on her way to stay for a few days. I should come after, unless he felt well enough to return to Chicago with her.

The next word I heard was two days later by mail, postmarked April. The folded thank you note read:

> *Thank you so much for all the help offered and given. The doctor said I will definitely have to get that thing in my chest. It might be done by the time you get this card. They really are not telling me how long I will have to stay here. Svetmana will come this weekend and if I am out, I will go to Chicago with her. LOVE, Juan*

The surgery was finally performed and Juan was now sporting a Hickman on that proud chest. He complained about a tight feeling in his chest while walking and the doctor said nothing could be done to correct it. So he was forced to hunch his shoulder a bit when walking. It broke my heart to see that proud walk of his yield to it.

The entire treatment lasted about four hours, which included injecting an equal amount of saline solution. At the beginning, Juan had to receive the treatment twice a day, which became quite time demanding. The period between the eighteenth and the twenty-third was a complete blank and probably because it was the most upsetting time of our lives. I cannot recall if Juan came in with Svetmana! I do know I was there the twenty-third and twenty-fourth because Juan had car problems and over three hundred dollars had been charged to my credit account.

Juan received weekly supplies of Gancyclavir, which needed to be refrigerated, so we went to Wal-Mart and I bought him a small insulated cooler for his long trips to Chicago.

As always, Juan seemed to take the terrible matter in good spirits. He did, however, complain about the time it took to administer the drug.

"Aw, Recharred, I 'ave to sit ond wait four hours each time I put the medication in. I am never gonna be able to work even if I could!" And there were side effects that were difficult for him to accept. His body became very weak and it confused him. After all, he always had an abundance of energy. And that was only one of the side effects. Nausea almost became an every day occurrence especially once he took his AZT. Fortunately, the duration was short. Yet, even with all this hanging on his shoulders, he still talked so proudly.

"Do you know, Recharred, is it not something? I am the very first person in this hospital to receive Gancylavir!"

My intentions were to return the first weekend in May until Juan called.

"Recharred, Endira called me last night, ond she asked if I had AIDS."

"Why did she think that all of a sudden, Juan? Did you say anything to Svetmana? I thought you told her you had an infection in your eye?"

"Recharred, Endira has a few friends in her church group who 'ave AIDS, ond she knows all the illnesses they con get. So I told her thot I do 'ave AIDS. Ond, Recharred, she was very compassionate ond understanding. She also said I should tell Svetmana. So, Recharred, she is gonna bring her here this weekend because she feels I should be the one to tell her. She also realizes I would 'ave trouble telling my parents…so she is gonna go thar ond tell them for me. Aw, Recharred, I don' know how I am gonna be able to do it! This is so ter-ri-ble!" We decided no one else needed to know. He then asked if I could refrain from calling during the weekend because it may be the moment he's telling Svetmana.

"I love you, Juan," I whispered after saying good-bye.

"I love you, too, Recharred."

"Recharred, I had a very sad weekend," were Juan's first words that Monday evening, "When I told Svetmana, she started to scream ond cry hysterically. She kept crying out whot was she gonna do when I die? Ond, Recharred, all weekend she cried ond kept saying, 'Whot am I going to do…I will be an orphan!'" My heart went out to Juan and I wanted to be there for Svetmana, but yet I couldn't help wonder…there she was again, only thinking of herself. What was 'she' going to do? She didn't cry for Juan because he is too young to die…no! She only thought of herself and the fact that he wouldn't be around to take care of her!

Chapter Fifty-Two:
New Support for Juan

Barry called Juan to inform him of the tragic news that Don had passed away, and he immediately phoned me.

"Ond, Recharred, Barry will be coming in from California to give the eulogy. You will also receive an invitation to attend. Recharred, I am not going to come in for it because I do not want to drive my car too much." It surprised me to hear how well Juan seemed to take it, although he may have broken up while on the phone with Barry. I really wanted to be with him at this time, but there was that distance again.

I wasn't able to attend the memorial either because our grand opening for the gallery was the same day, so I sent a sympathy card instead. I later talked with Marina.

"Don's sister had a recording of the time he sang 'Ave Maria' at her wedding, and they played it during the ceremony…and you know me, Richard, it is very hard for me to show any emotional feelings. However, I was very moved this time."

Juan was becoming quite an expert administering his medication and changing the dressing, which protected the sensitive exposed entry into the artery. In fact, changing the dressing was quite a complicated procedure that had to be handled in an absolute sterile manner. Juan had it down to an art as I watched closely each time.

"Recharred, watch me change the dressing so in case I need help you will be able to do it." So I stored every detail in my head. He was very well read on AIDS and was aware of the different medications used on each symptom. At times, I almost felt Juan was as knowledgeable as some doctors. He also continually urged me to read as much as I could on the disease and medications used to suppress the progression of it, and for once I did. However, Juan was always five steps ahead of me. Juan's complaints about nausea after taking his

AZT and the weakness that would encompass his body were mild compared to the fuss I had heard about others making with the same problem. His biggest complaints were about the time it took to administer the medications, especially when he had to do it twice a day.

"Recharred, whot kind of quality of life is this when all I con do is sit here all the time?" And all I could do to try to appease him was to remind him it was keeping him well. The Army was sending a nursing service to his apartment a couple of times a week to check his blood and levels, and to inspect the Hickman attachment to be sure it wasn't infected. Yvonne was from England and it was very evident Juan was someone special to her. In fact, she even gave him her home number should he have an emergency, and this wasn't something that was done. But then, who could resist the charm of this man.

Juan still was the same person even though he tired easily. He still managed to make me laugh while mimicking my Mussolini face, by hanging his teeth partially out on his lips, by passing gas in my face, or whatever else came across his mind. He still was that gem…a truly rare gem! He talked often about the disease…CMV and how it could harm him.

"Recharred, this disease con make me go blind. They really do not know how long this medication will suppress it because I could eventually get immune to it. Ond then whot happens? I do not want to live if I go blind…aw, no!" He'd discuss his living will, mentioning a lawyer who did them for his HIV support group. He'd also talk about all the money he owed me…about adding me on his insurance as one of his beneficiaries, and all the things he insisted would and should be done when he died. However, I still didn't want to face the fact Juan was very seriously ill and always insisted he discontinue this kind of talk.

Endira once again borrowed from me, giving me a postdated check for a substantial amount over the loan, and in order to change the subject one time I brought it up.

"I know, Recharred," he quickly replied, "because she called me again. She knows I do not 'ave any money but she keeps calling. I don' understand thot woman? She makes so much money ond still she cannot manage. She is lucky you 'ave been thar for her all these years, you know, Recharred."

"I know Juan, I know."

May continued on and both of us were traveling back and forth, although Juan sometimes preferred to take the bus because Larry offered to pick him up at the depot each time he took it.

Juan was again excited because Larry was taking him to see the musical, *42nd Street*.

He couldn't then stop raving about the wonderful tap dancing. He loved tap dancing and particularly large production numbers. 'Stepping out with My Baby' from the Astaire and Rogers movie was one of his favorites, and there he'd be singing it in one note.

Videos became an important part of our lives, especially Juan's, because there was so much time to fill. This meant a couple of trips to the library each week. At the same time, we'd do our usual sightseeing and end up at Union Station or the Market Place for those "wonderful Caribbean meat-filled pastry pockets, Recharred!"

Svetmana was spending the third weekend in May with Juan, so this meant I wouldn't be seeing him. It was Matt's birthday and I decided to see if he'd accept my offer to take him out for dinner. To my surprise, he accepted and I wondered why he wasn't spending it with his effeminate friend. There was no way I could afford it, but I felt I needed to make an impression on him, so I decided to put it all on my charge card. After I presented him with three dozen roses and a picture he had liked at the gallery, he enjoyed my extravagance with a dinner at Como Inn and a show at the female impersonator club, The Baton. The roses were bought from a wholesale house, so they were extremely inexpensive, but the restaurant tab hit my charge card for over eighty bucks, with another fifty at the Baton. Crazy, but that was me. He had been enthralled but I received another cold treatment when I called him Monday, though he informed me he was no longer seeing his nellie friend.

"It was just something I had to do," he replied once I inquired why he went out with the queen, "a fantasy I had to have, Rich."

My mind quickly flashed back to Daniel when I thought I wanted him. He also had his fantasies…one to have a dwarf because he had heard they had tremendous dicks. I remembered the day that fantasy came true. In one of my pursuits, I had been thrilled to find myself driving just behind his car. He had appeared to be seated alone in his car and I figured we could get together. When he pulled into a gas station, I had followed. It was then that I noticed what appeared to be a flock of hair bobbing in the passenger seat. I had thought it might be the head of a little kid. However, I had sped off quickly once I stretched up to get a better look. That head had been the head of his fantasy!

Daniel's other fantasy also came to mind…to one day have a horse! I had never thought he'd try something that impossible, especially since a horse would never allow it. Still, it didn't stop him from trying. I recalled the time he thought a horse would appreciate being accommodated by him. While in a stable, he had reached out to grab hold of a horse's tremendous tool, and I'm sure he would've been licking away or sticking his butt up had the stallion not reared up and neighed. And to the best of my knowledge, I believe the closest he ever got to this fantasy was someone hung like a horse!

My relationship with Matt was going nowhere because he continued asking for his space. My mind was totally consumed with it all, and I found myself attempting to find out his true feelings. He was still the very hot and cold person, making me feel extremely happy at times, but miserable for longer periods afterwards. I never felt he was telling the truth about places he was going without me, so I began chasing after him, staying up until the wee hours of the morning. I thought if I could catch him in a lie, it would be exactly what I needed to say it was over again. This was the only way I could end it because he continually talked of a future together and could be very wonderful when we were out antiquing or wherever. My chases, however, were never fruitful.

Ironically, Matt had a way of giving himself away each time I felt he was going to meet someone or to have a trick over. It had to be his own ego doing it because he was so proud of his conquest or excited about his date. He'd tell me an old friend called and wanted to get together. Once you knew Matt, an old friend meant…an old trick because all of his old tricks were now friends. And all of these friends were on his Christmas card list…about two hundred or so. He'd say he wasn't going to see the friend who called. However, the following day, he'd call to tell me he was going to see his daughter or, staying late at work, I'd drive by his house to see his car parked in its space and the lights on in his apartment. Then, to go even further, once I rang his doorbell…no one would answer. Or he might have told me he wanted to sleep in early that evening…and then his car would be nowhere in sight. Still, I kept trying and hoping for those few shining moments we had once upon a time, thinking they'd return. By no means did Matt stop being curt or discontinue blaming me for making wrong turns. They continued and in fact grew in numbers, but I still held on because I felt we had the love of the century…Matt just didn't realize it.

It came to mind that maybe the reason Matt is this way is because I haven't told Juan we are once again resuming a relationship. So I made the decision to tell Juan, but to be certain he was aware that nothing would ever hinder our friendship. I felt sure Matt was going to be pleased when I told him because it was exactly what he'd been trying to get me to do.

Matt had talked so much about going many places together after our initial meeting at the bar. Even after I told him I'd never be able to afford it, he always assured me.

"Don't worry, because, Rich, I have enough to pay for both of us, and I want to share things with you." Surprisingly, after telling him my glorious news, I stood there in shock listening to his reminders.

"Rich, how can we have a relationship when you don't have any money?" What I said meant nothing to him. And when I went on to explain why I had no money, he shocked me even more.

"Rich, that is your problem…not mine, because I could care less." I was absolutely stunned, but still an idiot because I allowed the relationship to continue! He had to think me an idiot, too, since we did go on. His idea of sharing was very clear while antiquing. He'd easily spend two hundred dollars for one trinket after another for himself, and never think of buying me a token item. In fact, it was always me who ran back to a booth to buy a chicken or rooster he decided not to purchase, even though I couldn't afford to do it. Matt still continued to be curt…manic at times and selfish all the time, and even though I'd be knocked down, I'd still get up and ask for more. My one consolation…I never did tell Juan what I intended.

Juan continued going with Larry to see one show after another, raving excitedly about them to me each time. Svetmana was even invited to join them on one occasion. Juan had so much time on his hands that he began recording music on cassettes from the radio or LP records and I insisted he make a copy for the gallery. He had talked so much about the movie, *Dances with Wolves*, and once I took him to see it with passes from Jacque, he couldn't thank me enough. However, he somehow sensed I had seen it before with Matt.

"Who did you see thot picture with before, Recharred?" he teased. "Was it with thot Matt? The one with the curly locks ond bleached blond tips?"

"You know, Juan, once you move here," I said quickly to change the subject, "I will be able to get passes all the time for us to see movies."

"Be sure you tell Jacque how much I appreciated her passes," he said, obviously elated that he'd be seeing so many movies. "You know, Recharred, as soon as I begin to receive all my disability ond retirement pay, I will 'ave to take you somewhere special." I couldn't help think but of Matt and the many times I took him to free movies, and never did he offer to reciprocate. In fact, one particular time, he wanted to see a movie but I wasn't able to get a hold of Jacque.

"Well, that's okay, Rich," he merely said, "I will just go by myself, or maybe I can find someone else to go." And I made sure I went along just by taking from Peter again.

Juan and I made another one of those quick decisions when I drove there. After only half a day, we returned to my house for the sixth and seventh of June. Amanda stopped in the second day and after having a hell of a time, we decided she should stay over. We could then ride with her early in the morning to Indianapolis because she had a couple of deliveries on the way.

"Because then I will be able to spend Saturday and Sunday with you, guys, and I can drive you back later that night, Richard."

Amanda had already been told about Juan's condition about a month earlier after I begged him to allow me to tell her because I knew he needed more support from those who loved him…. At that time, she surprised me by showing up after I gave her a last minute invite to stop by for leftover spaghetti. I wanted her to eat before saying anything about Juan. I mixed her a cocktail while the spaghetti was heating.

"How is everything going with Matt, Richard?" she asked, aware that I was still seeing him. Of course, this brought on my frustrations and I quickly enlightened her on everything.

"I am surprised to hear that, Richard, after what I saw that night at the bar a few months ago. He was so attentive and caring," Amanda said, completely bewildered.

"I catch him in lies constantly, and you know what? He lies himself out of those, too!"

"Richard, it sounds as though he is very selfish and that he needs to have his ego lifted constantly. Why do you continue to see him if you feel he is tricking all over the place…and, Richard, if he is, I hope you are being careful."

"I don't know why I'm still seeing him or why I even picked up with him again, Amanda. I really don't know because I meant it when I broke off everything back in February. I guess he got me started again by being so nice."

"It's exactly that, Richard, because he knows how to bait you…so you will be available when he wants you. Richard, why are you clinging to him, especially when you say he totally disregards your needs in bed?"

"I don't know, Amanda, I guess I feel he loves me and that it will come out again, especially since he has often said all good things in a person's life take a long time to develop and that I should have the patience and give him space for now." Amanda just shook her head.

I changed my tone of voice at this time because I now had to tell her about Juan.

"Juan and I felt you should know his condition." This puzzled her.

"What do you mean, Richard? You said Juan was having severe headaches and they were affecting his eyes, and that is why he is receiving medication…to get rid of the infection?" I stood silent for a moment, looking at her and wishing I didn't have to go on…because she appeared more fragile than ever. Yet I knew I had to go on…Juan needed her support.

"Amanda, Juan is in the hospital because…because he has AIDS." Suddenly, my nose felt puffed, and in a moment, tears flowed freely down my cheeks. My eyes stood fixed on her and she seemed to appear smaller than ever…and so crumbled, as though all joy and life had just been completely torn from her. Oh, God, how I wanted to take those words back!

"Oh, no, Richard! Oh, God, I don't believe it!" she whispered, her voice quivering. "Oh, Richard, how did this happen? Oh, God, how did it happen?" She quickly took hold of my hand…squeezed it tightly, and looked despairingly into my eyes. It was as though she was begging me to tell her it was all a lie. However, she knew. My tears were too real.

I told her everything from the very beginning and we talked and cried for some time.

"It is unbelievable, Richard," Amanda then said in awe, "how this man remained the same funny…the same sexy…the same happy person! And you tell me he was diagnosed HIV back in 1986…and with full blown AIDS this last April! I don't believe it? Even now he still is the same lovable and happy person!"

"I know, Amanda…he is…he really is. The only thing that has changed is he doesn't have that energy anymore…that desire is there but he doesn't have the strength to fulfill these wants! And you know how he used to badger the hell out of me to go dancing all the time…and how we would dance our heads off! Aw, Amanda, how I wish he would be that way again…driving me crazy, pleading, 'C'mon, Richard, let's go cha- cha…'while raising his arms in the inimitable way of his." We laughed until tears flowed down our faces…and then we cried.

Juan sat in the passenger seat of her minivan once we took off for Indianapolis, and because it was loaded with artwork, I set myself on a box directly behind. It wasn't what someone would call comfortable, but I was satisfied just to see how happy Juan was as he talked with Amanda. It was very evident he was happy to be with both of us.

Juan asked Amanda if she could stop at the next exit and that he'd treat for lunch. We ended up in a Bob Evans. Since she was on a Jenny Craig diet, she just ordered a plate of plain noodles to throw the contents of her canned lunch over. I excused myself to go to the restroom and was told of the following conversation later by Amanda..

"You know, Amanda, I 'ave an insurance policy with the Army…so when I die thar will be fifty thousand dollars," Juan said once I excused myself from the table. "Recharred is gonna be surprised because I am gonna leave him ten thousand dollars. I owe him so much, Amanda. He has been so good to me, ond I want to leave him thot much because he has given me money through all the years I 'ave known him. I could never repay him. Aw, Amanda, he has been thar for me whenever I needed help…whether it was with money, or whatever. It is not enough, but I want to leave him something."

"That is beautiful, Juan, because Richard will really need something because his compensation is just about over."

Once I returned to the table, I noticed tears in Amanda's eyes but never questioned her, not wanting to continue anything sad.

Of course, once we arrived at her scheduled appointment, which was west of Indianapolis, she casually made mention that she was three hours late. Naturally, no one was there. We waited almost two hours for someone to arrive after she made some calls, and because it was so hot, Juan got quite tired from the sun. My heart was aching as Amanda and I were hanging the artwork because the memory of the many times Juan insisted he be the one allowed to select the places and to hang our pictures was so vivid in my mind. Instead, there he was, looking so tired and helpless, watching our every move…sitting in an office chair. I knew he'd give anything to be there next to us. I could just hear him insist.

"C'mon now, Recharred ond Amanda, let me do it because I 'ave a good sense of knowing where pictures look the best."

"You know, guys, my other delivery is on the other side of Indianapolis…about a hundred miles," Amanda said once we were on the road again, "so from here it will probably take three hours or more and that means we won't get there until about seven o'clock." I knew that would be much too late for Juan because we probably wouldn't get to his place until eleven or so, and then it took four hours for the treatment. Juan still insisted she drive there, not wanting to impose on her.

"No, I will just call from your place to tell them I will go tomorrow." I realized the town was also north of Indianapolis, and I was certain she wouldn't want to backtrack to Juan's. This meant Juan wouldn't have us there all of Sunday as expected. However, I didn't mention this to him for fear of spoiling his evening. After dinner, the three of us sat in the living room and talked while Juan administered his I.V. treatment. He insisted we watch a movie he had seen already because it was so funny, and he of course laughed as if he had never seen it before.

The evening turned into a hilarious riot because Juan was in the mood to mimic me. So there he was, mimicking every expression and stance of mine. I'd just stop laughing from one and he'd do my next expression. Amanda was giggling at a nonstop pace as though she was watching a Laurel and Hardy film.

"You two guys are so funny," she exclaimed once she caught her breath. "A person doesn't have to go see a movie comedy because when you're together, you're a show in itself."

"We are, Amanda? We really are?" Juan sighed in that boyish manner of his.

"Amanda, Juan mimics me all the time and I laugh each time even more than him."

"I love to mimic Blanche because he has such on expressive face. He should 'ave been in silent movies," Juan exclaimed. "Ond Amanda, I would not do it if I did not love him so much." It felt so good to hear Juan finally admit his feelings about me to Amanda…instead of constantly denying it like I was some kind of plague and then laughing.

"I've always told Juan he should've been an actor because he is so talented and funny, though I know he'd never go on stage in front of an audience."

"Yeah, I would probably shit in my pants."

"Well, both of you should have been in silent movies," Amanda remarked while rocking in her giggles.

Juan usually tried to avoid sleeping with me because of my snoring, but this time I felt he was actually looking forward to having me next to him for the night once Amanda retired to the den and sleeper I usually bedded in. I was a bit apprehensive because of my wild movements during the night, afraid I might accidentally grab at his Hickman. So it was a tremendous relief the next morning to see we got through the night without any mishaps and especially nice because Juan never complained of any snoring.

After breakfast, it was very evident Juan was becoming depressed realizing Amanda had to get going, and that I would be going with her. Suddenly, as if Amanda and I planned it, we simultaneously said:

Amanda: I've been thinking, Richard, why don't you stay here with Juan? I will go myself and then return to take you home.

Richard: I've been thinking, Amanda, maybe I should stay here with Juan….

Of course I stopped to let Amanda continue and when I glanced at Juan, he was glowing.

"I bet she never makes it back," I said to myself once she was on her way. Of course, she didn't fail my expectations. She called later in the day to say her destination was much further than expected and I told her not to worry about returning…that I'd take the bus home. She insisted on returning and said she'd call back later. However, she never did call back and I wasn't really surprised.

Amanda was one of the most giving and loving persons in the world, but definitely undependable! When she was with you, you were fortunate because she'd bend over backwards for you. She had a way of spreading herself too thin. I always thought if there were two hundred twenty-four hours in a day, she'd shine!

"Recharred, you are never gonna change Amanda…thot is how she is ond thot is all!" Juan always said, tolerating her tardiness more than me. "If she is with you, she will give you the world two hundred percent! But when she tells you she will be thar…you better pray she has not said the same to six other people!"

I was a bit worried about taking the bus this time because a new terminal had been built in Chicago, located in an isolated area slightly southwest of the loop. This meant I'd have to walk several lonely and dark blocks to the train stop, which was even scarier than the streets. Juan was even more worried and pleaded for me to leave in the morning instead. I wasn't dressed for the gallery and explained it to Juan, but he still insisted I leave in the morning because the subway waiting platforms had a notorious history of terror.

"Recharred, please call as soon as you are home…will you do thot, my darling?" Juan asked just before we entered the terminal. I assured him I would. He then shook my hand vigorously as I boarded the bus alongside the other passengers.

"Goodbye, old buddy! 'Ave a good trip home, mon! 'Ave a good trip home!" he shouted in that gung-ho manner of his. He was something else! Though once I was seated and looked through the window to see his face, I knew how he really felt.

On arrival in Chicago, I found the streets dark and deserted once I left the hustle-bustle of the new modern terminal, and to say I was scared is an understatement. I had to walk the five or six deserted blocks to the El station, and I was terrified! There I was, running like a scared rabbit, certain someone was chasing me, carrying a very bulky plastic bag containing my two down pillows and toilet case. The faster I ran, the more wild this bulky bag became, blocking any view of the darkness behind. No matter how hard I tried to look over my shoulders, there was this bulky, bouncing bag blocking it all. Finally, I reached the entrance of the station with the long descending ramp leading to the platform below. A sigh of relief echoed from my lungs. I made it through the lonely streets safely! Now, what was I to do once I made it down the ramp to the lonely platform?

Oh, God, I thought, *please let a train come real quick before some dope addicts come walking down that ramp!* I, unfortunately, wasn't able to tell if a train would soon arrive because of the curved oncoming track. So my frenzy continued. I felt sure someone would come walking down the ramp any second and attack me. I became even more terrified when, suddenly, my eyes spotted two people hiding behind an advertising sign at the opposite end of the platform! Or could it be just a shadow? No! I felt sure they were waiting for some jerk like me to appear so they could sally forth and do their thing!

My heart was beating like a drum, and I was sure it would pop out of my shirt any minute! A brainstorm suddenly struck. Why not take out my keychain? After all, a two-inch pocket knife was on the chain. It was one of those convenient gadgets with all sorts of mini tools attached. The tremendous two-inch blade was only one of the necessity features.

Suddenly, it appeared as though the two persons were walking slowly in my direction and I quickly flipped open the blade and pulled up the large bag of pillows to my chest, concealing the knife. I was ready to slit their throats if needed. I almost shouted a hallelujah when, surprisingly, a train arrived! I hurried on and sat on one of the side seats. No one would be able to attack from behind. I held on tightly to the pocket knife, which was cleverly hidden from view.

I started to breathe a little easier once I noticed two people sitting at the other end of the car with their backs to me. They had to be the two I thought were hiding behind an advertising billboard, and evidently harmless. Then two young black guys boarded the train and sat almost directly across from me. I began to breathe heavy again. I didn't know if the blade of the knife was facing the right direction should I need to swing it savagely towards an assailant's throat, but there was no way I could tell by feeling it.

"Oh, my God, what if the blade is facing the wrong direction," I thought, "and once I slash it against someone's throat that it will close on my fingers instead?" So I sat there in a worried frenzy, imagining all sorts of crazy things.

Fortunately for me, and I guess for them too, the train finally arrived at the end of the line…my stop. They went in the opposite direction, and it was after twelve o'clock once I entered my place. Just as I was about to pick up the phone to call Juan, it rang.

"Aw, Recharred, I am so happy you are home! I 'ave been so worried since you left because I knew you would 'ave to walk in thot bod area ond then 'ave to wait on thot lonely platform. Aw, Recharred, I cannot tell you how happy I am you are safely home." I immediately explained my defensive tactics and even though it was a bit tongue and cheek, he roared with laughter.

"Aw, Recharred, you are so funny…so funny!" but quickly composed himself. "Recharred, it is really not something to laugh about…you should not 'ave gone home tonight! It was much too dangerous…much too dangerous! Ond, Recharred, whot was a fuckin' two-inch blade gonna do if you swung it ot someone for Chris' sake?"

"I don't know, Juan! Probably get me shot after cutting off my fingers!"

Chapter Fifty-Three: Costly Mistakes

Juan's birthday was coming up the last Monday in June and I remember him calling the week before to tell me he was again invited by Larry to see a play on Thursday.

"Then, on Friday, I 'ave been invited by my old battalion to see *Oklahoma* ot the same dinner theatre you performed at," he went on to say, "ond that is not all, Recharred. Saturday night, I 'ave been invited as a special guest to a big 'Copa' party given by a gay business group. The party is to raise funds for the AIDS Hospice Center. Recharred, I am a special guest because I 'ave AIDS!" This threw me for a loop! He almost sounded proud. Though I realized how he meant it…because he would be a special guest.

I remember the mixed emotions I experienced. I was disappointed I wouldn't be going the weekend, and yet pleased since it gave me a chance to see Matt. I also remembered Matt has asked me to go on a gay cruise, and if I could meet someone Monday night to buy tickets. With that on my mind, I told Juan I wouldn't come until Tuesday. I should've gone Monday, especially since he was having a dinner party and had invited Phillip, Kent, and Larry. But, because something romantically seemed to be happening with Matt, I felt the tickets were more important.

Daniel had told me he and Stan wouldn't be going to their cottage in Michigan that weekend, so I asked if Matt and I could go. He obliged and we left on Friday and stayed to Sunday afternoon. Matt was very attentive that weekend and I felt we had something going. He had to be serious about me! We spent one of the evenings at the same bar and restaurant Juan and I went with Phil and Vic back in 1986 while on vacation. Yes, I had asked Juan to resume as lovers after we had made beautiful love while Phil and Vic were down on the beach. He had said it was more important to be good friends. I'll never forget the beautiful experience Juan made during that dinner…how he raved about that crusted Halibut! I cannot remember anything about my dinner with Matt. He just didn't have what it takes to make a dinner exciting enough to be a rare and beautiful experience. As usual, another thank you card arrived the following week with a special personal message written in it.

I telephoned Juan the morning of his birthday and was surprised to be greeted by an answering machine. I called throughout the day but didn't get an answer until that evening, and once I heard his voice, I sang my usual birthday greeting. He wasn't really happy once he realized I wasn't on my way, though he then tried to act as if it wouldn't matter even if I didn't show up the next day. I should've got in my car and headed there that very moment. But, I had to meet that girl for the cruise tickets later that evening. Of course, I never told Juan that. Arrangements were to meet at a halfway point, and the parking lot of the banquet hall Juan had worked as bartender years earlier turned out to be it.

I felt a bit of guilt as I sat waiting for the girl to show up in the banquet parking lot. Especially remembering the many times Juan walked happily out, wearing his bartender vest and counting his tip money, anticipating to see me because we were going out to 'cha cha'…and here I was buying tickets for an evening cruise I would spend with Matt.

Of course, though Juan had tried to make me think he could care less if I came, the phone rang very early in the morning. Like so many times before, I was pulled out of the shower to hear his happy and excited voice inquiring when I'd be there. I told him I'd leave as soon as I showered and dressed. As always, he rattled on while I dripped on the carpet.

Our joy at seeing each other was mutual, and why we ever wanted someone else I'll never know. He always was capable of making me feel so important in his life, and there was no exception this time as he talked excitedly about the big AIDS benefit bash.

"Ond the cocktail party Larry took me to before the affair was ot the home of two of his friends. Recharred, thar place was so unusual because it was two houses, side by side. Recharred, they had joined them together! Aw, Recharred, it was really bea-u-ti-ful!" Of course, every feature was described to the fullest.

"Well, they had a big cocktail party before the benefit ball, Recharred."

"Did you drink, Juan?" I quickly inquired. "You know you shouldn't be drinking alcohol while taking AZT and injecting Gancylavir into your blood."

"I know better than thot, Recharred," he quickly replied. "Thot is a foolish question to ask." Somehow I felt this was one of those little white lies he often told so I wouldn't harp on it. He also was proficient at it whenever purchasing something or spending money foolishly. I tried to go on about the seriousness of it, but it did no good. His excitement took over.

"Recharred, I am gonna 'ave to show you thar house tomorrow. We con drive by because I 'ave to go downtown to the social security office regarding my disability allowance."

After excitedly opening his birthday present, he continued to talk about the AIDS Benefit Ball. I was listening but couldn't help from wishing he had asked Larry to get tickets for me, too. It also came to mind that Juan had been the one who received the tickets. I realized he felt obligated to Larry because of the many shows he was taken to…and that was fine, but he should have had me with him, too. If only he would've thought of it and insist I come? I never would've refused him.

Once I asked about the answering machine, he immediately told me his nurse thought it was a necessary need and gave it to him.

"Was thot not nice of Yvonne to do thot, Recharred?" I agreed but knew it would be expected since he was such a charmer who also never complained to her about his illness or show any bitterness because of it. He was always just JUAN.

The next morning, we were kept happily busy. We drove by the homes that had been joined and along with that narration, Juan included a detailed and exciting description of the progress on the new downtown mall. We included a stop in the Market to have those delicious Caribbean meat-filled pastry pockets he loved so much. Our last stop downtown was to the social security office and thrilled once he heard his benefits would start in six weeks.

"Recharred, you do not know how relieved I will be once I start to receive my payments! Do you know I had to go to a company thot consolidates all my bills, ond ofter I pay them one check…they send my creditors small token payments."

Juan needed a few groceries and stopped off at Marsh's and I was shocked to see him do something he'd never think of doing before. He passed the cigarette rack and almost blew me over once he nonchalantly took a pack and quickly slipped them into his pocket!

"Juan, what the heck are you doing?" I whispered. "Are you crazy…what if you get caught? Aw, Juan, I'm not gonna walk with you because I don't want to be caught like the time I changed the price on a roll of tape!"

"I don' care, Recharred…I cannot afford to buy them. If I pay for them, then I will not be able to buy groceries ond I will starve. Is thot whot you want me to do, Recharred?" I never got a chance to answer and he was out of the store. I couldn't help but laugh. Here was Juan insisting he had to have them even though he didn't have the money. In a way, I think I understood his logic. He had AIDS, which was totally unfair…so why not have a free pack of cigarettes now and then, especially since his disability benefits were taking so long.

Juan didn't want me to take him out for a birthday dinner because he knew I was struggling to survive, too. However, I insisted on taking him to Marino's because just being able to sit across and watch the elegance and joy ooze from his body was worth it. And, besides, what difference if I added one more bill to my charge card, especially since so much was added to it for Matt's birthday, and then even more with a chicken teapot set for eighty bucks and a silk floral basket for another fifty while on the weekend.

It was nearing time to leave and again Juan was showing signs of depression, and made it clear he wanted me to leave in the morning. I tried to explain my reasoning. Parking lots near the gallery were very expensive. If I went home at night, I'd then take the train to the gallery in the morning, and the cost was only a fraction of parking lots. However, the fact was I liked leaving in the morning because Juan would leave for work before I started on my way, and I'd quickly run into his room to watch from the window as he cranked up his motor. He never realized I was watching as he lit up a cigarette while the motor was warming up, and there he'd be…inhaling deeply and blowing out the smoke. I remember, it always felt so good realizing he was part of my life…or better yet…he was my life….

"You know, Recharred, I think I will go out tonight because I do not want to be home alone," Juan said as I gathered my things.

"What do you mean you are going out tonight? You know you shouldn't drink. Juan, don't make me worry by saying crazy things like that!"

"I jus' wanted to see if you would change your mind ond stay, Recharred. I 'ave no intention of going out. Yes, I know you 'ave to be ot the gallery even though no one is buying…. I know you cannot expect Mario to sit thar all the time. Aw, Recharred, I wish you could be successful! You 'ave such a bea-u-ti-ful gallery." I couldn't help think of the many times Juan came into the gallery and how proud he'd make Mario feel, walking through holding a cup of coffee and raving about the gallery and the artists, and saying if he had the money, he'd fill his house with some of each artist's paintings.

It was 11:18 once I dialed Juan's number to let him know I was home, but instead of hearing his happy greeting I got his answering machine.

"That son-of-a-gun went out," I muttered to myself. "I should have known he was lying!" I was sick because this had to be suicide. I began pacing the floor knowing I had to do something and suddenly thought of calling his friend, Larry. It was late but I called anyway. It was evident he had been asleep, but still listened patiently. However, instead of going to Jimmy's Bar, he said he'd call to check if Juan was there. I thanked him but was disappointed he didn't offer to go to the bar, especially since it was only two blocks from his house. I was panicky! I should have realized not everyone is willing to get out of bed, dress, and go into the night searching bars for Juan.

I began getting angry with myself for not staying with him, especially after his comment. What was a few dollars for parking compared to the eighty-four dollars I charged on my card for Matt's birthday dinner, and the forty dollars in cash for the female impersonator show besides his gift and the flowers? This would have only been a few dollars, and would have been for Juan. If I added it to the sixteen spent for Juan's birthday dinner and the thirty-four for the shirt, I still would barely reach a quarter of Matt's total!

I began thinking seriously of driving back, but realized the damage would be done by the time I got there…that is, if I even got there alive? So I sat there in my nervous state dozing off at times, and the night moved slowly on.

After what seemed to be forever, a glow of daylight finally streaked through the window. I jumped up and dialed his number only to hear the answering machine again. Larry should be awake by now so I dialed his number. He had no word and my hysteria continued. As I reached for the phone to call Mario to tell him I'd be coming in late, it blasted out a thunderous ring. Juan's voice, upon answering, was heaven to hear though I was still distraught.

"Juan, where have you been?" I screamed, not giving him a chance to say more. "I've been a basket case all night worrying about you! Why did you go out last night, Juan, and where have you been until now?"

"Recharred, I did not go out drinking! A little ofter you left, I started to feel very sick. So I called the hospital ond they told me I should go thar, Recharred…thot they would 'ave to check me in person. Ofter driving thar, I was told I had to stay the night because the doctor would not be thar until morning."

"Why didn't you call me, Juan?"

"Recharred, you were on your way home ond I thought I would be back here to call you. I did not know I would 'ave to stay thar overnight. Then they gave me something to sleep ond I did not wake up until this morning." Juan's tone became somewhat sarcastic once I told him I was a bit hysterical since I never got a call from him.

"Well, Recharred, I was sick ond in pain ond I do not know how I was able to drive to the hospital. If you did not leave, you could 'ave driven me thar ond you would not 'ave had to worry all night." His sarcasm was short-lived and my conscience relieved once he went on. "They gave me something to stop the pain ond the doctor explained it as a medication reaction. Aw, Recharred, I am so glad thar was not another thing wrong with me…only a side reaction."

I soon realized this was only the beginning of many short stays at the hospital, which finally caused Juan to complain slightly about how tired he was of never feeling just right. However, he never preyed on it. The majority of the time, he was still the happy person I always knew. If he wasn't happy, he had to be a fantastic actor because he never made me aware of it.

The last weekend in June included the evening cruise and the Gay Pride Parade. Matt's constant attention really began to convince me this was for real. I never liked to wave flags for controversial causes, so the parade wasn't something I looked forward to. Matt, however, loved it, so I figured I should go along with his eagerness. I remember a strange feeling come over me as we stood watching the parade. I should have been excited watching the passing floats; instead, I felt guilty because I had lied to Juan about the weekend. I wondered what he was doing and didn't find out until a year and a half later from Larry. They had driven to Brown County State Park, south of Indianapolis, to see the location Juan had chosen to have his ashes scattered, a spot he had decided upon after driving there alone following his diagnosis of CMV. I know it was something he would have chose to do with me, but he was aware of my childish refusal to accept the inevitable.

Svetmana drove Juan to Chicago to spend a week the first part of July. His intentions were to split his time between his folks and myself. I had picked him up from their house the first day he arrived. Then it happened…something I'll never forgive myself for allowing to happen. Matt was aware Juan was coming in because I had asked him to refrain from calling the house during those times…that I'd call him during the day from the gallery. He seemed to understand. He also was aware that I hadn't told Juan we were dating again. So there I was, faced with a hot and cold person, and me thinking he was for real. My ego was determined to win him over…hoping that one day he would kiss the ground I walked on. In the meantime, I was actually making myself fall in love with him…or thinking it? I don't think I knew!

Juan and I were sitting on the couch enjoying our conversation. He had placed the telephone between us so it would be convenient to answer should his messages to friends be returned. Juan didn't say much the first time Matt called, even though I felt certain my manner was clumsy trying to evade questions asked of me. A few minutes hadn't passed when the phone rang again. Juan answered and handed the phone to me with a smirk on his face.

"It is him again, Recharred." I couldn't believe it after emphatically pleading with him not to call. So my answers to his nonsense questions were even more stupid, and I certainly couldn't call him down for calling, especially since Juan was sitting beside me. I finally managed to say good-bye, and from one look at Juan's face I saw he wasn't happy. He had chuckled in disbelief when Matt called the second time as he handed me the phone. Yet, because of all my stupid answers and Matt's apparent refusal to keep the conversation short, it was obvious he was agitated. As always, once agitated, I could expect sarcasm even though it would start in a sweet manner and there was no exception this time.

"Recharred, why is thot queen calling so much? Ond, Recharred, why are you so nervous?"

"What do you mean, Juan. I'm not nervous."

"Recharred, c'mon now, I 'ave known you for almost eighteen years…I know when you are nervous. Recharred, your face cannot lie." His interrogation continued and before long, a razor sharp tongue took over.

"Recharred, if you do not want me to hear…why don' you talk to him on your bedroom phone!" His jealousy was very apparent as he continued his fast-paced needling.

"Huh, Recharred? Why did you not go ond talk in your bedroom? You could 'ave done thot, Recharred…you could 'ave closed the door so I would not 'ave been able to hear your loving conversation…huh, Recharred? Why did you not do thot? C'mon now, Recharred, tell me why?" I insisted I had nothing to hide…that Matt and I were just friends, but he continued. This certainly wasn't what I wanted to happen. I wasn't sure where I stood with Matt and didn't feel Juan had to know anything until I was certain there was something sincere going on. The funny thing about it was when with Juan, I hardly gave Matt a thought. It was almost as though he didn't exist. I tried to explain it to Juan, but it only confused him more. I'm certain he didn't believe me but, finally, calmed down enough to seem to accept it. However, he continued to slam away at Matt in his best sarcastic manner.

"Recharred, I don' believe you are again going with thot queen? Even though it is jus' as friends, as you say, are you not embarrassed to walk down the street with him? I hope you are not bringing him to meet your daughters because Martina and Jacque would immediately know he is a queen, jus' by looking ot him with his curly locks thot are tipped with bleach blond. Ond, Recharred, he dresses so gay…so gay!" My plea in Matt's defense came off quite weak because those were the very things that had been bothering me about him. I had tried desperately to tell Matt these feelings, but never could get the courage because I felt he'd never consider any of it as constructive criticism. It certainly should've made me realize this couldn't be love. Juan and I loved each other and always took criticism from one another should we act overly gay in public. In the end, it only proved to make us respect one another more. It also brought to my mind Matt's personality in a gay bar in contrast to the times he was in a store or straight restaurant. While in a bar, he was always the very macho man. At a straight restaurant or wherever, if someone teed him off by committing a slight error, I could expect to see him blow up like an angry queen. And I never had the nerve to tell him how gay he looked.

Juan had finally laid his anger aside, but still had to give me a few mocking criticisms of Matt to be sure I was aware of his gay personality. So he again described the meeting in the forest preserves. Of course, his elaboration of the meeting forced me to insist he was exaggerating.

"Recharred, it is true. He was jus' keeping his beady eyeballs looking up…like a fairy. I know…jus' like those holy cards!" He then began to chuckle, realizing the opportunity to mimic Matt hanging from a branch, looking upward. This mockery wasn't something that should've amused me considering I had begun a new friendship with Matt. Still, I couldn't help but end up on the floor in hysterical laughter.

The following evening was another matter, however. I had specifically reprimanded and pleaded with Matt not to call again…that I didn't want to cause Juan any more stress. Well, he was either deaf or he just didn't care because, again, I was faced with another long lasting call while Juan and I sat on my couch. One leading question after another was asked of me, and there was no way I could sensibly answer any of them without Juan realizing there was more than just a friendship going on. I was confused, especially since Matt refused to make a commitment to me. It was certain. Matt wanted Juan to be completely aware of a relationship going on between he and I…and he accomplished it.

Juan showed all signs of awareness and in order to hide this hurt, he began acting as though nothing between us mattered. He was doing a slow burn and it was apparent he wanted me to think I meant nothing to him. His curt and arrogant manner continued, refusing to commit to spending any of the other days with me during his stay. I should've realized he wanted me to beg him as I always did in order to allow him to feel some restitution for being hurt. However, I felt he should realize he was the most important person in my life without saying it. No, he had to satisfy his anger instead.

"Recharred, I am gonna be busy tomorrow with Svetmana because we are going somewhere." I quickly inquired where they were going, only to hear more arrogance.

"It does not matter where I am going, Recharred…only thot I will probably be back ot her house too late to come here. In fact, Recharred, I do not know if I can even see you the following day, the Fourth of July, because my mother wants for us to do something." I tried reasoning with him but he just continued in that angry and arrogant manner he was such an expert at. After all…he had to make me pay for my sins. Juan always meant everything he said or did to badger me…but then again, he didn't mean it…if that makes any sense! In other words, as I have repeatedly said, his anger and badgering were always meant to test me…to see if I would give up what made him angry.

The entire evening wasn't a total bust, however. He slowly regained his charm and became his usual lovable self as we played 'Scribbage' while sharing one of the Chef Kitchen pizzas he loved so much. I felt better once he left for his mother's since he appeared to lay his anger aside.

I couldn't believe Matt's reaction once I reprimanded him for calling the house again. I tried to explain the stress it caused Juan only to hear.

"Hogwash, Rich, how can that give him any stress!" And the sad thing about it was I let him get away with his twisted rationalization.

Juan, however, didn't call in the morning. So I didn't hear his cheerful greeting or his laughter teasing me about getting me out of the shower. So I missed the laughter and the continued conversation. I tried reaching him at his mother's once I arrived at the gallery, but each time, I heard "no, Juan, no home." So I began calling at Endira's…receiving the answering machine each time.

During all of this, Matt called to ask if I'd like to join him to see the fireworks at the lakefront. I explained my tentative plans with Juan and that I hadn't been able to get in touch with him. I then said I'd let him know either way before leaving at six. Of course, this didn't make him happy and in his curt manner, managed to pressure me into calling him before five o'clock. And, again, I allowed myself to be a pushover. At about a quarter to five, I again dialed Endira's number. It was odd but I almost wished Juan wasn't back yet as I listened to the rings of the telephone…and probably because I was pissed he had kept me hanging all day…without any consideration for my feelings. And partly because I felt I shouldn't refuse Matt, especially since I was trying to start a relationship. This time, Endira picked up the phone.

"No, Richard, Juan and Svetmana haven't come back yet. I don't know when they'll be here. Do you want me to have him call you once he returns?" I told her she should have him call immediately because I wouldn't be at the gallery much longer. My excitement about the chance of being with Matt got the best of me and I called immediately. He quickly put on his charm to ask if I could leave immediately and come directly to his apartment…that we could stop for something to eat and drive back downtown for the concert and fireworks. So I never really gave Juan a chance to get the message from Endira.

I had never seen fireworks so spectacular and listening to the orchestra play the 1812 Overture made it even more fantastic. I couldn't believe how Matt seemed to appreciate my company and how he made me feel like I was someone important in his life. So I enjoyed the evening in spite of a couple of bittersweet moments thinking of Juan. My mind almost heard the sound of his 'Aws' each time a tremendous display was shot into the sky. So I felt guilty…feeling I had cheated him out of something beautiful. The only thing that appeased the guilt was that I finally realized Juan wouldn't have wanted to fight the crowds, and that we wouldn't have been there anyway. Surprisingly, Matt never got angry even while fighting the huge crowds to return to the car. Usually, I was blamed for something like that.

I cannot recall the happenings on the Fourth of July. I remember that Juan and I did talk about the fireworks and that I felt terrible once Juan expressed his feelings.

"Recharred, you did not wait very long ofter you talked to Endira because I came in about fifteen minutes ofter you called. Ond, Recharred, I called immediately ond Mario said you left about ten minutes ago. Thot means, Recharred, you only waited five minutes ofter you called. You never gave me any time to call you back!" I quickly asked if Endira had told him I left one message after another on her tape.

"Recharred, I even waited an hour ond called your house but you were not thar either," Juan said quickly while nodding a 'No.' "Aw, Recharred, how could you do thot to me? I wanted to go so badly." I realized he was trying to make me feel guilty and he was succeeding, even though he had to know his stubbornness was at fault. Still, I felt terribly guilty listening to him go on.

"Recharred, I wanted to go with you to the fireworks so badly because I read in the paper thot it was gonna be spectacular. Ond do you know, Recharred, I cried while I was watching it on television. My mother even asked why I was crying ond I did not know whot to tell her."

I didn't tell Juan I went with Matt to the fireworks. He guessed it, which opened up another can of worms. His nasty remarks continued, and yet he still made the evening enjoyable. That was what made him so exceptional. He could be hurt and angry but would never completely close the door to enjoying my company.

I tried to make amends, insisting we do something special the next night.

"I could call Jacque and have her get passes for a movie…how about doing that, Juan?"

"No, Recharred, I am going out with Marina tomorrow night…jus' the two of us." I quickly asked where and whether I could go along.

"No, you cannot go with us because I do not want you to be with me. Ofter all, you did not want me to go with you to the fireworks. No, you are not welcome, Recharred. Why don' you call thot queen with the blond curly tips, Recharred? I am sure he would love to go out with you tomorrow night. Why don' you do thot, Recharred?" I shook my head in disbelief.

"Juan, why are you being this way…you know we planned on spending Saturday and Sunday together…and that is what I really want…c'mon now, Juan?" My pleading did no good because he sat there as belligerent as ever.

"Well, Recharred, thot is not whot I want. You cannot come with us ond thot is final!" I still insisted and he wouldn't give in, continuing to antagonize me with one remark after another about Matt.

"Juan, don't you understand? I want to be with you! He asked me to go out tonight, but I told him I was going out with you!"

"No, Recharred, I will feel better when you 'ave a date with him ond then cancel it because you want to go out with me! Then I will be happy, Recharred."

"Juan, you are totally unreasonable?!"

"No, Recharred, I am JUAN!"

After he left for the evening, I called Marina and was told they were going to the Baton to see a drag show. I quickly explained the mess to her.

"So, Marina, I'm gonna go there myself and wait in the lobby for the two of you."

"Ratchard, what if Juan gets angry and won't go in with you? What will happen then?" I explained I would leave.

"But, Marina, I'm certain he won't get angry because I know Juan! He knew I'd call you if I really want to be with him. He needs to have me pay for my sins, as he always says…and he wants me to chase him because it assures him of my love for him." She understood my rationalization and agreed not to tell him my plan. I was a bit nervous for fear it would backfire but finally realized I had to depend on my inner feelings…that this was exactly what he wanted me to do, and the excitement was pouring out of my every pore! I somehow had to make Juan understand…that he was me!

It was obvious Matt was pissed, though he still tried to give the impression that he wasn't disturbed once I told him I was going with Juan to the Baton. I never told him the real plan. Because, after all, it was the 'space' he always seemed to desire.

I tried to persuade Juan once more Saturday afternoon when I called but he held his ground. I decided before letting on that I knew, to let well enough alone.

"Well, Juan, if that is what you want, have a good time."

"Yes, Recharred, thot is whot JUAN wants!"

My apprehension was getting the best of me waiting in the small lobby for them to arrive. What if once he sees me, he turns and walks out in anger? I finally forced myself to concentrate on my inner feelings…that this is what Juan wants me to do. And I suddenly began feeling like a kid waiting for his first date. It was very odd because Matt never crossed my mind. No, I was waiting for Juan. A thought suddenly came into my mind. What if they arrived early and were already in the club? After all, Marina always is on time. My fears were quickly snuffed out once I inquired whether their reservations were picked up to hear they weren't. So I continued my nervous pacing, sometimes stepping out into the street to see if I could spot them walking towards the club. Finally, there's Marina driving by, and beside her seated in the passenger seat...Juan! Her car turned at the corner and was out of sight.

My heart stood still for fear they'd never turn the corner, especially since Juan had looked directly at me in passing. The few minutes seemed like an eternity, but finally, there they were...'Mutt and Jeff' turning the corner...Marina, in high heels, towered over a head higher. The two of them looked so funny and I could've burst into laughter any other time, but not this time. It was what Juan always dreaded each time he went out with her. Once they were a few steps away, Marina acted out her role well, calling out in surprise,

"Ratchard!... How are you?" Juan didn't say a word, but this was a good sign.

"I'm fine. Hi, Marina...hi, Juan! Would it be all right if I go in with you?" Juan didn't smile but he quickly said something that made me realize he was happy to see me, because the only time his voice would be in this elegant pitch was when he was feeling good.

"It is a free country, Recharred...is it not? If you want to come here, thot is your privi-ledge. You 'ave a right to go anywhere you wish." We were seated at the bar, which were excellent seats since it was a raised area. Marina sat herself to Juan's left and it was perfect because the other stool was to his right. Juan continued in his elegant manner and I was pleased, realizing he was performing for me instead of ignoring my presence. He realized I knew his every mood and this was definitely a happy one. I also realized in order for his happiness to be complete, he had to then change into his normal self by laughing and talking in awe about the show. I needed that revelation, and once he began talking about the queens and mimicking some of their funny actions, it arrived!

My only concern was Juan was drinking vodka and diet coke. I also realized that this wasn't a good time to badger him about drinking. None-the-less it was like old times and I didn't want it to end. He was laughing and making me laugh, only to 'laugh' harder once he heard me react to his funny sayings.

"Recharred, I would really like to go out dancin' tonight. Would you like to go dancin', Recharred? It has been so long since we 'ave been dancin'." The thought of dancing again with Juan was wonderful. It had been so long...not since the evening I met Phillip and Kent. Besides, the activity would wear off the alcohol.

Marina chose not to join us and it was perfect because then she wouldn't have to drive the long distance to take Juan to his mother's. He could stay over my house, and then we'd be together on Sunday, too.

We headed for the car with Juan talking in that fast-paced manner of his. Of course, he didn't miss raising his arms and waving them as only he could to show how happy he was. In fact, he danced all the way to the car.

I felt so good and should have driven on to one of the bars on the north side without asking. Instead, I asked which one we should go to.

"No, Recharred, I want to go to the bars near your house because they both 'ave dancin'," Juan answered with a definite change in the tone and mood of his voice. It was definitely a tone of sarcasm, almost challenging. This was exactly what I didn't want to do since the possibility of Matt being there was so strong. I was quite sure this was exactly what Juan was thinking. He was very high, yet sober enough to be conniving. There was no mistaking his manner…yes, there definitely was some mischief in the air…and not in any funny way. It was apparent he wanted to see my reaction should Matt be there.

"Whot's the matter, Recharred, are you afraid thot the curly blond tips will be thar?" Juan probed, holding tight onto his sarcasm.

"Juan, he probably could be at one of them and I don't want you to be upset if you see him. C'mon now, Juan, will you promise me you won't get angry and make a scene? We're having such a wonderful time and I don't want it spoiled."

"Are you afraid he will see us together ond then he will know we were out tonight?" Juan inquired sarcastically. "Is thot whot you are afraid of, Recharred…is it?" I tried to explain how ridiculous his reasoning was but it did no good. He never listened when I told him I declined an offer to go to a movie with Matt telling him I was going to the Baton with Juan.

"Juan, why can't we just go on the north side and have a good time like we always did?" There, however, was no way I could change his mind.

My insides felt sick…I knew Juan, and certain a confrontation this evening with Matt could only be disastrous. All I could do was pray Matt decided on the Chicago bars this evening. Then, this could all backfire on Juan. I also realized that should Matt not be at the first bar that Juan would insist we move on to the other one. There was no getting away from it. Somehow, he was out to hurt himself and I couldn't understand his reasoning. It was almost as though he had planned it this way. But then I realized this couldn't be because I certainly knew when he truly was having a good time. This has to be the alcohol finally getting him to that state…like the many times after my episode with Ed many years before. The anger eating at his insides finally erupts with excessive drinking.

Juan decided upon the Nutbush and very apparent he's out to find someone once we entered. The happy mood was completely gone. My nerves were shot as I tried to casually case the place to see if Matt was present. Juan, though, was completely obvious. His eyes searched the room like a cat ready to attack a prey and because of it, refused once I asked to dance. His mind wouldn't consider anything but his original intentions…being the hunter! It didn't matter that he would be the one who was then hurt.

Matt was nowhere in sight once we entered the disco room, giving me some relief and I again asked Juan to dance. He didn't answer and just stood in one spot, his eyes searching the room. Finally, he nudged my waist.

"See, Recharred, he jus' walked in…did you not see him walk by wearing his very tight short shorts. Thar he is moving his hips like a queen," pointing him out, "Miss Big Hips!" And that's exactly what I saw him doing! What was I to do? It also never occurred to me why he didn't say anything as he passed? However, Richard always was a gentleman, and there's no exception this time…I must acknowledge him. Juan tensed up once I explained this to him.

"No, Recharred, you do not 'ave to go ond cater to him! Recharred, he saw you! He should 'ave greeted you! No, you do not 'ave to cater to him!" Juan screamed, "If you go thar, I am not gonna stay here! Recharred, I am gonna leave right now ond I want you to come too!" With that, he turned angrily and stormed out of the room and the bar! I didn't know what to do! I should have followed him, especially since Matt never focused in my direction. Instead, my body was hesitating in both directions. In a stupid and rash decision, I finally rushed over to Matt, clumsily took hold of his hand to shake, while he continued his hip movements not really seeming to care whether I was there or not.

"Hi, Matt, I'm here with Juan." I was bewildered when he didn't say a word and acted as though I was someone cruising him. "Juan just left and I have to go after him." My confusion doubled and without any further hesitation, I hurried out. In my turn out of the room, my eyes caught a glimpse of Matt still swaying his hips!

Juan was fuming once I reached him and so nervous he actually was trembling. I was miserable and tried to plead with him to calm down, but he raged on.

"There he was, Miss Big Hips with the bleached blond-tipped-curly hair! Ond thar you are catering to him! Recharred, you are so dumb! You make him take advantage of you…making him treat you like a fool!" It was impossible to settle him down or to have him even listen to any explanations because all he wanted was for me to drive him to his mother's. I tried to reason with him but my pleas were futile…so futile.

Juan didn't say another word as I drove except to object fiercely whenever I attempted to turn back towards my house, even threatening to jump out of the car. He refused to listen to anything I tried to say. My mind was swimming in every direction because I didn't want Juan to have any stress, and now it was completely encompassing him! I tried again to convince him to return with me once I parked. Instead, he jumped out of the car and slammed the door violently. I felt sure the window would shatter in a million pieces as it did years ago when he was angry with me, only this time my heart was breaking and all because of my stupid loyalty to people.

My drive home had to be one of the loneliest in my entire life, trying to comprehend why I didn't merely drive to the north side instead of asking Juan. He would have complained for a while…but just until we were in one of the bars and he realized there wasn't any threat of seeing Matt. I know once he heard the music we would have been dancing. Now, there wasn't any music and we weren't dancing….

Chapter Fifty-Four:
Believe as I

This had to be the first time in seventeen years Juan held onto his stubbornness for more than half a day because I wasn't able to reach him for several days. Each time I called, it was either 'Juan no home' or 'Juan cannot come to phone…do medicine now.'

I was a basket case because he didn't need this happening in his life. He needed me as much as I did him! So I'd leave my code name in hopes he'd finally call. I hated using another name…not now…everything was too important to be playing games. But my reasoning told me I should…he certainly didn't need another problem in his life.

To add to my depression, the landlord told Mario and me that we'd have to leave by the end of the month. We knew it was inevitable. After all, we hadn't paid rent for four months, and that amounted to thirty thousand dollars! We finally realized he had been more than patient and fair with us, and enough is enough. We had three weeks to dispose of everything, which meant we would be kept quite busy.

Juan finally answered his phone on the twelfth of July, and to my wonderful surprise, he was his usual charming and witty self. He was again the Juan I knew. He appeared to lay to rest his objections to my friendship with Matt. However, his way of acceptance was to completely ignore Matt even existed, and this was fine with me because I still was so unsure of where the relationship was going. Juan knew about the gallery and I believe this brought him around. He had too much compassion to ignore me at a time like this. In fact, he was hurting more than me.

"Aw, Recharred, how I wish thot I had the money because then you would never 'ave to worry. Believe me, Recharred…it would be yours."

I was very busy but still managed to drive those roads to Juan's. And he was still JUAN because he wouldn't let up once I began cooking in his kitchen, especially Italian tomato sauce. He'd go on endlessly reprimanding my messy cooking manner.

"Never, never am I gonna clean the kitchen before Recharred gets here!" he'd rant, even though he wouldn't have it any other way…he loved it!

Music was still so much a part of Juan and even though I was a singer and loved it myself…somehow while with him, it became more special! It was always there with us, especially while driving. It was always common to hear his praises for our compatibility.

"Recharred, I am so happy you like the same music as me ond especially Spanish music. I am so lucky to 'ave you in my life."

The bathroom was between each of the bedrooms at my place and since the beds were on opposite walls, when the doors were left open, I'd see Juan lying on his side reading his usual book before falling asleep. After biding him a good night, I'd throw a kiss. He'd roll his eyes but it was always obvious that he loved my attention because as I kept it up, he'd suddenly give me his double take and stare with his owl look. And then we'd repeat the scene again.

I really wanted Juan to move in with me once he returned to Chicago, but for the present, decided not to mention it to Matt. However, every time I brought it up to Juan, he'd refuse, insisting I didn't have enough room. I kept persisting because, for one thing, I'd help pay my mortgage and leave him enough money to do the special things he wanted to enjoy.

"Recharred, I would like for you to look for me. You know what I like, Recharred, so you con look around in your neighborhood because then I con go to the VA near your house. Or you con look downtown because then I con go to the hospital near there. Would you be so kind to do thot for me, Recharred?" I looked, though reluctantly.

I remember Matt harassing me because he felt I wasn't spending much time looking for one. Each time I reported the progress to Juan, he, too, was aware of my lack of enthusiasm. When questioned, I'd merely say I wanted him to move in with me. So he managed to do some searching with Svetmana, concentrating on the downtown area. This led me to believe she'd influence him in taking one because of the prestige…and then saddled with a high rent.

One morning, Juan called and again pulled me out of the shower, and even though I begged to call him back, he insisted on going on.

"Because, Recharred, I want to talk to you now because I am in the mood. When you call later, I might not be in the mood to talk."

"Aw, c'mon now, Juan, you're doing this on purpose! I know you…you just want me to drip on the rug!"

"Yes, thot is me, Recharred…thot is JUAN," he said, laughing in his contagious manner. "Recharred, thar are two places I want you to go see…they are near my old apartment on Eighth Street. Two high-rise buildings on the south end of Michigan Avenue," and after telling me the addresses asked, "do you think you can go thar today…would you please do thot for me, Recharred? You know whot I like, Recharred, do you not?" His excitement was so charming I could never refuse. He knew his likes were always my likes but still had to remind me in his little boy voice,

"No, I don't. What do you like?" I teasingly asked. Of course, he acted surprised.

"Aw, c'mon, Blanche, you know whot I like?"

"Then why do you ask, Juan, when you know 'I know' what you like?"

The buildings were only a block from each other and I found myself very disappointed after being shown apartments in the newer one. However, I was tremendously impressed once I entered the large foyer of the older building, and especially after being greeted by a very lovely and personable young Black lady. I was even more impressed upon seeing the apartments because, although the building was quite old, it had character and elegance, and I was certain Juan would love them.

I wanted Juan to come live with me very badly but somehow I got caught up in the same excitement that would always take hold of him after seeing an apartment he liked so much. I couldn't wait to call him.

"I know you're gonna get very excited about the way you want to decorate it once you see them, Juan,"

"I am, Recharred? Aw, I'm so glad you finally found something nice!" He made immediate plans to come in to see them.

"Recharred, Svetmana said she would like to come with us to see the apartments ond she is supposed to drive here to your apartment so we con all go together," Juan said as we were getting ready to leave for our appointment with the young lady at the building. But it was already an hour past the time and Juan was becoming quite nervous because he could not tolerate tardiness since he himself was always very punctual.

"Recharred, she is never on time for anything! I 'ave never seen anyone so irresponsible! C'mon Recharred, we will go ourselves. The hell with her! She is already over an hour late ond we cannot wait any longer because we are already late for our appointment." I quickly wrote a note with the address of the place to leave down in my lobby.

"Recharred, I don' know why you are writing a note," Juan quickly commented upon noticing my action, "we will probably be back before she arrives. Last time I was ot my mother's, she was to come with me somewhere ond did not show up until four hours later, ond I had gone ond come back already." I still left the note.

Juan began talking about Svetmana and her moods once we were on our way as he had done so many times before and there was such a feeling of despair in his voice.

"Recharred...you know I really don' like Svetmana. She really is a miserable ond nasty person." I didn't want him talk in this manner. He needed to have love in his heart at this time.

"Juan, you don't really mean that...you're just angry and disappointed in her now."

"No, no, Recharred, I mean it! She is really a nasty person. You know whot she did to me again, Recharred? The last time she came to my house she again started to scream ot me for no reason ot all…ond she again ran into the bedroom, slammed the door…ond then stayed there all night! She did not even come out to eat! She is so miserable! Ond then, Recharred, she does not want to work. She has cleaned my kitchen a couple of times when she was in a good mood…ond do you know how long it takes her? Half a day, ond she does not clean anything but the outside of the refrigerator and the stove…ond the sink! She does not clean the oven! How can it take anyone four to five hours to do thot?" I didn't know how to answer.

"Aw, Recharred, she does a good job, especially around the faucet of the sink…she uses a toothbrush ond gets all the grime out…I 'ave never seen anyone so slow…so slow. Recharred, she has disappointed me so much ond I know she will never change because her mold is made. The only time she has made me proud is when she drew that copy of the movie poster. I was proud because she did it for me because she knew I loved movies from the thirties so much. Recharred, she will be twenty-two years old ond thot is the only thing I 'ave ever been proud of her doing. It is a shame…really a shame." I was surprised to hear it took her over a year to copy it. I tried to persuade him not to swear at her whenever she was in one of her nasty moods and to finally stop being the one to apologize when she was the one who did something wrong.

"No, Recharred, I do not do thot anymore. Now she comes to me to say she is sorry."

"Well, then, Juan, you're too easy. I know because I've seen how you act once she does come around. Instead of correcting her faults, you make all over her like she did no wrong. So she's won! And she's gonna do it again because you never give her a chance to admit to being selfish or nasty whenever she gives a faint indication of remorse. You immediately start hugging her and before she can say anything else, you begin telling her how much you love her." He had no response to this and changed the subject instead.

"Recharred, you know John is pretty bad now. Do you know he also has CMV like me? He is very bad, though, because he is already goin' blind. His childhood friend is taking care of him. Thot is why he moved next door to her. He told me he is gonna put her as beneficiary on his Army insurance. So she will receive the fifty thousand when he dies. Do you know he told me he is still gonna 'ave the party in his new place around Christmas time. I don' know how he is gonna be able to do it because he can hardly see. But he still insists. I hope he can, Recharred, I really do." As Juan talked my mind drifted back to 1987…months after he and I had our wonderful trip to Boston and Cape Cod….

"Recharred, I asked Amanda ond Patti to come over tomorrow. John also called ond I asked him to come, too. You don' mind do you, Recharred?" I always got a kick out of his polite requests, even though he knew he didn't have to ask. Of course, John and I weren't bosom buddies but Juan liked him and that was enough for me. This was to be the first time Amanda and Patti were to meet John and once everyone arrived, we decided on eating Chinese out.

"Jesus, John really acts so feminine!" was Amanda's bewildered sigh once John excused himself from the table to go to the restroom. Of course, John had brought along his little hand puppet teddy bear, which only confirmed these traits. Juan quickly explained that he had asked him not to act so feminine many times, but that it did absolutely no good.

"Ond you know me, Amanda, when I am drunk it does not matter how he acts."

"Believe me, Juan…we know you," Amanda sighed with a smile.

I had suggested we go bowling after dinner because it was something Juan and I never did do together. All were in favor and it proved to be a ball, especially watching Juan try to fit his fingers in a ladies ball.

"Well, thot is a little better than the last time I bowled," Juan cried out after his first ball curved sharply into the gutter, "thot time the ball flew out of my hand ond went down the alley next to mine!" Juan never hit a 100 and mine wasn't much over while Patti soared. But, as always, Juan's praises of appreciation were there once the night came to an end.

"Recharred, we 'ave to do thot again…I really liked it…I really did."

Juan loved the apartments as I expected, and his constant charming chatter completely captivated the young gal. He was his usual self as he talked endlessly about every which way they could be decorated and that his daughter sometimes stayed overnight, explaining why he wanted two bedrooms. His excitement grew with every apartment and he finally decided on one of which there were two available…one with a lake view and one with a skyline view. We then agreed the skyline view would be best because the lake view would be so black at night. The application needed to be filled out and so we headed to the office. Juan's excitement was exhilarating.

"This is my official notice listing the amount I will be receiving in disability payments each month," Juan said, handing her his copy of the official document. "As you can see, I will receive twenty-two hundred dollars clear each month. So there will be no problem in paying my rent." I asked to see the document once she handed it back after making a copy to attach to the application. One statement in the form, however, bothered me. "The reason for eligibility to receive disability benefits is because Sergeant Sursedicius has contacted a viral infection." Once we left the office, I told Juan I was bothered by the statement…that they may discriminate.

"Recharred, I am sure they would never let thot influence their approval."

I then spotted Svetmana walking towards us as we were about to get in the car and quickly made Juan aware of it.

"See, she is late the same amount of hours as thot other time…four hours! Can you believe thot, Recharred?" Svetmana never walked fast in her life and there was no exception this time as we waited forever for her to approach.

"Hi, Daddy, I drove all the way to Richard's, so that's why I'm late."

"Aw, c'mon, Svetmana, when we left the house, you were already an hour ond a half late ond we 'ave been here for two ond a half hours! Too bad you cannot be on time. You missed seeing the bea-u-ti-ful apartment I rented." As always, she whined a mild apology, and as usual, Juan forgot his disgust and hugged her tightly. "Aw, my darlin', wait until you see how bea-u-ti-ful it is ond the great view I will 'ave of the city!" And again, as usual, she quickly broke away from him. And, again, Juan seemed oblivious to her apparent eagerness to escape his embrace, and joyously raised his arms instead.

"Aw, Svetmana, I am so happy…so happy!" His eyes were glowing as he again took hold of her to hug. She, on the other hand, showed absolutely no emotion whatsoever as she pushed herself from him.

"Oh, c'mon now, Daddy!" she whined, almost appearing to be ashamed because he loved her. I never understood it because this is what I always remembered Svetmana doing each time he embraced her during her life. Juan had to be one of the most affectionate and loving persons in this world…so this behavior of hers always baffled me? I never spoke of it to Juan and never really knew if he was aware of it. And I certainly wouldn't want to hurt him more by my reminder. His cover-up for her complaints about his embracing was usually said.

"Aw, but, my darling, I am so happy ond I want to show you how much I love you!"

We were going out for dinner and Juan insisted she join us and as Svetmana turned to walk towards her car, I said my usual, "Bye now," and immediately, she sarcastically mimicked my very words. Of course, Juan never noticed her obvious ridiculing and didn't say a word, so she felt content about making fun of me. Juan had the gift of making his mimics funny, but Svetmana's were exactly what she intended them to be…cutting and insulting! My daughters were young when they babysat Svetmana who was only four years old and they still complained about her rude manner and insulting ways. I also remembered the time Geena told me Juan had stopped by in the afternoon with Svetmana, who was then a teenager.

"I had my hair in rollers, Rich, and do you know what that Svetmana sarcastically asked? 'I hope you are not going to keep those on all the time we are here!' Oh, Rich, I wanted to smack her in the face…the smart alec!"

Exactly what I suspected…happened! I received a message to call the apartment complex and was devastated once the young lady informed me Juan had not been approved, trying vainly to give me one cock and bull excuse after another as the reason. I couldn't believe it and a slow burn began rushing to my head. Even though I realized this sweet girl probably had nothing to do with this decision, I still erupted.

"You know what I think? I think there has been some discrimination involved here…and damn it I don't like it!" This had to be the first time I ever blew up this quickly.

As usual, it began to prey on my mind and I was livid by the time I called Juan.

"Recharred, I do not understand why I did not pass the credit check because I had someone who works for the bureau see if my repossessed car is still on my record...ond he told me I was clear. So, Recharred...why?" I told him he should have never shown them his disability approval forms.

"Because, Juan, it clearly stated the reason you were receiving benefits...because you had contacted a viral infection. So what do you think they thought of immediately?"

"Thot I 'ave AIDS? Do you really think thot is whot they thought, Recharred?"

"Juan, I am sure of it! You will be getting enough money to afford the rent, and, besides, you were too nice to be refused. I am sure the girl gave you a great character reference. It was because they saw that statement on the form!"

My anger began increasing the more I thought of it...in the same delayed manner I always experienced during my life when I was insulted or taken advantage of. Those assholes were discriminating against Juan because he has AIDS! I immediately began talking excitedly.

"Juan, this is not right...not right at all! I'm gonna call there tomorrow and demand to see the manager! And Juan, once I see him, I'm gonna blast the hell out of him! Oh, he is gonna be sorry after I get done with him! Do you know you can have a good lawsuit against them? Oh, is he gonna know about that!"

"Recharred, I would never 'ave the nerve to do thot. I would accept their decision ond not say any more. Recharred, I am so happy to 'ave you on my side. You are so strong when you are fighting for something you believe in." A catch in my throat became quite evident.

"Yes, Juan, I believe in you, and you don't deserve this...because, Juan, you are someone who is sincere and honest...and because you have AIDS doesn't mean you are a criminal or a leper!" You can be sure Juan lightened my mood.

"I am so happy I 'ave Blanche D'Mella on my side!"

I arrived exactly at the appointed time and was greeted by a cowering manager and realized I certainly had him by the balls. I showed great strength as I talked seriously and calmly about Juan...about the beauty of this man...how well he always maintained every apartment and how his first concern always was to pay his obligations. I then spoke of the terrible disease Juan was so unfortunate to have...how unfair it was. My emotions finally took hold and I broke down in tears. I managed to compose myself enough to finish my complaint and was aware that, even though he was moved, it was quite evident the worry of a lawsuit was on his mind. Instead of denying my accusations, he humbly suggested Juan re-apply...that they would be happy to reconsider. I surprised him when I didn't jump at the offer.

"I will tell Juan, but I'm not sure he wants to live here anymore. He is a very proud man and couldn't live in a place once he knew he was being discriminated against." As I headed to leave the office, I slowly turned my head to him and stared. "You will, however, hear from us again, even though Juan does not decide to accept your offer!... Good-bye and thanks."

Juan really laughed once I explained everything that transpired and praised me for my strength. Unfortunately, we didn't move ahead with a lawsuit because everything ganged up on us...like my move out of the gallery and Juan's frequent but short hospital stays with one malady bout after another. He also was informed that his present lease was expiring October 31 instead of August 31 because of an error when filled out. It was all so consuming.

An accomplishment Svetmana could lay claim to and one I certainly commended her for was she made Juan realize he should give up smoking, and to do it cold turkey. Of course, he insisted I join him and I tried, but always seemed to resume while out drinking with Matt or whenever out chasing him in one of my fatal attraction pursuits. So when I craved a smoke while with Juan, I'd sneak into the bathroom or go on an errand. I had to realize I was only fooling myself since Juan had to be aware of my stupid deception.

"Recharred, you 'ave been smoking ond I thought you were quitting along with me? You know, you 'ave no willpower. Why can you not do it? If not for me...do it for yourself." He'd continue to plead and finally lunge for me, ending up in a hysterically funny struggle.

"C'mon, Recharred, give me those cigarettes because I am gonna tear them apart!" Sometimes he managed to wrest them from me and sometimes not...but we laughed until we were weak and that was what was important. It was really strange seeing Juan without a cigarette in his hand, especially since he always enjoyed them thoroughly while I didn't.

"Recharred, I would really like to help you move because I know you need it, but I am so afraid with this Hickman in my chest. Every time I strain a bit, it pulls ond hurts so much. Ond, Recharred, I get tired so fast...so fast. Do you understand, Recharred...do you?"

I wanted Juan to help more than anything in this world...because then he'd be well. I couldn't help but think of our many moves and how he managed to single-handedly set everything in place. My heart was breaking as I tried to control the catch in my throat.

"Juan, you know I do! Don't even question it because I know you'd be there for me. I thought of having you here just for company, but then realized you might forget yourself and pick up something heavy...so it is for the best. It will be fine, Juan, because Nicky has agreed to help one day and to let me use his truck for the rest of the move." I sat in silence after hanging up, wishing with all my heart that Juan would be there with Mario and me. That he'd be lightening our hearts and minds with one witty remark after another...and I cried...and I wished....

I never regretted anything as much as when I asked Matt if he'd help with the move. I couldn't believe he said it would spoil his weekend. And he kept reminding me about it...so much so that I felt uncomfortable throughout the entire day, wishing I'd never asked him. I was, however, grateful he didn't act in this manner when we delivered the furniture my sister, Geena, and daughter, Jacque, purchased. In fact, this was the first time Jacque was meeting Matt and I prayed he'd act as he always did in gay bars…very macho, and that she didn't suspect anything once she saw his curly blond tipped locks.

I was never so relieved once we finally finished because Matt made me absolutely miserable throughout the move. He had griped maliciously each time we were carrying a piece because I was moving too fast, or it was my fault he was scraping his hand against a door frame. During the entire day, I couldn't stop thinking of the many times Juan and I carried pieces of furniture while struggling because they might be slipping from our hands. Juan would make me laugh so much I'd almost pee in my pants. And, GOD, how we needed that beautiful diversion on this dreary day.

Somehow, Juan sensed Matt had been involved in the move and this was the only mention of him since his armistice.

"Whot did Mario say about him? Did he not wonder if he was a fag?" I completely ignored the question and decided not to mention going to Geena's or Jacque's or that Mario had asked whether he was gay the day following the first floor grand opening. Neither did I dare mention Matt's foul mood helping, because Juan surely wouldn't have let up on my stupidity.

The HIV support group Juan belonged to was conducting a special seminar and he decided to register in the course. I was in town the day of his second or third meeting and he insisted I join him that evening. I was not looking forward to it because the purpose of the course was to accept death. Juan was aware of my feelings because I could never hide my emotions from him. "Recharred, I know you do not want to believe I will die in the near future…but I do…ond I 'ave to come to terms with it."

"Juan, everyone is gonna die one day…we all know that!"

"Yeah, I know, Recharred, but I am gonna die sooner. I am not gonna live to thot ripe old age you think I am. No, Recharred, so I 'ave to face the fact! 'WE' 'ave to face the fact, Recharred!" Still, I would not face it and admit to it, continuing to hold onto my hope for a cure.

"Juan, I am twelve years older than you. I have to go before you because I wouldn't know what I'd do if you died before me." And while holding back tears, I pleaded, "How could I ever laugh again, Juan?" Juan immediately saw his opportunity to perform and contorted his face to look like a corpse.

"Jus' think Recharred, I will look like this." However, I wouldn't laugh. Of course, he continued to do it until I did. It was the same whenever he talked about going blind. He'd hold out his hand, helplessly, trying to find his way. Again, I refused to laugh, but he'd continue until I did.

I accompanied Juan to the meeting that evening and as we waited in the foyer for the moderator to arrive, he was his usual charming self introducing me to the others. Phillip and Kent were not present because I guess only those infected with full blown AIDS had signed up for the course. There were about twelve others…Black and White…AIDS did not discriminate. I found them all to be very friendly and warm, and could not seem to set it in my mind…that they were supposedly scheduled for early deaths. No! I completely put it out of my mind…especially regarding Juan.

The moderator invited me to join the circle, which pleased me since I'd have a problem hearing sitting on the sidelines. Everyone held hands as the moderator said a prayer and then he introduced a girl assisting that evening. They talked on the ultimate death each of the members were facing and the terrible burden of knowing they would not be living the long life everyone hoped for. They further explained that each and every one had to face it, but in a manner they, themselves, felt comfortable. I remember the serious and somber expression on everyone's faces, especially Juan, and as I watched him, a feeling of guilt came over me…because I was not also infected…that I was healthy….

"I want everyone to close your eyes and let yourself completely relax," asked the moderator, and then the assistant continued to say, "We want you to think of death…to imagine you have just died. We then want you to think of it as something beautiful and to picture yourself…to hold onto the pictures that come into your mind." The moderator then added, "Please, keep your eyes closed and let your mind take over. And please stay silent…we want it so quiet that we will be able to hear a pin drop." And it was quiet…so quiet I could almost hear the air stirring. I don't know how long we continued to keep our eyes shut, but I am certain it had to be quite some time. I remember trying to visualize a picture in my mind…but nothing would appear…and why? My only reasoning…I wasn't facing a death notice. I wondered if any of them felt as I. If they also believed they would be spared as I felt Juan would? It seemed like forever but finally the moderators asked everyone to open their eyes, and at the same time reminded them to hold onto as much of the vision as possible because, if they so desired…to share it with the group. I cannot recall any except for Juan's, and even at that, cannot repeat it word for word.

I can still see Juan sitting erect in his folding chair, describing every vivid detail with the aid of his hand and arm movements. What I do remember still remains in my heart because a feeling of pride came over me as I listened to his deep, clear, and resonant voice….

"It was very strange because I kept seeing one color ofter another as I walked from place to place. Ond as I approached each place, the colors became more vivid ond brighter. I remember the colors being very bea-u-ti-ful." If I recall correctly, Juan's vision was the only one the moderators attempted to fully interpret and together told him he was truly seeing something beautiful…that he was accepting his ultimate death.

The following week, I again accompanied Juan to the meeting, but this time was given a seat outside the circle. I had forgotten to bring my hearing aids and found it very difficult to follow. So it didn't take long to begin dozing off. Juan wasn't pleased once we left.

"Recharred, I don' believe you were falling asleep during the meeting! This was something serious ond I wanted you to hear it so you know I am accepting whot will happen to me." Juan seemed to understand once I explained everything, but still managed to scold me for forgetting my hearing aids.

I have to mention the time Juan called very excitedly about a barbecue Phillip and Kent invited him to and that the invitation was extended to me. It was impossible for me to go since it was the time of my move out of the gallery. I was so disappointed I had to refuse, and especially since I hadn't heard him this excited and happy for so long. My heart ached.

"Aw, Recharred, it is such a shame because they 'ave a nice backyard with a three-foot raised pool. I know you would love it because everything is so private ond we could relax ond be ourselves…. Aw, I wish you could be thar with me, Recharred…it would be so nice…so nice Recharred."… I couldn't help but think that Juan was reminding me of the Sunday afternoon we spent in someone's very private garden pool, when we first moved to Atlanta. It had been so beautiful since we didn't have to worry any neighbor might see us being playful lovers in the water. In fact, that afternoon had been one of the most beautiful days of our lives…we weren't worried about hiding our love. And even though everyone at the pool party was gay, this had to be the first time Juan consistently displayed his deep feelings for me.

"You know, Recharred, John has been very bad," Juan stated once I arrived. "He has been shittin' all over the house ond Mary has to clean up about two, three times a day. She told me John is almost totally blind now ond it is hard for him to move around because he moved thar when he was losing his sight…so he is not really familiar with the surroundings. Aw, Recharred, it is so sad…so sad."

"You know, Recharred, the movie, *Ghost*, is playing ot a theatre thot only charges one dollar to get in," Juan said once I arrived. "Why don' we go see it tonight…would you mind, Recharred? I 'ave read thot Whoopi Goldberg is so funny in it." Of course, I agreed. It also suddenly came to mind that in all the three years Juan lived here, we never had gone to a movie together.

"Isn't that something, Juan? Especially since we'd travel long distances to see a movie that was just released because you couldn't wait for it to come locally. And you wouldn't let up until we were on our way…sitting in the car very excited because you were going to see a much talked about movie, especially *Jaws*!… And then you didn't mind waiting in the long line to get in!" Juan laughed and then confessed.

"It is easier now to wait ond watch it once it is released on VCR."

Juan had imagined the movie to be a very funny ghost story from what he had read about Whoppi Goldberg's performance and wasn't prepared for the actual theme…a truly beautiful but sad love story of a young couple separated once he is tragically murdered by muggers. Juan didn't say a word once we walked out, which was totally opposite what I was accustomed to when Juan truly was happy he saw a movie. Once he began to talk, it was about the story line instead of the usual raving about the funny scenes. He could only think of the two lovers who were separated by death because of a twist of fate. The tears and sadness that were hers were preying on his mind and he was hurting. And mostly he talked about how sad, lonely, and frustrated the ghost was because he was cheated out of his life and his loved one, and I realized he was relating to it. This was the first time I had seen Juan depressed and truly angry about his illness…about knowing it was a matter of time and he, too, would die.

"I never expected it to be thot type of movie, Recharred," he cried out with a bit of anger in his sad voice. "I thought it was a funny ond scary ghost movie! I did not know it was about real people ond death, Recharred! If I had known thot, I would not 'ave gone to see it…because, Recharred, I do not want to be reminded thot I will die soon…ond thot I will die young, too! Because, Recharred, I want to live, as he wanted to live! I don' want to die, Recharred! Aw, Recharred, I am so angry…so angry…why did this 'ave to happen to me…why?" There was no answer I could give because I realized I couldn't again assure him of my beliefs…that a cure would be found! He didn't want to hear of my dreams at this time! He wanted only to wake and find this to be a bad dream. I cannot remember what I said, but my heart was breaking and I was silently praying and begging God to reconsider. If I had known what the movie was about, I would've never allowed him to see it…to have it tear him apart.

"Never, never Juan!"

So I finally realized Juan was putting on a happy face for me…that he, too, was praying for a miracle. He had to continue with his happy face because he had a dream just as I did! Yes, this dream belonged to both of us…and maybe now we will be heard.

* * * * * *

Juan finally laid his anger and depression aside to go on happily with our time together.

"Recharred, I talked with Barry in California the other day ond he asked if I would like to go thar for Thanksgiving…so whot the heck, I am gonna go. Ofter all I can pack enough of my medication in a cooler for five days. Do you not think thot would be nice, Recharred?'

"Oh, Juan, that will be wonderful because you have never been to California! Do you think Barry would mind if I came with you? Aw, Juan, I 'have' to be there as you 'aw' about everything! What do you think, Juan?"

"I don' think Barry would mind if you came, too…besides I want you to go with me." Of course he had to be certain I meant it and politely asked, "Do you really want to come with me, Recharred? Are you sure you do?" I let out a breath of disgust.

"Juan, why do you ask a silly question like that? You know I'd love it! By that time, you will be living in Chicago and we can fly from there." I had already decided Juan was going to live with me once he moved back and didn't want any arguments about it. He had tried to argue against it but once I insisted, it was all he needed to hear to have that glow of contentment on his face…and I knew I had made the right decision.

Juan then began talking excitedly about returning to Chicago, and it was so apparent he was happy to be coming to my house.

"Recharred, I want to go to so many places once I am back in Chicago. I want to really enjoy life! I want us to do so many things together…so many things we never could afford to do on a regular basis…to go to theatres…ballets…to go to the opera you love so much. Aw, so many nice places! Recharred, I really want to enjoy life while I am living!" I explained that I didn't know how I'd be able to afford any of it because I didn't even know if I'd have a job.

"Recharred, you will not have to worry…I will 'ave enough money to take you. I 'want' you to share all those things with me because you are the only person in this world I want to be with, ond I will be getting twenty-two hundred clear a month…ond since I will save quite a bit living with you…we can do all those things together." I looked at him and felt more positive than ever as I again reminded him we had time…and during that time, surely, a cure will come. Juan smiled, though it appeared to be a smile that graciously humored me.

"You know, Recharred, you are really gonna miss me when I die."

Chapter Fifty-Five:
Burrows and Memories

It was a wonder the highways to Indianapolis and back didn't have burrows from the many times I drove them during the months of August, September, and October. In fact, there were times I'd return home the same evening, and then head back the next day. And each time, I wanted to go…never did I feel I had to.

During those months, Juan only came to Chicago once and then I drove him. The hospital had given him an electric I-Vac pump to administer his medication and he didn't want to be away from it for any long periods of time, especially since the manual system didn't seem to work right after using the automatic. He also wanted to be home for his nurse when she came to check out his levels and to change his dressing. He looked forward to her visits and was still the charmer and captivator each time. It always seemed to appear as though Juan was Yvonne's favorite patient. There was no denying, she made him feel special.

Juan was quite proficient changing the dressing himself and I sometimes fetched things for him. He had such steady hands and would tease me once he saw mine shaking.

"Recharred, I don' know if you will ever be able to change my dressing because, Jesus Christ, look ot your hands shaking like a leaf!" He'd gasp once I handed him something else.

"My God, look ot your hands, man, they are trembling!" Of course, that wouldn't be enough because he then had to tease me, "Look ot yourself, Blanche, you are shaking like on old man!" His theatrics managed to go even further once finished and I sat next to him.

"Aw, c'mon, Recharred, move away from me," he'd say, sniffing in that exaggerated way of his and gesturing with his hands for me to move from him, "you even smell like an old man!" He was so believable, I almost thought I did smell, quickly whining in my defense.

"C'mon, Juan...what are you talking about? You know I don't smell that way?" Detecting my obvious distress naturally egged him to hand out more theatrics.

"Aw, Recharred, please move away from me," he'd gasp sniffing even harder and making queasy faces, "aw, Recharred, please move away from me...you 'ave thot old man smell!" He then shivered and added, "aw...ugh...you smell so bod, Recharred!" And he kept it up until I actually began smelling myself, only to see him finally end up in hysterical laughter, making me realize this was another one of his theatrical performances.

I had intended to go to Juan's the first weekend in August until he called to tell me Larry was taking him to see *Bye Bye, Birdie* at the Starlight Theatre, an enclosed outdoor facility. So I decided to make it Monday instead. Of course, this left me free to do my chasing after Matt. I didn't want to complain too strongly because I wanted him 'up' as much as possible. Besides I was happy for him because he was enjoying something he loved so much. I just wished I would've been able to go along. My mind reflected back to Atlanta, when we first moved there and had lots of money....

Juan had spotted an ad in the paper announcing a special series of eight Broadway musicals and said how wonderful it would be if we could send for tickets for the entire season. So I sent for season tickets because I could never refuse Juan, and at the same time also purchased tickets for Puccini's *Madame Butterfly* because then we could see the famous Fox Theatre. Unfortunately, all we ever saw was *Madame Butterfly* and two of the musicals. The others found us in front of the theatre selling our tickets during our bad times at the club....

Going into the second week of August, I became quite worried when Juan never responded to my messages left on his machine. In fact, I became frantic as the day went on. I was just about to call the hospital when the phone rang.

"Recharred, I hope you were not trying to call me because I did not stay home last night. Larry went on vacation ond will be gone until the twentieth, ond he asked if I would check on his cat every day or so to feed him ond clean the litter box. So I decided to sleep thar instead of driving home last night." After telling him how frantic I'd been, he went on to say it was possible he might stay a couple of nights more because Larry had cable television. He then said Svetmana was coming down for the weekend, which meant I wouldn't be able to go as planned.

So this left me free to see Matt and to go on with the guessing game. Of course, this only made my desire for him grow even more. I was still looking for the reciprocal relationship we once had and my ego just wouldn't let go until I proved he loved me, or that he was a whore. Unfortunately, neither one was surfacing, so I continued to dangle.

"Recharred, this is my last day to take care of Larry's cat, ond do you know they are 'aving a big outdoor fair on the grounds of the Benjamin Harrison home in honor of his birthday today!" Juan exclaimed in an early

Sunday morning call. "It is being sponsored by the Army ond thar will be free food ond drinks…ond tours of his home, Recharred. It is really supposed to be a nice affair, Recharred, ond it would be so nice if you were here to go with us…do you not think, Recharred?" His excitement got the best of me and even though I was planning to go three days later, I agreed on the same day trip.

The heat was horrendous, but Juan still had that way of making you forget it. The affair was really very nice…so much like a small town event and yet like a large garden party so reminiscent of ones we had seen in movies. The Army band was playing old forties songs much to our delight, and even nicer, Svetmana took off on her own. It was wonderful because I didn't have to listen to her sarcasm or nasty remarks about anyone who might be passing. One of the few times I ever remembered her being nice or friendly with me were when she used to cue me whenever I was rehearsing for a play. She liked acting and this gave her a chance to do a bit of it. In fact, it was the only time I ever remember her accepting criticism from me as I corrected her line deliveries.

"Recharred, this is real nice, is it not," Juan raved as we listened to the band play on…and it was…it truly was because I felt as though the two of us were walking the paths of yesteryears. Svetmana joined us for the tour of Harrison's home and as usual, Juan's awe for the history was awesome in itself.

Juan called a couple of times Wednesday morning to get my tail moving and I told him I'd call just before walking out of the door so he'd be certain I was on my way. I called exactly at 9:30 and walked in his place at 12:30, and as usual was greeted by the happiest person anyone could ever be fortunate to know—Juan. He had just finished his treatment.

"Aw, good, Recharred, you are on time ot last. Now, we can leave to go to Brown County right away. I made some sandwiches to take because I know how you 'ave to feed your belly." As he rushed me out I was informed he had to do his treatment a second time.

"So we 'ave to get going, Recharred, because I do not want to get home too late." He then asked for my car keys and said, "Recharred, I will drive thar because I know the roads better…then you can drive back because it is difficult for me to see well ot night. My eyes are very bad ot night. I hope I am not going blind already, Recharred?" This upset me.

"Aw, c'mon, Juan, don't talk like it is nothing to go blind. And don't think because you can't see well at night…that you're going blind. My father-in-law had that problem and would stay overnight at our house so he could drive home in the daylight…and he didn't go blind."

Juan was so excited because, at last, I was going to see Brown County State Park. As we neared the park, the scenery became more picturesque and Juan decided to stop and take pictures. I, of course, never liked to take a shot of scenery unless one of us was standing in the foreground. I spotted an outhouse on the other side of the road after he took a shot of me, and perfect because it was situated in a valley surrounded by a panorama of beautiful hills.

Juan decided I should take one of him with that background. The big grin on his face was perfect as he stood there holding his hands behind his back.

"Recharred, look how bea-u-ti-ful this is…ond it is nothing compared to the park! I cannot wait until you see it." As I looked at him I couldn't get over the glow on this man…or how handsome and strong he looked. He was so full of life! How could he be sick?

"Aw, Recharred, c'mon now! You spend money so foolishly ond then you complain about paying a couple of dollars to see something so bea-u-ti-ful?" Juan sighed once I complained in my penny-pinching way because there was a two-dollar entry fee. But it was true…that was me.

The park was truly beautiful…over 15,000 acres of wonderland! Somehow, though, everything looked familiar…as if I had been here before or dreamed of it. In fact, I somehow remembered complaining about the entrance fee before. I wasn't sure so I never mentioned it to Juan. I began taking pictures and usually, Juan objected to posing…this time, he didn't. We snapped one after another, not certain how they'd turn out because the sun had disappeared behind the high bluffs. The last spot we stopped to see was spectacular…Hesitation Point. Just before taking a shot of Juan, he raved about the beauty of the site.

"I jus' love it here! I could stay forever!" It never occurred to me what he really incurred.

Once we left the park, Juan insisted we drive into Nashville, which was only about half a mile down the road, the opposite direction we had driven in from. Before entering the main drag of the town, we stopped for gas and it was here I remembered all. We walked into the building to pay and, immediately, I recalled being there, because of the bakery counter just to the left of the door. Juan and I had been there when he first moved to Indianapolis on one of our sightseeing drives! Once I informed him, he also remembered.

"Yes, Recharred, now I remember buying those apple fritters for you! However, Recharred, we did not go into town thot time because we drove back the way we came." It certainly was odd that a bakery would be the thing to convince me I had been there before, especially since the sights were so spectacular in the park. I guess Juan was always right when he claimed, "Recharred, all you ever think about is to fill thot belly!"

Nashville was as quaint as Juan had said. A true tourist town filled with antique and collector shops, and housed in log-built buildings. I insisted Juan take a shot of me standing on the street, in front of the Nashville Playhouse and he abided but did it quickly because he again felt his old embarrassment of two guys taking pictures of one another. So when I tried to take one of him with the quaint shops as a background, he quickly declined and began to walk swiftly down the sidewalk, away from me. However, I did manage to get shots of his quick walk, swinging his arms strongly, with his back to the camera.

The only thing we had eaten all day was the sandwiches Juan had made, so I insisted on buying dinner.

"No, no, no, Recharred! It is much too expensive here to eat. I know because Svetmana insisted on it when we were here." My thoughts quickly figured the princess would do exactly that. Juan kept insisting we stop off at a MacDonald's but I wouldn't hear of it, and finally began seeking one out. Juan insisted on seeing the menus first in two very nice restaurants, and it was the same in both.

"Aw, Recharred, it is much, much too expensive here for you…never, never, never!" We finally came across a small place, which really didn't intrigue me because it looked like a neighborhood lunch hangout. However, the sign claimed they served 'home cooked meals' and we figured that might be better than any of the others. Juan didn't ask to see the menu.

The waitress indicated we could sit anywhere. That was no problem because there weren't any other patrons in the place. I realized Juan would never leave now. It'd be too embarrassing. So he continued on by charming the waitress with clever chatter. Once I saw the menu, I discovered it was more expensive than the others, and especially since the portions listed were so small. I ordered the fried chicken, which consisted of a small quarter portion and for sides they generously included one slice of tomato and two very tiny soft rolls…and all at a mere $8.95! I guess the atmosphere was included in the price? But I didn't care because Juan was excited about his special hamburger, "with lots ond lots of raw 'oonion' please, Ma'am." He also ordered a salad and seemed very satisfied with everything, so I wasn't going to spoil his pleasure by complaining about the prices and small portions. Richard, at last, held his tongue!

Juan's brows were rising and his eyes were sparkling as he took his first bite.

"Aw, Recharred, this is perfect…jus' perfect," and indicated so by kissing his fingers. God, how could anyone ruin that joy by complaining!

We continued to sit after I paid the check and as Juan talked on about the park, he suddenly noticed my hands resting on the table. My hands were never able to look completely relaxed…so they always appeared to be in a claw-like manner. Of course, he always made mention of them and performed some theatrics regarding their clumsy and ugly look. He was never one to miss out on a chance to mimic me, especially when he knew I always laughed hard after his performance. Besides holding his hand in an ugly claw form mimicking mine, he began contorting his face to look like the Lon Chaney silent film version of *Phantom of the Opera*. He knew he had a roll going because I couldn't stop laughing. So he kept teasing me.

"Whot's the matter, Recharred, with your hands…huh, Recharred?' And he managed to hold onto that Cheney face…so much so that I almost fell to the floor with laughter. This egged him on even more!

"Juan, your face is so ugly…aw c'mon now, my belly is hurting. Aw, Juan, I don't know how someone so handsome like you can make yourself so ugly! You look just like the phantom!" Suddenly a quick change of expression appeared. No one could appear more innocent and amazed.

"I do, Recharred? I really do?"

Juan suggested another route to return home and we were moving right along in good time, when suddenly there we were in the middle of a 'major' construction delay. The delays were frequent and as long as fifteen minutes each. It was very reminiscent of the snowstorm in 1975 back in Chicago when it took me seven hours to drive thirty-nine miles, only this time, the weather was hot and muggy. It didn't bother Juan…not until the delays got longer. He then became extremely agitated because he realized he had to administer a second injection before bed, and the process took four hours. His complaints continued and he had every right because this was also cheating us out of savoring the day, as he always enjoyed doing. I was getting very nervous because I knew he didn't need this stress, so I tried to change the subject. However, even though he calmed down, his spirits remained low and he once again spoke out about his illness, though not in the same angry manner as he did after seeing the movie *Ghost*. This time, he sounded almost as though he wanted to give up.

"Recharred, I am so tired of 'aving to sit ond wait for my medication to go into my blood. I am so tired of doing it every day now for five months! I 'ave to sit for eight hours every day, Recharred…ond I cannot do anything else! Ond, Recharred, do you know how weak it makes me? I 'ave no strength to do the things I loved to do. I cannot dance anymore like I used to ond you know how I loved to dance! Whot kind of quality of life is this?"

"Juan, you're still living well and you're still the witty person you always were," I shouted. "Don't say that isn't quality!" Still, his somber tone continued.

"No, Recharred, this is not living. I cannot do things while I am ot home. How can I ever think to go on a vacation again? Ond how I wanted to go to Santa Fe with you. I do not even know if we will be able to go to Barry's in California for Thanksgiving."

"Juan, we still can go there because we can pack enough medication in the cooler for five days! And we still can go to Santa Fe!"

"Yeah, I know, but whot kind of vacation is thot for you when you 'ave to sit around for eight hours waiting for me to finish?"

"Juan, you don't always have to do it twice a day…that has only been occasionally for about a week or so, and even if you do…so what? There still are eight hours and in that time, we can see and do so much! It's like you have a job for eight hours! Didn't we enjoy ourselves when we were both working? Juan, the most important thing is this medication is keeping you well and that is all I care about…more time to find a cure. I'm certain that's what you want!"

He finally laid his depression aside. However, his usual matter-of-fact attitude regarding his illness took over again. It was obvious he was feeling better. Yet, this matter–of-fact manner he used never made me aware of the seriousness involved. Listening to him casually mention he may very possibly go blind soon only tended to shove the crisis to the back shelf because it was delivered like a weather report. It never sank into my head because it was always down the road…five…ten years or so, and by that time, I was certain a cure would be found. Who knew?

We didn't get home until about eleven and as I feared, Juan insisted he was going to shorten his treatment, which meant he wouldn't be injecting the entire amount. No matter how I argued, he insisted.

The long wait finally led Juan into one of his playful moods. I hadn't smoked in front of him my entire stay because, supposedly, I gave it up the week before. Of course, it only lasted about two days and I was at it again. I just came out of the bathroom after smoking one and sat next to Juan. He then over emphasized one sniff after another.

"Recaharred, who do you think you are fooling? Me or you…whot do you say…huh?" I tried to act as though I didn't know what he was talking about and it only started him on his usual manner of fast interrogation.

"Recharred, I am no dummy…you know thot. Do you not know thot, Recharred, do you not…huh?" Instead of allowing me to answer, he went on, "So don' say you 'ave not started smoking again because I was not born yesterday, Recharred. I 'ave smelled smoke on you all the time you 'ave been here. I did not say anything because I wanted to see if you would tell me you could not wait to smoke again." He continued and finally held his hand close to his chest, as always when scolding me. He was so funny as he shook his finger in shame.

"Shame on you, Recharred, you 'ave no willpower ot all…no willpower. You are so easily tempted. Jus' like sex, ond then all you can think of is thot cock between your legs ond thot you 'ave to get your rocks off. Aw, Recharred, you are so bad…so bad!" Of course, this brought him down to hysterical laughter while I tried to remind him I had quit smoking eleven years when married and that my wife smoked one cigarette after another during all of it.

"I am just not ready to quit yet, Juan."

However, he did not yet want to abandon the harassment he was dishing out at me.

"You know, Recharred, thar will be a day you no longer will look younger than you are…ond then you will not attract the young guys anymore. Aw, Recharred, whot are you gonna do once your skin gets wrinkled ond begins to sag?" Naturally, both of us ended up in hysterical laughter as he tried to wrinkle his face and push his nose down and against his lips to give me a preview of what I might expect to happen.

Just prior to informing Amanda about Juan's illness, I realized I needed someone to confide in to give me support, and who could eventually be there for Juan, too. After all, Marina never communicated with me after I told her. I had figured since Juan told Hank while in his jealous anger the evening of the New Year's Eve party, I certainly had every right to break my promise and tell Daniel, and especially since Hank never so much as called to inquire how Juan was doing. It certainly proved Juan's statement of "Recharred, I like 'Hank' very much ond he is so much fun because he is so crazy…but let's face it…he is really jus' like the bar friends thot we had met and liked through the years. Once he goes home, you never hear from him."

Daniel certainly was the contrary. He kept in constant touch and I could always expect to receive advice should I bring up a problem, so I was certain I had made the right decision by confiding in him. Daniel also kept after me to convince Juan that he should tell him about his condition himself. When I finally was successful in convincing him to confide in Daniel, he was so pleased because of the tremendous support he got from him. Daniel talked so openly with him about his illness, and he liked that.

While we were talking, I mentioned Daniel had sent his very best, which pleased Juan to know he was thought of.

"I 'ave really found I like Daniel very much," Juan said after a moment of thought. "He is a bit crazy ot times ond wants his way, but when you think of it…so am I. The main thing is he is a very sincere person who cares, ond thot is whot is important. I was not sure when I first met him if I wanted him as a friend because his ideas on sex were a bit wild ond he seemed to be so gay. Remember thot time he invited me to come along with you for dinner ot his ex-lover's restaurant? I was so surprised because he hardly knew me ot the time, Recharred?"

"He is that kind of person, Juan. He knew we were close and made sure he invited you along. One thing Daniel has never been…is cheap." Juan began to laugh as he recalled, "I will never forget how he was talking as he drove us home thot night…I thought he was crazy!"

"You mean when he told us about the guy everyone in his old crowd was after?"

"Yeah, Recharred, the guy with the three-inch diameter cock! Remember he said he was ofter him for so long ond thot he finally was lucky to get him?"

"I remember, Juan…especially when he said he was determined to accommodate his three inches! I think that was the first time I ever saw you shocked, and when you didn't come up with some witty remark, I was certain of it."

"Recharred, I could not believe it! I could not understand how he could boast about it? I would 'ave been ashamed to tell anyone."

"Juan, Daniel has never denied being a whore…so it doesn't matter to him what anyone thinks of his escapades. At least he has always been honest about his wild desires. Maybe this guy came close to fulfilling his fantasy about a horse?"

"Aw, Recharred, thot is so funny!"

In spite of my objections, Juan cut the treatment short and headed for his bedroom. As he sat on the edge of his bed, he went through a ritual he had begun to do every night before retiring…to check his legs and body for any lesions that might possibly have broken out. Fortunately, none ever appeared like many other AIDS patients who were shackled with them. So I sat next to him in silence as I always did before going to my room, savoring the joy of being with him. As always, he remained quiet, intent on searching his body, and then suddenly he gave me one of his looks of "What are you doing, man? Are you strange or something?" Though, as always, it was apparent he relished my attentive gazes.

I started for my room, and just as I made the turn through the doorway I quickly poked my head back as I always did to say, "Good night, Juan...sleep tight," throwing a kiss his way. After a couple of seconds I poked my head in again in a very quick motion. Of course, there he is doing a double take and giving me his owl stare!

Juan was already doing his treatment in the morning.

"Recharred, you are so ter-ri-ble when you sleep!" he bellowed after a happy smile to see me. "You snore so loudly...aw so loud. You woke me up a couple of times...ond even ofter I closed your door, I still could hear it. You were so loud I wanted to put a cork in your mouth."

I insisted on making his special frittata for breakfast.

"Do you think you can make it like I do, Recharred?" I told him he could coach me.

"Yeah, Recharred, but then you are gonna make a mess in the kitchen ond I jus' cleaned it real good before you arrived. No, no Recharred...you are gonna make a big mess. I will make it myself." I finally convinced him I'd clean everything, because if he interrupted his treatment, he'd have to sit there longer.

While cooking, I noticed he again had put the vitamins away in the cupboard.

"Juan, why do you always put these vitamins I left out for you away in the cabinet? I can tell from looking at the amount that you haven't been taking them. So what if two small bottles sit on your counter? They don't make it look messy!"

"Recharred, whot is it gonna do for me? Do you think it will keep me alive? No, it will not, so it is a waste of money ond time."

"Juan, it's proven, vitamins keep you healthier...so please leave them out to remind you to take them?"

Once I tasted a forkful of my concoction, I found it wasn't near as moist as Juan's. So I wasn't too happy as I brought him a plate, yet hoping he might not notice.

"Well, Recharred, this is the official test. Let us see if you can make it as well as I do." He scooped a small forkful and placed it ever so gently into his mouth, and it was amazing how majestic he looked doing it! It was as though he was the official judge. Better yet, his air of elegance gave the impression of a king about to test a meal prepared by a new chef in the palace. I anxiously awaited his reaction as he slowly chewed the portion placed in his mouth. However, once he swallowed, I was given a look of woe as he shook his head.

"Recharred, yours is not as moist as mine. It is okay, but not as good as when I make it. Recharred, you 'ave to be sure to leave the cover on for enough time...otherwise it gets too dry." Of course, he went on to shake his finger in shame.

"It is too bad, Recharred…aw, too bad!" He was good at rubbing it in until he realized I was feeling bad, and then after a quick smile he added, "Recharred, you know I do not mean all thot…I jus' love to get your goat ond make you laugh. I love you too much to ever hurt your feelings. You know me…you know JUAN! Besides, you make so many more things than I do ond they are all superb…especially your lasagna!" And while savoring the memory, he shivered and added, "Aw…ummm, I con jus' taste it!"

Juan gave me all the latest information about everything going on in the city during our afternoon drive through town. We returned to his place about three hours before we were to leave for Larry's to go out for dinner.

"Recharred, I want you to hear what I recorded on these two cassettes," Juan excitedly sighed as he inserted one into the player. "Aw, Recharred, I cannot wait until you hear all the songs. They are all the ones we loved ond danced to since we met! You know how I always love to play them. Now, instead of playing each song individually, all I 'ave to do is play these two cassettes!"

Juan had always loved to mix records in the DJ booth whenever we had a slow day at the club in Atlanta (and there were many of those)…. In fact, he was really very good at it since his hands were always so steady. He also had no problem seeing in a very dim light. Whenever I tried, my hands were so shaky…besides the fact that I didn't see much in the dim light. I'd invariably lay the playing arm on the wrong groove or scratch the surface badly. This always brought Juan running.

"Recharred, whot the hell are you doing?" he'd shout. "Jesus Christ, you are not only blind, but you shake like on old man. C'mon now, Recharred, let me do it before you ruin all the records!" Being 'Mr. Music,' he couldn't tolerate abusing records.

I realized these cassettes wouldn't really show his mixing ability because he only had one turntable to work with, but I still knew his love for these songs would force him to lay them down as though they had been mixed. Juan stood there glowing and immediately raised his arms in that incomparable manner of his.

"Cha, cha, Recharred…wait until you hear all the songs!" So there we were, both standing as the music began, while Juan moved his hips to the beat in that subtle way of his. I was so pleased moving along to the beat with him because here was a succession of songs that were ours! Each song had a special meaning…some more…some less. And once I heard George McCrea's "Rock Your Baby," my mind immediately flashed to the first time I ever danced with Juan. In fact, the first time I ever danced with a man! I remembered how wonderful and proud I felt to see Juan before me, turning his head subtly from side to side, as if he was romantically teasing me! And oh how I remembered his beautiful blue eyes glowing in the black light.

They were all there! Every one we ever danced to—"Rock Your Boat," "Everlasting Love," "The Last Dance," "I Shall Survive," "Doctor's Orders," "Hot Nights," "Shame, Shame, Shame," "Gloria," "I Never Can Say Good-bye" (One I loved because it was exactly how I felt about Juan.), and "Fly Robin Fly" was one that always brought the memory of Juan dancing the line dance at the Closet…. One that Juan never could miss dancing to, which was "Love Hungover"; the Richie Family medleys of "I'll Be There," "It's Alright We Gotta Get Back to Where We Started From," "Ladybug," "Brazil," "Tangerine," "More, More, More, How Do You Like It," and the memory of Juan predicting them a hit after picking up the promotional record. Charo's "A Noches" was one Juan raved about constantly while doing his inimitable 'cha, cha,' and the reason the name was latched onto him at our bar. "Get Down Tonight," which was one I always thought too monotonous, but one Juan loved to do the line dance to…Barry White's wonderful songs brought me to tears, remembering how they described my feelings for Juan: "Lover," "Can't You See You've Changed Baby," "Make Up Your Mind," "Disco," "Where All the Happy People Go," "Nobody Is Somebody," "Y.M.C.A.," and Thelma Huston's 'Don't Leave Me This Way," which probably made Juan more excited than she because it was such a big hit. He did not miss including the wonderful Spanish hits *"Cumbalaya," "MaCumba, Macumba," "Muchachos Baia Baia Baia,"* and "I Go to Rio," and one of the last disco songs we remembered to be recorded and one we loved to dance to, "Memory" from *Cats*. Of course, "Rock Your Baby" was included on both cassettes….

What more could anyone want! Two cassettes loaded with one memory after another! Besides recalling simultaneously where we were when we danced to them so crazily. It was so special…so very special! Who could have so many songs in their lives that meant so much? Our reason…Juan was music himself, and even though he often denied it, he was a romanticist, just as I was. Memories meant too much to him not to be a romanticist. Otherwise, why did he always insist on controlling the records whenever we had a party once we got back together in 1985? And then he played nothing but these songs. And why did he record "Rock Your Baby" twice in this collection and even raise the volume halfway through the number? Of course…to be sure I was aware of it being played. Yes, Juan was a romanticist!

I was so excited after the last song and insisted on making copies immediately.

"Recharred, I will make you original ones ond get them perfect…ofter all, I 'ave nothing but time on my hands." I told him that was fine, but that I wanted a copy of these.

"Because after all, Juan, there were a few needle scratches you made on them, which proves you can do it as well as me."

I had just completed the last copy and Juan insisted I take my shower because it was time to head for Larry's.

"You know, Recharred, Larry always has cocktails…you are not gonna drink tonight, are you?" I assured him I would do him honor by not accepting and he added, "You know, Recharred, Larry got angry ot me because I told him he was an alcoholic. He does not jus' 'ave one drink or two when he comes home from work…he drinks all night. So I told him he is dependent on it ond he did not like thot I said thot. But, Recharred, I did not care because you know me, I am always frank."

"Well, Juan, you should know those who drink all the time don't want to be called down for it, or to hear they need it. At least you would admit to it when you were sober because you knew you had a problem once you started drinking."

"Yeah, but he will not even admit it then, Recharred...ond, Recharred, thar were times I had one drink ond stopped the rest of the night."

"I know, Juan, but only when you weren't in the mood to go out."

Larry did have a drink in his hand once we arrived and I decided to finish the roll of film we took to Brown County. Somehow, Juan got himself into a negative mood and I wondered why. I had asked Larry to pose with him. He obliged, but managed to ask a question that explained his sudden mood.

"Why, Recharred, so you can 'ave pictures of me ofter I die?" I tried to ignore it, but at the same time realized his illness was preying on his mind. However, this wasn't like him. He never complained about his illness to friends. Yet, as I thought about it, he may have been down because I was leaving for home after our dinner with Larry. I didn't know!

Once the film was developed, I was happy with those taken at Brown County, even though a few were on the dark side. I also liked the one of Larry standing close to Juan, holding tightly onto his shoulders. There was a huge smile on Juan's face. But once I looked at the picture Larry had taken of the two of us, it was very apparent Juan was edging away from me—and with a strained expression on his face. Sometime later, while showing Amanda the photos, we talked about the reason Juan always appeared so apprehensive and defensive while posing for pictures with the two of us.

"Richard, the reason Juan is at ease and smiling when he is next to Larry, or anyone else for that matter, is because they are just his friends and he hasn't any hang-ups about standing close to him or anyone else. He doesn't even mind having them holding their hands on his shoulders or waist. However, he loves you, and because of his sexuality problem, he cannot take a picture with you, especially in public. He is a very proud man, so he doesn't want to chance being called a faggot in public...for your sake as well as his. He has no problem with a friend." I realized that had to be true, especially remembering the many times he kept his distance from me each time pictures were being taken.

The only shot of the two of us standing close was the one taken by Gloria the night we were married. Unfortunately, we were always afraid to frame it and put it out in our apartments because of our hang-ups...afraid a family member would see it. So I kept it in the top drawer of my chest. However, after Juan separated from me in 1981, I was always worried someone from my family would discover it. At that same time, I decided upon erasing the wedding ceremony from the cassette Ted had made for us. It was truly a shame because I believed that ceremony was one of the most beautiful happenings in my life. However, my sexuality hang-up conquered, and it became one of my rash decisions...one I have regretted for all these years. Then, upon looking for the picture, it was gone too! I was sure Juan had taken it and destroyed it during one of his anger tantrums, though he'd never admit it.

I've often thought that I might run into our good friend, Gloria, one beautiful day. Since she had faded away from our lives, I'd ask if she had kept a copy of the picture she had taken of Juan and me that wedding night. It would be so wonderful to hear her excitement.

"Yes, Richard, I still have it and each time I happen to see it, I reminisce about how beautiful the two of you were together."

Juan continued his low mood once we returned to his house, and especially while I began to gather my things to leave. As usual, he didn't accompany me to my car, saying good-bye at the door and quickly shutting it. It has taken me all this time to realize the loneliness he had to be feeling each time I left. I should've realized because of the many times he had proven he never liked being separated from me through the run of a show. Now, he was faced with this dreaded disease…never sure what the next day would bring. He needed me with him to give him hope. Why I didn't decide to stay with him permanently for the few months left in his lease has tormented me to this day! Yes, I was working for a woman I met in a choir Matt and I had joined. While talking with her at one of the rehearsals, I found she was looking for someone to do painting and handy work and once she agreed to pay fifteen dollars an hour, I jumped at the chance to earn some decent money. The other reason, Matt had baited the hook well.

As I drove home, I kept thinking about Juan and how he was still the charmer…still the very excitable little boy he always had been…how, that afternoon, he insisted to take me to see the Starlight Theatre so it would be a way of sharing the times he went there with Larry. As we stood at the rear of the huge theatre, he raved on.

"Aw, Recharred, I really enjoyed *Bye Bye Birdie*…it was so lively…so much fun! Ond, Recharred, you remember I also saw *Camelot* here with Larry? Aw, Recharred, Judy Kaye was so good in it! Ond, Recharred, it was very well done. But do you know I got a little sleepy ot times?" I assured him it was probably because of the serious theme of the play…that it moved slowly at times but he still was puzzled.

"But, Recharred, you know I never fall asleep ot a theatre like you do…I guess it is because of all the medication I am taking ond because I lose my strength so much…I don' know, Recharred."

I returned home about midnight and as always, called Juan, only to hear his answering machine. I no sooner hung up and the phone rang. It turned out to be a collect call from Juan.

"Recharred just a while ofter you left I began getting an extreme headache ond it got so bad I called the hospital. Well, Recharred, I am ot the hospital now because they told me to come to the emergency room. I am gonna 'ave to stay overnight again, Recharred, because they want me to see the doctor when he comes in. So here I am again ond I hate it." I quickly assured him it was better to stay there. Juan returned home the next morning feeling great. However, they hadn't given him a reason for the extreme headache.

"Recharred, the Arts Council in town is 'aving a festival this Saturday ond it is supposed to be the most fantastic event of the year held in Indianapolis," Juan said very excitedly in a call that first week in September, "Larry says they have all kinds of entertainment...opera...dance companies...comedy groups...art displays! Aw, Recharred, it is only for that day. Do you think you can come here so we can go?"

Of course, I agreed but I can't recall why I didn't leave on Friday to avoid the necessity of getting up early Saturday morning to drive there. My only thought was that I wanted to be available to see Matt one evening of the weekend. If I did see him, the memory of doing anything special escapes my mind. And probably because my subconscious mind wants to forget it.

I left about six Saturday morning in order to arrive early so we'd have enough time to enjoy everything at the fair. Just as I turned onto 465 East from Route 65, I got that wonderful feeling, as always, because I knew I'd be seeing Juan's smiling face in about ten minutes. I had made good time and felt great because I'd be arriving ahead of schedule. Then, once I entered 465, there I was in a sea of cars moving at what seemed to be a snail's pace! Juan had failed to let me know about this major road construction. It was only about ten miles to Allinsonville Road, the exit to Juan's, and it didn't appear that I'd ever reach it. I finally decided to take the exit before, figuring I could head the half mile up to the street before his complex and then drive east. Well, I won't try to explain what happened because if I didn't know then where I was, how could I know now? I had probably been to Indianapolis well over a hundred times, but still got lost and finally had to call Juan for instructions. Juan was just about finished with his treatment and laughed once I tried to explain my dilemma. I was happy to see that Phillip was there, keeping Juan company and joining us for the affair.

We were on our way in minutes with Phillip following in his car.

My only regret...it was one of those blistering hot and humid days and I was concerned for Juan. He'd have to walk in the steaming sun. In fact, even though it was apparent he was very happy being with me, he seemed to lack his usual strength and liveliness. It was heartbreaking seeing him drained this way, but I certainly couldn't call it to his attention, especially since he didn't admit to it. So I kept my mouth shut and let the gnawing continue in the pit of my stomach.

We had to park quite a distance from the entrance and then walk some before getting on a shuttle bus. Still, Juan kept his excitement up. His excitement continued once we arrived at the entrance. Phillip was waiting there for us, and we were fortunate to spot him because the crowds swarming to gates were unbelievable!

The park was absolutely beautiful! It was as though we were at a world fair...stages and people everywhere! Phillip excused himself after a short while and went on his own.

This had to be better than a world fair! Never had we seen so many special attractions and entertainers for one affair!

"See, Recharred, did I not tell you how spectacular it would be!"

We located Larry in the art fair section and I was especially glad Juan never mentioned my usual gripes about paying the high entry fee. After some conversation, we were on our way, managing to find some shady areas to sit in the grass to watch shows.

"Aw, Recharred, here is the Kaleidoscope dance company! Aw they are so fantastic! You remember I saw them perform twice?" However, we couldn't see too well because all the seats were taken and there were rows of people standing in our way. Phillip suddenly appeared and took off almost as quickly.

"He probably wants to walk by himself so he can cruise," Juan said with a chuckle.

"He cruises when he has a lover, Juan?"

"Because, Recharred, they 'ave 'thot' agreement." I didn't say another word.

At about six o'clock, we came upon one of the main stages set in a very secluded area.

"Aw, Recharred, look how bea-u-ti-ful it is here?" A performance had just ended and we were told another would be starting in about half an hour featuring all the top opera stars of the city performing Broadway songs as well as opera. We were thrilled, especially since available seating was in the shade! Juan was his usual charming self, striking up conversations with those seated next to us. However, it was apparent Juan was not relaxed once the performance began. In fact, only two artists had performed.

"Would you mind, Recharred, if we started to find our way out of here? I am so tired…I really am. Please, Recharred, would you mind? I am so sorry to spoil your time, but I jus' cannot stay any longer."

"Juan, you're not spoiling my time by wanting to leave. I just thought because these seats were in the shade and because it has been too hot for both of us all day…that you might want to rest a while. Please, Juan, don't think you are spoiling my time…never could you do that…never!" I couldn't believe how humble he asked. How he was so worried about me and my feelings. I wanted to stay…yes, but only if he could enjoy it with me. My disappointment was because he had something in him that wouldn't allow him to stay. My mind kept thinking of the beauty of this man to still think of me. He was not spoiling my time because I told him enough times…that just being with him was all the pleasure and joy I could ever desire….

Chapter Fifty-Six:
Hospital Stays Increase

Juan was in the hospital for two very short stays in August and I could accept this, but September wasn't as considerate. If I wasn't working for Mildred so often, I may have thought of moving down with Juan for the duration of his lease. But this was all the money coming in except for the paltry sixty-three dollars a week I was fortunate to receive from unemployment compensation. It still wasn't enough and I was forced to make loans on my life insurance.

"Recharred, I 'ave been 'aving this ter-ri-ble high fever ond I called the hospital," Juan said in a call the morning of the twelfth. "I think I am gonna 'ave to go in again. They are gonna call me back to let me know." I realized I had to be up in order to give him a positive attitude.

"Juan, then you must go in so they can find out why you have the temperature."

"But, Recharred, I am getting so tired of going to the hospital…I really am."

"Juan, you only were in the hospital twice last month and they weren't long stays."

"Yeah, but, Recharred, I also go thar often for checkups ond I am tired of it."

"And, besides, Juan, you will get a few free meals," I quickly reminded him, trying to lighten up the situation. And it did work because he chuckled and I could tell he felt better.

Juan did go into the hospital, but this time he was in for about a week. He asked me not to go there because Svetmana was arriving and he didn't know how long she'd be there. We talked at least once a day and sometimes more using our telephone game, but now I'd first call the nurses' station to ask if he were available. If so, I'd tell them I'd be calling in ten minutes …and if they'd be kind enough to tell him to be near the public phone. Sometimes it worked and sometimes not.

Juan was diagnosed with pneumonia during this stay but still managed to be in an up-mood for all our conversations. His awed descriptions were amazing.

"Recharred, my fever was about 104 to 105 degrees ond they put me on this ice-bed…ond you know whot, Recharred? It really brought my fever down!" He was so 'up' I felt he was telling me about a party he had attended. Larry had been stopping by to see Juan almost every day, so I would call to get his opinion on his progress. With each call, I was told Juan was improving.

While talking with Juan Sunday he said Svetmana was returning to Chicago.

"Juan, I am coming down tomorrow to see you!" I sighed excitedly. "I feel terrible I haven't been there to see you and don't tell me I will then have to be at your apartment alone because you are in the hospital! I want to be with you at the hospital!"

"Aw, thot is great, Recharred, but guess whot? I may be discharged tomorrow…but probably in the late ofternoon."

"Aw that is wonderful to hear, Juan…but I'm still leaving early in the morning because then I will stay with you until you're discharged."

At 8:30, just before leaving, I called Juan and found him to be as chipper as ever. This I was certain of because he would not stop talking about everything and anything.

"Juan, if you talk much longer," I quickly reminded him, "I'll never get there!"

"Recharred, are you all finished painting ot thot woman's house?"

"No, Juan, I told Mildred I was going to see you in the hospital and would call her once I returned." Juan laughed and I realized why…because I had previously told him she was living alone and could sense she liked to have me around. And when I had told him Mildred made lunch for me and even dinner at times, always giving me a choice of entrees, he had raised his eyebrows and shook his finger.

"Recharred, she is ofter you."

I cannot say how beautiful the sight of Juan talking happily while gesturing excitedly with his hands meant to me as I stepped out of the elevator into his ward! There he was standing at the nurses' station, charming the panties off them! He looked so happy and my heart sang. He spotted me walking hurriedly down the corridor and turned my way.

"Aw great, Recharred, you are here, because as soon as the doctor comes, I will be released." From the glow in his eyes, it was apparent he was happy…happy to see me and happy to be getting out of the hospital.

"Aw, Recharred, I am so happy to be gettin' out of here. It has been too long a time. Ond, Recharred, thank you so much for comin'!" He continued talking excitably to them.

"Juan, why don't you change into your clothes," I interrupted, "because, then, as soon as the doctor discharges you, we can leave."

"Good idea, Recharred," and we quickly walked to his room.

"You know whot I call thot fat, blond nurse?" he questioned excitedly, "I call her 'Nurse Ratchat'…. You know…from *One Flew over the Cuckoo's Nest*. Recharred, she is so serious ond mean ot times. So I decided upon calling her 'Nurse Ratchat'…. Do you not think thot is a good name for her?" His giggles continued.

"I did notice she was on the cool side, Juan…but isn't that unusual for you? Usually, you charm the hell out of all the women." Juan stopped his giggling and shook his finger, "Not this time, Recharred…not with Nurse Ratchat."

Juan's car was still at home. Still, I never asked how he got to the hospital. Juan's chatter continued in his usual happy manner while I drove to his apartment, and I thought, *This is the Juan I know and love…he is never gonna change*. I hadn't made a time limit on my stay because I wanted to be sure Juan was completely well before I left. However, two days later, Juan got the bright idea to pack his medications in a cooler and head for my house.

"Recharred, I will jus' stay ot your house. I won't tell my mother I am in town. I feel very guilty in doing thot but I really want to be with you ot your house for a couple of days. Then you can drive me to the bus station because I know you 'ave to work for thot woman. I can call Larry because I know he will pick me up from the station. You will do thot, Recharred, will you not? Also, Recharred, would you be so kind to return these videos to Pharmor while I pack. They were supposed to be returned while I was in the hospital, so thar will probably be a late charge. Would you not do thot for me, Recharred?" While there, I decided to call Matt's office to inform him Juan was returning with me because I certainly didn't want a recurrence of calls such as the other time. I prayed he had sense to oblige this time.

As usual, Juan had the radio on in the car while happily talking and I was surprised to hear two ballads that had always been very meaningful to me in our early relationship…and they were played consecutively. These were "Precious Love," "When Will I See You Again," and 'You Make Me Feel So Good.' Of course, he had always said I was too much a romanticist whenever I told him how moved I felt each time I heard them. However, this time he seemed to really appreciate my sighs at hearing them.

Juan never liked American sports, especially baseball, and always totally ignored it, giving me a hard time each time I wanted to watch a game on television. He so detested the game that each time I tried to switch the radio in the car to hear the scores, he'd foolishly say they should bomb every stadium. I realized it was his way of protecting his stand on baseball but still reprimanded him for making such a horrid statement. Well, while changing the station, he momentarily stopped on one giving scores and I quickly begged for him to let me hear the scores. Atlanta was in the thick of the pennant race and since they had never won a championship, I wanted to hear what they did that day. He surprised me this time because he gave no objections. However, it is a shame Abbott and Costello never heard the following conversation, because I am sure they would have shelved their 'Who's On First' routine and used this one instead. And believe me, I had to do every contortion in my body to keep from running off the road!

Juan:	Whot do they want a pennant for, Recharred?
Richard:	Well, if they win it…then they will play in the World Series.
JUAN:	I don' understand…jus' because they win this pennant…this flag…they will be in the World Series? Recharred, I don' even know whot a world series is?
Richard:	Juan, I'm not talking about a real pennant…not a real flag. I mean the team that wins the most games in their league…then plays the team that wins the most games in the other league. Well now, it's not exactly that…because they have divisions. But, not to confuse you, I'll forget about the expansion teams and tell you how it originally was.
Juan:	Do some teams expand?
RICHARD:	Forget about the expansion, Juan. Just remember the winner of one league plays the winner of the other league, and they call this the World Series.
Juan:	aw, Recharred, I don' understand…it is all so confusing. Whot is a league ond how do you win?
Richard:	Wait a minute, Juan. Do you know how the game of baseball is played?
Juan:	No, Recharred, I never cared to know, but now I think I would like to know why everyone goes so crazy.
Richard:	Well, Juan, there are nine men on a team and they play another team of nine men.
Juan:	Then whot do they do with the league?
Richard:	That is something I will get to, Juan. For now, let me explain what the purpose of the game is and how it is played.
Juan:	Okay, Recharred, whot is the purpose?
Richard:	Naturally, the purpose of the game is to make more runs than the other team, and to do it in nine innings.
Juan:	In nine innings? Whot is on inning?
Richard:	Juan, that is when each team has a time at bat, and they are allowed three outs each.
Juan:	This is more confusing, Recharred, I don' understand whot these outs are?
Richard:	You know Juan…like when we play Scribbage…you have three minutes to make your words! Well, in baseball, each team has three outs per half inning and there are nine innings in a game!
Juan:	I don' understand these outs, Recharred?

448

Richard:	Well, then let me explain to you how a person makes an out or gets a hit.
Juan:	Now, you are really confusing me…whot is a hit?
Richard:	Aw, Juan, now I'm getting confused! Let me tell you about when a batter gets to the plate.
Juan:	A plate? Whot does he do with a plate? Is he gonna fill it with food?
Richard:	Aw, c'mon now, Juan! The plate is the home base of the baseball diamond. There is first base…which ends the first line of the diamond. And then there is second base…which ends the second line of the diamond shape. Then the next line leads to third base and then finally home base! And all of it forms the shape of a diamond, which is called the infield, and there's a player at each of these bases.
Juan:	This is more confusing because now you are talking about an infield ond I do not even know whot this diamond does?
Richard:	Diamond shape, Juan! Not an actual diamond! It is how the field is shaped…a diamond shape!
Juan:	Recharred, you do not 'ave to shout. I can hear you. I jus' do not understand whot all these lines are doing in the game ond why they are shaped to form a diamond.
Richard:	Because, Juan, that is what they call the playing infield and right in the middle of it is what they call the pitcher's mound.
Juan:	Why do they want a pitcher thar for, Recharred? So they can drink some water from it?
Richard:	No, Juan, it is not a water pitcher! It is a player…a man! And he is the one who throws the ball over home plate where the player is batting from. The player tries to hit the ball with a bat and if he does, he runs to first base and if he gets there before the ball, then he is safe with a hit. Oh, wonderful, I got that much in.
Juan:	Aw, c'mon now, Recharred, don' make fun? I jus' don' know why he wants to get thar before the ball?
Richard:	Because, Juan, that is the purpose of the game as I told you…to make hits…but most important is to score runs…more than the other team.
Juan:	I still do not understand these hits ond runs, Recharred?
Richard:	Juan, you understand a team has to have hits and they have to have enough of them to score a run, don't you?
Juan:	No, I do not, Recharred.
Richard:	Aw, c'mon, Juan! They have to run around all the bases and reach home for a run and they can only do that by getting hits…that is unless they are walked.
Juan:	Walk? Do you mean someone helps them walk?
Richard:	No, Juan…. If the pitcher throws four balls before he throws three strikes.
Juan:	You mean he throws four balls ot him? Why does he do thot?

Richard:	Juan, he does not throw four at one time. He only throws one ball at a time and it has to be in the strike zone.
Juan:	A strike zone? I don' understand? You mean they put this strike zone in front of the man?
RICHARD:	No, Juan, it is an imaginary area and only the umpire can decide whether it is a strike or a ball.
Juan:	You are confusing again, Recharred. How con he do thot?
Richard:	Juan, I think maybe we should wait until I can draw some pictures and diagrams because then I will be able to explain everything more clearly.
Juan:	I don' know, Recharred. It sounds like something thot is so stupid…Yes, Recharred, I think it is so stupid!
Richard:	Juan, it is not stupid. It is just a game of scoring runs. You know, like you score points when we play cards or when we play Scribbage.
Juan:	I still think it is stupid…so stupid!

It was a bit frustrating, but I must say, very funny. I never knew if Juan was pulling my leg since he was so serious and innocent in his questions. However, he did accomplish something he was master of…making me laugh, especially whenever I thought of it

It was very apparent Juan was overjoyed to be coming to my house because whenever he continuously mimicked me, he was happy. And he managed to do quite a bit of it, especially once we were in the slow elevator going up to my apartment. I was in thought and there he was, doing his Mussolini face…. And when I didn't laugh hard, he managed to drop his teeth. Again, I didn't laugh hard, so he let out a loud fart.

"Aw, c'mon, Juan, why did you do that? What if someone gets in the elevator now?" But it didn't matter to him because he just began giggling in that throaty laugh of his while reminding me of the time I ran to the refrigerator for an onion instead of appreciating the smell of his passed gas. And his laugh was always contagious!

His theatrics continued once we were in the apartment and he wouldn't give up until I became hysterical with laughter and that finally happened once he formed his hands in an exaggerated claw and distorted his handsome face to look like the Lon Chaney phantom. Once he felt I was entertained enough, he settled down and we talked.

We did quite a bit of driving just to be out. It also gave Juan the opportunity to talk to me more because I was directly next to him and not busy doing something in the house. At one time, he insisted on bringing up his eventual death and in spite of my objections, continued to say he was leaving me five thousand dollars of his insurance and that the car and all his furniture were mine.

"Juan, I do not want your furniture," I cried out, "I only want you to live...and I don't want five thousand dollars either! Do you think that is important to me, Juan? No...only you!"

"Well, Recharred, I told Endira to be sure Svetmana gives you the money from the insurance because I told her I owe you so much." I thanked God once he changed the subject.

While driving, I realized Geena's house was just a couple of minutes away and asked if he'd like to stop to see her.

"I love Geena very much, but I only want to be with you...not Amanda, Patti, or Daniel either...only you, Recharred." I said no more but thought he also undoubtedly didn't want to see Geena because she is totally unaware of his illness and knowing him, he didn't want to lie to her by saying he is fine.

"You know, Recharred, you are lucky," Juan said after some silence.

"What do you mean, Juan, why am I lucky?"

"You are lucky because you are so healthy, Recharred...you are really healthy." I didn't know what to say, especially after he looked so reflective. "Yeah, Recharred, I wish I was thot healthy." My heart ached and it was difficult to come up with a response. I realized he didn't say it because of jealousy. No, Juan and I never felt that way towards each other. We were always proud of the each other's fortunate attributes and success. No, I knew what he was getting at...he was a bit angry as well as sad, and was questioning the reason we couldn't be well together...to share our lives for years to come. It was what he always talked of, and now we were being cheated out of it. I realized, too, why he would never commit when asked to resume as lovers because I continued asking after that beautiful morning during our vacation with Phil and Vic in Saugatauk. After all, I knew he wanted me to beg...that he was waiting for the right time, but then that autumn, he was diagnosed HIV positive.

"It is not fair for anyone to be lovers with someone who has AIDS, Recharred," was something he always said afterwards.

We managed to do everything we loved those two days besides our drives...we played Scribbage while playfully arguing because one of us didn't turn the timer over.... We watched my *I Love Lucy* videos and there was Juan laughing each time she made a face taking 'Vitameatavegamin.' And doing the same while Lucy challenged the Italian woman in the grape mashing bin. Of course, he rewound them a second and third time, and laughed as hard each time. It was puzzling who was making me laugh each time—Lucy or Juan's cackling laugh?

We had to be in heaven because our joy couldn't be any higher, and I believe Juan's goal was to keep me in a constant roll of laughter. So he continued his mimics and if that wasn't enough, he concocted other things to keep me laughing. He was happy when I laughed even if he had to do something gross. He also realized I would object to anything gross, but in the end, I'd finally submit in helpless laughter once his innocent perseverance continued. So I realize I must include something many would consider as extremely gross, but by this time, everyone should be aware of the rare and unique logic of this man…that he was always on stage solely for me, no matter how ugly it made him appear…as long as I'd eventually break into uncontrollable laughter. So it never mattered what he said, or how he said it…or what he did, or how he did it because he just had that knack of coming out and smelling like a rose….

"Recharred, will you please come to the bathroom," Juan called out as I sat in the living room watching television. Once I got there, he was standing next to the john with a stupid and innocent look on his face, and there were his drawers lying down on his ankles! He looked like a cupie doll because his belly was sticking out as he just stared in my direction. He didn't say a word once I asked why he called, but merely turned his head and stared into the john.

"Aw, Juan, why did you call me to look at your crap in the toilet, for Chris' sake?" I yelled racing out of the room. "Why the hell are you doing something so gross like that!" I didn't get far because Juan clutched onto me, laughing uncontrollably.

"Whot is the matter, Recharred…huh? Whot is wrong?" I naturally tried to escape his clutches while trying to be aware of his Hickman.

"Aw, Juan, I think you are crazy! You are so elegant and you do something so vulgar like that?" It was crazy because he wouldn't let go as he continued to laugh and chant.

"Whot do you mean, Recharred? Whot 'ave I done…huh…whot 'ave I done?" I finally managed to make my way into the bedroom, with him on top of me holding tight and repeating his crazy questions while both of us landed on the carpet in a helpless laughing jag!

Juan had another quip he occasionally performed for me, and this visit was not void of it. Again, performed by Juan, even though it too was gross, came across as a theatrical comedy gem. He had just taken a shower and as he was about to pull up his pants, I entered the bedroom. His back was to me but evidently he was aware of my presence. Suddenly, he made a complete turn by quickly jumping around and landing on both feet at the same time while holding onto the base of his genitals! And there he was…waving them!

"You want thot, Recharred…huh? How would you like thot?" And he continued shaking them while keeping a stupid and crazy stare on his face.

"Aw, Juan, I think you are crazy," I quickly reprimanded, but still ended up in hysterical laughter along with him.

It was evident Juan was completely happy during the combined three and a half days we spent alone, and he wanted to be sure I, too, was enjoying them by his continued theatrics. I realized he didn't have to do this for me to totally enjoy his company and I am sure he knew it too, but I must admit they were always a fantastic added treat I was so fortunate to have in my life. Who could have so much laughter in their life and still be privileged to share the charm, intelligence, and sincerity of this man? No one could ask for more!

Everything had been perfect, but as usual, too short because Juan had to return to Indy late in the afternoon to get another supply of medication. Thankfully, he didn't get himself into a depressed mood that morning because he continued with his antics. I had been so busy, and as I always did when enjoying conversations with Juan or anyone, I'd put off relieving my bladder. So there I was, standing in the living room as he was finishing up his treatment, crossing my legs listening to his conversation. It didn't take him long to pick up on it.

"Recharred, whot is the matter...huh? Whot is wrong, Recharred...huh? Tell me, will you, Recharred...why are you bouncin' around like thot ond holding your legs in thot crossed position? Do you 'ave to pee or something...huh? Huh?" Then he began mimicking my position while making all kinds of exaggerated expressions of pain on his face until we laughed and then I almost peed in my pants! "Blanche, you are a grown man, so why are you always crossing your legs like thot when you 'ave to pee? For Chris' sake, you look like a queen!"

I wish I didn't have to once again relate something that completed these wonderful days Juan and I spent together, but, unfortunately, it happened and must be told. I also will never know why I allowed Matt to get away with it? I couldn't believe once I answered the phone, especially since I had specifically said not to call while Juan was there.

"Rich, I did not work today. I took a sick day. What are you doing?" I quickly told him Juan and I were just sitting in the living room talking and because I didn't know what else to say, I concocted a ridiculous conversation.

"So did you sleep late this morning?"

"Only to about nine thirty, even though I wanted to sleep longer because I stayed at the bar until closing last night. When is Juan leaving? Is he leaving soon? Maybe we can do something after?" I didn't want to linger in conversation since I knew Juan was aware Matt was on the phone, so I quickly added, "That sounds good. I will call you...okay? Take care now." Though I tried to appear nonchalant hanging up the phone, Juan's expression knew all.

"Well, who was thot?... Bleached curly locks?"

"Yes, Juan, he wanted to know if I might want to go to a movie with him later this week." Fortunately, he accepted my answer and we began talking happily again.

My heart jumped once the phone rang again; only this time, Juan answered.

"It is 'him' again, Recharred!" Juan related with a strong tone of sarcasm, handing me the phone. There was no way I could reprimand Matt with Juan next to me, so I just continued giving him double talk to his specific questions. However, I never was one who excelled in improvisation while sober and my nervousness had to be showing. Anyone else listening to my answers surely would have hung up, but not Matt. He just continued asking one question after another until I finally was forced to say good-bye and hang up.

Juan had been avoiding the fact that I was still seeing Matt, even though he had to be aware of it. He had just blanked it out of his mind and that was fine with me because even though I felt I was falling for Matt, I still wasn't sure it was ever going anywhere because of his refusal to commit, and especially since I really couldn't trust his fidelity. It was evident Juan wasn't pleased and before he could say anything, the phone rang again. I quickly picked up the receiver to hear Matt shout and reprimand me for hanging up on him before he had finished talking. I realized I couldn't respond, and merely listened as he shouted. Finally, he hung up, and as always my face betrayed me. Juan realized Matt, once again, had called and this time he was livid. My mind was swimming with disbelief! Why was Matt calling when I begged him not to? He had to know his calls would cause stress to Juan, and yet they appeared to be tailor-made to do just that! My face had to say it all and Juan had to be aware of it.

Juan couldn't control himself any longer. He began trembling as he rose from the couch, his face flushed with anger, quickly lashing out in a nervous quiver.

"Recharred, why is he calling you so much? If he is jus' a friend as you say, he would not be calling thot many times in a row? Ond, Recharred, I know you when you are nervous…your voice ond face tells all! I cannot believe how you were talking, Recharred? Nothing was making sense…nothing!" Juan had to realize he was quivering and in order to make it less obvious, slowed down and finally reverted to his nasty manner of badgering me,

"Recharred, casual friends do not call each other so much. Why did you not tell me you were going out with him all this time…HUH?…YOU KNOW YOU 'AVE EVERY RIGHT TO DO AS YOU PLEASE…SO WHY DID YOU NOT TELL ME?"

"Juan, what is the difference if he called me more than once? Friends do that." Of course, Juan wouldn't agree and held onto his anger instead.

"BECAUSE, RECHARRED, I AM HERE, OND HE KNOWS IT BECAUSE I AM SURE YOU TOLD HIM! YES, BECAUSE I AM HERE…YES, BECAUSE JUAN IS HERE!" There was no calming him.

"ARE YOU REALLY GOIN" OUT WITH HIM AGAIN…WITH BLEACHED BLONDE CURLY TIPS? ARE YOU NOT ASHAMED TO WALK DOWN THE STREET WITH HIM IN PUBLIC? AW, RECHARRED, HE IS SUCH A QUEEN…SUCH A QUEEN!" There was no way I could calm him as he continued to tear away at Matt. I was sick because I knew this was causing him so much stress…something I wanted to avoid so badly.

"Recharred, please drive me immediately to my mother's…I will call my daughter and 'ave her drive me to the bus station." There was nothing I could say or do to change his mind, and when I tried, he became angrier! The drive to his mother's house was a complete blank, and probably because I was in a stupor, knowing this should've never happened. Of course, my subconscious mind erased it from my head.

Once again, I let Matt control the argument in my attempt to reprimand him. I tried to convince him he was causing Juan stress only to hear, "Hogwash!" So there I was being controlled again, and all because I clung to a faded memory of our initial meeting and the few times he reciprocated in sex…and I guess my subconscious mind believed Juan would die, leaving me alone…and I knew I needed someone to be there for me. This could be the only explanation for allowing Matt to verbally attack Juan…for keeping the anger and hurt in my heart each time Matt tore away at him, and not really realizing who the important one was in my life. I really believed Matt would one day show compassion for Juan and at the same time love him. So I never objected to his nasty abuse of Juan. I'd just shut my mouth. It didn't make sense at the time, but I let it be…and I will never understand why.

There was no way I could talk to Juan because I received the same response each time I called at his mother's…"Juan no home now." I finally figured he should be home by this time and just as I was about to pick up the phone to call, it rang. I wish I could describe the joy I experienced once I answered.

"Recharred, you know I cannot stay angry with you, especially when you were not wrong. Recharred, you are so good ond always try to be so fair and loyal to everyone. I know thot is how you are, ond it is so wonderful to be thot way. You are truly a *Man of LaMancha*, Recharred, ond I know how good you are to me, ond you want to be thot way to everyone. Recharred, thot is not wrong ond I am so sorry for making you miserable. You are the most important person in my life because I know we are truly 'one person.'"

"Juan, I know that, but you get so stubborn and all it causes is stress…and you don't need that, Juan." He agreed.

"Recharred, it was jus' thot we were 'aving such a wonderful time together, ond when he kept calling, I could not control my anger because I felt he was purposely trying to upset me. So, Recharred, I could not help myself. Please, try to understand?" I felt Juan didn't need to know my feelings were mutual. How could I then ever get them to be good friends? So instead, I made an excuse for Matt.

"I truly understand Juan, but I think he was only bored because he had stayed home from work and I was the only one available to talk to.

Juan continued to talk in that charming way only he was master of.

"Recharred, while I was riding on the bus, I could only think of you ond how badly I treated you with my ter-ri-ble temper. You know I do not mean any of those mean things I say to you when I am angry. You know thot, Recharred, don't you?"

"Juan, I have known you too many years to think you have ever meant any of the nasty things said to me…even though they hurt when you say them."

Juan called the next morning and informed me, "Recharred, I am gonna 'ave to go back to the hospital because my fever is up again ond they want me to come in."

"Well, Juan, I'm gonna leave now so I can be with you. I will have to leave tomorrow morning because I promised Mildred I'd definitely be there in the afternoon."

"You really want to come, Recharred, for thot short time…do you really?" I quickly reminded him how many times I did it before.

"And besides any amount of time with you is like heaven."

And there he was again, talking excitedly with the nurses as I walked onto his floor from the elevator on my arrival.

"Guess whot, Recharred, my fever has gone," he called out excitedly, "but, unfortunately, the doctors want me to stay one more day to take some tests. Aw, Recharred, I am so tired of coming back ond forth to this hospital." I again assured him that it was the only way to help it.

I spent the entire day with Juan and we did manage to go down to the emergency entrance for a short while to enjoy some of the beautiful weather. Juan was his usual happy self and seemed to be enjoying the great day. However, suddenly he looked very depressed. It was very apparent because once he stopped talking, I knew something was bothering him, especially since he began walking listlessly around as though deep in thought. I knew he had every right to finally complain about his illness because he had held on stronger than I believe anyone else would have in his condition. He finally turned to me and raised his arms hopelessly.

"Aw, Recharred, I don' know.…Whot am I gonna do? I am always sick. I want to be healthy so bad." He repeated it, only this time the words caught in his throat and became a desperate plea, "Aw, Recharred, whot am I gonna do?" I wanted to have an answer…to again assure him he would be fine. I wanted to take him in my arms and hold him, but afraid of that foolish fear of being called faggots. Instead, all I could do was look him square in the face and give my assurance I'd always be there for him.

I stayed fairly late, taking off for home that evening instead of morning since Juan wouldn't be at home anyway. After talking several times on the phone once he returned home, I was back on the road to his house Sunday morning. Even though Juan's fever had returned, he managed to only tell me of it once, and that was only because he was baffled it was reoccurring. At the same time, he casually mentioned that a tooth was giving him some pain. I finally insisted he call the hospital to see if someone could check his tooth but upon calling, he was told a dentist wasn't available on Sundays. For the rest of the day he never complained again, but I was sure he was still having pain. He, however, wasn't going to ruin our time together by complaining. No, this wonder of a man was his usual charming and pleasant self!

It was evident Juan wasn't feeling well the next morning.

"Recharred, I did not sleep well ot all because this tooth was aching all night," he answered when asked how he felt, "ond I also took my temperature, ond it was even higher." I insisted he call the hospital. He did so and was told he would have to go to a civilian dentist. However, he was given a referral list and after calling the first number, he was surprised to hear the dentist agree to see him immediately once he was told he had AIDS.

"He did tell me the tooth could be causing the fever. Aw, Recharred, I am so happy because, maybe now I will finally get rid of my fevers!" It was amazing, he was in terrible pain…had a high fever, yet the thought of possibly being better after seeing the dentist put him in a wonderful and happy mood!

Juan's tooth was extracted and once we left the office, it was apparent he was tremendously relieved as he talked through the ice-pad pressing against the bloody gum area.

"Recharred, the dentist said my fever should go down now…thot the tooth was the reason it has been occurring on ond off." Juan took hold of my hand and squeezed tight.

"Aw, Recharred, I am so happy!"

"Me, too, Juan…me, too!" Juan called my attention to the fact the dentist had mentioned several of his friends were being treated for AIDS. "So, you see, Recharred, he was gay, too. I guess they are everywhere."

Juan's fever was gone and we were elated! Although I knew Juan had to be having some pain from the extraction, never did he complain the entire day. He was too happy to complain about something like pain from a tooth extraction because that would only spoil our day together and his joy because the fever was gone! The next day went by too soon and we were saying goodbye about nine in the evening. Juan got himself in his usual depressed mood and I tried to lighten his spirits by reminding him it was the beginning of October.

"And before we know it, the end of the month will be here and you will be living with me, Juan." I had already started the ball moving to have his medical records transferred to the VA hospital near my house and after reminding him of it, I added, "And besides, Juan, you know I am gonna be coming here regularly until that time."

It wasn't yet midnight once I arrived home and before calling, Juan decided to play my messages only to have my heart stop once I heard the first message.

"Aw, Recharred, ofter you left my fever came bock ond began to go up high again." I couldn't understand it! The dentist said the bad tooth was the reason for the fever. Why is it back again? "I jus' called the hospital," he went on to say, "ond they said I should come in. Recharred, I am jus' leaving for the hospital ond it is eleven thirty my time." I stood stunned and about to shut the unit when suddenly his voice came on very sadly, sounding almost desperate with a definite catch in his throat…words I have heard till this day.

"Aw, Recharred, aw how I wish you were here with me."

Chapter Fifty-Seven:
The Fever Persists

My anxiety got the best of me because I couldn't understand why his fever returned. I finally decided I had to call the hospital and once the nurse answered, she told me he was doing fine and if I called back in a few minutes, she'd get him to the phone. My heart was aching as he talked quietly, explaining he couldn't stay on his feet too long.

"Juan, I am gonna return there in the morning after I get some rest because I want to be there, and because you always get better once I am with you!"

"I would like thot, Recharred, but why don' you wait now because I talked to Svetmana ond she is coming tomorrow, ond Endira will be coming this weekend. So wait until they are gone. You know I want you to come, Recharred, but they will be staying ot my place now. Besides I will probably be home soon." I agreed but I was not happy about it. At the time, I never realized how this fever would persist.

The first two days, I called the hospital ten times but unfortunately wasn't able to talk because they wouldn't allow him to leave his room. So I'd attempt to get information from the nurses. A couple of times, Svetmana was there. However, I never really felt she was honest with me. I received more information from Larry because he was stopping by to see Juan almost every day. Phillip even called to tell me about Juan's progress after he visited him. Neither of them could explain the reason his fever wasn't subsiding. Late one evening, I called Juan's apartment and reached Endira. In a very casual manner of speaking, she assured me he was coming along, but that his fever wasn't showing any signs of subsiding. When I finally got to talk to Juan, I knew he wasn't doing well because his tone of voice wasn't his usual 'up.' He said Svetmana and her mother were leaving late in the afternoon the following Monday, and I quickly said I'd head there that same morning.

After working for Mildred that Sunday, I washed and dressed at her place because Matt had asked me to join him after dinner at a wedding reception for the son of our Pinochle playing friend, Carl. Of course, Mildred made dinner. It was odd because I should have been elated to join Matt, but somehow being with him meant nothing that evening. My mind could think of nothing but finally seeing Juan the next day.

It was raining very heavily the next morning and I decided to leave later in order to avoid driving in the rain during the rush hour traffic. I arrived safely in spite of the torrential rains that never ceased. Once I rushed into Juan's room, my heart ached at seeing him struggling incoherently on his way to the bathroom, and I knew he was still very sick…this time I wasn't greeted with that happy smiling face. Svetmana and Endira were just standing there, motionless, with their coats on…not attempting to assist him.

"Oh, good, Richard, you are here," Endira quickly said, "because we are just leaving." I said a soft hello but my focus was on Juan as he fretted in agitation. He almost appeared to be in a delirium as he shook his head anxiously in disbelief and anger.

"I don' know whot is wrong with me!" Juan cried out in anguish, "I don' know why I cannot get rid of this ter-ri-ble fever!" He was trying desperately to hold his balance and there was Svetmana and Endira just standing there coldly, not attempting to help him. I quickly washed my hands and tried to take hold of him while he continued his agitation, not really acknowledging my presence. My heart ached, realizing, HE HAD TO BE SO SICK NOT TO ACKNOWLEDGE ME! He suddenly began jerking his head every which way.

"I don' know whot is happening to me?" he cried out in desperate anger. "I don' know! But I am not ready to die yet! I AM NOT READY OT ALL!" A heavy weight came on my heart with this outcry, and I felt helpless. At the same time, I couldn't believe Svetmana never appeared affected by Juan's outcry, and that she decided to leave with her mother at that very moment! But I realized it was what I wanted because I knew Juan always got better once I was with him. My only consolation from hearing his desperate pleas was I knew he didn't want to die…he wanted to live and along with me, we were going to lick this thing!

I finally settled Juan down to realize my presence and then fall asleep. Once awakened, his fever subsided considerably. I managed to talk with the social worker regarding his transfer to Chicago while he slept and was told my constant calls to the AIDS nurse and the social worker there were proving successful because conferences were now in progress between the two institutions. Upon explaining this to Juan, he was almost his old self…he glowed.

The change in Juan was unbelievable those two days I spent with him! He was so much calmer and his fever was nowhere as high. I also found his stomach had shrunk some and that he had no appetite because no one evidently had tried to coax him to eat, so I began spoon feeding him while trying to divert his attention by talking about something entirely different. It was never difficult to find a subject when talking to Juan. And it was working!

The next day, I continued trying to divert his attention for each meal because he had been holding his lips tightly closed each time I raised a forkful, but with a diversion he'd forget and open wide.

"C'mon, Juan, you have to eat because you know what they say about feeding a cold and you will starve a fever?" was my only mention of eating.

"Yeah, but then they are talking about good home cooking, not this ter-ri-ble hospital food, Recharred." Was a reply I was glad to hear him joke about.

"Well, then, I will go to your place and get the dinner I put in your freezer to eat later. Remember I made my Italian pot roast the last time I was here, the day before you went into the hospital? So I'm gonna go get it so you can eat what you like."

"Recharred, I don' want you to do thot because then you will be gone for about two hours," quickly adding, "You know what, Recharred? Svetmana ate the portion you left in the refrigerator and told me it was delicious."

"Did you tell her I made it, Juan?" I couldn't believe she'd compliment anything I made."

I decided to leave about 9:00 P.M. that second day, much to Juan's displeasure, but I needed the money I was making working for Mildred. I also reminded him that Svetmana was returning on Friday and staying until Sunday.

"Aw, Juan, I also forgot to tell you that I talked to Amanda last night and she and Patti are delivering something in the area today and asked if they could stop in to see you tonight. I talked to the head nurse and she said it would be okay for them to come up even though it is late. So, Juan, you will have company later tonight."

Never in my life would I have ever believed Juan would be in the hospital for the rest of the month. So there I was returning home and I'd be off to be with him once again…sometimes the very next morning. I'd stay three or four days and then return home for a few, and then back again for a couple, and this continued throughout the month. I found I needed to be with him, and not because I had to…I wanted to be with Juan! And when I was home, the telephone always was so much a part of our lives…of keeping our communication with each other alive.

Juan finally began eating a bit on his own but when I was in town I'd make certain I was there for every meal, occasionally missing breakfast because it was served so early. However, I'd be sure to bring him something from home or a fast food chain. He certainly didn't like the hospital food and if he didn't have home cooking I felt his appetite would take forever to grow. So I started preparing some of his favorites at the apartment and bringing them to the hospital. However, he still wasn't eating with his usual gumption. It was going to take time.

Juan was near released a couple of times the middle of the month, but then the doctors would discover something else they felt should be checked, or his fever would return at an even higher degree. He was improving but there were days he was very ill with high fevers, and I found myself crying uncontrollably while driving to his apartment for a night of rest. And this crying would continue while sitting hopelessly on his couch begging God to make him well. I usually felt my prayers were answered once I arrived at the hospital in the morning, because Juan would be so chipper…and so happy to see me!

On one of my return trips, I was greeted by Juan's wonderful little boy aura.

"Aw, Recharred, you are here ot last!" Without a pause, he went on excitedly. "You know, Recharred…guess whot? They put me on the ice bed again because my temperature was going so high! Aw, Recharred, thot really brought the fever down fast!" I was so happy to see his smile and eyes lighting up because then it was apparent he was better.

"Recharred, it is so good to see you…I 'ave missed you so much."

"And, Juan, I have missed you so much, too."

It became very apparent that my persuasive powers were working because Juan began eating more, especially when I brought food from home. He wasn't eating as much as I wanted, but at least he was doing better. Yes, he was improving because he began razzing Nurse Ratchat constantly. He was bewildered, though, and bothered since she never responded with any laughter. This was Juan's way of trying to win her over, and she continued her curt manner and sour face. He was baffled, because never before had he failed to charm any woman.

I found Nurse Ratchat, or rather, Verna, to be a very pretty woman who, unfortunately, was saddled with an off balanced body. In fact, it appeared as though she was two people put together…the bottom half definitely the fat lady in a sideshow. I thought maybe this was the reason for her disposition…because she was unhappy with her body. But then I noticed whenever the nurses were cutting up, she also joined them in laughter. In fact, she looked very pretty when smiling. Her coldness towards Juan began irritating me to no end and I finally decided to discuss the matter with her. She was always very pleasant to me and I felt it shouldn't be a problem approaching her on the situation. I finally managed to find her alone while Juan was sleeping.

"Verna, I am somewhat confused about something. Juan is such a charming person and I have never seen him fail to win any woman over…or anyone for that matter once he wanted to. He is an absolute captivator, and yet he has not captured you with his charms. That's so unlike him, especially when I know he's trying so hard to win you over! Verna, everyone loves Juan when they meet him and he only kids people he wants to have on his side." She listened but held onto her sour expression, and I almost felt as though I was talking to a wall. However, I was going to settle this if it killed me because I knew I had to ease Juan's troubled and confused state of mind.

"Verna, has Juan been a pain…has he been too demanding? If he has, I cannot understand because he has always been respectful, polite, and humble to anyone in the medical profession." She still remained silent, holding onto her sour expression, and I felt like smacking her smug face because Juan didn't need this. However, I held my cool, and talked about AIDS…how the victims needed so much love! There was nothing more I could say, and just stared at her waiting for a word of compassion.

"Richard, I really liked Juan when he arrived the very first time," she said after a welcomed smile. "He was so polite and obliging…and also so appreciative. However, once his daughter began to visit him…he changed! He became demanding and no matter what I did, he was never satisfied…or she wasn't I guess. Richard, when you are here he is a different person. He is wonderful! But when that daughter of his is here, he is someone else. He becomes very nasty. Then you return and he is again pleasant. I guess I was confused and couldn't overcome their nastiness once you arrived."

It was hard to believe any woman could say anything against Juan knowing the charmer he was. Why couldn't she add up everything and realize who was causing this problem? I was certain Juan's illness wasn't making him do something he so despised about Svetmana. It had to be Svetmana badgering him until he was forced to torment Verna in the same nasty miserable manner he always said his daughter had exclusive claim to.

I slowly and clearly explained every character trait Juan had, and how Svetmana was the exact opposite, even as a small child. I went on to further explain how Juan always catered to her because of the guilt trip his ex-wife put on him.

"So, Verna, he had to be only appeasing her by giving in to her demands to complain. Believe me, that is not Juan."

"Richard, I totally understand now and I'm sorry," she sighed after a moment of reflection and a smile. "I didn't know this before. I assure you everything will be different now." This certainly called for a big hug!

I never tired being with Juan in the hospital even though I often stayed from nine in the morning to ten or so at night. After all, I never tired being with him before…why would I now? Juan was also receiving antibiotics for his pneumonia through his Hickman, and these tubes were always hanging to the side of the bed. In fact, they were so long they bunched on the floor. Then it happened. I was fetching something for Juan from his night stand when suddenly my foot caught onto one of the tubes.

"Aw, ow…aw, Recharred, my Hickman is killing me!" He continued crying out while desperately holding onto his chest. I stopped in my tracks, realizing it was I who was pulling on his tubing! I quickly untangled my foot from the tubes.

"Oh, Juan, my foot caught onto your tubes! Aw, how could I be so clumsy?" I was so terrified that I began trembling, almost afraid to look once Juan pulled up his pajama top to expose the dressing covering the Hickman attachment! There was no blood and everything looked intact, but I realized

I had to be sure! Once my foot was untangled, Juan stopped crying out in pain and quickly assured me everything was fine. Nevertheless, my trembling continued as I paced the floor in hopeless agony, not knowing what to do first!

"Recharred, calm yourself! It does not hurt anymore…please, don' worry because it looks okay." I continued in my panic, realizing I had to call Verna to be sure I didn't pull it from his artery, and quickly ran out while mumbling incoherently to myself.

"Recharred, you are being hysterical for nothing! Please do not act thot way!"

Verna returned with me and once she checked the Hickman attachment, she assured me that everything looked fine.

"Richard, you don't have to worry…so calm yourself." I sat there still trembling and exhausted from my hysteria once she left the room, not believing I was so clumsy. I shook my head and was almost in tears but once I looked at Juan's smiling face I tried desperately to return one to him. I felt he should've been a bit angry or at least concerned because of my negligent clumsiness…but no, instead, he just looked at me lovingly.

"Blanche, you are so dramatic all the time. You jus' 'ave to be more careful with those big feet of yours, my darlin.'" He then chuckled and assured me it was only an accident. Still, I couldn't contain myself…my mind wouldn't let go. What if I had pulled it out, and with it his artery as well? Oh my, God! I continued in my nervous state for some time until Juan finally took hold of my hand compassionately.

"Recharred, please forget about it? Now, ot least, you will be more careful, my darlin'."

Juan had asked if I could make arrangements to see the social worker in the hospital to make out a power of attorney for his personal belongings. I agreed because I realized he might not be there once his furniture was packed and put into storage. I, however, hesitated once he mentioned he also wanted his banking included in the document because I felt it would be admitting to his grave illness.

"Recharred, it is only to protect whot I 'ave in case something does happen to me! It does not mean it will happen! Aw, Recharred, you are the only one I trust. Would you do thot for me, Recharred? Please, my darlin'?" So I met with the social worker.

Juan's car had been in the parking lot during his entire stay and I made sure it was started every now and then in order to keep the battery charged. However, on that particular day, it went completely dead and I hustled out for a new battery.

On that same day, Juan was given a spinal tap to check the condition of his bone marrow and I will never forget when he described it to me.

"Aw, Recharred, you cannot imagine how it feels to 'ave a needle stuck into your spine. It is such a ter-ri-ble feeling. But I guess I will 'ave to 'ave it done regularly to check if my bone marrow 'as been infected. Ond, Recharred, it gives me such a headache, especially if I do not stay on my back." During the day, I realized he was having severe headaches. Yet, he never complained outside of the original mention. So he continued to talk and joke and it was apparent he was savoring the thought of finally returning to Chicago…and to live with me. So he held his pain to himself, not wanting to upset me. But how could I not feel his pain? We were one person. I remember thinking of my refusal to accept this illness as being fatal, but yet my apprehensions had to be buried deep inside of me, getting the best of my impossible dreaming that had always been so much a part of me.

I wouldn't leave that evening until the results arrived regarding his spinal, and once they did, his happy and glowing face were all I needed for my long drive home. They were there with me…his beautiful glowing blue eyes and those brows dancing happily.

The transfer to Hines VA hospital was approved, which meant as soon as Juan was discharged from the hospital, he would be able to move to Chicago, and we were elated because it appeared as though this would be happening any day. However, during the third week of October, Juan called.

"Recharred, my Hickman became infected ond had to be removed, so now thot means I will 'ave to stay longer ot the hospital to be sure the infection is totally gone."

"Aw, no, Juan, that is probably because I pulled it! Aw no, Juan!" He realized I was a basket case and immediately assured me.

"No, Recharred, it is not because of that…they told me it happens sometimes because of so much use. So please do not blame yourself!" I still insisted but he wouldn't listen.

"Another one will be connected, Recharred, but this time it will be put on the right side because, ofter all, I am a lefty." So this meant he would probably have to remain there another two weeks or so, which would take us to the end of the month and his lease. I wanted to go there immediately but was told Svetmana was arriving for the weekend.

"So, Recharred, could you come on the twenty-second, because she is leaving then…would you not do thot, Recharred?" I agreed, even though I saw no reason I couldn't be there the same time as she. After all, there were two beds in his apartment. However, he probably realized Svetmana's constant sarcasm towards me and didn't want me to have to contend with it.

The only thing good about staying home…I was able to finish much of the work I was doing for Mildred. Then again, I was available to be with Matt more often. In fact, I had been still trying desperately to stabilize our relationship and even though there were times I felt this is what he wanted, the game of guessing continued to go on. So there I'd be chasing into the night trying to catch him in an act of deceit. The only proof I ever came up with was when his car was somewhere it shouldn't have been. Yet, once I approached him about it, he'd merely concoct another story and even though any idiot would know that was another lie, I allowed him to get away with it. I really felt I loved and needed him in my life.

I made arrangements with Amanda to pick up Juan's antique desk, chest, and some pictures while I was still there because I realized I could never fit them in my car. She had told me she'd be in the area again and I felt it was a good opportunity to take advantage of using her minivan for things that wouldn't go in storage. I wanted Juan's room to look familiar, and with his own belongings, he'd feel more at home. She was happy to oblige. I told her I'd make arrangements with Daniel to meet at my place, so he could help carry everything up to the apartment. At the time, I asked how everything was going with her and Patti.

"There's peace between us, because, after all, Richard, we have the business together and I'm still living in her house. But, Richard, it will never be the same with us again…we are just friends and that is it." She then told me Patti was so demanding and never felt she was doing a good job with the business.

"She is always on my ass about it, Richard." I felt bad because Juan and I always thought they'd never break up. I decided never to tell Juan because it would break his heart. In Patti's defense I realized she had a full time job and could only be with Amanda for special deliveries. Although Amanda always meant well she, did try to do too many projects at one time. So there they'd be sitting, all unfinished…cluttering up the place. However, this was Amanda, as we always said. She has such a giving heart and if there were many more hours in the day, she'd reign like a queen!

It was wonderful to see Juan's happy face upon returning for four days and three nights. He was fine during the day but as evening approached his fever began rising and with it came depression and anxiety. So again I was crying uncontrollably driving to his apartment at night.

Happily, after the first night, Juan's temperature began to stabilize. However, if he wasn't to be discharged before the first of November, he'd definitely have to be transferred to Hines because his apartment had to be vacated and Svetmana and I wouldn't have a place to stay. I immediately began pressuring the proper authorities and was finally assured this would come about on November first. I wouldn't be returning until just before that day, so this meant there was much to do to have the move run smoothly. So besides sitting long hours enjoying Juan's progress, I was running all over the place getting everything accomplished and was my usual detail-oriented self being nervously sure things were getting done. Of course, Juan was not one to miss his chance to remind me.

"You know, Recharred, you thrive on running around like a chicken with his head cut off. Thot is thot Italian in you." It was so wonderful to see and hear him finally again do one of his mimics of me.

"Aw c'mona now, let'sa alla getta the salami onda cheesa onda runna for the train…c'mona everyona!" And there we were laughing ourselves silly!

While accomplishing all the necessary details, I happen to think about my down pillow I just had cleaned and fluffed, and how wonderfully plump it came out. I decided to surprise Juan and do the same with his favorite pillow and was lucky to find a place that would do it in one day. I never understood why he adored this pillow because I felt it had to be made of clay!

"Why the hell do you love this pillow, Juan?" I had always asked. "It feels as heavy as a sack of potatoes and when I punch in it, the indentation just stays like clay!" But he'd just take hold of it and while hugging it close to his face he'd sigh, "aw no, Recharred, I love it…I really do. It has been my pillow for years ond years. I jus' love it!" And he'd continue hugging it while smiling away. I also realized it should be cleaned for sanitary measures.

I was a bit disappointed the movers wouldn't arrive until ten, the morning of the first, which meant I'd probably be there for some time because everything had to be packed into boxes before going into storage. I was unhappy because the time set for Juan's transfer that day was the same time and I realized I wouldn't be at Hines once he arrived.

I went immediately to the hospital after picking up the pillow. Once I told Juan about the pillow, he appeared very concerned.

"Is it okay, Recharred? Aw, I hope it is okay because you know how I love thot pillow." I was a bit reluctant to tell him that some of the clay weight was gone, but once I did, I immediately reminded him that it needed to be done for sanitary reasons. He accepted my reasoning but still shook his head, uncertain he'd be happy once he saw it.

When I asked about breakfast, Juan replied that he ate almost all of it. I took out the bottles of vitamins from his night stand. It was so funny because Juan always insisted he didn't need them, yet he'd silently open his mouth and look so appreciative as I placed them through his lips. His appreciative stare in my face always gave me such a warm feeling.

Juan was so happy once I told him about his furniture being picked up by Amanda.

"Recharred, I do not know whot I would do without you," Juan sighed, clasping onto my hand. "You are so thorough. Aw, Recharred, you are so good…so good! God should bless you…He really should!"

"I have done nothing more than you would do for me, Juan…nothing more."

This had to be one of Juan's better days…but then again, he may have acted this way for my benefit because he never liked for me to worry. He then said he was scheduled for another spinal the following morning, and when I expressed my concern, he said it was because the last one hadn't been conclusive enough.

"They 'ave to check something else, I guess, Recharred, but I was told not to worry. You know, Recharred, I am giving permission to Dr. Andrias to do the procedure…. You know Elizabeth, the young intern. Recharred, I really like Elizabeth ond she has asked me so nicely if she could be allowed to do it, ond, Recharred, I know she is a caring person ond would not ask to do it if she thought she might hurt me. I trust her because she has such compassion…aw such compassion…ond I know she needs the experience. No, Recharred, I insist she do it. I want to show her I 'ave trust in her, ond she has been so good to me." I finally accepted his trust in her, at the same time remembering that it was Elizabeth who was instrumental in securing Juan's transfer after I made numerous pleas.

I excitedly informed Juan that I made one of my fast spaghetti sauces after arriving at his place and he immediately asked if I also made meatballs?

"Of course, I did, and sausage too. I had one of the nurses put it in their refrigerator. So now you will be able to have it for lunch." At that moment, Elizabeth came into the room to inform Juan that the spinal was set for ten thirty the next morning. I was pleased because I'd be here. Conversation filled the air as it did so often once she came in the room. I quickly asked if she'd care to share some of the pasta but was told she had just had lunch.

"Well, why don't you get a dish or something and I'll give you some to save for later?"

"Aw, Elizabeth, Recharred makes the best pasta sauce I 'ave ever had," Juan quickly added, "It is so superb! One day you will 'ave to come to his house ond have his lasagna because it is the best in the world!" I tried to explain Juan was a bit prejudiced but she insisted.

"No, I know he is probably right and it looks as though I am in for a treat."

While talking, I inquired if it was possible for Juan to get a pass to go to his apartment because he wouldn't see it again before being transferred. After reminding her the day was beautiful and sunny, she agreed and commented there should be no problem to arrange it. We continued in conversation and it was wonderful to again experience Juan talking in that fast excitable manner, and to see him glow once Elizabeth gave us her address.

"Aw, Recharred, she is so wonderful…is she not?" Juan sighed once she left to do her rounds. "I really like her so much!"

I suddenly realized Juan's Hickman hadn't yet been scheduled to be attached and voiced my concern.

"No, Recharred, they are not gonna do it here. They said it can be done once I arrived ot Hines." Again, I expressed concern about being without it for so long.

"No, don' worry, Recharred, because they said I need thot rest from the medication."

Juan dozed off and I could've gone into the lounge to watch television, but somehow never thought of it. Yes, he was still the ultimate in good company because even watching him sleep was always something that fascinated me. Once he awakened, he seemed to be thinking intently because he was fairly quiet.

"You know, Recharred, you do not 'ave to stay with me all these hours," he finally perked up to say. "Are you not bored? You must be bored because each time you are here you stay all day ond night. If you want to go somewhere, you should go."

"Juan, why do you say something like that? Where would I go when I can be with you? Juan, I have been with you at your house or mine for longer periods of time and I have never wanted to be anywhere else…why would I want it now? Juan, you are the joy of my life and I wouldn't be here unless I wanted to. You have never bored me and you never will. I enjoy being with you and always will! So please, don't ever doubt it!"

"You do, Recharred?" he sighed with a glow of satisfaction in eyes. "You really do?" I smiled, and then as if they were magnets, our hands softly and slowly met for a brief squeeze.

About three thirty, Elizabeth popped her head into the doorway to say everything was fine for the pass but that they wanted Juan back by eight o'clock. She then kissed her fingers.

"And, Richard, Juan was right…you do make the best pasta sauce! It was superb," and she fled on her way. It didn't take Juan long to dress compared to the time he spent saying his farewell to the nurses…but after all, this was Juan.

As usual, Juan directed me onto a scenic road leading to his apartment…one I had never been on and it was beautiful because the colors of autumn were brilliant.

"Aw, Recharred, how do you like how beau-ti-ful this drive is? We are still in the city, but yet thar is still so much natural beauty. Look at how the trees are bending over the road."

"They are beautiful, Juan. They almost appear as though they're forming an arch over the road. It's gorgeous, Juan!" It was certain Juan had seen many other places this beautiful, but as always, this was the best as his boyish awe continued.

"Aw, Recharred, never 'ave I seen anything like this…never…never!" Juan explained that he had come across the road on one of his frequent trips to the hospital, but never had seen it with such glorious color. I felt as though Juan and I were driving through a picture postcard…and no one else could make it as beautiful an experience as he.

Juan's awe continued, although there was something different this time in his behavior. I could see it and almost feel it. He was enjoying something he loved so much…but as though it was for the last time. It was there…unmistakably on his face and in the movements of his body. Almost a nervous apprehension grasping at all the beauty and storing it in his mind for fear those crystal blue eyes would soon deny passage through them. Juan finally spoke…not in an angry or sad tone…but as someone speaking seriously and straight forward about an inevitable occurrence destined to happen…one he was accepting, but only because he had to for his own peace of mind. I somehow knew before the first word was said, what I was about to hear, and I did not want to listen. But then I knew I could not refuse this time because he needed my support…my understanding. I turned slightly in his direction as I drove because I wanted Juan to be sure I was there for him. It was short, but to the point and with each word, my heart felt as though it was being crushed.

"Recharred, this is so bea-u-ti-ful ond you know how much I 'ave always loved driving in the country…ond cities, too. Ond you know, Recharred, it

Why Has All the Music Gone?

may not be long…ond I will never, never see them again…because thar is no doubt about it. I will be blind…ond everything will be black." There were no tears…just a stare of realization, and with it Juan took hold of my hand…and we held on tight.

Juan had not yet seen the pillow once we entered his apartment and once I handed it to him, it was very evident he was disappointed. He held it close, and gently squeezed it.

"Aw, Recharred, it is so different. It is not the same as it was because it is not heavy anymore." He wasn't the least bit angry with me…just a bit disappointed.

"Believe me, Juan," I assured him, "it will not be long and it will be as it was before."

"It will?" Juan sighed with that elfish smile cradling his pillow. "Aw, I am so glad."

I took out the Italian pot roast from the freezer, but after heating and serving it, noticed Juan was not showing any kind of appetite. I asked why.

"Recharred, I guess I am jus' too excited about returning to Chicago ond your house."

He was edgy and I realized the reason…the time had passed too quickly because it was almost time to return to the hospital. We both realized this would be the last time the two of us would be sitting together in his living room because we had reminisced about the laughter and joy we were so fortunate to have there. I will never forget two touching moments Juan gave to me the last fifteen minutes we sat there…never in my life will I forget!

Juan was sitting on the couch opposite the loveseat I was seated on, and I could feel the sad longing in his voice.

"Aw, Recharred, I wish thot they gave me a pass for the whole night…because then we would be able to sleep together tonight…thot would be so nice. Would it not be, Recharred?" I had never heard Juan say anything as tender…or as beautifully. I have often thought of that evening and my mind is so angry because I didn't think to call the hospital to request it. No, instead I realized he had to be at the hospital early for the spinal and merely agreed.

Juan took me completely off guard just as we were about to leave. It could not be more touching. He rose from the couch, walked slowly in my direction and sat directly next to me on the loveseat and suddenly he laid his head onto my shoulders.

"Aw, Recharred, whot am I gonna do?" he cried out desperately. "Aw, God! I want to live so badly…so badly!" He held onto me tightly and sobbed. My throat was so choked I couldn't even utter a word. I just held him close as tears flowed down my face…over my jaws and down my neck…and I couldn't control myself enough to stop them from flowing. I don't know how long we remained there as I softly and slowly caressed him, but it will live in my heart for always.

I couldn't remain with Juan long at the hospital because Amanda was coming to pick up his furniture and besides they wanted him to be well rested for the spinal. I cried hopelessly driving back to his place because the image of Juan pleading to live kept appearing before me.

To my surprise, Amanda arrived exactly on time. I included a few boxes, which held some of his favorite pieces of his elephant collection…several Southwestern pictures and the porcelain bust of an Indian and his squaw I had given him. I decided upon taking the brass bumblebee with me on the day of moving. We thought we were done when I suddenly thought of his bed frame. It was on casters and the one on the bed at home was not.

"Aw, Amanda, I think you should also take his bed frame because I want to be sure his spread hangs properly. You know how fussy he is." I needed a laugh and that is exactly what we did, especially after Amanda cried out.

"Jesus Christ, Richard, you are really thorough…you two make a beautiful pair!"

After calling Daniel to tell him Amanda just left, I noticed a message on Juan's machine. I switched it on immediately.

"Hello, this is John, if you are there, Richard, please call me no matter what time it is. I am up very late every night so please call me collect. I really want to know how Juan is doing. So please, don't forget to call."

I was completely surprised to hear how 'up' he was once I called, especially since Juan had told me he was almost totally blind. In fact his compassion and concern over Juan really tugged at my heart. Here was a man who was in worse shape, and yet showed unselfish feelings for a friend. I felt a bit ashamed because I had denied a friendship between the two of us to flourish. I also realized he was equally at fault, but I should've overlooked it and welcomed him into my heart. After all, he was also burdened with the same dreaded disease as Juan. He had reached out to someone to share his grief…and Juan took hold of his hand. I realized I should've calmly discussed the drinking parties he pushed Juan into instead of voicing my objections strongly. Surely, that was when he began resenting me. So all of this was mulling in my mind and I realized I had to make things right…that I had to show him I would also be there for him.

"John, I know you have been having a very bad time and I want you to know I want to be there for you, too. I know we have had our differences and I am truly sorry for them. I want you to know my heart is with you and if you need anything or want to talk…please call me. I really mean it, John, so will you please do that?" From the tone of his voice I realized he was appreciative and sorry for his ill behavior as well.

"Remember, Richard, I really want you at my party, too…it is going to be a real fun party."

A priest had come into Juan's room once I arrived the next morning to offer communion and just before opening his mouth to receive the Host, he looked at me in his little boy manner.

"Recharred, you want communion with me too…do you not?" he asked most candidly. I assured him I did and the moment I said it, he glowed as though all the heavens were shining on us both. I will never forget the wonderful look of happy anticipation as he watched the priest place the host on my tongue.

It was not long after and Elizabeth showed up with her team and asked if I could please wait in the lounge while the spinal was being performed. It seemed like forever as I waited and I will never forget the strange feeling going through my body. It almost felt as though I, too, was going through the same ordeal as Juan because an annoying tingling sensation kept running through my body, finally ending up in the pit of my stomach. I realized what I was experiencing and it only confirmed the idea that Juan and I we're truly one person.

"Richard, you can go in now," were the cheerful words I heard as Elizabeth poked her head suddenly through the doorway. "Everything is fine and Juan is doing well," and she was off down the corridor.

Juan was lying flat on his back as I quietly opened the door of his room, and there he was looking at me with his chin crumpled into his neck and his eyes and brows raised to get a good view as I approached.

"Aw, Recharred, how I hate thot so much…so much, Recharred!"

"Was it real painful, Juan!" I sympathetically but very stupidly asked.

"Recharred, jus' imagine a very long needle being stuck into your spine ond jus' staying thar a long time." However, it didn't take long to forget the pain. "Aw, but Recharred, this time it was not anywhere as painful as the last time. I am so glad I gave permission for Elizabeth to do the procedure. Aw, Recharred, she was so gentle…so gentle ond caring. She is so compassionate ond so sure of her every move." Then, as much as he could move his head in that position, approvingly nodded and sighed, "I think she is gonna make a wonderful doctor, Recharred. Do you not think so, too?" I agreed and he quickly and softly added, "You know whot, Recharred, she had tears in her eyes when she thanked me before leaving the room. She was so grateful for my trust in her. Aw, Recharred, she is so nice…so nice."

For most of the day, Juan was flat on his back and only mentioned having a headache once. I was sure he was still bearing it, yet managed to hand out playful hell to Nurse Ratchat each time she came into the room. He was overjoyed as she handed the same to him.

We had a taste for junk food that afternoon and figured it could be a good carefree meal to celebrate Juan's jubilance about coming home at last. I had passed a Hardy's that morning and told him I could go there since it was near the hospital.

"No, Recharred, I think you should go to the one downtown," Juan said quickly, "because thot one is in a ter-ri-ble neighborhood. No, Recharred, it is much too dangerous thar…. People are beat up all the time. I 'ave read about it in the paper. So please, Recharred, listen to me!" Of course, I didn't listen because what could happen in the bright daylight? Besides, I wanted to be back to spend as much time with him as possible.

I realized what Juan was referring to once I walked through the entrance door. It was lunchtime and the place was almost empty, except for two Black men standing at the napkin counter. To say they appeared somewhat surly and raunchy looking would be putting it mildly. They immediately turned my way. And to mention that I felt a bit nervous would also be putting it mildly, especially since they continued to glare at me. My order was quickly filled and while paying, in my nervousness, I dropped two twenty-dollar bills on the floor. While nervously picking them up, I noticed one of the guys nudging the other, and to say I was scared would again be putting it mildly. I quickly grabbed my order and change and headed towards the door. As feared, the two of them followed suit. Like an idiot, I had parked some distance from the entrance and just as I raced towards my car one of the guys called out. I couldn't understand and surely wasn't going to ask him to repeat it.

"I'm sorry, but I don't have time!" I yelled, running as fast as I could and at the same time taking out my key in order to have it in position for the lock. They stopped in their tracks once the mechanics of inserting the key…getting in and locking the door worked out perfectly! I was shaking in terror, yet managed to start up the motor. I figured if they continued my way in an attempt to break the window, I'd run them down! At last I was on my way, while they merely stood in their tracks looking bewildered.

I didn't want to lie to Juan and once he heard my story, he sighed and shook his head.

"I don' know when you are gonna learn, Recharred? Why do you 'ave to be so stubborn all the time?"

The weather was so beautiful that day and we weren't able to go out to enjoy it, but I must say it wasn't missed. Just being together was more than any fresh air and warm sunlight could ever do for us. Juan talked about his anxiousness to finally be able to listen to his Spanish stations again once he returned to Chicago. He raised his arms in that inimitable way of his to imaginable music and boasted how glad and fortunate he always has felt because I loved the music as well.

"How can I not like Spanish music? Besides, Juan, even though you cannot even hum a tune…you are music yourself. Have I ever told you…how once you walk in a room, I have always heard music? I mean it, Juan, you really make me hear music." Juan looked at me as if I was ridiculous and laughed.

"I do thot, Recharred, I really do?" he sighed in that charming little boy aura of his. After again mentioning that his intentions were to enjoy what life he had left to the fullest, and to share it with me, he became somewhat sentimental about his years in Indianapolis.

"You know, Recharred, I am gonna sort of miss this city, because, ofter all, it has been my home for the last three years." He then nodded his head in disbelief and continued, "It is funny Recharred, but I had lived here for over two years ond was so lonely. I missed you so much ond would not make friends with anyone. Then jus' this year I met Phillip ond Kent ond resumed my friendship with Larry. They are really good friends, Recharred, especially Larry ond Phillip. I will miss them." I quickly assured him we could drive back now and then to visit and our home would always welcome them…and he felt better. He, however, needed to assure me I was the most important person he wanted to be with.

"Recharred, I know I 'ave told you before, how lonely I was living here, ond how I would cry each time you left…but thot was how I felt. It was so ter-ri-ble to be alone ond I wanted you to be here all the time." I looked at Juan…a bit agitated with him, but probably more at myself for not realizing this long ago, but he had always put on such a good front that it probably never entered my mind.

"Why didn't you come right out with it, Juan, instead of beating around the bush all the time? Why didn't you just ask me to come live with you? You had to know me…that I could never refuse once you asked in that charming way of yours?" Juan shook his head as I went on, "Maybe I wouldn't have come immediately, but you know how things prey on my mind, and once I knew you wanted me with you very badly, I would've managed to work something out with my condo…probably renting it out…and I probably wouldn't have opened the gallery!"

I would not give Juan a chance to answer…I was hurting because of all these mistakes we made and I had to let him know my feelings. You should've known I wouldn't be able to resist. Why didn't you do it just after you moved here? You had to be the loneliest then? No, instead, you waited until I opened the gallery, and even then you still never came right out and asked…you just beat around the bush by taking me to see apartments and casually mentioning it would be nice if we lived there together…thot I could probably open a gallery there, when you knew I was completely broke! No, you never once said, 'Richard I am so lonely and want you to come live with me because you are the only one I would ever want to live with!'" I continued to dwell on it because the realization of what we had missed was hurting so badly!

"Juan, for Chris' sake, I gave up a booming business to move with you to Atlanta once you asked in that charming way of yours…and I would have moved to Argentina with you when you talked of it, but it was too late once you brought it up, because all the money was already gone! Juan, I left everything to be with you as a couple because I knew you wanted to be with me as much. And Juan, I have never regretted any of it for one moment, and even though I lost all my money…it did not matter because I would have done it again…just for all the wonderful and beautiful times I have been so fortunate to have with you! So why, Juan…why would I not make the simple move here?" I looked at him as tears fell down my face, waiting for some response.

"I don' know, Recharred," he responded his eyes tearing as well. "I guess I was so afraid to ask because I did not want to chance you would refuse." I shook my head sadly.

"Juan, when did I ever refuse when you asked sincerely and charmingly?" Juan smiled.

"Never, never, never, Recharred."

Elizabeth stopped in to say good-bye to me because we figured I might not see her when I came in for the move. The conversation was lively and during her short visit, we all agreed to keep in touch so she would be able to come over for lasagna dinner. We had become such good friends and I wanted it to be something lasting, not only for me, but for Juan, too. Oh, God, I prayed, let her be our friend for years to come.

"You know whot, Recharred, I think I know when I was infected with the AIDS virus." Juan said after appearing to be in deep thought. "I went out drinking one night ond got really drunk…ond the next morning, I remember waking up ond seeing this guy beside me. He looked so skinny with all his bones sticking out from his flesh. Aw, Recharred, I got so scared ond quickly dressed ond ran out of there before he awakened." I just stared at Juan, not knowing what to say and he finally said, "It had to be him, Recharred, I know it." My stomach felt sick, but realized I could not say much for fear Juan would prey on something that could not be changed. It could only depress him more thinking of someone who knew he was infected with this terrible disease, and yet went to bed with him, totally disregarding any precautions. I changed the subject, but could not get it out of my own mind and it has remained there to torment me since. I cannot to this day conceive how someone could be as brutal, and have cursed the person every time it enters my mind…damning him to never rest again and to burn in eternal hell! My anger against the alcohol Juan so freely consumed remains with me because he was a vegetable once he went over his limit. That limit had always been controlled by me and once I disregarded our marriage vows and permitted Juan to leave, 'I' was guilty too! Instead of overlooking his stubborn belligerencies when he was drunk and his jealous rages when he was sober, I should've looked at the majority of times when he was charming. So much of my anger has been towards my own self, because, had we stayed together, he would not have ever contacted this terrible disease. No, I had to let him go because I could then fulfill my ego with others. Oh, how many times I have wished I could turn back the pages of time. No, I could not bring up any of this to Juan now. No, I had to keep the hurt inside.

Endira had given Juan a Walkman, which allowed him to listen to many of his favorite tapes. He insisted I listen to its clarity and wonderful tone.

"Here, Recharred, it is jus' like you are in a room listening to a magnificent stereo." And he was right. However, my pleasure came from watching him because no one else could appear so natural dancing on his bottom.

There I was again saying good-bye, but this time realized it would be the last farewell we'd be saying to each other. Next week, Juan would be on his way home before I even left Indianapolis. Then, after a short stay at Hines, he'd finally be home with me! This time, tears of joy were falling down my face while driving home. It was much too late to call the hospital once I arrived home. I kept busy, however, because, strewn all over my living room were all the parts of Juan's desk, along with drawers belonging to his chest, besides everything else. I decided to put everything together and in place. Once finished, I felt so good because these were Juan's things in my house at last! Soon, he would be here, too.

Chapter Fifty-Eight:
Farewell to Another Era

I continually inquired about the spinal results each time we talked, only to hear he hadn't yet received them. He did say Elizabeth told him he shouldn't worry because the particular thing they were looking for very seldom occurs. I was certain Juan was getting more thrilled to be returning to Chicago with each passing day, but at the same time I noticed a bit of tiredness in his voice. It was bothering me but felt I should not bring the subject up unless he talked of it. He was trying desperately to keep up his spirits and yet, at times, the drop in his voice was so noticeable. No, he didn't need to hear I was aware of it.

Jacque and Gil had gone to Ireland to be married and had finally returned home. I had asked why when she informed me they were going there to be married and was told she already had a big reception for her first marriage and didn't feel she should obligate family and friends to give gifts again. She also added that Gil had so much credit in his frequent flying plan as well as relatives he's never seen.

I was kept quite busy that week...working for Mildred filled most of the time besides last minute arrangements for Juan's transfer. Of course, I was seeing Matt and even though it was apparent he wasn't in favor of Juan moving in with me, he still seemed to accept it. In fact, at times I noticed a definite indifference...as though he was relishing the opportunity to have some freedom from me. Then there were times he made me feel as though I was the most important person in his life. To put it mildly, I was confused! However, he was a specialist in keeping me hanging, which only made me desire him more. I was certain Juan and he would be great friends.

Matt had two telephone books in his briefcase that seemed to be his Bible, being sure I never looked through them. In fact, he often boasted they were filled with old tricks who were now friends. The list totaled almost two hundred! It sounded so unbelievable that he would remain friends with so many tricks, but he insisted they were. In fact, it comprised his Christmas card list he talked about so often. The thought of him sending these cards to keep himself on their minds for future encounters entered my mind, but shook it from my head, because surely, no one would keep in touch with so many tricks for that reason?

There were other books Matt guarded like miserly gold…these were books he wrote in every evening before going to sleep. These were miniature-sized diaries that he boasted would one day be written into a book. Should I be at his place once he decided to record his daily activities, he'd carefully guard his writing with his hand.

Vincent was a friend of Matt, and my meeting with him proved to be somewhat chaotic so I was forbidden to join them again. Now, Vincent was someone I had seen each time I had ventured into the forest preserves years earlier, and he had never failed to approach me. I had found him to be as repulsive as a preying vulture and always completely shunned him, not comprehending how anyone would permit him to touch them. It was obvious the years certainly had done him no favors. I recalled his widely spaced green and yellow rotten teeth in his vulgar and lecherous grin he'd give me and remembered how I wanted to vomit. Now, his present ill-fitting replacement bridge proved to be no improvement since they appeared as though they originally belonged to a giant and were forced into his mouth with a bulldozer. Vincent was short and pot-bellied; he always appeared as though he had slept in his clothing, and yet every time he walked, I felt he thought he was a Pierre Cardin model. However, I really suspected they were having sex…or rather Vincent was performing sex…whatever! Each time I approached Matt on the subject he would shout.

"Rich, look at Vincent…do you think I would want to be with him sexually? He just needs a friend! And in fact I brought him out of his shell." So I'd bite my lip, but yet still suspect. Matt was meticulous in his dress and I couldn't comprehend him even giving a casual thought to having sex with Vincent, or even to have this 'creep' next to him. Here was a complete intellectual bore with a boorish body to match his manner of dressing and usually one side of his shirt tails were being forced out of his pants by his pot belly. It certainly wasn't uncommon to see his long, sparse, and greasy strands of hair falling every which way on his head and face. I have to also call attention to this short, fat man and his slimy goatee, and how it made him appear so reminiscent of Luther. And once he opened his mouth to reveal these teeth, he looked like a caricature come to life! It was evident his plates were too tight because his words came out as though his mouth had just been stuffed with very hot mashed potatoes! I never could understand him!

Vincent did bestow many gifts on Matt and even though he was earning a fantastic salary and didn't need them, he still accepted each and every one. I certainly realized this because he readily accepted one after another from me even though he was aware I couldn't afford it.

There were times Matt seemed to be very compassionate about Juan's illness, urging me to be with him, and yet later would be sure to warn me.

"But, of course, I cannot say I will not be going out to the bars…and who knows who I might meet?" This proved how contradictory he was and almost made me feel as though he didn't care whether Juan lived or died. It should've been enough for me to finally tell him to get out of my life. Yet, I still imagined a great friendship finally blossoming between them…and Matt eventually worshipping the ground I walked on.

There were so many things irking me in my relationship with Matt, and I should've been able to talk of them freely. Instead, I always felt uncomfortable each time I approached the subject, especially since Matt would sidetrack the subject each time I tried and I'd find myself being reprimanded instead…and for something totally out of content. I truly believed Matt was manic because the slightest thing would cause him to blow up. I was also bothered because, even though his generosity was evident with extravagant tipping in gay bars and the fact that he allowed his ex-wife to miss one rent payment after another in his old homestead after re-mortgaging the place to pay off her share, he still showed no signs of reciprocating for all my home dinners and movie passes. In fact, I sometimes was the one to pick up a restaurant bill and add it to my charge card. So there I was believing I was deeply in love, forgetting the things that annoyed me…blocking all of them out by loving his infectious smile and the sound of his voice saying, "Hello there" once I answered his phone calls. I loved how he seemed to appreciate every time we were asked if we were brothers because of our strong resemblance to each other, and how he would be sure to comment, "Yeah, but he is the older one." I guess I also felt because he often called late at night asking me to come over that I was making some gain. Never did I think he had been out and wasn't successful! No, I was sure he wanted me.

"Recharred, Larry is gonna pick me up today because I can go out on a pass. He has a friend in from San Francisco ond I think they are gonna take me for dinner," Juan said as we talked on the phone Sunday morning. I thought it would be great and especially if the weather there was as good as it was here. However, I detected a lack of enthusiasm in his voice, and it bothered me…so I decided to try to bring him up with a reminder that he'd be back in Chicago by the end of week…and it seemed to raise his spirits.

Since I had to drive Juan's car back to Chicago, I planned on taking the train this time, and the only one scheduled wouldn't arrive until about eleven o'clock. I decided to ask Larry if he'd mind picking me up and once I explained everything, he agreed. I mentioned my concern regarding Juan's lack of strength and asked how he had been Sunday. He said Juan did seem to lose his energy after a while, but that on the whole his enthusiasm to do normal things was still great. We both agreed he needed encouragement in order to improve his desire to go on as always.

I took the train Friday, Halloween night, and couldn't get over how much more comfortable I was compared to the cramped seating I always experienced on the bus. My anticipation was overwhelming thinking of Juan finally returning to Chicago, and because of it, the four hours seemed to pass quickly and pleasantly. The train pulled into the station a little after eleven and my excitement grew stronger because I realized in a few minutes I'd be met by Larry, and once at the hospital, I could see Juan before driving his car to the apartment.

The lobby of the station was located beneath the tracks and while descending the staircase, I scanned the lower area for Larry. Suddenly, I received a wonderful surprise, because, immediately next to the staircase was none other than Juan! In my shock, I immediately thought, *Could he have been released from the hospital? Why would he be out so late at night if he wasn't?*

"Aw, Juan, it is so good to see you! But why are you picking me up? Did you get released?" Juan explained he thought it was much too late to impose on Larry, so he asked if he'd be able to leave the hospital for a short time to pick me up.

"Ond they agreed because the station is not far from the hospital, Recharred." We were on our way and I again noticed Juan seemed to be so tired. I finally realized it seemed to be a pattern…full of energy in the morning, but drained of it by evening.

"Recharred, it is so late ond I am a little tired. Besides, I want to get a good rest before the drive to Chicago tomorrow," he quickly replied once I mentioned coming up. I voiced my disappointment, yet realized he was right, and my eyes flowed with tears as I followed every step he took walking to the entrance, disappearing through the doorway.

It was strange considering the many moves we had had through the years…one would think I'd be used to seeing everything ready to be moved out once I finally settled in bed at three thirty. I scanned the rooms and a strange feeling came over me, realizing so much was going into storage…many of the artifacts I had given him or we had bought together…those we shared through the years…and my heart felt heavy.

I was awakened by the telephone the next morning instead of the alarm I had set and as usual, it was nothing new, because it was an 'up' and 'happy' Juan, which immediately put me in a happy frame of mind.

"Good morning, Recharred, did I wake you? Aw, I am so sorry, but you should not sleep your life away."

"You are so funny, Juan, ha, ha." However, this time I really wasn't the least bit angry because it was so good to hear him in this mood. He continued to talk happily about all the details of his departure in that fast paced manner of his and finally added, "Recharred, we will be leaving earlier than I thought. We are jus' waiting for another guy to arrive ond he should be here any minute." And then as he had done so often whenever anxious, quickly cut me off by saying, "Recharred, I think this is the guy now so I 'ave to hurry…bye now."

It was a typical November day…brisk and cloudy as I placed the last piece I was taking into the car. Since I had been getting in the way of the packers and movers, I decided upon spending some time in front of the apartment and couldn't help but reminisce once I looked around the area. Here it was, three years and two months since Juan had moved here. And oh, the memories that began racing through my mind. Even the parking spots directly in front of the walk to Juan's unit were a memory of the times I arrived and pulled in while hearing his stereo blasting…absolutely certain we were going out on the town that evening! I could also see Juan pointing to some car that shouldn't be parked there, because, after all, this was in front of his apartment and should be his parking spot…. And I could see us walking down the path towards one of our cars…Juan talking excitedly because he wanted me to see something so wonderful……and the picture of me peeking out from his bedroom window as he left for work, just to catch a glimpse of him lighting his cigarette while waiting for the car to warm up, and the wonderful feeling of love that always took hold of me as I watched him inhale and slowly exhale… The memory of Juan taking Max for a walk, or rather Max taking Juan for a walk was so vivid because he was so proud he at last had a dog. Even more vivid was the memory of Juan racing for the car when going out on the town, raising his arms in that inimitable way of his while holding a cigarette and a cocktail, shouting, "Cha, cha, cha, Recharred!" My eyes were moist once the picture of the evening Daniel, Stan, and I arrived to see Juan waiting in the cold, so happy to see me!

    I walked back to see how the movers were progressing, and as I entered the small vestibule, the memory of Juan putting his arms around me after Daniel and Stan had walked in came to mind. He had held me tight, smiling while saying, "Aw, Recharred, I am so glad you are here…I 'ave missed you so much!" That moment had been so special because Juan had never before shown his feelings for me in front of anyone, and I glowed with the memory. My spell was suddenly broken once one of the movers approached to ask for my signature.

    Everything was packed and ready to go and after returning his keys to the office, I sat in the car, taking a last look for both of us, while bidding farewell to another era.

Chapter Fifty-Nine:
The Hospital and Then Home at Last!

Juan was admitted at the fifteenth, the top floor of the hospital, and upon entering his room, I was greeted with a happy but somewhat aggravated mood as he rattled on about having to wait over four hours to be admitted. This didn't upset me in the least because this was the Juan I wanted…the man of fire and zest! And he was already handing out one witty remark after another to every nurse entering the room, so I was sure he was feeling good. I also realized one more reason he was so 'up.'

"Recharred, I was told my spinal proved negative…is thot not wonderful! Nothing could have been better news than that for me.

"Guess whot, Recharred?" Juan added, his eyes sparkling, "My sister is in from Ecuador! I called my mother once I arrived, ond ofter cryin', she told me Christina is here for eight weeks…until New Year's Eve. She was not thar to talk to, but it will be so good to see her. Ofter all, I 'ave not seen her since 1989." Immediately, one of his mimics of her was performed…placing his lower lip over the top one in an exaggerated expression of her toothless mouth. Of course, I laughed but reprimanded him, only to be given one of his wide-eyed looks.

"Recharred, you know thot is me…thot is JUAN! She does not want to keep her teeth in her mouth, so I let her know."

He then informed me that Svetmana was on her way with his sister and father to see him. His mother wasn't coming because her legs were giving her problems. He'd go to her place once he got out of the hospital. I told him I would then leave because I had a carload to empty and wanted to get his room in order. His head rose in that put-on arrogance.

"Thot is right, Recharred, you must do it properly ond bea-u-ti-ful for JUAN!" And that was the Juan I wanted!

As soon as everything was in order, I gloated because the realization was physically there. Juan was home at last! I checked his closet to be sure everything was meticulously arranged just as he liked it, and laughed realizing the mess mine was in. I stood there touching the top of his desk, realizing it needed refinishing, and immediately decided it would be done before he arrived home.

Juan's Hickman had not been reattached and yet he was in fantastic condition and spirits, which meant there was no reason he should remain in the hospital. We were finally told they wanted to familiarize themselves with his history and once they were fortunate to secure a time in the busy operating room schedule, it would be necessary to remain a while to stabilize the IV treatments. Neither of us was happy to hear this, but one consolation…Juan was again himself! So I'd be sure to be there at least twice a day for long periods of time. Besides working on the desk, I also had to be sure everything was sanitary and in order, especially my breakfast counter since it had become my catch-all and I knew how Juan despised mess like that. So I kept quite busy, also managing to see Matt.

"Guess whot, Recharred, I am to be the first to receive the new drug, Foscarnet! Is thot not something," Juan quickly said as I arrived, "ond you know, Recharred, I heard the director of the hospital gave instructions I should be given special care! You know I must really be an important case to get such recognition from the head of the hospital…do you not think?" Of course, I agreed, not really knowing if those actual words had been said by the director especially since Juan always was an excellent storyteller, and if it gave him pride and satisfaction, it was fine with me. Besides, I already knew how special Juan was and didn't need to hear it from someone else.

Svetmana and I were getting along fairly well even though she often managed to come up with her nasty mimics of some of my phrases. Juan was doing too well to let it bother me, so I just overlooked them. Christina was with Svetmana each visit and I figured she was the one responsible for pushing the princess to come as often in order to spend as much time with her brother as possible during her stay. It was evident Juan was doing well because he continually mimicked her once her teeth were out of her mouth…and she laughed heartily each and every time. If that wasn't enough, he was back to his mischievous self. He'd sit there with a blank expression, waiting for us to notice the foul smell he had considerately passed into the room. And once we complained, he'd end up in hysterical laughter, forcing each of us to join in.

The lounge was immediately next to his room, so we spent much of the time there usually playing our favorite game, Scribbage. Daniel visited on a couple of occasions, as did Amanda and Patti. Juan also told me Marina had been there to see him, and on one occasion I was surprised to see my brother-in-law, Frank, stop by, which caused a bit of apprehension on my part because of the body fluid warning sign on the door of the room. He left totally unaware, and to this day I will never understand why I kept his true illness from them.

The Hickman operation was finally scheduled and I decided to wait once Juan was wheeled out of surgery, even though informed it wasn't major. I still wanted to be there, smiling for him. I had expected Svetmana to be there also, but she was nowhere around. I was greatly surprised while waiting in the corridor for Juan to be wheeled out, when I recognized the doctor walking alongside the surgeon as she exited the operating room—someone I had tricked with a few times, years before. Raja broke away to greet me and after asking if I knew the AIDS patient, explained he had assisted in the operation. I informed him of our close relationship and at that time, Juan's doctor came over to tell me everything was fine.

I smiled broadly and received the same from Juan, realizing his spirits were up. He assured me later in the day that he felt great.

"In fact, Recharred, remember I always complained about the other one pulling...well, this one feels so much better, so I think the reason the other got infected was because it was not attached properly in the first place." He then informed me the special IV technician would begin refreshing his memory in changing the dressing along with teaching how to use the electric pump he would be taking home, "ond I think you should be here too, Recharred, so you will know how to do everything, too...would you not be able to do thot, Recharred?" Of course, I agreed.

I couldn't believe what he said after I told him about my old trick assisting.

"Yeah, Recharred, I knew immediately he was gay when he came to my room yesterday with the other doctors. Once I was lying thar completely nude, he kept staring ot my cock. So you know whot I did, Recharred?... I could not believe how his big black eyeballs were almost popping out of their sockets...so I realized here was another one, ond figured, aw whot the hell! So I grabbed my cock ond asked...you want thot...huh?"

"Juan, I don't believe you...you didn't really say that...did you?"

"I did, Recharred...whot difference does it make to me...I 'ave AIDS. He was drooling so badly, I decided to ask him if he wanted it."

"Juan, you are terrible...you really are!" I shook my head in disbelief. We laughed, but I never really knew if he was telling me a story in order to make me laugh! Yet, recalling my many embarrassments at late night breakfasts made me think...it was possible!

Mary Marie was a young, very lovely technician who began instructing Juan on the proper use of the electric pump, as well as refreshing his mind in absolute sterile dressing changes...and as expected, they took to each other like bread and butter. It was apparent each time she was with him.... It was always as though he was the only one in the hospital, and this shouldn't have been anything new to expect because Juan had charmed women all his life.

Barry and I had been in touch throughout Juan's stay in both hospitals and once I told him he was finally coming home Wednesday, the thirteenth of November, he was as thrilled as I. However, I was totally unprepared for his response once I mentioned Juan was still intending to visit him in California for Thanksgiving.

"I don't know if it would be wise for Juan to travel so far from the hospital, Richard. I really don't think it would be a good idea." I wanted to argue, because I felt bad, but figured I should hold my tongue. I really thought it would be wonderful for Juan…but at the same time, realized Barry had to be in favor of it before we'd feel comfortable. I decided not to tell Juan.

Juan was allowed a pass the day before his discharge, and where else would he want to go but to our house. Everything was spotless and in order and his bedroom looked perfect, so I was anxious for his reaction once he walked in. And when he did walk in, he immediately began strutting around in that floating manner of his when he was pleased, and exclaim in his wide eyed expression.

"Aw, Recharred, you must 'ave been straightening out for a week! Everything looks so orderly! You must 'ave really been busy, Blanche!" After promising not to leave all my papers on the breakfast counter again, he sighed, "I don' believe it, Recharred, because I know it only takes you one day to do thot."

Juan hadn't yet walked into his bedroom, and of course, decided to tease me again by strutting in that put-on regal manner. He stopped in his tracks at the door, completely awed!

"Aw, Recharred!… Recharred, it looks so bea-u-ti-ful…so bea-u-ti-ful! I don' believe it!" Then, once he noticed the desk, his sigh was even greater and in a manner only he could do so well.

"Aw, Recharred, you refinished the top of my desk! Aw, it looks so good…like a sparkling gem! Aw, thank you so much, Recharred…so much!" He went on praising my placement of pictures and finally decided upon teasing me again with, "I guess you con do things nice sometimes, Recharred." He didn't, however, miss mentioning his bedroom looking better than mine, which I merely told him I had intended.

Juan settled into his favorite spot at the end of the couch, looking so happy. I made sandwiches the way he liked and before we realized, it was time to return to the hospital. After reminding him of it, he slumped back into the couch, caressing it like a kid not wanting to leave his favorite movie.

"Aw, Recharred, I don' want to go…I want to stay here now…. Aw, why do I 'ave to go?" I quickly reminded him he'd be able to stay, starting tomorrow, and he smiled. He was so beautiful.

After six weeks in hospitals, Juan was coming home…and wouldn't you know it? Once the doctor finally issued his release, there he was, chatting on endlessly with the nurses. I finally managed to hustle him along and couldn't believe it when I heard one of the nurses call out, "Don't worry, Juan, we will be seeing you again!" I wanted to smash her face, but was glad Juan's excitement seemed to override the words she used so tactlessly.

Juan had informed me about Svetmana coming with his sister.

"Ond, Recharred, I would like to treat for dinner ond thought we con order from Rocky's. You know how I love their spaghetti marinara sautéed with mushrooms." I asked if he wanted to dine there, but as usual, he preferred enjoying it at home. He was so happy to be home at last! It had been his longest hospital stay…six weeks, and I was determined everything was going to be perfect tonight and always!

Svetmana and Christina arrived and everything was going well as Juan chatted on happily. He then suggested we should all take a ride to pick up the order instead of me going alone. I had given everyone a soft drink and just as we were about to leave, Svetmana held out her empty glass in a very profound and arrogant manner…making it clear and obvious this was what I could expect of her whenever visiting.

"Here, Richard, *you* don't have to worry about washing my glass because I will use the same one when we return."

Her message was well received because it was obvious what she meant by her impertinent statement…for me to be well aware that she had no intention of ever picking up after herself while here, totally disregarding the fact that this would be her father's home, too. Her brashness bothered me but I decided to let it pass, especially since Juan, again, seemed to be oblivious to her flagrant and obvious insinuation. However, this time, it was apparent he was too happy to even notice.

Juan suggested I drive Svetmana's car, so she sat in the back seat with Christina, teasing her continually during the entire drive. I couldn't believe her juvenile behavior, forcing Christina to act in the same manner. It was as though she didn't have the ability to hold a conversation and reverted to childlike pranks instead. Juan had appeared stumped at one time and finally commented on her childish behavior, but she still continued with her obnoxious teasing. In fact, I had noticed this behavior towards Christina many times while at the hospital, but never thought to remark about it to Juan, since I was sure it was only a passing fancy. It had always been obvious that she never contributed to any conversation except to boast how intelligent she was because she could unscramble the jumbled up letters in a puzzle within minutes.

The village had just completed a metered parking lot directly across from my condo, and knowing the limited parking on my street, I decided to call it to Svetmana's attention.

"They just built this parking lot, so it will be great for you when you come to visit your dad…and it only costs a quarter for four hours." I hardly finished when she suddenly began mimicking in outrageous fashion, even adding her own ridiculous sounds to them.

"Oh, reeeeally…reee-alley…oh, I don't believe it…oh-hhh my, oh, my-yyy…ohhh, that's wonderful…wonderfulllly wonderful!" And she continued these obnoxious sounds! Words I cannot even begin to try to sound out and put on paper. It was obvious she was making fun of me again in her nasty way of trying to make me feel as though these idiotic sounds were what I sounded like! I couldn't keep my mouth shut this time, especially since Juan was silent, and probably because her ridiculous behavior had him bewildered.

"Svetmana, why are you talking like that…being so sarcastic?" I inquired, barely managing to keep my cool. "Why are you always making fun of me?" She paid no attention and just went on with her nasty-sounding mimicking. I finally lashed out, "Svetmana, when are you gonna grow up, for Chris' sake!" This was all she needed to explode into a screaming rage.

"How dare you say that to me! What do you mean! I 'am' a woman! Who the fuck do you think you are! You are no one to me…. Do you hear me?…nothing but an asshole fucker!" She continued with every swear word she ever learned, which left me no alternative but to lash out at her.

"Svetmana, you should have had your mouth washed years ago! That is why you have no friends…you insult everyone and make fun of them!" This only infuriated her more.

"That's what you think! I have lots of fuckin' friends!"

"Aw, don't give me that because your father has told me repeatedly you have no friends because of your miserable personality!" She was a picture of a wild woman, stamping her feet on the pavement!

"I am going home! I never want to see you or be with you again!" This put me back to reality since I couldn't help notice the sad and bewildered look on Juan's face. This was his first day home after six weeks in the hospital and I allowed this to happen! I quickly calmed myself, trying to reason with her to set the unfortunate matter aside, but she would have none of it, demanding only to retrieve her bag from my apartment and leave. I really thought I could persuade her to stay by pleading for compassion.

"This is your Dad's first day home from the hospital…please forget everything and stay for dinner?… It means so much to him…please, Svetmana?" However, she would have no part of it and continued calling me a fucker as we started on our way up, and through it all Juan and Christina remained stunned!

I truly believed she'd calm down once she looked at Juan's face. I was convinced she wouldn't cause her father this stress and accept my apologies, but she just ran into the powder room to get her bag while continuing her screaming rage. It was like a nightmare and I wanted to awaken to find it was just that! Christina looked at me hopelessly.

"She should no talk to you like thot…it is not right ot all." I continued my pleas for her to stay for her father's sake, but it did no good. I finally begged Christina to remain…that Juan and I would drive her to her mother's but to no avail.

"I come with Svetmana, ond I should leave with her." It didn't make any sense, but it was happening! I felt as though I was living a nightmare, and there it was before me…Svetmana! And I needed to lash out at it!

"You've been nothing but a spoiled brat all your life!" With that, Svetmana ran down the hall to the elevator, screaming at the top of her voice!

"Fuck off! Fuck off! Fuck off!"

My pleas to Christina to stay did no good because once Svetmana called out to her, she followed into the elevator. To be sure she had dinner, I quickly handed her most of the order. Juan had stood stunned through all of it, but finally surprised me as he hurried angrily to the elevator to face her before it closed!

"Svetmana!" he shouted, "I want you to get the fuck out of my life!... Do you hear me!" The elevator door closed immediately and Juan walked dejectedly back into the apartment.

This was something that should not have happened! Everything was supposed to be perfect tonight because this was Juan's first day home from his long stay in the hospital. I was sorry Juan had reacted in this manner towards Svetmana, but he angrily insisted he was right.

"She deserved it!" Even though I was trembling as much as he, I realized I had to get him out of this state. He didn't want to eat anything, "Because, Recharred, I 'ave lost my appetite." I finally calmed him enough to eat some but his usual relish for that meal was gone. He finally accepted the scenario for what it was, since he was so accustomed to Svetmana's nasty personality, realizing she was wrong, yet still managing to reprimand me.

"Recharred, you are aware of her nasty ways ond should 'ave ignored her." I couldn't say anything to the contrary because I realized he was disappointed, and that I was the only one he could really reprimand. So I accepted it because if he didn't love me, he wouldn't have said a word. The intimidation received through the years from Endira had made it impossible for him to truly feel comfortable reprimanding Svetmana and sticking to it. By evening's end, he once again proved capable of laying aside his problems to enjoy me.

Juan was again his happy self in the morning, talking excitedly about plans to do many things together. He had already called his mother and was ready for breakfast, but he wanted to call Barry first to catch him before he left for work. Through the years, Juan always paced the floor while talking excitedly on the phone, but now he placed it on the couch, figuring it would be convenient to answer when seated there. I had left the room for a moment and wasn't certain whether he ever mentioned Thanksgiving, but figured I wouldn't bring it up. It was funny because even though he wasn't pacing the floor, he still managed to wave his hand excitably.

It didn't take Juan long to look completely acclimated to his new life out of the hospital. He was thrilled and it really showed.

"Recharred, I would like to go shopping for some clothes. I 'ave to celebrate my new freedom with some new shirts. Would you like to go with me, Recharred? You do not 'ave anything else you 'ave to do today…do you?" I assured him the weekend was his.

"And in fact, Juan, I'm gonna be with you most of the times anyway." It was apparent this pleased him and I was glad since these were my plans. I hadn't mentioned I'd be seeing Matt once or twice a week and usually only when Juan was with his family because I didn't feel it was yet necessary to tell him. He had to be sure I'd be with him every time he wanted me to be, and that I desired the same of him.

Juan was so excited shopping and insisted on buying me a shirt, too, surprising me with the same choice as his, but another color, which was something he never did before. We also did some grocery shopping and I had forgotten what a pleasure that had always been, because his excitement at making certain dishes was a joy to hear.

"Aw, Recharred, we are gonna 'ave to eat thar one night," Juan said excitedly as we passed a Tapas restaurant, "because thot is the rage now." His excitement continued as he sighed, "Aw, Recharred, we 'ave to get Amanda ond Patti to the new Latin ballroom. I 'ave heard it is really hot. Maybe we con get a big crowd to go like Lucille, Daniel ond Stan, ond Marina, too." His arms then went up as he sighed, "Cha cha cha, Recharred!"

"You know, Recharred, I am gonna buy some very sharp ond stylish clothes ond wear a pair of sunglasses," he sighed, looking so cute standing in that swaggering manner of his when he stood fully on one leg with the other out on an angle, "ond then go to the bar ond jus' stond thar ond make them melt!" With that, he lifted his chin in that regal pose, holding it for a moment and then suddenly breaking into laughter.

"Juan, you are crazy, why would you want to wear sunglasses with those beautiful blue eyes you have?" He quickly reprised the pose.

"Because then, Recharred, no one will know who I am…I will be the mystery man!" I laughed and he finally settled down to say, "Besides, Recharred, my eyes are no longer thot bea-u-ti ful…they are dull now."

"Aw, no, Juan, not when you smile," I quickly assured him, "not when you smile!"

This first week had to be the greatest and I was especially happy because Matt, at last, abided my wishes and didn't call! For everything to run smoothly, Juan and Matt had to be friends and I didn't want to chance spoiling it by not allowing enough time. Never did the thought of oil being incapable of mixing with water enter my mind!

My daughter, Jacque, had invited us to a special preview of a new movie with Bette Midler and James Caan called *For the Boys* and I was glad because Juan had not seen her for so long besides only meeting Gil once that Christmas in 1988. It was so wonderful watching Juan and Jacque kiss and embrace, while he talked on excitedly, thanking her for inviting him. He was so appreciative. Juan and I sat there mesmerized because of the nostalgic 'forties' music and we both loved Bette Midler. Unfortunately, Juan began to tire once the movie refused to come to an end, especially realizing he still had to do his treatment. However, he wouldn't embarrass Jacque by leaving before the movie had ended.

I arrived home from Mildred's one evening to hear Juan happily say Svetmana finally called to say she was sorry. I was glad, but at the same time baffled why it took so long knowing her father's health.

"But she said she will never speak to you as long as she lives. She told me she hates you, Recharred." Even though I had expected something like this from her, I wasn't happy and asked him why he hadn't demanded she apologize to me. He couldn't give a real answer and I realized he was grasping out again for a child to be there for him...and said no more. I realized it would make me available to see Matt, but still felt it was more important to have the air clear between us. Tension wouldn't do Juan any good and I certainly didn't want to feel uncomfortable in my own house, especially since I was so happy Juan was finally with me.

Amanda and Patti's business wasn't far from the house and I went there a couple times a week to help with marketing, in hopes that one or two leads would come through to earn some commission. Juan would laugh once I reminded him that Amanda still started one project after another...never managing to finish any of them.

Daniel never was one to let a lull occur in any conversation, whether on the phone or in person. So it was fun watching Juan trying desperately to get a word in when he stopped in for a visit. He could walk in and tell you everything going on in his life, in a non-stop flow of words, so it was a riot watching the frustration on Juan's face. It would seem like forever, but finally he'd stop, smile, and listen. Daniel mentioned that he wanted to throw a surprise party for Stan's forty-ninth birthday, which surprised me...because Stan never even remembered Daniel's. But Daniel was always sure to give him one each year.

"I know whot you con do, Daniel...you con 'ave the party here ond invite whoever you want! I think thot would be nice. Do you not think so, Recharred?" I naturally was never one to refuse a party and agreed, especially since I was so happy Juan was in a frame of mind to have one.

Daniel was never one to expect anyone else to serve their food and drink as Vic did when he held the party for Phil at Juan's apartment years before. Yes, he arrived with an abundance of goodies and beverages.

The evening of the party, Juan was his usual witty and talkative self, but my heart felt a bit heavy...because he remained seated the entire evening. I so missed that excitement of him playing one record after another insisting we all cha cha. After everyone left, he didn't rehash and savor the evening's festivities as always.

"I am so tired, Recharred," he said softly instead, "ond I am gonna go to bed.... You don't mind do you, Recharred?" Then as he headed for his bedroom, he slowly turned to say, "I jus' don' 'ave the energy anymore, Recharred."In fact, there were nights he'd retire before nine o'clock.

Because Juan was tired so much didn't mean we didn't have our wonderful times together, because he'd merely remain seated, and his catchy laugh would have me uncontrollably doing the same. I no sooner arrived home from Mildred's and he excitedly insisted I watch the movie *Switch* with him because he had seen it before,

"Aw, Recharred, it is so hilarious...Ellen Barkin is terrific ond funny! You know I really like her. She is so streetwise with her smashed looking face...so tough, but with a fantastic figure. You know, Recharred, she is the same type as Angie Dickenson was." Barkin was superb, but I'm sure it was Juan's catchy cackle that kept me rolling!

I had been seeing Matt, but almost always when Juan was with his mother or Svetmana. I still had to be sure of him, and his guessing game wasn't coming to an end...I felt he could be the love of my life even though he proved to be an egotistical hypocrite, as well as holding onto his other selfish traits. I, however, was sure these would change because he had given me so many indications he wanted our relationship to be lasting.

I was to see Matt and had informed him I was going to drive Juan to his folks before coming to his house because he didn't like driving at night and that it would only be a matter of about fifteen minutes later than the time we agreed upon. Again, he complained, insisting it would ruin his entire evening. I could never understand his impatience!

Juan was in an exceptional talkative mood as I drove and we were almost to his folk's.

"Recharred, I would like if you would stop ot this supermart before dropping me off because they 'ave lots of Latin condiments ond we con buy a couple of bottles of Sazon. Besides, Recharred, they carry the very good brand thar." I realized this would probably make me later than the fifteen minutes, especially since Juan continued talking while in the store. I was on pins and needles realizing what to expect once I got to Matt's, but managed to hide it. Yet, it made me angry with Matt as well as myself for allowing him to intimidate me in this way. I wanted to enjoy my time with Juan and shouldn't have subjected myself to become this nervous. I felt I covered myself perfectly because I would've been aware if Juan realized my nervousness. Yet I still wasn't certain since Juan always had this extra-sensory perception. I, somehow, think he realized I was going to be with Matt and decided upon not saying anything. Instead, he gave the excuse to buy Sazon...to see how far he could push me? And I think he was happy I didn't rush him. Still, I never should've had to go thru such stress.

John had been in and out of the hospital a few times and Juan had visited him.

"John is really in bad shape, Recharred. He is shitting all over the house. I feel so sorry for Maryann because thar is crap everywhere when she goes over to check on him." I didn't know what to say, but realized that Juan was subjected to the bacteria that had to be infesting the place and that was dangerous. However, he wanted to be there to support John and would do it no matter what, but I still felt uneasy because of his own weakened immune system.

"John is bock in the hospital, Recharred, ond he is very bod...very bod," Juan said a few days later. "I don' think he will pull out of it this time. I talked with Maryann and she told me he does not comprehend anything...thot he is in a semi-coma."

"Aw, Juan, that is terrible...I feel so bad." I didn't want to say much more because I realized what had to be going through his head...and I wanted to shout out…NO! But then he seemed to be accepting it because he showed no signs of faltering…of crying. And I was proud because I felt he was assuring himself it would never happen to him! He was just concerned about his friend. A friend who was very sick…and this wasn't going to happen to him.

Chapter Sixty:
The Seesaw of Rash Decisions

This had to be the real beginning of that seesaw...or the tug-of-war...or whatever one might call it, and I was right in the middle of it all! I was about to leave the house and this was the first time Juan was really aware of the fact that I was about to see Matt. I had tried to make light of it once I told him...merely stating that Matt had asked me to go to a movie. Svetmana was coming over and I figured this would be a good time to finally admit to it. One look at his face as I was going out the door made me realize he wasn't just depressed, but shocked as well. It was as though he hadn't been aware of the fact that I had been seeing Matt...and why now? To add to my distress, Juan's face continued to be there before me the entire evening, and because of it I cut the night short.

My persistence to continue this relationship with Matt wouldn't subside, even though my inner feelings felt he was playing around. But I wasn't the type to chug someone off without proof, especially since he had made accusations that I was only using him until Juan returned. I knew this wasn't true, so I guess I had to prove it. Oddly enough, I had two of these so-called proofs back in June, but let Matt control them. If this had happened to anyone else, Matt would have been given the old 'heave-ho' the very first time! But after all, I was Richard, probably better known as 'Mr. Give-All.'

The first occasion I had been out once again searching for Matt and decided on trying the Nutbush. The bar was packed but I managed to spot his back seated just before me. My happiness at seeing him was short-lived just as I was about to pat his back because, there he was holding hands with this baldheaded gent next to him. I was stunned, immediately backing off to a spot at the kidney-shaped bar, which would keep me from his sight. It wasn't long after and they began embracing and kissing passionately, almost making me think I might be treated to an X-rated movie. Of course, I downed three cocktails in non-stop gulps to finally walk over to stand directly behind them as they lingered on a kiss. And of course, my face was directly between the two of theirs once they broke from their passionate clinch! Once Matt came out of shock, I merely returned to my spot at the bar, my fury becoming more intense with each beckoned call from him. It was incomprehensible, actually expecting me to join them! So I finally walked out to my car. I know what I should have done. I should have immediately started the car and take off for home and forget him forever. But no, instead I sat in my car in a complete stupor. Here he was kissing someone passionately and I only got a peck now and then because he always complained his lips were chapped. I could imagine from what! Suddenly, there was a tap on the window. My first mistake had been when I didn't drive directly home, and my second was once I opened the door to let him in the car. It doesn't take much to guess my third mistake.

The second occasion…. Again, I was on the prowl looking for Matt, walking into the same bar to see him with the same guy, but only this time seated in the corner on the far opposite side of the bar. So I strategically positioned myself at another spot to watch the same movie again. This time, the fire in me had to be stronger than the alcohol I began drinking. Again, after being discovered for 'snooping' I accepted his stories, wiped away his tears, and went on with our relationship…or whatever he called it….

It was odd, but Matt had been receiving hang-up calls all hours of the day and into the night, always appearing to be so intrigued instead of upset. He seemed to enjoy the mystery of it, believing they were coming from some secret admirer. He even boasted.

"You know, Rich, I have sometimes shouted out for the guy to come over when no one answers." Of course, this didn't set well with me, but I still remained densely oblivious to what he was actually admitting about himself!

My feelings and love for Juan were still the same and I realized that would never change. However, the one or two times a week Juan was aware of the fact that I was seeing Matt became too much for him, causing his temper to flare up. He was still the same charming person and our wonderful times together continued…but now they were in the minority, far and few between these terrible flare-ups. In all of our years, Juan never allowed his nasty moods this much majority…but he was obsessed with the fact that I was continuing to see Matt. He was hurting, and because of it, I, too, felt a constant ache, especially after his repeated mentions of stress because I was well aware of what it could do to someone with AIDS. I had tried desperately to avoid causing any, but it was impossible to accomplish. So he'd shout out that I was causing him stress by refusing to discontinue seeing Matt. I then would try to reason with him…to give me time because my gut feelings had to realize Matt was playing a game.

"I just cannot tell someone to get out of my life until they give me reason, Juan!" But he just wouldn't rationalize anything I'd try to explain. He just remained stubborn and irrational, and admitted to it.

"I know I am being a bitch, Recharred, but I jus' do not want you to go out with thot flaming queen," and he continued his bewilderment as to why I was going out with someone so obviously gay...repeatedly badgering me with the same questions. I never answered because I didn't feel he had a right to demand I discontinue seeing Matt totally. It had to be my decision...and for a reason.

There were times Juan must have searched into his heart, realizing the deep love we had for each other and lay aside his anger to be the loving person I knew so well, and then I'd be so happy. I wanted it to be like that always, not realizing myself the anguish he had to be going through...the feelings of despair because I may not be there for him one day. I never thought of it since I knew that would never come about. So I longed for times like the day before Thanksgiving, which had only been about three weeks earlier. We had spent a beautiful day together and I wanted it to be that way each time. Juan was sharing another of those crazy holiday arrangements...this time at Endira's, along with his folks. He decided to bring a cake for dessert and we went to the bakery I always bought his birthday cakes. After choosing an absolutely scrumptious-looking one, he was looking to do something pleasant.

"Recharred, why don' we go across to the Dodge dealer I bought my car from to see if they 'ave the new Stealth. Aw, Recharred, it is so bea-u-ti-ful ond I would like for you to see it!" They did have one in the showroom...in red, and just looking at Juan's face light up, anxiously waiting for my reaction, would have been worth traveling across the globe to see it! He went on talking...or rather dreaming about the two of us being rich...to be able to one day buy one. The day had been wonderful, without any mentions of Matt. In fact, I never thought of him anyway when I was with Juan.

I was home with Juan more, but, because he realized Matt was still in the picture, he began refusing to go out with me to a movie, even ones we had planned to see. Instead of going with him to all the places he had talked about, he was doing it with Svetmana during the afternoon hours. I'd beg to see a movie with me, only to hear him obstinately refuse.

"Why don' you ask thot flaming queen with the curly bleached tips to go with you? I am sure he would love it!" To make matters worse, I began feeling very uncomfortable each time Svetmana came over, ending up in my bedroom sulking, finally running out to relieve the tension.

I was in misery because I was feeling guilty. This wasn't like before when I had to satisfy my sick ego to trick...not like when Juan demanded I needed to pay for my sins...no, not this time. This time, I was serious about someone I wasn't sure felt the same about me...yet *he* would not let go! So I kept pursuing. I was trying so desperately not to cause Juan stress, yet everything happening seemed to be filling his days with it! Because of it, I was miserable, but still couldn't let go of Matt. He had been giving me so many indications he wanted this relationship and I was certain he'd soon be kissing the ground I walked on, while understanding the love Juan and I shared. Being the person I was, I couldn't just give him the gate. There'd be no problem if he came right out to say he wasn't interested and could never love me in that way. Knowing myself I would soon lose interest, especially since my makeup would never allow me to love someone deeply once I realized they didn't love me the same in return. I even stooped so low as to suggest we meet on the sly, thinking that if he truly loved me, he'd agree to it. However, he would have no part of it, which should've told me something. It also should've made me realize he really didn't care whether or not Juan was having stress.

"Bullshit, he is not gonna have stress! He just wants his own way." I couldn't understand how anyone could be so cold and callous, but yet I let him get away with it.

I wanted to be with Juan, but many of the times I planned on it, he'd then call Svetmana and ask her to come over, forcing me to leave the house. He often made it unbearable because his continued badgering drove me up the wall! My only peace of mind was when I was out of the house. On one such night, he kept on with his badgering…insisting I leave to see Matt, and he wouldn't let up! Out of desperation, I finally rose and started for the door.

"Recharred, if you cannot stop seeing Matt, I am gonna 'ave to move from here ond get my own place…I mean it, Recharred! I cannot stay here ond watch you go out with him. I cry every time ofter you leave." This upset me tremendously because I knew he needed to be with me…. He couldn't go on his own! He finally calmed down, realizing I was tremendously upset.

"Recharred, I know I am being a bitch…thot I am totally unreasonable, but thot is the way it is. I jus' cannot take seeing you go out with him…ond I know you 'ave every right to, but I 'ave to be away from you so I con one day be friends ond accept him in your life. Do you understond, my darlin'?" I understood, but yet I didn't! He couldn't be on his own! He had to be with me and I needed to be with him! So again I calmly explained the doubts running through my head about Matt's feelings for me…that he had to give me some time. I finally felt that he was convinced he had to be with me. He seemed to accept my logic and for a couple of days, he was again the charming Juan I knew.

This charm was short-lived because Juan was allowing everything to prey on his mind and one evening, just as I was about to leave to see Matt, he arose from the couch, trembling!

"Recharred, I know you are goin' out with thot queen again. You don' know, but I 'ave gone to the bars near here…ond I 'ave talked with some guys thar. Do you know whot he is known as? Huh? He is known as the whore of Oak Park! Why do you want to go with him Recharred? He is such a whore, ond will leave you jus' as soon as the first new guy comes along! Recharred, he will never be true to you!"

I tried to explain we were just friends but to no avail. "Juan, I don't want to have him accuse me of using him!"

"Whot difference does it make, Recharred? You don' need his respect! Don' you care about how I feel, Recharred?" I glared at him not believing he could say that.

"JUAN, how can you say something like that? Aw, Juan, you and I are one person!"

"Aw, Recharred, I 'ave not been feeling well ot all lately," he cried out tears falling down his face, "ond I don' know how much more time I 'ave to live!" In that instant, I felt as though my throat had been clutched tightly…yet nervously thinking that he is just trying to scare me…yes that's it, just to scare me!

"Juan, that is not true…you told me the doctors say you have five or more years and we were sure they'd have a cure by then!" I was near hysteria! "NO! You have to have five or more years…you have to!" Juan began trembling, looking at me desperately!

"Recharred…Stress! Stress! It con make someone get sick very fast…very fast! Whot do you want to do…huh? DO YOU WANT TO DANCE ON MY GRAVE…IS THOT WHOT YOU WANT TO DO?"

I can't remember what I said…no…I can't remember because I was too upset to believe he'd think such a thing! I tried to plead with him to realize I loved him more than myself, but he was in a complete rage and wouldn't listen to anything said. He just continued to shout louder, demanding I get out of his sight. I finally realized I had to leave for his sake…to enable him to realize his rash statements and settle down. My mind was shattered as well as my heart and I immediately realized everything had to end with Matt, and it had to be cold turkey! It had been apparent on many occasions that Matt always seemed to have a knack at coming out on top in heavy conversations held at his place, and there was no way I would chance that possibility. However, I can't recall where I brought it up, but I managed!

The change in Juan was miraculous once he heard my decision to stop seeing Matt entirely. I must admit, even though it was wonderful he was so happy, I was a bit disturbed he'd been so demanding…that he wouldn't allow the time to find out for myself if Matt was truly a whore. However, I was certain I had made the right decision.

Then, it happened….

The following evening, Juan and I were enjoying being home alone. In fact, I hadn't given a thought to Matt at all, happy because it was finally over with him. We were both seated on the same couch of the sectional and the phone was set between the two of us because Juan had just made a couple of calls. Suddenly it rang and as Juan picked up the receiver; he spoke in that eloquently charming voice he was so capable of doing when he was truly happy…

"Allo, this is Juan, may I please help you?" Suddenly, the smile disappeared as he held the receiver out to me as though it were contaminated.

"It is him." A feeling of despair fell over me because I didn't know what to expect. I had already made it clear I wasn't going to see him again…that I had to devote myself totally to Juan. I had explained that I loved him but that I'd never be able to forgive myself if Juan thought I wasn't going to be there for him. I had gone on further to say I wasn't being sacrificed since I loved

Juan more than myself and wanted to do everything possible to keep him alive. I had even talked about my dreams of a cure and once Juan had rid himself of this dreaded disease…that we might find we needed someone else to fulfill our sexual needs, while still remaining as one person. I had told him that Juan and I could possibly resume as lovers…that I didn't know. But I had to be there for him even though he was being unreasonable…and that he had every right to be because he had AIDS and everyone with it was dying. So why was Matt calling?

I really wanted to take the call in my bedroom since I felt Juan didn't need to hear any heavy discussion Matt was so good at…but then again he might think I was playing games if I did. So I casually answered and was then greeted with dead silence. It was a ray of hope, thinking he had decided against talking. However, just as I was about to hang up, I heard his voice greeting me in a low despondent tone. I wanted to keep the conversation as light as possible and merely asked how he was doing? After another pause, he sadly expressed his misery, which confused me! He had always asked for his space and refused to commit, so why was he miserable? I decided I had to cut this short, realizing he'd go on endlessly, and before saying a quick good-bye and hanging up, I confirmed my decision again.

It was evident Juan was happy and satisfied with the way I handled myself, but two minutes hadn't passed when the phone rang again. This time, I answered, and my fears Matt again was calling were quickly confirmed as he pleaded to see me…that he needed to talk. I again tried to keep it light because I didn't want to see him. I knew how persuasive he could be, and I wasn't going to change my mind. My short conversation had to sound a bit awkward, yet Juan seemed to accept it. He did, however, shake his head unbelievably.

"Boy, he *is* persistent!" he exclaimed. I decided to say he was only disappointed we couldn't be friends because I didn't want him to think it was any more than that.

I decided to change the subject because I didn't want it to prey on Juan's mind. Ten minutes passed and I felt somewhat relieved, assuming Matt finally realized I meant everything. Suddenly the phone rang again and this time Juan answered, but not in that same charming manner. I was hesitant in taking the phone from him as he angrily handed it to me, but then I was Richard, and 'Richard' was a nice guy who never wanted to hurt anyone.

Matt continued his persistence and I went on to say there was no need for further discussion since everything had already been said, but he just wouldn't take no for an answer. I finally realized he would probably continue calling until he drove Juan crazy, and felt I should possibly see him the following evening to explain everything again. I wasn't the type to tell someone to get the fuck out of my life even though that was what was needed to be said. Juan wasn't happy with my decision, but after explaining I felt I owed Matt that much, and to please let me do it for my own peace of mind, he reluctantly agreed.

If ever there was an evening I could wish stricken from my life, this would be the one. To say it hurts to recall is the biggest understatement ever made.... If I had walked into an enemy campsite the hostile atmosphere would have probably been less than what I felt once I walked into Matt's apartment. I hadn't taken off my coat and just stood in the kitchen, leaning against the counter, feeling more than a bit awkward. Matt had answered the door wearing a long and angry frown and hadn't said a word, leaving me alone while continuing to walk from one room to another finishing up whatever he'd been doing. I wondered why I even came, and should've stormed out immediately at that time...but I didn't. Instead, I just stood there like some idiot. I had expected to have a quiet talk from his despondent manner of speaking the night before and was totally unprepared once he came storming towards me, demanding to know the reasons for my actions. I attempted to remain calm myself after his eruption, but found my voice shaking as I again explained everything. As soon as I mentioned "stress," he pushed his face into mine and shouted!

"Oh, what do you mean, Rich...STRESS! He is not going to have any stress! He just wants to have his way like a little kid.... Fuck his stress!"

I was in shock! No matter what I said did no good. He just stood there with clenched fists shouting one profanity after another, placing his face a breath away from mine and finally bringing his fist beneath my chin. It was as though I was living a nightmare! The hatred in his eyes was unbelievable and I became weary about remaining any longer since I remembered my feelings about him being manic and especially remembering the time I had gone to trick with his ex lover, George. His face had looked as though he had been gang beaten, and after I had asked what happened, was told Matt had mauled him during one of his jealous rages. I wanted no part of this, especially since my four front caps could possibly be knocked out. I wanted out and was certain I'd never return, and once he again accused me of using him while viciously calling me an 'asshole,' I raced for the door off the back sitting room! Unfortunately, I never made it, because, while reaching for the doorknob, he lunged at me and viciously pushed me onto the rattan chair directly next to the door! There I was, sprawled on the chair while Matt stood directly over me with a clenched fist...and in shock besides scared shitless!

He continued his vicious tone demanding, "Where the hell do you think you are going? I want to talk to you and you want to leave!"

To this day the rest of the evening is a total blank and I could never attempt to try to remember what was said. How he finally calmed down to talk...I'll never know! And we talked for three hours! Why I agreed to stay, even though he calmed down...I'll also never know! This I do remember: *He once again managed to talk me into seeing him—as always....* I went against my word to Juan, and by agreeing to it, I should have felt happy...but as I left, a terrible feeling of gloom came over me. I knew I had made the wrong decision, yet realized I was going to stick to it. It didn't make sense and the only reasoning I can now imagine...my subconscious mind realized Juan was going to die…and because I always needed to have someone by my side…I thought it could be Matt!

Juan was sleeping once I arrived home, and though I hated the fact that he no longer had the strength to stay up to hear what happened, I was relieved because how was I to explain this reversal, especially since I was so despondent? And yet, my heart yearned for the old days when he'd be laying on the couch waiting anxiously to hear all the details. Again, my mind will not recall what excuse I gave the next morning for remaining at Matt's so late, and I cannot remember if it was then that I told him I had reversed my original decision. So, again, I am faced with a blackout regarding one of my decisions I knew to be wrong even at that time.

I do recall that Amanda and Daniel had been talking to me about it. They realized that Juan was being totally unreasonable, yet strongly advised to heed his wishes. Daniel had been very positive.

"Richard, Juan does not have that long to live and Matt will still be around after he is gone…. Believe me, I know he will be willing to pick up again. You can count on it, Richard! Knowing you…you will never forgive yourself if you let Juan leave. I really urge you to reconsider." I realized Daniel didn't care much for Matt because he had often said, "Believe me, one whore knows another, and I know he is one."

However, I was really bothered by his statement that Juan didn't have long to live, when I had been repeatedly assured by Juan himself that the doctors were talking about five or ten years, which gave me continued hopes for an ultimate cure. This was really the factor in my decision to ignore his advice and warnings. Amanda, however, liked Matt fairly well, although she was completely aware of his roving eye, especially after he couldn't control himself and very obviously continued staring at her associate's basket the day I decided to take him to see her shop. She then called me that very night….

"Richard, James does not know I am gay and because he is all macho man, I certainly do not want him to know. So, please, tell Matt to keep his damn piercing eyes to himself! For Chris' sake, I thought he was almost going to go down on him." But again, I let her words slip from my mind, even though I also had noticed how he was mesmerized with James. A few days later we discussed the situation again.

"Richard, I like Matt well enough, but Juan has AIDS and he wants you to be with him. I don't want you to one day regret doing what you are about to do, and I know you will!" I tried to explain I still would be with him as much as I am now and even more, but all she could do was remind me Juan was being stubborn and just didn't want me to be with Matt. "And, Richard, we have all talked with Juan and know there is no way he will change his mind." I should've listened and heeded her advice…but I didn't.

Juan and I were seated on the couch once I finally broke the news. Again, my exact words are wiped from my head, but my heart and mind will never forget the words Juan uttered once he was told and my words afterwards. The bright glow was gone from his face and his shoulders were hunched, staring into space for some time and finally sighing,

"Well…it looks…like I lost."

"No, Juan, you have not lost me!" I cried out. "You could never lose me because I love you more than myself! Juan, I want you to live! I will never believe you will die soon! Aw, Juan, you have to be here all my life because I don't know what I would do if you die! But now you keep telling me you will die one day soon…so if you feel that way, don't you want to have someone there for me…to support me?" I couldn't control the tears from erupting.

"Yes, Recharred, I do want you to 'ave someone when I die, but not Matt."

"Why?" I cried out desperately,

"You 'ave Daniel, ond you 'ave Amanda!" he shouted, "ond they will be thar for you." I begged him to understand I'd be there for him always, but he refused to talk of it anymore.

The feeling had come to my mind many times…that Matt only wanted to beat out Juan in this tug-of-war and didn't care one bit about me. He hated Juan because he realized Juan wanted no part of him and this crushed his ego. But I'd chase the thought from my mind immediately. Now, here was Juan saying, he had lost. I could have also thought the same of him…that I was just a game to win. But I knew better because Juan had proven his love for me so many times, and in so many ways, each time he touched my heart.

So we continued with our lives and I decided to spend even more time with Juan. However, he still preyed on my terrible decision and would retaliate by being nasty. Still, he couldn't remain totally angry with me, and those times were like heaven.

He was in an exceptional good mood one day and I never thought this would happen.

"Recharred, I am gonna 'ave to move on my own. I 'ave to find an apartment. Please, try to understond why I 'ave to do it. I 'ave to finally accept this, ond it will help if I am away from you for a while. Then I will be able to have you bock in my life…. Please, understond, my darlin'?"

But I didn't want to understand! I knew he had to be with me because there was no way I could stay away from him for any length of time, and I tried to tell him this, but he insisted that was what he had to do. In fact, I found he had already been looking after receiving a call from an agent. I immediately realized Svetmana had to be pushing him into it just to get him to move from my house. I could almost hear her words bugging him.

"C'mon, Daddy, let's go look for apartments today…c'mon I want you to move from here!"

Daniel was almost as upset as I and pleaded with him to change his mind, but to no avail.

"Richard, I hope he is not serious about this because he needs to be with you. He cannot stay alone because that daughter of his will be absolutely no help at all, especially when he needs someone all the time," Daniel had said once we were alone. I simply informed him I would then go stay with him, only to hear him snap back at me.

"Yeah, then you will be there for him while he is not helping with your expenses…you are the one who needs financial help, so make him change his mind before he ends up signing a lease…because then he will be forced to move." I tried to explain money had nothing to do with my wanting him to stay, but Daniel still was concerned.

And we did have wonderful times, especially when Matt didn't call the house, but when he did, Juan and I were back at square one.

"Guess whot, Recharred?" Juan had excitedly exclaimed one day, "I am gonna go to an elegant formal affair ot one of the big hotels in Chicago! Endira's church is 'aving their annual Christmas formal ond she asked me to go with Svetmana. Recharred, it is supposed to be a very elegant dinner dance. Ond do you know whot?… I am gonna wear a tux! Endira said she will pay for my rental. Do you know this will be the first time I will wear a tux in my life?" I couldn't believe his excitement! It was like always…sharing his joy with me!

I had put up my small Christmas tree while Juan was out and once he returned home and noticed the gifts under it, he appeared to be annoyed.

"I see you 'ave gifts for me under the tree, Recharred. Well, I do not want anything from you ond will not accept them, so I suggest you give them to your curly bleached blond tips friend." I decided not to say anything and he just went on to say, "Recharred, I am not giving you anything, so bring them bock…I mean it!" I still ignored it.

My son, Nicky, had asked if I'd care to build shelving in his garage so I was kept quite busy before and around the holidays because it was quite a project. I especially wanted to do it because he had given me almost five thousand dollars just before Father's Day and told me not to worry about paying him back. I felt this was a show of appreciation. Because I was so busy, I hadn't gone with Juan the day he was fitted for the tux. However, I drove him to pick it up the day of the dance and insisted it needed to be taken in because his weight loss was mostly in his butt. So while we waited for them to alter it, he talked of nothing but the dance and wearing his first tux. He was so excited and I told him I wished I could go along, if only to watch his excitement through the evening.

"Recharred, do you think you con drive me to the hotel tonight? Would thot not disturb your evening?" I immediately told him it wouldn't, though I realized it would make me a bit late for my date with Matt. But I didn't care because I'd be with Juan, listening to his excitement about the formal…and that would be worth bearing the torment of Matt's abuse.

"You know, Recharred, you will 'ave to help me dress," he added, "because I know I am gonna 'ave trouble with those buttons."

While Juan showered, I decided upon calling Matt to tell him I'd be about forty-five minutes later, and as expected…he complained! I knew it was hopeless explaining Juan's night vision again, so I just let him go on complaining. Juan began dressing a little later than he should have and I realized I was going to be in trouble, but tried desperately not to show any anxiety. I was angry at myself because I always seemed to let Matt get the best of me. I couldn't understand how I allowed him to give me one nasty ultimatum after another, and why he always insisted I was ruining his entire evening should I inform him I'd be a few minutes or so late. And I heard the same tonight.

"Well if you're not here by eight fifteen, Rich, I am gone!"

The last thing I had to help Juan with was his bow tie, and I will never forget as we stood facing each other…I was trying desperately to straighten his tie to look nice, when I caught the blues of his eyes staring softly into mine. I didn't ask what he was thinking because I felt it was the same as mine…that this was the man I will always love.

I stepped back to get a full view once I secured the tie.

"Aw, Juan, you look so handsome…so elegant," and as I tried to hug him, he gently managed to edge free of my grip, while shaking his finger in shame in the manner he was so good at.

"Now, now, Recharred!" I just shook my head and laughed but managed to give him a quick squeeze anyway. I had film in my cheap camera and decided on taking a couple of shots.

"Why do you want pictures of me, Recharred? So you con 'ave them as a memory ofter I am gone?" I didn't think it was funny and merely reminded him that it was his first time wearing a tux.

Traffic was at a standstill the entire block before the hotel, and I guessed it was because of drop-offs. So Juan kept my mind busy with his excitable chatter and I stopped worrying about the woe I'd soon be getting from Matt. I wanted to share this night with Juan so badly.

"Well, I am off to cha, cha!" Juan sighed, raising his arms in that inimitable way of his once we reached the entrance. "Good night, Recharred. Thank you so much for driving me!"

"Good night, Juan, and have a wonderful time! I'll see ya."

It was almost eight fifteen and I quickly found a phone to let Matt know I was on my way, but there was no answer. Once I beeped my number, I found he had left a message informing me he was going out alone. The man had to be the most impatient and temperamental person I ever met in my life and I couldn't understand my loyalty to him. The evening ended in a fiasco because after chasing to a couple of places, I ended up sitting with him in his rear sun porch listening to him repeat one complaint after another. If I hadn't had to chase around after him I would have arrived at eight thirty, and for most people that is a perfect time to begin a Saturday evening. However, he insisted I had totally ruined his evening and just continued his miserable mood. He did not yet commit to me, but, at the same time wanted my complete devotion? I truly had to be the puppy dog Juan said I was to him because I listened to his manic complaints for five hours!

Juan was already asleep once I arrived home, which disappointed me because I wanted to hear his excited talk about the formal. But when morning arrived, I received my treat.

"Recharred, everyone of the single women thar wanted to dance with me!"

"Why would that surprise me, Juan? You are still the most handsome guy around and you still captivate every woman you meet!" Juan looked at me with that sheepish grin.

"I do? I still do?"

"Of course, you do, Juan. You always will!" What did he think, there was sign on his back reading, AIDS? No, he'd never look like he had AIDS...not with me around!

Juan had decided upon a truce...not to talk of Matt and ruin our times together, and I tried to keep him from calling when Juan was home. It was working out fairly well, though he still wasn't taking me along on all his outings. He was doing them with Svetmana instead. However, he had been going out during the afternoons and I was so busy at Nicky's while still working for Mildred, so it was some consolation. I did however realize if Matt hadn't been in the picture, Juan would have definitely waited for me to get home to do these things, and it hurt.

I again spent Christmas Eve with Matt because, as usual, Juan was going to his mother's. I think if all of this hadn't happened with Matt as well as Svetmana, I would've been asked to go along with Juan to his folks. They were well aware that he was living with me because they often called to ask how he was doing, and I knew they were very appreciative of my hospitality. They didn't know how much Juan and I loved each other and that it wasn't a question of hospitality, but one of pure love and concern. Juan was completely unaware that I spent Christmas Eve with Matt. I had been invited to spend it with my old friend, Gina, and her family and he had answered the phone when she called to hear me accept her invitation. What he didn't hear was when I called her to say I'd only stay a short while.

I arrived early at Gina's and sat in her kitchen as she fried all kinds of fish, and once I left, discovered my velour shirt had saturated the oils to make me smell like one, too! I also decided upon parking my car several blocks from Matt's house in case Juan decided to drive by. After Matt and I had dinner, we decided on going to midnight mass and since I was complaining of the fish smell, he insisted we stop off at my apartment to change. I couldn't believe he'd ask me to do something like that and quickly told him.

"What if Juan comes home early? I don't want the two of you to be confronted with each other." Matt saw no reason why he shouldn't be allowed to go up with me, and especially once I told him it would only cause Juan stress.

"Oh, bullshit to his stress!" I kept my mouth shut as he continued with his remarks...even at Christmas. However, I did sit in church smelling like a fish.

Juan made me very unhappy because he refused to accept my Christmas gifts, and no matter how I pleaded, he wouldn't break. He finally agreed to accept one gift because he knew what it was and he was out of it…a bottle of our favorite cologne, Paul Sabastian, which also included a porcelain of a flying Eagle as an added bonus.

Juan always had a full face with classic features of high cheek bones, and even though it was somewhat thinner, it wasn't really noticeable. However, when I received the pictures, the ones of him in his tux especially came out as though they were taken with an X-Ray because every bone seemed to stand out. Still, it didn't bother me because I knew he didn't look that way in person. He was 178 pounds and that was fine for someone just a bit over five-foot ten.

I had informed Matt I was definitely spending New Year's Eve with Juan and he didn't seem to mind. However, once I told Juan, he could only react sarcastically.

"Whot is the matter, does the old queen 'ave something else to do?"

I quickly assured Juan that wasn't the reason…that I told Matt I wanted to spend it with him. With that, Juan seemed to roll his eyes and appeared to be measuring the wishes of a casual friend.

"Well, I don' know if I will be able to be with you," and then to confirm his reaction to a so-called casual friend asking for a date, smugly added, "I will let you know, Recharred." I realized he wanted me to pay by keeping me hanging and that was fine with me. So I held my ground because I wanted to be with him. I finally forced him to give me an answer.

"I think I may be going to a big party ot Endira's or we might 'ave it ot my mother's." He continued to talk excitedly about the big party they were planning, which I was certain was totally exaggerated! Yes, I was sure he just wanted me to suffer, but I still didn't care as long as we ended up spending the night together. I was also angry because of Svetmana…if she had been on friendly terms, I'm certain I'd have been included in this so-called big party.

Daniel and Stan were going to Mexico for the holiday, and Amanda and Patti were going their separate ways, otherwise I would've invited them over. That surely would keep Juan home. I also suggested we go out for dinner and return home to spend the rest of the evening but Juan wouldn't give me an answer.

Juan still hadn't committed the morning of New Year's Eve, and I was off to work at Nicky's. It was early afternoon once I called Juan and was stunned to hear he was definitely going to his mother's…that the big party was being held there. I realized this big party probably only included his folks and Svetmana as well as Endira and her husband, Dan. Still, it would've been a big party for me if I had been asked to go…because, after all, Juan would be there! And when I asked to be included, he reminded me of Svetmana only too slyly.

"I am sorry, Recharred…why don' you see if the old queen con do something with you?"

I really had thought Juan kept me hanging just to suffer, and then finally agree to spend the evening with me. So I was shocked and very disappointed.

I really should've just stayed home alone, instead of deciding to call Matt. He hadn't made plans and we set a time to go for dinner and to Gentry's, an entertainment bar.

Juan hardly acknowledged me once I returned home from Nicky's and I felt very uncomfortable. I tried to talk to him, but he wouldn't answer. This wasn't something usual between us. No, we never had problems communicating. I finally mentioned I was going to dinner with Matt since he wasn't available, but received no response from that either. It was so awkward that I finally decided to take my shower and dress. Juan was still in the same spot, sitting quietly once I returned to the living room fully dressed.

"Aw, I see you are going out," Juan lashed out suddenly. "Whot, are you afraid to be late? Ond you 'ave not even asked how I am feeling?" I stopped in my tracks in disbelief!

"Juan, I tried to talk to you when I came in, but you completely refused to acknowledge my presence."

"Recharred, you should 'ave asked anyway. You jus' do not care how I am." Now I was certain he was reaching for something to pick on.

"Juan, how can you say something like that when you know how I feel about you, and how badly I want you well! What is wrong? Haven't you felt well today?"

"No, Recharred, I 'ave not felt well all day."

"Well, why didn't you say anything about it when I called today…why didn't you?"

"I did not want to bother you, Recharred."

"Aw, Juan, I don't believe it! Well I'm not going out tonight…I'm gonna stay home with you."

"No, no, no, Recharred, I am gonna go to my mother's. Endira will be picking me up soon…so you go out." I tried to reason with him to stay home, but I couldn't get anywhere. I finally left feeling very low, especially since I wasn't quite sure if this was one of his tests to see what I'd actually do. As I pulled out of my parking spot, I noticed Endira getting out of her car, so I realized Juan was telling me the truth.

The evening with Matt was pleasant enough because he remained in a good mood instead of spoiling it with one of his angry outbursts. However, we spent almost three and a half hours sitting on stools watching one performer entertain continually. He was great, but I never liked to sit in one spot while out, especially on New Year's Eve. Matt was sort of sedate all evening, so it really was a fairly quiet night. We just hugged each other at midnight, and at the time, my mind was on Juan, wanting desperately to telephone and wish him a Happy New Year, but afraid my call could possibly be upsetting. However, my decision was wrong again.

"Recharred, I thought you would 'ave called me last night to wish me a Happy New Year. Aw, Recharred, I felt so bod." I never knew if he totally believed my reason for not calling. Again, Juan couldn't remain angry once we spent the holiday alone. It was how it should always be…Juan laughing in that uncontrollable and contagious laugh of his…with me following suit. And who could make it better than the *I Love Lucy* shows going into 1992. Why couldn't he be this way all the time? A good answer to that question could most certainly be…why I had to be so caring…so concerned about feelings…and so loyal to everyone…?

Chapter Sixty-One:
Ond I Will Never Let Go!

In spite of my objections, Juan continued his apartment hunting once 1992 began. Even Daniel continually insisted he reconsider, but he held onto his stubbornness.

Matt was still giving me difficulties threatening to break it up every other day, especially when in his manic moods, and yet, even with all this, I still felt deeply in love with him…or I thought I was. I finally talked to Juan and told him I really felt a relationship could never happen between Matt and me, and even though I wanted the proof, I felt I needed to break it up.

"I will do it now, Juan…just as you have wanted me to do. I definitely do not want you to move out of here." I had given this much thought and was really sure Juan would be overjoyed. Instead, I was completely shocked as he flatly refused! I couldn't understand and continued pleading until I finally realized I was just going around in circles. He finally admitted his inner gut feeling felt I would go against my word…and there was nothing I could do or say to convince him that would never happen.

I found out much later from Daniel that he and Juan had gone to Chinatown together the beginning of the month. I was a bit surprised Juan hadn't mentioned it to me, but realized this was one of his ways of 'making me suffer,' by not sharing it with me. Daniel was always very candid discussing his disease, and most of the conversation was told to me.

"How do you feel about the fact you know you will be dying, Juan?"

"I 'ave accepted it, Daniel…I really 'ave, ond I believe I am ready for it. I do not want to die, but I know I cannot do anything to change it. I 'ave a disease thot is deadly, so I 'ave to accept the inevitable."

"How do you feel about Richard, Juan? What do you want for him after you die? You do know he is going to take it very hard because he will not believe you are going to die? He still talks about a cure."

"I know, Daniel, thot Recharred does not want to face the fact thot I am gonna die, ond I wish thot he would, because it is gonna be so hard for him. Daniel, I don' want to leave Recharred. I love him very much. For him, I wish I could live."

"Do you want Richard to be with someone after you die?"

"Yes, Daniel, I do! I want Recharred to find someone who really loves him…. But, Daniel, I do not want Recharred to be with thot Matt…. No, Daniel, not Matt!"

The first week of the year had not ended and it finally happened…Juan found an apartment. I was beside myself and no matter how I pleaded, he wouldn't change his mind. He had initially been very secretive about the location.

"Because, Recharred, I want to be away from you for a while." This didn't last a day. He finally couldn't keep it from me any longer, and once I heard the location of his apartment, I realized it was on the same street as Matt's, but about five blocks away. He then told me he hadn't yet signed the lease, which would begin the first of February. His appointment to sign was set for the end of the week and I figured there still was time to change his mind. Moving into a new apartment had always been thrilling for Juan and there was no exception now. I felt good he wanted to share this excitement with me,

"Recharred, would you like to go see my apartment? They are doing some repairs ond I know thar will be someone ot the place now."

The building was an older red brick three-story six flat and I was impressed with the large entrance hall and the nicely decorated staircase as we went up to the second floor. We were greeted with the smell of fresh paint as we entered the very large foyer. To the right was a lovely living room graced with chair rails throughout. In the center of one wall was a stucco finished, simulated fireplace built up on an angle…one you might likely see in a Mexican hacienda. I quickly commented how wonderful that would be for the Southwest decor he always wanted so badly. Also featured on another wall was a very quaint, built-in knick knack cabinet. Juan then led me back through the foyer to a small hall leading to the very large master bedroom, and the bathroom was off that same hall besides a linen cabinet. Back through the foyer again was another hall but quite longer, and a second bedroom on the right, also a good size. Once we walked down the hall and turned right, we were greeted with a large formal dining room. It also featured chair rails along the walls besides two corner china cabinets. Just off the dining room was a cabinet kitchen. Except for the kitchen and bathroom, newly sanded and polished hardwood floors were throughout the place. And there was an abundance of closet space. I was awed as much as Juan and almost felt it was ours instead of his.

"Aw, Juan, I just love it…it is absolutely charming! I want to live here with you!" In fact, during the entire time, my mind had been thinking just that…to eventually rent out my condo and move in with him. But then my mind remembered I had to talk him out of this because I didn't want him to move from my house.

Unfortunately, he did sign the lease…still, I continued trying to talk him out of the move, only to be refused. Juan had to go to Fort Sheridan to sign the release papers on his furniture and asked if I'd drive him. On our return trip home, he asked if we could stop for some kosher corned beef sandwiches in a delicatessen he'd been to when he worked at the fort. We decided upon sitting at the counter and while seated I noticed he suddenly appeared to look a bit melancholy. I almost felt he was thinking about his decision to move. I thought it a good opportunity to bring up the fact that it still wasn't too late to back out of the lease, but he just shook his head. I then again reminded him that I'd stop seeing Matt once and for all.

"No, Recharred, I am still gonna move," he sighed warmly. "Maybe one day we can move together…let me do this now, Recharred. I 'ave to learn thot I cannot always 'ave my own way."

During the last three weeks of the month, Juan had his ups and downs, and probably because he was fighting within himself. I knew him too long not to know his every mood and he didn't want this move to happen! But yet he wouldn't give in.

Jacque and Gil were having another preview…this one *My Cousin Vinny*. They had invited my family and I thought it would be wonderful because Juan had not seen any of them for so long. But he wouldn't go. Jacque and Gil were then holding a dinner party at a restaurant for the immediate family…sort of a belated wedding dinner. I begged him to go but he again refused. I finally realized his reason…even though he was maintaining most of his weight…he looked tired, and he did not want them to see him this way.

We did have our beautiful evenings together and every time I picked up his weekly medications from the hospital, his appreciation was overwhelming. As I have said, Juan and I were not doing any of those special things he had talked of doing together, so I was greatly overwhelmed when he asked if I wanted to go to the University of Illinois Pavilion for an ice skating extravaganza.

"Brian Boitano ond all the Olympic winners are performing, Recharred, ond Endira has three tickets." After I immediately accepted, he added, "Endira is gonna come here ofter work, so why don' you make a spaghetti ond meatball dinner, Recharred? Would you not do thot please?" Of course, I agreed, and when she arrived that evening, she didn't shut her mouth once talking about all her business deals Juan and I could have cared less to hear about. She did, however, manage to shove the spaghetti and meatballs through at the same time, not ever thinking ever to mention her pleasure eating them. She was like one of those businessmen you often see at a restaurant table talking endlessly with his associates, not realizing what they are even eating. I had fussed on a meal, and as usual, Juan charmingly complimented it and I wished I had a separate plate of hot dogs for Endira…she wouldn't have known the difference.

It was bitter cold and I dropped them off at the entrance of the stadium. Juan sat between the two of us and I think I had more pleasure watching his eyes sparkle with surprise and joy each time one of the stars accomplished a difficult jump or routine. I remember as I went for the car after the show, how my mind thought of the many times Juan and I ran through the bitter cold for the car…and oh, how I wanted him there with me now.

Juan arranged a party to go to the Baton, the female impersonator club, and was very excited about it. Amanda and Patti, Marina, Daniel, and Stan had confirmed to go with us and Juan was his old self anticipating a great time.

"Recharred, maybe we con all go out dancin' ofterwards," Juan had excitedly said. I felt great because he and I hadn't been dancing since Indianapolis, the night I met Phillip and Kent. However, shortly before everyone was to arrive, I received a call from Matt. He really didn't have anything specific to talk about and I couldn't again understand why he phoned, especially since I had told him not to call because I knew it might upset Juan. It was almost as though this was his intention, and I couldn't comprehend why anyone would intentionally disregard my wishes and upset someone?

Again, Juan's happy mood changed, as it had done so many times in the past once Matt called the house. Juan had to strike out Matt from his mind, as if he didn't exist, and once he called, he was again aware of his presence in my life and he couldn't cope with it, and this didn't make me feel proud of my relationship with Matt.

Daniel and Stan were the first to arrive and I was hoping Daniel's positive personality would bring out Juan's enthusiasm and wit, but he remained in his somber mood, occasionally throwing digs at me. Daniel was aware of the psychological difficulties Juan had been putting me through and he was never one to hold his tongue.

"Juan, are you being kind to Richard? You know there aren't many guys like him around. He has done so much for you, and he is still doing so much now. He is the closest person to you in your life, so I hope you are not treating him badly? You know, no one is gonna be there for you like him." It upset me to hear this, especially since I didn't want Juan to go deeper into a depression, and I quickly tried to change the subject. Juan, however, wouldn't let me continue and completely surprised me as he sat there calmly.

"You are absolutely right, Daniel. I know how much Recharred has done for me ond how much he is still doing. Yes, I know I sometimes treat him very badly…ond I really don' mean to be thot way…but I cannot help myself sometimes…ond once I realize it, I am so sorry." I quickly interrupted as Daniel continued to encourage Juan to appreciate me.

"Daniel, I have known Juan for almost eighteen years and I know he never truly intends to hurt me…he just has to be truthful about his feelings, and that is the only way he can show me! I know the appreciation he has in his heart just by looking at his face, and besides, I do these things because I want to, not because I have to…I always have!

"I am sure you know I am not a person who gets close to many people, Daniel" Juan interjected softly," but when I do, I really hold on tight…. I met

Recharred a long time ago ond found someone I could really love. I took hold of him," and as he choked up continued, "ond I will never let go."

Seating at the Baton was in narrow counter type rows directly in front of the stage, and our reservation held the very first one. Unfortunately, I was the first to enter thinking Juan would follow, but he allowed everyone to go in before him, which put us at opposite ends. Once I saw his reaction to my disappointed expression, I realized I needed to suffer! I glanced in his direction throughout the show and even though he appeared enjoying himself, I knew it wasn't the same Juan who laughed and came up with one witty comment after another while watching drag shows. That spark was missing and I didn't know if he was feeling ill or if his mind was on his move and Matt. I tried to bring myself up by ordering a couple of cocktails, but they did no good and I remained seated with a fixed smile on my face, but a heavy heart.

Another feeling of disappointment ran through my mind as we boarded Amanda and Patti's minivan. There was no mention of continuing the evening by going out dancing, and in fact, Juan was very quiet as he hunched his shoulders, appearing to be cold as he sat in the backseat. Conversation seemed to be limited even from Daniel, and before I knew it, we were saying good night to everyone.

Juan immediately headed for his bedroom to retire, and it was very evident he was troubled by his weakness. One glance and I realized what his mind had to be thinking.

"Aw, why, God, is this happening to me?" It had to be, because the same question was flashing before mine, while my heart tried desperately to deny Juan's serious illness.

Juan was in exceptional good spirits Sunday morning and talking continuously about everything imaginable during breakfast. Yes, this was the start of the day and after resting, he was again his happy self. He was so happy as he then went on to make his social calls, while including me in his conversations. I then went into the bedroom to make up my bed and once I returned to the living room, he was just placing the receiver of the phone in place. He seemed very chipper and satisfied.

"Does your friend 'ave one of those new ID phone systems, Recharred?" Exactly at that time, the phone rang and I quickly turned back into my bedroom to answer. It was Matt, and I was confronted with demands instead of his usual calm and happy greeting.

"Rich, did you call here twice in a row a few minutes ago?!" He took me by complete surprise and I naturally informed him I had not. It never occurred to me his question had anything to do with the ID system I helped him connect a few days earlier, and I was shocked to hear him shout out, "Well, then, it is that asshole Juan who has been calling and hanging up.... I should have known it!" As he continued in his frenzy, my mind began swimming with the thought that Juan had been the one calling all those times and if I had known, I certainly would have warned him about the ID, and I certainly would have immediately thought to tell Matt I did call, but had to hang up because my phone was beeping with another call coming in! How was I ever gonna get them to be friends!

"Rich, it had to be Juan since you have told me you didn't call" Matt shouted, continuing his anger, "because your number flashed twice in a row on my system! Oh, he is gonna be in trouble now because I am going to see my lawyer and charge him with harassment!" It was shocking to think he'd threaten to do such a thing, especially since he'd been so intrigued with the hang-ups, and after reminding him, he still denied it.

"Rich, I took snapshots of your number, which will be the proof I need!" I knew his behavior was ridiculous since he'd been so fascinated with these calls and seemed to be always looking forward to them, but now because he realized they were from Juan, his ego was shattered. He was especially bothered since he realized Juan was aware each time he invited the caller over. I finally assured him I'd talk with Juan to get some answers and call him back.

Excellent hearing was always one of Juan's God-given gifts, and I realized he was well aware of what was going on once I returned to the living room. His eyes did have a certain twinkle.

"Whot is the matter, Recharred?" I looked at him coyly since I knew he already was aware of the situation.

"Juan, I think you already know, because I'm sure you heard all of my side of the conversation." He tried to make light of it by chuckling and finally admitted to the calling after I informed him that Matt had just installed the system. Although I realized I'd probably do the same in a jealous anger, I tried to make him realize how foolish and small it made him look. It was apparent he was sorry he'd belittled himself even though he tried desperately to laugh it off, and by this time, I realized he was the one habitually making them, dating back to Indianapolis…just by looking at his face. He finally agreed to apologize to Matt. However, by this time, we were interrupted with one call after another from Matt and even though I assured him he'd get an apology from Juan he continued his vicious anger, abusing me with one nasty remark after another. The nervous manner of my voice was quickly apparent to Juan and it didn't take long for his face to show his dislike for the abuse I was receiving. And Matt continued with his calls! Because they continued, I finally realized Juan was beginning to have second thoughts about apologizing, or even admitting to making the calls. He didn't like the harassment Matt was handing me and he was going to make him pay!

The matter went on for days because Matt wouldn't let it drop. His anger became even more intense once I told him I wouldn't testify against Juan should he insist on going on with his ridiculous lawsuit.

"Why would you want to cause stress to someone with AIDS?" I insisted.

"Bullshit to his stress!" he replied like always. I tried to reason with him…that I'd probably do the same if I was jealous and especially if I thought I was going to lose someone should I be the one with AIDS, but he wouldn't listen.

"Matt, Juan had every intention to apologize, but now that you've made this into a federal case and won't stop harassing me, he's stubbornly refused...and, furthermore, he will not even admit to the calls."

I continued trying to persuade Juan to finally apologize, but because he was aware of the abuse I was receiving, he flatly refused. His irritation wanted revenge.

"Recharred, if he continues with this, I know where he works ond I am sure they would not appreciate knowing he is a faggot, especially since he is involved with so many young people! Recharred, I swear I will call thar!" I didn't like Juan making a threat like that, even though I realized he wouldn't carry it out...but I realized he had to strike back with something to protect me along with himself. I also realized they probably knew Matt was gay because he had told me the rumor had been going around about him some time ago, so it would be no big deal. However, I still didn't want Juan to do such a low thing, and he never did.

Matt also never did go on with his ridiculous lawsuit, but he never let it drop and continued calling Juan nasty names. My blind infatuation for him caused me to be angry with myself because each time his viciousness came out, I just bit my tongue.

"Recharred, do you think you con drive me to visit John tonight? He is in very bod shape ond looks so ter-ri-ble." Of course, I drove him and found John to be far worse. He was lying in bed almost appearing to be about to fall out of it as his arms dangled helplessly to the side. I hadn't seen him and was shocked because I wouldn't have known it was he. John was always quite overweight and even though he wasn't a skeleton, he had lost a considerable amount of weight. He just lay there babbling, waving his arms helplessly. I was sure he wasn't aware we were in the room as Juan tried desperately to receive some sort of response from him.

"John, this is Juan...Juan is here to see you.... Con you hear me, John? This is Juan." My heart was aching as I looked into Juan's face to see nothing but desperate concern. He stood in the middle of the room, appearing as though he was afraid to touch John, for fear he'd catch the same terrible illness, and this was fine with me because Juan didn't need to be in contact with any of the diarrhea bacteria. I felt helpless and didn't want to believe this could ever happen to Juan. He continued his pleas to no avail and I was pleased once he agreed to leave because the anxiety I was experiencing was almost about to explode, and I wanted out. I especially wanted Juan to leave because it wasn't something needed to keep him up. I felt as though my thoughts were forcing Juan to desert his friend, but I couldn't control my feelings. I didn't want him to begin thinking, *This could be me soon!*

I didn't say much once we were on our way out of the hospital because I didn't know what to talk about. I was confronted with someone dying of AIDS, and it was sad, but I still didn't want to think this could happen to Juan. It also passed my mind that Juan's reason for wanting me to go with him, were to make me finally realize what AIDS was about.

"Recharred, I would like to take a ride to the north side of the city," Juan pleaded as I pulled out of the parking spot, "down Broadway ond Halsted…would you mind to drive thar? I jus' want to see everything for old time's sake…do you mind?" And he reminisced as we passed many familiar places, but this time, he wasn't the lively person talking excitedly about the times we spent there. This time, there was a definite sound of melancholy in his voice. As we were approaching Little Jim's, Juan asked, "Recharred, I would really like to stop in thar…would you mind?" As usual, the place was jam-packed, and what made it more reminiscent was the doorman was the same guy with the obvious wig…the one Juan often mimicked as an owl. Of course, he didn't miss reminding me of it. I was just about to buy a couple of Cokes when Juan suddenly approached to say he'd like to leave. Once we were on our way home, I never asked why he wanted to leave so abruptly because my mind felt he may have been reminded of the guy he was certain gave him AIDS, and this was undoubtedly where they met.

A couple of days later, Juan received the tragic news: John had passed away. Juan didn't cry in my presence and in fact seemed to handle the news in a calm manner…as if it was something scheduled in the program. If he did cry, it was when he was alone. There was no wake, but John had previously arranged a memorial with a dinner afterwards. I had every intention of going with Juan until he said Svetmana was going with him and Marina, and that he thought it would be too uncomfortable for the two of us to be together.

"So I would rather not 'ave problems with Svetmana…do you mind, Recharred?" I did mind and felt bad I couldn't pay my last respects to John, but realized Juan didn't need any more stress, and reluctantly agreed to his request.

The day before the memorial, Juan approached in a very cold manner.

"Recharred, I would like for Svetmana to stay overnight the day of the memorial ond Saturday. Why don' you stay ot thot Matt's house those nights? I am sure he would love you to do thot." It was almost a demand instead of a request, and I really didn't want to do it because I realized Juan's reason was because he once again was reminded of Matt after I received several calls from him. In fact, I had not stayed over with Matt since Juan moved in, except a couple of times, and then faked headaches so I could return home. I never wanted Juan to hurt should I be out for the entire evening.

Juan had not yet returned from the memorial and I was particularly glad because I didn't want either of us to feel uncomfortable as I was about to leave. This wasn't something I wanted to do, especially since Matt hadn't seemed overjoyed that I'd be spending the two nights. I then discovered that I had forgotten something and returned, and just at that time Juan walked in the corridor with Marina. Svetmana wasn't with them and I asked why.

"Aw, she will be coming later. She could not make the memorial." From my reaction, Juan had to know I was disturbed because I would have then been able to go.

Marina greeted me quietly; otherwise, it was silent as the three of us stood on the slow elevator. Juan was holding a long stem rose directly next to his nose, appearing as though the sweet fragrance was his last remembrance of his lost friend. Suddenly, he looked out, and as though this was his last bit of wit on behalf of John, he said, "Well, ot least I got a filet mignon dinner on John."

I cannot remember what Matt and I did that evening or Saturday, so I am assuming he was pleasant enough. However, I was feeling very low and very guilty, wondering how Juan was doing. So I decided to call at the house Saturday evening and once Juan answered, I told him I couldn't stay away from him any longer and that I didn't want to sleep a second night at Matt's. He surprised me by reacting in a very happy and pleased manner. So I went home.

Juan continued to take Svetmana along to the movies and always was sure to rave about them to me. Yes, I had to pay. One movie he absolutely loved was *Fried Green Tomatoes*.

"Aw, Recharred, it is on absolutely bea-u-ti-ful movie! I loved it so much! Ond aw, how funny thot Kathy Bates was! You know, it is almost two stories in one." I managed to see it on my own and felt the same as he. I also realized how closely related the story of those two women were to my own life with Juan. The beauty of their relationship was one that could capture anyone's heart…no matter how their love was shared. It will remain one of my all-time favorites and each time I am fortunate to watch it, Juan will be there at my side.

Friday, the thirty-first of January arrived and unfortunately, this meant Juan was moving. I had already pondered the idea of eventually moving in with him, and was accepting this move in a better frame of mind. The storage company would be delivering in the afternoon and we were going to move Juan's things on Saturday.

"Recharred, you know ofter I move I will not be seeing you for a while because I need to get used to the fact thot you are seeing thot Matt." I objected but he went on, "Please let me do thot, Recharred? You know I will eventually be seeing you…we could never not be friends because we are one person, but I need it for now." It didn't make me happy. How could I accept something like that?

My prayers were answered that evening as Juan stood in the middle of the living room. I had just told him I'd be staying over with him for a few days to get everything settled, and he accepted it tenderly,

"Recharred, you know you are always welcome in my house. You con come anytime you want. You know I could not be away from you ond thot I do not ever mean any of those mean things I say to you." I was standing directly in front of him and could feel those words tugging at my heart. I moved to him and put my arms around his back.

"Aw, Juan, I also could never stay away from you."

I was surprised to see Lucille arrive Saturday morning to help. She had called several times inquiring about Juan's health; otherwise, we didn't see much of her. However, we were aware of the fact that she was attracted to Amanda and this would be a good time to be with her since she agreed to move Juan's things in her van.

Amanda finally arrived and it didn't take long to pack and load Juan's furniture and things into her minivan and get on our way. As soon as everything was in Juan's apartment, Amanda was off, because, as usual, she had promised to help someone else. Lucille remained to help and I was glad because the storage movers hadn't put to place anything.

Even though Juan kept talking excitedly about the new apartment I realized he was feeling so helpless because he no longer had the strength to assist with anything, and it was tugging at my heart remembering so vividly those times he single-handedly organized our apartments, and I am certain he was thinking of those times, too. But he still had his wit and managed to make our day a joy. And he still talked excitedly about the Latin dancehall.

"You know we should get up a good crowd ond go thar? How about it, Lucille, would you like to go with us ond cha, cha? It is supposed to be a blast!" Lucille agreed and immediately Juan took hold of her for a few steps.

I wondered why Svetmana was nowhere around but Juan told me his parents were also moving since their rent had been increased quite a bit.

"Ond this one is only a couple of blocks from their old place...ond, Recharred, it is jus' as nice, but the rent is as much as they were originally paying ot the old place...so they are lucky. Well, Svetmana went thar to help...I know they are gonna be in a big mess because you know how much she will help."

Lucille was a chain-smoker and lit up one after another, not realizing we were no longer smoking while with Juan. I was just about to bring it up to her when the phone rang.

"Richard, will you tell that damn woman not to smoke in the house because it is too dangerous for my dad!" sounded the screeching voice of Svetmana once I answered, and she hung up as loudly. It was the first time she had spoken to me in two and a half months! I wondered how she knew it since I hadn't seen her when we arrived at the house. I finally figured she had to be in the other bedroom when we arrived because I remembered the door had been shut. She must have seen Lucille smoking like a chimney while I was down at the van and beat it out of the house before I returned. I immediately asked Juan why he was allowing Lucille to smoke.

"Recharred, I don't want to sound like a fussy man to her." I finally told her myself and she had no problem with it. So we both went out onto the small back porch to smoke.

Lucille and I were lifting the occasional table in the living room to place an area rug Endira had given to him when suddenly, the glass-blown elephant set slid off and fell to the floor, breaking two of them. I was sick because this was the set I gave to him, and one Juan especially loved.

"Aw, Recharred, how did thot happen? Aw, I really loved thot set so much...aw, so much. Aw, why did thot 'ave to happen?" Juan was so upset because when I had given him the set, he had told me it would always be his favorite in his collection. Lucille's hobby was designing jewelry and immediately told him not to worry because she would take the pieces home and fix them. This brought a smile to his face. However, we never saw them after that and she never even brought up the subject. I realized she had good intentions but was probably too busy chasing after Amanda.

Once the furniture was in place Lucille was on her way, but now the chore of emptying all the boxes and putting everything away needed to be done...and they were strewn throughout the apartment, along with the pictures. It was a real mess and I was surprised Juan wasn't annoyed being in the middle of it all. It was time for his treatment so as he sat in the living room administering it, I went on with the unpacking...receiving one adoring glance after another from him. He *was* happy I was there with him.

Amanda had told us she would return later to drive us to pick up the upholstered rocker which was part of my old living room set...the one I had given his parents years ago. Their new place was too small for it so Juan figured he could use it in his large bedroom. Well, she was not arriving and it was getting late, so I figured we could drive there ourselves because I was certain it would fit in my hatchback. I was worried I'd have trouble carrying it down myself but was determined to do it. So we drove to his parent's old apartment.

My heart ached while struggling with it and I was angry...not because Juan didn't help but because he was too weak to help and my anger called out to God.

"Why does this beautiful man have to have this dreaded disease...why, God?"

Juan wanted to stop in to see his parent's new apartment and I'm sure he'd have asked to join him, but realizing Svetmana was there, didn't want to chance any repercussions because of her violent temper. I understood and before he said anything, I merely mentioned I'd wait in the car.

"Aw, Recharred, you should see 'their' mess!" he quickly said on his return. "Svetmana has not done a damn thing except to run out for something to eat! Recharred, she is jus' sitting down watching them struggle to put things in order. Aw, Recharred, I don' know about thot girl? I don' believe how she is!"

It didn't appear to bother Juan that the apartment wasn't in order immediately once we returned. He wanted me to spend time talking with him, so I wasn't able to work at a steady pace and devote complete attention to getting everything in order. I stayed over three nights and in this time we also did some shopping for groceries. As I think back, it was very possible he purposely delayed getting everything in order...just so I'd be with him longer. When he did place a chair to sit next to me, attempting to help with the unpacking, he couldn't apologize enough for not being able to do more. My heart felt so heavy as he pleaded forgiveness.

"Aw, Recharred, I am so sorry I cannot help like I would like to...but I am so weak."

I don't recall if it was Monday or Tuesday evening when I finally put up the last picture. I do remember I was so pleased because the apartment looked so spacious and elegant. It was that evening I definitely decided I'd eventually be moving in with Juan…that I'd rent out my condo. Even though I felt I was in love with Matt, I was certain this would be happening, especially since I was sure Matt's feelings for me weren't mutual, and that he needed to have his ego fulfilled with one guy after another. Yet, I still needed to have proof.

Endira had stopped to see Juan that evening and had remained in the living room with him the entire time I was finishing up. As usual, she refused to talk English in my presence and ignorantly went on in Spanish. She went on as if I wasn't even there, and never once commented on my decorating accomplishments or to even give any suggestions, which all added up to why Svetmana was the way she was.

"Do you know whot Endira told me, Recharred?" Juan said once she left. "She told me she has always loved me. Con you imagine thot, Recharred?" I just smiled because I knew that was easy enough, but still I recalled all her cheating Juan had told me about.

Chapter Sixty-Two:
Home Alone

All that was needed to complete Juan's apartment were some rugs and the following Sunday, he called to ask if I'd possibly go buy them for him.

"Recharred, I would like to go with you to buy them, but I am jus' so weak ond get tired so fast. Endira gave me a hundred dollars to buy an area rug for under the dining table, so I will give you some more to buy the others I need for the bedrooms ond the halls. I trust your taste. Will you please do thot for me, Recharred?" I really was surprised to hear it because Endira had already bought him a very modern table lamp for the foyer, besides the area rug in the living room.

After finding some remnants in equal sizes for the halls, I was very fortunate to find a very beautiful area rug in exactly the right colors he needed. I felt sure he was going to love it. He was sitting on the couch once I let myself in with the keys he willingly agreed I should have. His eyes were sparkling as he looked up while receiving his treatment.

"Recharred, you know whot? Svetmana has been in the kitchen for four hours cleaning…ond all she has managed to clean in all this time is the sink, the outsides of the cabinets, refrigerator, ond stove…ond I think the floor. Do you believe thot, Recharred? It has taken her over four hours jus' to do thot!"

"Juan, that is nothing new. You have told me that for years."

"Yeah, but, Recharred, she is a grown woman now!" I turned apprehensively towards the kitchen and Juan whispered she wasn't there because once she heard me call out to him as I opened the door, she ran quickly into the other bedroom.

"So you con go in thar ond see whot she did because I would like to know whot took her so long." I was especially interested in seeing it myself since I had cleaned everything when I put it in order just a few days earlier. As I turned to head that way, the doorbell rang. Endira and her husband, Dan, had just returned from church to pick up Svetmana to take her to dinner. As usual, the two of them went on talking like gangbusters saying absolutely nothing, but I was glad they showed up because now Dan could help lift the table to put down the rug. Once the rug was down, Juan came in the room rolling his IV unit alongside.

"Aw, Recharred, you picked the perfect one. It is beautiful ond goes so well with all the colors. Thank you so much." I couldn't believe Endira!... She never said a word about it. However, Juan mentioned that Svetmana had been cleaning the kitchen for four hours, and all she could do was rave about how wonderful it looked.

"Oh, Juan, this kitchen looks so beautiful and clean! Svetmana really did a wonderful job!" In fact, she wouldn't quit raving about it even though it looked the same the night she was over, after I had just cleaned it. I had to do every contortion possible to keep from laughing in her face after watching Juan give me one mimic after another of Endira's praises. I also wanted so badly to kick her in the ass, because she didn't say a word about the rest of the apartment, which I had spent the entire week getting in order, and which looked so elegant.

So Juan was on his own in his very large beautiful apartment, and to my happiness, instead of avoiding me, he was calling every morning, and in fact, every chance he got. Of course, I was doing the same. Unfortunately, many times I intended to be with him, I was told not to go because the princess was there and he didn't want any problems. She had started a project I knew would take forever, and that was to sew straight panels of a Southwestern pattern to hang on each side of the living room windows. Of course, Juan kept me abreast on her snail-paced progress, and we laughed each time.

A problem this caused...I couldn't be with Juan as much as planned and I knew he wanted me there. So he'd often tell Svetmana to go home and then call me to come over. However, I never knew beforehand, and there were many times I wasn't home or couldn't get there because I had to be somewhere else. So this meant he was home alone. It wasn't that I seldom saw him, because I still managed to be with him several times a week. It just meant some of the visits were cut short because her highness was about to return. I continued getting his Foscarnet or Gancyclivir or both from the hospital and would accompany him on his visits to the clinic. Sometimes, if I was late in arriving, he'd be gone already and I'd race to the hospital...search the parking lot for his Omni to be sure he was there, and then join him while he waited in the clinic. I will never forget one particular time I finally found the clinic he was scheduled in. He was sitting along with the others, but his head was dropping to his side, dozing off. Now, this was something he never did in his entire life...never! *I* was noted to do that whenever I sat for long periods of time waiting somewhere or even at a movie...but never Juan.

Juan still was up to his old tricks, getting me out of the shower and keeping me there dripping wet, because he was in the mood to talk. And he'd laugh. He also came up with something else that completely puzzled me at first. I was receiving messages on my answering machine, and once I played them back, would be surprised to hear a mush mash garble sounding as though the voice was coming from someone who came from outer space. It was evident actual words were mixed in with this garble, but I certainly couldn't make them out. In fact, they'd make me laugh hilariously…so I was baffled for some time. It finally dawned on me! Who could this be…but Juan! It had to be him because he loved outer space movies so much! I finally was sure of it and when I phoned him, decided to answer with his message. When I finally came on the phone, he was laughing hilariously…then innocently asking what that was. I insisted it was he, but he just continued laughing, weakly denying it.

"Whot do you mean, Recharred? Thot is not me. I 'ave not been calling." However, he could no longer control himself and admitted to it while laughing in his contagious cackle. I explained how baffled I had been to his amazement.

"I really fooled you, Recharred? I really did?"

"Yes, you did, Juan. I always told you to be an actor."

As we were driving out of the hospital complex after one of Juan's clinic appointments, we passed the Blind Center.

"Recharred, thot is where I will 'ave to live when I go blind," Juan remarked nonchalantly. I looked at him in disbelief.

"Aw, no, Juan, not while I'm alive! Besides, Juan, it is never gonna happen! Do you hear me, Juan…NEVER!"

Larry accepted Juan's invite to come up from Indianapolis for a weekend, which included Valentine's Day. I remember Matt didn't mind that I was going to a party with Juan on Saturday…a wear anything red party. Friends of Daniel had invited us after meeting the evening of Stan's surprise party in December. I gave roses to Juan and to Matt. This was the first time I saw Juan so pleased to receive flowers from me. Through the years, he always thought it too feminine a thing to do. I was particularly disappointed Juan didn't wear something red, especially since I recalled when he told me about an all-white party years earlier. He had raved on about it. I could still hear him sighing endlessly.

"Aw, Recharred, you cannot imagine how bea-u-ti-ful it was. It was in their garden ond all you could see was white against the vivid greens!"… I wanted that same Juan, but tonight, he appeared to be very tired after administering his treatment. In fact, it was a totally different Juan as he sat in an uncomfortable folding chair the entire evening at the party, only getting up to fill his plate. I sat between him and Larry and tried to be up as my heart ached. Even his wit seemed to be gone. I realized this wasn't an evening he was going to sneak some drinks as I did, trying to bring myself up. But as usual, they did nothing for me. I was too concerned about Juan. In a way, I wished the party had been held in the morning, because Juan was always so chipper then.

I spent part of the Sunday afternoon with Juan and Larry to show him some of the area, but then had to get home because the sauce had to be prepared for the spaghetti dinner that evening. I had invited Daniel and Stan also because I felt it would give a festive mood for Juan to be in. I knew Daniel would keep things lively with his non-stop conversation. Juan, however, surprised me because he said he felt too weak to sit at the table with us, and just ate while sitting on the couch. I felt terrible and wished I would've served buffet style because my heart was breaking to see Juan sit alone on the couch. Again, he tired and went home fairly early.

My relationship with Matt continued in the same hot and cold manner, but I still pursued, hoping he'd return to the person I originally thought he was. At the same time, I was sure he and Juan would be friends one day. However, I began parking my car several blocks from Matt's because of an incident that happened. On that particular evening I was in Matt's kitchen and just as I was putting a pizza in the oven, he walked in and shouted for me to look at the porch window, swearing that Juan was peering through it. I quickly responded but saw no one. I had quickly headed to the door repeatedly asking him if he was sure. I had opened the door calling out Juan's name several times, and continued as I ran down the stairway. And since I didn't receive a response, I had checked the alley, too. But no one had been in sight. I remembered walking dejectedly back up, realizing it had to be Juan…I had felt sick because this had been good cause for stress and that wasn't what he needed.

On another evening, I was dropping Matt off in the rear alley of his apartment and we sat in the car deeply involved in one of his heated and heavy conversations, which had him threatening to break up our so-called, "working on a relationship" involvement. I had discovered long ago he never meant it…that it was only his way of keeping me in gear to continually chase him. Suddenly, we were blinded by the bright lights of a passing car and Matt swore that Juan was driving the car. I knew the car that passed wasn't an Omni, but as I peered into the rear view mirror, I saw a larger red one make a right turn out of the alley…and Svetmana had a large red car! I didn't think I needed to mention this to Matt. Instead, I told him it couldn't have been Juan because the car was not an Omni. Still, Matt was convinced it was Juan and began threatening to call the police.

"Because, Rich, he is stalking my place and this is definitely a fatal attraction!" This again, lasted for days and I had to come up with one lie after another to keep him from doing anything hasty. Why I never told him to fuck off, I will never know! I guess I believed we were destined to have a beautiful relationship one day, and maybe it was because I wanted the little sex I was getting…Juan had mentioned to Daniel he no longer had any sexual desires because of all the medications he was taking. I want to believe it was because of my dream for a lasting beautiful relationship, and not because of sex…but who knows?

I mentioned these two incidents to Juan but received angry denials, which made me certain it was he. However, I dropped it because he didn't need any more aggravation. I also realized I was doing the same by chasing into the night searching to find Matt in one of his escapades. I was going through full tanks of gas driving through the night and early mornings looking for him…but each time would come home without the goods.

It was March and for my birthday, Matt took me to a country club for dinner because he had received a forty-dollar gift certificate from someone at work. I have to say the evening was a very pleasant one because he was very attentive and polite. However, just before my birthday, he had asked what I'd like as a present. At the time, I merely said not to worry about giving me something. I didn't believe he'd do just that…give me nothing! It should've told me something, because he put an important value on monetary things. I realized this from the evening we were with Carl and Frank playing Pinochle. Carl had received a stereo from Frank for Christmas.

"He must really love you to spend that much," Matt had said with great awe.

Juan hadn't given me a gift either, but I was aware he wasn't going to because of his financial bind before his disability payments came through. He had already decided to stop giving gifts because he wasn't able to get out like he wanted. However, Juan was aware Matt hadn't given me a gift.

"I don' believe it, Recharred…you mean he actually did not give you anything? Thot is ter-ri-ble." To me, monetary value never meant anything because I only wanted someone to go out of their way to maybe buy something very inexpensive I happened to have liked on one of our outings…or even take the time to make something special. I always felt it was a way of showing a person you were thinking of them. It was a bit ridiculous, but I actually went out and bought a flowered shirt for myself and told Matt it had been given to me by Juan. I wanted him to feel embarrassed, but I don't think it worked. Daniel also invited me out to dinner and asked Juan to join us. It was very apparent Juan was feeling bad because he hadn't been able to get something for me, but I told him I understood, and just having him well was all I wanted. He was fighting to stay healthy and this still bothered him. So he finally managed to take me out to eat twice for my birthday…once for breakfast and then one evening.

"Aw, Recharred, I 'ave to take you to this oriental restaurant on Lake Street for your birthday. Aw, I know you will love it because their Mongolian Beef tastes jus' like the one Mine Gen served." So I was not only treated to a dinner, but to the elegant presence and wonderful conversation Juan always was capable of bringing to a meal, and the wonderful memory of all the other times I had that pleasure. At the time, I know I didn't realize where this wonderful evening would stand in our lives. I couldn't help from thinking…it was always said a great meal brings out great conversation. Somehow, I could only think sitting down at a table with Juan to hear his beautiful conversation and to experience his charm would make any meal great!

Daniel called to ask if I'd like to go to a surprise birthday party for Lucille given by a few of her lesbian friends the third Saturday of the month. I agreed to go, but once I mentioned that I was going to ask Juan, Daniel said I wouldn't be able to because Marva and Julie would be there and that they do not want to be near anyone with AIDS. I couldn't believe anyone could be so narrow-minded and immediately knew this was Julie's doings because my mind flashed back to my housewarming party when she asked me to watch her glass while she danced.

 I was feeling bad because I couldn't ask Juan to go, but then realized his uncle, Nicolai, had come in from London to choreograph a special ballet and he had told me he'd be busy going to the theatre to watch them rehearse and to special receptions given in his uncle's honor. I was certain one of the receptions was being held that Saturday, so my mind was a little relieved. I know Juan never knew of the party and I was so happy because I realized he'd have been heartbroken to hear such a thing.

 I decided to ask Matt, and at first he balked because he totally disliked lesbians. I finally talked him into it but was worried because I realized if he were miserable, I'd be the one crucified. I was determined I was going to let myself go, to have a good time, and to also show Matt I was capable of making others do the same. I had told him so often how Juan and I were capable of making others have a good time, but I knew he never believed me. The evening turned out to be a total blast as I really let myself go, and along with a couple of the girls, had everyone in stitches, including Matt. In fact, Daniel screamed out for us to stop because his belly ached, laughing so hard. Matt was elated as we left and I think this had to be the best time he ever had at any party.

 Juan's uncle was still in town because the premiere hadn't yet been performed and unfortunately, I wasn't able to be with Juan much for over a week because Svetmana was sticking around like glue. After all, she would not miss being around socialites and celebrities. This was a feature she surely inherited from her mother. And even though I asked Juan to be sure I got to see his uncle, it never happened because when he was over, so was Svetmana. I hadn't realized Svetmana was leaving Juan alone to go to all these social affairs given for the ballet company and in fact the evening I stopped in to see Juan, I was aware he was going to a special reception for his uncle and wanted to tell him to have a good time. When I asked when he was leaving and where Svetmana was, I was told she had left already and he wasn't going because he was feeling ill. I was disturbed she left but still didn't know about the other times.

 On Tuesday, the twenty-fourth of March, I had met Matt for a drink at the Hideaway because he called to tell me he was stopping after work. We didn't stay long and upon leaving, asked if he wanted to come over for dinner…that I had made bean soup. He agreed, but said he wanted to stop off at home to change first. I was just about to enter my building when Juan pulled up to the curb, and as he lowered the window, he appeared bewildered and anxious.

 "Recharred, you know whot happened to me? I left the hospital ofter my appointment ond all of a sudden…I was lost! Recharred, I did not know where I was! Aw, Recharred, it was so scary!" I did not know what to make of it, especially since he sometimes liked to pull my leg…and I was hoping this was the case. However, I looked into his eyes and it was clear he was distressed and confused, so I immediately insisted he park the car and come up with me.

"I am okay now, Recharred, I want to go home," and even though I continued to insist, he still refused and suddenly drove off. I was beside myself and didn't know what was happening. Matt had said he wouldn't be over for at least forty-five minutes, so I waited a few minutes to call to be sure Juan arrived home safely. I decided I was going to his house to be with him…to call Matt and cancel, hoping Juan wouldn't give me any arguments should Svetmana happen to be there. My anxiety was relieved once Juan answered to say he arrived home safely. I told him I was coming over.

"No, Recharred, I will not be here long because I am going to the dress rehearsal of the ballet with Svetmana tonight." That was it. I could say no more except to enjoy himself. My head was swimming…something strange was happening, and I didn't know what!

Matt asked if I'd like to spend the night at his place and while driving, he cried out suddenly.

"Look, Rich, I think I just passed Juan walking in the opposite direction and he didn't seem to have a jacket on." My heart jumped as I quickly turned to look, but couldn't see anyone because Matt had been driving so fast. "Matt, turn the car and go back!" I shouted. "Please, will you turn back to see if it was Juan walking because he shouldn't be out in this cold damp air!" My mind was swimming because this couldn't have been Juan. He was going to the rehearsal? I kept insisting he turn back and should have jumped out of the car.

"I am sure I was wrong, Rich…it probably was not him." My mind was in a frenzy…not really sure if it had been Juan! Again, Matt intimidated me to remain with him…not allowing my mind to be at peace by checking it out, and at the same time, subjecting Juan to the elements of the damp weather, should it be he walking. And I allowed him to do it because I felt this was the love of my life!

I couldn't relax that evening, yet had to hide my feelings because I didn't want Matt to become manic. I did manage to sneak one call after another to Juan's, but never received an answer.

Juan beat around the bush when I called in the morning to inquire if it was he out walking, and insisted on talking about something else…so I still was unsure. He then called in the afternoon.

"Recharred, whot are you doing? Would you like to come over?" Once I asked if Svetmana was home, he told me she had gone out and did not say where. I decided upon bringing a container of my bean soup and held it out as I came through the door.

"Look, Juan, I brought you a bowl of the bean soup I made."

"You made it, Recharred? I don' believe it! The last time you made soup it tasted like dishwater!"

"No, Juan, it tasted like *dirty* dishwater! But while you were still living in Indianapolis, I tried making bean soup with escarole, and believe me, I finally was successful." After heating some, I brought a bowl to him while he was having his treatment. Juan raved as though it was a gourmet meal once he placed a couple of spoonfuls into his mouth.

"Aw, Recharred, this is superb! It is the best soup I 'ave ever had!" I again asked if he had been walking down the street and from the expression on his face I realized he was disturbed, which gave me every impression it was he.

"Recharred, I 'ave told you I was not walking last night," he insisted, "ond thot is thot! So don' ask no more." I decided to shut up and he then confirmed my impression once he said, "Recharred, Svetmana has been going out so much lately because she wants to be around my uncle and all the famous dancers…ond I really feel I should not stop her. So I 'ave been alone many times."

"Juan, why didn't you call me?" I asked in disbelief. "You know I would've come over to be with you!"

"I did a few times, but you were not ot home, Recharred." This upset me more.

"Then why didn't you leave a message? You always leave me messages and when it is something important…you don't! Juan, you know I always beep my machine! Aw, Juan, I thought you were doing all these things with your uncle because each time I've talked to you, I hear you're going to be busy with him! Do you mean you haven't been going all these times?"

"Recharred, I 'ave only gone once, ond then I was not feeling well ond had to leave. So I 'ave only seen my uncle when he comes here."

"Aw, Juan, and here I was thinking you were doing all these things with him!"

"I wanted to be able to do them, Recharred, but I 'ave not been feeling well ot all. I 'ave been so nauseated lately."

"Then, Juan, why didn't you tell me, for God's sake!"

"I don' know, Recharred…I guess I did not want to bother you." I again looked at him in disbelief!

"JUAN, YOU COULD NEVER BOTHER ME—NEVER!" Juan immediately changed the subject and began talking about his uncle and how ageless he was. I spent the day with him and once Svetmana arrived, I left.

When I called early Thursday morning, Juan was feeling fairly well.

"I hope I am feeling well tonight because I am supposed to go to the big reception for my uncle, ond then Saturday evening to the opening premiere of the ballet with his new choreography. Aw, but I don' know because I get sick so quickly all the time." I told him I was coming over immediately to be with him and he quickly replied that Svetmana was there now…that I should come tomorrow instead, but of course to call first. I was beside myself…angry because Juan was allowing her to get away with her demands that I should not be there when she was! I was also angry with myself for allowing her to intimidate me as much! I COULD NOT BELIEVE ANYONE WOULD BE THAT SELFISH! It was inconceivable to think she'd rather her father be alone than with someone she realized he loved.

Matt called that afternoon and asked if I'd like to come over to spend the night after his racquetball session. It was past the time Juan was to leave for the reception, but I decided to call before leaving for Matt's. I prayed I'd not receive an answer, but instead, heard the receiver being slowly picked up. I then heard Juan speaking in a barely audible voice.

"Juan, didn't you go to the reception tonight?"

"No, Recharred, I 'ave not been feeling well all day, ond now I 'ave started to vomit."

"What did you eat that made you sick, Juan?"

"Recharred, I did not eat anything since this morning."

"What do you mean you have not eaten since this morning? Didn't Svetmana fix something for you?"

"No, Recharred, she rushed out early this ofternoon because she wanted to stop home before going to the reception.... You know how slow she is." I could not believe she left him in his condition.

"Juan, why did you allow her to go when you were so sick? She should've taken you to the hospital! What's the matter with her, for Chris' sake! Why didn't you call me?"

"Recharred, she was looking so forward to it," he sighed after some hesitation, "ond besides, she can't help me anyway. Ond I 'ave been too sick to even pick up the phone." I was near hysteria.

"It doesn't matter if she can't help, Juan! She should've stayed or she should've called me! Your life is more important than her foolish pride! I'm coming there now and I'm gonna bring you something to eat! You have to eat, Juan!"

There wasn't anything in the refrigerator I could bring, so I stopped off at Popeye's for a chicken dinner, and when I arrived, he was lying in bed looking so weak…so sick.

"Recharred, nothing comes out when I vomit but bile…because I 'ave not eaten anything all day. But I keep getting these ter-ri-ble spasms." I softly ran my hand over his forehead trying to give him some comfort…to show I was now there for him…and my heart was breaking.

"Juan, I brought you a chicken dinner…maybe it will help if you eat something." He took hold of it, but quickly set it on the night table and raced for the bathroom. I followed behind as he threw himself on the floor and began heaving violently, desperately trying to hold his head steady over the toilet, and nothing was coming out but bile. I held firmly but gently onto his forehead with the palm of my hand, trying to calm his trembling…to soothe him, but he kept gagging while attempting to make more come out. It had always been difficult for him to vomit…he'd only gag. Even the time after Svetmana's birthday years before, I had to stick my fingers down his throat so something would come up. But this time, Juan was not drunk and didn't have the alcohol to throw up…no, this time, there was nothing to throw up, and I couldn't understand why he was having these terrible spasms.

Once we returned to the bedroom, I insisted on taking him to the hospital.

"No, Recharred, I feel much better, I really do." I still insisted but he would have no part of it and I knew there was no way I'd be able to force him.

"Well, then, Juan, I want you to try to eat something because you cannot go without eating."

"I will Recharred…later."

I decided I was going to stay with him and to call Matt to cancel, but figured I should call Endira first to let her know, so she could tell Svetmana not to come. I certainly did not want her coming in screaming at me like a crazy person because Juan would only get worse. Once Endira answered, I explained everything and she immediately told me Svetmana had stopped there after the reception and was already on her way to Juan's. This upset me because I didn't want to leave Juan, realizing I should've called immediately upon arriving. Juan asked what Endira had said as I sat holding his hand.

"Maybe you should go then, Recharred," he sighed once I told him, "ond I will see you tomorrow."

"NO, Juan, I'm gonna stay with you until just before she gets here, and Endira said it will probably be about half an hour. I don't want you to worry about it, Juan, because I will leave just before she gets here." My nerves were shot thinking about how she intimidated him even when he was so gravely ill. It was just a bit past the half hour and I could tell Juan was getting nervous, so I gave him a hug.

"Please, don't forget to eat the chicken, Juan…and please, if you feel you have to go to the hospital to call the house." I stood at the doorway, lovingly taking him in.

"Thank you so much, Recharred…you are so good." But I did not feel good…because I was leaving Juan…and he was sick.

I was extremely late arriving at Matt's and even though he went through his manic spasms, I didn't care. However, I allowed him to get away with his sly and nasty remarks.

Matt left for work shortly after six and on my way home, I drove past Juan's, praying desperately he was better. I really wanted to stop in but afraid Svetmana would wake and go into a tantrum. I was expecting to see her car as I passed the alley leading to Juan's parking spot, but it was nowhere in sight. The thought quickly came to mind that she may have parked on the side street next to the building, but I had to be sure and made a quick u-turn to check…but again, it was nowhere in sight…only Juan's red Omni. I became panicky!

"Aw, God! Don't tell me she never came! That son-of-a-bitch Endira must have lied!" I quickly parked while thinking it was possible Svetmana took Juan to the hospital, but then I had asked him to call the house and when I beeped, there were no calls.

I was a bit apprehensive after knocking on the door as a warning, because I didn't know what to expect. I immediately knew Svetmana wasn't there because the door of that bedroom was open and there was nothing but her mess. I still didn't yet know if Juan was there because usually he called out my name once he heard the door latch. So I called out softly, not to startle him in case he hadn't heard the door. He finally answered in a weak voice as I walked towards his room, and once I walked in, Juan was lying on his side with his knees up in a cramped position.

"JUAN! JUAN!" I anxiously called out, "didn't Svetmana come here? Endira said she was on her way! I don't believe she lied about something like that!" Juan just looked up hopelessly and appeared almost incoherent.

"I don' know where Svetmana is. She never came!"

"JUAN! JUAN! WHY? Why didn't you call when she didn't arrive after I left? Aw, God, why didn't you call, Juan?" I was angry at Endira and Svetmana, and at the same time with myself because I let them walk all over me again. I also was angry because, what if Juan did call the house and received my machine...he may not have even left a message figuring I may be at Matt's! Yes, I should have called. Instead, I allowed Matt to again intimidate me because I was afraid of upsetting him.

"AW, I am so sick, Recharred...so sick."

"Well, I am taking you to the hospital, Juan. There are no ifs, ands, or buts about it! You have to go to the hospital, Juan!" This time, he didn't give me an argument but insisted he had to take a shower first and that there never was hot water at this time.

"So let us wait, Recharred, please...because I would like to be nice ond clean when I go thar." The chicken dinner was still sitting on the table and I quickly took it and threw it in the garbage. Upon returning, I tried to persuade him to go immediately, but he still insisted. 'Because, Recharred, I know how the hot water is in this building...everyone gets up early to take thar showers ond when I want to take one before going for my clinic appointments...thar never is any. Recharred, whot difference is another hour...please?" So I agreed, but my anger at Endira and Svetmana was getting the best of me so I decided to call their house. I wanted her to know how caring her precious daughter was besides cussing her out for lying. Though I wasn't sure Svetmana hadn't actually left from the house but I didn't desire to hear any of Endira's terrible Latin temper, because I had already experienced it.

"Endira, I am at Juan's now and I left last night because you told me Svetmana was on her way," I shouted once she answered. "Well, she never arrived and Juan has been vomiting all night! So I am taking him to the hospital now!" She tried to make weak excuses and I felt like telling her Svetmana probably went to her bull-dyke friend's house instead, and had undoubtedly been going there constantly because Juan has been left alone so much. But I bit my tongue.

Juan hadn't eaten for almost twenty-four hours and I realized he had to have some nourishment. I decided to make some tea and give it to him with plain crackers to avoid the chance of any more vomiting. As I waited for the water to boil, I kept thinking of how I allowed Matt to intimidate me...how

I felt like a lackey, allowing him to take control even though I had such strong beliefs…and I didn't know what to do about it!

Juan obliged by taking a few sips of tea along with a bit of cracker, but then wanted no more. So I insisted he take his shower.

"Because, Juan, you have to get some antibiotics in you."

"No, Recharred, I know it is not yet hot enough because I 'ave gone to the clinics many times without taking one." I went into the bathroom and found the water barely warm, so I began pacing nervously. I was also very concerned because Juan was so disoriented…so confused. His manner of talking was almost childish…like the many times after drinking when I finally got him home, lying on top of him in hopes he'd fall asleep. Though this time drinking had nothing to do with his manner…certainly not this time, so why is he so disoriented?

Oh, God, I thought, *what is happening?* My only consolation…he finally stopped vomiting.

Then exactly what I didn't want…happened. Svetmana came through the front door, walked to the bedroom and just stood at the doorway. I was so angry with myself for calling Endira because not only did I not need her presence, but realized she'd cause Juan stress by creating a scene with me. I hadn't seen her for over two months and couldn't believe the weight she had gained, and her manner of dress and makeup. Juan had told me she was a great fan of the movie *Misery*, and here she was, a carbon copy of Annie, even the same hairstyle. She looked twenty years older than her age!

Of course, Juan greeted her pleasantly, not even asking why she never showed up at night. Once he asked how the reception turned out, she gave me a sharp look, almost snarling.

"I will tell you after *he* leaves!" and then turned to leave the room. "Well, I am not leaving," I quickly and nonchalantly called out bringing her to a halt, "because I am taking your father to the hospital!"

"I don't want you to take him! I will take him!" she screamed, taking a step towards me.

"He should've gone last night, but there was no one here to take him," I said, trying to keep my cool. "Well, I'm gonna take him because I want to be next to him when he takes a shower so there's no chance of him falling." That possibility didn't give her cause to be concerned, only my insistence brought her to hysteria while stamping her feet.

"Who the fuck do you think you are! You're not even family!" she screamed, waving her arms wildly. I couldn't take any more of her tantrums. I had tried to be calm for Juan's sake, but now I wanted her to know what she was doing to him!

"I am just as much family to Juan!" I shouted, "and besides if you're so much family, why have you been leaving him alone so much, especially when he's very sick and when I could've been with him! What do you want? Do you want him to be alone all the time!" This brought her into a rage and she finally screamed out an ultimatum!

"Daddy, it is either me or him…make your choice!" She just stood there waiting for him to answer and I couldn't believe she'd demand this of her father? She had to know the love we shared and how much he adored her! There should be no choice to make! It was unthinkable she'd cause him this stress! Juan stood there confused, not heeding to her demands, trying to reason with her instead. She finally stormed out of the house, slamming the door behind, screaming hysterically!

My heart was aching for Juan as he stood in one spot appearing so helpless and bewildered, trying desperately to reason this out.

"Whot is going on, Recharred? Whot is the matter with thot girl?" I didn't know what to say, but that I was sorry I didn't control my temper, while assuring him she'd finally reason it out and be back to apologize to him…but he just stood there baffled.

Suddenly, we heard the front hall door opening and she came in like a raging maniac, her body trembling wildly!

"I am gonna kill you! I am gonna kill you!" She stood at the doorway of the bedroom, stamping her feet, demanding, "YOU HAVE NO RIGHT TO BE HERE! Do you hear me…NO RIGHT! And if you don't leave, I am gonna kill you!" Juan was completely bewildered and tried to calm her in his usual soft manner he always pleaded with her.

"Svetmana, please don' be this way…please, my darlin?" But she'd not stop her demands. I tried to sit calmly on the bed because I realized the state Juan was in and I quietly begged her to realize what all this anger was doing to him, but this only infuriated her more because she realized I wasn't going to budge. Her father's feelings meant nothing to her and she went on in her rage. I finally couldn't take any more of her theatrics!

"Listen, I am not your father and I am not your mother!" I lashed out rising from the bed, "who you try to fool with your theatrical hysteria, just so they feel sorry for you and give in to your every demand! And for Chris' sake, I don't come over because I think you are here, not wanting to cause him any stress watching you in a rage! And then you're not here anyway! You don't even make sure he's eaten! Don't you realize he never wants to impose on his precious princess because he doesn't want to upset you? So he tells you not to worry! Anyone with any sense should realize that! So he goes without because he's too weak to do it for himself! All you care about is yourself!" Her nasty rage continued to scream throughout my flare-up, but once I made the last statement, she ran out of the room and down the hall towards the kitchen.

"I am gonna kill you!" she screamed and her hysterical sounds continued to bellow throughout the apartment! I could also hear rummaging through the drawers of the kitchen cabinets, evidently in search of a weapon. She returned, just as I expected…empty handed, which firmly convinced me her psychiatric problems were pure theatrics.

She did, however, run towards me, swinging wildly, while screaming every profanity. My only defense was to extend out my arm in an attempt to keep her swings out of reach. Finally, she ran out of the room. My hopes that she again left the apartment were quickly snuffed out once I realized she'd slammed the door of the other bedroom since her loud screams came from that direction.

Juan was completely bewildered, which only added to his present confusion, and he just stood in a pathetic trance.

"Recharred, I don' know whot is wrong with thot girl?" he finally uttered. "She is so nasty," and then he looked at me sadly but with compassion and sighed, "Maybe, Recharred, you should go. I will be able to get to the hospital ond you con come thar later. Please, understand, will you please, my darlin?'" He stood there appearing so helpless and sad and I didn't want to leave, but realized he didn't need any of this hell.

"Okay, Juan, I will do it for you," I sighed, raising my arms hopelessly, "but I don't want to because I want to be with you to be sure you get to the hospital safely." I then reached out to hold him close.

"Recharred, I will see you later ot the hospital. Please, understond, Recharred?"

"I do, Juan, I do…but then I don't!"

So again Svetmana broke Juan's heart with her selfishness…because of her inability to love or to be loved, and finally because of her jealousy of me. She was incapable of having the strength to be there continually for Juan, and yet, hated me because I did. She'd rather see him alone…. It did not make sense!

Chapter Sixty-Three:
Trying Desperately to Join Hands

Juan had been admitted to the same private room on the fifteenth floor he had back in November. Antibiotics were already being administered through his Hickman, but he was still very ill. In fact, those first few days I found it quite difficult to communicate easily with him because he also seemed to be so disoriented. I was also confronted with Svetmana on occasion, which didn't help matters, though she'd usually completely ignore me and sit in a corner of the room reading. When she did give me some attention, it was either one foul look after another, or she'd storm out of the room in audible anger. Fortunately, she'd not return.

A few days passed and the antibiotics had to be working since Juan was a bit more himself, even though he often was having trouble remembering, which gave me cause to be concerned. Another thing that concerned me was he was having problems with his balance, feeling dizzy once he tried to walk a few steps. I finally realized this had to be because he hadn't been out of bed for over a week. I decided I'd be there every morning to shower and shave him, and then walk him after he'd eaten his breakfast in order to gradually regain his strength and balance. He, however, continually refused to eat, messing everything on his tray until most of the food ended up on the floor. I then decided I was going to spoon-feed him as I did in Indianapolis, occupying his mind with conversation not related to food. After all, I managed it when he stubbornly refused to eat in the hospital in Indianapolis, and he came through with flying colors.

Svetmana had gone through another of her outbursts, storming out and leaving Juan in a disbelieving stupor.

"Recharred, I am afraid she will never change. All she cares about is herself." He was feeling fairly well that day and I felt good about it. He was lying on his side, as he always did, and seemed to be deep in thought, when he finally looked into my eyes to say something I will never forget. There were only nine words, but one look at his beautiful blues and I was certain of the sincerity in those words.

"Recharred, please don' leave me?...ond keep me well." I looked at him tenderly as moisture filled my eyes.

"Juan, I will never leave you! I couldn't if I wanted...because you are me! And I am gonna do everything I can to keep you well. Juan, you have to get well...you have to!" He smiled tenderly.

"I will try, Recharred...I will try to stay well."

I tried desperately to divert his attention from eating whenever feeding him, but it was a slow process, even though there seemed to be some improvement each day. I began bringing food from home...those he liked, but even though he ate more, I still felt it wasn't enough to bring his strength back to normal. When I brought chocolate bars, his eyes would light up.

"Aw, good, Recharred, you know how I like cha-co-lot!" And most of the times, he'd finally finish them by breaking one piece off after another.

Juan's improvement continued at a very slow pace but I was still concerned because he was having problems remembering who had been there to see him, even the same afternoon. I realized he needed physical exercise in order to also help him mentally, and tried to walk him each day, which was quite an ordeal to talk him into. I began writing out his checks for bill payments and since he'd given me his personal power of attorney on that document in Indianapolis, I could've recorded my signature with his bank, but I didn't think it necessary. I decided to leave his checkbook and statements in the drawer of his night stand to make it convenient, because I was there so often. On one particular day, I made out a particular check.

"Look, Juan, this is your last payment for the car!" His eyes just glowed.

"I don' believe it! I never thought it would be still running!"

Juan was rational most of the times, but realized he was having memory lapses.

"Recharred, I would like you to 'ave my power of attorney for healthcare. I know you don't believe I need to 'ave someone...but you 'ave to admit my memory may cause some problems...please, my darlin,' you are the only one I trust. Will you do it for me?"

I finally talked with the social worker on the floor and he advised me to definitely do it. He then informed me staff members were not allowed to serve as witnesses. I decided on asking Daniel to witness the signatures and he agreed but said that Stan would have to come with him because they were invited out and that he knew he'd be anxious to get on their way. I also realized Stan didn't like to stay long visiting Juan because during their visits, he seemed to be on edge while keeping his distance from Juan. He almost appeared as though he was afraid to touch Juan for fear he'd catch AIDS.

I had just begun to read the form aloud in order for Juan and myself to clearly understand everything when Endira walked in the room in her usual nonsensical manner. Of course, I discontinued with the reading since I

Why Has All the Music Gone?

certainly didn't want to be intimidated with her opinions, especially since she seemed to think she had the right to control Juan's needs, on the basis of being Svetmana's mother. This may have been accepted since Svetmana had never matured into a woman and was presently under the care of a psychiatrist, which made her totally incapable of making critical decisions on behalf of Juan. However she had to be totally aware of Juan's relationship with me throughout the years and should have gracefully backed off. My problem was I was allowing her interference because I didn't want any more outbursts by Svetmana to destroy Juan. So I'd allow myself to be continually intimidated by the two of them.

She went on endlessly with her usual boring talk and it was evident Stan was tapping his foot impatiently, which naturally gave Daniel reason to give me one look after another to get on with this thing. I finally decided to interrupt her useless chatter to explain everything, and once I continued with the reading, she quickly snatched the form from my hand.

"Oh, let me see that form! You know you have to be very careful with one of these, because if the wrong thing is checked, a person can keep someone going on with their life when there is no hope." I wanted to spit in her face to insinuate I'd not follow Juan's wishes. Yes, my heart would break but I wouldn't want Juan to be a helpless vegetable. However, I'd never withhold food since that would give him the strength to want to live. She then managed to admit that Svetmana would go into a tantrum should she know I had the power of attorney for Juan's healthcare.

I tried to explain that her objections didn't matter since this was what Juan desired, but suddenly noticed he was becoming disoriented again, and realized there was no use going on with it at this time. I did not bring it up again because I was too busy concentrating on keeping him well and my beliefs were still strong about him returning home soon. He was going to lick this, as he had done before!

Juan still had his confusing moments during this initial two weeks in the hospital, and Endira was aware it was happening. She shocked me another evening when she again came in like gangbusters, totally unaware of Juan, to immediately sit down to fill out a card. I didn't realize what she was up to until she finally said she was going to cosign on Juan's bank account just in case he needed someone to sign for him. Juan was disoriented that evening and really didn't know what was going on, and I should have immediately objected. Juan in his right mind would never allow her to have access to his checking account because he was definitely aware of her mismanagement of money…and if she was in need of any, she wouldn't hesitate in taking it for her own use! It was inconceivable to think she had the nerve to take control of his financial affairs since she'd been nothing to him for eighteen years! Again, I did not mention it or that I had his signed document giving me power to make deposits and withdrawals in his account and in my shock only thought to say that I was writing out his checks and that he is signing them.

"That's okay," she said casually, merely flicking up her wrists, "you can still do that."

I realized Svetmana's behavior towards me wasn't doing Juan any good…that he had to know we were both there for him…hand in hand. I also wanted to truly be someone close to her…to forgive all the years she shunned me and be someone to love because she had been so much a part of Juan's life…someone he accepted to be his daughter because he needed that in his life. I thought if I could somehow explain the love Juan and I had for each other, while reminding her of his deep love for her, I'd be able to finally break the barrier between us. Just before Easter I mailed this letter to her…

Dear Svetmana,

I know there is one common bond that we both share, and that is the strong love we both have for your father. And nothing will ever change that or his equally strong love for us. Yours is a wonderful father-daughter love that God blesses. I will never forget how many times during the years I have known Juan, when he would tell me how lucky I was to be able to raise my daughters and sons, and to be with them during their growing up years. He missed that so much. All he would talk about is that he wanted to see you grow into a beautiful woman and to one day walk you down the aisle to a happy marriage. He was so worried this would not happen, when over five years ago, he was diagnosed with the dreadful HIV virus. I told him he would be here to see it happen, because I never would believe he would come down with AIDS. I was sure a cure would be found. I refused to talk about it because this could not happen to Juan! At the time, they were saying it would probably be about five years until a cure was found. All that had to be done is keep his mind off it and to keep him healthy, to survive the five years. Then the dream started to shatter when they began adding years to a possible cure. Still, I refused to accept anything would happen to your dad. NO, not Juan! And I still won't believe it, and I know you feel as I do. That is why we bring his favorite foods to him.

I go to the hospital two or three times a day to try to build his body to the strong one he had, and I guess, just to be near him, and at times, I would like to do this side by side with you. I know this would make your dad happy, and that is what we want more than anything in this world!

I don't think there are two friends any closer than your dad and me. The love and respect we share is very rare. We have often spoken about our love, realizing we are closer than brothers or even twins. We read each other's minds, so in fact, agreed we are one! I don't think there is, or will ever be anyone who makes me laugh as he does, and our friendship has been unequaled by any of the great ones.

The eighteen years I have known Juan have been the highlight of my life, and I would not trade them for millions, and the only thing I would ever want to change is this dreaded AIDS that he has! That is one thing that makes me so angry with the world! I don't understand it and never will! I know if he did not have it, he would be enjoying the simple things of life he loves so much...like driving into the country...disco dancing...listening to music...going to movies...watching the horror flicks...reading, and just rattling on in conversation. He has never had illusions of grandeur because all these simple things have been enough for him in this world.

I guess that is why my love and respect for him grew into a bond that will never break. And this wonderful friendship and love helped solace my broken dreams of becoming a star, because I had found someone and something better. Someone who would make me laugh and to be with...and not miss the other. A simple undying love and friendship. Oh, Svetmana, your dad is the joy of my life and I pray it would be me instead of him because I know he would wish the same, if it were me who was sick. But, by God, I will not give up and I know you will not, either. But I need to be hand in hand with you, holding your dad's hand. He needs our hope.

*Always,
Richard*

I prayed it took hold of her heart because I needed her alongside me giving hope to Juan.... He had to know she felt the same as I, to give him the will to live by being sure he was being exercised daily, and not just sitting there accepting his ultimate death. My prayers were answered a couple of days before Easter when I found a note tacked on the wall of his room informing me she would be taking her dad to see his parents for the holiday. I was so happy and made certain I arrived early enough Easter morning to shower and shave him before she arrived. Once she arrived, I was pleased to hear her wish me a happy Easter. She did not say much more, but I felt it was a start. However, Juan's balance was very unsteady and decided he didn't want to leave the hospital. I was very upset about it and surprised it didn't seem to bother Svetmana because she just told him she was having brunch with her mother and would stop off to see her grandparents later. I had hoped she'd remain with him for the afternoon because I had purchased tickets to see a play with Matt; otherwise, I'd have canceled my outing for the day. I reluctantly left feeling terrible because I realized as soon as I was gone, Svetmana would do likewise.

Juan was having one of his fairly good days, not experiencing any of those dreaded memory lapses, and it was so good to hear him talk on incessantly. Suddenly, he looked into my face with compassion and said something that again touched me.

"Recharred, you know, I am so sorry for all the aggravation I 'ave caused you…for being so nasty. I am truly so sorry!"

I took his hand and sighed, "Juan, I know you never mean the nasty things you say," I sighed taking hold of his hand. "I have always known! I know you love me and that is what is important…and you know I love you. I always have and always will!"

I brought in the title of Juan's car and I couldn't believe how his eyes lit up because it was paid up at last! The doctors usually came in to see Juan while I was there in the morning, and I was happy to hear them repeatedly say that he was doing well and would soon be released to go home! My one concern was Juan never seemed to be overjoyed hearing he'd be going home at last. It always seemed to go over his head, as if it wasn't said at all? The doctors finally became aware of these memory problems and began asking if someone would be with him all the time. I never knew how to answer since I realized I'd have to get a job soon because my unemployment compensation was running out, and I couldn't depend on Svetmana being with him while I was at work.

I was slowly getting Juan to eat more and even though it was only small portions, he still was increasing his intake. Svetmana began leaving me notes so I'd know how much he ate for her, and I decided to do the same. I was finally successful in getting him to eat half and sometimes three quarters of his meals, but disappointed once I read her notes informing me he ate three forkfuls of this and two of that. I wanted to explain how to sidetrack his attention, but afraid I might again put her on the warpath. I was often having difficulty getting Juan to walk and exercise, and realized the reason? I was the only one doing it…because that really took an effort.

The doctors had been continuously inquiring if someone would be with Juan all the time after being released and because nothing positive was being said, they wouldn't commit to a discharge date. I didn't want this to continue because I realized Juan had to get out of that hospital. It could be his only motivation to go on. I finally decided I was going to have him come to my house, or stay at his permanently. It was the only possible solution! I had to tell them.

Svetmana was standing alongside Juan's bed when I entered his room the day I was to tell the doctors of my decision.

"You know what my dad has?" she quickly said. "He has syphilis!" I looked at her in shock as she continued, "and he has to receive penicillin for ten days!" I didn't want to believe it! I immediately remembered when he had told me it was possible for the AIDS virus to reactivate the syphilis he had years ago…AND I WAS IN DESPAIR! I COULDN'T UNDERSTAND WHY HE HADN'T BEEN MONITORED FOR IT WHEN HE CAME IN ALMOST THREE WEEKS AGO. IT SURELY HAD TO BE ON HIS CHARTS! THESE DOCTORS HAD TO KNOW WHY HE WAS ADMITTED! HE WAS VOMITING AND HE WAS CONFUSED! OH GOD…NO!

I checked on the final stages of syphilis and when informed…severe vomiting and the brain deteriorating, I couldn't breathe! But I had to believe in them. I had to believe these Indian and Pakistani doctors knew their profession. I tried to get some answers, but it was like talking to a wall. I finally realized I had to put it out of my mind…to pray the penicillin would eliminate any possibility of any of these stages to continue. I had to lay aside my fears of negligence….

Juan seemed to be improving with all his medications and multitude of pills and tablets, and I wanted to believe my fears were wrong. As I entered his room, he was sitting on the edge of his bed, wearing his earphones.

"Aw, hi, Recharred, do you mind if I jus' listen to this last song? It is so good!" He then quickly took them off and insisted I listen for a minute to confirm what he meant, waiting anxiously for my reaction while his eyes sparkled. The minute I agreed, he put them back on and began swaying on his seat to the music, smiling away.

I began stopping in his apartment to be sure everything was fine, and upon seeing all his belongings and record collection, my throat would swell. I could see him standing at the stereo playing one song after another, and I could see those eyes sparkling along with his big grin. Then I'd look around and my heart would ache because during the two months after he moved there, he really couldn't enjoy it because his world seemed to revolve between the couch, the bathroom, and the bedroom.

I had heard from one of the doctors that they were considering performing a biopsy on Juan's brain, which caused me concern. However, they finally decided it was too much of a risk.

The IV technician, Mary Marie, began teaching Svetmana and me how to change the Hickman dressing again, so I felt relieved since this meant Juan would soon be going home. I was so glad for Mary Marie, because she really seemed to take Juan to her heart. She treated him like he was someone special, and he felt so good about it. She even seemed to go out of her way to be there for him.

Juan was doing better and because they needed a private room for someone, he was transferred to a four-bed ward in the same unit. I was sure this would disturb him because the others may keep him from sleeping, but he surprised me and didn't say a word. Mary Marie was instructing us one day.

"Recharred, you don't have to worry about learning now," Svetmana quickly said, "because I can teach you later." Juan gave me a look I thought would make me burst into laughter, but I managed to keep a straight face. I decided not to tell her I already knew more than she'd ever saturate, but figured I'd pacify her by accepting the offer.

Svetmana was talking to me more and I knew Juan was happy. There had been talk of Endira's brother-in-law serving as power of attorney for Juan and I was glad Svetmana accepted my opinion that it was ridiculous to have someone Juan hardly knew have control of his life. Especially since Juan only met him about two times and had always told me he felt ill at ease with him. I held my breath, but she finally agreed.

"However, Richard, I don't believe you should do it…I don't think you would forgive yourself if you had to make a decision to stop life support. I know I wouldn't want to do it." She then went on to do and say something that also shocked Juan, suddenly embracing me while saying, "I'm sorry, Richard, for being the way I was." I was speechless, but Juan wasn't.

"My, God, whot are you doing?" Juan exclaimed his eyes widening, "I thought you hated each other?" I knew the way Juan meant it because he knew I could never truly hate anyone. He was referring to Svetmana, but figured for her sake he'd include me.

"Oh, Daddy, I don't hate Richard," which called for a hug from me, but it would have been nice to hear her say she loved me.

I tried to interest Juan in reading or to play Scribbage, but these weren't his priority. Instead, his main desire seemed to be to lie in his bed to rest or to sleep, and he never talked of going home. He did show interest in watching the game shows on television, even beating the contestants in the Wheel of Fortune. He continued to be his bright and witty self on occasion, but even at that, he still didn't talk of home, which had always been his main topic of conversation during his previous hospital stays. So I was concerned. I was managing to get more food into him, but realized he had to be exercised by others besides me. He began accepting the exercise easier each time I worked with him. So I put up a note for any visitors to do it, but never knew if they did because it was a real effort to persuade him. He could be very belligerent even to agree to walk to the shower. But I would not give up.

He then began roaming the halls late at night, or even during a quiet time, and would finally be found sleeping in an empty bed along the way. The staff was concerned and they finally decided upon transferring him to the same private room since it was directly in front of the nurse's station. One nurse thought to tell me, "Richard, whenever you are here late at night, he never seems to do that," one nurse commented. "He will sleep through till morning." So I decided to also make late night visits, cutting time I might be with Matt. It never seemed to bother Matt anyway. It was also funny and wonderful each morning because as I walked into the room, Juan usually had just awakened and he'd immediately cheerfully greet me.

"Aw, you are here, Recharred…good!" Or he might say, "Aw, Recharred, you are up ot last," almost as though he had it in his mind that we were living together and I had just awakened. I hated this confusion, but even with it, he was so charming.

Daniel was the only friend I was certain to visit him on a regular basis and that was usually twice a week…sometimes more. I knew Marina had been there but hardly ran into her, and she wasn't communicating with me by phone. I also was constantly after Amanda and Patti to visit while helping at their shop, but never knew if they were there when they said they'd go…because as always Amanda always spread herself thin. To this day, I'll never understand why I didn't want my children and family to visit Juan. I guess I WAS STILL AFRAID FOR THEM TO KNOW HE HAD AIDS! I now realize his mind would've been kept pleasantly active, and that was what he needed.

On one of Daniel's visits, he told me he still talked candidly with Juan about his illness, and assured me that he had a long life yet to live…that I shouldn't be concerned.

"Because, Richard, even though he is forgetful, I know he is nowhere near dying." He then went on to tell me what Juan had asked.

"Richard, Juan asked if you were still seeing Matt since you have been at the hospital so much, and then he said, 'I don't think he is seeing him anymore' and if he was not right. So I told him I didn't know but that I didn't think you were. And then he smiled as if he was so satisfied and happy. Was that okay to say, Richard?"

"Aw, yes, Daniel, thank you so much! Please don't ever say anything about Matt!" At that moment, I realized I was just going to bide my time with Matt because I certainly was going to make a home for Juan once released from the hospital! Juan never mentioned Matt again.

I finally managed to find a part time job as a salesman in a furniture outlet store, working about sixteen to twenty hours a week. There wasn't any commission involved, so I was only bringing home about sixty to ninety dollars, which was a drop in the bucket to what I needed to survive, especially spending money with Matt. I didn't want to put in more hours because I wanted to have my time with Juan…. I had to build up his strength and if I wasn't there, it wouldn't happen. So I thanked God for my wonderful sister, Geena, who was slipping me fifty or a hundred every now and then. Mike had given me quite a bit in the past, but he was in the middle of a separation and his business was suffering because of it. However, Nicky came up with a bundle…in fact, a great big *bundle*…forty eight hundred, and told me not to worry about paying him back. I insisted I would one day. He insisted I pay off my charge card because my balance was just about that and felt it was foolish to pay so much interest. I decided to keep a few hundred for living expenses and paid the rest on my charge card. I was also lucky to have a daughter and son-in-law with so much heart even though they had bills raising two children, because Martina and Don were sending a hundred and fifty once or twice a month. If I didn't have these beautiful people in my life, I don't know what I would've done! My only regret is that I sometimes used some of this money on entertainment with Matt or to buy him a gift.

Endira called to ask if I had exercised the power of attorney for Juan's healthcare and once I said I hadn't, she told me she'd then do it. And, again, I did not say a word! Here was this woman, who was nothing to Juan for eighteen years, and suddenly she is controlling not only his money but his life! I then discovered Juan's checkbook missing from the drawer, along with all the statements, and once I asked him about it, he was unaware they were gone. I was infuriated but had to control myself because I didn't want to upset Juan. I knew exactly what had to go out in payments, including his rent, and once I called the bank to inquire what his balance was, I was told three hundred dollars. Juan was receiving twenty-two hundred in disability payments each month, and once his bills were paid, he should've had at least twelve hundred left. So Endira had already begun, and there was nothing I could do but put my legal power of attorney in effect, and that would only cause a mess at this time, which Juan didn't need. So I kept my mouth shut which only made a fire burn within me.

All of this wasn't enough because then Endira asked if I'd put the car in Svetmana's name because the one she was using was requiring one repair after another and costing them quite a bit. It was as though I had been smacked with a bat! I couldn't believe this sweet-talking woman! She was picking like a vulture before anything happened! I wasn't sure what Juan would say, since I couldn't rely on his memory and figured I should sign it over because I didn't want Svetmana on the warpath again. I also thought it possible that she may possibly demand the hospital restrict me from seeing Juan, and I couldn't let that happen! *Oh, my God*, I thought, *I have to be with Juan!* I certainly couldn't tell Endira that Juan had always told me the car would be mine should something happen to him because it would make me appear mercenary, especially since monetary things meant nothing to me…only Juan's life mattered.

Once I explained everything to my daughter, Martina, Daniel, and to Amanda…each of them said I should have my head examined if I signed the car over to Svetmana. Fortunately, Juan was rational enough to ask and he was emphatic.

"No, Recharred, I do not want you to do thot! Leave it in your name as I 'ave said!" He then surprised me by saying something I never expected to hear. "You know, Recharred, I do not trust Svetmana, as well as Endira." I asked his reason, but he said no more.

One of the nurses came into the room while Juan had his earphones on listening to music, and I was glad he had them on because he hadn't been using them much. She asked what he was listening to and suddenly he raised his arms in that inimitable way of his while moving his bottom to the timing of the music.

"Cha, cha, cha!" he shouted. I cannot begin to say how my heart swelled seeing him do that once again, even with the bit of the crossed left eye the CMV had begun to effect. It was heartbreaking to see this happening, but if that would be the only thing it would effect, it did not matter. In fact, it sort of gave him a happy madcap appearance. I was just happy the music hadn't gone…it was still there in him.

I usually started at eleven in the morning when I worked, so this didn't hamper going to the hospital to shower, shave, and feed Juan. Breakfast was served at seven and I made sure I was there at that time, and usually, I'd bathe him after. In this way, we could walk the corridors once he was nice and fresh. He did, however, still give me problems about walking. But he seemed to be improving. This didn't mean I always left happy, because there were still times I would cry while driving from the hospital.

Svetmana hadn't seemed to be upset about the car and we went on leaving notes regarding Juan's consumption of food. Still, I didn't feel this was accurate enough to be sure his every meal was covered. I decided upon making out a chart because in this way, everything would be included—walks, bathing, and food consumption, and then even the nurses could mark the specific time of the day with the activity…or whatever. I really felt this was the only way we could really get Juan on the way to recovery. I spent half a day drawing it up as Juan watched like a little kid, continuously asking me what I was doing. For the first few days, it seemed to be working because when I saw no one was there, I made sure I was.

Endira continued her rude ignorance each time she visited Juan. Instead of talking English, she'd converse in Spanish, and it was really bothering me. On one such occasion, she'd been talking excitedly and it was apparent Juan was becoming quite disturbed. She never stayed long, usually coming in like gangbusters and leaving the same way, and once she left, I asked what she was talking about because I couldn't believe how upset he became and I needed to know how to settle him. I couldn't believe the insensitivity of this woman once he explained everything! She had actually been going on endlessly about a cousin of hers who had tried to commit suicide, and another friend who had been mugged by intruders! This was a highly educated woman who didn't have a shred of common sense in her head! I finally realized what Juan always talked of, that she was, indeed, insensitive and totally selfish.

I entered Juan's room one day and was shocked to find the chart missing from the wall, and once I asked what happened to it, he was totally bewildered. I had an idea why it might be gone, but shook it from my mind. I didn't want to believe someone's ego and pride was more important than Juan's life! I had realized most of the activities had been marked off by me…in fact, five to six times more than Svetmana, but this shouldn't have mattered as long as it was getting done. It was common knowledge that I was ten minutes from the hospital, whereas, an hour for Svetmana, so it should be understood. This was not a game. This was Juan's life at stake. I finally asked Endira and she again flicked her wrist, as if it was a mere trifle.

"Oh, Richard, we don't need a chart, we know what Juan is eating and doing," and went on talking about something else as if my concern was nothing! I knew it had been tossed in the trash and all I did was bite my tongue and call her a fuckin' asshole under my breath…but what good did that do?

She never fed Juan…she never walked him…how could she do those things when she only stayed about fifteen minutes? But she didn't have to be there any longer, I realized that. She just wanted to make her appearance on behalf of her precious princess!

So Svetmana was once again my enemy, and when she did agree to talk to me, it was only to respond to my inquiry regarding the chart, by saying I should've just continued with the notes. I tried to reason with her that the chart was more thorough, but I knew her only thoughts were that I was showing her up. I tried to explain that hadn't been my motive…that my only concern was to get Juan well, but it did no good. She was only concerned about her pride.

I found her manner of getting back at me inconceivable. She no longer left any notes, and once I asked the nurses if she had walked Juan, I was told she had not…and in fact, that she had screamed at them hysterically in the room for one thing or another.

"And we don't think that is good for Juan, Richard." I was then confronted with something even more unbelievable! Each afternoon when I arrived, I was confronted with a room of darkness because the blinds would be drawn, and Juan would be covered with blankets up to his chin! Once I inquired about it I was told that Svetmana, or that she and her mother, had just left! Each morning the doctor had told me Juan had to walk for exercise and needed to know night from day, and here they were completely ignoring it! It seemed as though they were giving him the last rites! I was going crazy, and I finally talked with Mary Marie to ask if she'd explain all of this to Svetmana. The blinds were then no longer drawn, but I still was the only one walking Juan.

Juan wasn't receiving any physical therapy and I couldn't understand why. I continued bugging them about it and finally managed to convince them he needed it in order to strengthen his mind. The head doctor in physical therapy was scheduled to interview Juan and I made certain I was present. She agreed with me that physical exercise also benefited a person mentally. However, this wasn't one of Juan's better mornings and because of his confusion, the interview didn't go well. I tried to explain that he wasn't always this bewildered but it was evident she wasn't pleased with the cooperation given to her. I waited anxiously each day for a Juan to be scheduled for therapy…but a program never appeared on his chart.

Anne usually was Juan's day nurse and we'd continually tell her she should get into the comedy circuit because her one-liners would bring us to hysteria. What made them even funnier, they were always told with a dead pan expression. Of course, her presence would always motivate Juan to cut up whenever he was stable. She had just connected his IV treatment one day and immediately after leaving the room, blood began backing into the tubing. I quickly fetched her and as she began to change the syringe and tubing, I left to make a call. When I returned, I received the shock of my life once I saw the exposed blood-filled syringe and tubing sitting on Juan's tray table! Anne was nowhere around and when I looked down the hall, she was nowhere in sight! I couldn't believe she left it exposed?

There were miscellaneous items intermingled with all of this on the table and someone easily could've accidentally pricked themselves with the bloody syringe while reaching for something! She wasn't too pleased once I got her in the room to dispose of it, especially after expressing my distress. And her comments were certainly not one of her dead-pan wisecracks.

I was never one to report anyone for negligence, but I felt this time it was necessary because Juan could've reinfected himself with the AIDS virus, or the cleaning person…or anyone for that matter. I decided to discuss the matter with the head nurse, but at the same time not reveal the person…merely requesting she have a general meeting in regard to precautionary measures. I even decided I wouldn't tell her the day it happened, so she could not pinpoint any particular nurse. I didn't know if this was right, but I certainly didn't want a job jeopardized, and I realized Anne would never again be negligent in something so serious.

I believe this matter was instrumental in Juan's transfer to another ward on the fourth floor because the staff was much larger. I didn't mind this because I realized Jenny was one of the nurses in the ward. I had met Jenny years ago through Daniel when he took me to her New Year's Day food bash. I took Juan the following year when I received my own invite. I felt this could be a good move because I was certain Juan would receive special attention. I had last seen her at Lucille's party, which was the first time in years, and during this time her longtime companion had died of cancer.

Juan hadn't been transferred yet and I was trying to get him to eat his lunch, but this wasn't one of his cooperative days. Suddenly Endira again came in like gangbusters with Svetmana following, and behind her, Juan's dad. It had probably been over sixteen years since I last saw him and realized the years managed to rob him of that robust vigor. It was evident he looked lost and deeply concerned. I was pleased to receive a nice greeting from him. It was then evident Endira didn't think it was right I should be feeding Juan since his dad was present. She quickly edged me away.

"Here, let me feed him, Richard, I am a woman!" I thought, what difference does it make that I am a man…and besides, she had never fed Juan before! I wanted to vomit in her face for making it appear I was doing something abnormal! I was surprised to hear a comment from Svetmana even though she managed to insert some sarcasm.

"Oh, Mom, let Richard feed Daddy. *He* knows how to do it." However, Endira insisted, and instead of placing the food in his mouth, she just kept rattling on about nothing! I began getting extremely nervous and finally walked out of the room to stand near the doorway so I could still see if Juan was eating. She got all of two forkfuls in him, and then gave up while talking in Spanish as if she was the chief in charge, finally leaving hurriedly with Svetmana and Juan's dad following. I took a deep breath of relief and returned to resume with the feeding.

As I sat there smiling with every forkful and looking at Juan's appreciative face, I could not help from thinking that this was the fourth week of May! The ninth week and the longest hospital stay for Juan, and as he smiled, my heart prayed.

"Please, God, aw, please, let him come home soon?"

Chapter Sixty-Four:
A Voice So Priceless

We finally got Juan settled on the fourth floor that afternoon, a spacious room that had apparently been a two-bedroom. Jenny came on duty at three and once I talked with her, I was told she had already been aware Juan was coming down the day before. I was happy Juan remembered her once we began talking because it had to be at least five or six years since he had gone to her house.

"I remember you well, Jenny.... You had all thot food on the table ond you kept bringing more all day long!"

"Remember, Juan, you kept going into the kitchen as she was cooking, telling her and Penny to come into the living room so they could have a good time with us?"

"Aw, yeah, I do. I also remember Carol was thar. I had always seen her in the building where I worked, ond suspected she had to be one of the gang. Do you still see her, Jenny?"

"Oh, yes, we are good friends. In fact, you will probably be seeing her because she often comes to meet me after work and we go for some drinks."

"Aw, thot will be nice," Juan sighed with a big smile.

I had a chance to talk with Jenny out in the hall because I wanted to know about the ward.

"Rich, in this ward we can devote more time to patients who need it because there is a larger staff and besides, most of the rooms are single ones, so there is never a problem taking care of them." She then went on to say, "It will be great here for Juan, because if you're not here, you can be sure he'll be fed by one of us." This was like music to my ears, and then she continued to tell me she was going on vacation beginning in June, "and, Richard, I will be gone most of the month and once I return, I'm scheduled to work in the west ward for a while, but I know I will be poking my head in to see Juan every chance I get. However, you'll not have to worry because most of the nurses here are very compassionate…so they'll take care of Juan. There are a couple of lazy ones, but don't worry, I'll get after them."

I was caught completely off guard once she asked if I was aware that his daughter and her mother were going out of town today and would be gone for a week! I was shocked!

"What? What did you say? Did you say they're going out of town?" Jenny immediately assured me a message was left in the office, putting me further into shock. "They are going out of town and did not tell me so I could spend more time here? I don't believe what I am hearing!"

"Richard, I figured you didn't know anything about it…that's why I told you. Richard, we all know about the problems you are having with his daughter. Believe me, word gets around in this hospital, and we know she is a bitch."

I was furious thinking about it, but I didn't want to bring it up to Juan. I realized he had probably been told, but with his memory lapses, never had said anything about it. I finally couldn't control my emotions any longer and left the room to attempt to catch Endira at her office because I remembered her mentioning she had to hurry there. I wanted to tell her how cold and insensitive she was and again was cut short during the call with her non-stop casual manner, as if it was no big matter.

"Richard, I am going on a business trip and decided to take Svetmana along on a little vacation to get away from everything. So I am going to take a few more days to do some things with her while we are there." Before I could say more she rambled on, "Don't worry, Richard, my husband, Dan, will be going to see Juan, so everything will be fine." I was again receiving that flick of the wrist treatment, as if it was nothing important, and she immediately cut me off with her hurried, "I really have to hurry now, Richard. I will talk to you when I return…bye." And she hung up! I could not believe this selfish woman! She cared nothing that Juan would be left alone when I thought Svetmana would usually be with him! She knew I realized Dan worked late and couldn't be there until about eight thirty or nine!

I finally passed their insensitivities out of my mind to realize it was really a blessing…because now, I'd have Juan all to myself the entire week and wouldn't have to be subjected to intimidation from Svetmana or her mother.

I should've moved in with Juan because I spent all my free time with him that week, and it was beautiful! Juan was the best he'd been since he entered the hospital…everything…his mood and temper, and even his condition seemed to improve. I couldn't help thinking back to Nurse Ratchat, when she told me how miserable Juan was when Svetmana was with him. I wanted her to stay away from him forever because, now it was as though Juan was in a convalescent ward, growing stronger and relaxed every day. Yes, he still had his memory lapses, but they were not as frequent.

"Recharred, you want to receive communion, too…do you not?" Juan always asked in his typical little boy aura each time Father Jerry or one of the other priests came into the room to offer communion. I'd assure him I did. I'll never forget the wonderful expression of anticipation as he watched to be sure the communion was placed on my tongue. Even with his frequent crossed left eye, he looked so alive with love and happiness! And each day, when it was time to take his pills, he'd be like a little kid opening his mouth wide, waiting for me to place them on his tongue one at a time.

"When am I ever gonna finish all these pills? I am so full!" he'd ask in the same impatient manner a little kid would do.

Dan did come almost every evening, but it was always very late and he never stayed long because he hadn't yet eaten. I liked Dan very much and so did Juan. However, he always talked on endlessly about something totally boring to us…and most of the time it was something we knew nothing about. So if we were forced to listen, all we could do was twist our bodies, nervously praying for him to finally stop his long-winded sentences. He was a very good man and I never understood how he managed to tie up with Endira. Dan was also a very religious person and insisted on saying prayers for Juan before leaving. This always seemed to please Juan, because, since his illness, he had turned closer to God…and I felt this was good.

I had written my phone number on a card for Juan when he initially was admitted to the hospital because I realized he was having memory problems, figuring it would be a great reminder. However, my phone wasn't waking me in the morning, as it had done so many times through the years…and my heart was breaking because of it. In fact, Juan never called anyone, even when I suggested he call his mother because she refused to come to the hospital to see him lying ill in bed. I missed it terribly because no one can imagine the joy I experienced through the years each time I heard the beautiful resonance in his happy-sounding voice. I couldn't bear the thought that I may not hear that voice again in my life and especially couldn't comprehend that I'd never see him again in my life should he eventually die. So I went on with my hope, but I guess deep in my heart I knew he'd leave me one day, and I think this may have been the reason I continued with Matt…. I realized I needed someone to be there for me. I also believe the thought of never hearing Juan's voice again prompted me into bringing my small portable cassette to the hospital to record our conversation without Juan's knowledge. I wanted it to sound natural, and at the same time not have Juan suspect I was recording.

It was dinner time and Juan was a bit mischievous and didn't want to cooperate. So as I was trying to feed him, he kept giving me a hard time…in fact teasingly razing me to get my goat. Much of it may not make sense because many of the words were mingled with distortion from the cheap set I used, but they're words I'll be able to hear always. And what made it so precious was his voice was the one I heard so many times after finally getting him home from a night of drinking…that voice that was so innocently childish and so devilishly belligerent.

I was having a difficult time feeding him and each time I raised the fork to his mouth, he'd push it away and the food would fall to the floor. It just happened again and I was upset.

Juan: Hmm? Whot happened...whot? (As I try to explain, he interrupts) It is not important to eat. (Our conversation continues, and just as I again try to gently push a forkful through his lips, he complains) Don't push in my face....push in your face! Thot's more in your family...not mine! Jesus Chris' why are you so cruel? (I pout) Now, you are gonna stond thar for an hour...right? (I begin to shuffle the tray around to make it easier to feed him) Wha' are you gonna do now? You are so nervous! Recharred, you are so cruel to me!

Richard: Didn't you say to me, don't leave me and keep me well?

Juan: Well, now, I 'ave changed my mind because you are very cruel when you feed me.

(I try a forkful again) Aw, aw, it is gonna fall on the floor! (He pushes it from his mouth and the food falls again to the floor. So I begin pacing trying to position myself in a good spot) Whot are you doin'...goin' bock ond forth...goin' bock ond forth...hmm?

(Jenny enters the room and immediately realizes I am having problems feeding Juan and asks what is going on.)

Richard: He won't eat.

Jenny: Why won't you eat?

Juan: I don' wanna eat...so spicy...so mushy! I'm so full, so full. I am not hungry now. Sometimes when you eat too much, you are full...right?... Correct? (Jenny begins feeding him. Conversation continues but I found it impossible to make out on the tape. I do remember Juan continuously kidding her with laughter throughout. I also remember Juan telling her he did not like me and she responding with a laugh. A long conversation continued and I finally mentioned his pills were always found on the floor if no one immediately assisted in being sure he took them.)

Richard: So, Juan, I will hold the pills (He objects.).

Jenny: He says you don't take them by yourself...you forget they are there.

Juan: Aw, I do? Aw, I see.

Jenny: Until you get them all down...you have to be watched (continues to feed him). The Bulls are playing tonight.

Juan: Aw, they are?

Jenny: Gotta watch the basketball game. There's your coffee. You can pick it up and drink your own coffee...here.

Juan: I'm full. It is funny how full you con get. You know I am full...thoroughly full, you know. Are you a grandma?

Jenny: Yeah, nine times.

Juan: (shocked) Nine times...whot 'ave you done?
Jenny: I have three kids.
Juan: You 'ave nine grandchildren? (Continues asking the same question) I'm on a diet.
Jenny: No, you are not on a diet. It is important for you to eat.
Juan: How are you doin', dear?
Jenny: I'm doing fine.
Juan: You gonna retire soon?
Jenny: Not yet. Not for a few years. (I was talking quite a bit after that, but because I was not near the recorder, everything was impossible to hear. The next morning, I decided to try again and started the tape as I just lathered Juan for a shave).
JUAN: WHAT ARE YOU DOIN'?
Richard: I am gonna shave you (Juan began talking at a very fast speed, making it impossible to make out until he slowed down)
Juan: I wanna get outta here. I wanna go home.
Richard: (completely shocked) You want to go home? That's the first time you said that...you never say that!
Juan: I never said I did not want to go home...never, never, never!
Richard: I want you to go home, too!
Juan: You think I want to be here, huh? You think I want to be here?
Richard: Well, you never say anything about going home! I want you to go home. I want you to come to my house. You want to come to my house?
Juan: No matter where (begins talking about shave).
Richard: Does it feel good?
Juan: So, so (continues to talk as I finish).
Richard: You know what I got? I brought the clippers.
Juan: Whot?
Richard: I brought the clippers...the nail clippers!
Juan: Whot are you gonna do?
Richard: To do your toenails.
Juan: (as I begin) Ouch!
Richard: Does it hurt?
Juan: Yes...ouch!
Richard: Why does it hurt?
Juan: I don't know why it hurts? (Continues moaning as I cut)
Richard: Now, I am gonna do the little one.
Juan: (Pointing to toe and innocently asking) this one?
Richard: The little one. (I then said a word I believe my dad made up in Italian, meaning the littlest one) Pittiberille!
Juan: (Again pointing) this one?
Richard: Yeah.
JUAN: OW! YOU DON'T KNOW WHOT YOU ARE DOIN'? YOU DON' KNOW WHOT YOU ARE DOIN'! OW! YOU

	CRUSHED ME…YOU ARE SO CRUEL! IT IS VERY PAINFUL! JESUS CHRIS'…SO PAINFUL! PLEASE BE CAREFUL! OW! I DON' KNOW WHY IT IS SO PAINFUL! PLEASE, BE CAREFUL, OKAY? OUCH! OUCH! YOU ARE HURTING ME! WHOT ARE YOU DOING? I DON' KNOW WHOT YOU ARE DOIN', RECHARRED. YOU GO SO LOW…OW, OW!
Richard:	Juan, I don't want to hurt you. I would never want to hurt you! (He continued complaining and I could not understand it. I finally finished and began talking about a Spanish woman who came into the store and bought a mattress and spring) She paid $458…some in cash and part on her charge.
Juan:	She paid thot much? Four hundred bucks…thot was dumb! She was a dumb person…a dumb person!
Richard:	No, she needed a new mattress and spring because her old one was squeaking.
Juan:	(with a twinkle) She couldn't do her job, huh? Right? (Juan then talked of some pain he was having) I don't know why? (I wheeled the chair over to the bed) Where are you going?
Richard:	I am gonna take you out.
Juan:	(Belligerently) Why? I am not ready to go…I am not ready to go! You know I am not ready to go…I'm not ready! You 'ave to check with the doctor…okay? I told you many times you 'ave to check with the doctor! No! I told you a million times, you 'ave to check with the doctor!
Richard:	I did.
Juan:	Whot he say?
Richard:	He told me to take you out. He said to "take him out for a ride!"
Juan:	You lie! You 'ave to check with the doctor! I need to know! I need to know…okay? (I went out of the room and returned in a couple of minutes) You talk?
Richard:	Yeah, (overemphasizing) you have to walk in the halls every day!
Juan:	You're the doctor! (I wheeled Juan out of the room)

As I listened to the tape end and the noisy silence, I swear I could hear the sound of heartbeats…?

Chapter Sixty-Five:
So Many Crises, Yet Happy Forty-Ninth, Juan

Unfortunately, the week went by very quickly and I realized Svetmana had to be back. Before leaving work at six, I decided to call the hospital to check if she was there, and was told she was not. I decided to go and feed him. I began to feed him as soon as I got there and, unfortunately, she walked into the room. She greeted her father but didn't acknowledge me. I felt a bit uncomfortable and decided to ask if she'd like to feed her father, because it would lighten the air if I recognized her as family. I quickly discovered my mistake because, as usual, she fiddled with the food and Juan wasn't eating anything. Her mind just wouldn't realize she should try to divert his attention from it. Because of it, I began twitching nervously while sitting behind her. It was as though she was once again cleaning the kitchen and everything would soon be cold and Juan would never eat anything. After about a half an hour, I couldn't take any more and left the room, expelling a slight huff in my voice. I was angry at myself for allowing her rudeness to again intimidate me and probably because I thought she could have the power to bar me from seeing Juan! After a few moments, she came into the hall in a huff.

"You feed him!"

However, by this time, the food was cold and no matter how I tried, he wouldn't eat, besides feeling completely agitated! I couldn't believe it as she sat there watching me once she returned. There was a smirk of satisfaction on her face because I was failing to get Juan to eat anything! She was actually daring me to fail! It was obvious in her smug expression! I couldn't comprehend how anyone in this world could find pleasure in knowing I failed to get a sick man to eat! AND TO FEEL SATISFIED! She couldn't possibly be part of Juan!

This had to be what he had meant all these years! Where did she come from to be so willing to sacrifice Juan…just in order to call me down?

It didn't take long for Juan to occasionally react belligerently whenever I wanted him to walk, especially after Svetmana had been there earlier. Daniel finally got a job, but still managed to visit once or twice a week. Juan needed activity and this meant he had to have visitors more often. I finally decided I wanted my kids to visit him, especially since Jacque had been continuously asking to go…I also wanted Geena to be there, too, because he loved her so much, but he suddenly began saying obscene statements, even following with vulgar actions, and I was never sure when it might happen. It was shades of yesteryear, when he had drank excessively. Out of nowhere, he'd shout one vulgar statement after another. Only now, he began taking hold of his genitals, waving them wildly and shouting!

"Do you want thot big cock…huh? Who wants thot cock?" It didn't matter if one of the nurses happened to walk in because he'd continue. I'd try to cover him with the blanket, but it would only make him worse. He also occasionally did it while I showered him, and even though there was no problem there since we were always alone, I still realized this was not the mischievous Juan that had often done this to make me laugh. Yet, I still believed he'd wake in the morning from his night of drinking and be that wonderful charming Juan? Once he behaved in this manner when Amanda was there, I knew I didn't want to chance that the same would happen with Martina, Jacque, and Geena. So I kept them updated with his condition, although never revealing his true illness. No, Juan had brain cancer…?

Yes, Juan was forgetting things, especially when they just happened, and he began roaming the halls again. However, as disoriented as he was at times, he still maintained his excellent knowledge by retaining so much about the world he had always read about. We were watching the Miss Universe pageant as we did so many times through the years because it was one of his favorites, always boasting that South American beauties always dominated the pageant, which proves "thot Latin women are really very bea-u-ti-ful people." This time, however, the winner was Michelle McLean, a beautiful woman from Namibia. Once I voiced my ignorance to where Namibia was, he immediately raised his brows.

"Recharred, you mean you do not know where Namibia is? You know, you should be ashamed of yourself! You really should read more, Recharred." He then went on to explain exactly where it was located in Africa.

I kept in touch with Larry in Indianapolis and Barry in California and even though Juan had been doing so well, he again began going in and out of memory lapses, and along with them, he'd be very weak and always wanted to be in bed…so I was forced to give them unhappy reports. Whatever it was that was running through his brain seemed to go on a rampage at times and he'd be completely confused, childlike, or belligerently agitated…and there was nothing I could do! I tried to convince as many of our friends to visit him because I thought the activity of conversation could help. He seemed to be the most content lying in his bed talking with me, but I knew he needed to be active and I tried desperately to achieve it because he had to win this battle…he had to!

I continued his walks, even though he asked continuously to return to his room. Each morning, I'd weigh him after his shower and was always pleased that he was maintaining a weight of 168 to 172 pounds. He'd be completely adorable at times while walking with his arm through mine. Should there be another patient sitting in the corridor, he'd happily wave and say, "Hi!" He didn't look like an AIDS patient because the only place he really lost a substantial amount of weight was in his butt. Why would I possibly think he was going to die soon of AIDS?

Juan then became plagued with loose bowels and because of his old habit of passing gas whenever he felt the urge, he'd mess in bed. There were times he couldn't hold it for one minute while trying desperately to make it to a toilet, only to be unsuccessful in the attempt. However, he realized this was happening and would feel terrible because of it. It wasn't as though he was unaware it was happening. I kept reminding him that he shouldn't pass any gas when he felt the urge…that he should remember to do it while on the toilet.

"Aw, I forget, Recharred," he'd say, "I will remember next time." But his memory would not allow him to do this. I realized fresh fruit wouldn't help this condition and decided to refrain from bringing any, as I had been doing every morning. Finally, it seemed to stop, but would then start again. So we had to realize this was going to be an on and off condition.

If I were to tell everything as it happened, I realize I cannot go easy on myself…because I was living a life outside the hospital even though my total hours there daily ranged from six to ten, and which always seemed to pass like fleeting moments. So this meant I was spending time with Matt under those same absurd conditions, so similar to a hot and cold running faucet…one moment hot…turn it quickly and immediately cold! Usually, I cut the evening short to be with Juan, and he never seemed to mind. He had to realize I was going to the hospital each time, but never said anything. In fact, I think he liked his freedom. It never occurred to me he'd ever go out after changing for bed and writing loyally in his diary! I often wondered what he was writing, but even though I had many opportunities to read through them without his knowledge, I never did, because I realized this was something private. He often boasted that I'd read them one day because he knew a woman who agreed to take the diaries and write a book. I often wondered what could be so interesting to write an entire book?

My subconscious mind had to believe Juan was going to die, because I tried desperately to hold onto Matt, even though he was still playing his game. I needed someone to be there for me because the fear of Juan never returning home was buried deep within me. I prayed for Juan to be well enough to come home to my house so I could end this torment with Matt once and for all, but I couldn't bring myself to end it. My subconscious mind wouldn't allow it because it was telling me I needed someone there…that I couldn't be alone. So I again heard the same thing when I asked for a commitment.

"Rich, I am not ready for it. There are too many problems yet in your life with Juan."

"What difference does my devotion to Juan make?" I sighed in disbelief. "You have known that from day one, and you accepted it!"

Without any feeling whatsoever he said, "Well, we'll see, Rich, maybe after Juan dies." I glared in shock at the coldness of this man!

"You have to get something straight, Matt," and while raising my voice in anger, "I DO NOT WANT JUAN TO DIE! I WANT JUAN TO LIVE WITH ALL MY HEART! IF JUAN DIES, I DON'T KNOW HOW I WILL BE ABLE TO TAKE IT! NO! YOU HAVE TO WANT ME NOW, WHILE JUAN IS ALIVE!" I continued glaring in disbelief.

"Matt, by saying something like that, you make me believe everything I did for you was in vain!" I should have discontinued seeing him, but instead, I let him again double talk his way into my life.

Matt had a master's degree and always boasted his high IQ, and yet, he was capable of this.

"Rich, I hope you wash properly when you leave Juan? You know it is very easy for you to get infected with the AIDS virus, and also, Carl told me he and Frank will never come to your house because you are taking care of Juan." I looked at him in disbelief!

"I don't believe you, Matt! You have so much more education than me…and you make a statement like that? Yes, Matt, I wash my hands when at the hospital, but I wash them when I enter Juan's room! Because, Matt, he is the one who is susceptible to germs I may carry on them! Juan's immune system is next to nothing because his T cells are probably all gone now!" This didn't even affect him. He held his smug expression so I began screaming, "I cannot get AIDS by touching Juan or by washing and feeding him! I can even hold him close and kiss him and I will not get AIDS!

"MATT, I WISH I WOULD BE ABLE TO TAKE THIS AIDS FROM JUAN!" I pleaded hopelessly, losing all control, "BECAUSE I WOULD DIE FOR HIM! HE WANTS TO LIVE SO MUCH!… So much!" Finally, a realization occurred to me and I cried, "I really don't know if I have anything worth living for if Juan dies!" Of course, he took all of this lightly to merely say I was crazy for thinking such a thing.

Svetmana happened to come in the room as I was trying desperately to coax Juan to walk with me and instead of some urging, gave into his stubbornness by continually insisting I leave him be. I wanted to remind her of Mary Marie's assurance that Juan was in dire need of exercise but realized she'd consider my remarks as reprimanding. So she again managed to intimidate me, which in turn always inhibited me from talking normally and I'd lose all the charm I usually was capable of using to convince Juan. I had left the room to fetch something when, suddenly, she came storming out into the hall.

"Richard, I think it will be better if when you are coming here to call and leave a message on my tape, so I will not be here at the same time!" I agreed, but realized it would inhibit me from coming on the spur of the moment. She continued in her nasty manner to say, "I don't know why you have to be here all the time, telling me what should be done! YOU ARE NOT FAMILY!" She had to know I was closer than anyone, but her jealousy wouldn't admit to it. I should have told her I was closer than family, but again I avoided it.

"I feel like family with Juan! We have been so close and he's always said we are really one person!" Of course, this brought on an extremely smug expression.

"How would your kids like it if you were sick and in the hospital and my dad kept telling them how to take care of you?" I glared at her in shock.

"Svetmana, if he were asking them to do what the doctors advised, they'd welcome it! Besides, they love your dad, and especially because they know *I* would want him there! In fact, if he wasn't there, my family would be disturbed!" Nothing I said would move her to compassion and she continued to grasp for anything to attack me, and finally lashed out!

"Well, I don't know what you want! I think you are trying to get his money!" I stood there in shock, trying to comprehend this incredible accusation! She had to realize Juan never had any money I could want...that he owed me thousands! I immediately thought she must be referring to the Army insurance policy of fifty thousand dollars! Yes, this was what she was referring to, and she used it to cover up the hatred and jealousy for the love she knew Juan had for me! My voice almost trembled as I tried to reply.

"Svetmana, I don't want any money! All I want is to pray for Juan to get well! Svetmana, I want him well again and strong! Svetmana, I would trade places with him, so he could live!" She just stood there coldly, looking at me with hatred and scorn.

"Well, he is not going to live! He is gonna die, because, Richard, THIS IS THE DYING WARD...THAT IS WHY HE WAS BROUGHT HERE! TO DIE!" I became almost incoherent as tears began rolling down my face, trying desperately to deny her cold and vicious statement.

"No!... I talked with Jenny, and she told me everyone does not come here to die! Aw, Juan has licked so many things, AND I WILL NOT GIVE UP!" I then began hopelessly pleading, "Aw, Svetmana, we have to be there for him together! Oh, God, I DO NOT WANT JUAN TO DIE!" She just stood there, looking at me coldly.

"Well, he *is*.... Face it, Richard." I didn't want to believe her cold and unfeeling manner and kept rattling on about a miracle, but she merely turned away and finally stormed out of the ward and into the elevator. I stood there trembling as tears continued down my face, wanting to believe so badly she was wrong...that she had to be wrong! Finally, after composing myself, I walked to Juan's room, wiped away my tears, and straightened my shoulders. I then walked in and stood alongside him. I smiled broadly.

"Hi, Juan, did you miss me?"

I made certain to leave messages on Svetmana's tape whenever sure of going, which was almost every morning and for dinner. There were no problems late in the evenings because she never showed up at that time. It would then provoke me whenever I called to talk with Juan's nurse during lunchtime to find she left after being there about fifteen minutes, or that she never even showed up. If not working, I'd go and chance she'd not show up…and she never did.

Juan was to move to 409, a smaller private room where he could be watched closely since it was directly in front of the nurse's station. The evening before Juan was to be transferred, Endira's husband, Dan, stopped in. Juan had been quite agitated and wasn't willing to cooperate in any way. He had just told me he had to move his bowels badly and as I tried maneuvering him to the bathroom, his equilibrium was so bad he couldn't stand on his feet. I should've called for the nurse to bring a bedpan, but thought he could make it. I struggled desperately, but because his head was probably swimming, it was as though we were battling. I had expected Dan to assist, but he just remained in one spot observing the chaotic struggle.

"Recharred, I cannot hold it." Juan kept screaming, "I cannot, Recharred!" Then, while almost slipping from my grasp, he messed in his pajamas and the bathroom floor. I tried to wash him clean as he floundered helplessly, trying desperately to hold onto me…WHILE DAN DID NOTHING BUT WATCH! I was trying to steady Juan and my heart was breaking because I had never seen him appear so pathetic and ashamed! Dan still did nothing but glare in pity. After cleaning Juan, I managed to drag him into bed. Dan was obviously disturbed and quickly decided to leave. He, however, said prayers and I went down with him to have a smoke. What I really wanted was to ask if Endira was responsible for the majority of Juan's pills being eliminated from his daily medications.

I liked Dan because he was so polite and giving, and his sincerity seemed to be genuine. However, I became quite disturbed once he began discussing Juan's condition. Once he mentioned it was degrading to see Juan live in such a way, I retaliated!

"Because he has some accidents?… It's not like he doesn't know or care that it's happening. He just cannot control it at times. And the times he messes in bed is because he forgets he is having a problem and then decides to let out some gas! He is not having any pains…he is not suffering! It is his memory that is causing the problems and if he had continuous exercise, it would've helped his mind! But no! Svetmana just wouldn't try to help him, and now she is hardly here! When she does come, it is only for fifteen minutes or half an hour! Do you know most of the pills he was taking are no longer being given to him! They weren't life support…they are medications and Juan never requested medications be withheld. Endira designated herself as his power of attorney in healthcare, much to my distress, and I would like to know if she is the one responsible for discontinuing them? There were fourteen pills and capsules and now he is only receiving four!" Dan quickly denied knowing anything and said something I was shocked to hear!

"We do not like seeing Juan so degraded, and as far as Svetmana and us are concerned, 'Juan' is dead…he died some time ago, because he is no longer himself!" I stared in disbelief!

"Who are themselves when they are sick in the hospital! What do you mean Juan is already dead? He is as alive as you and I! He still has intelligence…he can watch Wheel of Fortune and come up with the answers before the contestants. He is just forgetting and I am sure that can be corrected if we all cooperated to give him therapy!" I was in a state of hysteria because he wouldn't agree and I felt they were all waiting for Juan to die, and the sooner the better!… I shouted in my realization!

"I know what your dear wife Endira's motive was for all the token gifts to Juan…so she could gain his trust and then control his life! She is nothing to Juan and because of her lazy and crazy daughter, she thinks she can control his life! They want him to just lie there and die…that's what they want! And then she got Juan to allow her to cosign on his bank account! She doesn't know, but I checked on his balance and most of it is gone…all SPENT!" This brought him to a fury!

"I love my wife and I don't appreciate hearing you say things about her!"

"Yeah, because you know they are true…. She wants him to die and will not even pray for him to get better…even for a miracle! Juan is not suffering and I am not gonna give up trying to make him well!" Dan broke from my near clutches, quickly entering his car and starting it up!

"Well, I am not coming here to see Juan again!" And he drove off swiftly as I stood there trembling, not wanting to believe any of the things he had said.

As far as I knew, Dan never did return, at least when I was there, and I was with Juan most of the evenings. I am sure he never mentioned our heated discussion to Endira since she never brought it up.

I managed to corner Juan's present doctor and once we were in the office, asked about the discontinuance of most of his medications. He had been assigned to Juan just before Endira and Svetmana went on their trip and I remembered them coming out of his office. All the other doctors always conferred with me, but I seemed to be avoided by this one. In fact, he gave an impression of being very cold with one of his statements.

"You tell me you do not want Juan to look and suffer like an AIDS patient…well, we decided by taking away all those medications, it will be better for him now, because he will not linger on like a typical AIDS patient." I was silent realizing I had no say. But my question was answered once he said 'we.'

I stopped in Juan's apartment as I often did to check everything and was stunned because they had begun clearing out some of his accessories! The two large carpets and lamp Endira had given him were gone, along with many of my Southwest pictures. And other things were scattered around, as if they would soon be on their way out. It took me a few minutes to get my bearings because I couldn't believe they were doing this! I realized I could put my power of attorney into effect, but again felt it would only cause a big mess. I decided to take a lighter view of it, because now he would be able to return to my house if they were liquidating the apartment. I felt I had to take the things that meant something special to Juan and me through the years…because they certainly had to be crazy to think they could keep them! Again, I was angry because she never confided in me. The first thing I took hold of was the brass bumblebee and the porcelain Indian sculpture. I then decided to take the antique side table I had given Juan to use because I could always picture him raving on about it after I refinished it, and about three pictures. There wasn't really any monetary value, only beautiful memories, and I was determined we would be enjoying them together at my place. I left a quick note explaining everything, and ended it by explaining that I am keeping these things at home for Juan to hold until he leaves the hospital, because as far as I am concerned, they will always belong to him…and then I wrote that I would return for other things.

    I did return, and much to my surprise, the front door was bolted from the inside! I decided to try the back door and found that lock had been changed! It again took me a few minutes to get hold of myself to realize they were trying to strip me of my meaning to Juan…to make me feel as though I was nothing in his life! Again, I did nothing…never told them. I wanted to tell Juan at a time he'd comprehend, but decided it would only upset him.

    I did return a few times because I thought she may have forgotten to bolt it if she stopped there. However, once I'd try to turn the doorknob it'd only release the sliding bar, and then open no further. So she'd always be aware that I'd been there. Finally, a note tapped onto the wall in Juan's room informed me she'd call the police if I tried entering again. If I had given it any thought, I should've allowed her to do just that since I could've put my power of attorney into effect. On that note, she also included a postscript accusing me of eating the kolachkys she brought for her father, and to stop eating his food…to eat my own, actually insinuating that anything free, even a hospital meal, appeals to me. She actually believed these things which only proved she had never matured.

    "Dad, Endira called me today, and she told me some things I want to talk to you about…but in person because I don't feel I should talk about them on the phone. Why don't you come over for dinner tomorrow and we can talk about it after…when the kids are in bed," Martina had said once I returned her call. I agreed, but was disturbed Endira had called my daughter because I felt it concerned Juan.

    "Dad, why didn't you tell us Juan has AIDS," Martina softly asked while Don was putting the kids to bed. Don returned to the family room as I nervously explained everything Juan and I had agreed upon and both of them quickly agreed,

    "Dad, we love Juan and him having AIDS would have never changed that…you should have told us." I made all kinds of excuses and Martina finally said, "Dad, Endira talked about so many things and I tried to tell her I was very busy with the kids, but she kept going on and on. Dad, I know Latin women, and they do not like to be told they are wrong, especially when I told her I knew Juan told you to keep the car! So use kid gloves on her, because she has a temper!" Martina suddenly tried being as compassionate as possible as she went on to say, "I knew Endira's motive when she told me she realized you had to have your time with Juan…that it was important for you to be with him." We continued talking and I was certain I'd always have their love. I went on to tell them about Juan's forgetfulness, his bowel problems, and his terrible belligerency at times. I felt like a terrible load had just been taken from my heart and finally asked Martina if she'd come to see Juan…that I wanted her to see him. We agreed to make a time to do it. Martina then called a couple of days later.

Dad, I love Juan very much and I don't know if I want to see him in this condition. I know you have to realize he is going to die, Dad, because no one survives AIDS. I want to remember Juan as he always was. I went to California to see my mother-in-law before she died and I can't get the way she looked out of my mind. Do you understand, Dad?" I told her I did, but I don't know if I did…because I was still praying for a miracle….

I called Endira to ask if we could meet. She agreed and asked if I could come to her office because there was a coffee shop in the building. I was very explicit when asking why she thought it was her duty to tell one of my children Juan had AIDS…that when they were told, I should have been the one to tell them. I also went on to say there was no reason they had to know as long as I did not keep from them that he was gravely ill. The temper Martina alerted me about immediately exploded loud enough that everyone in the small room had to hear.

"Well, my daughter knows, why shouldn't yours?!"

"Svetmana is Juan's daughter; that is why she had to know." Suddenly, the subject changed.

"I have to tell you Juan's father resents you because he thinks you were the one who made Juan spend all of the twenty thousand he made in the stock market in 1974." I almost laughed in her face to think it was coming down to money again.

"Endira, when I met Juan that was almost gone, and if you recall he spent the remaining amount on that trip to see his sister in South America, taking Svetmana and his mother and flying first class. In fact, he had no money when we went to Atlanta to open our business. We both had equal shares and I put his share into the business which was twenty-two thousand dollars. Well, all that was lost and in all these years, I never brought it up to Juan…. I always figured it was my loss." She then brought up the car again,

"I know I cannot do anything about the car because it is in your name, but if you do sign it over to Svetmana, I will be sure to give you thirteen hundred dollars…because I saw a note in Juan's handwriting which stated he owed you that amount. And I told Svetmana, it is the right thing to do." This was unbelievable! She was distributing Juan's insurance and he's alive! I wanted to vomit in her face! What a dealer! I felt nothing but contempt for this woman! Still, I realized I needed to control my emotions in order to explain what money meant to me.

"Endira, Juan owes me a few thousand more than that amount, and I have never cared if I ever got it back…especially now! All I care about is that he gets well! The car is probably not even worth much, and I was going to put it in Svetmana's name…but once I asked Juan if that was okay, he told me I definitely shouldn't…to leave it in my name." She then did one of her flicks of the wrist, since her conniving wasn't working.

"Well, what are you going to do about all the money Juan owes you?" She really needed to be pitied.

"Endira, I'm not really worried about it. I'm praying for Juan to get better, and if my prayers are answered…maybe he'll one day be able to pay me back? The money doesn't mean anything to me…if it did, I would've surely insisted he include me in his insurance when he talked of doing it so many times. In fact, Endira, Juan told me many times that he told you to be sure to give me five thousand from the insurance, and I always told him there would be no need because I only wanted him to live!" She just sat there looking dumbfounded.

"Well, Richard, he never told me to do that." No matter how I brought her down, this woman could not be belittled or ashamed. She knew what she wanted…because, after all, should Juan die, Svetmana would receive fifty thousand dollars from his insurance…and that amount could help get her out of so many financial messes.

Parting was friendly; after all, she was satisfied once I said the money didn't matter. Now, she wouldn't have to worry about lawsuits against her daughter's God-given rights.

It has always taken so long for some things to penetrate into my head, especially when someone was conniving and taking advantage…my Don Quixote traits, of course. It had not occurred to me until this moment, as I write, that Endira always was panicky when she was in a financial mess, and would do anything in order to borrow from me!

Juan still continued his charming ways regarding receiving communion together and happily greeting me in the morning…especially since I think he really imagined we were living together. He, however, always pleaded to lie down on anything that might be around if I was walking or wheeling him in the chair, and in fact would actually set his body down across the armless waiting chairs in the lobby. He was always telling me how tired he was.

I will never forget the evening Juan was lying on his back in bed, instead of his usual side position, and probably the reason he began hallucinating while staring into space. He always seemed to be describing a dream as he went on explaining how beautiful everything was…almost as though we were somewhere we had never been…maybe even another planet?

"Aw, Recharred, we are thar ond it is so bea-u-tiful...so bea-u-ti-ful! Ond, Recharred, it is only you ond I thar...only you ond I."

Tests were continuously being performed on Juan...the MRI didn't show anything more developing and his eye tests were also proving satisfactory. Yet, Juan always seemed to be bothered by brightness. Whenever I took him out in front of the hospital, he'd continuously squint his eyes looking with one eye after another. I could never figure his reason for doing it. Whether he was testing to see from each eye, or if he felt bewildered to his whereabouts he would never give me an answer.

After some persuasion, I still managed to get him to the shower and then hear his pleas to lie in the bathtub in the room...that is, not to bathe but to sleep in it. So I'd be sure to keep our distance for fear he'd drop himself into it and hurt himself. He finally discontinued groping himself while in the shower and the bed. In fact, he had stopped for some time. There were times, though, he'd spread his legs while in the shower to release a loose bowel movement.

"Aw, Juan," I'd plead, "why did you do that? Why didn't you say something before we came in here?" But he'd not say a word and just stare at me in one of his owl looks. I was glad it was summer because I'd usually get sopping wet trying to steady him on his feet. I finally decided to sit him in the shower chair and he seemed to appreciate it very much because there were so many times he sat there and pleaded like a kid while sighing.

"Recharred, do you mind if I jus' sit here ond let the water run over me?" I would agree and he would continue to sigh loudly while saying, "Aw, Recharred, it feels so good...it really feels so good! I could stay here forever...aw, it feels so good ond warm! Thank you so much, Recharred, for letting me stay in the shower a long time! Thank you so much!" It was a chore wiping him because his balance wasn't good, but he always managed to try to help as I guided him to another chair. And I angrily thought to myself, *This is a man who knows he is having a problem and wants to help himself! How the hell can anyone say he is already dead?*

Juan was maintaining the weight of 168 to 172 because I wouldn't give up spoon-feeding him because his unsteady equilibrium caused him to drop much of his food when he tried feeding himself. I understood what Jenny meant when she said there were a few lazy nurses because each time they were attending him, if I wasn't there, they'd leave him to feed himself. Betty was the only one I could depend on and Jenny had assured me she had as much compassion as she. However, she wasn't always his nurse. So I tried to be there for lunch, too, whenever I didn't work. Jenny was returning in about a week, and I'd be certain he ate, even if she wasn't his nurse.

Juan's forty ninth birthday was approaching the fourth week in June and I began planning a party for him. I became a bit anxious because I felt once I left my message on Svetmana's machine, I'd receive complaints because I wanted to be with him in the morning, afternoon, and evening of the day. My original plans were to bring him to my house that evening so it could truly be a wonderful surprise once he saw everyone. However, once I talked to the head nurse and doctor about my plans, they advised against it and told me I could decorate the lounge area instead.

I ordered the cake from the Italian bakery he loved so much and Daniel said he'd bring balloons to decorate the area, while Amanda agreed to supply a snack tray to munch on. After leaving a message on Svetmana's machine, I never heard any rebuttals, so I felt relaxed in my plans. The guest list included Daniel and Stan, Marina, Amanda and Patti, Lucille, Carol, and Jenny, if she could make it because she had just returned from vacation....

I was scheduled to work that day, but called to tell them I couldn't be in. I only stayed with Juan a short time that afternoon because, as he always told me, "Thar are things to be done, Recharred." I had already brought flowers in the morning and ran around crazy doing last minute things. I finally remembered I hadn't gotten a gift for Juan and it wouldn't be a birthday party for him if he didn't have something from me to open. Would everyone look at me as crazy if I gave him a shirt because they'd naturally think he could never wear it? I didn't want the party to be sad.... No! I wanted Juan to be happy and there could be no sad faces from anyone! Then, it came to me...Juan had really turned to religion and he didn't have a cross on a chain! Yes, he had given me the silver one, the very first gift he ever gave me! The one that was lost the night I had the fight with the drag queen in Atlanta. So I raced for the department store and found a gold one I was certain he'd have chosen. I was so broke and realized I couldn't afford a fourteen-carat chain, too, so I purchased one of those electroplated gold ones and figured I could buy a real one later. I purchased a card I thought befitting and once I arrived home to get ready, I decided to write something special before signing my name. I realized I couldn't be too mushy because it would be read by his family and everyone else who happened to visit him. I felt this expressed my feelings for Juan perfectly...

> *Though times may change so many things, the happiness that your friendship brings will never change, because they're treasured within my heart....*
> *Always, Richard*

I hurried along like a chicken without its head because I had taken so much time deciding which cross to buy, and once I arrived, it was already time for Juan's dinner. I noticed even though Juan seemed to be content, he was fairly quiet. He ate most of his meal without giving any problem. A vase of roses was sitting on the windowsill, so I figured Svetmana did stop by for his birthday, which gave some feeling of satisfaction, even though I knew she only stayed a short while. A feeling of deep regret came into me as I thought how wonderful it would be if she were with us to celebrate Juan's birthday.

I decided Juan wasn't going to be at his party wearing just pajamas, so I looked in the closet and got out the shirt he'd worn to the hospital. It was the flowered one I had given him just before Christmas, and I knew he wore it often because he loved it so. As I helped put it on, my mind was saddened to think it had been three months since this was hung in the closet. He looked great once I finished sprucing him up. Suddenly, he appeared to be upset.

"Aw, God, Recharred, I 'ave to go badly…aw, I cannot hold it long!" I tried desperately to get him to the bathroom in time, but he could no longer hold it. At that time, Lucille arrived and I motioned for her to leave the room, but said to call the nurse immediately. Betty was on duty and between the two of us, managed to get Juan in bed without any more mess. Betty decided it might be wise to put a diaper on Juan in case it happened again. It broke my heart to see him lying there, quietly cooperating. My heart ached as I thought, *Why, oh, God, why?*

I called Lucille to the room and after she hugged and kissed Juan, it made me feel so good to see the broad smile of happiness on his face, even though his left eye was crossing so badly. Lucille handed him a birthday balloon and a gift wrapped box, which I realized had to be chocolates. She then mentioned she had been to see him about a week before and that he asked her for a cigarette…and that she gave him one that he smoked. I was shocked but informed her he was not to smoke even though I inwardly was pleased he asked to do something he had done for so many years. I brought my cheap camera and decided to take one of Lucille with Juan, and when she sat on the bed next to him and put her arm over the headboard, he grabbed onto her warmly and smiled. She then took one of the two of us.

Almost immediately, everyone arrived, except Jenny and Patti. Patti had called to tell me she had to go out of town on business and I realized Jenny probably wouldn't be able to make it. Everyone brought Juan flowers and balloons and even though they were all so beautiful, I was wishing they were shirts and such. Daniel kept the conversation lively, as usual, and I finally decided to wheel Juan into the lounge so the party could commence.

Everyone kept the chatter lively and that was what I wanted, but found I couldn't really do the same. I had a fixed smile on my face but my heart was breaking because Juan was so quiet, and the terrible fear was going through my mind that this was the last party I'd be giving him. Yet, he seemed to be content as he glanced from one to another, taking everything in. The catch in my throat persisted and I tried to hold off the tears that kept running down my face so Juan wouldn't notice…but they just wouldn't go away. So I kept wiping them with my hand while continuing to smile. I wanted this day to last forever because he looked so happy, even though he couldn't contribute to the chatter as he always did before. I took pictures of the crowd standing behind him as he sat before the decorated table trying to smile broadly.

I was overjoyed when Juan popped a couple of pepperoni pieces into his mouth from the tray Amanda brought…and all on his own! It was a small thing, but to me, it was a complete joy! I tried to run everything as always for his parties and finally decided on opening the gifts, which were not many because of the flowers and balloons. But he did have cards to open and as I read each of them, he listened so carefully, appearing to be in awe at each word. I then handed my gift to him, deciding to read the card before he took off the wrapping. I will never forget his face listening intently to what I read because by that time, everyone was chatting amongst themselves and he was trying desperately to hear every word.

The awe on Juan's face as he fondled the gold chain and cross was indescribable! He sat there holding it as though he didn't believe this was for him. He looked at Amanda in awe.

"Recharred gave this to me?" After Amanda nodded her head, he innocently asked, "whot should I say?"

"Just tell him thanks, Juan," Amanda answered as she patted him tenderly on the shoulders.

It was time to light the candles and Juan sat there very seriously taking every word in as we sang…

…Happy birthday to you…happy birthday to you, happy birthday, dear Juan! Happy birthday to you!

He gave a hardy blow along with me, though I don't believe he needed my help to extinguish the candles. Everyone continued the chatter while eating their cake, and still, Juan remained quiet. I made certain he had a piece of his own birthday cake and was pleased he allowed me to spoon-feed him.

Juan kept touching his cross as it hung from his neck and I finally asked Amanda to take a picture of the two of us, and when she did, he beamed proudly while holding it out so the camera could see!

I realized he was tiring even though he hadn't mentioned it. I made sure the nurses had some of his cake, and asked Marina to wheel him to his room. The party was over because everyone had left, and the two of us were alone again. I took his shirt off, settling him in bed and he seemed so content to be there once he sighed a breath of relief. It was apparent he was again very pleased I had given him a party from the glances of appreciation I was receiving. There weren't the endless raves about all the fun had, as he had done so often before…. No, this time I know there had to be a great deal of bittersweetness going on in his mind…because it was going on in mine.

Chapter Sixty-Six:
A Lonely Feeling?

I continued leaving messages on Svetmana's machine, only to be disturbed because whenever I called the hospital from work to find out if Juan had eaten, and talked with Jody, who was his frequent day nurse, I'd hear that Svetmana didn't attempt to feed him and only stayed a few minutes or didn't show up at all. I began realizing it was true…that in her mind, Juan was already dead and she was just biding her time. And my heart was aching. My innermost feelings also told me Jody wasn't feeding him as she said…that she was leaving him to feed himself because she always seemed to be double talking while explaining what he ate. Especially since the one time I walked in unexpectedly. It was a little after the lunch period and I found Juan's tray of food barely eaten, or better yet, in a mess as though he had scrambled everything attempting to eat. Once I had approached her on it, she gave me a load of double talk. That was the reason I called the days she was his nurse because I no longer trusted her.

I continued trying to keep Juan's body active, exercising his legs back and forth as he lay in bed. He never complained about it and I was pleased because it seemed to make him more alert. At the same time, I was angry that the staff didn't do this from the beginning…and that they avoided the question every time I brought it up. I tried to be there more even though my family and friends were telling me I'd make myself mentally and physically sick.

"C'mon, Juan, let's take a walk down to the second floor canteen and have some cookies and coffee…okay?" I asked late one evening. I figured it was late and we'd have the place to ourselves. He gave me a bit of a hard time, but finally allowed me to help him from bed. We walked to the elevator with his arm through mine for support. I wanted him to feel good that we were sitting together in a booth once more, because it had been so long since we enjoyed talking to each other in a restaurant. I guess I was looking for a miracle…to have Juan sit opposite me once again talking in that charming way he so captivated me for so many years. But instead, he sat there looking very apprehensive and somewhat bewildered, and the extent of his conversation only amounted to pleading to return to his bed. I finally heeded his wishes and we walked slowly to the elevator.

"Aw, Recharred, I 'ave to go…I 'ave to go ond I con't hold it!" There wasn't a bathroom around and as I desperately guided him to the elevator, he messed in his pajamas. And he felt ashamed again. Fortunately, only a couple of specks managed to fall on the floor, and I wiped them with a few napkins from the canteen. It was apparent he was relieved no one was around.

"Richard, I have asked Juan's daughter to buy him some slippers because the ones he has are almost like tongs and they flop on his feet," Jenny had called to my attention. "I asked her sometime ago and she has never bought them. I think if he has slippers like shoes he'll not walk so much like an old man, shuffling his feet in very short paces." I quickly said I'd buy them and the next day after I put them on him it really did help the shuffling. He was definitely capable of taking longer strides.

Alexis was a very pleasant black nurse who often attended Juan, and she did a good job because she seemed to have compassion. I arrived one evening in time to feed Juan and it was obvious he was quite agitated. Alexis came into the room and immediately explained the reason he was so upset.

"Richard, late this afternoon, his daughter was here and she called to tell me Juan had to move his bowels very badly. I quickly ran to the room and tried to help Juan to the bathroom, but he became very belligerent and started fighting with me. He wouldn't cooperate at all, and as I struggled with him, he just let loose all over himself and the entire bathroom floor. It was a real mess!" As I listened in despair she went on to say, "The slippers you bought are a real mess, but I will take them home to wash. Richard, his daughter did absolutely nothing to help but to scream at me that I was mishandling him. Then she stormed out, screaming down the halls as she left the floor." I tried to briefly explain how Svetmana was, but didn't want to say much because Juan was lying there looking so down…so desolate. I immediately washed my hands and went to him to take hold of his hand.

"Hi, Juan, what happened today? Why wouldn't you let Alexis help you to the bathroom?" He looked at me sadly.

"I don' know, Recharred, but thar are times I am so agitated…so nervous…ond everything seems to be rushing ond burning in my head. I don' know why I get thot way." I looked at him tenderly, while squeezing his hand, not wanting to believe this again had to do with Svetmana's presence…. No, it had to be a coincidence…it had to be something more and I almost found myself wishing they had performed the biopsy on his brain…and why were all his pills taken away?

I no longer could bring him fresh cut-up fruit or stop off at the bakery to get him some fancy pastry, because of his bowels. It hurt because it was such a delight to see him reach into the bowl and pop a piece of melon into his mouth. I missed the smile he'd make once he'd squish down on the piece of melon. I did, however, continue to stop off at the Burger King for sandwich breakfasts for the two of us, because he always liked them so much.

Juan's agitation at times gave the staff some concern because he was pulling at things on his body, making it necessary to put added bandages over his Hickman to be sure he didn't pull at it. I also arrived one morning and one of the nurses handed me Juan's cross and chain.

"We found this on the floor this morning. Juan must have pulled at it during the night and it fell. We really don't want to be responsible for it so we think you should hold onto it." I finally decided I'd take it each night when I left and return it on Juan in the morning. Juan just looked at me lovingly as I explained everything.

"Would that be okay, Juan? I don't want it to get lost." Juan smiled tenderly.

"Recharred, it is the same if you wear it or I wear it...because we are one person." No one...no one in this world could ever touch my heart as many times as this wonderful man!

Deena's granddaughter was getting married and it was to be held on the day before the Fourth of July and when I told Matt I'd not be able to go again to see the fireworks, it didn't seem to bother him. I did manage to talk with everyone at the table after dinner at the reception, but there was something definitely missing...that spark that always glowed in me whenever I was at a wedding with my family wasn't there. I couldn't cut up as I always did because my thoughts were constantly on Juan...and I wondered if I was ever again going to be happy. The DJ played a set of disco numbers from the '70s and I sat there reminiscing about the many times I saw Juan out on the floor before me turning his head from side to side. And once "Rock Your Baby" played, my heart was aching, and I wondered if music was ever going to be in my life again. I couldn't take any more and finally told my family I was leaving to go to the hospital because I promised Juan I'd bring him a piece of wedding cake.

"Juan, look, I got a piece of wedding cake for you," I said as I washed my hands. He was so happy to see me.

"Was the wedding nice, Recharred? Did you see all your children ond family?" I nodded my head and he asked, "How was Deena? Was she the proud grandma, Recharred?"

"Yeah, Juan, they all said to say hello and sent their love." Juan surprised me by doing one of his wonderful mimics of Deena.

"You know what, Juan? They had a DJ instead of a band and I couldn't believe when he played all the disco songs we loved! Aw, Juan, it was so great to hear them and I kept thinking about all the times we danced to them. Aw,

Juan, I want to dance with you again. Will you promise me we will dance to all those songs again?" Juan smiled and answered softly.

"I promise, Recharred, I promise."

My plans were to spend the afternoon with Matt on the 'Fourth' so I could be the entire morning with Juan. Usually, Juan's dad was brought by Endira and Svetmana on Sundays, so I assumed he'd be there on a holiday. Juan did eat all of his breakfast, but seemed disoriented and quiet. I decided to take him for a long walk through the hospital in his wheelchair, and he gave no problems when I helped him into it. The hospital corridors went on forever, so we had quite a walk. Juan was receiving his IV treatment at the time and didn't say much. He just seemed to be looking at nothing. I began fighting with myself because I didn't want to leave him since my thoughts kept recalling the wonderful 'Fourths' we had together. I kept trying to convince myself that I should call to cancel with Matt, especially after seeing one sign after another that invited patients and their guests to a picnic in the auditorium. I wanted to take Juan and spend the day in its entirety with him. Then my loyalty to Matt, or anyone for that matter, kept telling me I shouldn't disappoint someone on a holiday. However, when I mentioned the picnic to Juan, he didn't seem to know what I was talking about. I was torn between leaving and staying and finally decided to leave since I felt sure I'd be confronted with Svetmana and the others should I stay.

Matt was very pleasant that day and suggested we go to a nearby suburb to see a parade his loyal friend, Vincent, was marching in. I brought along some sandwiches and after the parade, we sat in a local park, enjoying one of the rare pleasant conversations with Matt.

I'd immediately take the gold chain and cross from my neck each time I entered Juan's room and replace it on him. What made it so special was the expression on his face as I was very close to him. His eyes glowed with appreciation and I think the whole idea of doing this made him really feel as though we were one…because that is exactly how I felt.

It was Wednesday morning and Juan's balance had to be at its worst, because I had a terrible time trying to get him into the wheelchair to take him for his shower. He had no control of his footing whatsoever. It was even worse getting him in and out of the shower chair. But yet, I didn't want to face the fact that his brain was faltering…that it was refusing at times to command his body functions…or maybe I didn't realize? I don't know which! My thoughts kept asking God when enough is 'enough!' I didn't realize this would be the last shower I'd be allowed to give Juan…that they would sponge bathe him in bed thereafter.

That evening, I was determined to take Juan out in the grounds so we could watch the sun set together. It was a beautiful breezy evening and felt it would be good for him. As I sat on the bench with his chair just before me, I talked about the nice fresh breeze, but he wasn't really paying attention. He just kept looking out in all directions turning his head quickly while squinting his eyes. There was that beautiful sky up there, with all the colors Juan loved so much…and he wasn't aware of it! All that was on his mind was to lie down in his bed. I finally gave into his pleading and headed back to his ward.

It was as though I had given him a bucket of gold once I helped him into bed to snuggle comfortably on his side. He couldn't thank me enough. He seemed so content and suddenly he noticed the pen tucked into my shirt pocket.

"Recharred, con I please use your pen?" I was stunned because during this entire hospital stay, he had never had any interest in reading, let alone writing?

"Do you want to write something, Juan?" I asked. He nodded his head.

"Yeah, I do, Recharred." I was so excited as I headed for the nurse's station.

"I'll get some paper from the nurse, Juan." I was actually trembling at the thought of him wanting to write! A prayer being answered!

Juan positioned himself to lie on his back once I handed over the pen and paper along with a magazine to write on and he positioned his pen about to write.

"Juan, why don't you write something backwards?…You know? Like you always wrote for me to try to figure out before placing it in front of a mirror." Juan looked at me surprised.

"You want me to write something backwards for you, Recharred?" I very affirmatively assured him by nodding my head.

"Yes, I do, Juan. Please write something backwards for me?" Juan didn't hesitate and placed the pen in position to write, so I assumed he'd write his initial thoughts…only now in reverse. But his hand was shaking and I was praying he'd be able to do it. Oh, God, if he can do this, I thought, who can say he is losing the use of his brain? However, his strokes appeared to be scratchy instead of the wonderful rhythm and flow he always was so capable of doing while writing one sentence after another. It was very brief and he handed me the paper quietly.

"Here it is, Recharred." My heart stood still as I looked at the scratches on the paper. I felt sure he had failed this time. Juan looked at me inquisitively.

"Are you not gonna take it to the mirror, Recharred?" I reluctantly walked towards the mirror and held the paper up to it.

(PLEASE TAKE REVERSE SIDE PAGE 572 TO MIRROR.)

MEDICAL RECORD	PROGRESS NOTES
DATE	

My eyes sparkled and my heart jumped for joy....

Aw, GOD, HE HAS NOT FORGOTTEN...NOT MY JUAN!

It was a bit shaky "I love you" but it was there and I was overwhelmed. Juan was supposedly losing his memory...and he had no balance left in his body! But yet he still remembered he loved me! AND HE WANTED ME TO KNOW HE HAD NOT FORGOTTEN! I was so choked up with emotion that the tender words I said to Juan escape me totally. This man had touched my heart so many times in our lives together, and with this tiny achievement, he proved once again he was still capable of holding onto it tightly.

It should've been all I could ever want from this beautiful man...but I wanted more. Not for me alone, but to show them Juan is alive and doing well! So I handed the pen and paper back to him.

"Juan, will you write more?" Juan slowly took hold of the pen.

"You want me to write something else, Recharred?" He asked in such an innocent tone. I looked at him with tears running from my eyes and gently answered,

"Yes, I do, Juan, yes I do." Suddenly he seemed to be nervous, but he still was determined he was going to write something more for me. His hand appeared awkward and the pen was placed immediately under the word 'you,' in fact much too close. His hand was trembling terribly and I was certain he was having one of his attacks and didn't want him to continue. I quickly said to forget it but he continued, struggling desperately to write something more for me. I realized his brain again was refusing to send any messages, but that the love in his heart for me was trying desperately to overcome any refusal. I didn't have an immediate chance to place it in front of a mirror because I had to comfort Juan until the attack subsided. I realized I had asked too much once I did place it before a mirror. He couldn't tell me what he had intended to write, and I have never been able to figure it out. My one consolation...his heart was really trying to overcome a problem he realized he was having with his brain. Maybe an expert can one day read these words that were written backwards...?

(PLEASE TAKE REVERSE SIDE PAGE 574 TO MIRROR.)

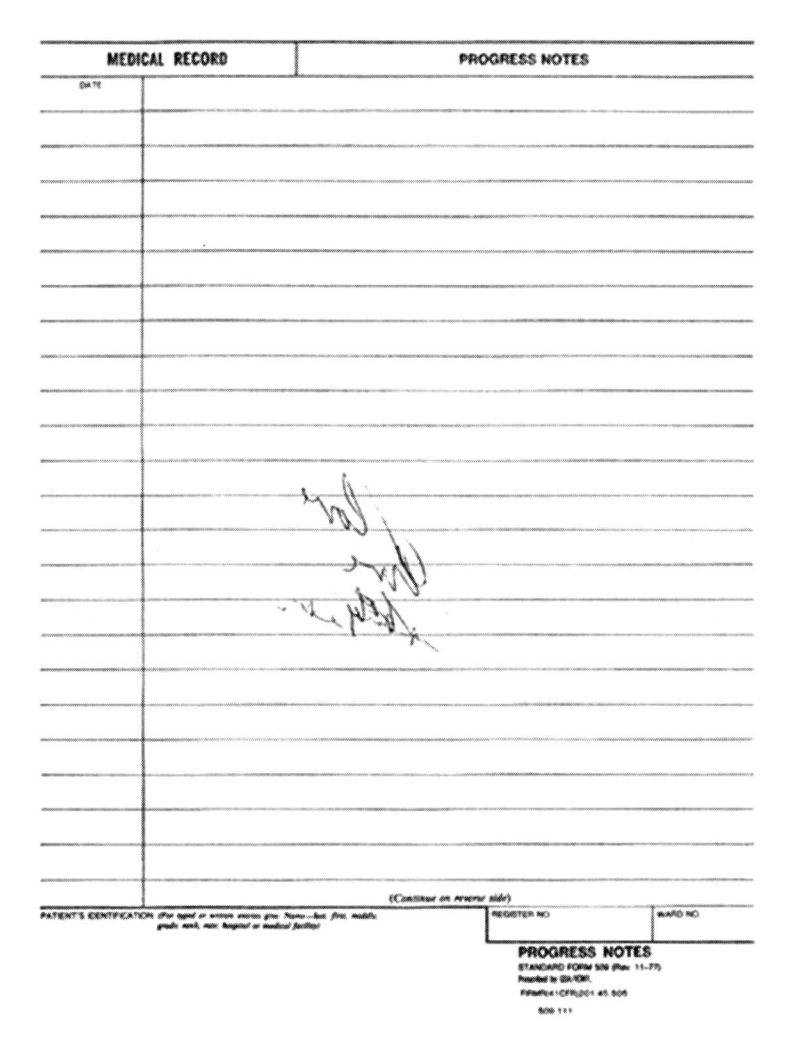

I was determined Juan wasn't going to just lie in bed constantly, and no matter how I had to struggle, I'd finally get him in the wheelchair going for a short ride. He was so dependent on me and it broke my heart…especially one particular time as I stopped to talk to one of the nurses. He lost sight of me, and suddenly began frantically looking in every direction until I finally made my position clear. It was such a small thing, and yet it gave him such fear…and each time it is recalled, my heart aches again.

Matt had begun a vacation the last two weeks in July and was going to spend it doing short little trips. He had been after me to show him Indianapolis and continuously put him off since I realized Juan would be everywhere. I finally couldn't refuse any longer and our one day excursion was planned the day following the evening Juan wrote the special note for me. We left once I returned from shaving and feeding Juan. I was determined I was going to make the day pleasant for Matt by not outwardly being depressed...just to swallow everything. And swallow I did, because, everywhere we went...there was Juan!

Matt had been quite nice that day, which surprised me tremendously, and once he asked to join him for a two-day trip to Galena the following week, I began considering it. Daniel assured me I needed to get away.

"Richard, you definitely have to get away from the hospital for more than a day.... You don't have to worry about Juan because he will be fine. He is nowhere near dying." This always provoked me to hear him say that, but finally I agreed to go.

I called the hospital Saturday afternoon after being there in the morning and was told Svetmana hadn't shown up again. I decided to chance going, praying I wouldn't be confronted with her. In fact, I was happy because I realized I wouldn't be able to come that evening because Matt and I had been invited for dinner at Carl's. Frank would be there also and pinochle was slated after dinner, which would make a late evening...and too late to go to the hospital.

It was time for Juan's haircut, and after much difficulty, I finally managed to get him in the wheelchair. But he continued pleading to return to his bed. He had begun having speech difficulties, and it was particularly garbled on this afternoon, making almost everything impossible to understand. This only added to the agitation Juan was already having and I didn't know how to make him realize my hearing problems didn't help. I was glad once Daniel dropped in for a visit, because his non-stop chatter kept Juan alert while keeping his mind off his speech difficulties.

While I continued cutting Juan's hair, Daniel asked who had been doing mine because he realized I couldn't afford to go to a shop. I responded by telling him I had been trading haircuts with Hank for some time.

"And as you know, he is so hyper...so I always got the worse end of the deal. But that wasn't the real reason I discontinued with it, because even though he and Dick took me to dinner a couple of times...Hank never once called Juan after I told him he had full blown AIDS back in April of 1991. Juan loved him so much, and no matter how I begged him to call...he never did! So I realized I didn't need a friend like that. He proved to be what Juan always said of him...that he was one of those bar friends...friendly at a party or the bar...but then disappears afterwards."

While walking Daniel to the elevator, I mentioned going with Matt to Galena.

"We are gonna leave as soon as I return from shaving and feeding Juan Monday morning, and we aren't gonna come back until Tuesday evening. Do you think you can be here both days to spend some time with Juan?" Daniel was very pleased.

"Good, I am glad you are getting away for a couple of days because you need to be away from here. You have been here too much! Don't worry, I will come both days."

I also called Amanda to ask if she'd do the same and she agreed, yet I still remained apprehensive about going for two days.

Juan remained quiet the rest of the afternoon, wanting to sleep constantly, and each time he awakened from a nap, smiled broadly once he saw me sitting alongside. I had inquired if Svetmana had been there, becoming extremely angry upon hearing she hadn't. It also bothered me that Juan was so quiet, but what was I to do? I stayed longer just to be with him.

Carl and Frank mentioned they were going on a four-day trip to Vegas in September and asked if we'd like to join them. I had no business in agreeing because, besides not having any money, I should've realized I'd never leave for a place so far away especially should Juan be living at my house. However, I wanted to prove to Matt this relationship was something serious. I realized I could back out later, especially since deposits were refundable if canceled. I also wondered if Matt might offer to take me, or at least lend the money, but he never did. So I didn't know why I agreed to go. In fact, Matt never even thought of lending money to pay any of my bills. Daniel was the one to do this when he took me to dinner one evening and suddenly began writing out a check, and then handed it to me.

"Here, Richard, is a check for five hundred dollars...you do not have to worry about paying me back because you need it. You have no money and a mortgage to pay besides other bills." I refused to take it and only agreed after insisting I'd one day pay him back. It took years to repay the four thousand to Geena that she sent to get Juan and I out of the mess in Atlanta, so five hundred should be no sweat. It bothered me that Matt never thought to offer a loan, especially since he made over eighty thousand a year.

As Matt was driving home from Carl's, we were a bit confused which exit to take off the expressway, and I made the mistake to suggest the very next one. Much to my regret, I immediately realized I should've kept my mouth shut, because it proved the wrong one, which didn't please him. Since no cars were in sight, I suggested he make a u-turn to get back on the expressway...but no, he wouldn't consider it. He preferred blasting off at me instead with one angry demeanor after another! It didn't make any sense! Still, he refused to stop his ridiculous behavior, and my only conclusion was that he had to be 'manic' and his obvious jealousy of Carl and Frank's devoted relationship had to spark the explosion. He even included them in his vicious remarks.

"I am so tired and sick of playing with them.... It's no fun because they always have to take the bid!" I tried to suggest he talk to Carl about it.

"Because you are best friends and there should be no problem telling him you are bothered because of it.... Friends should be able to do that." But he wouldn't consider it, and even decided to criticize the dinner.

"And that meal was terrible! How could Carl serve it! It was so dry!" I was confused since he knew absolutely nothing about cooking, and besides, I felt it wasn't dry. Yes, his problem was jealousy, and because he wasn't capable of loving, it made him angry to see them so happy and in love.

Matt continued calling me down with one threat after another until I had enough!

"For Chris' sake, I don't even want to go out with you anymore! I have never seen anyone like you! It is over as far as I am concerned!" I was fuming and didn't want to say more, but he continued with his nastiness. I was certain this was what I wanted and couldn't understand how I put up with his split personality for this long, especially after I vowed it wouldn't happen to me again after twenty-two years from my wife! Maybe Juan wasn't far off when he said years earlier that I was a masochist? However, I always insisted I was not…that I only believed people were basically good and could be changed.

It was very apparent that he actually expected me to beg for forgiveness—for *his* vicious temper! Then we could spend the night together and he'd have *his* satisfaction in bed. I held my stand, however, and he sped off in anger. I also realized I'd be able to go to the hospital in the morning…that there'd be no chance of him intimidating me into not going should we be together. I had left him one Sunday morning to be with Juan and I never heard the end of it. And this was someone who told me he was one of three who cared for a friend who died of AIDS?

Of course, Matt called again in his pleasant manner Sunday with the reminder that he was taking me to see *The Buddy Holly Story*. I realized I shouldn't decline this momentous occasion of generosity. And again, we resumed whatever it was we had going. He did, however, cancel Galena, which gave me some relief. The evening ended early enough to see Juan.

I was just about to leave for the hospital Monday morning when Matt called to ask if I wanted to go to Longmeadow, a quaint little shopping village of log cabins and gardens. I always felt it was a place that ladies and old women loved, but accepted the invite and said I'd be to his house after I returned from feeding and shaving Juan. Again he tried to intimidate, mixing a bit of nastiness with his sad tones.

"Well, by the time you get here, it will be too late to go!"

I was forced to cut my time with Juan, not wanting to start the day badly with Matt, so it was obvious that his intimidation worked. Juan was very quiet again and I assumed he felt it best to remain quiet since I was still having difficulty with his garbled words. It didn't seem to bother him that I was leaving earlier than usual because his only thought was to sleep. I asked Jody to be sure he ate his lunch and told her I'd call in the afternoon. I realized I didn't have to worry about dinner because Jenny was on duty and in his ward tonight. I took hold of Juan's hand, squeezed it gently.

"I will see you later, Juan…be good now. I love you." He looked at me tenderly.

"Okay, Recharred, I will see you…okay?" And he closed his eyes to sleep.

Matt again surprised me and was very pleasant that day as I tried desperately to hide my concern for Juan. I called from a public phone that afternoon and was told Juan was doing well…that he was very quiet and sleeping most of the time. I was also told Svetmana hadn't been there but that a gentleman was with him for a couple of hours, which I realized had to be Daniel, and I thanked God for him.

We returned to Matt's early and took in a movie. He then asked if I could stay over,

"And then we can go to Galena just for the day tomorrow morning, Rich." I didn't really want that. I wanted to make it to the hospital that evening and if I stayed over I wouldn't be able to see Juan until Tuesday night. I didn't know how to say no, realizing I was trying to make this relationship work, and finally remembered Daniel and Amanda still thought the two-day Galena trip was on, so they'd be with Juan. I called Jenny and was told Juan was still quiet, but doing well.

"So, Richard, take this time to relax a bit. You need it." Even with that, I felt a terrible guilt…that I was deserting Juan.

While waiting in Matt's car for him to cash a check before leaving for Galena in the morning, a terrible lonely feeling came over me as I thought of Juan and the dreaded illness. I had been informing my family and friends Juan wasn't doing well and that it was a matter of time, and yet, I WOULD NOT BELIEVE IT MYSELF! But this morning, a chill was running through my body because, suddenly, the realization of my words to everyone was appearing to be a reality and punching me in the face…that possibly Juan was nearing the end of his life! I tried to wipe it from my mind but the swelling had already begun in my head, nose, and throat…and tears were falling down my face, when Matt returned to the car.

I quickly wiped the tears from my cheeks while turning away, but he noticed them.

"Have you been crying, Rich?" I continued holding my head to the side.

"I was just thinking about Juan and I got all choked up. Aw, Matt, I don't want anything to happen to Juan!" I finally got myself together and said, "I'm sorry, I will be okay now," and he seemed to have some compassion.

But I wasn't okay that day…my insides were being torn apart as I continuously was reminded of Juan and the time we visited Galena with Vic and Phil in 1986, and his casual mention during the drive home. His innocent voice never realized the dreadful reality!

"Aw, the Army has decided to test everyone for the HIV virus…. I think thot is a good idea. Do you not think so?" And no one really answered because it wasn't something we had to worry about in our lives. And I kept hearing it the entire day. I was thankful Matt was very pleasant that day because I'm sure I would've blown him apart had he been nasty again.

It was bothering me because I hadn't called the hospital and it was past four thirty. Then Matt suggested we have dinner somewhere because we had only eaten the sandwiches I brought. I really wanted to be on our way, but figured I could use the phone in a restaurant without him knowing…because I actually was still afraid to do it in front of him because he always said I was spending my life doing things for Juan. I didn't want to ruin his vacation by upsetting him with something he mysteriously thought as foolish and especially since he had been so nice the entire two days. I didn't want to hear him again shout out why the hell I have to be there all the time and ask where his daughter is. I always tried to explain it didn't matter if she was there or not…that I still would go, but he never understood. I figured he may realize one day and come to terms with it.

It was almost five thirty once we walked into a restaurant and I was particularly pleased upon noticing a phone in the outer foyer. I excused myself from the table and just as I was about to pick up the receiver I noticed an out of order note attached. So I was forced to continue with a fixed smile on my face. I do not know why I felt intimidated, especially since he was totally aware of my devotion and love for Juan! We were out on the street by seven o'clock and I was elated once he suggested we get on our way since we had a three-hour drive home.

"Oh, good, we are almost at my place because I feel as though I am gonna burst! I have to go very badly." Matt laughed while pulling alongside the curb in front of my building, and I quickly shuffled out.

"Why don't you go up and do what you have to do, and then drive over to my place after, Rich?" I didn't want to go to his place because it was almost ten thirty and I wanted to go to the hospital to see Juan, but I agreed. I figured I could then call to say I'd not be over. I was angry with myself as the slow elevator began moving towards the sixth floor and audibly yelled out why the hell I didn't just tell him I was going to the hospital!

I grabbed the phone on the way to the bathroom and immediately dialed Daniel's number. He didn't seem to be concerned about anything, assuring me Juan was doing well.

"Richard, he was just a little quiet today," and again insisted, "Richard, this is nowhere near Juan's time to die, so please don't worry." He then said Amanda had called to tell him Jenny called her because she thought I should be there with Juan. This bothered me and I immediately informed him I was going anyway.

"Richard, you really don't have to go now because it is too late!" I still insisted my intentions were to see Juan, no matter what time it was. I became disturbed as I hung up because I couldn't comprehend why Jenny would call Amanda if Juan was doing well? Suddenly the phone rang, and once I answered I heard Amanda sigh.

"Oh, good, Richard, you are home! I was afraid you were gonna stay overnight in Galena, and if you didn't answer now, I was gonna call every hotel and motel in Galena to find you. Richard, Jenny called earlier to tell me she thought you should be at the hospital with Juan." I quickly explained that Daniel felt Juan was doing well but that I still had intended to go to the hospital anyway. We hung up and I felt confused…a little concerned…but in no way was I frightened. Nothing was going to happen to Juan.

Without traffic, Hines Hospital was about a five to ten minute drive and before leaving, I called Matt to tell him I was going to see Juan…that Jenny had called for me. As I started for the hospital, my mind was not thinking this was something serious since Juan had licked so many things before. I was going to stop for cigarettes, but then suddenly my mind began…or maybe it was my heart…telling me to get to the hospital…to get to Juan…and to get there quick! The few minutes seemed like an eternity as I sped to the hospital while continuously repeating, "Nothing can happen to Juan! No, not my beautiful Juan! Not this man I met eighteen years ago and who has become my life!"

As I drove the long roadway leading into the parking area of Hines Hospital, I refused to believe Juan could be in critical condition. In fact, I was sure if there was anything seriously wrong, it certainly would be something that would pass, as all the others had in the past. There wasn't any problem finding a parking space because there were always plenty late at night. After parking, I quickly got out of the car and half ran and walked to the emergency entrance since that was the only one open late at night. Upon entering, I hurried down the corridor and turned swiftly down the hall leading to the elevators, finding one ready to go. That same feeling of loneliness, along with apprehension came over me as I pushed the fourth floor button! The thought that something could really be wrong with Juan came into my mind, but I quickly dismissed the feeling, especially since he had survived all the other crises. This wasn't Juan's time, especially since Daniel had been so sure. I decided I had to be sure Juan would be fine…I'd stay with him all night. This would make him rest better, if he knew I was there with him. Besides, he had asked so often if I was going to stay the night, but I never saw reason to, because most of the time, after staying late, I'd return early in the morning only to find him still asleep. So I'd awaken him with a gentle pat, and as usual through all the years I've known him, he'd wake with a smile and greet me.

"Aw, Recharred, did you jus' get outta bed?"

"Oh, God, let him be okay," I prayed once I left the elevator and turned towards 4 East. I was there in seconds, and there he was…looking so weak and helpless, cuddled on his side in his bed that was raised to the usual one quarter sitting position. Jenny was at his side with her back to me and appeared to be feeding him. A terrible ache clutched my heart once I saw Juan's beautiful blue eyes so watery…as though they were begging for help. I didn't know if he saw me even though his eyes seemed to waver in my direction, and I managed to force my usual happy greeting, but this time in a choked up voice.

"Hi, Juan."

Jenny immediately turned my way and with a definite expression of relief.

"Oh, good, Richard, you're here!" I quickly stepped to the sink to wash my hands and my mind was swimming with guilt.

Oh, God, why? Why did I go and leave him alone today? My mind flashed to the lonely feeling I had while waiting in the car for Matt to cash his check, and the apprehension I had the entire day…. It had to be telling me something, but I did nothing about it! Aw, no, God…NO!

As I stepped to take Juan's hand, Jenny moved aside and explained that he hadn't eaten any of his dinner because he was having trouble swallowing…choking on solid food.

"So I have been slowly squeezing water through his lips with this medical syringe, Richard, and he seems to be taking it very well. He really seems to be very eager for each tubeful!" As I held onto Juan's hand, I wasn't sure he could see me because his eyes were so watery and weak looking. Yet, I knew his eyesight was still excellent because he had been to the doctor the Friday before and they said his eyes were doing well.

"Can you see me, Juan," I asked and he gave me a wonderful nod of the head. I was hesitant in asking if he knew who I was, hoping he wasn't confused. Still, I pleaded repeatedly.

"Do you know who I am, Juan?" He would shock me by managing to muster up as much an expression as possible to show me I was stupid to doubt him! He then finalized it with that tone in his voice that ridiculed me for thinking he didn't know me.

"Recharred?" he finally uttered after some struggle to get the word out. And yet, he still managed to let me know how stupid I was to think other than that in his inflection of the word. It was so good to hear him say my name, and to give me hell with his old spunk! It was evident he was happy I was there and I was certain everything would be fine, like the other times. I should have taken him in my arms and told him how much I loved him and how much I wanted him well, but then there was that 'society' and walls might tell.

I felt he was responding to everything, so maybe he will eat for me. I pronounced every syllable as I asked, "Are you hungry, Juan…? Are you hungry?" This time, he surprised me by nodding very anxiously, as though he hadn't eaten in days! Never was he this anxious in all the months he'd been in the hospital! My heart felt as though a heavy weight had been lifted, but in my excitement, my nerves created a trembling throughout my body…and I tried desperately to control it because I didn't want him to think I was scared. At the same time, Carol came in the room as she often did when she and Jenny were going out. She quietly said hello and patted Juan to let him know she was there. She then asked how he was doing and I assured her.

"He's gonna be fine, Carol, just fine, but he hasn't eaten tonight and he just told me he is hungry. Do you think you can go out for something, Carol, because I really don't want to leave him." Carol agreed and just as I was about to tell her what to buy, Jenny interrupted.

"I don't think Juan should have anything solid, Richard, because he has been choking…I'm afraid, especially since there isn't a doctor here tonight. I don't think we should take any chances." I agreed, but I felt he still could have soup and sent Carol to the canteen.

Juan always enjoyed Ensure and I realized he needed more nourishment besides a cup of soup, so I pulled over the tray table, snapped open one of the cans sitting on it, and told him I was going to feed him it before the soup. Juan nodded his head in approval. He was so weak, but still managed to show so much gratitude. I knew he was pleased I was with him. I could see it in his eyes! I was angry with myself because I hadn't been there since the morning before! The other nurses weren't like Jenny; they didn't have her compassion—but she was only with Juan for the dinner meal. Hence, I couldn't be sure he ate the other meals while I was gone! I had told them I'd be gone for over a day and was assured he'd be fed. But I could never depend on it since the many times I arrived late for lunch to see his tray of food getting cold and no one in sight.

My hand was trembling as I started to gently squeeze the syringe containing drops of the Ensure through his lips, so I steadied it with my other hand. It was taking so long because the syringe didn't hold much; after all, it was meant for medication…not food. But Juan was helping by sucking in with his lips. I couldn't help from thinking, *Oh, God, he looks like a hungry baby!* His eyes were so watery and sad and I prayed silently.

"Please, God, please make Juan well…please, dear God, don't let anything happen to him!" I continued squeezing the syringe slowly, not wanting him to choke if too much flowed into his mouth. If he sucked in, he could handle it, and he was doing it! I thought maybe he could drink from a straw, especially since he was sucking the syringe. So I inserted one into the can, placing it to his mouth and asking to suck in…and he tried hard…but couldn't do it. He was too weak to draw through a straw? He was trying desperately, but he didn't have the strength! I was trembling even more as I continued to feed him with the syringe, but I kept talking, assuring him that he was going to be okay. Yes, I was sure of it, and yet…I was trembling?

Carol had already brought the soup and I asked if she would find Jenny to ask for a clean spoon because I didn't think it wise to use the syringe, and once she returned, I had just placed the last of the Ensure into Juan's mouth. It was apparent he was still eager for more because he was opening his mouth anxiously. After explaining that he had finished the Ensure, I assured him I was about to start with the soup. His eyes were swimming in tears, but they still managed to convey his appreciation. His eyes always told me all, and especially when he was happy to be with me! Juan very eagerly accepted every spoonful as my trembling hand placed each of them to his lips, and he had no problem swallowing which made me certain everything was going to be fine!

I don't think I ever felt as close to Juan as I did during these moments. I was his lifeline…and it was apparent he realized it and was grateful.

After the last spoonful, Juan eagerly opened his mouth and once I asked if he wanted more, he nodded his head very affirmatively, but this time, he placed his finger into his mouth and sucked on it very loudly. Oh, God, he wasn't able to talk but he found a way to show me he was hungry.

Oh, my God…oh, my God, my heart cried out! Carol returned and I asked if she'd mind going for more soup. I assured Juan that Carol was going for more soup and from his wonderful expression, it was apparent he was pleased.

He continued to lay on his side as I went on talking. I wanted to keep his spirits up as well as mine, and while cradling his pillow, he appeared to be aware of every word I uttered. I kept squeezing his hand tightly to let him know I was there for him, and I was certain he was aware of what I was telling him. I wanted him to realize I was intending to stay the night and quietly told him so.

"Because I want to be here to help you lick this like all the others." Upon hearing these words, a feeling of relief—of contentment—appeared to come over him and he slowly moved himself until he was lying flat on his back, appearing very sleepy as his eyes began slowly closing. He wanted to sleep and I assured him he should, if that is what he wanted—that I would be there beside him. Carol returned with the soup, but it was too late…Juan wanted to sleep.

Jenny came into the room to say good night and at the same time, Carol told me she had talked with Amanda.

"And she asked if you wanted her to come stay the night too, Richard?" I told her to tell Amanda I felt Juan would be fine, but if she wanted to come later in the morning, I'd like that.

"Tell her thanks for me, Carol." Jenny and Carol hugged both of us, assuring me everything would be fine, and Carol reminded me to call if I needed her.

I continued holding onto Juan's hand as he settled in a position on his back, assuring him it was fine with me. The fact that Juan usually lay on his side or stomach when he wanted to sleep, somehow never entered my mind. I moved the chair over so I could sit while holding his hand and Juan turned his head slightly in my direction. He apparently realized I had let go of his hand, and once I took hold of it again, he opened his eyes partially, as if he was checking to be sure it was me there beside him. Then, with an expression of contentment, Juan turned his head back to lay flat and slowly began drifting off again. I squeezed his hand gently.

"I'm here with you, Juan. You know I will not leave you." I continued squeezing his hand gently to assure him I was there, and again, he slowly turned his head and barely opened his eyes to focus in my direction. Once satisfied that I was there, he turned back to fall asleep. Surprisingly, he did it a third time and finally must have been assured I wasn't leaving him, and fell into a deep sleep.

It had to be only a few minutes when, suddenly, his breathing became very heavy and laborious! OH, MY GOD…NO! A terrible chill touched my heart because I immediately remembered my father breathing that fast just before he died! I was scared, but still wouldn't believe this could be the end! My father was ninety-two years old and Juan was only forty-nine. He surely has to be stronger than my father?

"Oh, God," I prayed, "he has to overcome this, please!" I sat there helpless and petrified, holding onto Juan's hand firmly while squeezing it continuously! That night, Nurse Marianna walked in and stood behind me, rubbing my shoulders consolingly. Neither of us said a word. My eyes wouldn't leave sight of Juan.

"I'll bring you some coffee, Richard," she whispered. Juan was still struggling to breathe once she returned to set the coffee down on the tray table. She again placed herself behind me and continued rubbing my shoulders gently. We were silent; the only sounds that could be heard were the struggling gasps coming from Juan, trying desperately to inhale and exhale.

"He's doing well, Richard, he's not like the others…everyone usually perspires very badly." My heart stood still, confused to what she meant…and too afraid to ask? Something terrible was happening, yet I did not want to believe it!

After a few moments, Marianna left and I was alone with my wonderful Juan. Suddenly—LIKE A MIRACLE—just as quickly as his breathing became difficult, Juan began to breathe quietly and normally! I leaned apprehensively towards him, as I had done so many times before, to be certain he was breathing, since he was always so quiet while sleeping. The terrible beating of my heart gradually subsided once I realized he was fine! HE WAS BREATHING IN HIS SAME QUIET, NORMAL MANNER…AND I THANKED GOD FOR HEARING MY PRAYERS!

I continued holding onto Juan's hand. Much of my worry was relieved, but yet I was still trembling. I tried to stop it by assuring myself Juan didn't look like an AIDS patient. He was one hundred seventy pounds…just slightly below his normal weight when I had him on the scale a week before…there's no worry now! I decided I had to calm myself so he wouldn't detect it by the touch of my hand. I took a cigarette from the pack and the coffee Jenny left, and stepped into the nurse's social room. However, I only remained a couple of minutes, quickly extinguishing my cigarette to return to Juan. I felt much better because he looked so quiet and peaceful. But yet, as I sat there holding his hand, I could think only about how strong he had always been…so full of life and laughter and how he never wanted an evening of fun to end! And I thought of how unfair all of this was! I sat there unable to take my eyes off him, while my thoughts kept remembering the wonderful eighteen years I shared with him…the trials and tribulations…but mostly the joy and laughter…the music, and the love he brought into my life.

Chapter Sixty-Seven:
The Inevitable Shatters a Dream

The night should've been long, but somehow it wasn't...and maybe because I again was with Juan. The chairs weren't very comfortable because the backs were not very high. Because of it, they weren't very conducive for sleeping. I did doze off a couple of times, but once my head bobbed, I was awake. I never let go of Juan's hand the entire night, holding mine directly over the top of his, and never did I give a thought that he never moved it!

Juan's sleep had been peaceful the entire night and just before dawn, I must have finally dozed off more than a few minutes by bracing my head with my left hand, because I was suddenly awakened by the chatter coming from the nurse's station. I looked at my watch to find it was seven o'clock, and I realized breakfast would be arriving within the hour. Juan still looked so peaceful, breathing quietly, but suddenly I became concerned realizing he hadn't changed his position the entire night, which he seldom did anyway. However, I remained concerned because he never stayed flat on his back the entire night. He needed to be awakened and shaved before breakfast arrived, especially since I wasn't here to shave him the day before. I realized I had a job facing me since I needed to get Juan back to eating comfortably, and to not leave until it was done...and to be there for every meal, even if I had to move in!

I let go of Juan's hand, gently touching his arm, but he wouldn't awaken and I was suddenly afraid again. This wasn't like him, since he usually awakened immediately to cheerfully say, "Aw, good, you are up already, Recharred." He always opened his eyes, and now he continued to keep them shut? He, however, was breathing fine so I assumed it wasn't something to be concerned about. So I nudged him gently again.

"C'mon now, Juan? It's time to get up because I want to shave you before breakfast." This time his lids split lazily, just enough to see his blues, yet not focusing. No matter how I urged, he wouldn't acknowledge me and just continued to be totally unaware of my pleas. I decided to begin, realizing the lather would be refreshing and surely awaken him. Somehow, while trying to awaken him, his head had turned to the left, away from me, and I began on his right side…and still his eyes wouldn't focus! My body began trembling as I continued pleading with him to awaken and to please turn his head for me to lather his other side. Still, he wouldn't budge. It was as though he was fast asleep with his eyelids partially open.

I tried to turn his head ever so carefully to lather, but it wouldn't budge! It was as though he was forcibly holding it in that position?

"Please, Juan?" I pleaded quietly. "Will you turn your head towards me so I can do your left side?" But he wouldn't acknowledge. His eyelids remained half open, refusing to focus. My trembling became worse as I finally took hold of his head with both hands, gently but firmly turning it in my direction. Suddenly, he began breathing laboriously again, and I was terrified! OH, GOD, WHAT DID I DO! I then remembered his heavy breathing had finally stopped after a short while…so this had to be the same…it will subside and become normal again. Yes, I was certain of it! All I wanted to think of was Juan had to look good, so I went into the drawer for the electric shaver and did his left side very quickly.

By this time, Juan's breathing was becoming worse as he began struggling desperately to breathe! To this day, I will never understand why a nurse never returned after Marianna left the room while Juan was struggling to breathe? I began pleading desperately to get some sort of response, assuring him he was going to be okay, but he continued struggling for air. I then could hear a continuous rasping in his throat and it wasn't a voluntary forced action—it was something crackling within him! Suddenly, his head heaved forward, and a gusher of brown liquid began shooting out in continuous spurts from his mouth! OH, GOD, HE IS GASPING FOR AIR! Terrified, I ran out to the nurse's station!

"Jody! Jody! Please, please come quick because Juan is vomiting terribly! Please, hurry, Jody!" She followed and then immediately pleaded with me.

"Richard, I am gonna have to suction his throat out and it is not a pretty sight, so why don't you stay out of the room until I'm done?" I was hesitant but finally agreed and at that moment, a well-dressed gentleman approached to ask if he could have a few minutes with me, introducing himself as Dr. Creedon.

I was in a stupor as he guided me into an office adjoining the nurse's station, and once seated was informed he was a psychologist…that the staff had requested he talk to me because they were very concerned about Juan and myself. I immediately explained my problem with Svetmana, and my fear that I wouldn't be allowed to be with Juan. I talked about her inability to cope with it, but yet hating me because I was there with Juan.

"Doctor, she would rather he be alone and that is why I am always so afraid of upsetting her because I need to be with Juan and he needs me to be there for him. So I am always afraid she will demand I be barred from the room." Dr. Creedon looked at me compassionately.

"That will never happen, Richard. You would never be barred from being with Juan. Everyone in this hospital knows you or has heard of you, and they know how you have cared for Juan all these months. Believe me, Richard, you would never be barred from Juan's room." The relief I experienced was tremendous, yet regretting all the intimidation I allowed Svetmana and Endira to hand me.

"Doctor, I am gonna keep on trying to make Juan well…. They want him to die…but, Doctor…I want him to live and I am gonna keep fighting!"

"At that moment, a man dressed in the usual green hospital garb entered the room, seating himself alongside Dr. Creedon, immediately informing me that he was from the infectious disease unit. He gave me his name, but I never caught it because of his quickly spoken Pakistani accent. I had never seen him before, but that was nothing new, since a different doctor was attending Juan every week. I cannot remember much of what he said because of my difficulty in understanding his accent, and especially since my head was swimming. I do, however, remember the very first thing he said: that Juan was comatose….

That one word clarified all the confusion I experienced throughout the night. I also remember the last thing he said…that there was a new patch that could possibly help Juan's condition, but that he was not sure the pharmacy had them on hand since they were so new. I remember pleading desperately to do their best to secure it, and once assured, I left the room, anxious to see if Jody had finished.

Jody had finished because the door was open, and as I stood at the entrance, my heart shook and my body trembled once I saw Juan struggling desperately to breathe through the oxygen tubes placed into each nostril. His bed was still positioned at a forty-five degree angle and he on his back with his eyes partially open, but not focused.

I took hold of his hand, praying it would, somehow, settle the trembling going through my body. Breakfast had arrived, but in my heart, I knew he was going to miss this meal. My mind would not comprehend that this was my strong Juan gasping for every breath!

I had seen Juan in so many sorry situations throughout our lives, but never this helpless, and my heart was breaking! His gasping was so strong that the tubes kept slipping from his nostrils, and as I gently pushed them back, I continually assured him he was going to be fine. To this day, I cannot recall everything I said because my heart was being torn apart. I do remember Jody coming into the room, telling me the pharmacy did not have the patches, and I seem to recall her then saying they were sending out for them. I continued pleading with Juan to get better…to come out of this, but it was not happening. Three and a half hours had passed since I had been awakened by the chatter coming from the nurse's station, and yet it seemed like only moments. Then, suddenly, all my prayers were shattering before my eyes once Juan began to perspire profusely! OH, GOD, NO! PLEASE GOD…DON'T LET IT BE!… But the perspiration continued to pour from his pores…and I BEGGED FOR MY PLEAS TO BE HEARD!

Juan continued struggling…and SUDDENLY—SUDDENLY, HE JERKED UP AS THOUGH HE HAD BEEN STRICKEN WITH A SEVERE PAIN AND SALIVA POURED FROM HIS MOUTH! Terrified, I quickly hurried to the doorway, calling out for Jody! She responded immediately and I definitely wasn't going to leave Juan again should his throat again need to be suctioned. I quickly hurried to the other side of the bed, squatting down to take hold of him in my arms. Unaware of her actions since my eyes were focused only on Juan, I finally looked up pleadingly to Jody for help, only to see her motionless with a stunned expression! My face was next to Juan's and once I quickly turned to him, I felt the pain of a dagger thrust into my heart because his heavy breathing had ceased, but he wasn't breathing!

"JUAN'S NOT BREATHING! HE'S NOT BREATHING!!" IT HAS TO BE THE SAME AS LAST NIGHT…YES…YES…HE HAS TO AGAIN BREATHE NORMALLY!… Then…as I held him cradled in my arms, searching desperately for a breath…his head dropped, his face immediately next to mine…and suddenly, his beautiful blues WERE STILL….and I heard Jody's voice.

"He's gone, Richard." I held him close and tight. They had to be wrong.

"NO! NO! NOT MY JUAN!! YOU'RE WRONG…YOU HAVE TO BE WRONG!" I continued screaming uncontrollably, begging for something to be done because Juan could not be gone! Allison, the nurse practitioner, quickly entered the room and immediately placed a stethoscope to Juan's chest as I audibly prayed for her to hear a heartbeat! My eyes anxiously pleaded with her, praying incoherently until she finally looked at me sadly.

"Juan is dead, Richard." I took Juan in my arms, sobbing uncontrollably, crying for him to come back!!

* * * * * *

In my entire life, I never felt the anguish my heart was now experiencing! Never did I believe Juan would be in my arms without a breath in his body, and the beautiful blue of his eyes…so still! No, I did not want to believe it and continued screaming, and the only words I can remember hearing were when I heard Allison ask Jody to shut the door. Allison tried desperately to console me, but I could not be consoled!

Jody and Allison left the room, closing the door after them and I was alone with Juan. I began rubbing his arms, his shoulders, and his face…and they were SO WARM. I took his hand in mine, squeezing it tightly, praying he return one to me...but it would not happen. It was nearing eleven and I wondered where the time had gone since trying to awaken Juan at seven?

I don't remember how long it was before Dr. Creedon entered, and as he tried to comfort me, I just wept uncontrollably on his shoulders. I wanted to truly trade places with Juan because he had to be better off than me, and I knew how badly he wanted to live...how much he loved life. I remember a thought coming to my mind, wondering why Svetmana was not there. Why she had not been called! My heart needed to be comforted by her and at the same time, to comfort her. But I did not know what to expect and I just prayed this could unite us? But for now, Juan was mine...and no one could change that.

Dr. Creedon left me alone with Juan, and I continued in my grief, talking hopelessly while he lay before me, looking so peaceful and beautiful. Again, I do not recall how long it was before Dr. Creedon returned to inform me Svetmana had arrived...that they had intercepted her and asked to wait in the lounge. He also informed me she was not yet aware that Juan was gone and if I could possibly leave the room and go out to the grounds.

"The nurses will clean Juan and straighten up everything, and you can return and stay with him, Richard." I became panicky because I felt Svetmana may create an unnecessary scene because of my presence, which would be a terrible insult to Juan. I also wanted to keep the cross I had given him for his birthday...to wear it next to my heart always. I was never certain if she realized I had given it to Juan and did not want her to take it. I began trembling uncontrollably as I gently lifted Juan's head to remove the cross, not wanting to believe it would be my last time! All I could picture was the awe in his voice and on his face when he asked Amanda, "Recharred gave this to me? Whot should I say?" He was so quietly happy that evening...and I wanted that night back. There could never be enough words to describe my heartbreak once Juan's head nestled lifeless against my cheek.

I decided upon taking the flowered shirt, his coat, shoes, and slippers since they were the last things he wore. Svetmana would never give me any of his clothes as remembrances and once I explained this to Dr. Creedon, he said I should take them to put in my car. I caught a glimpse of Svetmana sitting in the lounge area, looking anxiously towards Juan's room upon cracking open the door and quickly shut it. Anxiously, I expressed my concern of the possibility she may go crazy accusing me of stealing...no, this could not happen, not while Juan lay there! Dr. Creedon then explained he would take Svetmana and her friend into the office before I left.

After putting Juan's things in the car, I walked hopelessly around the lot, trying to comprehend that he was never again going to see a beautiful sunny day such as this one...the twenty-second of July 1992. I felt as though I was going to explode and finally returned to the ward. The door to Juan's room was closed, but I was told Svetmana was gone...that she only stayed a few minutes.

"But you can go in, Richard, because everything has already been done."

As I opened the door…there he was, lying on his back. They had lowered the bed to a horizontal position while raising it to a much higher level. And there was my Juan…lying with his hands folded on his waist…with fresh folded sheets and a blanket. They had closed his eyelids, but somehow, the left eye had partially opened…and there was the beautiful blue that were his…only his. I never realized how empty and lonely I could feel until this moment!

How I wanted to shut my eyes and open them again, to find all of this to be a bad dream! I stepped to the bed, sobbing uncontrollably.

"Oh, God…God…why?… Why?" I wanted to believe Juan could hear me and I continued talking to him…questioning why he had to leave! He was still warm as I rubbed his hands and arms and kissed his face, and I wouldn't close his eyelid because I was certain he could see me. Oh, how I wanted both eyes to open…for the blues to sparkle, and to hear, "Aw, you are up, Recharred?" Oh, God!

How much time passed I cannot recall, but suddenly one of the nurses entered to tell me 'she' was back…for Juan's personal belongings, and if I'd mind leaving the room for a while. I walked slowly for the door and upon opening it, there she was…standing directly to my left with her nellie boyfriend who had recently been accompanying her on her short visits to the hospital. I looked at her and then to him, and saw nothing but scorn. I raised my hands hopelessly, wanting desperately to approach her…to take her in my arms and hold tight for Juan…to comfort her and be comforted in return. But she just glared at me coldly and backed away. So I walked slowly to the lounge area and sat there in a trance. After a few minutes, one of the nurses informed me she was gone.

The compassion given to me by Endira's husband, Dan, was overwhelming once he arrived, allowing me to sob uncontrollably on his shoulders, while trying to assure that Juan was now happy. After saying prayers, Dan, left to pick up Juan's dad and I again was alone with my Juan. He hadn't been gone long when the door suddenly opened and Amanda walked in apprehensively. She apparently hadn't been seen by the nurses and was totally unaware of the grief she was about to see. She took one look at me and then turned her head towards Juan, uncertain of his state….

"No, Richard, he's not gone…is he?" She reached out for me, her body trembling, crying out, "No, not Juan?" And once she was in my arms, it felt as though she was crumbling away. We cried together for some time and I continued stroking Juan's arms and face, wanting him to know how much I loved him. Amanda finally asked if I had called anyone to inform them of Juan's death, and I said I hadn't. "Well, Richard, it should be done…give me the numbers and I will call." I gave her the numbers for Martina, Geena, and Daniel, figuring they could call all others.

Once Amanda returned, she said Daniel was not home from work yet, but that Stan said he'd come to the hospital.

"Your daughter, Martina, asked if you could call her when you are up to it…and when I talked with your sister, she said she wanted to be here with you and would come immediately. I then called Matt and he also asked if you could call him, that he was worried since he hadn't heard from you all night."

Shortly after Stan arrived, Jody entered the room to explain they couldn't really allow us to remain much longer because it was four hours since Juan had passed away. I explained that his father was on the way to the hospital, and could we remain until then, and she reluctantly obliged. About twenty minutes later, Dan entered and asked if Juan's dad could have some time alone with his son. I looked at Juan, not really realizing this was to be my last time with him…. That I would never see him again! There was my mind again, not realizing something as final! They began hurrying me out of the room and I stood there beside Juan, and he looked so peaceful and I remembered how I always tried so desperately to get him to sleep so he wouldn't sneak out to the bars again. I remembered his wonderful mood once he awakened the next morning…never showing a sign of a hangover! How he could dance while the stereo blasted into the night…and who never seemed to tire because he never wanted the fun to end. So I guess my mind still couldn't comprehend everything, feeling HE WILL WAKE IN THE MORNING! And I quickly hugged and kissed him.

"I love you, Juan…I'll see you."

* * * * * *

Amanda reminded me that Geena hadn't yet arrived and we walked to the lounge area to wait. Amanda and Stan tried desperately to give support, holding their arms gently around my waist, assuring me Juan was at peace now. I didn't respond to any of their questions, since my mind could only think about Juan lying in that room and the grief his dad must be bearing. I wanted to join him…to comfort him and be comforted in return, but there again was society slapping me in the face…afraid to be called down for loving a man. I wanted to share this terrible grief with someone of Juan's own blood…who loved him as I did. So I merely sat there clutching onto a little bag I had stuffed his broken bridgework into, along with his toothbrush, pocket comb, and the electric shaver I had used to shave him. Evidently, Svetmana didn't want these things as remembrances…but I could never forget how many times he dropped this broken bridgework from his mouth, letting them hang there until I laughed.

I sat there in my stupor, knowing something terrible had happened, but probably not realizing the finality of it, and no one could ever imagine that this might take years to sink into my head. Yes, my mind continued to dream…that Juan would awaken and I'd hear him.

"Blanche, where are you? I was only foolin' around!"

Geena arrived and explained she had somehow forgotten where the hospital was located and after embracing me, realized I would not take my eyes from the door of Juan's room.

"I think it would be a good idea if you got home, Rich." I insisted I needed to place a couple of calls before leaving, and once we walked to the corridor, Jenny was arriving for her shift, quietly and tenderly embracing me. My eyes continued to focus on the door to Juan's room while seated on the bench, placing my call to Martina and crying together.

"Dad, you knew it was going to happen. Juan had AIDS, Dad, he's at peace now. Please be happy for him!" But I couldn't understand and didn't want to understand. She continued trying to console me and apologized for not being able to be with me, and I assured her I understood…that she had two small children.

"Dad, I loved Juan very much and you have to realize he wouldn't want to continue living the way he was." There was no reasoning with me since I knew he hadn't been in any pain…it was his memory and once a cure arrived, he'd be cured! We finally said good-bye and Martina assured me, "Dad, you will always have us…we love you very much!"

I was very apprehensive in calling Matt because of the hatred between him and Juan, and guilt was already beginning to harbor within my mind. But again, it was the proper thing to do. Matt expressed his sorrow, but I couldn't help resenting how he always talked so freely about Juan dying. He even thought to reprimand me again for not calling him sooner! He then asked if I wanted him to come over to the house. I explained that we were on my way there, not really feeling hospitable towards him at this time, especially since he didn't insist to be with me. In fact, my mind was swimming with the memory of the day Juan had cried out to me.

"Recharred, I don't want you to cry on Matt's shoulders when I die!"

So I merely answered by saying, "You do what you want, Matt…you are welcome to come if you want." He explained that Vincent was coming over in a while…that they wanted to take in a movie.

"So I will stop in later tonight, Rich." I shook my head slowly in disbelief. Juan is lying dead in that room…I am in terrible grief…and Matt was going to a movie?

Stan immediately pressed the elevator call button once I had hung up to continue in my trance on the door to Juan's room. At that time, his father and Dan walked out and I wanted desperately to walk back to the room…to be with Juan again, but I was quickly hustled into the elevator instead. Before the elevator door closed, Juan's father walked slowly in, followed by Dan. Here was a man who had always held himself so robust…so proud! He now appeared to be a lost soul. I wanted to take hold of him…to cry with him, but he kept his head low, never looking my way. No one said a word and in a few moments, the door opened to the ground level.

I don't remember who drove my car, but recall turning in my seat as we drove the long road out of the hospital grounds, to look up to the fourth floor of the hospital...and the window of Juan's room. My mind could think of nothing but that Juan was there alone, and I wanted to return...to hear him say, "Aw, Recharred, you are up ot last...good," and to see that smile linger on his face. I had to realize Juan was lying there...that he was gone forever...but somehow, it wouldn't sink into my head...that this was something real...that all the music was gone?

* * * * * *

Epilogue

I was "Richard" and no one could ever have imagined how much my grief and mourning for Juan would grow with every passing day. It always took forever to realize I had been insulted, or why I hadn't won a certain audition, so how could anyone ever expect me to instantly believe Juan's passing as something final and real?

Daniel, Carol, Patti, Lucille, and Wally eventually arrived at the house, and along with the others, tried valiantly to keep my spirits up. I continued in limbo…or shock…or whatever…. I don't think my mind thought this to be something real. And this had to be the most tragic happening of my entire life.

Amanda insisted we order from Rocky's in honor of Juan because he loved their spaghetti marinara sautéed with mushrooms. Carol volunteered to pick it up. I hadn't eaten for twenty-four hours, but could only manage to down a few forkfuls. There wasn't that smile of approval with every forkful I was so used seeing from Juan. Everyone suggested I go to my bedroom to rest a while. However, it bothered me hearing the cheerful chatter coming from the living room, even though I understood their reason—to keep my spirits up. No one gave a thought to the fact that I always had a one-track mind…and no matter what they said or did, it would be thinking only of Juan.

I could not remain in bed long since my head was swimming with one thought after another of the fatal day. I asked Daniel and Amanda to call all those friends who might be just returning home from work, and this included Larry in Indianapolis, along with Phillip and Kent, Barry in California, Arthur and Jake, and Marina. Daniel reminded me about Vic and Phil, and I also realized Hank should be called. Daniel informed me that he would be staying the night and that Amanda would be with me the following evening.

Geena was very concerned about me and I realized her confusion was partly responsible. I had told Amanda to be sure she told everyone not to talk of AIDS since she did not know Juan and I had been lovers. HERE I WAS

STILL HIDING THE FACT THAT JUAN HAD AIDS AND HE WAS LYING DEAD!

Geena did, however, tell me, "You know, Rich, I really like your friends. They are wonderful!"

Matt arrived late, just before almost everyone was about to leave. He stood in the center of the living room looking very uncomfortable and finally, I rose to be embraced while he expressed his regrets. During the conversation that followed, I guess he thought it proper to mention to everyone how hilariously funny the movie was? He also appeared annoyed once he heard Daniel was staying the night with me.

The phone was answered and handed to me even though I had said I didn't want to talk to anyone. I was taken by surprise to hear Endira's voice.

"I'm so sorry, Richard. I want you to know I realize how you must feel." No one could possibly know how I felt! And worse yet, how time would make everything even lonelier.

I found it inconceivable to imagine that Matt actually felt I'd be back to normal in a few days, and I resented him for being in my life. He'd stop in to see me and although he always seemed to be considerate and compassionate for my feelings, I never felt they were real. The length of his visits were kept at a minimum, especially once I called him down for expecting me to agree to his tasteless suggestions to jump in bed with him. So he would go on his merry way. The guilt I was harboring was the real reason for my resentment towards him. I felt I had robbed Juan of time to live because of his stress over my refusal to stop seeing Matt. Yes, I had always thought Juan had so many years yet to live…long after this fancy I had for Matt would be long gone! But Juan was gone now and this guilt was growing within me, along with a loneliness I never imagined!

On one of my counseling sessions at the hospital, the social worker did say I should realize I did more than any spouse ever did for their loved one in that hospital, but I still couldn't let it alter the low-esteem I held of myself.

"Richard, you did more for Juan than anyone could ever expect from the closest person in their life! Richard, all of us here at the hospital really believe Juan waited for you to be with him before he died! He made certain of it, and Richard, that is something beautiful! I do not think I have ever even seen a loving and devoted wife do as much as you did for Juan! So hold that in your heart, Richard, and be proud!" Even with that praise, it still continued to prey on my mind…that my ego-related adventures were initially responsible for Juan coming in contact with this dreaded disease.

None of this depression and guilt was doing my relationship with Matt any good and I was seriously thinking of putting an end to it, even though he finally began popping occasionally for dinners besides being so attentive while with me. Jenny begged to reconsider.

"Because, Richard, you don't know how lonely I am since losing my loved one. Richard, you have to go on with your life, and I believe Matt could make you happy." But I couldn't concentrate on the relationship.

Juan's memorial mass was being held at Endira's rich Episcopalian church just off the Magnificent Mile in Chicago. Juan was raised Catholic but hadn't been a member of any church and his parent's parish wouldn't consider holding it there. I had seen the notice in the paper, but Endira still called to remind me. At the same time, she thought it fitting to inform me Juan's parents had began insinuations that I was the cause of Juan being gay, which eventually caused him to be infected with the AIDS virus. I couldn't believe this woman! She was digging the dagger deeper into my back when she was totally aware that Juan had been gay before meeting me. However, this only added to my guilt, because of the improbable possibility he could have returned to the straight world had he not met me.

Daniel kept advising against my appearance at Juan's memorial, suspecting someone would go berserk. However, I insisted I was the closest person to Juan and would never consider not going, especially since I hadn't been included in the last visitation before Juan's cremation.

Daniel had tried desperately to have me included at the chapel, but to no avail. Upon talking with me on the phone, he had suggested I call the chapel myself to explain everything. I went completely hysterical once I had been told it was too late…that Juan had already been cremated! My hysteria caused my body to lose all control and I cannot recall how I had finally managed to place a call to Daniel while screaming incoherently that Juan was gone…that I would ever see him again! Daniel had rushed over, staying the entire day and evening.

I begged Endira to talk to Svetmana…to allow me to be included in the scattering of Juan's ashes…even though I didn't know if I could bear to see an urn, knowing it contained the remains of my beloved Juan. Yet, at the same time I realized I was a man of rituals, and needed this to accept that he was gone.

"Richard, you have had your time with Juan. I think it is Svetmana's turn now and I believe she does not want to share it with you." I could not believe this because my daughter had neglected to tell me everything when Endira called her while Juan was in the hospital.

"Yes, Dad, I don't know how it slipped my mind, but Endira also told me at that time that Svetmana had known about Juan for years because she had gone through his drawers whenever she stayed at his apartment and he wasn't home…and, Dad, she found his medical papers that stated that he had been tested positive with the HIV virus." Svetmana had known since 1987, and yet, she never made any attempt to have 'her time' to be with Juan! How many times he told me that he hadn't heard from her for months! And how she made him miserable with her crazy screaming for no reason at all, and then remaining in the bedroom the entire evening after slamming the door behind her! She had always been too busy being consumed in her own being! And now she was calling the shots because of a birth certificate, leaving me out in the cold. I even mailed a beautiful letter with my request, but heard no response.

Matt had offered to accompany me to the memorial, but thought it necessary to inform me that it was for my support only…not Juan. I saw no reason with that attitude and declined his offer. It was inconceivable to think he was still harboring his anger for the calls Juan had made. He couldn't find it in his heart to finally make peace with Juan…and it was sad. My daughters, Martina and Jacque, insisted they were going with me, as well as Amanda. Unfortunately, Patti couldn't make it since she had invited guests to her lake house. Geena had tried desperately to make it before we left, but because Frank was using the car, she had no means of transportation, and we had no time to pick her up since Amanda was late in arriving. I had left messages on both Nicky and Mike's tapes, but I was disappointed they didn't show up. Daniel and the others decided to wait for the memorial I was planning.

"Richard, I believe you are making a mistake by going!"

Just before the four of us entered the small chapel of the large church, Marina arrived and I introduced her to my daughters. It was odd, but it didn't bother me realizing they may wonder about her falsetto voice and height. I was disappointed entering the very lovely chapel, since there were so few in attendance. Svetmana was seated in the front row with her friend, alongside of Endira and Dan, and Juan's father. His mother was not present and I realized her physical condition along with her present mental hysteria was obviously the reason. Endira's mother was there, and I was very pleased to see Juan's old co-worker from the National Guard recruiting office…his wonderful black friend, Joel Lend! The other few were obviously Endira's socialite friends, who attended because of Svetmana. I was so disappointed because Juan deserved more!

I felt so alone because I hadn't been consulted about the services or anything regarding the plans. It was as though I was a casual friend instead of the closest person in his life…and it hurt. I needed these rituals and Svetmana and Endira had cheated me from them. When Juan had had his will drawn, he went to my nephew, an attorney, and after returning, had told me he appointed Endira as his executor. I had been hurt at the time and asked why I wasn't appointed since she hadn't been anything to him for eighteen years.

"Recharred," he had replied, "I did thot because she can then communicate with my parents. You would 'ave trouble understanding them, ond they would 'ave trouble understanding you. Recharred, she will be fair, I am sure she knows how close we are." Yet, I wondered.

I had also been told by Endira that the service had been changed to a mass, celebrating Juan's life, which meant his ashes would be present. But they were nowhere in sight. Martina and Jacque sat at each side of me while Amanda was next to one of them. They rubbed my shoulders continuously, but I couldn't be consoled. My world had ended! JUAN WAS GONE! HIS BODY NO LONGER EXISTED…AND I NEVER WAS ALLOWED TO SEE HIM BEFORE HE WAS CREMATED! And now his ashes were not there and I felt Svetmana meant for me not to see them! I couldn't come to terms with the fact that this was Juan's memorial mass!

Svetmana walked to the pulpit to read a eulogy to Juan. It was short and even though I couldn't concentrate on her words, she did appear to be affected as she nervously almost whispered the words. Or it possibly was a case of stage fright?

Endira's husband, Dan, then read a passage from the Bible. Dan was a very religious man and never one lost for words, but this time his words were all choked up. Just before the service concluded, Svetmana's friend approached our pew to invite us for coffee and refreshments afterwards in the hospitality room.

I sat in a trance once the mass ended and Amanda and my daughters respected me by remaining silent and in place…to give me my time. I had no intention of coping with Endira and her phoniness and once I rose and turned towards Marina, she was gone. I felt bad since I never had a chance to talk with her. Just as we started for the rear exit, Endira reentered from the hall they had exited.

"Richard, wait a minute," she called out, immediately approaching to insist we join them for coffee. Not wanting to embarrass my daughters and Amanda by refusing, I agreed to attend.

As we headed down the long corridor towards the lounge, we saw Svetmana sitting on a bench laughing while talking with her nellie friend. She rose once we approached and Martina, Jacque, and Amanda, embraced her to offer their condolences. Surprisingly, she approached me and put her arms around my shoulders as I tenderly grasped unto her back, sobbing.

"Aw, Svetmana, I loved your dad so much…I love him so much." Svetmana continued her embrace, and her response seemed obviously cold.

"I know, Richard, I know." Tears began flowing and I could only speak in a whisper.

"I want to be there for you, Svetmana…just as your dad would be…. Let me be there for you!" She never responded, and I later figured she had to be repulsed at the thought of my audacity to think I could replace her father…. I was sorry I hadn't mentioned how desperately Juan also loved me.

I did get to finally embrace Juan's father and talk of visiting him and his wife, and was given every impression I'd be welcome. I also had the opportunity to talk once more with Joel and again hear of all the laughter and joy Juan gave him during the years they worked as partners. Svetmana never came into the room, and Endira was her usual self, mixing useless chatter between the four of us and her few socialite friends. It was also heartwarming to meet a gentleman who was really out of Juan's past, a co-worker of his when he was a librarian at the university back in 1975-76. And it was wonderful to hear him speak so highly of the pleasure he always experienced working alongside Juan.

I was determined my memorial mass for Juan would be one he'd be proud of, and it kept me quite busy, because after all, 'there were things to be done.' My obsession to have everything perfect was almost as though he'd be present. I returned back to work and while there, couldn't get Juan out of my mind, especially when staring down the furniture-filled aisles. There he'd be…walking towards me, excitedly raving about certain pieces of furniture! In fact, there was nowhere that I didn't see Juan or reminded of him.

Father Jerry was very supportive, managing to locate a small chapel in a priest's home to hold the memorial, and it wasn't far from my apartment. I was especially pleased once he agreed to officiate in the celebration of Juan's life because he had talked to him many times when serving communion at the hospital. I decided to include a picture of Juan on the memorial card I was having printed, and because the most recent and best shot was the one I had taken of him with Larry of Indianapolis August of 1991. I had them make an enlargement of his face only. I received many sympathy cards from family and friends and decided to use a verse from the card sent to me by our friend, Marina. It had moved me to tears, especially since it was almost as though it had to be composed with Juan in mind….

> *A butterfly lights beside us like a sunbeam.*
>
> *And for a brief moment, its glory and beauty belong to our world.*
>
> *But then it flies on again, and though we wish it could have stayed, we feel so lucky to have seen it.*

I had been calling various support groups and finally received a call from one of their volunteers informing me of his availability to listen anytime I wanted to talk. Mark was his name. As it turned out, Mark was very helpful the evening of the memorial, August 13. He distributed the cards and ushered everyone to their seats, and most importantly…he did a fine job of playing the songs on the cassette player.

Juan's old friends, Arthur and Jake, arrived at the same time as Daniel, Jenny, Patti, Wally, and Lucille, also bringing a friend who had met Juan at one of their parties. Marina never showed up and I later realized that I never called to inform her of the change of date. Stan wasn't present, having to work that evening. Our old friends, Vic and Phil, arrived. Unfortunately, I had never called to inform them Juan was ill. Vic was very compassionate as we spoke, wishing I had called so he could've visited Juan. I was sorry myself, but once I saw the still arrogant expression on Phil's face, I understood why I hadn't. Juan certainly didn't need to be confronted with another person with a heart like that!

Father Jerry was a bit concerned since I insisted on holding up the start, especially after Carol arrived and said Amanda was on her way. Matt walked in, looking very uncomfortable as he placed himself in the last pew. I knew Juan would have laughed at the thought of waiting again for Amanda to arrive, and I could hear him saying, "Recharred, you know Amanda is never gonna change." Father Jerry began showing his anxiousness, which only added to mine since he had told me the priests living there retired very early in the evening. I finally agreed to start and at that moment, Amanda hurried in. I could almost see the glowing smile on Juan's face.

"Don't Cry for Me Argentina" filled the chapel and as I listened, I couldn't take my eyes from the picture I had framed to place on the altar railing...the one I had taken of Juan just before reaching the gate of Brown County State Park, when he managed a great big grin while standing on the road with the outhouse in the distance. Next to it, I had placed a vase of eighteen roses, one for each of the beautiful years I was privileged to share with Juan. Larry had sent a beautiful azalea plant, and another floral basket had arrived from Juan's Army company in Indianapolis, and these were alongside my roses.

The music was perfect because Juan had loved that musical so much, especially since it always reminded him of his childhood years and how his mother would tear Eva Peron apart...that she was the biggest whore in the country! And how he would laugh each time he talked of it. And I could just see him shaking his head in approval, sighing, "Recharred, thot song was a perfect choice!" During the Offertory, I had decided on the recording of me singing "Lonely," a song I wrote. Juan had loved it so once I played it for him years before. He had raved about it endlessly. I also realized these would be my feelings for the rest of my life. Father Jerry spoke very well, even though he only knew Juan from his several visits with him in the hospital. He asked if anyone would like to say a few words and the only one who could control his emotions was Daniel.

It had taken me days to compose my eulogy to Juan, deciding upon reading the eight typewritten pages for fear I would break up into tears should I try to talk without it. Juan and I never talked about our marriage to friends of recent years and before beginning to read, I brought it to their attention. I tried to include everything about Juan, knowing darn well it would be an impossibility to include everything without going on forever...but I believe that although my voice choked up, I still managed to capture the joy and excitement he continually brought to my life.

The memorial mass concluded and Juan's favorite disco songs were played. I felt Juan again would have been proud of my tribute to him, yet I still couldn't come to terms with his passing. Almost everyone accepted my invite to the house for refreshments.

My grief and mourning continued to grow, and even though Matt showed some compassion, my resentment towards him continued to brew within me. He had always just given me enough to keep me hanging...and I began feeling responsible for causing Juan stress. My children, as well as my sisters and brother-in-laws, were giving me tremendous support, but I just couldn't get it out of my mind. Daniel couldn't be with me often, but called every day, trying desperately to bring me up. Matt began coming over almost every day; however, he was completely baffled why I wasn't laying Juan to rest, and since I had absolutely no interest in sex, he'd be on his way. I joined support groups, but nothing seemed to lessen my grief. Svetmana refused to contact me after receiving my letters begging her to allow me to share this grief with her, and I also wrote a letter to Juan's parents. I even had it translated into Lithuanian, praying they may understand.

Larry had suggested I begin a quilt in Juan's honor when we talked, and once a woman minister I met at one of the support programs also mentioned it, I immediately began designing and creating one. And I did feel close to Juan the many hours of the days and nights it took to finally create one that seemed to depict his life perfectly. I included everything he loved—dancing, music, reading, sightseeing, also reminding everyone that we were truly one person forever.

I was surprised to receive a message from Juan's mother on my tape, asking to call her, and upon calling, I made arrangements to visit them. Even though English communication was not good, I did find they were very bitter with Endira and Svetmana since there had been very little contact with them. As expected, I was told Svetmana was already spending the fifty thousand-dollar insurance money foolishly. I had previously learned I wasn't included in the policy when Daniel insisted I call the Army insurance office.

"Richard, you have to call…you haven't a penny to your name and have devoted all those months to Juan…and, Richard, he told not only me, but Amanda as well…that he was leaving you five or ten thousand because he owed you so much! And you have to claim it in order to receive it!" I wasn't really interested in money, but finally consented to call to appease Daniel. However, upon calling, I was told no concession was made in my name. I tried explaining to Daniel after he became quite angry with Juan.

"Daniel, Juan never expected to die this soon! He talked of five…ten more years to live! So all I care about is that his intentions were to do it. He just never got to it and once his memory started failing, it was too late. Just knowing he wanted to do it is enough for me because I KNOW JUAN LOVED ME MORE THAN ANYONE IN THIS WORLD…and Daniel, that is what matters!"

At the time, I had also explained how shocked I was when I did call the insurance office.

"Do you know what she said, Daniel? After telling me no changes had been sent to them…she went on to tell me they had, however, received a letter from Juan dated in May, informing them to be sure the present beneficiary was not changed…and to accept no changes even if he later requested one! Do you believe that? Juan wasn't capable of writing that letter at that time since he couldn't concentrate on anything because he was losing his memory! It didn't take long to realize who was responsible for writing it to be certain Svetmana remained sole beneficiary."

I visited Juan's parents three times and felt I could possibly finally accept this tragedy since his mother asked if I could also be her son, which would make me work hard at keeping them happy. But then Svetmana began visiting them, probably realizing I had been there. From what I could make out in my phone conversations with Juan's mother, Svetmana had begun telling stories about Juan and I…that it was my doing that he was gay…which naturally meant I was the reason he caught AIDS. So even though Juan's mother wanted me there, she couldn't go against her husband's wishes to not see me again. So what was I to do? He spoke very little English and I also realized how narrow-minded he was from what Juan always said about him.

I began writing letters to everyone…for answers…for understanding, and at the same time found they were keeping Juan alive in my heart. Near the end of September, I began writing the story of this fabulous man, especially since I could feel his presence carefully guiding me to be sure I wrote the right words.

I had written to his uncle in England since I needed to share the wonderful stories about Juan with someone who loved him dearly. It could be the only way to help my grief. My beliefs were confirmed once I received a reply and read these passages:

> *Juan was a person I was always very happy to be with and he never missed an opportunity to come see my premieres while I was in Bloomington. Of all my family, I felt Juan to be the nearest and dearest.*
>
> *Your letter touched me to the bottom of my heart and I was moved. I do not think that I have ever encountered such a human love and friendship during the whole of my long life.*

I then needed to know the final cause of Juan's death—if it was listed as AIDS or something that had been infected because of his immune system, and decided to write to the director of the hospital. At the same time, I commended the staff for making Juan feel so special. I was thanked for my touching letter once I received a reply. She then referred to Juan's primary doctor and gave reasons for death in two separate paragraphs:

> *It is his opinion that the immediate cause of death was due to the progressive infection of the nervous system by the Human Immunodeficiency Virus. He, too, remembers your friend as being a special and gentle person….*
>
> *The cause of death was due to a cessation of the brain's ability to adequately control life-sustaining physiologic functions, such as breathing and heart rate. Remember that death is only a temporary parting between loved ones, and once again, someday, you will be together again.*

As I read and reread the letter, I couldn't get the fact that syphilis had reactivated in Juan's body. I had to be sure this wasn't because of my foolish suggestion years ago to have separate nights out? So I took up her suggestion to talk to one of Juan's primary doctors, and was assured by her that it was a dementia caused by AIDS. To this day, however, I still am not sure!

When I finally completed the quilt, I made a time to meet the minister since she agreed to take it with her to Washington, D.C., for the national display of the entire collection of quilts. Before handing her the folded quilt, I held it tightly against my heart, knowing this would be the last time I could cradle it in such a manner.

On my last visit, I had been told by Juan's mother that his ashes had already been scattered in Brown County and I was devastated, realizing all my pleas to Svetmana had been in vain. I realized Endira had been continually double talking, handing me one lie after another and my mind was livid. I decided I had to disassociate with her and Svetmana once and for all, and began composing a letter that would surely be the closing chapter. I wanted her to realize how meaningless she and her daughter had succeeded in making me feel, and how lonely and empty I had become because of it. In my anger, I lashed out in every possible way, wanting her to realize Juan and I knew everything about each of our marriages...especially the infidelities we were subjected to by our wives. I included my beliefs regarding Svetmana's mental stability...that her only problem was being totally selfish, which never allowed her to love anyone or even to be loved in return...and that she was too consumed in her own being.

I expressed my total disbelief in their vicious contempt for my continual caring of Juan. Included in the letter were my cutting remarks regarding her ruthless maneuvers to control Juan's life by gaining his trust with small gifts, only to take them back before he died, and all while controlling his bank account.

Several in my family besides Daniel read the letter, advising me to drop the matter and I finally agreed to set it aside.

I had finally gone to bed with Matt, but felt extremely guilty after the few times, finally realizing a relationship could never flourish under these conditions. Matt had been invited to his deceased father's university to accept a special honor being decreed upon him, and was very excited about it. I finally decided I wasn't being fair to him…that I'd have to stop seeing him entirely. Against Jenny's advice, I decided to record a tape and mail it before he left for the weekend, so it would be in his mailbox once he returned. In the recording, I explained how my depression wouldn't allow me to go on with this relationship…that I needed to resolve the guilt within myself and maybe then we could get together one day.

Amanda stopped by Sunday night in one of her rare visits, realizing her reason for avoiding me was due to my constant depression, and as expected, the phone rang later that evening. I figured it had to be Matt and allowed the answering machine to take the message. It continued to ring all night and with each call, I heard recorded sad and desperate pleas to see me to get an explanation for sending the tape. Still, I was determined to go through with this. However, I felt sure he'd eventually drive over to check if I was home, and upon mentioning this to Amanda, she decided to head on her way to avoid being involved in any embarrassment.

The doorbell did ring shortly after Amanda left and I was forced to buzz Matt in since his words over the intercom were not ones I felt anyone who might happen to be in the foyer should hear. Matt walked into the apartment as though it was the end of the world, appearing totally baffled with my actions, while informing me that he'd only stay a short time.

"Please, Rich, let me be the one to decide when I have had enough of this depression you've been in?" The short time turned out to be another one of those heavy and long discussion he so excelled in. My intentions had been serious to end whatever relationship we had, especially since Daniel had told me Juan's statement while in Chinatown. But here I was again allowing him to confuse my decision, giving me second thoughts by thinking he has to truly love me to fight so desperately. However, I didn't give him a total commitment.

"Matt, let's see what happens. For now, I will continue seeing you."

The following Saturday, I decided to drive to Brown County, realizing how ironical the timing was. I had taken the train just a year before on the same day to see to Juan's furniture and to drive his car back…on Halloween. I didn't know exactly where Juan's ashes had been spread, and just drove from one place I remembered Juan liking to another. It was a very dreary autumn day and many of the leaves had already fallen, so I had much of the areas to myself…and the quietness of being alone really made me feel Juan's presence.

I brought along the memory cassettes to play that Juan had recorded, almost believing he'd call out to thank me for playing his tape. I had begun listening to the Spanish station while driving and after hearing a group called Mazz, I fell in love with the song "No Es Amor," purchasing the cassette. I knew Juan would have loved it and this was to be my farewell…to leave him be at rest…but on the way home, I felt it was not going to happen.

The following Saturday, Matt and I were invited to Wally's for a housewarming party for a condo he and Don purchased. I had assumed food would be served since he always had an abundant table at his parties…so I didn't eat before. However, only a spinach dip, which was almost gone when we arrived, and another completely wiped out dip bowl were on the table. I hadn't done any drinking for some time, in fact since before Juan died, and after having two or three drinks, my system apparently couldn't take it. I was later told I got nasty once Matt approached to demand I cool it after overhearing my discussion with Stan regarding how I was coping with Juan's death. I never remembered any of my words and actions but was told by Matt the next day that I had been tearing him apart and that he and Daniel finally drove me home. Of course, he informed me that he went to the bars. I had already found out that he had been having sex with others since my lack of desire. When I had asked him if he had been abstaining to give me time, he quickly inferred I must be crazy to think he should do without.

A few days later, I had decided to finally begin visiting my agents again and spent most of the day going from one to the other in the city. I ended up stopping in a bar for a couple of drinks and this time felt a nice buzz. My spirits were the best they had been in some time and I finally began yearning for Matt, realizing he had to care for me very much to put up with my behavior. I headed home to tell him I was finally ready for a relationship…that Juan would always be in my heart, but that I had come to terms with his passing, and that I needed someone to love…who loved me.

Matt was not home but I spotted his car once I checked out the Nutbush bar. I walked in excitedly, anxious to tell him my revelation, but as I approached, I noticed an obvious, quick shuffle of hands between him and the black guy next to him. My mood immediately changed and any buzz I had was completely gone. He, however, had quite a buzz and happily introduced me to Don, who had quickly and conveniently engaged in conversation with the guy on his other side. Matt insisted on buying me a drink but I refused. I somehow forced myself to mention I had something very important to tell him, but he showed no interest whatsoever. It was apparent he was having too good a time to find out what I had to say. And it didn't bother him once I said I was going home as he merely said a quick so long…see you later. I was confused while driving home…not only since he showed no interest in my news, but because he almost appeared to be interested in this Don, when most of his comments about blacks had always gave me the impression that he was a bigot.

"You know, Rich? All niggers should be hoarded into a boat and sunk at sea," was a statement he had quoted on occasion. However, I finally recalled the tail end of his statement, "that is, except those with big cocks just for me!" So I suddenly understood.

I decided to go to his house the very next evening to explain the revelation I had experienced…to tell him I wanted this relationship to work. I was mortified to see how unaffected he appeared after hearing my so-called important news! He merely went on to say he'd see how things fell into place…that he had a date for dinner Saturday evening. Upon asking with whom, he brushed me off by stating it wasn't important since I didn't know the person anyway.

"I met him at the bar election night and have been with him twice, sexually." I left bewildered, not understanding how he had suddenly changed! It had only been a little over a week since he begged to reconsider my decision to discontinue seeing him! Was he playing some kind of game? It almost appeared to me that he was only concerned because I injured his ego…that he had to be the one to drop me? But still I refused to believe it!

I decided to write a letter, explaining everything in detail, especially because I could never really express myself to him in person since he always managed to confuse me by going in different directions. I called from work to ask if he could meet me during my lunch and he agreed. My plans were to read the letter to be sure he didn't just set it aside, and if he truly had sincere feelings for me he certainly would cancel his date after hearing what I had written because it wouldn't make sense to go out with someone else if we were in a relationship? Again, to my mortification, he reacted in the same manner, insisting on going through with this date.

"Matt, don't let everything I did for you go in vain! Please consider that I did not give you up to be with Juan…DON'T LET ME HAVE DONE THAT IN VAIN! Let me believe I did it for something I thought was beautiful…or could be beautiful!" However, my pleading did no good…this guy was hot for that date.

I played cards that evening at Geena's with my brothers and sisters and did quite a bit of drinking, feeling it would relieve my tensions. Once I left, I decided to stop in the Nutbush, feeling Matt may stop there with his date after dinner. I was sure it would give me a chance to see the guy. My feelings were correct because there he was. However, I was totally shocked to see him seated at the bar with the black guy he had been shuffling hands with…Don! Fortunately, their backs were to me and hadn't noticed my entrance…they were too busy holding hands and laughing again. I began drinking excessively and finally ended up immediately next to them and when he totally ignored me, a few nasty remarks were sent his way. He quickly rose to leave, his friend following suit as I continued my remarks. He, however, completely ignored them, taking his friend by the arm and exiting quickly. I lost no time following, catching him about to get in his car, and continued my harassment…calling him down for his lies…ridiculing him for the bigot he was, yet forgetting his hatred for the sake of a big cock! I was fuming and cannot recall a word he retaliated with, but he did jump into his car and immediately sped on his way. I immediately ran for my car and sped like a bat out of hell for his apartment, figuring that was where he was headed.

I never saw his car before me as I raced to his place, but managed to arrive in the alley just as he was about to pull into his parking spot. Once he caught sight of me directly behind, he did not pull in. Instead, he got out of the car and stood there listening to me repeat everything I wanted Don to realize as Matt's feelings about blacks. I continued shouting at the top of my lungs and he retaliated with the same while running to my car. It was obvious he was more concerned about losing the big dick than the neighbors hearing all the nasty business.

"Well, he is much better than you are in bed!" he shouted.

I quickly retaliated with, "Why, Matt, because he has a big cock? Is that what you consider being better? I know that has to be your criteria because that is all you ever talk about…big cocks!" I had no control over my emotions and he should've realized this from the very beginning, and lose me by driving away. Instead, he stood there screaming himself since it was apparent he realized sex with a big dick would not be in store for him this evening. I saw it as an opportunity to remind him of it, and he suddenly began punching at my face through the open window of the car, swinging viciously with each quick punch! I actually saw flashes of light with each blow! Finally, I managed to swing open the door in order to get out and defend myself, but as I did, he ran for his car and sped away! I was furious and because of it, I really didn't grasp that he actually was beating my face to a pulp! Those were not slaps, but fists jabbing into my face.

I was determined to catch him and was right on his tail and finally led into the police station parking lot! I cannot remember everything shouted…only that he was going to have me arrested.

"What for…because of my verbal abuse?… How about if I charge you with assault and battery?" And, with that, I slapped him as hard as I could in the face, and he naturally returned one to me, but using his fist instead. I saw stars…almost feeling one in my mouth! But once I moved my tongue I realized it wasn't a star but one of my front capped teeth! This called for a kick into those small balls of his because his arms were longer than mine and he kept holding off my blows! We finally ended up in a wrestling match on the asphalt and immediately separated by Don. After more shouts, I took off!

My anger was so intense that I returned about an hour later to ring his front doorbell because I wanted him to see what he had done to my face and tooth. He finally came down the front hall in his robe and refused to open the door, shouting out that I was a fatal attraction. My one consolation…Don wasn't there; otherwise, he would've never left the bed to answer the door. Shouting continued and after accusing him of killing Juan, I left.

I then spent over two hours being treated and having x-rays taken at the VA emergency room. I remember lying on the table in a trauma as the technician took one picture after another…trying desperately to understand how someone who continually insisted we were working on a relationship be responsible for something like this? I also realized I should never have voiced my feelings in such a violent manner, and yet I didn't think I deserved a mauling. And my mind kept thinking of Juan…of what I had done.

My face looked as though I had been in the ring with the Manassa Mauler…a fat lip, multiple bruises, and two black eyes to compliment everything! I was forced to tell my family I was mugged near the house, because how could I tell them this was done by a friend? I was determined it was finally over. I would never see Matt again. The stump of the cap had been completely broken, so I was faced with a nice dental bill to correct the hole in my mouth.

So what did I do? I began having second guesses about severing relations with Matt, realizing I had provoked the entire scenario. I needed someone in my life and still felt he was the one. So I practically fell on my knees, pleading for forgiveness. And believe me, he made me crawl, never thinking to apologize for knocking out my tooth, especially since it caused me so much expense.

Endira finally made arrangements with me to pick up the special mementos I had given Juan, namely the Southwest pictures and especially the bedspread, which I wanted badly because it was something that had been so close to him. Daniel came with me since I wanted him to confirm that Juan had always said for me to keep the car. But then he became involved in a conversation with Dan and I realized his confirmation was a lost cause.

I was extremely shocked, but held my cool, once Endira insisted I needed to sign a document prepared by an attorney, giving up further claims to anything in Juan's estate in order to receive these special items. I later realized she had to be aware that I had every right to make claim, but judged me from what she'd do instead. It then began to prey on my mind and I was certain I had to mail out my letter to her, severing any possibility of a reconciliation ever. At a later date, I also mailed a copy to Svetmana, realizing she'd never allow a relationship between us to flourish anyway.

Daniel was again having a surprise birthday party for Stan, only this time for his fiftieth. Wanting it to be special, he had invited about fourteen for dinner at an expensive French restaurant, and to follow it with cocktails and a show at the female impersonator club, The Baton, which would be costing him a small fortune. Matt and I hadn't yet had our big battle when Daniel originally informed me that he was having the party. So I had extended the invitation to Matt since I felt Daniel meant me to do so. Well, I had unfortunately told Daniel all the details of the terrible battle shortly after it occurred, and he in fact had seen my battered face. When he realized we had resumed our relationship, he wasn't happy to hear that I had previously extended the invite.

"No, he is not welcome…only you!" No matter how I pleaded, Daniel wouldn't change his mind and went on further to demand, "and if you do not come yourself, you can consider our friendship over!" He then went on to shout, "Richard, he is never gonna commit to you, and if he does, he will never be true. *I* know…because one whore knows another!" I tried to explain the same as I did to Juan…that I needed to find out for myself if Matt was never to be trusted, but it did no good. Daniel stood firm. So I couldn't tell Matt he wasn't welcome since it would certainly break up any possible friendship that might blossom between him and Daniel. Instead, I told him I didn't feel in the mood to party.

Monday evening after the party, I decided to bring my present to Stan and to also apologize for not attending the party. Daniel was his cordial talkative self, but with a sense of distance, apparently to remind me that our friendship was in jeopardy. I tried explaining my reasons again…that I felt I needed Matt to be there for me, especially since he was the only one coming around on a steady basis. This didn't set well with Daniel since he thought I was inferring he hadn't been giving me support. Even after I explained how much I appreciated his support by calling almost daily, that I still needed daily companionship, he merely smiled smugly.

"Stan, what do you think about Richard not coming for your fiftieth birthday party?" he inquired. Stan sat there with an expression I might see on Fred Flintstone's face as he tried to think of an answer. Once he finally came up with an answer it was as though some child was retaliating against another and I sat silently appalled.

"Richard, if I had known you would not be coming to my fiftieth birthday party, I would have given more thought about visiting Juan in the hospital…because after all, you only have one fiftieth birthday!" I COULD NOT BELIEVE HIM! AND FURTHERMORE I COULD NOT BELIEVE DANIEL WOULD CONDONE SUCH AN IDIOTIC STATEMENT!

I should have gotten up, taken my present, and spit in his face for imagining one birthday party more important than Juan's life! At the same time, I should have reminded him that he was there just a few times and each time he managed to keep his distance from Juan, and that he threw one look after another to Daniel to remind him they should be on their way. Oh, how I should have stampeded out of there! However, I was again too much of a gentleman and sat there swallowing it. And my courtesy was all in vain, because Daniel stopped calling and our friendship was over. I had felt we had something special but I finally realized he had stopped seeing Phil and Vic after they, too, failed to attend one of his parties for Stan…and the same with Brent and Cary before they moved to Arizona. And I thought, *Boy, he must really worship that big dick!*

Even though Matt continued with his space, keeping me groveling after him, he finally agreed to spend two nights at a downtown hotel starting Christmas night, and I felt we had something going at last. This seemed to help alleviate some of the sadness from missing Juan. This had to finally be something real for him. I needed to be loved and it appeared Matt was finally going to fill that void in my life.

The two days were going as I had hoped, with complete attention from Matt. However, we cut the second day short to attend Carl's mother's wake. I was quite surprised once Matt decided to leave the chapel after only a few minutes.

"Because, Rich, I want to visit Bob at the hospital." Now, Bob was someone I had never met, someone he was going out with before me, and each time I asked to meet him, he'd say the guy didn't want to meet me because he still loved him. So he'd spend time with him at odd hours of the day and night. I never knew what to make of it because when discussing it with Carl, he had informed me that he never met him either. Matt had told me Bob was about thirty-five and looked very much like his old lover, George. Well, now Bob had AIDS and was in the hospital and Matt would visit him at night, sometimes as late as eleven o'clock. I never understood how he was allowed to visit that late and he'd always tell me Bob had permission from the hospital, and I'd accept it.

I was a bit disturbed because Matt again was cutting an evening short going to the hospital, instead of making time to go at normal visiting hours. I couldn't fall asleep and it was already one in the morning. I decided upon checking to see if he was really going to the hospital, especially since I had previously waited in front of his apartment other times and once he returned at two in the morning, was told he had just come from there…. There had been several occasions Matt called in the wee hours of the morning complaining of being very sick, and I'd run to be with him. So I wanted to see if he'd do the same for me and faked being sick by leaving one desperate plea after another on his message machine. He wasn't returning my calls and I decided to drive by his place, and there was his car in the parking place and the lights on in his apartment. I decided against ringing the doorbell and went home to call again…but received the machine instead. I just sat there in a stupor, not wanting to believe he'd been out carousing…especially after the two days I thought as a new beginning? Two thirty arrived and my phone finally rang. I decided to let my machine take it since I had just left a message informing him that I was so ill that I was leaving for the hospital immediately. I heard Matt's voice say, "Rich, I am really worried about you. I hope everything is okay with you? Please call to let me know how you are?" And just before he hung up, I was sure I heard another voice call out, "Hey" or something to that effect. I was awake the entire night lying on my bed in a trance and he never called again until about seven in the morning, and I again did not answer.

What really bothered me was he never knew how sick I might be, or if I was lying dead at my place, and he just went on with whatever he was doing! I had included a key for my place in my Christmas gift and during the entire night, he never gave a thought to checking if I was still alive! It was well over an hour since the phone rang and I suddenly heard a key turn in my latch. I lay still in bed as he stood at the doorway calling out my name. He never approached and I felt he was afraid I may be dead. As it turned out, I was the one reprimanded for making him turn back while driving to work. I guess his conscience finally began working. That evening, we discussed it and I accepted what had to be one lie after another, which placed me again at square one.

Matt continued his late night visits to see Bob once we went into 1993, and I resumed my fruitless chases to find him, which really went into the wee hours of the morning. On one of such chases, I began drinking quite heavily and met Ron and Barry at the Hideaway, a couple we played cards with a few times. Ron was an avid follower of Matt, who seemed to idolize him. In fact, after leaving their house one evening, Matt had told me that Ron had been playing footsies with his crotch under the table,

"No wonder he was sitting so low in the chair?" Well, I finally had to leave the bar because everything began spinning and I did not want to collapse on the floor. The next thing I remembered was Matt nudging me as I lay passed out with my head on the steering wheel. I cannot recall our conversation, but this I do remember...Matt walking arrogantly away from the car and into the bar, leaving me to get home on my own! Somehow, a flying carpet must have got hold of my car to get me home!

The next day when I questioned Matt why he didn't ask Barry or Ron to follow him driving me home in order to return with them, I couldn't believe his response.

"Rich, I am not responsible for you...that *is* your problem." And I dropped it again to continue in my pursuit, especially after he managed to lay out some sweet bait.

All these outlandish acts on my part only caused Matt to refuse to go to the local bars during peak hours, also demanding I only drink soft drinks. Whenever visited by Vincent, I was told I could not be there, which only made me watch the house until the wee hours of the morning, once he left. I wondered how Matt was surviving since he arose before six in order to get to work! I'm sure it was at this time I realized I had to be hitting my head against a brick wall...that Matt would never change, and my depression became greater as my grieving for Juan increased. I wanted music and there was none around because as much as Matt liked to go to concerts, he seldom desired it on any radio, especially while driving. I wanted music and I wanted to dance, but Juan was gone and I felt I would never do it again. I couldn't understand how my life was so filled with music...and now suddenly it was gone? So I continued listening to the Spanish station whenever driving alone and I really seemed to feel Juan's presence.

My depression continued, and since my analyst couldn't prescribe drugs, I was referred to a psychiatrist in the hospital, but even with my loyal attendance and the Prozac she prescribed, I still continued to grieve. I began harboring a tremendous guilt since it was almost obvious I had deserted Juan for someone who really never wanted me. I wasn't improving and in fact, I was getting worse and my doctor asked if I wanted to be admitted into the hospital for observation. I refused, certainly not into a mental ward for fear I'd never be released.

I hadn't been seeing Amanda often, unless I stopped in her shop on the way to work or back, and once I quit my job because my nerves caused me to lose my temper and quit, it was even less. On one of her visits, we talked about my love for Juan and at the same time my feelings of love for Matt. I told her Juan was probably right when he kidded me about being a masochist because I let Matt get away with so much, even allowing him to ignore me in bed.

"Richard, I know you have repeatedly denied being a masochist and I truly don't believe you are. I just think you are someone who loves very deeply when you love someone! And you cannot believe anyone is truly bad. You loved Juan very deeply and there were times you let him take advantage of you…but Juan had a beautiful heart and really cared about 'your' feelings so I understand why you accepted it from him. You two should have never broken up because you had something special! And because of it, now that he is gone, you cannot get over his death. You then met Matt while Juan kept refusing to commit again. Then because Matt showed you some beautiful love in the beginning, you fell deeply in love with him. Even though Juan was number one in your life, and you realized that would never change, you still needed emotional and physical love. Matt gave you every impression he felt this way at the beginning and so you have clung to the hope he will again feel it is important, and so you let him abuse and batter you. I don't believe Matt has the beautiful heart Juan had, but I cannot say because I really don't know him that well. But from all I see, he only cares about himself…so, Richard, he may never feel that way about you again." She was very logical but I still had to see for myself.

A portion of the Names Quilt was being displayed at Loyola University on the far north side of Chicago for three days and my request to have Juan's included had been granted. I attended alone the first day and was accompanied by Geena the second because I had recently told her, besides Deena and Dino, that Juan had died of AIDS. My nephew, Dino, accompanied me on the last evening because he had become a wonderful support in my grieving. It was odd, but for all the years Juan and I went to the bars, we had never come across young Dino at any of them, and since, I had run into him several times. He was also supportive in my distress regarding Matt, even though he could not understand my logic in continuing with him.

Once I located Juan's quilt the first day, I went no further. It had been months since I gave it to the minister to take to Washington D.C. and it really affected me. I couldn't believe I was standing there looking at the quilt I made…and that it was in memory of Juan! In my grief, I tried to convince myself that he was gone, along with all the others whose names were memorialized on quilts…never to return again. I stared at the image I had sewn on of Juan dancing, my heart aching once I saw those arms of his raised in the inimitable way he had. And I cried out to him, "Aw, Juan, why did you have to die and stop all the music?

I probably had been there for over two hours, when a young gentleman approached to say a few words of comfort. He introduced himself as Bucci and told me he was from Nigeria and a seminary student at the university. He then went on to tell me in his distinct accent that he was one of the volunteers helping to comfort those grieving.

"Would you like to come to the lounge ond sit with me a while to talk, Recchard?" I agreed and he very politely asked, "Recchard, please have a seat, ond can I offer you some cookies ond coffee?" Again, I accepted and once he asked about Juan, I went on to tell him about my grief and the unique relationship we had. We talked for some time and I discovered Bucci to be very comforting and sincerely compassionate as he spoke so eloquently.

"Recchard, you have to believe thot you will one day see Juan again, and when thot happens, your life together will only begin," and as he handed me a book, he went on to say, "here, I want you to take this book of psalms and read the passages I have marked. I think you will then be comforted enough to realize Juan did not die in vain."

I then explained the situation with Matt…his selfishness…his split personality…his coldness…his carousing, and the guilt I was bearing since everything I did now seemed in vain.

"Recchard, I myself had many, many problems when I was much younger. I was very bad…very bad indeed, and all I ever thought of was myself. I took advantage of girls…not caring about their feelings. Believe me, Recchard, I was very bad and never thought I was doing wrong. Then, suddenly, I realized there was a better life out there…that what I was doing was indeed wrong. My selfishness kept me from thinking they were wrong. Then, something happened to me and I somehow found God. Thot was when I discovered other people had feelings, too. Do you understand what I am saying, Recchard?" I shrugged my shoulders in an uncertain manner as he went on to assure and convince me, "thot everyone is not all bad, Recchard…thot there is also good in everyone…it just has to be helped out, and 'I' was helped by someone. You must be patient ond be there for this Matt, and the goodness will come out one day."

It had been refreshing to meet someone like Bucci…someone so compassionate and understanding. I never saw him again, but he called on several occasions to be sure I was doing well and to give some words of encouragement.

Even though I realized my Don Quixote nature gave Matt every benefit of a doubt, I began thinking of what Bucci had said, that maybe he had this goodness buried deep inside and I should try to help bring it out. I talked with Matt about what Bucci had said and even though he didn't outwardly admit his wickedness he still managed some words.

"See, Rich, everyone is not all bad, so I do have some good in me." So I began thinking that maybe he did realize I was someone special…someone he didn't want to lose. It especially was apparent whenever I decided upon ending whatever we had. He never seemed to want me call it all off.

"You leave now, Rich, and you're history," was what I'd hear each time. And since he excelled in heavy discussions, I'd change my mind. So I always figured there had to be a hidden love for me...that it would eventually surface.

I always thought I was beginning to break the barrier whenever I reminded him, "Matt, you don't realize what you have in me...the years have taught me loyalty to the person I am committed to, because I have learned from my many mistakes. I now realize when you love someone so much and their life is more important than yours...then you do not want to chance losing that person by carousing around for extra excitement." At the same time, I'd assure him, "Matt, even if we never become lovers, I'll always be there for you." I really felt he couldn't control himself because of his inability to love and that he needed my help, often commenting, "One day you will be sorry, Matt."

I almost felt my relationship with Matt was one of love-hate, especially since my anger while chasing after him during his mystery outings found me desperately crying out to myself that the wrong person got AIDS!" This would only continue my depression and guilt...feeling I truly caused Juan stress by refusing to discontinue seeing Matt...and now it seemed all in vain!

I kept running into my nephew, Dino, at the bars each time I was out in pursuit of Matt and he always turned out to be supportive once the music brought on the joy I was so fortunate to receive from Juan, and my guilt would torture me. My sister, Deena, had brought up Dino in a good religious home and he felt as I always had...that there is no such thing as being promiscuous once you are attached to someone. And he certainly couldn't understand my persistence in continuing on with Matt.

"Uncle Rich, why don't you get involved in some groups and meet people instead of chasing after a dream?"

As I had mentioned, Matt always seemed to tip me off whenever he had a date with someone. Evidently, his sexual excitement always managed to betray him. Suddenly, out of the clear blue sky, he'd sigh something like...you know what I love, Rich? I love to be in bed nude with someone, drinking wine and smoking. I think it is so sexy!" This was my first knowledge of this desire, but it did make me realize something had to be brewing in the near future.

I had never made lasagna for Matt, probably since it was Juan's favorite and I felt as though I'd be betraying him. I finally decided there had to be no more hatred where Juan was...that he had to forgive by understanding Matt's problems. So I informed him I'd make it for Easter. However, Matt insisted we go out instead, and I said no more.

I had just begun working part time cutting hair again and excused myself from a customer to call Matt to see what he wanted to do that evening because it was the Saturday before Easter, which I always considered special. He was in a hurry and said I should call as soon as I got home, to plan something. He was in very high spirits when I called.

"Rich, I have one problem tonight because my cousins who live downstate called to let me know they were coming up tonight to see the early night game at Sox Park and they asked if they could stop by for a visit after to see all my collectibles." I couldn't hide my disappointment.

"That doesn't mean we can't have dinner together, Rich. In fact, I will take you to dinner!" I accepted but explained how I had wanted to go to the new piano bar opened by the old owners of Dandy's. "Well, Rich, we can still go to one of the bars in the neighborhood after dinner for a while." *Yeah*, I thought, *when the place is empty!* But he was so up…so accommodating…that I had to go along with him.

Matt continued his 'up' mood once he arrived and I couldn't believe how charming he was. He was almost the same as when we first began going out. He was so happy and excited when he handed me an Easter basket filled with little chickens and goodies, along with a couple of other gift wrapped boxes. I was overwhelmed and touched receiving all this attention and didn't want to believe it was only to appease me for not being able to spend the entire evening with me. But then again, that was fine, too, because it showed he cared, which was better than Greeks bearing gifts. He then caught me off balance.

"So we're gonna have lasagna dinner tomorrow…right, Rich! That will be great!" I decided not to remind him he declined the offer, especially since he seemed to be looking so forward to it. I'd just have to do my shopping late this evening.

We sat in an empty bar after dinner and Matt continued to be very up…in fact almost as though he was excited about something. Then, it occurred to me…he didn't seem to be concerned as to how far the Sox were into the game to be sure he'd be home for his cousins. He could have checked by asking the bartender to put the game on television, but it didn't seem to matter. It was as though he knew exactly the time his three cousins would be at his house. A thought passed my mind…possibly, it was someone else coming over, and immediately, I remembered the wine and smoking! I was positive this was what was about to happen and my insides were sick.

Immediately after he cheerfully dropped me off, I got into my car and sped for his house in another direction. I was determined to find out once and for all if he was lying to me, because I wanted this to be the last time I would ever chase after him! Matt's apartment was near the corner, so I parked on the cross street in a spot I often did to watch the front of his building in order not to be seen. The game had been over for some time and still three people never approached his building. I finally decided to drive to an outside phone, which was only about a block away to call and once I asked if they had arrived, he immediately said that they got there about half an hour ago and that they loved his collections. I stood there for a moment in shock, knowing darn well his cousins weren't there and would never arrive, and his real guest could possibly not be there for some time. One thing that was certain, Matt wouldn't answer the phone if he had a guest over for sex, and would prefer to wait patiently alone for someone he was hot to trot. I was also not sure whether the person would enter from the front entrance or the rear since his friend, Vincent, always went up his back steps. I really didn' want to think this was true…that

Matt could have cared less about Juan when he repeatedly assured me he did not trick around while he was dating someone…forcing me to continue with him against Juan's wishes! In my stupor, I decided upon going on with the dinner. Ask me why?… I have no idea!

It took me some time to shop because I kept talking to myself incoherently. I finally decided upon giving Matt one more chance, and when I called, he said his cousins were still there. I then said they were probably going to leave soon because they have a long drive to get home, and why couldn't I come over after and do something special because he always hates to waste Saturdays?" But he insisted he was too tired and wanted to go to bed as soon as they left. Yeah, I thought, with his guest!

How I managed to make my sauce and prepare the lasagna, I will never know! However, I couldn't relax and decided to head towards Matt's again. It was past midnight and his living room lights were still lit. I decided to ring his doorbell, especially since I could be a friend just stopping by late on a Saturday night. He never answered and after making a call from that same outside phone, only to receive his machine, I drove back again to find his living room dark. I was livid, realizing I had to get proof tonight, and decided upon going up the rear steps to peer through his kitchen window. So there I was standing in the same spot Juan had been that time, and I was doing the same…spying. It was after one and if Matt was asleep, the place would be dark. But instead, the lights of the kitchen and the dining room were dimmed very low and this is how Matt liked them when he was feeling romantic. And, suddenly, as I peered through the window, there on the kitchen counter, I saw an opened bottle of wine!

I sat on the couch like a zombie the rest of the night and at sunrise thought of returning to his house, but after a moment realized he would never answer the doorbell. I was anxious to see how he'd react once he saw me since he had to realize I was the one calling and ringing his doorbell! Instead, I decided upon waiting for the supermart to open…to then buy a small Easter plant, which would give me an excuse to stop by so early in the morning. Being the shrewd detective that I was, I decided to go the back way in case he may be in the kitchen for water or juice as he often did, and he'd be forced to open the door once he saw me through the window.

This was exactly what happened, because as I rang the doorbell, he was entering the kitchen clad only in his briefs…and he had to let me in! Nothing was mentioned about the phone calls or the doorbell, and I decided not to say anything myself. It was apparent he was savoring the evening and not wanting to spoil it by fighting with me. There they were as my eyes scanned the kitchen…an empty bottle of wine lying in the trash basket…and two wine glasses and a dirty ashtray sitting in the sink! I didn't say a word as a strange feeling of relief came over me. He had to think I was some sort of idiot to think he was putting something over on me. But I guess I was some sort of idiot anyway. If that wasn't enough proof, once I used his bathroom, I peered into his bedroom and there on the messed up bed, along with his pillows…was mine, which was always stored in the closet. I didn't say anything, even after I walked into the kitchen and he used the bathroom, and once I returned to his bedroom to talk, found my pillow suddenly missing. I realized I HAD FINALLY CAUGHT HIM…NOT IN THE ACT, BUT WITH PROOF ENOUGH! I then sadly thought about how it was two years too late.

I decided to go through with the dinner…it was too sacred a day to spoil by discussing Matt's sexual sicknesses. I went through the motions with a fixed smile, realizing Juan was right again…that Matt was the whore of the town, and everything I did was in vain.

I had to settle everything once and for all and invited Matt for leftover lasagna Monday night, and after dinner, approached him with the entire business. He was actually shocked I brought it up since he evidently thought he had put one over on me again! He stubbornly refused to discuss it and stormed out in a huff! I really think he was still savoring his sexual delights, not wanting me to spoil it with my angry tones. This certainly had to be the first time he didn't want to discuss the problem in order to change my mind.

I managed to get together with him at his apartment during the week and he finally easily admitted to his Saturday evening affair. I was informed that he met Lon at the bar…that he also reminded him of George.

"Looks like anyone that looks like your last lover, George, can expect to have an affair with you!"

He then said there was nothing serious between the two of them…that Lon had a lover who did not satisfy him in sex, which brought a disgusted nod of my head.

"But I love having sex with him and I am gonna continue having it anytime I can!" Finally, he admitted to having sex with others throughout our relationship, "but, Rich, not as many times as you may think." I glared at him despairingly.

"Matt, it does not matter how many…all that matters is you have lied to me continually! And Matt, sometimes that can even be accepted if a person knows they are truly loved by someone who needs these extra affairs?" I then stared directly into his eyes and asked, "Matt, do you love me as I have loved you? In fact, have you *ever* loved me in that way?" Suddenly, an expression of embarrassment came over him. Almost as though he felt cornered!

"Rich, I love you very much," and after some hesitation, "but I haven't loved you like that…I don't think I ever have." I sat there in shock…NOT WANTING TO BELIEVE WHAT I JUST HEARD! HE HAD PRESSED ME CONTINUALLY WHILE JUAN WAS LIVING…AND NOW HE IS FINALLY TELLING ME THIS? I just continued staring in disbelief, trying desperately to grasp onto what he just told me! I glared out into space and back again to him, trying to somehow utter some sounds, finally managing to overcome the terrible catch in my throat.

"Matt, why didn't you tell me? I continuously asked you for the truth, and you assured me that was what you were telling me? MATT, WHY DID YOU MAKE ME BELIEVE WE WERE WORKING ON A

RELATIONSHIP…THAT THE POSSIBILITY TO BE LOVERS WAS SOMETHING YOU WERE STRIVING FOR…WHY DID YOU CONTINUE TO KEEP ME HANGING? I DON'T UNDERSTAND!"

"I felt funny about telling you, Rich. I thought it would happen one day." I continued glaring at him in total disbelief, trying desperately to comprehend his logic. To actually think he felt 'funny' to tell me…but that it didn't bother him knowing he was causing Juan so much stress! He didn't care if Juan lived or died! I could not believe anyone could be this selfish…to keep me around just for his own convenience! Just to have the satisfaction of beating out Juan! How could anyone have so much hatred? He had to be sick, and I had to be sicker for not listening to everyone and giving him every chance to prove his love! The conversation continued and is a total blank, but even though I remember realizing it was finally over with him, I still didn't realize the scope of what he had just confessed to…and somehow why I did not spit in his face!

I was ravaged after that evening and after much time and thought, I realized this man had to have a terrible sickness…and because he denied it totally, he desperately needed help to truly realize what he had actually done. I had to overcome this hatred I was feeling because I never felt this way in my life, and I didn't like it! I decided to accept him as a friend…that maybe he could fill some of the void in my life, and at the same time finally realize what he had done to Juan. At first, I was hesitant but then there was so much forgiveness in my heart that I knew I had to help him. Juan was gone and if I deserted Matt, it wasn't going to bring him back. After all, there had to be no more hatred in Juan and he had to realize Matt's problem and respect me for being there for him.

My mind was finally at ease in my discovery that my feelings for Matt were no longer what I had imagined for so long…because I didn't love him! But I needed a friend as much as he. At the same time, I knew I would never love anyone in that way again…that I would only add to my pocket of empty tricks. I felt certain that I'd never find anyone to fill my heart as Juan did…that mold had been broken and if I tried with someone else, I'd only start comparing.

So Matt and I became friends, meaning we needed other friends.

Wally had always been receptive to socialize, so once he called to ask if I liked to play Canasta, I accepted and brought Matt along. Matt seemed to look forward to our Canasta nights, even suggesting I call to get together if I hadn't heard from Wally. However, my resentment towards Matt continued and would brew uncontrollably at times. So it took a great deal of work on my part to make this friendship something worthwhile. I will also admit to eventually having occasional sex with him…but only as an outlet. Never did they mean any more than adding to that pocket of mine. This is not to say he didn't try to once again get me in fold, and when he'd mention how horny he was, I'd merely remind him to call one of his "old friendly tricks." I had finally put him in the right place in my life, which only added to my depression and guilt, realizing I was two years too late.

I continued seeing the psychiatrist, trying to get some explanation why I was so much like the character I played on stage? Was Don Quixote and I one and the same person?

I had told Matt I would always be there for him as a friend when he needed me, and he began calling late at night whenever he was bothered with someone in his family, or did not feel well.

Matt then began experiencing severe cramps in his abdomen and would call, begging me to come over. I would oblige, trying to soothe him by rubbing his belly. However, this usually led to having sex and I was confused if his pains were only sex urges because he hadn't been successful in picking up someone at the bar that evening?

In the beginning of June, his doctor ordered an upper GI and I accompanied him to the hospital for the test. However, his doctor never called with the results and I insisted he call instead. He was told everything was fine but was very confused because he still was experiencing cramps after a meal.

It was very apparent Matt was bothered because I was not pursuing him for sex, even though it was apparent he appreciated my friendship. I needed a friend and I tried to explain this to him, but I knew he was looking for more, and that was probably to get me in the fold once more…and that certainly would never happen again! I had been able to be myself with Daniel by constantly kidding him about the whore he was, and now I finally was able to do the same with Matt. He never appreciated it, but I felt if he was going to accept my friendship, he'd need to know I always spoke the truth.

I kept my depression and guilt regarding Juan to myself. Unless I had to hurry somewhere in the mornings, it was very difficult to get myself out of bed. I felt if I was asleep, the reality that Juan was not around would be lost. The bed was some sort of refuge. I began to write the story of my life with Juan and it almost felt that he was there guiding my words.

Matt was still complaining of occasional abdominal pains after eating, never sure what was causing it since it was so erratic. He called the third week in June.

"Rich, I'd really like for you to come over to be with me because I really haven't been feeling well at all." I insisted he call his doctor, but he kept putting it off, and this bewildered me since he usually went in for a checkup every three months. In fact, he was a health fanatic, so why was he hesitating?

He claimed to be feeling fine once I arrived, but said it was only because he didn't eat anything. I tried convincing him he had to eat, just not anything greasy. However, he didn't really want to discuss it because his motive for asking me over was then apparent once he nervously asked just what our real relationship was. He had asked this same question many times, but in different ways and each time, I told him exactly how I felt.

"Matt, I have told you many times…we are friends and that is all! Good friends, because I need one as much as you do! But that is all it is. I have finally realized you never loved me and it has finally made my feelings for you completely disappear! You are finally in the right place in my life and you should be happy about it since you never wanted the other…and I am also happy about it." I continued explaining everything in detail again but it was apparent he didn't want to accept it, continuing on with his nervousness. But I did not care! I now realized it was over with him and I wasn't going to allow it to happen again!

Matt finally agreed to eat something, but when he chose a Granny Smith apple, I objected since it wouldn't be a good digestive thing. But he insisted and after a half hour, he was once again having abdominal pains, and they progressively got worse. I tried to convince him to call his doctor, but he continually refused. He finally pleaded for me to stay the night and I agreed only if he'd call the doctor or go to the emergency room in the morning should his pains persist The pains didn't cease and he finally gave me the home number of his doctor, who was a friend of his. However, it was past midnight and upon calling, I encountered a rather disturbed 'friend' for waking him so late at night…quickly hanging up after telling me to take him to an emergency room. But again, Matt refused and was especially hurt because his 'friend' gave me such a curt answer, besides not insisting he talk with him.

I am not sure whether Matt's pains had subsided or not, but I was taken completely by surprise once he amorously laid his head on my stomach. He continued to surprise me once he lowered my shorts and began to give me oral sex. . I felt a bit uncomfortable, realizing his motive…but then accepted it for what I wanted it to be…one to add to my pocket.

Even though he was feeling fine the next morning, I insisted he call work to tell them he would not be coming in…that we were going to the Maple Park Hospital emergency room even though his doctor did not practice there. What followed was a nightmare! The CAT scan taken diagnosed a large mast in the lower bowel area…suspected to be a malignant tumor! Matt had always been deathly afraid of the word "cancer", since his mother had died from it shortly after his birth. He was devastated, especially since he had been such a health addict, never really experiencing a headache in all of his life!

Matt was very well loved by his colleagues at work and I understood since he always reminded me that he did not fuck where he ate. His diagnosis almost appeared to be national news, bombarded with calls, cards, and flowers, along with constant visitors upon being immediately admitted into the hospital. All of them pleaded with him to go to the Houston Cancer Clinic, but he wouldn't heed their advice, which was the first wrong decision made. The house doctors—Moss, an oncologist, and Montage',, a surgeon— assigned to Matt were supposed to be tops…that is, according to a couple of staff nurses at the same hospital. Along with his sexual attraction for Dr. Moss, he consented to go along with their insistence to have a major biopsy operation in order to know how to properly treat it should it prove to be cancerous. And they felt almost sure that it was. All of his colleagues as well as myself and his daughter, Terri, pleaded with him to get a second opinion. Even Carl, who had lost his wife to cancer and was well read on cancer insisted, but Matt refused.

"I trust my doctors, and they are supposed to be the best!" I thought, *What else would these nurses say if they valued their jobs?*

I became very confused because Matt latched onto me as though we were lovers, expecting to have me there constantly. Every time I left, he insisted I return quickly. Of course, Vincent was there, but he still asked me to return immediately. Carl and Frank were also supportive and I had expected it since Carl had been a close friend. However, I really commended Carl's loyalty in spite of a sorry bit of news I heard when I joined them for dinner the evening before surgery. They had been aware of the problems I was having with Matt, not yet knowing I was finally over him, and after telling them, Carl told me the bit of news.

"What do you think of a friend who propositions your lover?" I was then told that on a couple of our pinochle sessions, as we were about to leave, that Matt, while hugging Frank, had whispered in his ear to call him sometime to get together! How do you like that for a friend?" It didn't surprise me since I already knew Matt had no scruples or morals when it came to getting sex.

Surgery was scheduled for seven thirty in the morning and Matt had asked for me to be there, along with his daughter, Terri, who was taking the day off. I felt a bit awkward since he was practically labeling me as his lover to everyone, which wouldn't have bothered me if that were the case. However, it no longer interested me, but I realized this was no time to upset him and was there early enough to see him wheeled into the elevator. It was a long wait and I wondered why his daughter had not yet arrived when it was almost one o'clock. Carl had called and left messages to call him to be updated, but no word from Terri. I suddenly glanced out the front entrance of the lobby to finally see Terri sauntering up the staircase, sipping casually on a soft drink. Alongside her were her roommate and mother. Her manner was as though she was out window shopping and I couldn't believe she had taken off work and was only now arriving, and at a snail's pace at that. After hearing her dad was still in surgery, she asked his room number and left with the others to make some calls. It was almost as though she was going to a party because the fact that her father had been in surgery over four and a half hours didn't faze her whatsoever.

As soon as they left, *I* was the one called by the surgeon to be informed of a mass as large as a cantaloupe touching the lymph glands and the colon...and that it was so entangled with his organs that it was impossible to remove except for the portions needed for the biopsies. He explained that it appeared to have been growing for at least eight or nine months and certainly had to be cancerous.

"But we will know once the biopsy report comes through." He didn't seem to have many encouraging words to say except that you can never tell and we just had to have faith in God. I realized if Matt knew it was spreading, he would lose all hope and I begged the doctor not to tell him it had spread to vital organs.

"Because as long as he knows it is cancerous and that it is very large…he will know it is something serious, Doctor." The doctor said if he asked he would have to tell him.

It was confirmed by the oncologist to be a Lymphoma cancer and that if you have any cancer…that is the one to have because it is the most treatable. Six chemo treatments three weeks apart were scheduled and would begin as soon as Matt recovered from the surgery. When I arrived the next morning, I asked the surgeon what he told him.

"He did not ask, so I did not tell him.' It was difficult for me to believe this after Matt had badgered us so much, but I accepted his answer.

Suddenly, Matt thought I was the sun…and the moon…and the stars, even preferring my company to Vincent or his children. In fact, he wanted me to be with him constantly.

"I can only take them for so long, Rich…I want to be with you." He then told me he loved me, adding, "Maybe we can work on that relationship again, Rich. Since I have come down with cancer, I feel different and I am sure I want to spend my life with you." I cannot say the thought of him using me didn't pass my mind because it most certainly did! It was obvious he wanted to be sure I'd be there to care for him…I'm also sure he was thinking of the caretaker I was for Juan. I must say he did have a way of appearing so sincere! However, there was no way I could bring myself to refuse and say these things when he was so ill. I was certain I could never love him again.

"Matt, no matter what, I'll be there for you and take care of you to be sure you get well." But he wanted more…he wanted to be lovers.

"But I don't expect you to accept now. I just want us to be lovers once I lick this thing and am well. I will prove to you then that I do love you!"

"Matt, we'll see…okay?" and he was satisfied.

Matt asked me to continue driving his car while he was recuperating. He realized since my Prizm was sold because I couldn't keep up the payments that I couldn't always rely on Juan's car with over a hundred thousand miles on it. I wanted to drive to Brown County, Indiana, in honor of Juan's birthday on the twenty-fourth, and I didn't want to take Matt's car on such a long trip unless I asked first, and he willingly obliged. I decided upon asking Geena to come with me and she agreed. My intention, at the same time, was to finally tell her the truth about my relationship with Juan. She had to know, because, since realizing my capability at capturing the unique character of Juan in his remarkable story…that it had to be published, and I certainly wouldn't want her shocked once she read it. Yes, I was going to finally do something I swore I would never do, and that was to tell her and Deena, along with my kids…and I felt that was all they needed to know.

It was a very hot and humid day as we sat on the picnic bench at Hesitation Point. The last time I saw Endira the evening I needed to sign the release, she had told me this was the area Juan's ashes had been spread. It then came to me that this was the place I took a picture of Juan, also recalling his statement saying he could stay at this spot forever. We had just had a piece of the birthday cake I had saved and frozen from the party I gave Juan in the hospital. The day had been very emotional for me and my emotions were also affecting Geena. I finally attempted to get up enough nerve to tell her, and by her expressions, it was apparent she knew what I was about to say. But I still couldn't bring myself to tell her I was gay! I struggled desperately but I finally managed to tell her without using the word "gay." I cannot recall my exact words, but she began crying very audibly, taking hold of my hand despairingly.

"Rich, I was afraid you were going to tell me something and I didn't really want to come today! We all knew you were carrying on too much about Juan's death, and that it was more than just a good friendship…but I didn't want to admit to it. I even wondered about the initials, JR, as the prefix on his car license plate…and because the car was in your name, we figured you picked those initials because they were the first letters of your names." She continued holding tightly to my hand, crying uncontrollably.

"Geena, that only was a coincidence…and to tell you the truth, I never realized it." She continued holding tight while crying.

"Rich, I love you very much and I don't understand how this happens…because I don't understand it? But I love you and will always love you!"

It had been a very touching but beautiful day because I knew I didn't have to hide the love I had for Juan anymore. My tears continued that afternoon and Geena finally seemed to relax and accept my story.

"Juan had to have been the luckiest person in the world to have someone love him as much as you do, Rich." I smiled but I knew I had to be the luckiest person for having Juan love me as he did. And Geena has continually made sure I know how much she loves me, because to this day, whenever we talk or part, she tells me she loves me. So I am the luckiest person in this world because after another emotional meeting with my daughter Jacque, and then Deena and Dino, I again have had the same assurance of love and support.

I was very apprehensive about telling my sons since they were men…not sure how they'd accept it. However, I was greatly surprised once I got up enough nerve to tell Nicky to receive complete understanding and love. And to even hear him tell me I had to now lay Juan to rest.

"And, Dad, why don't you find someone to be with now? You can't continue to grieve over Juan, and besides, knowing Juan, I know he'd kick your ass and tell you to get on with your life!"

Unfortunately, every time I tried to tell Mike, something would come up and I'd not be able to discuss it. I was also worried about upsetting him because he was having such a hard time with his finances since his divorce, and it was almost impossible to keep him still long enough to tell him. I also hesitated in telling Martina because she was expecting her third baby, and Jacque thought I should wait. I had thought she realized it from her conversation on the phone with Endira, but now I wasn't sure…unless she tried to avoid talking of it to protect me? Somehow, due to the chain of events,

I have never approached either of them about it, but I am certain they both know because of another happening I could write a book about.

Matt was being released from the hospital on a Saturday, and besides having to work that day, I had a family function going on at night.

"Well, Rich," Matt said once I informed him of the function, "I can have Vince pick me up and stay with me, but can you please come and spend the night? I really want you to be with me all night." I had already told him I'd stay over a few nights to a week to get him oriented at home, so I agreed to be there afterwards.

I wasn't out as late as I thought and once I arrived at his place, I decided not to ring the doorbell in case he was asleep. He had given me his keys when he went into the hospital and I tried to turn them as quietly as possible in order not to awaken him because his bedroom was immediately in front of the front door. Matt's bed was in full view as I opened the door, and to my shock, I was confronted with his totally nude body except for the binding around his abdomen, sleeping! There was no reason he should be naked and it still would be okay, but there beside him on the bed was Vincent, sleeping but fully clothed! Suddenly, Vincent awakened and clumsily scrambled to rise, trying desperately to hold his balance. Besides being shocked, I was embarrassed and decided the only thing to do was leave. So I immediately apologized and went out the door, closing it quickly. What he did with Vincent or anyone else shouldn't have mattered to me since we no longer were involved in a relationship. However, it bothered me since I didn't think I should've been subjected to a front seat. It was somewhat disturbing since Matt had presumably poured his heart out to me? So I went out and got drunk.

Once I returned home, I discovered Matt had filled my answering device with one message after another, pleading for me to come back, and the calls even continued throughout the night, but I refused to answer. I realized he was telling one lie after another once I did answer in the morning, but gave assurance I'd keep my promise to stay with him for the week. Matt tried to make me feel ashamed for not being with him the first night he returned from the hospital, but I refused to allow him to succeed in doing so.

"Matt, Vincent was here with you and I didn't want to intrude on your privacy."

"Rich, I just got home from the hospital after a major operation, so how could I have sex? And besides, I have told you repeatedly that I have never had sex with Vince! Look at him? Do you think I'd have sex with him?" I shook my head despairingly.

"Matt, it really doesn't matter to me. That's your business." Yet I truly don't understand because he's so repulsive and it makes me sick even to think of it!"

"Rich, I just got home from a serious operation…why would I want sex?" I just glared at him.

"Matt, I believe you'd have sex on your deathbed if you had the chance!"

I really didn't get much sleep that night because he kept waking me throughout the night roaming audibly throughout the apartment. Even though he had no problem sleeping while lying flat in his bed after Vincent serviced him, he complained it was impossible when he went to sleep for the night. It was over a week and I finally told him, for my own health, I had to return home to sleep in my own bed. I assured him I'd come every morning to prepare breakfast and do the same for dinner. Vincent came almost every afternoon, but he still couldn't be with Matt all the time because his wife also had cancer. However, I sometimes thought he was with Matt more than his wife. He'd take his laundry home to wash and occasionally fix him one of his specialty dishes and always was sure to let me know it was only for Matt once he handed me the dish, like I'd relish eating his cooking.

So it began…Matt took hold of me and wouldn't let go. Besides driving to his place each morning to make breakfast, I had to do it again for dinners. He wanted me there constantly and even though I felt he needed exercise badly, he still refused to do anything to help himself…even refusing to walk to the bathroom to urinate. So I'd be emptying the urinal constantly. Vincent, however, wouldn't agree that Matt needed to exercise and would wait on him hand and foot every time he was there. And Matt expected me to do the same…and I was there the majority of time. Inwardly, it was eating away at me since I never intended to be his Florence Nightingale. It even provoked him to think I went to work for only three hours to cut hair. It didn't matter that I sometimes made as much as fifty or sixty dollars, which I needed badly. I also wouldn't hesitate in voicing my disturbance about his kids not offering to help except for a one-hour visit once a week! And it irritated me more because he refused to ask them to be there for him! On one such evening, when I clearly expressed my anger, Vincent happened to be there and dumbfounded me when in his hot potato-filled voice, he garbled his opinion.

"Well, we Anglo-Saxons do not expect that of our children!"

What did he think I was?…an Italian scum because I expected family to do something for their 'loved' ones! The absence of his children was especially eating away at me because it was still very vivid in my mind how Matt constantly voiced his complaints because Svetmana wasn't with Juan as much as I…that she should be there for him! And she was probably with Juan ten times more than Matt's kids. Even when I said that they should be with him…just to be with him…he still never asked.

Matt pleaded for me to accompany him to his chemo sessions and again I obliged. The treatments were proving to be successful, especially since the tumor had shrunk to a tenth of the original size after just one treatment. Matt was elated and even though he began losing most of his hair, he was too happy to allow it to bother him. He just went out and bought a very expensive wig from someone Vincent suggested, the same person who had made one for his wife. It was too much hair, and probably originally a woman's wig. It was nothing like his own and even though his daughter felt he looked ridiculous, he was satisfied and continued to wear it. So I never said a word because he was happy with it and felt that was what mattered. He continued with the treatments and was told he could finally return to work on a part time basis in August. He was so happy since it was the beginning of their new year and he had planned on retiring at the end of it.

Matt's weight still hadn't returned to normal, realizing it would be some time after his sessions before that would happen. So he accepted it. With this slow improvement, he stopped talking about our relationship, and, in fact completely forgot he even suggested we work on it again once I casually mentioned it! I said no more since I realized I'd never again allow that scenario to happen to me anyway. Yes, it was very apparent Matt was a man who knew how to keep things convenient…for himself. So I continued spending all my off time with him…still preparing dinners at times, and driving him on trips he felt were too long to do alone. And he resumed stopping off alone at the bars after work for a soft drink or two…or whatever?

Then the balloon exploded…Dr. Moss was on vacation and when Matt was examined after his fourth treatment by the very young associate in the clinic, he completely ignored the doctor's suspicion that a strange growth seemed to be felt in his abdomen. In fact, he was extremely disturbed with him and once Moss returned, he informed him that he didn't want to be examined again by his associate. Moss didn't confirm the same once he felt his abdomen after the fifth treatment, which only confirmed Matt's decision about the associate doctor. He had been convinced he had the best doctor! However, shortly after that treatment, he began experiencing abdominal pains again after he had eaten, and upon being examined by both Dr. Moss and the surgeon, Dr. Montage, they were certain the tumor was again growing at a tremendous pace. Precious time had been lost since the associate doctor told Matt of his suspicion. Because now a CAT scan was taken, revealing a very large mass in the abdomen! The surgeon didn't want to operate again but was overruled by Moss. He insisted it needed to be done and left it to Matt for consent.

Matt asked for my opinion and I quickly explained that it had to be his decision…that I couldn't make it for him. Before he told me his decision, I was certain what it would be. He confirmed my belief once he said he'd go with the wishes of his oncologist. However, he realized I wasn't in favor once he looked at my face.

"Matt, I don't know why he wants to have you cut up again? They already know the mass is there from the CAT scan? They couldn't remove it last time!"

"Well, Dr. Montage did say he might be able to perform a bypass of the bowels that are blocked." I couldn't say more…he had made up his mind.

I arrived early the day of the operation, and again, none of his children were present. My fears of a quick open and closed operation were confirmed once I was called to the surgical lounge within the hour. The prognosis wasn't good! The mass was the size of a soccer ball and intertwined through his organs. After quietly asking if a bypass had been performed, the doctor sort of hesitated then quickly said that he had. I wondered how it was managed in so short a time?

Matt's condition began going down very quickly, losing more weight. The new incision was so badly performed that it wouldn't heal and puss continued to flow from certain areas. He was so completely obsessed with his illness, and especially with his appearance.

"Rich, look at me! I look like an AIDS patient!" And I guess he did, but he had originally been tested for the HIV virus in suspicion of an AIDS-related Lymphoma…but results were negative. Juan had been an AIDS patient, but once his eyes went still forever, you would have never known…he looked beautiful.

Matt's wonderful oncologist insisted he wasn't giving up, recommending three choices for other treatments, which would begin after he had recuperated from this last useless operation. Matt decided to go with a bone marrow transplant instead of another type of chemo or radiation, which meant he'd need to go to a major hospital. But he still needed to gain back some of his strength and this was going slowly because of his problems eating. His weight continued to go down until he eventually looked like a walking skeleton. He didn't walk that much so he'd sit in his lounge chair, almost resembling a ghoul. Matt and I had been taken for brothers many times, and now there was no resemblance because one would think he was in his nineties. Even though the doctor explained the risks, he still thought there was every hope and since he realized time was of the essence, set sights for admittance shortly before Christmas with the transplant just before that date. Matt's blood was otherwise very healthy, so a donor wasn't needed…they could use his own. A series of radiation treatments prior to actual admittance were required, which took Matt by surprise since it wasn't mentioned at the initial meeting. He wasn't pleased.

I was then pressured to make a decision I never thought he'd dare to ask, once he begged to stay at my house until admitted into the hospital. I hesitated, only to hear him cry, finally realizing I had promised to be there for him and it would be much easier than running back and forth, especially since he'd certainly be calling daily to prepare meals along with other things. However, after a couple of weeks at my house, his sister called, offering to come in town to take care of him for about five days and he agreed to return home, yet still insisting I be there for every dinner and anytime he knew I wasn't working.

A Hickman was then connected since he had to receive so many blood transfusions, and this again increased my depression, bringing back the many times I watched Juan change the dressing. Yet I did my crying alone, knowing my depression wouldn't help Matt.

Matt then threw me for another loop, begging to live with me once his transplant was completed, and we had been informed the recuperation period could last a year or more? I couldn't believe he actually expected this of me? Yet I had to hide these feelings since the slightest hesitation would have him crying uncontrollably. I finally appeased him somewhat.

"We'll see, Matt, once you are in the hospital…we'll talk about it."

Just before his sister arrived, I had it out with Vincent once he called to inquire about Matt. I decided upon bluffing him by inquiring why he had continued having sex with Matt when he was completely aware that we were supposedly working on a relationship at the time. He finally cleared up a matter I had wondered about for so long once he answered in his usual arrogant, mush-mash voice.

"That is between Matt and me!" And if that was not enough, he continued his nasty arrogance until I finally lost my temper to say he no longer would be welcome at my house should Matt return, even while I was in the house!

Matt was well aware that my loyalty to him was only platonic, yet he continually questioned me about our relationship and upon hearing me repeat it again, would cry out.

"Then there is no hope of ever loving me again," he would say, finally crying hopelessly. I realized he couldn't be allowed to continue in this depression. I had to appease him and decided to assure him that he had every hope I'd one day love him again…all he had to do was get better…and then show me he loved me. I had no fear here since realizing once he was better, his feelings would be the same as always. But I wanted him to get better…for himself! I was certain it was over for us…but it possibly could give me some satisfaction just knowing he finally had realized how cold, cruel, and ruthless he had always been, and repent. He looked at me pleadingly, tears rolling.

"Oh, Richard, I love you so much, and I pray to God that He gives me a chance to prove it to you! Oh, I pray He does, Richard, because I love you so much!" And I wanted to believe since he needed that to get better…to believe in himself and mean it! I did think to ask about Vincent and he again denied any sexual encounters, which caused me to lose my temper.

"Matt, will you finally stop lying! You have cancer and you are battling for your life! Aw, God, STOP LYING ONCE AND FOR ALL!" He stood silent, a grave expression on his face at the realization…and said no more.

Matt entered the hospital about a week before his scheduled time, having terrible pains. It was the last night his sister was to be with him and she called a short while after I had left to ask me to return again. The two of us sat in the emergency room while he was having his blood tests…she cried in bewilderment.

"Oh, I cannot understand why Terri and Randy are not here! They should be the ones taking care of their father…my children would be here for me."

I remained in a terrible depression throughout the holiday season, constantly reminded of Juan each time I walked through the halls. Presbyterian-St. Lukes had been the emergency room Juan always went to when he was having anxiety attacks. I saw him everywhere. I somehow thought I managed to keep my depression to myself until Matt talked of his doctor.

"Rich, he is also gay and his lover died of AIDS. I told him about Juan and that you were having a very bad time with all this. I told him I hope I can make you happy at last." I smiled, trying to appreciate his remark, but my heart was aching. Matt had also requested that Dr. Challig be his permanent doctor instead of rotating with the others. You see, he was also attracted to him.

Matt received good news...the transplant had grafted and everything appeared fine, and his spirits were the best that they had been! It was Christmas Eve and I returned late in the evening after being with him earlier. I had always controlled myself, giving full attention to Matt even though I had been crying hopelessly, thinking of Juan each time I drove there and home. However, this time, I couldn't control myself and the tears would not subside. Matt was aware of my desperate attempt to hold back tears and questioned me tenderly.

"You really did love Juan, didn't you, Rich?" I looked up, surprised, as tears continued rolling down my face.

"Matt, I always loved Juan...you knew that...didn't you? You knew I wanted him to live more than anything in this world! He was me, Matt!" It suddenly dawned on me that I shouldn't be this depressed in front of him...that I had to keep up his spirits.

"And I loved you, Matt. I thought we could have something beautiful, but you didn't want that. I kept trying until you finally told me you never felt that way." Matt began crying, apologizing for not realizing his feelings and crying out in desperation.

"So there is no chance for me, is there, Rich?" I realized he needed compassion.

"Matt, there is every chance...you just have to get better and show me you do love me...my love for you is probably buried under all the hurt."

Since Matt's bone marrow had grafted ahead of schedule, he was to be released the middle of January with a clean bill of health. Attributing to this early release was his otherwise healthy physical condition. However, he still looked like a skeleton and I was sure it was because of his second operation. All the patients in the unit were required to walk the halls for exercise, wearing medical masks, and outside of losing every bit of the hair on their bodies none of them were as fragile looking as he.

I had been assured by his nurse that I only needed to use common sense in keeping the house sterile, and with continual pressure, finally agreed to have him come live with me. So, again, I gave Matt my room since I couldn't bring myself to allow him to sleep in Juan's bed. Still, his kids just visited for a couple of hours on Saturday while I was at work.

A CAT scan and examination had been scheduled three weeks from the discharge date, and even though Matt wasn't gaining weight, he was eating everything I put on his plate, and I tried to increase the amount gradually. Suddenly, a couple of days before his scheduled appointment, he began again experiencing pains, causing him to be in a state of confusion and totally despondent. The evening before his test, he took my hand to feel his lower abdomen and, to my shock, I felt a very obvious large, hard bulk? In fact, I didn't really have to feel since the bulk of it was protruding from his flesh. I had a terrible feeling go through my body, but I wouldn't dare say anything to him. I tried assuring him that it was only scar tissue, especially since the last operation had been so badly botched up, as though they were in a hurry to close him. Matt accepted it to be scar tissue.

"Rich, the cancer can't be back after they injected enough chemo to kill me!"

I specifically begged Dr. Challig to call that evening since Matt was hopelessly anxious, but never heard a word. I only meant him to call with good news, figuring that after receiving almost a quarter of a million dollars, they would use some discretion and compassion to inform him in person should the results be bad. The phone wasn't ringing the next morning, and I figured that could be good news because at least we hadn't been called to go in. I was just about to leave for work when suddenly, it rang. Matt almost went hysterical as he screamed for me to answer, and when I did, I heard his doctor's voice say the results were not good. I never expected to hear this on the phone, but there was no way I could stop him from continuing because Matt was directly behind me, waiting apprehensively for my reaction. The doctor went on instead to say the results were very bad. By this time, Matt was trembling!

"It is bad, isn't it, Rich? IT IS BAD!" He finally insisted on talking to Dr. Challig and I was forced to tell him to pick up the phone in the living room. I couldn't believe the coldness and lack of compassion in his voice once Matt came on the phone.

"Matt, I am afraid I have bad news. The mass is back and is very large." Somehow, Matt kept his control.

"What does that mean, Doc?"

"It means you have two months to two years to live." Matt was silent, and upon looking into the living room, a grave realization of horror seemed fixed on his face. I immediately asked why there was such a large span of time.

"Well, we talked to his old oncologist and he thinks Matt can begin a new type of chemo treatment...and the two years is only if that is successful. We are turning Matt over to him and he will be calling to set up an appointment." And that was it, as he flatly said his good-bye and hung up. I was certain they also failed to accurately diagnose, instead, referring to the lump as scar tissue. That protrusion had never disappeared.

Matt began staggering hopelessly around the room, crying out that he was going to die. I ran and took hold of him, trying desperately to comfort him, but it didn't help as he continued sobbing uncontrollably. The goodness in my heart couldn't allow me to leave that day and I remained home to be with him. That evening, he insisted we watch the soap opera awards...not because he was a fan or cared who won...only because he wanted to watch some glamour. And he sat the entire evening hardly uttering a word.

I went to work on Saturday because a friend of Matt who had been staying with him while I worked was again coming over. I received a call from an office friend of Matt to tell me Matt had called her to ask if she could call his daughter to ask if she would come visit him,

"So, Rich, I told her to get her ass out of bed and go over to be with her dad because he is dying!" However, I later was told she didn't arrive until three and then only stayed an hour.

Matt had eaten the sandwich I left for lunch, only to vomit it up and continued vomiting bile throughout the night. I tried reaching a doctor in the bone marrow clinic the entire evening since we were told all we had to do was pick up a phone in any emergency…but to no avail. It wasn't until Sunday morning that I finally reached the head doctor at his home and was told to bring him directly to the bone marrow unit. A tube was immediately inserted into his nose, down to his stomach, in order to drain the bile and after a while he began feeling much better.

He then told me he had decided against trying another chemo…that his body was too ravaged and would never tolerate it…that he had already informed Dr. Moss of this decision, which meant he had two months to live. He then asked if I'd allow him to stay at my house once released…that Dr. Moss had told him his hospital had a wonderful hospice center, and would be there to relieve me whenever needed. I didn't know what to say. He had taken hold of me as though we had been lovers for years! However, I realized I wouldn't be capable of bringing myself to refuse.

His ex-wife visited that day, along with his son and daughter, and I managed to talk to her about the situation…to explain that I'd need help and that meant she should talk to her children about it. She was very compassionate but she still didn't want her daughter subjected to something like that and felt I shouldn't be either.

"And you shouldn't have to be responsible either…he should go to a home because he has the money." But I realized this was something Matt had definitely said he didn't want to do and merely told her I couldn't refuse.

My daughter, Martina, wasn't pleased with my decision to bring Matt to my house.

"Oh, Dad, why are you going to do that? Do you want him to die in your place?" But I merely told her my heart wouldn't allow me to do anything but that. I had to give him some quality of life before he died because I would never forgive myself if I refused. And she understood. I received the same reaction from Carl and others, but gave them the same answer.

Once I transferred Matt to the Maple Park Hospital Tuesday, I called Dr. Moss.

"I want to give Matt some quality of life these remaining two months," he went on to say, "so since I realize he is having quite a bit of discomfort from that tube going down his nose for drainage, I have ordered it to be taken out and surgically insert one directly into his stomach." At the time, I didn't realize he was again ordering Matt to be surgically opened. Matt's son, Randy, waited with me the following day, thinking the operation was in progress, only to find that he had been in complete agitation waiting in a holding area for hours for the surgeon to return from an emergency call. Matt had been receiving nourishment through his Hickman while at the other hospital, but he was now in hospice and IV feeding wasn't allowed, which meant thirty-six hours had passed.

A surgeon I hadn't seen before entered the room we were waiting in and shocked me once he explained I'd have to learn how to feed him and that it took a total of six hours for each feeding.

"Do you mean that a feeding tube was connected?" I quickly asked. "How is he to be drained if it takes that long to feed him?" The doctor went on to explain that he could also be drained with the tube.

"But it has to be done quite some time after he is fed, and his feeding today cannot begin until about midnight." I sat there with my mouth gaping. *This will never work*, I thought. How could Dr. Moss have been so evasive in his explanation of the procedure?

Matt was very irritable that evening and had every right since he hadn't had any liquid past his lips for days. I arrived shortly after nine thirty Thursday morning to find him very agitated and uncomfortable...and his coloring, very yellow. He was having a bit of difficulty with his speech and when I couldn't understand, he'd get even more irritable. He was being fed through the tube since midnight and I wondered about the drainage of his bile? He suddenly began to cough desperately, and once he began gagging, I grabbed hold of the bucket from the tray table, while trying desperately to hold onto his head for support. Just as I held it under his chin, he began vomiting! And the bile wouldn't stop as it gushed out in one long spurt after another. He looked so helpless and my heart ached for him as I screamed out for the nurse. She finally came into the room.

"Why hasn't he been drained! I don't understand why he hasn't been drained!" I was asked to leave the room once an aid came in to help clean him. As I stood in the hall, I could hear Matt screaming hysterically in pain! This was unbelievable! It was like a nightmare!

I was told I could return to the room and upon entering, saw an oxygen tube inserted in Matt's nose, and when he tried to talk his speech was completely distorted...and there I was with the memory of Juan again. And when he began struggling to breathe and partially closing his eyes, I was further reminded of that terrible day with Juan! It was happening again, and I should've known what was in store...but I still wouldn't admit it. A short while after, Vincent appeared at the doorway and didn't say a word, probably realizing what was going on. He then walked into the room and sat in the background, and before realizing, he was gone.

Once I was assured Matt was in a coma, I was told he still could hear everything. She then suggested I call anyone I thought should be there, and that afternoon, his daughter arrived with her mother...and shortly after, Randy and his wife. Carl arrived in the evening, as well as a good friend of Matt from work. Everyone took turns holding his hands and it was apparent he was aware of everything going on as he helplessly moved his arms about. Randy told me his brother would be getting a lift into town in the morning, and that Matt's sister would be arriving also.

Everyone left by nine o'clock and I was left alone with him. Uncertain if I should remain or go home to get a few hours sleep before returning by five to see the doctor, I finally decided on the latter.

I didn't get to bed until about midnight and before laying down my head, I called the hospital to inquire how he was doing. His nurse informed me he was resting well, the same as when I left. It seemed as though I had just fallen asleep when I was awakened by the phone.

"Is this Mr. Mella?" After responding, she quietly went on, "I am sorry to have to tell you, but Mr. Matter passed away." I was in a state of limbo as I dressed and drove to the hospital.

I arrived at the hospital in minutes and upon entering his room, saw Matt, motionless, lying at peace…and I finally cried.

I received something from Matt's kids I should've gotten from Svetmana—that is, respect and compassion. I realized they had to think Matt and I were lovers, and I didn't want to say anything to the contrary at this time. So I agreed to accept their invitation to be included in the funeral arrangements because Matt had already told me his desires…and I felt they should be carried out. I was surprised even further when they asked for approval on each and every detail. Matt had given me a list of pallbearers and asked if I would sing. At the time, I had been surprised he hadn't included Vincent as one of the pallbearers, and I thought it might have been a last gesture to me. However, I did ask him to serve because I felt he had been loyal to Matt for so long and it was the right thing to do. Matt had also insisted he not be in the casket without his wig. The kids agreed to my suggestion to have the funeral procession of cars pass his place of work, because Matt loved it dearly.

I was again surprised to see my children pay their respects because each of them probably only met Matt once. Mike was the only one who didn't attend, but had intended to until he received out of town guests. Deena had only met him casually once and attended alone because we were hit with the devastating news that Dino had the same cancer. Her son, Dino, also managed to show up. As I thought of it, they probably also assumed I had something going with Matt. To my knowledge, only two of the hundreds of old tricks that he always boasted of as good friends attended. Geena and Frank attended the funeral as well, and were surprised to see police cars guide the route.

"Rich, that had to be the most beautiful funeral I have ever been to," Geena said afterwards. "He really went out in style!"

So in my sorrow, I now realized I was definitely alone. Whether I could have fallen in love with him again, I will never know. I had laid aside my hatred because I needed a friend, and being Richard, I could never really hate anyone. I do know that my heart went out to him every day I saw his ravaged body sitting on my couch looking fifty years older than his age. My heart went out to him because his whole world had ended before his eyes each time he looked in the mirror. He had tried to be so sure of himself all of his life and suddenly became a wasted man. My heart ached because I believed he went to his death believing he was being punished by God for being so bad. I really do believe it since he said it constantly.

"Rich, I haven't been that bad. Why is God doing this to me? I haven't been that bad." And he kept repeating it, so he had to be aware of how he had used people. He just didn't want to ever admit it…to say he was sorry. I'd try to convince him that God never took vengeance on anyone…that He looked at everyone as good people…and was always forgiving. But Matt still never thought to ask for forgiveness. I believe it was on his mind constantly and it was so sad, because no one should go to their death thinking that. I wanted to believe that Matt was with Juan…holding hands at last, as friends, and that there was no such thing as hatred any longer.

Two days before Matt passed away, he had asked what I wanted of his after he passed away. I told him I didn't want anything but for him to get better, but he then said he wanted me to have his car because Juan's had so many miles on it. I didn't want to talk of it, but he still insisted. I wanted to think it was a gesture of love, but I wasn't sure since Carl had told me he had asked Matt while I was out of the room Tuesday night what he was leaving me after he died, and that he seemed disturbed that he should ask.

"I think he was upset because he probably never even gave it a thought. I finally told him he should think about it because you have been the one there taking care of him…not his children." So I didn't know if he offered because of embarrassment or not? Of course, he died before his last will could be changed, and it wasn't anything I'd bring up to his children. It was then ironical because the car was given to me by his children. I asked Randy if his Dad had said anything about it.

"No, we just wanted you to have something to show our appreciation for doing so much for him."

I did manage to take Matt's diaries, along with other things I realized would upset his children. Since Matt always boasted about having a book written about his life, I felt I had every right to read them. I cannot say I felt honored as I read…no; instead, a feeling of revolting repulsion came into my body and has remained to this day. As I read, it was apparent anything Tom Jones ever accomplished in sex was dwarfed by the deplorable exploits Matt managed to excel in! I stayed up until the wee hours of the mornings reading one page after another of the ten years he managed to record in his diaries, and what I had suspected he had done was only a minute fraction of the quantity of sex he so readily achieved. I usually had problems keeping awake when I read at night, but there was no sand in my eyes these evenings. I had realized he had roaming eyes and that he always talked about sex, but never imagined his entire life revolved around it! The diaries definitely appeared to be dedicated solely to the amount and type of sex he was successful in acquiring. He almost always rated them for the pleasure he received, and even if he had only been with someone a couple of times, if the guy had a great body and well endowed, he would insert a notation: "I think I am falling in love with him."

I was right about the evening he came home from the hospital...he did have sex with Vincent, noting that it was great. In fact, there were many times with Vincent he had sex a total of three times in one visit! He even had sex with him the day Juan died.... He had met Vincent six years earlier at the forest preserves and they had been having sex from the very beginning...even during his so-called attachments to someone. I found there were times I dropped him off or left his place, to read Vincent then came over and did not leave until four or five in the morning. I wondered when he slept.

I didn't take the time to count, but it was very possible Matt had sex with Vincent more than anyone else. I never realized the scope of his statement, "Rich, you really have not had sex until you are blown by someone who wears dentures and takes them out to blow you!" This doesn't mean he didn't have sex with others because he had written each name into his books, and if they were sizable enough, he most certainly would mention it! And these names went on endlessly! There were times he recorded seeing Vincent at the adult bookstore, but too involved himself, blowing others. It certainly clarified something...why he always complained of chapped lips or canker sores. As mentioned, I didn't count the times he had sex with Vincent since I was stunned with the realization of the total of all encounters! Matt very capably managed this by systematically adding each one as he went along by listing the increased total on each page...which came to a grand total of over thirty three hundred! All I needed to do was count the star markings he had drawn on the daily ledgers to verify, which were his code designating he had sex!

My long hours of reading finally enlightened me...there never was a Bob in his life! Yes, there were some occasional ones, but not the particular one who was madly in love with him and eventually came down with AIDS! He had to be someone he concocted for his own satisfaction! I finally figured it out by studying the times I remembered he told me he was going to see him, and each time he had either gone to the Bijou theatre or an adult bookstore. The Bijou featured triple X-rated male films and darkened back rooms for convenient sex at a mere fourteen-dollar fee. The same convenience was offered at the bookstores for an added cost. It didn't take long to realize his own personal code each time he went to see Bob—it meant the Bijou or bookstore! Another frequent haunting ground was the forest preserves. Yes, he often picked up men at the bars, but this was too time-consuming. At the Bijou or bookstores, it was like instant sex, because otherwise, why would anyone go? I discovered these were his every day activities when off from work, and during the late hours of almost every night...even returning several times in the course of a day! I really wondered when he slept.

I cannot say this didn't break my heart, because it did! If only I had realized the scope of Juan's angry cry, "Recharred, he is known as the whore of Oak Park!" I do not believe Juan even realized the scope? I finally understood why Matt always boasted about having a book written from his diaries. He had to be proud of his life and I guess this pride made him desire to share it with everyone, as he shared his body. He was an avid collector, but

I never realized his biggest collection was men! So the sadness had to be even greater as I remembered his cry.

"Rich, I don't think I will ever have sex again because all those radiation treatments have made me impotent!" His world was gone....

I wanted to be angry with Matt, but at the time I couldn't...realizing his sickness...that his mind was twisted about the real values of life. I had suspected he was out seeking men...so what is the difference between a few dozen and thousands? It is still the same. The only difference is now I understand him more. He was out to prove to the world that he could have more sex than anyone, and no matter who it was...he was proud because he had conquered and it made him feel important and wanted. I couldn't find it in my heart to hate him after I read all the diaries since I was never capable of truly hating—even after meeting his old lover, George, at the bars a few times, to be told the reason he didn't attend Matt's wake or funeral was because he felt he wasn't deserved of his respect.

It was the same once I met with his supposed first lover, Ron, who had come into town. I needed some answers and he agreed to meet for breakfast. In our conversation, I was told they had never been lovers...that he only agreed to have Matt live with him because he needed a place to stay once he divorced.

"Matt always wanted to be lovers, but I constantly declined." I then realized why Matt always refused to allow me to be present when he met Ron at the bar on his occasional returns to the city. I was stunned after telling him that I had forgiven Matt...that I knew Juan had to also realize he had a sickness and had now taken hold of his hand to be friends...to hear Ron firm's statement.

"I don't think they are in the same place!"

I also spoke with his ex-wife to hear her belief that Matt was two people...one loved by everyone he worked with, and another who was a miserable wretch in his personal life, often throwing her dinners at the wall and violently blaming her for *his* wrong decisions. I felt it was a pity he couldn't have reversed roles, but understood why from his often statement.

"I don't fuck where I work." I guess he preferred to fuck everyone over in his private life instead.

Still, I could not despise this man since he was now dead. I realized he wasn't capable of loving anyone since he was so consumed in his own being. Yes, he loved me and he loved Vincent, but because we built his ego by bestowing him with gifts and affection. In fact, he loved everyone he encountered sexually since this same ego was inflated or because he was taken with their well-endowed body.

I wanted desperately to believe he truly meant everything when he pleaded to me.

"Rich, do you think I will ever go back to the life I led? Never! I think God gave me cancer instead of AIDS...as a warning, because there are cures for it! No, Rich, I will never go back because I have learned my lesson!" And there were those, even while he was still living, who believed he'd never change…that once cured…would merely revert to his old ways. There was no doubt in the minds of Carl and Frank, especially after the tumor began to disappear during treatment and Matt conveniently forgot his pleas to me to resume our relationship. I still wanted to give him the benefit of the doubt. I needed it for my own salvation, and gave a year of respect to his memory. And I was angry, not for myself, but for him…especially since he truly never experienced the beauty of being loved and loving deeply in return!

I am angry with his doctors, because after securing his charts from the hospital, there was one lie after another. The surgeon botched up in the first operation and had to return Matt from the recovery room to the operating room in order to reopen his incision again to correct it, and never thought anyone had to have knowledge of it. My suspicions had been correct when I wondered if he actually had a bowel bypass on the second operation because none was performed. His doctors were aware that he was gay because, in his charts, they wrote he had admitted to it. It bothered me as I thought of how evasive his oncologist had always been when discussing anything with me, assuming I was Matt's lover, especially after reading he had talked to Matt's partner regarding procedures. An ill feeling enters my body, recalling the attraction Matt had for his doctor, prompting him not to seek a second opinion, and how it proved to be his final demise. However…he had finally realized it when he told Carl the Tuesday before he died.

"I made a lot of wrong decisions." At the time my mind felt, and continues to truly feel these doctors were playing God, and no human being ever has the power to do that!

So I am left alone with my guilt…with my grieving for Juan, still believing he'll come back to me one day. Matt died a year and a half after Juan, and it is now near two years since he passed away. I put Matt to rest some time ago, wanting desperately to believe he truly meant it when he vowed he'd never return to his old ways…that he truly loved me in the end. I needed it because it meant everything I sacrificed with Juan wasn't in vain. I needed Juan to realize it, too, and to take him by the hand, knowing I could've been happy with Matt. I wanted to be certain that he'd have filled my life with some joy. I wanted to remember the winning smile of Matt…the charming way he'd say "Hello there" when he called?

I tried for a year after he died to hold this in my heart, because I needed it for my peace of mind, and at the same time, realized no one should go to the grave despised. However, I was Richard, and wrong doing against me have always preyed on my mind…and the following year, I was tormented with them. So I no longer visit his grave and have tried to put him out of my mind. Every now and then a bitter feeling of resentment comes over me as I think of how he used me and the precious time I lost with Juan. A strong belief also enters my body…that Juan could've had more time if I wasn't the loyal person I always managed to be. A terrible thought comes to my mind…that God was aware Matt would never live up to his vows to me, and that He denied his prayers to recover! But yet I've always known God didn't take vengeance on anyone! So I have tried to believe that, instead, He did it for me...so I'd no longer be hurt. I will never know, and should really believe Matt meant his vows because it would bring me peace of mind. Whether I'll ever be able to believe this, I don't know. I do know I should try, since it could help me to go on with my life. So I must say, "Matt...peace be with you always."

* * * * * *

My intentions had been to end my story of the legacy I was privileged to receive from Juan, shortly after he was taken from me. The chain of events that eventually transpired while still writing, however, brought on the realization that I needed to continue since everything was so much a part of my life with Juan...the last years before he died and my grieving afterwards. I also realized I needed to include all the aftermath, as *my* legacy to my children and family, to completely understand their father and brother. To also realize I was not some gullible and stupid jackass who allowed everyone to walk all over him, but instead...truly a Man of LaMancha!

I'm not sure whether my grieving and guilt over Juan will ever end? Sometimes, I want it to end and remember all the wonderful memories...and then...sometimes I feel it should continue...and maybe the reason is to be punished for all my wrong decisions, even though I am well aware that Juan was equally as guilty for the same reasons. I am not sure? I know I will never stop missing and loving him, and pray I will one day see him again. I want to believe so badly that, once we die, our spirits live on forever. So I need to believe Juan lives on and that he will always be there beside me, and sometimes I really do feel his presence because I hesitate doing something I know he disliked for me to do! But yet, there is this terrible fear racing through my head that, once we die...there is nothing! That the mechanism ceases to function!

"Aw, God," I shout out, "No! JUAN CANNOT BE GONE! NO, JUAN CANNOT HAVE CEASED TO FUNCTION?... NO, ONLY HIS BODY...IT HAS TO BE ONLY HIS BODY! JUAN HAS TO LIVE ON!" So I try desperately to revert to all the religious teachings I was taught throughout my life...to realize why we were put on this earth in the first place! I know I have to believe this...and I try...I try....

* * * * * *

Every story has an ending, but that doesn't necessarily mean that after the last word is written, the story has ended. On the contrary...love continues to live on, and if I've managed to have multitudes from all walks of life reach this point...then I'll have accomplished a great deal...to set aside some of the bigotry. Maybe then some of my sadness will finally end, because, at last there'll be others to share my grief since they'll feel part of the beautiful relationship Juan and I were so fortunate to have.... If I have managed to bring a realization to these people, as well as my beloved family...that a love between two men can be something created in heaven, whether it be sexual or the deepest of friendships, I may then find peace in knowing Juan did not die in vain. Circumstances in our lives helped mold us into the persons we were, and because of it, our meeting was inevitable. I will never believe that the love and respect Juan and I had for each other could ever be something wrong! Both Juan and I were never proud to be gay, and if we had the choice, we would have chosen to be straight...but one thing that was certain...WE WERE PROUD OF OUR LOVE FOR EACH OTHER!

    I began writing a couple of months after Juan died in my arms, knowing I needed to record the many beautiful memories racing constantly through my head and heart, for fear my memory would lose them as I grew old and forgetful. I needed to also do it in order for those dear to me to understand my grieving...and the guilt I have been bearing. I completed the story a year and a half later and then a third writing three and a half years after Juan's death. If it hadn't been for Margot, the social worker at the VA hospital reading my first drafts as I wrote them, I probably would not have realized I had a story so beautiful...and one that needed to be shared with the straight world. There has never been a time during all of my writings, even this last one nineteen years later...that I have not felt Juan's presence, guiding my every word.

    Many of my original drafts were written in long hand while at the park Juan loved to sun in, just across from our Harvard address and I chose to do the same once I had been ready to write the conclusion of my testament to this wonderfully unique and beautiful man. As I sat there, I could see Juan lying on his towel...reading! Every now and then, I'd picture him raising his head to me as I sat on the bench in the shade...to read something! I could actually hear myself begging him to allow me to read it myself.

    "Because, Juan, I cannot understand everything you say when you read...YOU ALWAYS PRONOUNCE EVERY LETTER IN EVERY WORD!"

    I sat there smiling at the thought of parking the car in front of our old apartment, just before walking across the street to the park...I had glanced down the alley...and there was JUAN! Yes there was JUAN...as drunk as could be, chasing after me, and calling out.

    "RECHARRED! RECHARRED! I AM GONNA GET YOU!" Only to fall on his face! And he never even cried or complained after realizing blood was pouring out of his mouth!

    I thought of the movie Juan loved so much, *Fried Green Tomatoes*, and how much it had remained one of my favorites. I continually think of a line Jessica Tandy said that haunts me to this day. I believe it went something like this....

"A heart can be broken, but unfortunately, still continues to beat." So I realize I am forced to live on and hold onto my memories. I don't know if I am right in making them a living part of my life, but part of me is gone and I feel I need to hold onto these memories in order to feel whole again. I am sure I will never be the same person I was those years with Juan, but know I need to accept my life and live it for him.

* * * * * *

The words of this story have all been Juan's words as well as mine, and are as vivid in my mind as they were nineteen years ago when I started the work. And sometimes I find myself dictating these memories to Juan as a reminder that his spirit is still present…because it will never fade from my mind…. Juan…I see you every day, Juan, and I hear your cackling, contagious laugh……so much so that I almost join in as I always did!… Juan, the many times I look at a couch and see you lying on your side reading, or rattling on with some story…they are still in my mind. Your hysterical belly laughs while watching *Lucy* make her faces after taking her spoonful of 'Vitameatavegamin' will always remain in my heart…and how I unbelievably always joined in even though I had seen it a hundred times before. That inimitable way of yours, holding up your arms, smiling and calling out, "Cha-cha-cha," will always be there before me, even as I close my eyes! Juan, no one could ever do it like you, because no one has that same beautiful sparkle in their eyes!

You must know every time I am driving alone that I'm not alone!… I feel you there next to me, and I hear you rattling on about the bea-u-ti-ful scenery! I really can! Aw, the many times when we visited a new city to hear you excitedly sigh, "You know, Recharred, I would not mind living here…would you not like thot, too, Recharred?" Aw, Juan, how I wished we had moved to each of them! I also have to tell you, Juan, that each time I sit in a restaurant, my pride is overwhelming once I realize how privileged I had to be to have shared so many tables with you! Juan, you are so charming and elegant, and watching you lift a fork had to be one of the most magnificent and elegant sights ever to behold!

Do you know how many times I have thought about the times you mimicked Danlye's walk? I never laughed so much in my life! I think there were times I almost peed in my pants! Aw, Juan, you were so funny…so funny! I always said you should've been on stage. You have that rare gift!

I still wonder about the helium-filled balloon I let loose in this park, the autumn after you left me? I wanted it to fly up to Heaven, and as I watched it go higher and higher into the sky, I felt it had reached you…because, Juan, it completely disappeared from sight! I hope someone else didn't get it because I had inserted my recipe for lasagna in it.

Do you remember when we did the *Andrews Sisters* at the club? I'll never forget how drunk you and John were, but I knew that was the only way you'd go on stage. I can still see you shaking your finger to the 'No, no, no!' Aw, Juan, you were so funny and the place went up for grabs, especially after you turned the wrong way and bumped into me. I must admit I was a bit disturbed you didn't remember my choreography, but relieved once I saw you didn't need it…because you were a star!

You know what else I think of Juan? Those times I didn't want to go out drinking…and there we were, sitting in the kitchen while you were drinking…and then suddenly there you were begging me to have one so we could go out dancing. You'd then walk over, lift the glass to my mouth and gently pull down my lower lip so you could pour easily into it…and all while pleading, "Aw, c'mon, Recharred…drink…drink, so we con go out ond 'ave such a good time!" And there I'd be, already tipsy after one drink to hear you laughing and saying, "You know, Blanche, you are such a cheap drunk. One drink ond you are already drunk!"

Remember the onion, Juan? How hard you'd laugh each time you thought of me putting it to my nose after you passed gas? And how you'd wrestle trying to get the match from my hand, calling out, "No, Blanche, if you light thot match, I will tell Deena on you…c'mon now, Recharred, if you do thot, I will tell her…thot you sleep with men!" And I can't get over how you laughed as hard each time!

You must know I finally told Jacque, Nicky, Geena, Deena, and Dino about our real relationship…and you know what? They were so wonderful and loved me just as much! I am so sorry I didn't tell them years ago when I thought of doing it…because I was so proud of you then as always. You were right when you always said I was so lucky to have such a wonderful family…because that is what they are! Do you know what Geena said when she realized my heart was breaking? She said Juan had to be the luckiest person in this world to have me love you so much. Well, I told her I was the luckiest person in this world to have *you* love me the way you do! As you already know, Dino and Deena are now with you and my consolation…they have to be laughing at all your antics, especially mimicking Deena!

I have never really told Martina everything since she was pregnant with Martin at the time, and Jacque felt I should wait. And now they're all grown. Aw, Juan you were right, because Martina has made a wonderful and caring mother!

I have, however, realized I am loved by all of them…after all, you know the nice guy I have always been and how could anyone hate me?

Juan, I am trying so hard to remember you as you always were, and not while you were in the hospital and ill. There is, however, one time I will never forget in the hospital...and that is the last time I fed you. The love and gratitude on your face will live in my heart forever because you truly made me feel like I was your lifeline. Never did I feel as close to you as that evening. I truly felt as though we were one...and if I could have gone with you or traded places, I would have done so gladly.

Juan, I can never begin to tell you how much it has meant having you in my life...no, never! I cannot ever thank you enough for giving me so much...so much of you! I *know* I am the luckiest person in this world to have had you in my life! You left me a legacy I will cherish forever and I want to believe we will be together again ...to be sure you never let go! I don't know if you realized how much it meant to me when you said those words? You cannot imagine how you touched my heart...and how my heart will never let it go.

Juan, do you remember the beautiful harvest moon...remember...?

Well, I have looked for it constantly...but never have seen it again. No, never that large. I have finally reasoned it out...and that is because you are not there beside me.

I had been told your ashes were spread at Hesitation Point in Brown County State Park, and returned each year on your birthday to recall your excitement when you sighed, "Is this not bea-u-ti-ful, Recharred? I could stay here forever!" I had a picture taken of me the very first time and do you know what I saw once it was developed? AW, JUAN, YOU HAVE TO KNOW! Because there you were! Not your actual image, but in the trees, the LEAVES FORMED THE IMAGE OF YOUR FACE, MIMICKING ME WITH YOUR EXPRESSION OF MUSSOLINI! I KNOW YOU HAD TO BE RESPONSIBLE FOR IT...I KNOW! It was your way of telling me, "Recharred, get thot sad face off ond live for me!"

So, Juan, if I do and there is a heaven, will you wait for me? Please, Juan...please, don't ever get so involved up there...that you forget me! Please, be there for me...so we can join hands and be happy again? I am trying so hard to again believe we have an everlasting life awaiting us! My thoughts are so mixed up because it has been hard for me to imagine all the souls who have departed since time began...but I want to believe it, and I try to think of how it will be once I enter the gates of heaven.... My mind imagines all these arms reaching out to touch me...to welcome me along as I begin to walk the path into heaven...that my mother will be reaching out to hug me...and my father will be there, too, along with Dino and Deena and my two brothers!

AW, JUAN, IT HAS TO BE, BECAUSE I WANT TO HEAR MUSIC! AND I WANT TO BELIEVE! I WANT TO SEE YOU AT THE END OF

THE PATH AND HEAR GEORGE McCRAE'S 'ROCK YOUR BABY!!!" And JUAN, THE MIX OF MUSIC WILL BE FANTASTIC BECAUSE I'LL HEAR THEM ALL! All the songs we ever loved—"Everlasting Love"... "Doctor's Orders"... Barry White's songs..."Gloria'..."The Richie Family"...along with all the Spanish and English ballads we loved so much! Aw, Juan, you will be so happy and so will I! ...JUAN, aw, Juan, I don't know if I ever told you...but whenever you walked into a room, I heard music, and I want to hear it again! JUAN, I CAN SEE MYSELF RUNNING TO YOU AND SUDDENLY THERE YOU ARE WALKING IN THAT PROUD MANNER! ....AND THEN JUAN.......UP GO YOUR ARMS! So, please, please don't ever let me again have to ask God...WHY HAS ALL THE MUSIC GONE?